BETWEEN TWO KINGS

ALSO BY LINDSAY STRAUBE

Split or Swallow
Kiss Of The Basilisk

BETWEEN TWO KINGS

LINDSAY STRAUBE

Arcadia

First published in Great Britain in 2025 by Arcadia
an imprint of Quercus
Part of John Murray Group

1

Cover and internal design © 2025 Sourcebooks
Cover design by Antoaneta Georgieva/Sourcebooks
Cover images © Malgorzata Maj/Arcangel, Viorel Sima/Adobe Stock, Verity Corvo/Arcangel,
Benedek/Getty Images, Yulimuli/Getty Images, Historic Images/Alamy, Fine Art Photographic/
Getty Images, Patti McConville/Alamy, Diem/Adobe Stock, Cat'chy Images/Alamy, Kurt SPK/
Getty Images, YUSHENG HSU/Adobe Stock, Olesia/Adobe Stock, Dana.S/Adobe Stock,
incamerastock/Alamy, Igor Ustynskyy/Getty Images, Shutterstock

A CIP catalogue record for this book is available
from the British Library

HB ISBN 978-1-52944-588-6
TPB ISBN 978-1-52944-589-3
EBOOK ISBN 978-1-52944-590-9

Printed and bound in Great Britain by Clays Ltd, Elcograf S.p.A.

MIX
Paper | Supporting
responsible forestry
FSC
www.fsc.org FSC® C104740

Papers used by Quercus are from well-managed forests and other responsible sources.

Quercus
Carmelite House
50 Victoria Embankment
London EC4Y 0DZ

John Murray Group
Part of Hodder & Stoughton Limited
An Hachette UK company

The authorised representative in the EEA is Hachette Ireland,
8 Castlecourt Centre, Dublin 15, D15 XTP3, Ireland (email: info@hbgi.ie)

This book is for anyone who has ever had to choose.

ABOUT THIS BOOK

Nothing I write here could possibly prepare you for this book. Whatever you think is about to happen, I guarantee that you are wrong. The best thing to do is take a deep breath, steel yourself, and dive in. And after this book inevitably breaks you, pick up the prequel in order to heal.

Oh, and get your tissues ready. You're going to need them.

Content warning: this book contains sexual scenes of an intense and graphic nature. For a full list, please visit www.oxfordlemon.com/triggers.

CHAPTER ONE

••●—✳—●••

TEM HAD NEVER BEEN FUCKED AGAINST A TREE BEFORE.

They were alone in the forest, but it didn't matter—Tem would've let Caspen fuck her with a crowd present. His hands gripped her hips, her legs wrapped around his torso. The stars above them, the grass below them—it was all the same. Basilisk and human, predator and prey. The soft lines of Tem's body blended with Caspen's until they were one being rather than two. She was immeasurably *full:* of desire, of want, of cock. They were almost there, climbing the perennial slope of pleasure she'd come to know so well. Caspen's mind intertwined with hers. Smoke rose from his shoulders.

Let me see it, Tem.

She wanted him to see it.

Show me.

She would show him.

Caspen's entire body was pressed against hers, the great expanse of his chest anchoring her to the tree. There was no escape, and Tem didn't want to anyway. Her orgasm slammed into her so sharply that her vision went black. By the time it returned, Caspen had finished too.

They lay on the forest floor afterward, panting, their bodies soaked with sweat. Despite the frigid night air, Tem felt as if she were burning up inside.

"What's happening to me?" She gasped when they finally drew apart.

"You are adjusting." Caspen was equally out of breath. Tem had never seen him so winded.

"But why now? It was never like this before."

"Now that you have transitioned, your basilisk side has awoken."

"Awoken?"

He shrugged, and a drop of sweat rolled down his shoulder. "I do not know another word to describe it."

After a moment of thought, Tem found the word actually worked quite well. But she found herself wondering if she would ever feel fully adjusted. It had been a week since they'd gotten married, and she felt no closer to mastering her basilisk side than she'd been when she first transitioned at the lake. Instead she felt completely out of control, her body an open flame.

"If that's the case, why can't I transition the way you can?" Tem asked as they walked back to the caves. They'd been hunting in the forest for hours, and she hadn't been able to turn at all; she'd only managed to transition once since her first time, and even then, she'd only been able to do so with Caspen's guidance in her mind. He'd practically *pulled* her into her true form, his assistance barely enough. Transitioning felt just out of reach.

"You are new to this, Tem. It will take time."

"But I've done it before. And you do it so easily."

"I have been doing it for a very, very long time. You will get there."

"I hate being weak."

"Weak is the last thing you are."

Tem tried to believe him. But it was difficult when there was evidence indicating otherwise. She was a Hybreed. She was supposed to be a powerful creature, and instead she could barely transition. The flow she'd found just a week ago was now nowhere to be found, and she was beginning to think that the first few times were flukes. Now she was relegated to the sidelines, like a child who had played too hard and needed to rest. It was pathetic.

"I should be getting better, not worse."

"You will get better, Tem. You will master it. You need only learn how."

By the time they returned to their chambers, Tem was almost convinced. But any thought of transitioning disappeared the moment she saw the letter on their bed. Caspen read it first, his expression indecipherable as he handed it to Tem. Her throat went dry at the three neat lines of script:

Temperance Verus,

The king requests your presence at the castle this evening.

A carriage will be sent for you. Come alone.

Tem turned the paper over, half expecting to see an additional note. There was none.

"Come alone," she whispered.

Caspen took the letter and tossed it into the fire. She knew he was merely disposing of it, but somehow the act felt significant.

"It should not surprise you," he said.

"What shouldn't?"

"That he wants you to come alone."

"Oh," Tem said again. "Right."

It *didn't* surprise her, exactly. But it made her nervous. Tem hadn't seen Leo since the wedding. Surely, he had found Evelyn by now. Surely, they were together. The thought made her sick. She looked up at Caspen.

"Doesn't it bother you that I'm going to see him?"

Caspen raised an eyebrow. "No. It does not."

She couldn't understand his apathy. How could this pivotal event be of no concern to him? "But *how*?"

Caspen shrugged. "You chose me," he said simply.

She stared at him. That was technically true; Tem had chosen Caspen. But it wasn't because she didn't love Leo. It was because she wanted *more* for Leo. And in doing so, she had accepted less for herself.

"Tem," Caspen murmured. "You do not have to go."

Of course he would say that—closure with Leo was of no importance to Caspen. What was her love for the human prince—now king—in comparison to her blood bond with the basilisk? To Caspen, his marriage to Tem was the only legitimate union. But not to her. Besides, Tem *wanted* to go. She needed to see that she'd made the right choice—that Leo had found Evelyn, that he was happy now.

"I have to go," she said carefully. "He and I are technically still married."

Tem did not voice the rest of her thought, which was that Leo could not marry Evelyn if he was still married to Tem.

Caspen shrugged again. "Then you shall go."

This entire affair was of little interest to Caspen. Basilisks didn't have paperwork; they didn't concern themselves with human legalities. But Caspen understood human customs, and if there was anything he supported, it was Tem closing this chapter of her life.

Tem looked down at her naked body. "And just what am I supposed to wear?"

The corner of Caspen's mouth twitched. "We will find you something."

"Something" turned out to be rather difficult to find. The dresses Caspen had given her during the training were custom made, Tem learned, and it would take days to make another. Basilisks were always naked. Hours of searching led them to a single floor-length silk robe. When tied with a braided tassel, it marginally resembled a dress. Its plunging neckline was hardly appropriate, but Tem didn't care. The outfit was the least of her worries.

Caspen walked her to the cave entrance but didn't follow her to the path. Instead he kissed her, and Tem felt the tendrils of his mind brush against hers. His grip tightened. Perhaps his earlier nonchalance had been feigned; perhaps he wasn't as unbothered by this process as he led her to believe. But Tem could do nothing about that now. The only way for Caspen to have her all to himself was to let her go to Leo and end their relationship.

A moment later, he released her. Then he disappeared back into the caves.

Tem waited alone for the carriage, which arrived just as darkness fell. She didn't recognize the stable boy; it wasn't Henry or Peter, which disappointed her. It would have been nice to see a familiar face. Instead, she resigned herself to staring out the window. It was nearly winter; autumn had flown by in a heartbeat, and there was a sharpness to the air that made her shudder with anticipation. Winters were long and dark in the village. She wondered whether they would feel different beneath the mountain. It would be her first winter away from the farm, away from the chickens, away from her mother.

But Tem didn't mind. She wanted nothing more than to assimilate into basilisk society, to finally feel like she was truly home. Caspen wanted that too. She could sense it every time his eyes met hers. He was always watching her, gauging how well she was adjusting, checking to make sure she still belonged to him. Sometimes Tem wasn't sure if she did.

Her thoughts turned to what was to come. She had no idea what to expect tonight, but it was imperative that the evening go well. There was far more than just her marriage with Caspen at stake. In the aftermath of the violence at her and Leo's wedding, tensions between the humans and the basilisks had never been higher. If they couldn't find a peaceful way to coexist, things would only get worse.

But the thought of just coexisting with Leo was impossible. One week ago they'd been in love. They were *still* in love—at least, Tem was. The ache in her chest was evidence enough of that. But was Leo? He had agreed to share her. *That* was what Tem wanted. But then the wedding happened, and something had changed within her— some thread of selflessness had tugged on her heart when she'd looked in Leo's eyes after she'd crested him. It wasn't fair for him to have to share her. Not when he wanted all of her. He'd told her that himself once: *"I want all of you. Or I don't want you at all."*

Tem sighed, leaning back against the seat. The memory of their wedding plagued her—the way Leo had looked at her as she ascended the stage, the way they'd kissed when she'd crested him. It was a memory she cherished, a moment she thought of in the dark hours of the night when Caspen was asleep beside her. She remembered other things too, from the night they'd spent in his bed: the way he tasted like honey, the way he'd worshipped between her legs, the way he'd murmured her name while his cock was inside her.

The carriage seemed suddenly too small. Tem was unquestionably turned on. Ever since she'd transitioned for the first time, the line between simply existing and arousal had become desperately thin. All it took was the mere thought of sex to make her wet. And when she thought about Leo, it took even less. Something in her body craved him beyond explanation. It was different from the way she craved Caspen. With Caspen, her desire was primal and raw, visceral, consuming her like a hungry animal. With Leo, it was slower—a glowing coal that smoldered deep within her chest. She could not rid herself of it. She wasn't even sure she wanted to. Just the thought of being close to Leo was sending her into a frenzy. Tem leaned forward, cradling her head in her hands. She had to get it together.

"Miss?" The footman's voice interrupted her thoughts. "We've arrived."

The carriage door opened, and Tem accepted the hand offered to her. The stars were bright overhead, the last sliver of the harvest moon glowing beneath the freckled sky. She stared up at the castle's foreboding turrets, dreading what came next. No part of her wanted to walk inside those doors. This was no longer her home.

Now it was Evelyn's.

Tem paused before the entrance, her hand on the doorknob. Was Leo on the other side? Was Evelyn? He'd told her to come alone—did that mean he would be alone too? When she opened the door, however, Leo was not on the other side. Instead, Lord Chamberlain greeted her with a subdued smile.

"Temperance," he said calmly. "How are you this evening?"

"Oh," she said, clearing her throat. "I'm fine."

He nodded. "Please, follow me."

Tem did so, following him through the foyer and into the parlor, where Lord Chamberlain gave her a curt nod and bowed as he left the room. Tem wondered about the formality. Did her status as queen of the basilisks give her some respect in the royal castle? Or did he merely pity her for what was to come?

Tem needed a drink.

She scanned the room for alcohol, her eyes landing on a golden tray holding a faceted crystal bottle filled with whiskey. She crossed to it immediately, pouring herself a healthy dose and downing the entire thing. The liquor settled her nerves, but just barely. The parlor was hot; suddenly the stupid robe was too tight.

Tem looked up at the paintings on the walls. Dozens of faces stared back at her— all royals, all long dead. It was clear that Leo's icy-blond hair had been passed down through generations. Even when his male ancestors had married brunette women, the children somehow ended up blond. Her eyes traveled over the sea of angular faces, seeing Leo in every single one. One man had Leo's slate-gray eyes, another his thin, elegant fingers. Finally, she spotted Maximus.

Tem crossed to his portrait, still clutching her whiskey glass. The former king was standing in what looked like the library the Frisky Sixty ceremony had taken place in. A thick golden cuff glinted on his wrist. Tem wondered where Maximus was now, whether Leo had allowed him to roam free or imprisoned him for his crimes. Before she could follow that thought, someone cleared their throat. Tem whipped around at the sound.

There, in the doorway, stood Leo.

He looked just the same. Tall, slender, wearing an impeccably tailored velvet suit. His hair was just as she remembered it, white blond and slicked back. For some reason, Tem had expected him to look different—older, somehow. But the only thing that had changed was his eyes. They were hooded, as if he hadn't been sleeping properly. Tem didn't want to think about what could be keeping him up at night. He was wearing a wedding ring, and she wondered suddenly whether it was the same one he'd married her with. Tem still wore hers—she hadn't taken it off since their wedding. Surely, he would ask for it back. The thought killed her.

"Tem."

Just her name, but something inside her awoke at the sound of his voice—something impossible to ignore.

"Leo."

Just his in return.

Tem remembered Caspen holding her and Leo's heads together, sealing their bond with a kiss. She wanted to kiss him again now. Tem immediately suppressed the thought. Leo was not hers anymore. Not only did he belong to someone else, but Tem herself had told him to go. She didn't feel as though she was allowed to miss him when she was the one who had sent him away in the first place.

Leo's eyes traveled over her, lingering on the diabolically low neckline of her robe.

Tem set her whiskey down, afraid she might drop it.

"Thank you for coming." His tone was oddly formal. She couldn't stand it. "I wasn't sure if you would."

Tem frowned. "Why?"

He tilted his head. "Because you're…with him."

Tem didn't know how to respond to that. Just because she was with Caspen didn't mean she was going to ignore Leo's existence. She was the one who'd made him promise they would see each other again.

"I'll always come when you call," she said quietly.

He didn't reply. Tem rather wished she'd had more to drink, but perhaps it was better this way. There was no telling what she would do if she was drunk. Even without the influence of alcohol, she felt uncommonly warm. And every time she looked at Leo, she only felt warmer.

"Are you…?" Leo began but stopped.

"Am I what?" she prompted.

"Happy?"

It was an impossible question. How to answer? Of course she was happy with

Caspen—she always had been. But part of her yearned for Leo—*ached* for him. It was a part as real and as prominent as the part that loved Caspen. She couldn't help it, couldn't control it. It simply *was*. Rather than answer, Tem decided to ask him the same question in return:

"Are you?"

Leo's gaze was unwavering. The intense eye contact was beginning to test her. She wanted to cross to him, to cup his chin in her hand, and pull his face to hers. She balled her hands into fists, resisting the urge.

"Happiness is an indulgence," he whispered.

Tem had no idea what to make of that answer. Was he saying that he wasn't happy? Or that he was, but it had cost him something to become so? She didn't know, and she couldn't fathom asking. Instead, she asked the thing she'd come here to find out: "Did you find her?"

Tem expected an immediate response, but none came. It was a simple question. She already knew the answer. Still, she needed to know for sure—needed to hear him say it.

"Yes." His voice was tight when he said it.

Tem nodded. She could think of nothing else to do. On the one hand, she was glad Leo had found Evelyn. That's what she'd ordered him to do, after all. On the other hand, she felt a wave of jealousy so severe, it nearly ripped her breath from her chest. A thousand terrible images flashed through her mind: Leo touching Evelyn, kissing her, saying her name instead of Tem's. It was revolting.

There was only one more thing she wanted to say to Leo—one thing that weighed heavily on her heart. Tem knew she shouldn't say it—had no right to say it. But she needed him to know it anyway. "I miss you."

Leo's eyes narrowed. There was no mistaking the desire in them—pure, animalistic craving that matched the craving in her. But pain flashed across his face, and Tem immediately regretted her words. She hadn't wanted to hurt him.

Leo opened his mouth, then closed it. Not for the first time, Tem wished she could read his mind the way she read Caspen's. Instead she could do nothing but wait—and pray. She was helpless, as she always was with Leo.

It seemed like an hour went by before he said, "That will pass."

Something inside Tem wilted. This was a version of Leo that she wasn't used to—a version that was distant and cold. She understood it. But she hated it.

Leo crossed his arms, cutting himself off from her. "So, shall we get on with it?"

"Get on with…?"

"The annulment."

So that was why she was here. Tem should have expected this, should have known that after Leo found Evelyn, the next logical step would be to marry her. But she couldn't bring herself to speak. So she simply nodded.

Leo cleared his throat and gestured at the door. "After you."

Every step toward him felt like it was taken underwater. Tem moved as if in slow motion, sensing every rise and fall of his chest—every twitch of his pulse. She could hear his heart rate speed up as she got closer, her basilisk side wide-awake and wanting. The moment she smelled his cologne, her nostrils flared, and she stopped. He smelled like summer—like a warm breeze over an open field. But there was another scent mixed with his. Sickly sweet, like vanilla. The whiskey turned in her stomach. It was *her*. Tem was sure of it.

She was still frozen in place.

Leo stared at her, his posture stiff and guarded. "Tem...?"

At the sound of her name, she looked up into his slate-gray eyes. He was so close. They were breathing the same air, their faces inches apart. Was she imagining it? Was he leaning in?

"Your Majesty? Are you ready?" Lord Chamberlain stood in the doorway.

Leo snapped immediately out of it, shaking his head as he turned toward his uncle. "Yes. We're ready."

Tem resented his use of the word *we*.

"The annulment must be administered by the former king, as he was the one who married you." Lord Chamberlain gestured with his hand. "If you will both follow me."

Tem's steps synched with Leo's as they descended the stairs to the dungeon.

She stared straight ahead, her eyes locked on the back of Lord Chamberlain's head, acutely aware of Leo beside her. His hand was almost brushing hers. Should she touch him? Better not. If she touched him, she wouldn't be able to stop.

By the time they reached the door to the dungeon, Tem was stiff with cold. It was freezing down here—far colder than she remembered. Everything in her wanted to shift closer to Leo, to drape herself against him and feel his warmth. It was a carnal need, one that took all her strength to resist. Lord Chamberlain was fiddling with the door; it appeared to be stuck. Tem tried desperately to concentrate on anything other than the heat emanating from Leo's body, but it was impossible. Her basilisk side clawed for dominance, forcing her to listen to her instincts. It was no use. She had to touch him.

Against all logic and will, Tem extended her hand toward Leo's. Her mind screamed at her to stop. But her body moved of its own accord, brushing just the tip of her pinkie finger against Leo's. The moment their skin touched, Leo froze. Electricity exploded across her skin. A barrage of memories flooded her mind so forcefully that she bit her lip to keep from crying out.

They were in his bed, naked, the night before their wedding.

"Be still."

She would be anything for him.

"Say it. Say you want my cock."

She would say anything for him.

"You were made for me."

Nothing could be more true.

Was Leo remembering it too? Was he seeing what Tem was seeing—the two of them together, the way they were supposed to be? Tem expected him to pull away, but he didn't. Instead, after a debilitating pause, his finger moved too. It trailed along the length of hers, brushing all the way up to her knuckle. Tem savored the vibration that coursed up her arm at the contact.

Something inside her called to him. Something predatory and instinctual and undeniably inhuman. Tem had to have him; she needed to kiss him and taste him and press her skin against his until she—

"After you," Lord Chamberlain said.

They both jumped at the same time, yanking their hands apart. The dungeon door was open, its gaping darkness beckoning.

Tem's heart was pounding so fast, she found it difficult to breathe. It was as if she'd just exchanged something vitally important with Leo—as if some element of his body had transferred itself to hers, and vice versa.

She didn't dare look at him. Instead she stared straight ahead as they entered the dungeon, stepping into the darkness together. It was just as she'd remembered it: dimly lit and brutally cold. But this time, it wasn't her father in the cell at the end of the row. It was Leo's.

Maximus was slumped against the stone wall, his blond hair tangled, his eyes closed. He looked nothing like the proud king she'd come to know during the courting contest, and Tem found she enjoyed the sight. He was right where he belonged, reaping the consequences of his actions in the place where he had caused others so much pain. Seeing him in the same cell her own father had once occupied was an incredible victory and one she knew she owed to Leo. Tem wondered how soon after the wedding he'd put his father here. She could only imagine how that must have felt for him.

"Father," Leo barked. "Wake up."

Maximus's eyes opened slowly. They traveled first over Leo before settling on Tem. He let out a low, humorless laugh that cut into her like a blade.

"Not who I expected," he said, his voice hoarse.

"We need you to witness our annulment," Leo continued as if he hadn't spoken.

Maximus laughed again. This time it descended into a tortured cough. "Pathetic," he said, his eyes locked on Leo's. "Even for you."

"Enough, Father."

Tem looked at Leo. It wasn't his usual sharp comeback—he sounded tired. She wanted to reach for him again.

Maximus shrugged, and it was then that Tem noticed he was manacled to the cell floor. It seemed a particularly cruel way to keep him—he couldn't stand, and his shoulders were permanently hunched. It was a personal touch; there was no need to restrain him within his own cell, and Tem knew Leo must have ordered him to be kept that way. She wasn't sure how to feel about this revelation. She knew Leo was capable of cruelty—all men were. But it wasn't his instinct, and it certainly wasn't his preference. Had his experience at the wedding hardened him? Was he no longer the twenty-year-old boy she knew?

There was no time to wonder about this. Lord Chamberlain produced a piece of paper from his jacket pocket, and in the dim light of the dungeon, Tem caught the words *dissolution of marriage*. She felt the sudden urge to fight back tears. *This* is what would unbind her from Leo? It seemed so stupid, so *worthless*. Tem stared at the piece of paper. It was so simple—nothing more than ink on a page. Signing this would do nothing to change the way she felt. It wouldn't soothe the fiery need that threatened to drown her whenever he came close. Nothing could soothe that—love demanded to be felt.

"Ladies first," Lord Chamberlain said as he brandished the paper at Tem.

Numbly, Tem took the quill and signed her name. She took specific care not to touch Leo's skin when she handed the paper to him. Then he signed his name too. Lord Chamberlain passed the paper and the quill through the bars, into Maximus's outstretched hands. He took his time signing it, first reading every word as if he were savoring the experience. Tem couldn't exactly blame him. Surely, this was the highlight of his day. When he was done signing, Lord Chamberlain retrieved the paper and tucked it away into his jacket. The moment it disappeared, Tem felt even colder.

They were just about to leave when Maximus said, "Well, Thelonius? Has it been hard?"

Leo stopped in his tracks. Tem stopped too.

"Has what been hard?" he whispered.

"Knowing the truth."

Leo's fists clenched at his sides. Tem looked from him to Maximus, wondering what was going on. She was missing something—clearly there had been a previous conversation between father and son.

Leo's answer was a single word: "Yes."

Then he turned on his heel and left.

The journey back up to ground level was silent. It wasn't until they were once more in the foyer and Lord Chamberlain had bowed away that Leo finally turned to face her.

"Tem," he said quietly.

She paused, her hand already on the front door. Was he going to address the way they'd touched earlier—the electricity that had passed between them? Or was it entirely one-sided?

Before she could spiral, Leo continued: "I wish for us to have dinners."

Tem blinked. "Dinners...plural?"

"Yes," Leo said, a shadow of a smile twitching his lips. "Dinners, plural."

"What sort of dinners?"

"Every Sunday night, you and Caspen will come to the castle and dine with me and Evelyn."

A chill ran down Tem's spine at the sound of her name. It was the first time she'd heard him say it. She wondered once again whether Evelyn was here, just upstairs, perhaps in Leo's bedroom. Her presence permeated the walls.

"But...*why*?"

Leo rolled his shoulders as if they pained him. "Because we need an avenue in which to discuss how our two kingdoms can coexist. I thought dinner might be pleasant."

Tem was still having trouble grasping the concept. Her *and* Caspen? *Here*? It was absurd. Dinner with Leo and Evelyn would be anything but pleasant. She couldn't imagine a worse way to spend a Sunday evening.

"Leo—" she began.

"We have to work together, Tem. Otherwise this will all fall apart."

She sighed. She knew he was right. They were attempting to break a centuries-old pattern of strife between their kingdoms. It was necessary work. But the thought of sitting so closely with him and Evelyn was abhorrent. She didn't want to see them together, didn't want to observe how Leo looked at her the way he used to look at Tem. That was a special kind of torture—one that not even Tem deserved. When she didn't answer, Leo leaned in.

"There will be excellent food," he said quietly. "And ample dessert."

The smallest of smiles broke her face. The memory of feeding him the chocolate soufflé in front of his father sprang immediately to mind. "In that case, we'll be there."

Pure joy flitted across his face, so quickly Tem almost missed it. A moment later, it disappeared, smoothed over by a careful mask of indifference.

Leo nodded. "Very well," he said. "I shall send a carriage."

Tem nodded too. It was all she could do.

There was a silence as they looked at each other, and Tem remembered all the conversations they'd had in this very foyer. The one after their first date: *"I'm not going to kiss you. Instead I'm going to picture everything I want to do to you without that dress on. And I'm going to pretend that someday you'll let me do it."*

The one where she'd asked for his trust before taking him down to the dungeon:

"You can't tell him I'm showing you this."

"I will not tell him. You have my word."

Tem would take either of those conversations over the one they were having now. She no longer wanted to be in this castle—it hurt her to stand here among all the gold. But there was one more thing she needed to ask him.

She held out the hand with her wedding ring. "Do you want this back?"

Leo's eyes flicked to her fingers—to the slim silver band that had belonged to his mother. Tem expected him to answer immediately, but he didn't. Instead, he stared at her raised hand, his jaw tight, his own hands behind his back. Then, he said simply, "No."

Then he turned and left her.

Tem stood in shock as Leo ascended the steps to where she knew his bedroom was. Was Evelyn waiting for him? She wanted to vomit at the thought. How different this interaction had been from her previous nights at the castle, during the competition to see who would be his bride. Back then, Leo had constantly pursued her, his sole goal to marry her. Now that marriage was annulled.

Tem looked down at the marble floors, staring blankly at the tiles laced with gold. The whole castle felt poisonous to her now, as if the walls themselves were trying to strangle her. She should leave. But somehow, standing here, she still felt close to Leo. She wished she could run up those stairs after him. It didn't matter that Evelyn was there—it didn't matter that there were a hundred reasons why she shouldn't. Tem wanted to fall into Leo's arms and never leave him again. But she couldn't do that.

She may have won the competition for Leo's hand in marriage, but she'd barely had any time as his wife. None at all, really. It would have been a good marriage, of that much she was sure. Leo would have taken care of her, ensured she never wanted for anything.

And yet.

A life in the castle with Leo would have been a life without Caspen. A life without the addictive rush of danger and lust that only a basilisk could provide. Tem remembered the heat from the dream the night before she went into the caves for the first time. Caspen's heat. She didn't know much, but she knew she would die without that heat. Tem had duties now—obligations and promises to people other than herself. She belonged to Caspen and her quiver and every single basilisk beneath the mountain. She was their queen. She would not let them down; she would not let it all fall apart. Even if it meant missing Leo—even if it meant feeling incomplete every day for the rest of her life. Her future was decided.

It was time to return to her husband.

CHAPTER TWO

••●❋●••

T HE RIDE BACK TO THE MOUNTAIN WAS LONG AND COLD, BUT TEM BARELY FELT IT. When she finally returned to their chambers, Caspen was in their bed. He sat up immediately when she entered. "How did it go?"

In reply, she kissed him.

She was desperate, somehow, as if she needed to prove to herself that what she had with Caspen was enough. And of course it was. It was as easy as breathing with him. His hands slipped to her waist, ripping off her robe before pulling her on top of him. But instead of setting her on his cock, his hands gripped her thighs, guiding her so she was straddling his face, his mouth between her legs.

Tem gasped as his tongue found her center.

They'd never done it like this before—him on his back, her thighs clamped over his shoulders, bracketing his jaw. His tongue was on her clitoris, teasing it before he gave it the gentle pressure of his teeth. Tem had no idea how Caspen didn't suffocate beneath her. Every time she tried to lift herself, he yanked her right back down, his fingers digging deep into her hips as he held her against him. His moans were guttural; he drew just as much pleasure from this as she did. Tem couldn't believe the ferocity with which he devoured her, as if he were tasting her for the very first time.

His head tilted back, coaxing her forward. Tem angled herself so there was no more space between them—nothing stopping the orgasm that bore down on her like an avalanche. Undeniable power surged through Tem as she rode his face the same way she rode his cock, knowing that as soon as she was done, she would ride that too. Her fingers threaded into his hair, holding him against her, seeking salvation.

Come for me, Tem. Come on my tongue.

Gone were the days when such a plea would have scared her. Now Tem knew there was nothing Caspen wanted more than to taste the part of her she never imagined could bring another person pleasure. Now she knew he needed that part of her just as she needed every part of him.

His hands squeezed her ass hard. Tem was losing her mind on top of him. The very last of her inhibitions abandoned her as she threw her head back in surrender, allowing him to take her where she so dearly needed to go. Caspen didn't relinquish his grip as her climax spread. Instead his fingers tightened on her ass, holding her against him as he drank down every last drop of her. When at last he pulled away, he trailed his tongue over her clitoris. Tem was so sensitive that she gasped, then leaned down to kiss him, tasting herself on his lips.

Now turn around.

Tem did so without question. Caspen moved behind her, centering himself between her legs and pushing them open with his thighs. Strong hands grasped her, lifting her hips and exposing her even further. Then he gave her is cock.

Caspen was less gentle than he used to be. And Tem liked it.

Every thrust was merciless, filling her completely. She was split open—a raw nerve. Smoke twisted in her hair, pulling it back and arching her neck. A hiss filled the cave as Tem cried out shamelessly, her moans an endless intonation of pleasure just for Caspen.

It was simple like this. It was right. Caspen took what he wanted from her and gave her what she wanted in return. There was no explanation, no rationalization. They were beyond words, and Tem had never been so happy to be speechless. The sound of his cock sliding in and out of her was the only thing she cared to listen to. The feel of his breath on her back was the only thing she cared to feel. She wanted only to *give* and *take* and be enraptured as she deserved.

Beautiful, Tem. So beautiful.

Tem barely heard him. The air was unbearably warm; sweat coated her chest.

Look what happens when you do as I say.

He showed her with every thrust. It was her reward—the prize she won for compliance. But she wouldn't let him take charge that easily. It was her turn now.

Tem pulled suddenly forward, sliding herself up his cock so he was barely inside her. She moved her hips tentatively, testing the distance. When she was nearly empty, she paused. Caspen gasped as she slid herself back down his cock, taking all of him in one go. Tem held still, snug at the base, before moving again.

Up. Down. Then back up again.

She went slowly—*so* slowly—to make sure he would see it. The visual would be incomparable for Caspen. Tem knew from his presence in her mind that he was captivated by this, watching every single inch of his cock disappear into her before coming back out again. She arched her back, accentuating the angle, working herself all the way up to the tip.

She stayed there—just on the head—using tightly controlled movements until she knew she was dripping all over him. With a strained groan, Caspen yanked her all the way down his cock and held her there.

Enough.

Tem smirked. She'd won their little exchange, and she knew it. If Caspen thought he was in control, he was wrong. Tem had always been able to push him to his limits, to force him to recognize her power. That would not change no matter how many orders he gave her.

For a moment, they were both still. The air was sweltering; smoke swirled along the edges of her vision. Caspen slid his palms slowly over her hips and up her back, squeezing the curve of her waist until he reached her breasts. Then he squeezed those too. His fingers twisted in her hair, pushing her into the mattress. His body pressed against her with immovable weight. Just when it became too much, he pulled them both upright so she was on his lap, her back against his chest. Tem turned her head to look into his black eyes. Scales were crawling steadily up his neck, turning his skin to armor. Then he began to thrust.

They were building toward it now, each of their bodies acting of their own accord. Tem moved her hips to match his rhythm, taking his cock as deep as she could while his fingers found her clitoris. The combination of sensations took her straight to the edge. But just before she came, Tem did something she'd never done before.

In her moment of climax, she shielded her mind from Caspen, closing herself off so they were no longer connected. Tem wasn't even sure why she did it—pure instinct, pure intuition. If Caspen noticed, he didn't say anything. Possibly because he was too busy having an orgasm.

As soon as he pulled out, she pulled him back in.

"Again," Tem said.

It was never enough.

She had him over and over until they were both soaked with sweat and out of breath. Tem had once thought that Caspen's sexual appetite was unmatched. But now hers was just as insatiable, if not more so. The thought of going a night without sex legitimately scared her.

You never have to go without sex, Tem.

He was still inside her.

What do you mean?

I mean you are free to sleep with other basilisks if that is what you wish.

She looked up at him. He pulled out slowly, trailing kisses down her throat as he did it.

Won't that bother you?

It will not.

At the incredulous look on her face, he laughed.

"I have told you before, Tem. You are mine. Whether you give your body to another does not change that."

"You say that now, but…"

"But what, Tem?"

She pictured Leo—his blond hair, his dexterous fingers. Caspen had only mentioned sleeping with other basilisks, and the specificity was not lost on her. "Do you really mean it?"

"Of course." He said it calmly, as if it were an irrefutable fact.

Tem nodded, although she couldn't fathom sleeping with anyone else—except for Leo. The moment she thought it, she glanced at Caspen to see if he had heard. Her mind was still shielded, but he continued: "You may find that your basilisk side demands it eventually."

That Tem could fathom. Basilisks lived in a permanent state of arousal, always being tempted and teased. Tem had had more sex in the past week than she'd had in her entire life, even during her training sessions in the cave. Caspen was always *right there*. Tem needed only to look at him and he would grow hard for her, needed only to take a step in his direction in order to mount him.

Caspen loved it. The spark of pride in his eyes was unmistakable every time Tem reached for him. She knew basilisks respected this—understood it and encouraged it. Basilisks belonged to each other in a way humans could never comprehend. Still, Tem couldn't believe how often they had sex. She woke up wanting it. She fell asleep still wanting it. She was completely feral, like a wild animal. Even Caspen could barely keep up with her. She was constantly, untenably, desperate for more.

Perhaps Caspen was right. Perhaps, given the right basilisk, Tem would be tempted. There were many things about her body that she no longer understood. Sometimes it felt as if someone else were controlling her. The hunger that burned within her was an unquenchable thirst. Tem would do anything to slake it.

"Is that what you want?" she asked. "To see me with someone else?"

A small smirk twisted his lips. "Only if that is what you want."

She sat up, looking him right in the eye. "But is it what *you* want?"

The smirk deepened. "I would not mind it."

"You wouldn't *mind it*?"

He laughed outright. "I am a basilisk, Tem."

It was all he said, but Tem understood. Caspen was not like the human boys she'd grown up with, the ones who were raised to enter into monogamous relationships with their wives. Caspen was something else entirely—wild and free, beholden to the customs of his people just as Tem was beholden to hers. The fact that he wanted her to sleep with other basilisks may be baffling to her, but it was far from baffling to him. For Caspen, it was the norm. For Tem, it was incomprehensible.

"How can it not matter to you?" she insisted. "How can you not be jealous?"

His fingers trailed gently down her stomach, raising goose bumps on her skin. "I would only be jealous if you slept with someone you loved."

Guilt prodded her. There *was* someone she loved. "*I* would be jealous if you slept with anyone else," she whispered.

Caspen smiled. "I know you would. And that is understandable, given that you are part human. But I told you, Tem, there is no one else I want."

He said the rest gently into her mind: *My body and my heart belong to you.*

She kissed him, and he kissed her back. When they drew apart, he said:

"I care only that you are loyal with your heart."

Tem stared at the silver ring on her finger. Caspen hadn't asked about it. Possibly it didn't matter to him—basilisks wore no rings, and their matching gold claw necklaces were evidence enough of their love. But it mattered to Tem. And she couldn't bear to remove it.

Tem leaned against his chest.

For a long moment, they simply lay there. Eventually, she asked: "What's your favorite thing about me?"

Caspen smiled, and she saw the barest trace of his fangs. "That is easy: your mouth."

She rolled her eyes. "Be serious."

He laughed. "I am always serious." He traced her bottom lip with his finger. "Your words are sharp." He looked her in the eye. "Your opinions even sharper."

Before Tem could roll her eyes again, he asked, "What is your favorite thing about me?"

She considered her answer, thinking of all the things she loved about Caspen. She also loved his mouth, although it certainly wasn't because of his opinions. She loved how sure he was: how steadfast and *solid*. But most of all she loved the way he loved her: unconditionally.

"Your devotion."

Caspen smiled. "It is easy," he whispered, "to worship you."

Then he kissed her. His tongue moved against hers, tracing the mouth he loved so much. When they were done kissing, they simply lay there, watching each other, until their eyes began to close. Eventually, Caspen's breathing slowed.

Tem watched the great plane of his chest rise and fall rhythmically as he slept. She had always drawn comfort from Caspen. He was her protector; he would never let harm befall her. He was perfect in every single way. But Leo had ensnared her in a way she hadn't expected, and Tem was having great difficulty shaking him.

She'd tried to do the right thing, tried to give him what he deserved. But in doing so, something had broken within her. A tiny piece of herself had walked off that stage right alongside Leo, and that piece had called to her ever since, no matter what she did to distract herself. It felt as real as a physical sensation, compressing her chest, making it difficult to breathe. Tem would never forget the way her mind exploded with sensation when her pinkie brushed against his. Was it an aftereffect of the crest? Tem knew nothing of such magic and, quite frankly, was too afraid to ask Caspen. She couldn't even bring herself to mention the Sunday-night dinners for fear of what he might say. But that was a problem for another time.

Besides, Tem was not the only one keeping secrets.

The night after the wedding, the basilisks that had been kept at the castle for bloodletting had returned to the caves. Tem didn't know whether Leo had freed them or if they had come of their own accord. The basilisks were all directed toward Adelaide.

"Why are they going to her?" Tem had asked.

"She is exceptional at healing," Caspen had explained. It was a shorter response than the ones he usually gave. He had been distracted, his eyes searching the weary line of basilisks as they staggered into the caves, their hands cradled against their chests.

"Are you expecting someone?" Tem had asked.

Caspen's gaze had flicked to hers, his expression returning immediately to neutral. "No."

Too late, Tem had realized she should have asked a different question. Had she asked *Are you hoping to see someone?* she might have gotten a different answer. Part of Tem wanted to follow up, to insist that Caspen tell her who he was searching for. But the other part feared what he might say. Could she really blame him for having a past when it was Tem's present that threatened to undo them? Her husband had lived a long life. He was the Serpent King, and he had earned that title. There was no point in holding his past against him. She hoped he would offer the same grace to her.

Eventually, Tem burrowed herself against Caspen and slept.

The next day they headed to breakfast together. Meals were held in the banquet hall, an enormous room where hundreds of basilisks gathered throughout the day. Basilisks ate at any time they pleased, whenever they were hungry. The lack of schedule was disorienting for Tem. Even their sleeping schedules were completely random—Tem only just now realized that Caspen had been catering to hers. If anything, basilisks tended to be nocturnal.

The food was different too. Basilisks primarily ate fish and wild game, which they caught while hunting in their true forms. Meals eaten under the mountain were similar to the dinners Caspen had served her during the training process—cured meats and cheeses, nuts and dried fruits, the occasional loaf of bread. Basilisks were partial to chocolate, she learned quickly.

"It is bitter," Caspen said. "But also sweet."

"You could describe a basilisk that way."

"Yes," he said. "You could."

At first, Tem had assumed that the banquet hall would be the one place where she wouldn't witness any sex. But she'd been utterly wrong. Not only did basilisks have sex at mealtimes, they incorporated anything and everything on the table within arm's reach. Chocolate was spread on and licked off various body parts. Utensils were used to stimulate all manner of erogenous zones. When it became too much, Tem simply closed her eyes.

We do not have to eat here, Caspen's voice came to her, amused. *It is not required.*

I'm fine.

You look as if you might faint.

I won't.

Your eyes are closed.

I'm just resting.

At the dining table?

Yes.

A rather odd place to rest, my love.

Maybe for you. For me, it's necessary.

It is all the same to us, Tem: eating and sex. There is no difference. Both are basic needs. Both must be met.

Do they have to be met right now?

We do not believe in delaying our gratification.

Tem thought back to last night, when she'd made Caspen wait for it.

You do.

She felt another wave of his amusement.

Only when it comes to you.

And why am I so special?

Because with you, the reward is worth the wait.

Tem opened her eyes just so she could roll them. But she was no coward; this was her life now, and she had better get used to it.

The woman beside her was pleasuring her partner. Tem watched them for a while, observing the way they both moaned in unison. Eventually, the woman mounted the man. But to Tem's surprise, she did not begin to ride him. Tem turned to Caspen.

What are they doing?

The woman was sitting on the man's lap. They were clearly *involved*, but her body was completely still. He didn't thrust, and she didn't move.

They are simply experiencing each other.

But what's the point?

Pleasure.

Of course. That was the point of everything here.

Caspen's voice came to her again: *Do you wish to try?*

Tem hesitated. She didn't know *why* she hesitated, but she did. They were surrounded by basilisks here. They were in public. Even though she'd been through the ritual, which was just as public as this, somehow that was different; even when the basilisks had lined up to touch her, they'd retreated right after. But here, they were seated on a bench with basilisks on either side of them. Tem couldn't imagine touching Caspen in such proximity to others. But larger than her doubt was her curiosity, and it was that, as always, that won out in the end.

She didn't need to say a word.

Caspen was already lifting her onto his lap, pushing her legs open so they rested on either side of his. Her back was against his chest, his cock already hard and ready for her. He eased Tem onto it slowly, working himself inside one inch at a time. When he was fully inserted, he squeezed her hips.

Now what?

Now you sit. And you do not move.

It was a curious thing to simply sit there. Tem was used to variance—to the incessant retreat and advance of Caspen's cock in her center. But this was an entirely different sensation. She wasn't used to holding his full length inside her for any extended period of time. Barely a minute had passed, and she already wanted more. Tem moved her hips instinctually, desperate to feel that addictive rhythm. She wanted to ride him, to slide up and down his cock and relieve herself of the gnawing wave of heat that was clawing its way up her back. The moment she tried, Caspen gripped her waist, holding her in place.

I said you do not move.

Tem squirmed. Moving was all she wanted to do. It was impossible just to sit here— she had no idea how the other woman was accomplishing it. How could she be expected not to grind on him, to move her hips and take them both to climax?

It is an exercise in restraint, Tem.

But Tem had never been good at restraint. Caspen was the one who had endless patience, and he was demonstrating it now. He held her still, his body unbearably warm, his chest pressed against her back. Tem didn't often consider the size difference between them, but now, perched on his lap, she felt just how *big* he was behind her. Caspen was carved from stone—his body hard and sturdy and immovable. The heat from his skin seeped directly into hers, and Tem felt a single bead of sweat form between her breasts.

Caspen trailed a finger up her stomach, brushing it through the drop and lifting it to his lips. Fire erupted in Tem. All she wanted to do was *move*—to apply friction, to feel his cock pump inside her. The thought of it alone made her even wetter than she already was. She could feel it dripping onto the bench beneath them.

Patience, Tem.

This is ridiculous. And a waste of time.

That is your opinion. I am rather enjoying myself.

Tem squirmed again, and this time Caspen's hand went to her throat. He held her face to his, pressing a kiss to her lips. His tongue teased hers. Still, Tem wanted to move. Still, Caspen held her in place.

I can't believe people do this.

Do what?

Just sit here. I'm so…

Needy?

She blushed. *Yes.*

I like when you are needy, Tem. It is one of your finer qualities.

Tem rolled her eyes. Caspen's fingers traced her jaw, then her neck. He brushed along her collarbones, touching one and then the other. Tem wasn't used to him being so reserved during sex. But were they having sex, really? Tem didn't know what to call what they were currently doing. She was just…sitting there. While he was inside her. It made her feel deeply connected to him, like they were joined at their most fundamental point, not two beings but one.

You feel so good, Caspen.

As do you.

You feel so good it almost feels…bad.

Caspen skimmed his palms up her body, cupping her breasts and squeezing. He rubbed her nipples between his fingers until they were hard, tender points. It was almost beyond what Tem could handle. He was molding and forming her body into whatever he wanted. His lips brushed her neck, and she felt his teeth nip her skin.

More, she begged.

No.

Please.

Good things come to those who wait.

His fingers resumed their slow, sensual teasing on her nipples. Tem strained against his touch, arching her back and pushing her breasts into his hands. At her desperation, Caspen's amusement only increased.

Sit still, Tem.

Tem did as she was told.

The moment she sat still, Caspen rewarded her with one single, hard thrust. Tem yelped at the sudden change, crying out in surprise and pleasure, aching immediately for more. But he didn't let her have it. Instead one hand moved from her breast to her clitoris, rubbing in a steady rhythm. Tem was lulled into a trance by the motion, content finally to let Caspen take control.

He didn't thrust into her again, but his other hand reached forward, dipping into a jar of honey on the table. Caspen swirled his fingers slowly through the honey before bringing them to Tem's lips. She opened her mouth, lapping the honey with her tongue, turning her head so he could see her doing it. When the honey was gone, Tem sucked gently on his fingers before taking them all the way down her throat until he said:

Kora.

If this was a game, Tem knew she could beat him at it.

She moved her hips an infinitesimal amount, shifting barely an inch at first. The great expanse of his chest was behind her, keeping her upright, preventing her from doing anything sudden. But Tem went slowly, teasing him just as he had teased her, arching her back in order to take him deeper. It was just like what they did last night, only this time they were not alone. Tem knew people were watching, knew everyone could see where she was sitting. A low thrum of approval vibrated over the table. It was one thing for basilisks to have sex in public—it was another to watch their king and queen do it. They were their leaders; they set the standard. It was an honor to do so and not one Tem took lightly. She knew they looked to her for guidance, that she held a position some thought she had not earned. She strove to be worthy of it now, with Caspen inside her, for everyone to see. Tem understood this was a way to prove herself, that those who doubted her ability to thrive would have no choice but to accept her if they saw how good she was at this.

Her body moved in earnest now. Tem grabbed the edge of the table, holding on for stability as she took herself there. Her palms were sweaty; she could barely keep her grip. Caspen's hands were on her hips, jerking her forward, his entire body rigid beneath hers. Her orgasm came like a lightning bolt, sudden and bright, taking the air from her lungs. Caspen came too, his teeth pressed against her neck. Tem was breathless. Caspen's chest rose and fell with hers, in sync even as their heart rates slowed. Caspen kissed her on the cheek.

You did well, my love.

Tem smiled. Then she kissed him back.

It wasn't until they left the banquet hall that Tem found she could think clearly again. When they passed through the courtyard, it was bustling with activity. Basilisks congregated around the fountain, arranging an elaborate tower of goblets.

"What's going on?" Tem asked Caspen.

"They are preparing."

"For what?"

"For mating season."

"*Mating season?*"

"Yes." Caspen smiled. "It is a time when anyone who is not partnered will seek a mate. It happens every winter."

Tem took a moment to process this. Basilisks were already amorous on a regular day—look what had just happened at breakfast. She couldn't imagine how they would act during a time when their sole purpose was to find a mate. "And what exactly does mating season entail?"

"There will be a series of events to celebrate."

"Such as?"

"They are rather difficult to explain."

Tem sighed. It didn't matter whether Caspen told her; she would find out soon enough. "When will the first event be?"

"Tomorrow."

So soon. Tem had barely begun to adjust to basilisk culture, and now there was an entire event to consider.

As if on cue, Caspen said: "You can always tell me when it becomes too much for you."

Tem frowned. She didn't like his wording—*when* instead of *if*, implying that it was only a matter of time before it became too much for her. The last thing she wanted was Caspen thinking she was incapable of adjusting to his world. "It's not too much. It's just a lot. There's a difference."

And there was so much more. Tem had barely begun to scratch the surface of basilisk culture. There were a thousand unanswered questions, and never enough time to ask them. "When will I learn how to petrify?"

To her surprise, Caspen frowned. "You will not learn to petrify."

"Why not?" Insecurity cut through her. "Don't you think I can do it?"

"Of course you can do it."

"Then why won't you teach me?"

They reached their chambers and sat on the bed.

When Caspen didn't answer, Tem insisted, "I want to learn."

He shook his head. "You will not learn from me."

"But *why*?"

"Tem." He looked her in the eye. "It is a terrible thing to take a life."

"But you do it all the time."

Darkness flashed over Caspen's face, and Tem knew immediately that she'd struck a nerve. He looked away. "I do it only when necessary," he said quietly.

She reached for him. "I didn't mean to offend you."

Caspen placed his hand over hers. "I am not offended. It is true that I have had more than my fair share of kills. But you must know I do not relish it. I regret most of them, and I do not want the same for you." He paused, staring into the fire before whispering, "I would not have you become a monster."

Tem's grip on him tightened. "You're not a monster."

A grim smile twisted his lips. "Perhaps not to you."

The fire crackled. Neither of them spoke.

Tem tried to see where he was coming from. She supposed it made sense that Caspen wouldn't want her to feel the same regret he did. He wanted her to retain this last strand of morality. But it was not his decision to make. And it didn't change the fact that she wanted to learn how to do it. It was a part of her that was still undiscovered—something all other basilisks knew how to do. Tem didn't want to be the last to know. Not again.

She waited an appropriate amount of time before asking, "Can't you teach me how to do it on an animal?"

Caspen shook his head. "Petrification is not effective on animals. They are our peers. It is only for—"

"Humans. Right. Of course." Tem sighed. She should have known that would be the case.

Caspen brushed a curl from her face. "I did not mean that as an insult, love."

Tem sighed again. "I'm just tired," she whispered. "One minute I'm doing just fine, and then the next…"

Caspen watched her patiently, his eyes softly holding hers.

"I just feel like I'm splitting in half," she finished quietly. "It's overwhelming."

He leaned in, pressing his lips gently to her cheek. "Of course it is overwhelming. You are going through something of great significance. Anyone would feel as you do."

Tem gave him a sad half smile.

"Perhaps you should visit your parents," he murmured.

Whenever life beneath the mountain became too much for Tem, Caspen insisted she visit her parents. Kronos and her mother lived on the outskirts of the village, in a small cottage with a beautiful backyard, without a chicken in sight. It was quiet there—specifically, it was quiet in her mind when she was there. Caspen always left Tem alone when she went there, as if he could sense she needed a full break from basilisk life. Her human side craved solitude after hearing all the voices in her head and feeling too many bodies around her. Tem was grateful to Caspen for insisting she have it.

"You're right," she said. "Perhaps I should."

—•◆◆◆•—

That afternoon, she found her mother in the garden tending to the vegetables and Kronos seated at the kitchen table.

"Temperance," he said, as she walked in, his face breaking into a slow smile. "What brings you here?"

Tem had only visited a few times, and she was still getting to know her father. He always spoke deliberately, his words flowing like a slow-moving river.

"I needed a break," she said simply.

He nodded knowingly. "Yes, I can only imagine."

Pride stiffened Tem's spine. "I *wanted* a break," she rephrased.

"Of course. There is no shame in wanting a break."

Shame was all she felt.

"The mountain can stifle even the strongest basilisk, Temperance. It has a mind of its own. I would never subject your mother to it."

Tem could understand that. A human probably wouldn't survive it.

"But don't you miss your people?"

Her father raised his shoulder. "Occasionally. But I spent many years alone. That is what I am used to now. Were I to return, I do not think it would ever feel the same."

Tem nodded. She could understand that. Still, it seemed like an inevitability that her father would miss his old life.

As if he'd read her mind, he said, "Daphne is my life now."

Tem looked out the window to the garden, where her mother was pulling weeds. She thought about her parents' union and how much it took for them to be together. "Would you have made her do the ritual?" she asked.

To her surprise, her father laughed.

"What's so funny?"

"I could not have made your mother do anything," he said. "Back then or now. You are just like her in that way."

Tem allowed herself to laugh too. It was a blessing to see herself in her mother and

26

an honor for her father to equate them that way. "You know what I mean," she insisted. "Did you want her to do it?"

Kronos sighed. "I wanted *her*. And if that meant she had to do the ritual, then yes. I would have requested it of her."

"Would she have done it?"

His mouth twitched. "I doubt it."

Tem wondered what it said about her that she had.

"The ritual is ancient," her father continued. "It is considered standard practice for any human who wishes to marry one of us. But your mother did not adhere to our traditions."

Tem couldn't blame her.

"Why did you do it?" Kronos asked quietly.

A beat passed. The birds twittered.

Tem thought back to her decision to participate in the ritual—how she'd decided to do it after seeing Leo mobbed onstage. She remembered the fear that clenched her heart at the sight of him throwing his hands up to protect himself from the advancing villagers, how scared she'd been until Maximus had pulled his son from the stage.

"I did it for Leo."

At the look of surprise on her father's face, she elaborated.

"Caspen had just broken the truce, and the villagers were revolting. I thought if I was accepted in basilisk society, I would have some power to keep Leo safe."

Another silence. Tem knew her father was processing her answer.

"Do you not find it odd?" he asked carefully.

"Find what odd?"

"That the man you did the ritual for was not the man you are now married to?"

Tem had never thought about it that way. She shrugged. "I would do anything for Leo."

"And for Caspenon?"

"For him too."

"Are you certain?"

His question stopped her cold.

Tem couldn't ignore what her father had just pointed out: that on a basic level, Caspen's request hadn't been enough of a reason for her to do the ritual. It had taken Leo's life being in danger for her to finally decide to do it. It wasn't something Tem had considered until now. The thought made her bristle. "Why would you ask me that?"

Kronos raised a gentle hand in surrender. "I am merely wondering."

But now, Tem's brain was turning. She wondered if perhaps that was the point of his question. It felt like he was warning her. "*Why* would you ask me that?" Tem said again, firmly this time.

A pause. Then: "The heart is a curious thing, Temperance," Kronos said carefully. "It cannot be reasoned with."

"What do you mean?"

"We cannot choose who we love. Our hearts choose for us."

"I love Caspen."

"I know you do. But you also love Leo."

Tem closed her eyes.

"Temperance. You must be careful. Basilisks are free with their bodies but not with their hearts. It is a dangerous thing to love two people. You need to prepare yourself."

Tem didn't want to hear how it was wrong to love two people. It was her reality, and it wasn't going to change anytime soon. They'd agreed to share her. Was that a lie? Had Caspen merely said that to get Leo to stop the bloodletting? Leo had seemed genuine in his promise, but was Caspen? Supposedly he couldn't lie, but he could certainly bend the truth to suit his needs. She'd seen him do it many times before.

A sliver of doubt pierced her chest.

Had Caspen *really* agreed to share her? They'd never had to contend with their arrangement since Tem had ordered Leo to find Evelyn. If she hadn't sent him away, the three of them would be in a very different circumstance right now.

"Tem?" Her father interrupted her thoughts. "What is it?"

"I don't know," she whispered.

"Talk to me, child."

There were a thousand things she could say. But for some reason, only one gnawed at her heart. "I think I made a mistake," she whispered.

She couldn't say any more. Not when she wasn't even able to face it herself.

Kronos placed a gentle hand on her shoulder. "It does not matter what you did wrong, Temperance. It is how you choose to fix it that defines who you are."

She'd tried to fix it by sending Leo away. That had been her solution, and it had been a terrible one. It was merely an attempt to avoid dealing with the real issue. Her love for Leo wasn't going away. She should have known it wouldn't fade even if *he* went away. Tem wanted to confide in her father, to tell him that it hurt to think about Evelyn with Leo, that resisting the draw of their bond was painful for her, if not downright impossible.

Her next words slipped out before she could stop them. "Do you think Leo still loves me?"

Kronos sighed. A moment later, his hand touched her chin. "How could he not? You are easy to love."

Caspen was the first person to make her feel as if that statement were true. *Caspen* was her first love. And yet she could not shake Leo. No matter what Tem did, no matter how many times she had sex in the caves, Leo was always there, in the back of her mind, calling to her.

"Sometimes it doesn't feel that way," Tem whispered.

Sympathy softened Kronos's face. "The ones who love you need no coercion to do so."

For some reason, tears threatened to fall. Her father leaned closer.

"Look around you, child. You are not alone."

Just then, her mother entered the kitchen. "Tem, are you staying for dinner?" she asked, her hands covered in dirt from the garden.

"No." Tem shook her head.

There was someone she needed to see.

CHAPTER THREE

⸻ ✳ ⸻

T HE HORSEMAN WAS NEARLY EMPTY, AND THAT WAS JUST FINE WITH TEM. GABRIEL was in their favorite booth, surrounded by empty beer glasses. The moment she saw him, a part of her relaxed.

"My *dearest* Tem." He pressed a kiss to her cheek as she slid into the booth. "How are you this fine evening?"

"Can't complain."

"I can. They're charging me for drinks again."

"They're supposed to do that."

"Not if you're cute. It should be a rule that you drink for free if you're cute."

Tem smiled. His good mood was contagious, lightening the darkness that was plaguing her heart. They hadn't discussed anything of substance since the wedding. Tem knew he was waiting until she was ready to talk about it, respecting her boundaries as only a best friend could. But they both knew Tem owed him an explanation. She'd rehearsed her speech a thousand times: how to explain that she was a Hybreed, how to tell him what she'd done to Leo, how to reveal the most vulnerable parts of her. She'd avoided it out of fear—or possibly shame. But her father's words ran through her mind, and Tem knew she did not need to weather this storm alone. Gabriel had always loved her, and he deserved to know the truth.

"Gabriel," she said quietly. "There's something I have to tell you."

He threw his arm around her. "Well, let's hear it, then."

Tem bit her lip. Was she really about to do this? If she was to confide in him—to reveal this deepest, most essential part of herself—it could change their relationship forever. But Tem would rather it change than continue living a lie.

She told Gabriel everything.

Every secret she had harbored for so long, every sin she had kept close. Everything that had happened over the past few weeks came spilling out of her in a torrent, landing at Gabriel's feet. He listened silently, his eyebrows slightly furrowed, his hand loosely curled around his beer glass. When Tem was finally done, night had fallen and the Horseman was beginning to fill. Gabriel looked her in the eye. He smiled.

"What's *that* for?" Tem asked in bewilderment. Rather than react with horror—or, at a bare minimum, shock—Gabriel was grinning widely at her. He was almost on the verge of laughter.

"I always knew you had it in you."

"Had *what* in me?"

"The gall."

"But aren't you…surprised?"

"No, dearest. I'm not surprised."

Tem stared at him blankly. "You're not surprised that I'm half-basilisk?"

"No."

"Or that I did the ritual?"

Gabriel's grin widened. "No. Although I'm a little jealous you got to fuck Caspen's father."

She smacked his arm. "Be serious, Gabriel."

"I *am*, Tem. I can only imagine the gene pool of that family."

That earned him another smack. Gabriel simply chuckled into his beer.

"Aren't you…" Words failed her. "Disgusted? Or at least…worried?"

"Disgusted?" Gabriel let out a deep, mirthful laugh. "Tem, dearest." He pulled her closer, pressing his lips to her cheek. "I was beginning to think that you were entirely boring. That would disgust me far more than what you just told me."

With one simple sentence, her soul unfurled. Of course Gabriel accepted her; of course Gabriel still loved her. There was nothing that could come between them—he was not so easily deterred. He required no coercion to love her.

"As for being worried," he continued. "Should I be?"

Tem bit her lip. "I don't know," she said honestly.

"Hmm." He considered her, his head tilted. "Something tells me you'll be fine."

"And why do you think that?"

"Because you are far more capable than you think you are. You always have been."

Tem considered this. She wasn't sure if it was a compliment or not.

"What *does* surprise me," Gabriel said quietly, his expression sobering, "is that you waited until now to tell me."

Tem sighed. She remembered the night not so long ago, in this very booth, when she'd been about to tell Gabriel everything. Then Leo had shown up, and things had taken an unexpected turn. Now she wished things had turned out differently. What would have happened if Tem had confided in her best friend that night? It would have made everything that came next so much easier. If she'd had someone to talk to, she wouldn't have had to face so many decisions on her own.

"I waited because I was afraid," she said honestly.

"Of what?"

"Of what you would think of me." Sometimes Tem didn't even know something was true until she spoke it out loud, and the moment she said it, she realized how deep that fear truly ran.

"Tem." Gabriel leaned in. "You're my best friend. Nothing could ever make me think any less of you."

Tears were imminent. "But I've done bad things, Gabriel. Really bad things."

"You did your best with the circumstances you were given." He clasped his warm hands over hers. "That's all anyone can hope to do."

Tem just shook her head. She didn't deserve his patience and understanding. Not after everything she'd kept from him. "I'm sorry," she whispered.

"I know."

For a moment, they simply looked at each other. Tem studied the face she knew so well, marveling at how beautiful Gabriel had become. The gangly awkwardness of childhood was long gone. He was a man now, and somehow she'd missed it.

There was one more thing she had to tell him. "Being friends with me is risky, Gabriel. I…don't want you to get hurt."

To her surprise, his mouth quirked into a smile. "How dangerous are we talking?"

She gave him a half-hearted shove. "I'm *serious*. You know basilisks can petrify humans."

"Pishposh."

"And they're constantly…"

Gabriel raised an eyebrow. "Constantly what, Tem?"

Tem blushed, remembering the banquet hall that very morning. "They're constantly having sex."

Gabriel's face lit up with glee. "*Are* they, now? *Do* tell me more."

"They do it all the time. It's how they gain power and how they determine who ranks highest in their society."

"Sounds like my kind of society."

"Shut *up*. It's…obscene. It's all they do."

"In that case"—his face brightened even more—"you should set me up with one."

"Absolutely not."

"Oh, come on, Tem. I could finally find someone who matches my stamina. Stable boys just aren't cutting it these days."

"This isn't a joke, Gabriel. My world isn't safe for humans. I don't want you anywhere near it."

Despite her warning, Gabriel was still smiling. "I think it's rather unfair that you get to attend sex parties all day while I waste away washing dishes in the castle. You should let me come to one."

"*That's* not happening."

"Tem, you've *got* to take me."

"To the *caves*?"

"Yes. Immediately, if possible."

"No, Gabriel."

"Why not? If there are snake sex parties happening, I take it as a personal insult that I'm not invited."

"There are no *snake sex parties*," she hissed.

"*Pah*." He flicked his fingers dismissively.

"Gabriel," Tem put her hands on his shoulders. "I'm not attending any sex parties, and you wouldn't be safe at them even if I were. I mean it. It's dangerous under the mountain. I would never put you in that position."

A sly smile curled his lips. "I've been in all sorts of positions, Tem. And I especially enjoyed the dangerous ones."

Tem rolled her eyes at that.

"*Fine*," he said finally, tapping the tip of her nose. "We'll put a pin in that for now. But promise me this: no more secrets between us." Gabriel looped his pinky finger around hers and kissed it. Tem did the same. "From now on, we tell each other everything."

Tem smiled. For once, it was a promise she wanted to keep. "No secrets," she agreed. "From now on."

It was nearly morning by the time they left the Horseman. Gabriel disappeared with a jaunty wave, crooning a church hymn as he rounded the corner to his cottage. On the way back to the caves, Tem thought about what her father had told her: how basilisks were free with their bodies but not with their hearts. Guilt clenched her stomach. Only Tem knew the truth—that her heart did not fully belong to Caspen. Her feelings for Leo would not go away. With time or otherwise. She couldn't do this forever. She couldn't lie.

She thought about what Gabriel had said as well, how he wasn't surprised that any of this had happened to her. How could that be true? Tem couldn't fathom a world in which anyone was unfazed by such news. But if nothing else, it spoke to Gabriel's perception of her. He thought she was worthy of the life she was now living. So perhaps she was.

When she reached their chambers, Caspen was by the fire. She crossed to him, touching his shoulder gently. It wasn't time to bare her entire heart to him. But confiding in Gabriel had given her the courage to at least broach the subject that was most urgent.

"Leo wants us to come to the castle every Sunday night for dinner."

The words were so quick, she almost wondered if he heard her. Tem closed her eyes as she said them, bracing for impact. A long pause followed.

"Why would he want us to do that?" Caspen sounded calm. But just barely.

"He wants us to try to get along. It will give us a chance to figure out how to run our kingdoms together."

Silence. Tem opened her eyes.

Caspen was staring purposefully into the fire, the flickering flames reflected in his pupils. "He is naive."

The words were sharp. Tem touched the tips of her fingers gently to Caspen's chin, pulling his face back to hers. "Maybe so. But he's also hopeful. And so am I."

His expression was unreadable. He seemed to be holding back.

Tem soldiered on anyway. "He abolished the bloodletting, Caspen. And he wants to include the basilisks in discussions moving forward. That's more than Maximus was willing to do."

Caspen held her eye contact for a long moment. He blinked, slow and reptilian. Then he said, "It is still not enough."

Tem knew it wasn't enough. At a minimum, reparations should be made for the pain the humans had caused the basilisks over the centuries. Dinners did nothing to fix the problem on a granular level. A weekly meal was the bare minimum Leo could offer them. But he was offering nonetheless.

"He's trying, Caspen," Tem whispered. She was keenly aware of the thoughts she was harboring in the back of her mind—of the wedding ring still on her finger.

Caspen's reply was short: "I will decide later."

Tem sighed. It wasn't the answer she'd hoped for. But there was no arguing with him when he took that tone; he was as immovable as the mountain itself. She had no other choice but to wait until he was ready.

"Come," Caspen said, cutting off any other thoughts. "It is time for mating season."

Tem had completely forgotten about the event today. She still had no idea what it was, and she was still too afraid to ask. But she followed Caspen out into the passageway, joining the stream of basilisks to the courtyard. By the time they arrived, the courtyard was already full. The large circular room was packed; it was the most basilisks Tem had ever seen in one place. The last time she'd seen such a crowd was during the ritual, and that had only been the Drakon quiver.

Tem was still getting used to the presence of so many nude bodies. Not to mention being constantly naked herself. More than once, she found herself instinctually reaching for her sleeves or her collar, only to remember there was nothing there.

She stayed by Caspen's side as they entered the crowd, dodging throngs of basilisks engaged in conversation and...other activities. The clamor of overlapping voices reminded her that basilisks lived in constant community. Even Tem's mind was no longer a refuge. There was no privacy here, no isolation. No matter where she turned, Caspen was in her head.

I do not have to be.

She smiled, knowing he had heard her. *I like having you in my head.*

That is nice to hear. But should you ever need solitude, you need only ask for it.

Caspen's voice was not the only one in Tem's head. Snippets of other basilisks' conversations flashed through her mind as they crossed the courtyard—arguments, declarations of love, words conveyed in the heat of pleasure. The latter occurred more times than Tem could count. She was just about to close her eyes to get a reprieve when suddenly, a male basilisk approached them.

He looked vaguely familiar, but before Tem had a chance to place him, he leaned in to kiss her. She yelped audibly, lurching backward in surprise. The basilisk halted immediately, looking questioningly up at Caspen.

"She is not used to our customs yet," he said. "She means no harm. Let her adjust."

The man bowed and walked away.

"What was *that* all about?" Tem asked, staring after him.

"There is no cause for alarm. He was merely greeting you."

"*Greeting* me?"

"A kiss on the lips is the proper way to greet the queen. It is a way to honor your position."

Tem frowned. "If that's the case, then why hasn't anyone else tried to kiss me?"

Caspen laughed. "It is only when a fellow member of the council wishes to address you directly. It is like a handshake to us."

Considering what happened at council meetings, Tem wasn't at all surprised that a kiss on the lips was on par with a handshake. Now the man's familiarity made sense. Tem had seen him before...when his head had been between her legs. The memory made her blush.

Thankfully no one else tried to kiss her as they continued their lap of the courtyard. Everywhere they went, people parted for them, sometimes bowing, other times simply staring. More than once, basilisks fell to their feet before them, having sex right in the middle of their path. It was becoming somewhat of an obstacle; every time it happened, they had to step around.

"What are they doing?" Tem asked after the third couple fucked in front of them.

"They are hoping you will join them."

"*What?* Why would they want that?"

"Because it would be an honor."

Tem looked up at him. "An honor?"

Caspen's hand, which had been resting on the small of her back, brushed up her spine. "You are the highest-ranking woman in our society. It is a revered position."

Tem wrinkled her nose. She hardly felt worthy of that position.

As usual, Caspen read her mind. "You survived the ritual, Tem. The king gave you his blessing, as did my quiver. You have earned your place. If you wish to join them, you are free to do so."

Tem couldn't believe that.

"You are the queen, my love. You are entitled to anyone you want, at any time."

Her eyebrows shot upward. *"Entitled?"*

"Yes."

"That's ridiculous."

Caspen let out a small sound of amusement. "You are reacting like a human."

"I *am* a human."

"You are *part* human, Tem. You must remember that basilisks do not share the same customs."

"What customs?"

Caspen's head tilted slightly to the side, as if considering what to say. Finally, he settled on "Consent."

Tem looked at him in disbelief. He let out a soft laugh.

"I know what you are thinking. And it is not what I am saying."

"Then what *are* you saying?"

"I am saying that it is normal for us to touch one another without asking permission first. Consent is assumed unless stated otherwise."

It was the exact opposite of how humans navigated sex. She knew basilisks were different—that their culture revolved around sex in a way she was still getting used to—but assumed consent was a foreign concept to her.

"So is everyone going to assume that I want to…"

"No." Caspen shook his head. "You are the queen. It is different for you. And for me."

"How so?"

"Our status means we are expected to initiate. We are allowed anyone we want, at any time. We need only make our desires known, and they will be fulfilled."

"But that's *unbelievable.*"

"Perhaps to you. But to us, it is natural, and it is the way things have always been done."

"Are you telling me your father just walked around and…slept with anyone he wanted?"

"Yes."

"And that was just…allowed?"

"Not only was it allowed, it was considered an honor to be chosen by him."

Tem crossed her arms. "And is that what you're going to do?"

Caspen smiled. "No. I am not."

"Are you sure?"

"I am very sure."

Tem frowned. While her human side didn't like the idea of Caspen sleeping with anyone else, the last thing she wanted was to prevent him from participating in his own culture. If she stood in the way of such customs, she ran the risk of him resenting her.

Caspen took her hand in his. "I have told you before, Tem. There is no one else I want."

She shook her head. "You say that now, but you might want someone else eventually. I don't think I can—"

He pressed his lips to hers. *I will not want anyone else. Now or eventually.*

The words were exactly what Tem needed to hear. But they were hard to believe, especially after what he'd just told her about how basilisks viewed sex.

If you don't want anyone else, why wouldn't you expect the same from me?

The kiss deepened. *Because you are new to my world, Tem. I wish for you to experience all that is available to you.*

But if you—

I have already experienced everything there is to experience, Tem. No one else compares to you.

You've experienced…everything?

A smile tilted his lips. *Everything.*

Tem pictured Caspen with a man. It turned her on. Caspen smiled, and Tem wondered why the thought of Caspen with a man turned her on yet the thought of him with a woman was terrifying. In her heart, she knew it was because she was afraid he would compare her to another woman. But he himself had told her that no one else compared. Perhaps it was time she started believing him.

They continued their walk.

Most of the basilisks mingled joyfully in the middle of the courtyard, but several stayed along the perimeter, their arms crossed, clearly displeased. One group of men stared at Tem with such vitriol that she recoiled, pressing herself against Caspen.

"Who are they?" she whispered.

Caspen followed her gaze. His jaw tightened. "They are Senecas."

"Why are they looking at me like that?"

"Because you are married to a Drakon."

Tem understood how her father's quiver—*her* quiver—might disapprove of her marriage. Surely, they expected her to marry a Seneca. Still, some solidarity would have been nice. Tem already felt out of place here; it was difficult to face rejection from her own quiver.

"Many of the Senecas chose to leave with Rowe," Caspen continued. "Those that remained are still wary of our union."

"Where did they go?"

"The sea," he said. "Basilisks originated there."

Something fell suddenly into place. *You smell like the sea.*

Caspen told her that long ago. Tem had thought nothing of it, never considered that it might have any sort of significance. Was that why she was so drawn to the salt spray on her mother's dresser? Had it reminded her of her true home—not the cottage where she was raised but where her family originated? And how did her mother acquire the salt spray? Had she been to the place where basilisks originated? Tem wanted dearly to explore that train of thought, but they'd reached the center of the courtyard, and something else distracted her. An enormous tiered fountain stood before them, made of off-white marble. Snow-white liquid spouted from the top before cascading down the tiers in shimmering waves. Even from here, Tem could sense the richness of the substance as it poured from the fountain. It looked like white gold.

"What's *that*?" she asked.

Before Caspen could answer, a man approached the fountain. He was fully erect and—Tem realized with a jolt—touching himself. She watched in shock as he leaned over the edge, still stroking his cock. He finished a moment later with an anguished groan, releasing his cum into the base of the fountain. It joined the rest of the liquid in a great swirling pool.

"Oh," she said simply.

Caspen laughed. "It is an elixir made from our essence."

Tem's eyes fell to the tower of goblets stacked next to the fountain. The man who had just ejaculated in the fountain reached for one before holding it under the highest tier. He filled it to the brim before downing the entire thing in one gulp. Tem was too shocked to react—too shocked to even blink. The man filled the goblet again before turning and disappearing into the crowd.

"The fountain itself serves a purpose," Caspen continued as if nothing remotely out of the ordinary had just happened. "It transforms our essence into an intoxicating substance."

"Intoxicating?"

"Yes."

Tem frowned, trying to understand. "So…you drink it to get *drunk*?"

By now they had reached the fountain, and Caspen lifted a goblet from the tower beside it. "Yes, Tem. We drink it to get drunk."

"But…" She tried to find the words to express her astonishment, but there were none. She settled on "I swallow yours all the time and I've never gotten drunk."

A possessive smile split Caspen's face. "That is different. What you swallow is my essence in its rawest, purest form. This"—he dipped the goblet into the flowing stream, filling it—"has been transformed by the fountain."

Tem realized that for all the times she'd drank wine with Caspen, she'd never seen him get drunk—the alcohol didn't affect him the way it affected humans. It made sense, Tem supposed, that basilisks needed such a substance to get drunk. They drew their power from sex, after all. A direct infusion of cum in its purest form was probably the only thing strong enough to do the trick.

Caspen raised the goblet to his lips and drank.

Tem watched as his pupils widened and smoke curled over his shoulders. She thought about the bloodletting—how through alchemy, basilisk blood became something else entirely. Was this magical fountain really so different from the magic Caspen had used to create the claw? Merely a process, nothing more. A transformation.

"I want to try it," Tem said.

Caspen's eyes slid to hers. He hesitated.

"It is strong. You do not have the tolerance for it yet. Even I must pace myself."

But Tem would not be so easily dissuaded. Clearly this was an essential part of basilisk culture, and she was trying to assimilate. She was never going to fit in unless she did the things all other basilisks did.

"I want to try it," she repeated.

To her surprise, Caspen smiled. "So stubborn."

In response, Tem held out her hand. Caspen handed her the goblet, and she raised it to her lips. The elixir had no smell whatsoever. A single mouthful lingered in the bottom of the goblet, and without a moment's hesitation, Tem tilted it back and poured it down her throat.

"Tem?" Caspen said. "How do you feel?"

Tem could barely hear him; it was as if he were talking to her through a wall. For all the times she'd gotten drunk at the Horseman with Gabriel, this was ten times stronger.

Her head spun, her vision blurred. She was already warm, but the elixir made her *hot*—her cheeks flushed immediately as her center ached. Without touching herself, she knew she was wet.

"Caspen," Tem gasped, her hand darting out to touch him. He stepped closer.

"What is it?"

"Now."

A heartbeat passed. Then he was inside her.

The moment Caspen slid his cock between her legs, Tem felt peace. It was truly that simple between them—it always had been. Nothing was better than this; nothing brought her more clarity. Caspen sat on the edge of the fountain, holding her on top of him. Basilisks were watching, but Tem ignored them. The only thing that mattered was enjoying this moment with Caspen. She gave him her full attention, expecting the same in return. Tem moved her hips, grinding on his cock at exactly the pace she needed. Her wetness was spreading; it was all over their legs. Caspen slid his fingers up her thighs, pressing them against her clitoris. Tem moaned as he did it.

The elixir was unlike any alcohol she'd ever drank; there was no comparison whatsoever. She was stimulated and sensual and *free*, as if all her inhibitions had been removed at the exact same time.

Caspen. Look at me.

She wanted him to pay attention—to crave her so deeply, he could think of nothing else. He looked at her, his eyes endless black pools.

Tem.

He was completely entranced; she was all he could smell, all he could feel. Tem reached behind him, extending her fingers so they dipped into the waterfall of elixir. The liquid was warm; she knew instinctively that it was the exact same temperature as her body. When she pulled her fingers away, they were dripping. Her other hand wrapped around Caspen's neck, pulling his face up to hers. Tem brushed her fingertips over his mouth, spreading the elixir onto his lips. Caspen's eyes were wide, focused on nothing else but her. He ran his tongue over her fingers, tasting the essence of his people.

Tem kissed him so she could taste it too.

Their tongues slid against one another, matching the pace she set with her hips. Tem drove herself down on his cock as quickly as she could, desperate to get what she knew she could take from him.

Deadly little viper.

Tem was *very* close now.

She rode him faster, to the point of panic. Caspen's hands were all over her—gripping her skin and tangling in her hair. All she wanted was more: more touch, more words, more Caspen. There could never be enough of him—not in this lifetime or the next.

You have me, Tem. You—

Tem squeezed his neck. Without another word, he came.

She came too, throwing her head back in ecstasy, soaking up everything Caspen's body had to offer her. By the time he lifted her off his cock, Tem was breathless. Wetness ran down her legs, and she didn't bother cleaning it up. It was all the same here, and she knew before the evening was over, she'd probably have sex again. There was no point in removing the evidence of her last congress when the next one was right around the corner.

They stood together, still dripping with each other's sweat.

"Impressive," a voice said. "But rather swift. Are you losing your stamina, Caspenon?"

Tem turned to see a man approaching them. He was nearly as tall as Caspen and just as imposing. Beside her, Caspen shifted so he was between them.

"Tem," he said. "My brother. Apollo."

CHAPTER FOUR

⋯⋅✳⋅⋯

TEM SAW THE RESEMBLANCE NOW—APOLLO HAD THE SAME DARK HAIR, THE SAME strong jaw. He looked even more like Bastian than Caspen did. He had his father's cock: impossibly thick at the base. Tem flushed at the sight.

"Nice to meet you," she said.

Apollo took her hand in his, raising it to his lips and kissing the back of her wrist. He lingered for far too long, murmuring his next words against her skin. "The pleasure is entirely mine, Temperance." His voice was smooth, like caramel. He dropped her hand, glancing at Caspen. "She is beautiful," he said. "You did well."

"Her beauty is none of my doing."

Tem blinked. She knew that tone—it was the same one he used with Leo.

Apollo's handsome face slid into a cunning smile. "Of course," he said easily, turning back to Tem. "I meant no offense. Your beauty is your own. And what beauty it is."

Tem nodded because she didn't know what else to do.

Silence fell, and none of them broke it. Instead, Tem watched as Caspen and Apollo stared at each other, clearly having a conversation in their minds. She tried to hear what they were saying but couldn't. Caspen was blocking her. That wouldn't do at all. Tem said the first thing that popped into her mind:

"Do you seek a mate?"

The brothers finally broke eye contact, both turning to look at her.

"Why would I do that?" Apollo asked back.

"Caspen told me that's what mating season is for."

A slow, sultry smile slid over Apollo's lips. "I do not seek a mate."

"Why not?"

"I do not desire one."

"Then what do you desire?"

Somehow, the question felt significant. Tem had meant in general, but something about the way Apollo's smile deepened made her feel like she'd asked something else entirely.

"Pleasure," he said simply.

Another silence. Beside her, Caspen shifted but didn't say anything. She got the impression he was watching their interaction to see how it would pan out. Tem wasn't sure what he expected. Apollo made her feel...precarious. As if at any moment, she might tumble.

"If you don't want a mate, then why are you here?"

"I am here because mating season is an opportunity to experience everything my people have to offer. Surely Caspenon told you that."

Tem could read between the lines: Apollo was saying he was here to have as much sex as possible. "That seems wrong."

Apollo raised an eyebrow. "How so?"

"What if someone develops feelings for you?"

He tilted his head. "Then I will let them down easy."

"What if *you* develop feelings for someone?"

To her surprise, Caspen laughed. She looked up at him in bewilderment. "What's so funny?"

"My brother is incapable of developing feelings. He is only capable of deceit. He manipulates, and he lies."

"I thought basilisks couldn't lie."

Caspen's lip curled into a sneer. "My brother finds a way."

There was such vitriol in his words that Tem nearly recoiled. Clearly there was a history here, one she did not understand. And if she knew Caspen, he was never going to tell her.

"Lies are deception," Apollo said smoothly. "And I think you will find I am always truthful." His gaze slid to Caspen's. "Some might say to a fault."

Tem had no idea what to make of that. The conversation had quickly gotten beyond her, and she was quite ready for it to be over. Before she could express this, Apollo gave her one last lingering look before turning and leaving without saying goodbye. Tem glanced up at Caspen, who was staring after his brother with his eyebrows furrowed.

"What was that about?"

"I do not know what you mean."

"I *mean*, what's with you two? Are you...on good terms?"

Caspen rolled his shoulders. "We are not on bad terms."

"That's not what I asked."

"We are not on bad terms," Caspen said again, harsher this time.

Tem gave him a look. She didn't believe that for a second. Another question was on the tip of her tongue: "Was he flirting with me?"

Caspen sighed. In that sigh Tem heard the burden of brotherhood and the weight of their past together. "He was."

"He shouldn't be doing that."

"He has every right to flirt with you, Tem."

"Well. I'm not going to flirt back."

Caspen finally looked at her. "I cannot stand in your way if you did."

Tem frowned. "Seriously?"

He nodded. "Yes. My brother has first rights to you."

"And what are those, exactly?"

"They are an ancient basilisk custom."

Tem rolled her eyes. The last thing she needed was another ancient basilisk custom. "But what does that *mean*?"

"It means if I were to die, Apollo would be given the option to court you first, before anyone else. He would be expected to marry you in my stead."

Tem blinked in disbelief. "That seems like it shouldn't be allowed."

Caspen gave her a small smile.

"Everything is allowed here, Tem."

It was then that Tem remembered the ritual. Did she really expect siblings to respect one another's relationships when she had slept with Caspen's father to prove her worth to his quiver?

"I would never marry your brother."

"That is your choice. But you should know he will expect you to sleep with him."

"*Why?*"

Caspen's lips twitched into a smile. "To ensure your compatibility in the event that I die and he has to exercise his first rights."

"Well. You're not allowed to die."

The smile widened. "I shall endeavor not to."

"And I won't be sleeping with your brother."

"It is not mandatory, Tem. I am simply telling you that he will expect it."

"He can expect nothing from me."

The smile widened. "That is your choice," he said again. Then he kissed her on the forehead. "But he will pursue you unless you tell him not to."

Tem shook her head. "Can't you just tell him for me?"

"It would have to come from you. That is the only way he will respect it. Otherwise he will think I am trying to keep you from him."

"But you *are* trying to keep me from him."

"No." Caspen shook his head. "I am not. You say you do not want him now, but you may change your mind in the future. And if you do, I cannot stand in your way."

Tem turned his words over in her mind. She knew that Caspen liked it when she adhered to basilisk traditions. But she was having a very difficult time wrapping her head around how it could possibly make no difference to Caspen were she to sleep with his brother. The concept of first rights was completely foreign to her. It was almost as if siblings were considered interchangeable.

"Tem," Caspen said gently. "Do not let this overwhelm you. You have many things to learn."

His words only made her feel worse. Because he was right. There was *so* much to learn—so much that Tem was bound to get wrong. She lived in a constant state of terror, afraid that she was going to offend someone or insult Caspen by refusing to do something. It was like learning an entirely new language in just a few days. Her brain hurt from trying to process so much information, and she was tired of feeling out of step in her own body.

Do you wish to return to our chambers?

Tem looked up at Caspen, who was looking down at her with his brow furrowed. He was worried about her. He wanted her to adjust, and she wasn't adjusting quickly enough. Even Caspen, with his seemingly endless patience, would surely grow weary of playing teacher.

I do not mind teaching you, Tem. It is not a burden to me.

Of course he would say that. But even if it was, he wouldn't tell her. And Tem would always wonder whether he would secretly tire of her. There were a thousand things to remember and no hope of remembering them all. Tem was overwhelmed, and she was tired. But she was also determined.

"Do you wish to return?" he asked again, this time murmuring the words against her cheek.

"No," she said firmly. "I want to stay."

She recognized the flash of pride in his eyes. "Good."

They kissed. This, at least, she did not need to be taught.

"Caspenon," a voice bloomed beside them. "Aren't you going to introduce me to your wife? Or is that honor reserved only for Apollo?"

They pulled apart to see a man watching them. Unlike most of the other male basilisks Tem had seen, who were built like warriors, this one was slim and wiry. He was also tall, his height only accentuating his thinness, as if he had been stretched.

"Tem," Caspen said. "My youngest brother, Damon."

Tem raised her eyebrows. She couldn't believe she was meeting so many members of Caspen's family tonight.

"Oh," she said. "Nice to meet you."

Damon took her hand and kissed it. Unlike Apollo, his lips didn't linger.

"Nice indeed." He tilted his head at Caspen. "She is beautiful."

Tem almost laughed. Did these brothers know any other compliments? "You're beautiful too," she said without thinking.

Damon raised his eyebrows in delight. "Am I? How kind of you to say."

It was true; Damon was stunning. Tem decided right then that she liked him. She could tell this interaction pleased Caspen too; he was almost smiling.

"Has my brother given you any trouble tonight?" Damon asked.

Tem looked up at Caspen. "No. Not yet."

"I do not mean Caspenon," Damon said with a wink. "I mean the one who is likely to give you trouble."

Clearly Apollo's reputation preceded him.

"No," she said again. "I can handle him."

"Can you, now?" Damon clapped Caspen on the shoulder. "You picked a strong one."

Caspen looked down at Tem, his eyes full of pride. "I did indeed."

With that, Damon swept away. He was the second basilisk to leave without saying goodbye. Apparently farewells were not part of their ancient customs.

As soon as he was gone, Caspen pressed his lips once more to Tem's. The kiss was just beginning to deepen when Caspen pulled suddenly away, glancing over his shoulder as if he had heard something. Several male basilisks were gathered in a group, staring in their direction, clearly discussing something.

"Caspen? What is it?"

He was still looking at them when he answered, "Dissent." Before Tem could ask what he meant by that, Caspen turned back to her and said, "I must address this. It will not take long. Can you manage on your own?"

Anxiety closed Tem's throat. She was all alone here; Caspen was her only lifeline. But she couldn't cling to him forever. There was no future for her under the mountain unless she could manage on her own. So she said, "Yes."

Caspen pressed a quick kiss to her forehead before turning and heading for the group of men.

Tem scanned the room, prepared to find someone—anyone—to talk to. Not even five seconds passed before someone appeared in front of her.

"Temperance," the woman said.

"Hello," said Tem because she didn't know what else to say.

The woman sneered. "*Hello*? Is that all you have to say to me?"

So they were skipping the small talk. Lovely. "What else am I supposed to say to you?"

"You could start by apologizing."

"For what?"

"For being here."

Tem crossed her arms. "I have just as much of a right to be here as anyone else."

"Do not make the mistake of thinking you are special," the woman snapped. "Caspenon has had every woman under the mountain, including me."

A blush rose on Tem's cheeks. Her first instinct was to be embarrassed or even angry. But she'd already known that Caspen had slept with nearly everyone in this room. If this woman thought that information would hurt her, she was wrong. A part of Tem actually reveled in it. Caspen had been with everyone and he still chose her. It was an honor—an accolade to add to Tem's list of accomplishments. She took pride in her status, and she would not be talked down to by this woman or anyone else.

"None of those women mattered to him," Tem said. "Including you."

"You should abdicate," the woman hissed.

"Abdicate?" It was a ludicrous idea. Tem was insulted she'd even suggested it. It was true she was new to the throne and new to basilisk culture. But she had earned her place. Caspen had said so himself. "The day I abdicate is the day I die."

The woman leaned in. "Then let us hope you are not destined for a long life."

"Enough, Evangeline."

The voice belonged to Adelaide. She emerged from the crowd with her arms crossed, looking as perfect as ever. Sharp fury flashed over the woman's face before being replaced quickly by disbelief.

"Have you lost your mind, Sister?"

The moment she said it, Tem realized how unnervingly similar the two women looked. They had the same regal shoulders, the same flawless hair. It was a wonder she hadn't noticed it before.

"Temperance is here, and she is our queen," Adelaide continued. "We owe her our allegiance."

Evangeline scoffed. "You are the rightful queen. We owe her *nothing*."

"Enough," Adelaide said again. This time Evangeline simply turned on her heel and disappeared. Adelaide looked at Tem, her expression sympathetic. "My sister is angry. I apologize for her actions."

"It's fine."

"Temperance." She touched her shoulder gently. "I mean it. I am sorry."

Tem was struck by her sincerity and also by the physical contact. Adelaide knew better than anyone what it meant to be with Caspen. She'd been engaged to him before Tem, after all. Her apology meant a lot, even if Tem wasn't in the space to hear it.

47

"Thanks," she said quietly.

Adelaide dropped her hand. "You may find she is not the only one with opinions about your queenship."

Tem glanced at the group of men, some of whom were still looking at her. "What about them?" she asked. "What do they think of me?"

Adelaide followed her gaze. "They would not have any woman in charge."

Something occurred to Tem, and she asked it before she lost her nerve: "Have there ever been two queens?"

"Yes."

"And two kings?"

"Yes, although not as often."

"Why not?"

Adelaide gave her a small smile. "Men do not share."

Tem almost smiled too. That was certainly true. Women were raised to share their time, their attention, their love. Men kept everything for themselves.

"Are you enjoying yourself tonight?" Adelaide asked presently.

What a question. This night was already bizarre and it had barely begun. Tem had no idea whether any part of it had been remotely enjoyable. "It's…a lot."

"A lot?"

Tem shrugged. "So much happens here. I feel like I can't keep up."

"You will adjust," Adelaide said. "It may take time."

The same thing Caspen had said to her. But was it true? "Is every night like this?" Tem gestured out over the courtyard at the piles of copulating bodies.

Adelaide smiled. "Not quite. This is mating season. Everyone is especially…ferocious right now. You chose a particularly volatile time to join our society."

Tem sighed. She hadn't chosen the timing at all. "So they're not usually like this?"

"No," Adelaide said. "They are not."

That made her feel slightly better. Adelaide shifted closer.

"Temperance," she said quietly. "I can imagine that your time here has not been simple."

Tem snorted. That was putting it lightly.

"Should you ever need guidance…or a friend…I am available."

Tem raised her eyebrows. A friend? Adelaide was the last person she thought would offer something of that sort. Friendship wasn't something Tem had expected to find in basilisk society and certainly not from Adelaide. But who better, really, to understand what she was going through? Adelaide was once engaged to Caspen. Adelaide was a Seneca, and she deeply understood her quiver's plight. There were stranger things, certainly, than a friendship with her. Tem was smart enough to recognize when she was being offered an olive branch and was brave enough to take it. She'd considered Adelaide an enemy at first. But perhaps that wasn't true at all. Perhaps they were allies.

"Thank you," Tem said, suddenly self-conscious. It was difficult for her to accept help, especially from someone like Adelaide. But she found she was deeply grateful for it. Basilisks did not often extend graces. If Adelaide was choosing to be kind, Tem was glad to receive it.

"Of course," Adelaide said.

A silence followed, but it wasn't uncomfortable. Instead, the two women stood together, watching the revelry taking place. Nearly everyone was having sex. Mostly in pairs, but sometimes in groups. For the first time, Tem saw a full range of basilisks, particularly older ones. Tem realized she had never seen a baby basilisk and had no idea how they were born.

"Are there any children here?" Tem asked.

Adelaide smiled. "There are not."

"Why not?"

"We do not raise them here. It is unsuitable for the young."

Tem stared at the writhing naked bodies before her. Unsuitable indeed. "Then where do you raise them?"

"Out in nature. They are born as basilisks and transition into humans when they come of age. Once they are able to assimilate, it is safe to bring them near the villagers without worry they will lose control and violate the truce."

This was fascinating to Tem and answered most of her questions. But she found she had one more: "When do basilisks come of age?"

"One hundred."

Tem blinked. She'd always known Caspen was ancient, but she hadn't realized that a century was the *starting point*. Surely, he was far beyond childhood by now. Her eyes slid to Adelaide, who was watching her with a smile, as if she could already predict her next question.

"How old is Caspen?"

"Perhaps you might ask him that."

"Perhaps I might not," Tem muttered.

"We are not shy about our age, Temperance," she laughed, touching her shoulder again softly. "But I know Caspenon, and he would want to tell you himself."

Tem sighed. It was hard to wrap her head around the fact that everyone here was over one hundred years old. They all looked so…youthful. Even the basilisks who were clearly older—who had hardened faces and traces of gray at their temples—were beautiful. Humans wilted as they aged. Basilisks seemed to do the opposite.

They watched the crowd some more. Every once in a while, someone walked over to release themselves into the fountain. Tem spotted Apollo, entangled in a web of women. The moment he made eye contact, she blushed and looked away.

"Do you know Apollo?" Tem asked. "Caspen's brother?"

Adelaide shifted, glancing down at her. "Of course. Why do you ask?"

"Caspen said he'll try to sleep with me."

The basilisk smiled elegantly. "That is likely true."

"Well. I don't want that."

Adelaide's smile only widened. "It is not such a bad thing, Temperance," she murmured. "To have two men fall at your feet."

Tem had no idea what to say to that, so she said nothing. Eventually, the silence lingered, and Tem felt the need to break it. "Do you have anyone falling at your feet?"

Adelaide gave her a devious look. "Always."

Tem perked up immediately. If Adelaide had been engaged to Caspen, the son of the king, who was a suitable match after someone of such high ranking? "Who?"

Adelaide leaned in. "Can you keep a secret?"

Tem raised her eyebrows. "Yes."

She leaned even closer, and Tem felt the thrill that only gossip could bring forth.

"Cypress has been in my bed the past seven nights."

Adelaide pointed across the room. Tem followed her gaze to see Caspen's sister. They had the same dark hair, the same regal stature. She was a stunning woman and a fitting complement to Adelaide. Tem could imagine they looked beautiful together.

"Why is that a secret? I thought everything was allowed here."

Adelaide shrugged, straightening. "Men are curious creatures, Temperance. They are petty, and they are stupid."

Tem snorted.

"It is true, is it not?"

"It's completely true."

Adelaide laughed too, far more elegantly than Tem. "Caspenon is protective of his sister, as he should be."

Tem frowned. "Sister? I thought he had two."

"Agnes is dead."

Adelaide said it so bluntly that Tem had no idea how to respond. It didn't feel like the right moment to press the topic, so she didn't. Instead, she waited until Adelaide spoke again:

"Besides, he does not fully trust me."

Tem looked up at her. "Why not? He was going to marry you."

Adelaide shrugged. "A marriage does not guarantee trust. I am a Seneca. He is a Drakon. We are on opposing sides. He was right to be wary."

Tem was a Seneca too. Did Caspen trust her? "Can…I trust you?" Tem whispered.

Adelaide looked at her. "Yes," she said. "You can."

For some reason, Tem believed her. Another question occurred to her—one she was almost too afraid to ask. But she asked it anyway. "Are you…angry with me? For… taking Caspen?" Tem wanted to finish her sentence with *from you* but decided against it.

To her surprise, Adelaide smiled. "It is not possible to take someone who wishes to stay."

It was a typical basilisk answer—more riddle than response. "But are you angry?" Tem repeated. She needed to know.

Adelaide turned to her, placing a gentle hand on her shoulder. "I am not angry, Temperance. Caspenon and I were not compatible, and I know he would say the same. Our future would not have been a happy one. I am at peace with the way things turned out."

Tem nodded. She felt immeasurably lighter.

"And I am glad he found you," Adelaide finished quietly. "You two are meant to be together."

Sharp guilt pierced Tem's chest. She wanted to believe Adelaide more than anything. But she was also breaking the one rule the basilisks held sacred—she was doing the *one thing* she wasn't allowed to do: have feelings for someone else. Was she truly meant to be with Caspen if she was still in love with Leo? Only time would tell.

Despite Tem's anxiety, she was enjoying this moment here with Adelaide. It was feminine and fun and light. Almost as if she were talking with Gabriel—as if she had found a new confidant. For the first time underneath the mountain, Tem felt truly safe. It was a wonderful feeling, and she savored it.

"What else should I know?" she asked, eager for more basilisk secrets.

"Hm," Adelaide said with a smile, looking out over the crowd. "Let me see." She pointed to a group of women in the corner. "They are king chasers."

"What does that mean?"

"It means they will pursue the Serpent King at any cost. It is their dream to seduce him all at once."

Tem wrinkled her nose. *That* wasn't going to happen.

At the look on her face, Adelaide laughed. "You have nothing to fear, Temperance."

Tem looked at the group of women. They were stunning. "How can he possibly resist them?"

"Caspenon does not favor the desperate."

Victory flowed through Tem. She watched as the women preened and giggled, all of them looking over their shoulder at where Caspen was standing, still talking to the group of men. The sight gave her a curious mix of jealousy and pride. Part of her was thrilled. It made her feel special that someone so desired had picked her. The other part of her was irrationally angry.

Adelaide seemed to sense this, because she said, "He will not stray."

Tem glanced up at her. Were her emotions really so transparent? "How do you know?"

"Because he only wants you."

Even after everything they'd been through, Tem found that hard to believe.

"Do not underestimate your power, Temperance."

"What do you mean?"

"You hold more sway over him than anyone else."

"Sometimes it doesn't feel that way."

"But it *is* that way. Beyond a doubt. I have never seen him like this. Nobody has."

"What was he like before me?"

Adelaide smiled. "Rather insufferable."

"Really?"

"Yes. His ego was unprecedented."

Tem supposed she could imagine that. Anyone with a father like Bastian would surely take after him.

"You have tamed him," Adelaide continued. "He is…more careful now."

"Careful with what?"

"His life."

Tem frowned. "What do you mean?"

There was a pause as Adelaide tossed her hair over her shoulders.

"Before you, it did not matter to him whether he lived or died. He was always the first to step into a fight. Now he refrains. I know it is for you."

"Why would he refrain for me?"

"He wishes to keep you safe, Temperance. He views it as his duty."

Tem processed her words slowly. She couldn't imagine another version of Caspen, one who was rash and impulsive and reckless. Those were qualities she possessed, not him. Tem was struck once more by the fact that he'd lived an entire lifetime before her—that while her adulthood was largely shaped by him, his had not at all been shaped by her.

As if on cue, Caspen chose that moment to return.

His eyes flicked first to Tem's, then to Adelaide's, his brow furrowing in concern.

"Tem?" he said before he even reached her.

"I'm fine," she said preemptively.

Caspen's face softened but just barely. He looked once more to Adelaide, and his eyes narrowed. "If you are filling her head with lies, I will—"

"I'm *fine*, Caspen," Tem insisted. "Will you calm down? Adelaide and I are friends now."

That got an amused laugh from Adelaide and a distressed grunt from Caspen, who pursed his lips but didn't press the issue.

"How did it go with…" Tem didn't know how to address the group of men he'd been talking to. "Them?"

Caspen sighed, and his expression darkened. "The Senecas are angry. They feel I am corrupting one of their own."

"The Senecas consider me…one of them?"

"Yes," Caspen said. "They do."

Tem couldn't fathom that. She wanted nothing to do with Rowe or anyone associated with him.

"To add insult to injury, you are a Hybreed."

"Excuse me?"

He smiled. "What I mean to say is that your status as a Hybreed makes you an asset. And since you are a Seneca, they feel they are owed your allegiance."

Tem wrinkled her nose. She'd never felt like much of anything, and now she was an asset?

"The Senecas know that your basilisk side can draw power from your human side," Caspen continued. "Once mastered, your power would be…limitless."

Tem blinked.

Limitless.

It wasn't a word Tem had ever heard in conjunction to herself. She remembered how she'd been able to crest herself at her wedding—how she'd do anything to feel that invincible again. Something within her fluttered at the thought.

"Limitless?"

"Yes."

"What does that even mean?"

Adelaide's eyes flicked to Caspen, as if asking for permission.

"Just tell me," Tem barked.

"Tell her," Caspen said.

A moment passed before Adelaide spoke. "If the legends are true, it means you can channel Kora."

"*What?*"

Tem blinked. The basilisks thought she could *channel Kora*? It was an absurd belief. Kora was a goddess—she could not be channeled through someone as insignificant as Tem. She looked down at her hands. Twelve freckles on each palm. Three beneath every finger except her thumbs. Tem flexed her fingers, wondering what she had done in a previous life to deserve this.

"Such power is unimaginable, Tem," Caspen said. "The Senecas covet it."

"Why do they care? I thought they didn't support mating with humans."

"You are not a human. You are a Hybreed, and they feel I have taken you from them. They will not forgive it. Nor would I expect them to."

"Well. That's their problem."

"They are rightfully angry," Adelaide said. "Bastian used you against your own quiver." She glanced at Caspen. "That was wrong of him."

Tem thought about her first council meeting, where the Serpent King had touted her as a weapon. *We have a Hybreed*, Bastian had said. The implication was that the *Drakons* had a Hybreed. But the Drakons had never had her. They'd only discovered her. There was a difference.

"But Adelaide is a Seneca," Tem said. "You said that marriage was arranged to bring peace between the quivers. If I'm a Seneca, and we're married, shouldn't that bring peace too?"

Caspen gave her a grim smile. "Any hope of peace was nullified when I...punished Rowe."

Tem flinched at the memory of the mangled mound of flesh where Rowe's cock used to be. Punishment indeed.

"So what does that mean?"

Both basilisks looked first at each other, then back at Tem. It was Caspen, finally, who answered.

"It means that Rowe seeks to retaliate. We must be ready when he does."

CHAPTER FIVE

———•◦✳◦•———

Before Tem could wonder how Rowe would retaliate, a murmur swept through the courtyard. Everyone turned to watch as a large mattress was set down in front of the fountain. It was not unlike the mattress Tem and Caspen had used for the ritual, and she wondered briefly if it was the same one. As soon as it was in place, two basilisks emerged from the crowd. The woman was tall, the man even more so. They were stunning, as all basilisks were, and when they reached the mattress, they stood beside it and waited. The crowd fell silent.

"What are they waiting for?" Tem whispered.

Caspen's lips dipped to her ear. "You."

Tem's eyebrows rose. "*Me?* Why?"

"They expect you to bless their marriage."

Tem was already blushing at the sight of the beautiful basilisks before her. If Caspen was about to tell her that she was supposed to join them, she would not survive it. "I thought you said basilisks don't have weddings."

"We do not."

"Then how do I bless their marriage?"

"You will witness their union as a married couple."

Tem blinked. "What?"

"You are the Serpent Queen, Tem."

Tem stared up at him. "I need a little more detail than that, Caspen."

He let out a soft chuckle. "Every mating season, any couple whose marriage is bound by blood has the opportunity to be blessed by the Serpent Queen."

"Why only marriages bound by blood?"

"Because they are considered sacred in the eyes of Kora."

"Who blesses ours?"

"No one. You are a Hybreed. That means you do not need anyone's blessing."

Again, Tem felt a whisper of possibility at the prospect of such power.

"When my mother died, the blessings stopped," Caspen continued. "Now that we have a queen once more, they can begin again."

Tem frowned. She didn't know exactly how long ago Caspen's mother had died, but even if it was mere years ago, it seemed incredible that only this couple had since bound their marriage by blood. Caspen had said that the blood bond was rare, but Tem hadn't realized it was *that* rare—that there was just one other couple who were joined the same way she and Caspen were.

Tem shook her head in disbelief. "Can't someone else do it?"

"It is your duty as their queen."

The concept of duties was not unfamiliar to Tem. She was used to the chores and obligations of life on the farm. But *these* duties were bizarre to her. The most responsibility she'd ever had was feeding the chickens. She certainly wasn't ready to bless a marriage.

"It's my duty to *watch them have sex*?"

"Yes."

"But what if I don't want to?"

"You…do not have to," he said slowly.

Tem narrowed her eyes. "I don't believe you."

Caspen sighed. "It is true that you do not have to. No one will force you, including me. But it would not be wise to refuse. They will view it as an insult."

Of course it would be viewed that way. Every custom that directly railed against her human side was a mortal insult to the basilisks if she refused. There was no neutrality here, no way to stay in the middle. She was always choosing a side.

"It just seems so"—Tem searched for the right word, settling finally on—"invasive. Won't I be intruding?"

Caspen shook his head. "You must dispel your human notions of sex, Tem."

"I know that. But still."

"They *want* you to watch them."

She gave him a look.

"We do things differently here. You know this."

Tem did know this. "Any other duties I should be aware of?"

Caspen's mouth twitched. "Nothing comes to mind."

Tem rolled her eyes. *Surely* there were more. And surely, they would surprise her. But that was the nature of her life beneath the mountain. She'd come to expect the extraordinary. "So I just…watch them? And that's how I bless them?"

Caspen looked suddenly apprehensive. Dread filled her stomach.

"Caspen," she insisted. "How *exactly* do I bless them?"

"You need only watch them. But it is also customary to enjoy yourself."

"What's that supposed to mean?"

"It means you are welcome to…indulge."

"Indulge in what?"

Finally, the truth came: "You may touch yourself if you wish."

Tem blushed. For all the times she'd pleasured herself, she'd never done so while watching two people have sex. The entire concept of *using* the couple as inspiration was absolutely foreign to Tem.

The courtyard was still silent. The couple was still looking at her. *Everyone* was looking at her. Tem was suddenly self-conscious and moved their conversation to her mind:

I don't understand. How is that a blessing?

Technically, it is not. In order to bless them, you must climax to the sight of them.

WHAT?

It is to show your approval.

Tem didn't even have a response for that. Perhaps no response was sufficient.

Why did everyone have to be so *involved*? It had required an entire ritual for her to be with Caspen. And now this couple sought her approval. Even when Tem was on the other side, in the position of power, these traditions baffled her. It seemed unbelievable that she would be so enmeshed in everyone's personal lives. Tem hardly felt worthy of such responsibility. But she also understood that the basilisks were a community. They made their decisions together. Everything was a group effort, a group project. There was no point in resisting this, just as there was no point in resisting anything else that happened here.

So Tem stepped forward.

The moment she moved, the crowd parted for her, and she approached the couple with Caspen at her side. They bowed first to her, then to Caspen. Tem didn't know what to do, so she simply nodded in return. The couple smiled. Then they stepped onto the mattress. A moment later they were kissing.

Out of the corner of her eye, Tem saw Caspen take a step backward. She understood his retreat. This was her duty; they sought Tem's blessing, not Caspen's. Still, she wished he would stay by her side. Standing here alone with so many eyes on her was extremely nerve-racking.

You may kneel, Tem. Or do anything that feels comfortable.

But nothing felt comfortable. Everything felt open and exposed and public, as if the most vulnerable parts of her were about to be laid bare. It was one thing to witness casual sex in the passageway or the banquet hall. It was another thing entirely to see it three feet away, solely for her pleasure, and with the expectation that she would touch herself to it. It was too intimate—too personal. For all the times she'd seen basilisks having sex in the past week, it had never been like this, never seeking her approval.

The woman's face was flushed. Tem felt much the same: warm and turned on, as if she were watching something she shouldn't be. She remembered how Caspen had said she wasn't intruding, and she tried to believe it. But as soon as the man began to enter the woman, Tem couldn't help but close her eyes.

Open your eyes, Tem.

I can't.

You must watch.

I'm too nervous to watch.

There is nothing to be nervous about.

Says you.

Says everyone.

Everyone is watching me watch them. I can't do it.

Empathy flowed from him to her. *I understand. But no one is judging you.*

Tem was still wrapping her mind around the fact that *she* was judging *them. I feel like I'm intruding.*

You are not.

What if I don't do it right?

There is nothing to do but watch.

But that wasn't true. He'd told her that she needed to touch herself—that she needed to climax in order to bless them. Her approval of their marriage was directly contingent on that event, and if it didn't happen, everyone would see her failure.

I can't do this. I'm nobody.

You are their queen. A moment passed. Then: *You are* my *queen.*

Caspen believed in her. Caspen knew she could do this.

Tem. My love. Open your eyes.

Tem opened her eyes.

The couple was now fully intertwined, staring adoringly into each other's eyes with every thrust. Tem thought about their blood bond—how they were bound together on a magical, unbreakable level. It was the same bond she shared with Caspen, and it was immeasurably special.

Just watch them, Tem. Witness their love. It is beautiful.

Despite Tem's nerves, it *was* beautiful. There was nothing more beautiful, really. What could be better than watching two people who were in love express that love to each other? It was no different than what she did with Caspen every night. It was no different than what she'd done with Leo. Sex was beautiful. Sex was everything.

The couple was clearly obsessed with one another; they kissed at every opportunity, cradling each other's faces and pressing their lips together tenderly. Tem saw the way they looked at each other like they were the only two people in the world. It was humbling to witness such devotion. Tem wondered suddenly if this was how she and Caspen had looked like during the ritual.

We looked better.

Tem rolled her eyes. Caspen was still in her head, watching from behind her. Eventually, under the protection of his steady presence, Tem relaxed. She still hadn't touched herself—hadn't even moved from where she was standing. But she felt ready now to *indulge*, as Caspen had so eloquently put it. And she wasn't going to do it from here.

Slowly, so as not to disturb the couple, Tem stepped forward and knelt on the edge of the mattress. The moment she did so, a wave of approval crashed into her mind. It wasn't just from Caspen; Tem felt it from all over—everyone in the crowd who was watching her wanted her to do this. Their hunger was staggering.

She touched herself tentatively at first, hesitating only due to the acute awareness that everyone was watching her. Tem had been watched before, but this felt different from the ritual. Back then, Bastian had been involved, and she'd had a clear task to complete—one that Caspen had taught her to do. But this time felt more nebulous. This time the approval being sought was her own.

The couple was enamored with each other, and Tem was enamored too. She synced her motions to theirs, fingering herself in gentle, forgiving strokes, pretending that she was the only one in the room. Her basilisk side was turned on. But her human side couldn't comprehend that the couple was *having sex for her.* Every time she thought about it too hard, her throat tightened and her heart sped up. She glanced around the crowd for a distraction. To her surprise, she found one. Apollo.

Everyone was watching the couple. But Caspen's brother was watching her.

When their eyes met, Apollo's mind brushed against hers, and Tem fought the urge to recoil. She didn't let him in. She couldn't. Instead she threw up a barrier—the same one she'd used against Caspen—to keep him out. His gaze dug into her like a knife, hot and insistent, unrelenting in its intensity. He wasn't touching himself—no one was—that act was reserved for the Serpent Queen. But his cock was hard, and without thinking, Tem's eyes trailed down his body to look at it. It looked so much like Bastian's. The resemblance was uncanny. Like father, like son.

With a gasp of surprise, Tem came.

The moment it happened, the crowd erupted into cheers. Caspen picked her up by the waist and spun her around before setting her down and kissing her straight on the mouth. Tem kissed him back, squeezing her eyes shut tight, willing herself to forget what she'd just seen.

The couple was beaming; it was clear they were overjoyed by her blessing. Only Tem knew the truth: that the couple had not made her come at all.

"Now what?" she asked, still breathless.

Caspen smiled. "Now we celebrate."

Celebrating, of course, meant sex.

Everyone around them was already doing it; the crowd was breaking off into pairs and groups, their bodies overlapping in an endless wave of skin. Caspen pushed her down on the mattress, and Tem wrapped her legs around him. She knew many were still watching, and she knew she didn't care. She might even have preferred it at this point. Her basilisk side was alive and well, filled with the communal joy that her blessing had brought to the couple.

Caspen spread her legs, but she stopped him before he could enter her.

"Wait," Tem said.

He paused. "What is the matter, Tem?"

"I…" Tem began. She looked up at him, and her throat seemed to close.

At her expression, Caspen took her face in his, pressing his lips to her forehead. "Talk to me," he murmured.

For some reason, tears pricked her eyes. "Am I good enough?"

Caspen frowned. "Good enough at what?"

"This. Everything. You."

His frown deepened. "Me?"

"Yes. One day I'm nobody and then suddenly I'm queen of the basilisks. It's…too much."

"Tem." Caspen pulled her closer. "You have nothing to fear. You are doing beautifully."

"How can you say that? I can't transition without help. And even then I can barely—"

"Tem," he cut her off again, pressing his forehead to hers. "Enough."

She stared into his golden eyes, trying to understand the fondness in them. "How can you always think the best of me?"

"Because you are the best of me," he said simply.

His words floored her. It was impossible to believe that she could make a centuries-old creature *better*.

"You are more than good enough," he murmured against her cheek. "You are perfect."

Tem smiled. Caspen smiled too, pulling her closer.

Are you ready?

Yes.

Unmistakable approval lit up his face. He kissed her on the lips.

Caspen thrust into her relentlessly, and she took him deeper and deeper. He was right; they did look better. Tem knew it by the way basilisks watched them *enviously*, as if they yearned to step up and join them. But for now, they belonged only to each other. There was no daylight in the courtyard—no way to know how much time had passed in the endless tangle of limbs and liquids and frenzied breathing. They lay on the mattress between climaxes, draped in each other's arms, the celebration raging around them.

"I can't believe this is what your life is like," she whispered against his skin.

"It was not nearly so enjoyable before you arrived."

Tem giggled. She looked out over the basilisks. "How late will it go on?"

"Quite late."

At the look on her face, Caspen said, "We can take a break, if you need one."

Tem hated to admit that she did. It was all too much—the bodies, the moans, the movement. She didn't want Caspen to think she couldn't handle it. But the truth was that she couldn't.

Come, Tem. We will rest.

His hand found her waist, lifting her up off the mattress. Tem knew it was not in Caspen's nature to take a break. But she appreciated that he did so for her, leading her to a quiet spot at the edge of the courtyard. They looked out over the chaos together. All around them, basilisks were kissing and laughing and having sex. Tem couldn't help but think about how much Gabriel would love this.

"Caspen?"

"Yes, my love?"

"How old are you?"

He bristled. "I do not think my age is relevant."

"Well, I do."

"I am older than you."

"I'd already guessed that, actually."

He didn't reply.

"Tell me."

"No."

"Why not?"

"Because you are too eager to know."

Tem didn't have the energy to push him. Instead she moved the conversation to their minds:

I like Adelaide.

Do you?

Yes. She's a girl's girl.

I do not know what that means.

It means she would choose me over you.

His arms tightened. *Who could blame her?*

And I would choose her over you.

She felt him smile. *Is that right?*

Yes.

Should I be insulted?

It's a compliment to her, not an insult to you.

In that case, I will allow it.

It's not up to you to allow. But good to know.

He pressed a kiss to her forehead.

Tem continued: *Adelaide said you used to be insufferable before me.*

Is that so? How kind of her.

She said it with love.

I very much doubt that.

She also said you had a big ego.

Now that…might be true.

Tem was getting sleepy. Caspen seemed to sense this, because he said, "We do not have to stay."

"Are you sure?" The last thing she wanted was to leave early, especially if it might cause insult.

"Yes."

"I don't want to offend anyone."

"You have done the opposite of that tonight, Tem." He kissed her temple. "You did well. They will all be pleased."

Tem smiled at his words. It was all she wanted, really—to please the basilisks, to please Caspen, to please herself. If pleasure was at the forefront of basilisk culture, then what could be a nobler goal?

I'm ready to go.

Very well. Let us go.

He lifted her into his arms. It was only once they returned to their chambers and Tem collapsed onto the bed that she realized how exhausted she was. She dearly wished to sleep. But there was something on her mind. "Caspen," she said quietly. "How did your mother die?"

He shifted her in his arms but didn't answer.

When the pause drew on, Tem leaned in close. "You never talk about her. Why?"

The last time Caspen had withheld information about a death, she'd learned he'd crested Rowe's father. It stood to reason she was slightly anxious for his answer. Caspen was silent for a long time. Tem was used to waiting him out, and she did so now.

Eventually, he answered. "She died right before my father came into power." His tone was matter of fact. Removed.

Tem contemplated the significance of that timing. "But *how* did she die?"

Caspen sighed, and Tem watched the sharp rise and fall of his chest. "My father killed her."

Tem sat up straight. "*What?* Why?"

Caspen sat up too, and they looked at each other in the flickering firelight. "She betrayed him."

"How?"

"She slept with another."

Tem frowned. "But I thought that basilisks don't consider sex to be cheating."

"We do not consider *meaningless* sex to be cheating. But my mother was in love with the basilisk she slept with."

Tem's father's words returned to her suddenly: *It is a dangerous thing to love two people. You must prepare yourself.*

"Basilisks may be free with their bodies, but we are not free with our hearts," Caspen said quietly, repeating what her father had told her. "If you are bound to someone by blood, it means you have committed your heart to them. By falling in love with someone other than my father, my mother betrayed that bond. By sleeping with that person, she broke it."

A horrible feeling was forming in Tem's gut.

Caspen continued: "When they slept together, he retaliated by killing her."

Tem stared at him in shock.

"I saw it myself."

"But how could he do that?"

"He did not have a choice."

"I don't understand."

Caspen shifted, propping himself up on his arm and looking down at her. For some reason, dread pierced her. "There is nothing more sacred than the blood bond," Caspen continued. "It is our greatest tenet. Blood bonds are done in honor of true love—in the name of Kora. They are bound by magic bigger than us."

Tem remembered how Caspen had described the blood bond to her: *It is an ancient magic, and it is irreversible.*

The dread intensified.

"If the blood bond is broken, a curse is put into effect."

"What curse?"

"Whoever was betrayed must kill the betrayer. My father did not want to kill my mother. But he had to. The blood bond forced him to."

Tem was in awe. It was a horrible thing to hear. She couldn't imagine what that must have done to Caspen's family. She felt a sudden surge of sympathy for Bastian but quickly suppressed it. She would not pity such a man.

"Couldn't your father resist?"

Caspen shook his head. "It is impossible to resist such magic. Blood bonds are sanctioned by Kora—just like the ritual, or any of our other traditions. He was bound by a magic greater than himself."

"But if your mother knew what would happen, why would she sleep with the other man she loved?"

To her surprise, Caspen smiled. "Would you be able to resist sleeping with me?"

Tem would not. But Caspen was not the one she had to resist sleeping with.

What he had just told her was horrific. She couldn't imagine a worse scenario than his father killing his mother. And to witness it himself was unthinkable.

"Why didn't your mother just keep it a secret?"

"She tried. But the curse was triggered the moment she slept with her lover. The curse told my father."

Tightness. It was all Tem felt. Encroaching on her chest, squeezing her lungs.

"We cannot lie," Caspen whispered. "There are no secrets between basilisks."

"But doesn't it…*bother* you?"

Caspen sighed deeply. "Of course it bothers me, Tem. It is a horrible stain on my family. But in basilisk society, my mother is the one who was in the wrong. My father was merely enacting justice."

"But that's…"

There were no words for it, really. It was awful. And terrifying. And a little too close to Tem's situation for her liking.

"Aren't you…worried about…me?"

Caspen looked down at her. "And why would I worry about you?"

Tem rolled her shoulders uncomfortably. "Because of…everything that happened… with…"

For some reason, she couldn't bear to say Leo's name.

Caspen let out a dismissive laugh. "No. I am not worried."

It was then that she remembered Caspen's attitude toward Leo—how he never called him by his name, only referring to him as "the human prince"—how he didn't consider

Leo to be his equal. Tem and Caspen had a blood bond, a connection Leo couldn't hope to replicate. Caspen probably thought that was proof enough of her loyalty. It was a viewpoint that was understandable, given the basilisk mindset. But it was wrong.

"But why not?" Tem asked before she could help herself.

"Because you sent him away."

That was true. But it didn't mean she'd fallen out of love with him.

"You accepted the blood bond," Caspen continued. "That means you chose me."

That phrase again. *You chose me.*

"But," Tem said carefully, "I love you both."

It was the same thing she'd said in the cave the night they'd agreed to share her. But now Tem wondered whether either of them had really agreed at all. What would that arrangement have even looked like? She couldn't have been queen of both kingdoms. It was a problem without a solution—one that *she* had solved in the only way she knew how—by sending Leo off to find Evelyn.

Caspen's eyes narrowed. The room seemed to grow colder as he said, "You love *me*."

Tem could barely hold his gaze. It felt like he was giving her an order. It was true that she loved him. But she loved Leo too, no matter how unfathomable that was to Caspen. There was nothing else to say, so Tem didn't say anything. But in the late hours of the night, she lay awake.

What would happen if Tem slept with Leo? Would Caspen kill her? Would his family praise him for doing so? She touched the golden chain around her neck. It had always felt like a gift, something that bound her to Caspen. But now it felt like an anchor—a shackle with no key. Tem couldn't believe the cruelty of the curse. It seemed to go against everything basilisk culture had taught her: that everything was shared.

Everything except for hearts. Caspen's mother hadn't been able to resist hers.

Could Tem?

CHAPTER SIX

---✦---

THE LETTER CAME THE NEXT MORNING.

Caspen read it first, his brow furrowed, before handing it to Tem.

Temperance Verus,

Your presence is requested at the castle for dinner tonight. A carriage will be sent for you.
Bring your husband.

She glanced up at Caspen, who looked indifferent. But her heart was racing.

The letter was only addressed to Tem. And her "husband"? It was an awfully formal way of addressing Caspen. Neither Leo nor Caspen seemed to be able to address the other directly, either by name or by title. But no amount of avoidance would change their circumstances. And if everything went accordingly tonight, this would be the first of many more Sunday-night dinners.

"Will you go?" Tem asked.

Caspen was watching her, his expression carefully controlled. "Why should I?"

"Because it's a chance at peace."

Caspen snorted. Of course he didn't agree. But it was true whether he liked it or not. Cooperation and compromise were the only way forward.

"And what will happen if I do not attend?"

Tem really wasn't sure how to answer that. If Caspen refused to come to these dinners, Tem would be forced to attend them alone. She couldn't think of anything worse. "Please, Caspen," she whispered. "I can't do this alone."

He stared at her for a long moment. "I will go," he said quietly. "For you." Then he pulled the letter from her grasp and tossed it into the fire, just as he'd done for the annulment summons. His warm hand covered hers. "Come," he said. "We have duties to attend to."

His wording was not an accident. Tem knew he was placing emphasis on the fact that her place was here—that her duties were to the basilisks, not the villagers; that the *we* in question was her and Caspen, not her and Leo. Tem didn't need the reminder. She knew what she had chosen; she knew what her life entailed now. But that didn't make it easier to live it.

Tem laced her fingers through Caspen's, allowing him to lead her through the passageway and toward the courtyard. They passed many basilisks along the way, all of them parting to make way for the couple. If Caspen was powerful before, he was nearly a god now. Basilisks bowed to him as they passed, bending for him in a silent, worshipful wave. Tem saw firsthand how they respected his status and how they respected hers in turn. A week ago, it would have been disconcerting to have so many eyes on her. Now Tem savored it. It was an honor to be with someone like Caspen, to be chosen by the Serpent King.

They spent the day overseeing the setup of the courtyard in preparation for the second event of mating season. It was not unlike curating a wedding, choosing decorations and sampling food. Always, Caspen deferred to Tem, although whether it was because he didn't have an opinion or because he valued hers more, she had no idea. Either way, whenever someone asked them their preference, Caspen would wait until Tem answered first before saying, "As she wishes."

And thus the day passed quickly.

By the time it was evening, anxiety had taken over Tem. When they walked out of the cave together, she was nearly on the edge of panic. The night was cold, and although Caspen had procured Tem a proper dress this time, she shivered in the thin fabric, her hands clenched into fists. Caspen took her hand, relaxing her fingers and intertwining them gently with his. He seemed to be resolved to the situation, displaying far more composure than her.

"You must relax, Tem."

"I *can't*."

"Of course you can. Focus on something else."

But there was nothing else to focus on. The impending events of the evening were pressing in on her in a horrible wave, threatening to drown her.

"How are you not more nervous?"

Caspen raised his shoulders in an easy shrug. "There is nothing to be nervous about."

Tem rolled her eyes. It was such a typical Caspen answer, she didn't know why she'd bothered asking. Of course Caspen wasn't nervous. Caspen was ancient. He'd seen and done things Tem could only imagine, and at this point, nothing swayed him—not even this. But Tem was extremely swayed. She was nervous and frantic and all she could think about was what it was going to be like to meet Evelyn for the first time, to see her with Leo, to see them interact. Tem had no idea what to expect. Would Evelyn hate her? Tem could understand if that was the case.

But would Tem hate Evelyn? Perhaps that was the more relevant question. It was impossible for her to truly hate anyone who made Leo happy. That was the point of her sending him away, after all. But Tem couldn't ignore the dull jealousy that tightened her chest at the thought of the two of them together. Even though it had been her choice—and it had been the right one—she couldn't help but feel some form of latent regret. What if it had been a mistake? What if Evelyn wasn't right for him? But that couldn't be. From the way Leo had talked about their love, Tem knew she was. And Leo deserved someone who would love him the way Caspen loved her: wholly, purely, and without competition.

"Tem," Caspen said as they climbed inside the carriage and sat side by side on the velvet bench. "Relax."

"I can't."

"Let us try to enjoy dinner."

Nothing could be more impossible. Tem was not about to *enjoy* what came next. She wouldn't enjoy meeting Evelyn and watching her with Leo. She wouldn't enjoy seeing the woman who was now living the life Tem thought she would have. She wouldn't—

Caspen's hand slipped into the slit of her dress. His fingers dipped between her legs.

"What are you doing?" she gasped.

"Ensuring you enjoy dinner."

When he touched her clitoris, she moaned, arching her head back.

"No, Tem," Caspen whispered. "Do not make a sound."

Tem bit her lip. The driver was *right there*—just beyond the partition—close enough to hear them. Normally Tem wouldn't care who heard. But the last thing she wanted was for word to get back to the castle—back to Leo—that she'd been intimate with her husband on the way to the dinner. It wasn't the type of rumor that would encourage friendly relations between their kingdoms. Instead Tem burrowed her face in Caspen's shoulder as his fingers went deeper, biting the fabric of his shirt to keep from crying out. A steady stream of praise trickled into her ear:

"So good, Tem."

Soft words to accompany soft touches.

"So perfect for me."

Caspen was always commanding. But now he was gentle, his lips against her skin, his hushed words for her and her alone. They had limited time in the carriage, but Caspen was in no hurry. He fingered her slowly, with lyrical rhythm, caressing her center with intention and care. Never going too deep—never letting her moan too loudly.

It was a pleasure to be touched like this, to experience the stunning ascent toward imminence, to feel nothing but resplendent pleasure. Tem wished they were back in their chambers. She wished she could kiss him and ride him and bring them both to climax. The carriage was too small for everything Tem wanted him to do to her. Their capabilities were constricted by these four walls, their brilliance dulled by circumstance. If Tem had her way, Caspen would fuck her *in front of* the driver. That was all that mattered to her: being seen. Being *perceived*. There was nothing more clarifying than having a cock between her legs.

Caspen's eyes were turning black.

Tem stared into them, losing herself in the endless pools, imagining what it would be like to drown in them. His power was intimidating, even now. And yet, Tem wondered if she could match it. She wondered, somehow, if her allure was equal to his. He was the one who'd initiated this, after all. He was the one who pulled her closer.

"Caspen," she whispered.

In reply, he trailed kisses down her neck. His teeth found her dress strap, pulling it from her shoulder to expose her breasts. His mouth moved lower, sucking the tender peak of her nipple into his mouth. Tem was unbearably warm. She wanted him *right now* or else she would die.

Patience.

Tem had administered torture in a carriage once before. It was entirely different to be on the receiving end—to have someone know her limits and push her to them—to be at the mercy of the hard man before her.

Caspen worked her nipple between his teeth until tears formed in Tem's eyes. He was sucking *so* hard. She was on the brink of crying out, but she couldn't make a sound. He'd told her not to, and she would be patient; she would be good. Finally, he relinquished his grip. The moment he let her go, he switched to her other breast, the contrast so swift that Tem let out a yelp of surprise. Did the footman hear it? Did Caspen even hear it? He was so engrossed in what he was doing, she wondered if he even cared anymore.

Tem wanted to make him proud—to show that she could follow instructions. It had never been easy for her to obey. But she molded herself to him now, arching her back so there was as little distance between them as possible. Caspen rewarded her with a low growl. If she could just touch him back—if she could wrap her fingers around his cock and stroke him the way he liked—perhaps he would have her right here right now.

She cupped her hand over his trousers, squeezing the bulge between his legs.

Caspen pulled away. He was withholding himself from her, refusing to give in.

I am not going to fuck you in a carriage, Tem.

She whimpered her displeasure. Didn't he know how much she wanted this? How open and ready she was to give him whatever he was willing to take?

"Please," she whispered, pressing her lips to his neck. "Just a little."

"Just a little what, my love?"

"Just fuck me a little."

Caspen let out a murmur of a laugh before driving his fingers deeper. "No."

It was all he said, and Tem knew his decision was final. There was nothing left to do but give herself up to him—to *this*. His motions were purposeful now, drawing her toward release.

"Caspen," she gasped. She was almost there.

But Caspen's fingers were slowing.

Not only was Caspen not going to fuck her but he had no intention of letting her come *at all*. It was the ultimate distraction—the only way to force her to focus on something other than what was about to happen. Instead of worrying about Evelyn, she would worry about *this*: the incessant need that rendered her helpless. Tem would spend the entire evening aching for it.

"*Caspen*," she said, a reprimand this time. "Don't you *dare*."

In response, Caspen withdrew his fingers even more. Tem gasped with displeasure, pulling him back toward her. But he only retreated farther, raising his hand tauntingly between them, her wetness gleaming on his fingers.

"Patience," he said again.

Tem pouted. She wanted him to keep touching her. It was *all* she wanted, even if she knew he wouldn't do it. She'd been so good for him, so *perfect*, and this was her reward? It wasn't fair at all. But there was nothing else she could do.

In the pause that followed, they watched each other, their minds entwined. Caspen's eyes were black, the gold completely gone. Tem couldn't believe they were about to go into the first of many Sunday dinners this disheveled and enamored.

Slowly, Caspen's fingers returned to her. But still, he didn't let her come. Instead Tem felt a familiar sensation—one she'd felt many times before. She moaned as a claw formed—this time from her own essence—sucking in a sharp breath as it grew into place. The tip cradled her tightly, pressing against her tender clitoris. A pulse came. Tem closed her eyes with a shudder. It was nearly enough to come. But not quite.

On second thought, perhaps she *would* enjoy dinner.

Gently, Caspen removed his fingers, raising them to his lips and slowly licking them clean. When he was finished, he slid the straps of her dress back up her shoulders, covering her once more. Then he kissed her. Tem threaded her fingers through his hair, pulling him closer. She needed him *so* badly. Naked, raw, over and over again. The urge to mount him was so strong, she found herself pressing against him again, harder this time, willing him to give in. But this was Caspen. He never gave in.

Besides, they had arrived.

They exited the carriage together, hand in hand, Tem still thinking desperately about how a moment ago the fingers she was holding were inside her. But as soon as they entered the castle, any thoughts of sex fell away. Caspen stiffened immediately at the sight of all the gold. It was everywhere—laced into the tiles of the foyer, painted into the wallpaper. The first time Tem had come to the castle, she'd been impressed by such wealth after a lifetime on a chicken farm. Now she found it horrible, knowing the wealth had been created by the blood of basilisks.

"Right this way," the butler said. They followed him through the halls to the same dining room Tem had waited in before the Frisky Sixty. Tem tried not to look at the door that led to the library, where all the girls had disrobed for Leo. She tried not to remember the way he'd kissed her against the other side of that door—the way he'd waited to turn the hourglass until the very last second.

Will you keep me around?

For as long as you'll let me.

"Tem." Caspen's voice broke her from her memories.

"What?"

"Would you like a drink?"

A butler was brandishing a tray of champagne at her.

"No," she said, even though her throat was dry. "Not champagne."

"She will have a whiskey," Caspen said.

The butler nodded, then disappeared.

In the middle of the room was a round table surrounded by four chairs. Tem stared at the seating arrangement, unsure how to proceed. The shape of the table perplexed her: it implied equality, as if none of them were more important than the others. She hoped dearly that that would remain the tone of the evening. Rather than make an executive decision, Tem opted to remain standing. Caspen seemed unconcerned with his surroundings, his gaze trained only on her, his expression calm.

You must relax, Tem.

But Tem couldn't relax. It was the absolute last thing she could do. She was here—in the castle—and she was about to meet Evelyn. Nothing could have prepared her for this.

When she didn't reply, Caspen squeezed her hand.

I am right here, Tem. Lean on me.

Gratitude rushed through her at his words. Caspen was right; that's what he was here for. *I will go for you*, he'd said. Tem understood that meant he was here for her—to support her and to stand by her so she didn't have to face this situation alone. She squeezed his hand in return.

When the butler returned with Tem's whiskey, she downed it all in one gulp. A wave of fire was just hitting her sternum when she heard "Good evening."

Tem didn't need to turn to know the words were spoken by Leo. But she turned anyway to see him standing in the doorway, his long arms crossed. He looked closed off, as if he were protecting himself from something. Perhaps he was.

"Thank you for coming." His gaze flicked to Caspen. "Both of you."

Caspen didn't respond, and Tem could only nod. Her lungs seemed to have stopped working properly; it was nearly impossible to draw air. Beside her, Caspen squeezed her hand again, but she hardly felt it. All she could focus on was the person who had just appeared behind Leo.

Dark-blond hair the color of honey. Round, pink cheeks.

Evelyn stepped forward slowly, resting her hand on Leo's shoulder. Her white dress was conservative; not an inch of skin was showing. She looked, for lack of a better word, innocent. The polar opposite of Tem.

"It's so nice to meet you," Evelyn said, extending her hand.

Tem stared down at it, unable to move.

Shake her hand, Tem.

But Tem couldn't. To shake her hand would mean to accept the situation, and nothing could be more impossible. Shaking her hand meant succumbing to civility. Tem couldn't fathom anything worse.

It was Caspen, finally, who stepped forward first.

His movements were smooth—no trace whatsoever of the avalanche of anxiety Tem herself was feeling. He took Evelyn's hand in his, shaking it once before dropping it. Evelyn flinched as he did so. At the sight, a wave of satisfaction replaced Tem's anxiety. Of course Evelyn was scared of Caspen. She *should* be scared of him. Caspen was probably the first basilisk she'd ever seen in person, much less actually touched. And if Evelyn feared Caspen, it meant she feared Tem too. The thought gave her courage.

When Caspen dropped Evelyn's hand, Tem stepped forward. She inserted herself directly into Evelyn's space, looking her straight in the eye as she extended her own hand. Evelyn had the good grace to control her expression as she raised her hand and shook Tem's. The moment their skin touched, Tem fought the urge to recoil. Evelyn's hand was sickeningly cold, as if she were ill. Her palm was clammy—like a fish—and Tem wanted to gag. Instead she released her as quickly as possible, resisting the instinct to wipe her hand on her dress.

Not a word was spoken; Tem couldn't have if she'd tried.

She knew what was coming next, knew Leo was about to approach her. But she couldn't bring herself to look at him—couldn't even raise her gaze to meet his. The last time she'd seen him was the annulment, when their hands had touched by the dungeon door. Would they touch again? Would he try to shake her hand, as Evelyn just had? Last time, Tem had felt something seismic within her—a shift of such gargantuan significance that she didn't dare contemplate it now. She could not experience such a sensation in front of Caspen. He would see it all over her face. To her surprise, Leo didn't reach for her. Instead, he bowed his head and said, "Tem."

Before she could decide how to respond, he straightened, extending his hand to Caspen.

"Caspen."

Tem half expected Caspen to ignore him or possibly rip his head off. Instead he shook Leo's hand, his expression eerily calm. His mind was closed off to her; Tem couldn't tell what he was thinking. If there were ever a time when she wished to know how he felt, it was now. How could he possibly be this calm? The last time the three of them were together, Caspen had held Tem and Leo's heads together so they could kiss as she crested him. Their circumstances couldn't be more different now. So much had changed in such a short period of time.

The two men dropped their hands.

An awkward moment of silence followed, in which Tem and Leo stared at each other. He looked the same as he had when she saw him just days ago: weary, as if he hadn't been getting enough sleep. Tem didn't dare imagine what he was doing instead of sleeping. Was he telling Evelyn to sit still on his cock, as he had once told Tem? Was he gripping her hips with his hands, holding her in place so he could look at her? Was he—

"Shall we eat?" Evelyn broke the silence.

In reply, Caspen's arm wrapped all the way around Tem. She was used to him touching her, but this felt significant. Almost as if he were protecting her—holding her together—ensuring that she did not break. He steered her toward the table, pulling out a chair and waiting for her to sit before he sat too. Tem was exactly opposite Leo, affording her a perfect view of him as he pressed his lips to Evelyn's cheek. Uninhibited rage surged through her mind. It retreated an instant later when she reminded herself that she had chosen this. She had *ordered Leo to do this.*

Tem stared at Leo. He stared right back, his expression open and wanting. A vein throbbed in his neck. How could he look at her like that while Evelyn sat right next to him? Then again, Tem was looking too. But her situation was different; *Caspen* was different. He knew she had chosen him. He knew that was all that mattered.

Leo's finger was slowly tracing the stem of his wineglass. Up, then down, then back up again. Tem watched the motion, imagining what it would feel like against her skin. Was he doing it on purpose, to taunt her? If he was, it was working. Evelyn didn't even seem to notice. She was carefully adjusting her sleeves, readying herself for the meal.

Just as the butler placed their dishes in front of them, the first pulse came.

CHAPTER SEVEN

⸺•⊶✵⊷•⸺

T
EM GASPED IN SURPRISE.

Leo's eyes immediately narrowed. Tem wanted to moan. But she couldn't make a sound—couldn't move an inch. Nobody except for her and Caspen knew what was happening between her legs right now at this very dinner table. The pulse grew slowly, bathing her core in warmth and bringing a flush to her cheeks. Her nipples were hard, and the sensation of them against her dress was enough to send her mind into a frenzy. Tem wanted to be naked. She wanted to fuck someone—*anyone*—who could bring her relief.

Did Leo know what was happening? He'd seen her turned on before; he knew what it looked like, would recognize the signs. Or perhaps he had forgotten about that part of her, disregarded it as quickly as their marriage. It didn't matter anyway. The pulse continued to grow. Tem let out a quiet gasp as it reached an unprecedented rhythm. It was almost *vibrating*. She had never felt anything like that on her clitoris before, and the urge to jerk her hips against the chair was so strong she nearly passed out. Tem reached for her whiskey glass before realizing it was empty. She needed a distraction, and Caspen wasn't helping.

Without thinking, she said, "Evelyn."

Her tone was sharp—far sharper than it should have been.

Evelyn's round eyes became even rounder as she looked up at her. "Yes?"

"Are you glad to be back?"

It was a loaded question. But Tem didn't care. She needed to focus on something other than the hot, aching pulses between her legs. And some latent part of her also wanted to remind Leo that the only reason Evelyn was back was because Tem had made it so.

"Of course." Evelyn squeezed Leo's arm. "We're so lucky we found our way back to each other."

Another pulse. Stronger this time.

Leo was watching her, but she could do nothing about it. In fact, she *wanted* him to watch her. It only turned her on more to imagine that he knew what was happening—that he was picturing her naked just as surely as she was picturing him.

"Then why did you leave in the first place?"

A horrible silence fell. The pulses stopped.

Even the butler froze midmotion, his arm awkwardly extended to hand Leo another wineglass.

Evelyn's face pinched into an unpleasant expression. She looked at Leo, who was looking only at Tem. Then she said, "I didn't want to leave."

She is lying.

Tem's head snapped to Caspen's. He said it casually, as if he were stating a rather boring fact. But that fact was everything to Tem. *How do you know?*

He didn't reply. Perhaps his interest had already waned. But Tem's interest was very much piqued, so she asked once more, "Then why did you?"

It was rude to repeat the same question mere seconds later. But Evelyn still hadn't answered it. "I was…misinformed."

Tem blinked. So did Leo. "What's that supposed to mean?"

Beside her, Caspen's hand touched her knee. Tem knew what he was saying: *Relax.* But she was about to get the answer to a question she'd wondered about for far too long, and she could not be relaxed about it.

"On the morning Leo and I were supposed to run away together, I received a letter."

Tem straightened. Caspen's grip tightened. "What kind of letter?"

Evelyn turned to Leo. "Did you not tell her?"

Tem turned to Leo too. "Tell me what?"

A tenuous silence fell. In it, Leo's jaw twitched. When he didn't answer, Evelyn said, "Leo wrote me a letter telling me he no longer wished to be with me."

Now Tem was truly confused. As far as she knew, Leo had waited for Evelyn in the graveyard behind the church on the morning they were meant to leave. When she hadn't shown up, *he* had been the heartbroken one. Was that all a lie? Had Leo played her? Doubt curled in her stomach. His pitiful story about Evelyn had tugged at her heartstrings. Such a tale would have swayed anyone. Now, for a terrifying moment, Tem wondered if it had all been false.

"Why would he do that? He loved you."

"I didn't."

The words were spoken by Leo, and Evelyn bristled the moment he said him. At her reaction, he clarified.

"I didn't write the letter."

Tem frowned. "Then who did?"

"My father."

The pieces clicked slowly into place. Tem remembered what Maximus had said to her in the foyer after she discovered the bloodletting: *I have corrected my son's mistakes before. I will not hesitate to do so again.* The letter was his way of correcting Leo's mistake, of ensuring he didn't end up with a lowly village girl. But something about Evelyn's story didn't sit right with Tem.

In the silence that followed, she tried to pinpoint why she felt so angry. It was irrelevant whether Maximus had been the one to write the letter. What was unfathomable to Tem was the fact that Evelyn would have left Leo after reading it. If she and Leo were so in love, nothing should have been able to drive her away. Tem knew if Leo had broken up with *her* via letter, she never would have accepted it. She couldn't understand how Evelyn could have taken such a note at face value—not when her entire relationship was at stake. At the very least, she should have shown up to the graveyard to hear it from Leo in person.

Before Tem could say as much, Evelyn finished wistfully, "When I got the letter, I could think of nothing else to do but to flee."

Something flickered in Leo's eyes. Doubt.

Tem's eyes shifted to Caspen, whose expression was unreadable. Sometime in the last few minutes, the claw had begun to throb again. It was beginning to make her lightheaded. She clenched her fists in an attempt to focus, asking, "So why didn't you come back?"

Evelyn blinked slowly. She placed her hand gently on Leo's arm. Her power was quiet but no less present. Tem could feel it in the way she watched her every move at the table—sense it in the way her eyes flicked to Leo whenever Tem looked at him. She was watching—*waiting*—protecting her king.

"Are you implying something?" she asked quietly.

"You said the letter is why you left," Tem said just as quietly, keeping her voice steady despite the erratic pulses between her legs. "But you didn't say why you stayed away. So why didn't you come back?"

Across from her, Leo took a sip of his whiskey. Caspen didn't move.

"I was heartbroken, of course," Evelyn said. "I didn't think Leo wanted to see me ever again. As you can understand, I was devastated."

"No," Tem said. "I don't understand."

Evelyn raised an eyebrow. "What don't you understand?"

"Do you have it?"

Evelyn frowned. "Do I have what?"

"The letter."

Leo glanced at Evelyn. Tem wondered suddenly whether he'd asked her the exact same question. If she knew anything about him, he had.

"I burned it," Evelyn said primly.

"Why? Seems like something you would hold on to."

Evelyn tilted her head. "And why would I do that?"

"So you could show it to Leo. He has a right to see what his father was saying on his behalf."

"That letter represents a terrible memory for me. I did not wish to see it ever again."

"But if Leo—"

"Tem," Caspen cut her off. "Enough."

The pulses stopped too.

Throughout this entire exchange, Caspen had said nothing. But he chose to speak now, and for once, Tem fell silent. She was taking this too far, and she knew it. But she couldn't seem to stop herself. It was a bizarre story; Evelyn's reaction made no sense to her. If Leo had tried to break up with her using a letter, she would have marched right up to the castle to confront him face-to-face. Clearly, Evelyn had done no such thing. How could she let Leo go so easily? From everything Tem knew of their relationship, he'd truly loved her. To be loved by Leo was a privilege—an honor. And Evelyn had thrown that away. Why?

Caspen's voice was suddenly in her mind:

It is not your responsibility to speak for the human king.

I know that. I'm just trying to figure out why—

Their relationship is none of your concern.

Tem had nothing to say to that. Leo's relationship with Evelyn was very much her concern. She was the one who had *orchestrated* their relationship. Concern was *all* she felt when she looked at them, and not just for selfish reasons. Tem needed them to work. She needed Evelyn to be the love of Leo's life. Because if she wasn't, everything she'd sacrificed was for nothing.

Apologize.

Tem looked at Caspen in disbelief. It wasn't a suggestion. It was an order.

No.

Tem. You have offended them.

She had to physically stop herself from scoffing at that. Perhaps she had offended Evelyn, but Tem could tell from the look on Leo's face that he'd wanted to ask the same questions she was asking but hadn't. Was he suspicious of his newly returned love? Of the truth that might come out if he pried too hard? Relationships were built on trust. Leo had made Tem swear never to lie to him. Clearly he'd made no such demands of Evelyn.

"Forgive me," Tem said stiffly. It wasn't an apology, but it was the most she could manage.

Evelyn immediately gave her a slow, saccharine smile. "There is nothing to forgive," she said smoothly. "Of course you're curious about what happened. Anyone would be, in your position."

Tem didn't like the sound of that. Her position? And what position was that, exactly?

Before she could ask, Evelyn clarified: "As someone who was formerly engaged to Leo, I can understand how you feel."

Tem very much doubted that Evelyn understood how she felt. It was an impossibility. And Tem hadn't just been *engaged* to Leo—she'd been married to him. It was a specific distinction, and one that Evelyn had purposefully ignored. She was diminishing their relationship, attempting to minimize what they had together. Tem felt a wild urge to retaliate, to say something that would remind Evelyn just who she had been to Leo. Instead, she raised her hand and slowly brushed a curl from her face, positioning her fingers so that the slim silver band on her ring finger flashed in the candlelight.

Evelyn's eyes narrowed. Leo's widened.

Tem knew full well that the gesture was not lost on either of them. It was a dangerous thing to do, but Tem was feeling dangerous. Nothing about this conversation had satisfied her. She was in no mood to indulge it any longer.

"Of course," Evelyn continued, her eyes boring into Tem's, "now that I'm back"—she threw a meaningful glance at Leo, who was still staring at Tem's hand—"we can't wait to get married."

A knife twisted in Tem's stomach. Of course. Her marriage to Leo had been annulled for the express purpose of clearing the way for a marriage between Leo and Evelyn. The villagers needed a queen, and Tem was no longer an option. Her human side knew this was for the best. Her human side was almost happy for them. But her basilisk side growled in jealousy, and beside her, Caspen squeezed her leg once more.

He asked the question on the tip of Tem's tongue: "Are you not already married?"

Leo shook his head, snapping back to reality. "Evelyn wants a wedding."

"*We* want a wedding," Evelyn said, squeezing Leo's arm. "And we're going to plan it together. I want it absolutely perfect."

Tem stared at her blankly. Their kingdoms were on the brink of war, and she cared about planning a wedding? It was a perilous time. The truce was in flux and there had already been bloodshed. The fact that Leo had had two wives in the span of a week would not be received well. The right thing to do would be to marry quietly and get on with the task of ruling the kingdom. The path forward was clear to Tem. How could it not be clear to Evelyn?

The right thing to you and me is not necessarily the right thing for them.

Tem rolled her eyes. *Don't pretend this makes any sense.*

I did not say it made sense. Only that it is what they think is right.

It's what she thinks is right. Leo doesn't want this. You can tell.

Leo is a man. If he does not agree with his wife, it is up to him to express that to her.

Tem knew Caspen was right. He was painfully, logically, right. As always. *This dinner was a terrible idea.*

To her surprise, amusement seeped from his mind to hers. *I think it is going rather well.*

Seriously?

Yes. I had expected you to throw something by this point.

Tem shot him a look, which he returned. Then to her surprise, he smiled, leaned in, and kissed her. For a moment, all was right with the world. The table disappeared, and all Tem knew was Caspen's lips on hers. The claw pulsed gently, warming her once more.

Evelyn cleared her throat. They pulled apart reluctantly, and Tem looked over to see Leo glaring at her with complete and utter rage. It scared her so much that she nearly recoiled.

Caspen's mind tightened around hers: *He is angry, Tem. Do not hold it against him.*

Why are you suddenly playing peacemaker? You've been far too reasonable tonight. I don't like it.

He let out a quiet laugh under his breath. *Because it is in my best interest for this dinner to go well.*

Well, it's not going well so far.

It might go better if you focused on something other than your anger.

Tem sighed. He was being insufferable tonight. Then again, so was she. And only one of them was making this dinner more difficult. *There's nothing else to focus on.*

Shall I give you something else?

The claw pulsed. The pulse built. Before Tem could react, Caspen turned back to Evelyn.

"When will you be wed?"

Tem knew he couldn't care less about the answer. But he was the only one making conversation, and they both knew it was safer than her chiming in at this point. Tem had nothing whatsoever to add to a discussion of their wedding. Nothing *positive*, at least.

"On Mother's Night."

Tem frowned. "But that's—"

"Lovely," Caspen finished.

Evelyn smiled at him before returning to her chicken. Tem stared at Caspen in disbelief.

Mother's Night occurred on winter solstice and was widely believed to be Kora's birthday. Gods weren't born exactly. But it was said that Kora descended from the heavens on Mother's Night, many millennia ago, to bestow fertility on the women in the kingdom. She gave the gift of life, and the villagers had honored her by having children ever since. It was unbelievable to Tem that Evelyn would dare to hold her wedding on such a blessed day. There could be no greater insult—no exercise of ego more shameful than thinking your nuptials deserved to occur on Kora's birthday.

Lovely? How dare she?

She is merely excited.

She's delusional. Has she lost her mind?

It is not for us to have an opinion on her wedding.

It's their *wedding. And I have a hard time believing Leo supports this.*

Clearly he does; otherwise, he would have said.

This is ridiculous.

This is none of our concern, Tem. They can do as they please.

Tem had nothing to say to that. She stared at Leo, who was picking at his food listlessly, pushing vegetables from one side of his plate to another with a golden fork. He hardly looked like a man who was doing as he pleased. He seemed more like a captive in a cage.

Another pulse came, and Tem closed her eyes. Caspen was sending them faster now, and Tem was having trouble sitting still. This had all seemed like a great idea in the carriage—back when she thought she could control herself during dinner. Now that she was sitting here, soaking wet and squirming in her chair, it all seemed rather ridiculous.

Caspen. Please.

Was she begging for less? For more? Tem had no idea anymore. All she knew was that with one final pulse, her core clenched and intense relief slammed into her. Tem had never come quietly in her life. But she did so now, clamping her eyes shut as her release traveled through her in a shuddering wave. She squeezed her thighs together as tightly as she could, deepening the sensation as she gripped her seat with both hands. Her mind cried out for Caspen's, seeking his presence and immersing herself in it. In moments like these, she remembered that while she may be wearing Leo's wedding ring, she belonged to the man beside her.

"Tem?"

A voice floated to her through the echoes of pleasure.

"Tem?"

There it was again. Pressing and shrill.

Tem finally opened her eyes to see Evelyn staring right at her.

"Are you well? You look a bit flushed."

Of course she looked flushed. She'd just had an orgasm.

But there was no polite way of saying that, so Tem said, "I'm fine."

Leo was staring at her again. Was it her imagination, or did he look flushed as well? Leo knew how Tem looked when she came. He would recognize it now, right in front of him, at the dinner table. And if he did, how would it make him feel? Jealous? In the darkest corner of her heart, Tem wanted him to be jealous. But perhaps he was indifferent—immune to her charms now that his new wife was by his side.

When nobody said anything, Evelyn spoke again. "And how are your parents, Tem?"

Tem's parents were the last topic she wished to discuss so soon after climax. And how did Evelyn know about them anyway? Had Leo told her about them?

"They are fine."

"It's good to hear they are unaffected."

Tem frowned. "What would they be affected by?"

"The food shortage, of course."

"What food shortage?"

Evelyn glanced at Leo, who took a dangerously large gulp of his wine. "Haven't you heard?"

Obviously Tem hadn't heard. She was no longer a resident of the village; she wasn't privy to the daily happenings in town. If there really was a food shortage, she would have at least expected Gabriel to mention it. But he'd said nothing, and neither had her parents.

"No. I haven't."

"Oh." Evelyn tilted her head innocently. "I see. Well, as I'm sure you can imagine, things have become…difficult for our kingdom lately."

More silence.

"How so?"

Tem expected an immediate reply. When the pause went on, it was Caspen, ultimately, who answered: *She is referring to the bloodletting.*

Understanding shot through Tem. Of course.

"The *shortage* has been difficult," Evelyn said.

Beside her, Caspen stiffened.

Tem wondered briefly whether she meant the food shortage or the shortage of blood. One glance at the loaded golden plates before her told Tem it was probably the latter.

"There have been protests," Leo said quietly. "The villagers are angry."

That was no surprise. The villagers were already angry before her marriage to Leo.

Jonathan's and Christopher's deaths had violated the truce, and they wanted justice. Abolishing the bloodletting—a move that appeared favorable to the basilisks—was the last thing the villagers wanted. Leo was in a dangerous position. And Tem had put him there.

"That's…unfortunate," Tem said stiffly. She didn't trust herself to say anything else.

"What's unfortunate is that our people will be affected by this," Evelyn said over her glass. "Don't you think?"

The comment seemed innocent at first glance. But it was anything but.

"*Our* people," Tem said with pointed emphasis, "have already been affected by this."

Beside her, Caspen's energy was changing. Tem was not the only one who had to be careful controlling her temper. If Evelyn was implying that the bloodletting should continue, Caspen was sure to lose his good attitude. That was the absolute last thing that Tem needed to happen at this dinner.

Caspen's voice cut into her mind: *How dare she?*

Now Tem was the one to place her hand on Caspen's knee. This was all wrong—Leo had agreed to end the bloodletting. They shouldn't even be talking about this.

She should watch her tongue. Or I shall remove it.

Caspen. You can't hurt her. She's the queen.

Caspen turned to her, looking straight into her eyes. *You are the only queen I answer to.*

Everything else fell away as he looked at her. Tem saw his fierce pride, his unwavering commitment. Her basilisk side unfurled beneath his gaze, immediately drawn to him.

She turned back to Evelyn, shrugging with an ease she did not feel. "Sounds like you need to find a way to make money."

"We had a way," Evelyn said. "But Leo stopped it."

Tem's mouth fell open.

Leo's gaze remained on his wine, but a muscle in his jaw twitched.

"You could always ask for a loan," Tem snapped.

"And who would we ask?"

"The other royals. There were certainly plenty at *our* wedding."

Another jab. Tem was truly out of control now, but she couldn't help it. This conversation was making her furious, and she was dangerously close to losing her temper.

"The other royals are feeling the loss too. Our economy affects theirs."

"That's too bad."

Enough, Tem. Caspen's voice was tight. His anger matched hers.

I hate her.

She is not important enough to hate. Now that is enough.

Tem slumped in her seat. She felt suddenly exhausted, as if she'd just run a mile at full speed. Across from her, Leo seemed paler than usual. He really wasn't looking well, she realized. The more she and Evelyn argued, the more it hurt Leo. Caspen was right. It was enough.

Thankfully, at that moment, the butler appeared with dessert. The final course was consumed in silence, all four of them staring down at their plates as they ate. Caspen barely touched his. Tem couldn't blame him. This dinner had been, all things considered, an utter disaster. All she wanted was to leave the castle as quickly as possible.

But just as they were rising from their seats, Evelyn said, "Tem? Can we talk alone?"

CHAPTER EIGHT

··•●✳●•··

TEM GLANCED IMMEDIATELY AT CASPEN, WHO STARED BLANKLY BACK AT HER. "Uh. Why?"

Evelyn gave her that sugary sweet smile again. "I thought it would be nice to get to know each other."

"Why?" Tem said again. After the dinner they'd just had, she knew plenty about Evelyn already. And none of it was remotely good.

Evelyn's smile widened. There was no joy in it. "Because you and Leo were…close."

Tem knew she'd purposefully chosen not to say the word "married." Always diminishing. Always deflecting. "I see," said Tem, even though she didn't. She couldn't think of a single rational reason why she and Evelyn should get to know each other. She'd rather hoped they would never have to speak again after tonight.

Tem looked at Leo, who was watching the two of them with his brow furrowed. Had he suggested this? Surely not. He couldn't possibly want his former wife and his future wife to get to know each other. It defied logic.

"Perfect. Then it's settled," Evelyn said. "We'll have some girl talk. Boys, will you excuse us?"

She didn't wait for an answer. Tem didn't have time to wonder what the men were supposed to do while left alone in the dining room before Evelyn turned on her heel and walked into the library. With one last desperate glance at Caspen, Tem followed, feeling as if she were walking toward her grave. The moment she entered the library, memories crashed over her like a wave. Leo sprawled in the leather armchair with lipstick on his neck, his hair mussed. The taste of whiskey when he'd kissed her. The hourglass was still sitting on the desk, the delicate flakes of gold piled in a mountain at the bottom. Did Evelyn have any idea what had happened in this room? So many lines had been crossed here—so many things had been said. This was where Tem had allowed herself to kiss Leo without thought of the consequences, where she'd indulged in him for the first time on her own terms. How things had changed.

"So," said Evelyn as she sat in one of the leather chairs. "How are you feeling, Tem?"

Tem remained standing. And silent.

"Please." Evelyn gestured. "Sit."

It was the last thing Tem wanted to do. But she also didn't want to prolong the evening, and she had a feeling Evelyn wouldn't let her out of this room until she'd gotten what she wanted out of this conversation.

So Tem sat.

Evelyn leaned in. "I imagine you're feeling quite overwhelmed."

That was certainly one way to put it.

"I know *I'm* feeling overwhelmed. There's just so much happening with the wedding."

The stupid wedding again. Tem resisted the urge to roll her eyes. She was beginning to get whiplash from the way Evelyn changed her personality. One moment she was cold and dismissive, the next she was fostering a false sense of intimacy with her "girl talk." Tem hated it.

"Besides," Evelyn continued. "I'm dying to know more about you. Leo's so secretive. I thought I'd go right to the source."

Now Tem was beyond confused. Leo, secretive? He was anything but. He wore his emotions on his sleeve, to the point of inconvenience. There was nobody in the world who was easier to read than Leo.

"Well…what do you want to know?" Tem asked. She had no idea where this conversation was going and was starting to wish she'd never allowed herself to be dragged in here. She could have resisted—she could have screamed. How could Caspen let this happen? Or worse, Leo? They were both at fault. She would reprimand them later.

Evelyn leaned forward. "Did you love him?"

Kora. That was certainly getting straight to the point.

Tem noticed how Evelyn used the past tense—how she didn't ask *do* you love him? It was an interesting distinction, and one that framed Tem's relationship as something of the past no matter which way Tem answered. She decided to simply respond with the truth: "Yes."

Evelyn's eyes narrowed. "How long?"

"Excuse me?"

"How long did you love him for?"

That was a trickier question to answer. It implied there was an end to her love. But the truth was that Tem still loved Leo. She always would. "Why do you want to know that?"

Evelyn shrugged in an attempt at nonchalance, but the gesture came off stilted. "I'm just interested in your history."

"Our history shouldn't matter to you."

Tem's tone was a little harsher than she intended. But it was true—*Evelyn's* history with Leo was far more impactful than Tem's. Of the two of them, Evelyn was the one who had deeper roots with the current king. Tem should be curious about her, not the other way around. And yet Tem found that she didn't want to know anything about their history. She'd much rather pretend they didn't have one. That, at least, was easier than picturing the two of them together.

"Of course it matters," Evelyn said. "You were important to him."

Again, past tense. Tem couldn't know for sure, but she would bet everything she owned that she was still important to Leo. He was still important to her.

But enough was enough. Tem didn't owe Evelyn any details about her feelings for Leo, past *or* present. Evelyn was not in charge of this conversation just because they were in her home. Tem decided to take matters into her own hands.

"Where did you go?"

Evelyn crossed her arms defensively. "When?"

"When you decided to leave Leo."

Tem could play with language too. She was purposefully framing Evelyn's actions as her own choice, not one that was influenced by some letter.

"I went to a neighboring village."

Tem frowned. The closest village was less than a day's journey away. She couldn't believe Evelyn had been so near yet hadn't been tempted to return.

"And yet you never came back? Not even once, just to see him?"

Evelyn's eyes narrowed. "I thought Leo wanted me to stay away."

This again. But Tem was done believing it. "But surely you would've tried to return at least once, just for a chance to change his mind, to ask him if he was really sure?"

Evelyn shrugged. "I didn't want to risk it."

"No? I would've."

A testy silence fell. Then Evelyn said, "The letter was quite convincing."

"And yet you destroyed it."

"It was a painful memory for me."

"So you said."

Evelyn leaned forward. "Have you ever been broken up with, Tem?"

"No. I haven't."

"Then you can't possibly imagine what it feels like."

"I can imagine I wouldn't accept being broken up with via letter."

"Even if I had come back, his father wouldn't have allowed us to be together."

"I wouldn't have accepted that either."

"Then you don't know Maximus as well as I do."

"And how well *do* you know him?" This time Tem was the one asking pointed questions cloaked in innocence.

But Evelyn was clearly done playing games. She stood, crossing to the liquor shelf and gesturing at the bottles. "Shall we have some champagne?"

"I don't drink champagne."

"Oh, you must. It's fabulous."

Tem opened her mouth to protest again, but Evelyn was already pouring her a glass. She handed it to Tem, who took it with a grimace.

"This is our best champagne," Evelyn said. "Worth its weight in gold."

Tem looked down at the sparkling liquid with disgust. Anything worth its weight in gold was hardly worth anything to her. She'd bet that each sip probably cost more than her childhood cottage.

"Try it," Evelyn insisted.

Tem raised the glass to her lips and took the world's smallest sip. It tasted like dust to her.

"Well? Isn't it delicious?"

Tem set down her glass. "Were you ever planning on coming back? After Maximus had died, say?"

Evelyn raised her eyebrows. She took a delicate sip of her champagne. "That's quite morbid, don't you think?"

"Not really. Everyone dies."

Another sip of champagne disappeared down her throat. Then: "Life here was… difficult…as I'm sure you know."

Was Evelyn referring to her own life in the village? Or was she attempting to relate to Tem, referencing her childhood on the chicken farm? Tem was surprised she knew anything about that, considering Leo was supposedly so secretive.

"Yes," said Tem stiffly. "I can. But surely being just one village over was no less difficult?"

Was it her imagination, or did Evelyn avoid eye contact at the question?

"Well." She played with the flute of her champagne glass. "It wasn't…so bad."

Tem's senses pricked. Had she met someone? Was that what made life one village over not so bad? Had she fallen in love with a man who wasn't Leo? But if that were the case, why had she returned? It would have been impossible to leave a new husband without making a scene.

"And what wasn't so bad about it?" Tem prompted. She even raised the champagne to her lips to look like she was drinking it.

Evelyn shrugged, still looking down at her glass.

She was avoiding the question. There was something going on here, and Tem was determined to figure out what it was.

"I know if it were *me*," Tem said pointedly, "I'd want to check up on Leo, just to make sure he hadn't moved on."

Silence.

"Then again, if I'd moved on myself, I wouldn't care whether he had as well."

A razor-thin pause. Evelyn's eyes met hers. "Is that what you think? That I moved on?"

"I don't know what to think."

To her surprise, Evelyn let out a small laugh. "I didn't move on, Tem."

The way she said it made it seem like it should be obvious. But nothing about this conversation was obvious. Evelyn was proving impossible to figure out, and Tem was tired of talking in circles. She leaned in. "Then why did you leave? What did Maximus write in the letter? Did he threaten you?"

"Of course not. A king would never stoop so low."

Tem snorted. A king certainly would. "What, then?"

Evelyn slid her finger up the flute of her champagne. She didn't answer.

Tem stared at her blankly. What could be worth leaving Leo? She herself had only done it because she'd assumed he'd be better off with Evelyn. An assumption, she was rapidly learning, that was a categorically false one.

Still, Evelyn said nothing.

In the silence, Tem's brain worked furiously. Why had Evelyn really left? She didn't believe for a second that a letter would have done the trick. Not if she were truly in love. It wasn't *enough*. It didn't add up. There had to be another reason.

How much did Evelyn know about their current circumstances? Did she know that Tem was the reason they were even sitting here—that Tem had been the one to order Leo to find her? Tem would have thought it would've been the first thing Leo told her. But according to Evelyn, he was secretive. He was keeping things from her. He was lying.

But Tem didn't care whether Leo lied. She cared whether Evelyn did.

Perhaps it was all an excuse—the letter, Maximus, all of it. It was Evelyn's way out—her story to tell so that she didn't seem like the villain. Her lie.

Tem leaned in.

"Do you want to know what I think? I think Maximus never wrote you a letter. That's why you don't have it."

Evelyn's lips pursed. She didn't reply.

But Tem couldn't stop. "I think you wanted to leave him. I don't know why—that's between you and Kora—but I think you were too much of a coward to tell him, so you left town. When he came to find you, you made up the story about the letter so he would take you back. And now you're looking to me for support, to corroborate your lie. But I won't do it."

Evelyn still didn't reply. She was watching Tem with shrewd intelligence, analyzing her. "I'll tell Leo," Tem said.

A cruel smile tilted Evelyn's lips. Finally, she spoke. "Will you now?"

A tenuous silence fell. The two women stared at each other.

"You don't know my story," Evelyn continued, her voice dangerously low. "And you'd better be absolutely sure you're right before saying anything to Leo."

Despite herself, Tem faltered. Evelyn hadn't confirmed her theory. She'd only smiled in that creepy way—hardly an admission of guilt. Tem had no *proof* that she'd left Leo of her own accord. Only suspicion. And she could not go to Leo with a suspicion. It wasn't enough. It would ruin everything, and what if Tem was wrong? What then?

Evelyn leaned closer. "He might have been yours once, but he began as mine and he is mine again now."

Fury built in Tem like a storm.

"You think you know Leo, but I know him better," Evelyn continued. "And I always will."

"If you hurt him, I will—"

"What will you do, Tem? *You* are the one who hurt him. You left."

"You left too."

"I came back."

Tem had nothing to say to that, no way to counter her argument. It didn't matter, ultimately, whether Evelyn only came back because Tem had stepped aside. She was right—she had come back.

Tem stood abruptly. "This conversation is over. And I won't be meeting with you in such a way again. Good night."

With that, Tem swept from the room.

CHAPTER NINE

———•◦❋◦•———

Caspen was waiting for her in the foyer. It was odd to see him there, surrounded by the gilded castle walls, his ethereal beauty outshining even the gold in the tiles.

He looked up as she approached, his eyes dark with worry. "Tem. How was it?"

"Horrible," she answered honestly.

A pause. "Do you wish to discuss it?"

Tem shook her head. It was all she could manage. So much had happened tonight that it was impossible to distinguish which event was most worth discussing.

Caspen's hand found her waist. "Shall we go home?"

Home. Under the mountain.

"I can't."

Caspen frowned. "Is something wrong?"

Tem just shook her head again. "I'll meet you back at the caves."

Still, Caspen hesitated. His fingers tightened around her waist. "I know this was difficult for you tonight," he said quietly. "But you can always speak to me about it."

When she didn't answer, his voice dropped even lower:

"About…him."

Tem felt the sudden urge to cry. She didn't want to speak to Caspen about Leo. It was the last thing she should be talking to her husband about.

"I know it is hard for you, Tem. You are not used to…sharing."

It was true. Basilisk culture had prepared Caspen for the situation with him and Leo. But Tem was not prepared. Tem was being torn in two. Her deception had begun already, when she'd shielded her mind from Caspen during sex. Something told her that was only the beginning.

"Please, Caspen," she whispered. "Just let me go."

Without another word, he did.

They took separate carriages away from the castle.

Tem watched as Caspen's carriage wound into the darkness, toward the mountain. Their connection was closed; Tem had thrown up a barrier as soon as they'd parted. At first she thought of heading to her parents' cottage. But at the last moment, she asked the footman to take her into the village.

The Horseman was crowded. Gabriel was in their favorite booth, as he always was. Except this time when he looked up to see her, his smile was just a moment delayed. "Tem," he said. "What are you doing here?"

It wasn't his usual greeting. Usually he called her "dearest" and kissed her on the cheek.

"I needed a drink," she said. "What are you doing here?"

Tem expected him to make a joke about needing a drink too. Or perhaps needing some action. Instead his eyes shifted to the bar, where a group of men were gathered. Tem had seen them before; they were regulars. Vera's father was among them, along with Jonathan's older brother, Jeremy.

"Gabriel?" she prompted. "What's going on?"

He pursed his lips. Tem knew he was remembering their promise—how they'd sworn to be honest with each other. "There's meant to be a protest tonight," Gabriel said finally.

A protest—the very thing Leo had mentioned at dinner. Tem hadn't wanted to believe him. She stared at the villagers gathered around the bar. These were men she'd known since childhood. They were peaceful people. Tem couldn't imagine them protesting.

"About what?" she asked, although she felt like she already knew.

He shrugged. "Money. Food. Everyone's starving. There's nothing to go around. Even your old farm is running out of eggs. Trust me, I checked."

"You…checked?"

If Gabriel had checked her farm for eggs, that meant he was suffering too, that her best friend in the entire world had been affected by her decisions—that she'd inadvertently hurt yet another person whom she loved.

"I'm fine, Tem. I work in the castle, remember? No food shortages there." But something about the way he said it sounded bitter.

"What do you mean?"

Gabriel shrugged, avoiding her eyes. "Our soon-to-be queen eats well."

It was all he said. But Tem knew exactly what he meant. The royals were not suffering; they never would. The consequences of Tem's actions would land squarely on the villagers—the people who deserved it the least. Evelyn would not feel the pain of constriction; her stomach would not tighten with hunger. Tem thought of the dinner she'd had just an hour ago—roasted chicken, golden potatoes, luscious greens. Gabriel was right. The new queen ate well.

"What can be done?" she whispered.

Gabriel shrugged again before taking a tight sip of beer. He didn't answer, and he didn't have to. Tem's eyes slid once more to the men gathering at the bar. Protesting was the only way to retaliate, the only way for the villagers to make sure their voices were heard. But it created a precarious situation for Leo. Protests, no matter how peacefully they began, were just one slip away from violence.

"Gabriel," she said. "This is dangerous. Whoever got you into this doesn't have your best interests at heart."

His eyes narrowed. "*I* got me into this, Tem. It's my choice to be here."

"I know, but—"

"I got everyone else into it too."

A moment passed as Tem understood what he was saying. "*You* organized this?"

"People are angry, Tem. I'm one of them."

Tears pricked her eyes. Things were going so very wrong. Everything was supposed to be fixed now that the bloodletting was over; that was supposed to make everything better. But it had only made everything worse.

"I work in the castle, Tem," Gabriel said. "I see it firsthand."

"Gabriel," she said slowly. "What exactly have you seen?"

Gabriel rolled his shoulders. His normally relaxed posture was stiff, his arms crossed protectively. He didn't look her in the eye as he answered. "I see how they eat, how they live. I see that they're still drenched in gold while the rest of us starve." He paused, and his next words came quietly. "And I saw how they freed the snakes."

Tem's heart thudded in her chest. "What do you mean?"

Gabriel finally looked at her. "You know what I mean."

For the first time, Tem heard accusation in his tone. She wondered what he'd overheard within the castle walls. Did he understand that it was ultimately Tem's plea that had freed the basilisks? The last time they were here, she'd told him she was half-basilisk. He'd been understanding then. Would he hold it against her now? Tem and Gabriel had never faced a crossroads in their friendship, never reached a point where their ultimate goals were at odds. Now Gabriel was protesting the very thing Tem had begged for—the thing she knew was right. It felt deeply unfair that a win for the basilisks was a loss for the humans. It always would be.

Tem raised her hand, cupping his cheek. "We said no more secrets," she whispered. "We promised each other, remember?"

Gabriel sighed. "I remember."

Tem opened her mouth to say something else, but a cheer from the bar cut her off. The men were heading toward the door.

Gabriel stood, and Tem stood with him. "What are you doing?" he asked.

"I want to come."

Gabriel shook his head. "It's not safe for you."

"Then it's not safe for you either."

"Just go home, Tem. Please."

She shook her head. "If you're going, I'm going. That's final."

A tiny smile split Gabriel's face. "You are rather stubborn tonight, dearest."

Tem rolled her eyes. "Every night."

With a sigh, Gabriel hooked his arm through hers. Together, they joined the crowd and filed out onto the street.

Tem had no idea what to expect. Energy was high—the men were whooping and yelling and clapping each other on their shoulders. There were no women that Tem could see, and she wondered if their husbands had forbidden them to come the same way Gabriel had just tried to do to her. Most of the windows around them were dark—it was after dinner, and the children of the village were asleep. As they approached the town square, a chant formed. Three words, over and over:

"Kill the snakes! Kill the snakes! Kill the snakes!"

A horrible chill slipped down Tem's spine.

It was the same thing the villagers had chanted after the Passing of the Crown. That day had been a tumultuous one; several men had stormed the stage, putting the prince and his family in danger. Tem still remembered the way Gabriel had leapt into action to protect Leo on her behalf. Afterward, Leo had shown up on her doorstep and she'd wiped a drop of blood from his cheek. They'd kissed, and Tem had decided his family's sins were not his own. But the villagers were not so easily persuaded. And who could blame them?

The chanting grew louder as they rounded the corner to the town square. Gabriel's arm was tight in Tem's as they crossed the cobblestone square and reached the church steps. But they didn't climb them. Instead, Tem saw a dozen soldiers stationed in front of the enormous wooden doors. They were dressed in armor stamped with the royal insignia: a snake dueling with a rooster.

"They've been here ever since your wedding," Gabriel said over the chanting. "Protecting the church."

"Why?"

"The royals built it."

Tem stared at the church, at the statues of the gods. It was Kora's house of worship, and it was supposed to be sacred. It was also the nicest building in the village. Surrounded by thatched huts, its marble walls stood out like a sore thumb. Tem glanced around the crowd, which was far more than a dozen people. The guards were outnumbered.

"Gabriel," she said. "What are they going to do?"

"Send a message," he said simply.

Dread pierced her. The men were in a frenzy. Even Gabriel's lanky frame couldn't shield her from getting jostled.

"You should get out of here," he said in her ear.

"What about you?"

"I have to do this." His words were laced with deeper meaning.

"No." Tem shook her head. "You don't."

"Just stay here, Tem. Please. I need you to be safe."

She opened her mouth to reply, but Gabriel was already gone. Tem watched his shoulders as he moved through the crowd, corralling the men toward the church.

What happened next was a blur. One moment the crowd was stationary, and the next, they were moving, surging toward the guards. From her standpoint on the sidelines, Tem could see the panic in their eyes as the villagers descended upon them in a merciless wave. If it wasn't for Gabriel, she would have run away. Instead she watched as he guided the crowd, directing them so they were pushing the guards to the right side of the church. At first, Tem thought they were clearing a path so they could enter. Instead, just one man ascended the steps. He wore black gloves on each hand and held a wooden bucket. When he reached the middle of the steps, he knelt, plunging his hand into the bucket and pulling out what looked like mud.

"*Hey!*" one of the guards cried, pointing at him. "Stop that at once!"

But the kneeling man ignored him, leaning over the steps to spread the mud onto the marble. Just then, the wind turned, and Tem's face twisted as a foul smell brushed against her nostrils. It wasn't mud. She would have recognized that stench anywhere— she'd grown up with it clinging to her clothing, lingering in her hair no matter how much she washed it. She knew exactly what the man was spreading all over the steps of the church.

Chicken shit.

It was unimaginable—such a horrible desecration Tem couldn't wrap her mind around it. She covered her nose with her sleeve in an attempt to keep the smell out, but nothing could block such a stench. It was then that Tem realized the man was writing something. Two words, smeared across the smooth, white marble of the church steps for everyone to see:

Feed us.

Tem stared at the dark brown letters. It was a desperate plea, a clear symbol of how the villagers felt about the food shortages, not to mention the murders of Jonathan and Christopher. They would never forgive such an act of violence, especially not when it had broken the truce. Nor should they. Caspen had gone unpunished. And since he was not available to reprimand, they would choose the next person in power: Leo. The villagers didn't know that Leo's kindness was the reason they were starving. They didn't know he tried to do the right thing, that his choices were born from a desire to do what was best for Tem's people as well as his. All they knew was that their king was lenient in a way that previous kings hadn't been. All they knew was that the food on their tables had become scarce, that their clothing was fitting looser. They attributed such detriments to the royals, to the snakes, to Leo. But really, they were Tem's fault. She was at the center of it all; she had called for the bloodletting to cease. She had begged Leo to choose.

Tem understood their anger. But to put it on the steps of the church was unfathomable—she had never seen such a horrible display of disrespect. And yet, they had every right to do so. The royals were supposed to protect their subjects. They were not supposed to sequester themselves in their castle while everyone else starved.

No sooner was the man finished than the crowd dispersed. The villagers sprinted in every direction, scattering down side streets before the guards could decide who to run after.

Gabriel's beautiful golden hair was suddenly before her. His lip was cut.

"Come on." He grabbed her hand and pulled her down the nearest alleyway. They ran together all the way to the edge of the village, only stopping once they'd nearly reached the wall.

"Gabriel," Tem panted, nearly doubling over as she caught her breath. "That was—"

"Amazing," he said.

She looked up at him. Inexplicably, he was smiling. "Dangerous," she insisted. "That was *dangerous*, Gabriel. What if someone had gotten hurt?"

"We all knew the risks."

"You can't ever do anything like that ever again. You could lose your job. What if one of the guards had recognized you?"

"The guards don't come inside the castle."

"Still, you—"

"Tem," he said, placing his hands on her shoulders. "Stop. I came up with a plan, I organized everyone, and the plan worked. *I* did that."

Tem stared up at him in disbelief. His eyes were bright, his face lit up. Clearly this made him feel alive. Somehow, despite herself, Tem found she understood the feeling. Gabriel had just discovered that he was good at something. Tem of all people knew how empowering that could feel. She just wished that the thing he was good at wasn't protesting the royals.

Gabriel pressed his lips to her cheek. "You had better go."

There was nothing else to say. A moment later, he was gone.

Tem followed the winding path among the trees, her heartbeat finally settling as silence fell. Here in the quiet, she allowed herself to reflect on what she'd just seen. The villagers were furious. It was not ideal. Their ire reflected what Evelyn had said at dinner: *It's unfortunate that our people will be affected by this.*

Will be. As if the effects were not already in motion.

Feed us.

Tem couldn't stop picturing those horrible, streaky words. To write something in such a blasphemous way beneath the eaves of Kora's home was a sin beyond what Tem could comprehend. For the first time, fear slipped through her. Not so long ago, things were different. Not long ago, it was Maximus who would have reaped the consequences of rebellion. Now those consequences fell to his son.

By the time Tem returned to the caves, she had resolved to talk to Caspen. He was the one who had killed Jonathan and Christopher; he was the one who would have a solution for this. Yet when she reached their chambers, he wasn't there. A cursory search revealed nothing. He wasn't in the courtyard, and he wasn't in the banquet hall. Tem was about to give up looking when she heard a voice behind her.

"All alone tonight, Temperance?"

The voice belonged to Apollo.

CHAPTER TEN

——•◦✴◦•——

H E WAS LEANING AGAINST THE WALL OF THE PASSAGEWAY, HIS ARMS CROSSED, HIS expression unreadable. She was struck once again by the similarities between him and Caspen—how they shared the same broad shoulders, the same strong brow. But Apollo's beauty was harsher than Caspen's. He resembled his father more than he resembled his brother, and every time Tem looked at him, she couldn't help but think of Bastian.

"Looking for someone?"

Apollo's mouth was turned up at the corner. There was no one Tem would be looking for other than her husband. He knew this, and she knew it too.

Still, Tem answered, "Have you seen Caspen tonight?"

Apollo stepped forward, his arms still crossed. His cock was half-erect, thick and straight and glorious. Tem had removed her dress already, as had become habit when returning to the caves. She was suddenly acutely aware that she was naked.

"I saw him yesterday. Does that count?"

"No," said Tem. "It doesn't."

"Shame." He smiled wider. "I wish I could be more helpful."

"Are you ever helpful?"

"Occasionally. For example, I know where Caspenon is right now."

"Excuse me?" Tem snapped. "You just said you hadn't—"

"You asked if I had seen him tonight. Not if I knew where he currently was. You should know by now that basilisks take pride in the details, Temperance."

If it was possible to roll her eyes even harder, she would've. Apollo was infuriating. But that was not surprising. What *was* surprising was his willingness to help her.

"Fine." She crossed her arms. "Then where is he right now?"

Apollo smiled. "And why should I tell you that?"

"Because he's my husband. And I want to know."

"Only one of those reasons is compelling to me."

Tem didn't bother wondering which one. "Just tell me, Apollo," she said. "And then we can both get on with our evenings."

"And what if I do not wish to get on with my evening?" Apollo murmured, stepping *far* closer than was appropriate. "What if I wish to linger here with you?"

Tem looked up at him—the familiar golden eyes, the same smooth, warm skin. Apollo's heat radiated off him just as Caspen's did, enveloping her. But she would not be seduced by it.

"I don't care what you want," she snapped. "*I* want my husband."

"Perhaps I could be what you want for the night."

"I'm *taken*, Apollo."

"There are many types of relationships, Temperance. I have no doubt we could find an arrangement that everyone is happy with."

"I'm already happy with my arrangement, thank you very much."

He smirked. "If you insist."

"I do insist."

The smirk deepened. "You do not need his permission to do what you want, you know."

"And how do you know what I want?"

"Please," he laughed. "I can sense it."

It reminded her of what Caspen had said in the caves. *You are afraid of me. I can sense it.*

Was Tem afraid of Apollo? She wasn't sure. She was certainly wary of him. But that didn't necessarily equate to fear, and it would be wrong to interchange the two. She was still getting to know him. And what she knew so far was decidedly aggravating.

When it became clear that Tem wasn't going to indulge him, Apollo said, "Your husband is hunting."

Tem frowned.

"Ah," Apollo whispered. "Are you surprised he would seek sustenance without his bride?"

"Of course not. It's just…"

But it *was* a surprise. There was no denying it. Tem had always hunted with Caspen—ever since she'd come under the mountain. It was their routine, and it was special to do it together. But considering how dinner had ended, she couldn't exactly blame him for going off alone. She'd gone to the village to see Gabriel, after all. It was only fair that Caspen unwound in whatever way he saw fit.

"You are hurt," Apollo said quietly, interrupting her thoughts.

Tem blinked. "What?"

"You have a bruise." He raised his fingers and touched them gently to her cheek. "Just here."

Tem hadn't even noticed—it was probably a remnant of the rowdy crowd. She swatted his hand away. "Don't touch me."

Apollo dropped his hand. "Bruises are complex," he said with a smirk. "Like you."

Tem rolled her eyes. It wasn't the first time a Drakon brother had tried to compliment her, and it certainly wasn't the most flattering. To say she was complex was like saying the sun was bright. It was hardly a groundbreaking analysis, and it would not soften her to Apollo.

"Your observation skills leave something to be desired," she said.

"Do they?" Apollo arched an eyebrow, stepping even closer. His smile grew so wide, it looked as if it might split his face. "And what do you know of desire?"

Not for the first time, Tem deeply regretted the words she'd just said. Apollo took everything as a challenge. Everything was a taunt and a tease, and Tem was tired of it.

Or was she?

The night had been a heavy one. But for some reason, this moment wasn't. For some reason, she felt oddly at ease with Apollo, as if she were playing a game that she was good at. So instead of recoiling when Apollo's mind brushed hers, Tem savored the feeling, noticing how similar his presence was to Caspen's. Both were overbearing, yet they were not the same. Whereas Caspen was rigid, Apollo was loose. As if he existed in the space between what was right and what was possible.

Anything is possible, Temperance.

And just as quickly, her resistance returned. *Not for us.*

We are meant to sleep together. Surely, my brother told you.

He told me you would try.

And what would you do if I did? It is mating season, after all.

I'd tell you no.

I am trying right now.

They were standing a foot apart. They weren't even touching. Yet Tem knew what he said was true. This was Apollo's first flirtation. He was testing the waters to see how she would react. What happened next was up to her.

Well. You're failing.

Am I?

Yes. Miserably.

That got a laugh from Apollo.

Is it such a crime to wonder what you think of me?

I don't think of you at all.

His face twisted into a smile. *You wound me.*

Nobody could wound you.

I beg to differ. You, of all people, are up to the task.

Don't flatter me.

It is not flattery. Merely fact.

The way he said it made her blush. The conversation was becoming too real—too intimate. Tem had to create some distance. So she said out loud, "I don't want to hurt Caspen."

Apollo let out a soft chuckle, speaking out loud to match her. "My brother and I have done this dance for centuries, Temperance. It would be a mistake for you to think you are the first person to find yourself in this position."

And what a position it was. Tem understood what Apollo was implying: that he and Caspen had done this before—that she was not the first to come between them. But Tem had no desire to repeat history.

"I'm loyal to him," she insisted.

"No one said you were not. Do you consider this conversation disloyal?"

"I consider it a nuisance."

"Is that so? Your heart says otherwise."

"My *heart*?"

"I can hear it beating, Temperance. It speeds up whenever you look at me."

Tem looked pointedly at the ground. Caspen had told her the same thing the first time they'd eaten a meal together. *Your heartbeat*, he'd said. *It is irregular.*

"My heartbeat is none of your business."

"And yet, it beats so loudly, I can hear nothing else."

"Well, stop listening."

"You are rather difficult to tune out, Temperance."

Tem didn't know whether that was a compliment, and quite frankly she no longer cared. The evening had not gone at all as planned. She hadn't expected to talk to Evelyn, hadn't expected to witness a protest in the village, hadn't expected to run into Apollo. It was late and she was alone with her husband's brother, and nothing that was happening right now felt even remotely within her control.

She shook her head, trying to clear it. "How can you speak to me like that?"

To her surprise, Apollo laughed. "I like the way you blush when I do it."

Tem resisted touching her fingers to her cheeks. She didn't need to touch them to know that they were warm. Apollo just made her so...*flustered.*

"I'm blushing because I'm angry. Not because you're flirting."

"Are you, now? Fascinating. I have never heard of an angry blush. You must be the first to experience it."

"Then I guess I'm the first."

"How thrilling," he said, tilting his head. "To be such a trailblazer."

Tem rolled her eyes. There was absolutely nothing to be done with him. He was *unreasonable*. She couldn't believe he would act this way, especially when he knew she was married to his brother. It didn't matter that basilisks did things differently. This wasn't the way to do things. She should leave. She should tell him good night and walk away. So why didn't she?

The truth was that she didn't want to. Tem *wanted* Apollo to listen to her heartbeat—to continue standing far too close to her. It felt right to be in his vicinity. Here, in the quiet of the passageway, Tem knew temptation. She understood what it meant to look at Apollo and want to touch him—to want him to touch her. She remembered the first night of mating season, how the couple had fucked on the mattress before her— how she hadn't come until her eyes had met Apollo's.

But it didn't matter. He wasn't Caspen.

"This belongs to your brother," Tem said firmly.

"*This?* Are you an object?"

She frowned. "No."

"And yet, you belong to my brother. That implies ownership."

She shook her head. It was difficult to refute Apollo's point when he was standing so close. Despite Tem's best efforts, her gaze kept dipping to the thick stem of cock between his legs. Something glistened at the tip: a perfectly round drop of cum. Tem had never seen such a thing before. When Caspen came, his cock was either inside her or down her throat. She'd never seen an erect cock that was already seeping cum.

Apollo followed her gaze. His mind returned to hers. *That is for you.*

I don't want it.

Is that so? Then why are you staring at it?

Tem's eyes snapped back up to his. *I'm not staring at anything.*

It is yours to stare at. I do not mind.

Of course he didn't mind. He *wanted* her to stare at it. He wanted her to do plenty of other things too. Tem knew she should retreat—knew she should remove herself and go to bed. But she was frozen in place, entranced by Apollo's intoxicating words. He was not unlike Leo in that way. Both were talented with their mouths.

Apollo was mere inches away, his head tilted down, his lips mirroring hers.

Do you wish to taste it?

Desire clawed at her. What would it be like, she wondered, to raise her finger, brush it along the tip of his cock, and taste it? Would it taste different than Caspen's? Or even more intriguing: Would it taste the same? Oh, they were in dangerous territory now. This was *not* what Tem had expected to do with her evening. But her husband was gone, and his brother was here, and his cock was hard and ready and leaking for her. Her basilisk side practically roared with pleasure at the thought of taking Apollo to bed. Why shouldn't she indulge?

Tem hadn't even realized she'd raised her hand until Apollo's presence surged in her mind. He gripped her temples, squeezing everything out except for him.

Touch it. His grip tightened.

Tem nearly blacked out.

Taste it, Temperance. It is yours.

Tem was unbearably hot. Her hand was still raised, her fingers an inch from the tip of his cock.

Taste it, Temperance. Put my cum in your mouth. Slide it across your tongue. Swallow it.

The passageway seemed to swim around her. Her throat was tight.

It is only a matter of time before you give in to me. So give in now.

But she couldn't give in. To give in would be to listen to her basilisk side—the side she was still learning to tame. The side that sinned.

To sin is to live, Temperance. I know you want me. So taste me.

Finally, it was too much for Tem. She looked Apollo straight in the eye as she said, "If you say one more word, I'm going to slap you."

Apollo's eyes flared. He leaned in, his breath against her blushing cheeks as he whispered, "Please do."

Something within Tem just snapped. She'd had enough of this evening—enough of Apollo and his games and his insistence on making her *feel something* when that was the last thing she wanted to do. So she slapped him.

Tem threw everything she had into it—every ounce of frustration she'd been feeling the last few days, every deep, tortured worry she'd harbored since beginning her time under the mountain. All she wanted was to *Shut. Him. Up.*

The moment her palm made contact, Tem felt a release not unlike a climax. It traveled from her body to his, and she was sure Apollo must have felt it too. The exchange of energy was powerful—it reverberated through the passageway like a physical force, ruffling her hair and shaking dust from the walls. Apollo's head whipped away. Then he turned back to her slowly.

Even though she'd just slapped him, he looked at her as if she'd kissed him. And perhaps, in his opinion, she had. The slap was as good as a kiss. Both were an exchange of power. Both were a passionate, raw reaction. The slap only confirmed that Tem was out of control with him, that she was unable to resist her emotions. She'd thought she was drawing a line between them, but now she realized she was doing the exact opposite. By the way Apollo was smiling, he surely realized it too. She had slapped him, yet he had won.

A red welt was forming on his cheek. Tem knew Apollo was barely injured, if at all; it had done nothing but make him happy. He was smiling at her with utter triumph in his eyes, as if he knew exactly what he'd finally managed to provoke. There was no doubt he had won their little exchange. It was his intent to tease her, to push her to her limit, and he had succeeded.

"Aren't you going to heal yourself?" Tem snapped. She could think of nothing else to say.

Apollo smirked. Even with the welt, he was devastatingly handsome. He touched his fingers to his cheek. "I would rather have a reminder of you."

Tem was already wet. But his words made her wetter. "And *I* would rather forget this happened."

"Would you? And why is that?" The welt on Apollo's face was spreading. Tem could clearly see the impression of her wedding ring. When she didn't answer, Apollo continued, "Is it because you are afraid of what we could be?"

That was not a question Tem was remotely prepared to answer.

"Or is it because you are afraid of what we already are?"

For some reason, vitriol built within her. Tem didn't know whether she was angry at Apollo or angry at herself. At this point, it didn't matter. She couldn't stand his smug expression, how clearly he reveled in his victory. It was time to end this.

"We're nothing," she snarled. "*You're* nothing."

For the very first time, a shadow of hurt flashed in Apollo's eyes.

It was gone so quickly Tem wasn't even sure she saw it. But it prompted her to say, "I'm sorry—"

"No," he cut her off. "You are not. And I do not want you to be sorry anyway. You are justified, and you know it quite well." He stepped closer, and Tem's cheeks flushed. "To accept your apology would be to comfort you."

They stared at each other, inches apart, both breathing hard.

Finally, Apollo whispered, "Do not come to me for comfort, Temperance. Come to me when you want me to fuck you the way my brother will not."

With that, he turned and disappeared.

Tem was left alone, too stunned to move, her heart pounding in her chest. Apollo was *impossible*. There was no other word for it.

And yet.

Flirting with Apollo was a thrill she hadn't felt since flirting with Caspen: the appeal of the forbidden, the promise of more. The possibility of destruction. There was something about the other Drakon brother that drew her in, that tempted her. But Tem could not afford to be tempted. If she gave in—if she surrendered to her instincts and let

Apollo fuck her—it would risk her relationship with Caspen. And nothing could make her do that. Tem didn't believe him no matter how adamantly he claimed it wouldn't bother him if she slept with his brother, and it wasn't worth it to find out whether she was right.

Caspen was in their chambers by the time Tem returned. A wet leaf was stuck to his shoulder, dirt along his back. He looked up when she entered.

"Tem." His eyes flicked down her body, and not for the first time, Tem wondered if he could sense what she'd just been doing. "Where were you?"

"Where were *you*?"

"Hunting."

"Without me?" Tem tried to say it casually, but her hurt must have showed on her face because Caspen crossed to her and cupped her chin in his hand.

"I had to transition," he said quietly. "I did not want to strain you."

Tem nodded. It wasn't fair of her to expect him to accommodate her pace when it was so much slower than his. It wasn't until now that she understood how often Caspen had to hunt, that he required a steady supply of sustenance beyond what was available in the banquet hall. She could not blame him for going alone.

"I did not mean to leave you," he said quietly.

"I know."

A long moment passed before his expression suddenly hardened, and he leaned in. "You are hurt." Caspen's fingers brushed her cheek.

Tem winced as he made contact with the same spot Apollo had touched earlier. A cool pulse bloomed beneath her skin, and she knew Caspen had healed her. She wondered suddenly why Apollo hadn't. "Nobody hurt me," Tem said quickly. "I promise."

"Then why are you bruised?"

She heard the fear and fury in his voice—knew he was remembering the time when she had come to him desperate and scared, right after Jonathan and Christopher had tried to touch her.

"I went to the Horseman with Gabriel," she said, trying to decide in real time how much to tell him. "And there was a…protest afterward. It became violent."

"A protest?"

"Yes."

"A protest for what?"

But how to explain it? On the surface, the villagers were protesting the royals, lamenting the sudden drop in food now that the bloodletting had ceased. But a deeper undercurrent ran through their unrest, and ultimately, their wrath was directed at the basilisks—at Caspen.

"Without the bloodletting, there isn't enough food to go around," Tem said carefully.

Caspen listened with barely restrained anger. It radiated off him in waves, pushing against the edges of her mind. "They should have thought of the consequences before cutting my people open."

Tem had nothing to say to that. In Caspen's eyes, the punishment fit the crime. "Jonathan and Christopher are dead," she continued, keeping her voice as calm as possible, knowing that it was Caspen who had killed them. "The villagers are angry."

Caspen snorted. "Their anger is of no concern to me."

"It should be."

"And why is that?"

"Because they're already protesting the royals. If they don't get the response they want, they may take matters into their own hands. They may direct their anger here."

Another snort. "Do you truly think the villagers can hurt us?"

Tem thought about the bloodlust she'd seen in their eyes—the way they'd stormed the guards on the steps of the church. She thought about how good Gabriel was at organizing. "Yes," she said quietly. "I do."

The first war between the humans and the basilisks had been won with mirrored shields, after all. It was the humans, at the end of the day, who had prevailed. Why couldn't they do so again?

"If that is true, you should not have gone in the first place."

"I didn't *mean* to. It just sort of happened—"

"You should know better than to endanger yourself when you are the queen."

"But I—"

Caspen placed his hands on either side of her head. "I love you," he whispered, his breath fluttering over her face. "But I cannot protect you from every threat."

"Nothing's going to happen to me," she insisted. "I promise."

"You cannot make such a promise."

Finally, Tem understood what this was about. Caspen was scared for her. He'd seen his family and his people get massacred by the humans for centuries. Now, with tensions rising, he didn't want the same thing to happen to her.

"I'm fine, Caspen. It's Gabriel that I'm worried about. And my parents."

Caspen shook his head. "Your parents are under our protection. They will not be harmed."

"And Gabriel?"

Caspen pursed his lips.

Tem squared her shoulders. "He's my best friend, Caspen. I don't want him to starve because of me."

"He will not starve."

"How do you know?"

"Because I will always protect those you love, Tem. And if you believe otherwise, you do not know me at all."

The fire crackled beside them. Tem didn't know what to say to that. She knew Caspen would protect her. But she didn't always believe he'd protect the people she loved. Especially when the people she loved wanted to hurt him.

Caspen sighed, and some of the tension left his shoulders. "I will not let anything happen to them," he finished quietly. "I promise."

Tem couldn't meet his eye. She had heard many promises in her life. Mostly by men. She hoped dearly that Caspen would keep this one. A moment of silence passed. Caspen's fingers traced her face again, touching the spot where the bruise had just been.

"You must be careful," he whispered.

She sighed. "I *am* careful. It was just an accident."

He shook his head. "If they try to hurt you, I will turn the entire village to stone."

Rather than comforting her, this statement did the opposite. "How can you say that? Wasn't once enough?"

"You belong to us now," Caspen said firmly.

It was a truth Tem wasn't yet ready to acknowledge.

When she didn't reply, he whispered, "You must protect yourself, Tem."

"How? You won't teach me."

The words just slipped out. Caspen's eyebrows rose, then furrowed. "Petrification is not protection."

Tem just shook her head. This was not an argument she was going to win, and yet she wanted to argue it anyway. "Why not?"

Tem wasn't even sure why she was pushing this. She'd never given much thought to petrification—it was technically murder, after all. And Tem had no desire to be a murderer. But she *did* desire to learn everything there was to know about her basilisk side. If Caspen wanted her to protect herself, this was the best way to do it.

"But what if I need to do it someday? What if I'm in danger?"

"You will never be in danger when I am with you."

"But you're not always with me."

Caspen hesitated, and she knew she had him. It was impossible for him to protect her all the time—more impossible still if he was going to be absent for long hunting periods, as he had been tonight. Indignation rose suddenly within her.

It was unfair of Caspen to withhold such pivotal knowledge. Every other basilisk under the mountain knew how to petrify. But not Tem. "What do you expect, Caspen? That I'll never petrify anyone?"

He didn't answer.

Tem stepped closer. "You can't keep this from me forever. It isn't right."

"Enough, Tem. We will discuss this another time."

"But—"

"I said that is enough."

Tem pursed her lips. She wasn't only upset about the petrification. That was just one problem in a growing list of things that were pressing in on her like an avalanche— Evelyn's obstinance, the protest she'd seen tonight, Apollo's advances. It was becoming too much, and it had all just begun.

A moment of silence fell as they stared at each other. Tem raised her hand and gently brushed the leaves from his shoulder, savoring the warmth of his skin beneath her fingertips. Caspen closed his eyes as she did it, and she knew he was savoring it too. This was all it took with Caspen: one touch, and she would forgive him. It didn't matter that they were out of step, that things were rapidly reaching a boiling point. All that mattered was that they were together now.

Tem drew him into a kiss.

The moment it deepened, he pulled away. "Not now, my love."

She couldn't believe he was denying her sex. It was unheard of. "Why not?"

"Because we are already running late."

"For what?"

"Mating season."

CHAPTER ELEVEN

—•◦✦◦•—

A RE YOU SERIOUS?"

"Yes, Tem." He smiled, pressing his lips to her cheek. "I am."

Tem shouldn't have been surprised. It didn't matter to the basilisks that it was the middle of the night. For them, it may as well have been daytime. But for Tem, it was bedtime, and she yawned widely as Caspen grasped her waist and pulled her into the passageway.

The mountain was alive with activity. Basilisks streamed by on either side of them, all headed for the courtyard. As they entered, Tem saw the decorations she had chosen to adorn the space. It was a small thing, but it gave her pride, showed that she had contributed somehow, even if it was just on the surface.

Caspen's lips touched her ear. "I must check in with the council," he murmured. "I will return in a moment."

Before Tem could protest, he was gone. She looked around the courtyard, desperate to find a friendly face. Mercifully, her gaze fell on Adelaide. She was sitting on a bench alone, drinking a goblet of elixir. When Tem sat beside her, immediate ease flooded her chest.

"Temperance." Adelaide smiled. "Good evening. To what do I owe the pleasure?"

To what, indeed? There was really only one thing Tem wanted to tell her: "I slapped Apollo."

Adelaide's eyebrows lifted. "May I ask why?"

"He wouldn't stop flirting with me."

Adelaide laughed. "Yes. He tends to do that."

"Well, I'd like him to stop."

"Would you?"

The question reminded her of her conversation with Apollo and she knew the truth was not black and white. "I...don't know," she said honestly.

Adelaide smiled. "Apollo is complicated."

"He seems pretty simple to me."

"If he seems that way to you, then you have underestimated him, and that is your mistake."

There was a pause, and they both stared at the crowd of basilisks.

Tem shifted so she was facing Adelaide. "Complicated how?"

Another pause. Adelaide seemed to be considering what to say next, and Tem wondered about the origin of her hesitation. "He is…reckless. It has gotten him into some trouble in the past."

"What kind of trouble?"

"Apollo likes to take what is not his."

"What has he taken?"

"Something that belonged to Caspen."

A twinge of understanding sparked in Tem. She remembered what Apollo had said to her: *My brother and I have done this dance for centuries, Temperance.*

"Something? Or someone?"

Adelaide smiled but didn't reply. For a moment, neither of them spoke.

"They loved the same woman, didn't they?"

Adelaide looked over at her. "Yes, they did."

A dull pulse of jealousy ran through Tem. "What happened?"

"They had a falling-out," Adelaide continued. "It did not end well for any of them."

"But who did she choose?"

"You would have to ask Caspenon that."

Tem fell silent, processing this. She wasn't about to ask Caspen anything. "But…" Tem said slowly. "Caspen is with me, and Apollo isn't with anyone. So what happened to her?"

Adelaide's voice became quiet as she said, "She was taken for bloodletting."

A memory came to her of Caspen searching the line of basilisks returning from the castle, as if he were expecting someone. Had he been looking for his previous love? What would he have done if she had returned to him that night?

"I don't want to be in the middle of them," Tem whispered.

"But you are," Adelaide said simply.

"But I—"

"It is an honor to be pursued, Temperance. They desire you. You should take that as a compliment."

But was she truly being pursued? This didn't feel like pursuit. It felt like a competition—a game she hadn't agreed to play. And who would win? Not Tem.

"The Drakon brothers are complicated, Temperance," Adelaide said. "They lived long lives before they met you. You cannot expect to rewrite their history."

But it wasn't their history that Tem was concerned with. She only cared about their future. "I would never choose Apollo," Tem said firmly. "Caspen knows that."

Adelaide shrugged. "We are basilisks, Temperance. You can have them both."

Tem had nothing to say to that. They sat in silence for a while, watching the activity around them.

Eventually, Adelaide said, "I must admit I am envious of you."

Tem stared at her. "*Why?*"

"I have dreamed of slapping Apollo many times. As have others, I am sure. I am pleased someone finally did it."

That information surprised Tem. Then again, perhaps it didn't. Apollo did plenty of things she considered insufferable. He deserved to be slapped for them. "Did he ever…try to…?"

Adelaide gave her a significant look. "Sleep with me?"

Tem nodded. That was pretty much exactly it.

"Yes," Adelaide said. "He did."

"Oh."

Another question occurred to her, and she asked it before she lost her nerve: "And did you…?"

"Sleep with him? Yes. I did."

"Oh."

Tem didn't know where to look. She settled on staring at her hands, which were clasped on her lap.

Adelaide leaned in. "Caspenon would have you think he was the only one upset by our match, but I was not thrilled either."

"He never mentioned how you felt." As soon as the words came out, Tem realized how they sounded. "Sorry—" she stammered. "I just meant that—"

"I am not offended, Temperance." Adelaide's tone was kind. "I know what you meant. And I am not surprised he did not mention it. I doubt he wanted to mention me at all."

Given the way Tem had reacted to their engagement, she could hardly blame him. It seemed silly now, to have been so jealous of their union. Perhaps her basilisk side understood it on some level—perhaps she was adjusting to their customs.

"I slept with Apollo to be vindictive. But also because I wanted to. And if you were to do the same, no one would blame you."

That wasn't true—Tem would blame herself.

Adelaide seemed to know what she was thinking. "It is different for basilisks, Temperance. To be with both brothers…it is expected. Apollo has first rights to you. That is no small thing. He will expect to exercise them. Caspenon may expect it eventually too."

Tem continued to look at her feet. The thought of sleeping with Apollo was tantalizing; the fact that she was *expected* to do so was baffling. It was difficult for her human side to comprehend such a thing. She had been raised to view marriages as strictly monogamous. Sleeping with your husband's brother was considered cheating, point-blank, period.

"They are quite similar," Adelaide said presently.

"Who?"

"Apollo and Caspenon."

Tem scoffed. They were *nothing* alike. "How so?"

Adelaide paused, gathering her thoughts. "Caspenon is passionate," she said slowly. "He feels things deeply. Apollo is the same way."

Tem snorted. Apollo didn't feel *anything* deeply. He was as shallow as a puddle.

"You may not believe it," Adelaide said. "But it is true. Apollo is merely better at concealing it."

Tem couldn't wrap her mind around such a concept. All she could see was the differences between them: the way Caspen protected her, the way Apollo chided her. One brother cared; the other did not.

"Caspen is better than Apollo," Tem said firmly.

Adelaide tilted her elegant head thoughtfully. "In what way?"

"He wants what's best for me."

"And you think Apollo does not?"

Tem looked up at her. "I *know* he doesn't. He's constantly trying to corrupt me."

Adelaide let out a laugh. "You give him too much credit, Temperance. You are not easily corrupted."

It felt like a compliment, so Tem took it as one. "I can't let him win," she admitted.

"Then you need only deprive him." Adelaide smiled conspiratorially. "He wishes to sleep with you. That much is obvious. If you withhold yourself from him, he will never stop pursuing you."

Tem considered this. Did she want him to pursue her? Leo wasn't pursuing her, and Caspen already had her. Why shouldn't she indulge in the very thing that basilisks were known for indulging in? It would be a lie to say that she didn't like it when Apollo flirted with her. It turned her on her axis, as if she were a planet and he were a new gravitational pull. Perhaps that was exactly what she needed: lightness, levity, flirtation. Caspen would be proud that she was assimilating so well into basilisk culture. He might even encourage it. He *had* encouraged it.

"And you are wrong," Adelaide continued.

"About what?"

"About Apollo's intentions. He does want what is best for you. We all do."

With that, Adelaide stood and walked away.

Tem started after her in bewilderment. It was an uncharacteristically straightforward thing for a basilisk to say. *We all do.* But who, exactly, was "we"? Caspen and Apollo? Or had Adelaide meant it in a broader sense, implying that all basilisks wanted what was best for her? It had never seemed that way to Tem. It had always felt as if basilisks wanted something *from* her.

And what, exactly, was best for her anyway?

Tem knew it was Caspen. But sometimes, in the depths of night, she wondered if that were really true. Before she could ponder further, he appeared.

"Tem," Caspen said, extending his hand. "You must stand. It is about to begin."

Tem didn't bother asking what "it" was. Instead, she allowed Caspen to guide her to the steps at the edge of the courtyard. From this vantage point, she could see basilisks gathering around the fountain. They conversed intently with one other before dispersing into a circle.

"What are they doing?"

"They are forming an ouroboros," Caspen explained. "A sacred shape to us. It is infinite and represents renewal."

"But what's the point?"

"By participating in the ouroboros, we honor the cycle of our people. Mating season will result in many unions and will likely produce the next generation of children."

The circle was growing—morphing into a large loop that surrounded the fountain.

"What do you mean by…participating?"

Caspen touched her waist.

"The ouroboros is a symbol of unity. It is meant to connect us. Members from each quiver will join the circle in opposing positions."

"Opposing—?"

But Tem saw immediately what he meant. The basilisks in the circle were beginning to lie down in a specific sequence. The first lay on their back. Once that basilisk spread their legs, the next basilisk lowered their head between them. Behind them, another basilisk was on their back, positioning themselves between the legs of the first. Over under, over under. A simple pattern. Women connected with women, men connected with men, and vice versa. Everywhere, all along the circle, mouths went between legs, forming a living chain.

Caspen continued calmly, as if what was happening before them was completely normal and not absolutely unbelievable. "As each basilisk finishes, they will leave the ouroboros. The ceremony will end once everyone in the ouroboros has climaxed."

Everyone was gathering into the circle—everyone but them.

Tem looked up at Caspen. "Aren't we going to join?"

Caspen looked down at her, a mix of surprise and caution in his eyes. "Do you... wish to join?"

When faced with a direct question, Tem found she had no idea how to answer. The ouroboros was intimidating, to say the least. But there was also a logic to it. Some part of Tem understood the symbolism, understood how this was a unifying act for the quivers. In the ouroboros, they were all one. She wanted to be part of it. But after the night she'd just had, she didn't know if she could.

"Tem," Caspen said gently, breaking her from her thoughts. "It is not required. You do not have to if you do not wish to."

She shot him a look. Was this like the ritual, where she didn't "have" to do it, but if she didn't, the consequences were catastrophic?

"No, Tem," Caspen said, addressing her thoughts. "Our culture revolves around pleasure. If observing will give you more pleasure than indulging, that is exactly what you should do. This is not a requirement. I promise you do not need to participate."

But Tem *did* want to participate. She wanted to join in and be a part of this basilisk tradition. The shame she felt from her inability to transition clung to her like tar. If this was a way to assimilate, it was imperative that she try.

"I want to do it. I'm a Hybreed. I can handle it."

Pure pride brightened Caspen's eyes. Tem knew he liked it when she acted like a basilisk, when she made an effort to reach what he considered to be her full potential.

He cupped her face in his hands, brushing his lips against hers. "Hybreeds are rare. But you are rarer still." He was gazing at her with complete sincerity.

Tem had always been struck by the way Caspen looked at her—like she was capable of achieving miracles. And perhaps she was. "But I don't want someone else's cock in my mouth," she said quickly.

To her surprise, Caspen smiled. "In that case, you shall only have mine."

Only then did Tem realize that if she and Caspen joined the ouroboros, it would mean *he* would be pleasuring someone as well. Someone would be straddling his face, completing the circle.

Tem looked up at him. He was watching her calmly, and she knew he had already come to the same conclusion and was waiting to see what she would do. But even Tem didn't know. In the pause that followed, Caspen said simply, "You may pick the person, if you wish."

Tem found it significant that he respected her decision to join the ouroboros—and instead of suggesting they not participate, he was tailoring the situation to her, ensuring she had a say in what happened next. Relief, then anticipation, then excitement rushed through her. She remembered what Caspen had just said, basing her choice around his words: *Our culture revolves around pleasure.* But who would bring her pleasure? Tem thought of the fantasies she'd had of Caspen and Leo—the visions that she only entertained late at night, when her mind was closed off to him. She scanned the courtyard, searching for someone who fit those visions.

Eventually, she found him.

The basilisk was slim, with long, wiry arms. His white-blond hair was slicked back, a single tendril falling over his forehead. He moved with a confidence that was deeply familiar to Tem: a confidence she missed. She missed his tall frame, his long fingers, his blond hair. She missed the way he smelled like summer and the way he used to tilt his body toward her whenever they talked, as if to absorb as much of her presence as possible. But Leo wasn't here. He never would be.

"Him." Tem pointed.

Caspen followed her gaze. Perhaps it was her imagination, but Tem could have sworn she saw understanding pass over his face. Then it disappeared. He turned to her. "You have one more choice to make."

Another realization struck. Someone would be pleasuring *her.* Tem closed her eyes. Suddenly the air felt warm. Was she really about to do this? Or was it too much, too soon?

"Tem." Caspen's voice came to her in a murmur. "Choose someone who makes you feel safe."

When he put it that way, the choice was easy. Tem opened her eyes, looking up at him. "I choose Adelaide."

Caspen raised an eyebrow. For a moment, Tem wondered if he would be angry. But he said, "Very well. Do you wish to ask her, or shall I?"

"I'll ask her."

The words came easily, and Tem didn't question them. She wanted to do this herself—to claim her decision. Caspen nodded, turning to leave.

"Wait." She grabbed his arm. "You said that when someone finishes, they leave the circle."

"That is true."

"So…" Tem paused. She struggled to put it into words, settling on the same thing she'd said before: "I don't want another cock in my mouth."

Caspen smiled. Tem knew he would understand what she was saying: if he finished before she did, he would leave the circle, leaving her to pleasure the very basilisk she'd chosen for him. And if Tem finished before Caspen did, Adelaide would be pleasuring him. Neither was ideal.

"I will time my climax with yours, Tem. We will leave at the same time."

"Can you do that?"

His smile widened. "I can try."

Tem rolled her eyes. She had little to no faith in Caspen's ability to time his climax for the exact right moment. Even for him, that would require an unimaginable amount of self-control. But it was too late now. He was turning again, heading for the tall blond basilisk. The gravity of the situation set in as Tem watched him walk away. She was really doing this. She was going to be part of the ouroboros. It was time to find Adelaide.

She was at the edge of the courtyard, observing the proceedings.

"Temperance," Adelaide said as she approached. "Would you care to watch the ouroboros with me?"

"Um," said Tem. "Not exactly."

Adelaide raised an eyebrow. But the words were impossible to say aloud. So she said them with her mind instead: *I want to join it.*

Adelaide's eyebrows rose even higher. *I see.*

And...I want you...to join...with me.

Tem dearly hoped Adelaide understood what she was trying to say because there was no way she could actually ask her to do this. In the silence that followed, panic rose.

Only if you want to—Tem continued quickly—*if it's going to cause any trouble with*—

She cut herself off, suddenly remembering Adelaide's relationship with Caspen's sister. Of course Adelaide wouldn't want to do this with Tem. She was just about to bury herself ten feet beneath the ground when, to her relief, Adelaide's beautiful face broke into a smile.

"Of course I want to. I am honored, Temperance."

Relief swept through her at the sincerity in her voice. In moments like these, Tem remembered that she was a queen—that being with her was an honor, just like Caspen had said. It was a difficult concept to wrap her head around, and one she doubted she'd ever get used to.

"Great," Tem said, and meant it. Then anxiety set in.

Adelaide placed a comforting hand on her shoulder. "I understand this must be overwhelming for you."

"No, it's not that. I mean, it is, but..."

The truth was that Tem wasn't ready for a repeat of the council meeting. If Adelaide climaxed before she did, she would leave the circle and Tem would have no control over who would taste her next. What if it was someone she didn't feel safe with? What if it was one of the Senecas who was angry about her ascent to the throne? What if it was Apollo?

Adelaide held her gaze steadily, and Tem remembered why she'd chosen her for this in the first place: she trusted her. And that meant she could be vulnerable.

She tried to put it into words: "I…only want to be with you and Caspen." Tem didn't dare say any more.

What she really wanted was a favor and a big one. She needed Adelaide to make sure that Tem climaxed at the right time. If she was going to join the ouroboros—but only be with Adelaide and Caspen—it was imperative that she finish before Adelaide did.

"I can bring you there first, Temperance."

Tem was beginning to wonder whether this whole thing was a terrible idea. The possible ramifications of the ouroboros were very, *very* real. She had zero desire to see Adelaide's mouth around Caspen's cock. But Tem would rather her than one of the king chasers. At least she knew Adelaide wouldn't use this as an opportunity to take Caspen from her.

Put your mind at ease, Temperance. No one could take Caspenon from you, least of all me. You forget that I am pursuing a different Drakon sibling.

Tem smiled at that. She was still nervous. But she'd meant what she said: she trusted Adelaide.

The energy in the courtyard was rapidly changing, the chatter dying down around them as conversations devolved into moans. The ouroboros was forming; it was time to take part. Before Tem could wonder where to go, Adelaide took her hand in hers. They walked together toward Caspen, who was standing next to the blond basilisk. On either side of them, basilisks were lying down, arranging themselves into interlocking links. Tem marveled at the continuity. The ouroboros was alive—a living, breathing thing that swelled and rippled like water.

Are you ready Temperance?

Tem looked at Adelaide, who was looking calmly at her. *Yes.*

Adelaide nodded before glancing at Caspen. His eyes were on Tem's, and they were already turning black. The blond male basilisk stood regally by, waiting for them to begin, his arms relaxed at his sides. Without another word, Adelaide made the first move. She crossed to the nearest basilisk, who was lying on their back, an open end to the chain. Adelaide lowered herself over their face, her eyes rolling momentarily back in her head as the basilisk's tongue made contact with her center. Tem became immediately flushed at the sight. When Adelaide opened her eyes, she beckoned to Tem, who couldn't seem to move.

Tem, Caspen's voice said quietly. *It is your turn.*

His hand found her waist, giving her a gentle push. Tem moved forward in a trance, anticipation pricking every inch of her skin. She lowered herself to the ground in front of Adelaide, the stone hard beneath her back, sending a jolt down her spine. Slowly, as if not to scare her, Adelaide leaned forward, taking Tem's thighs and spreading them open. The moment their skin touched, a wave of calm enveloped Tem, and she knew it was Adelaide's doing. Behind Tem, the blond basilisk was getting in position. There was only Caspen left.

The Serpent King was the last to join the circle—the final link in the ouroboros. He approached Tem slowly, looking down at her with silent authority. Tem looked up at him, seeing him in all his glory, slowing her breathing as he lowered himself. Caspen slid his hand behind her head, lifting her face to the correct angle. Tem opened her mouth, allowing him to feed her his cock one inch at a time. As soon as she was full, Caspen leaned forward, and she knew he was about to take the blond basilisk in his mouth. The thought made her weak with arousal.

Just then, Adelaide's voice whispered in her mind: *Temperance, I am going to begin.*

Tem couldn't nod. Instead, she closed her eyes, surrendering to the ouroboros. A moment later, Adelaide's tongue found her center. The moment it did, the circle was complete—Adelaide between her legs, Caspen in her mouth. Tem had never felt so connected, so *whole.* She was one with the basilisks; she was one with her people.

Adelaide's touch was different from Caspen's. *Very* different.

Men were hard. Everything about them was aggressive and overbearing and *sharp.* Women, on the other hand, were soft. Adelaide's tongue was tender and intuitive. She tasted Tem slowly, with utter care and devotion, understanding exactly where she needed stimulation the way only a woman could. Tem had thought that Caspen knew her body. But he knew only what he could see, what he could feel. Adelaide knew what she needed because Adelaide needed it too. Even when Caspen pleasured her, it somehow still felt like he was *taking* from her. Adelaide was only giving—only bestowing pleasure.

Such an experience wasn't new to Tem—she had known the touch of a woman before, during the council meeting when all the members had kissed her. But this was nothing like that. Those kisses had been routine, almost clinical. This was almost unbearably intimate, as if Adelaide was giving her a deeply personal gift. Tem felt utterly safe in Adelaide's care. When her mind caressed Tem's, she accepted it willingly, letting her stroke her in more ways than one.

Time passed, or perhaps it didn't. One by one, basilisks began to climax. One by one, they left the ouroboros. Tem felt each orgasm as if it were her own, losing herself in a state of communal pleasure. She slipped into complete peace, thinking only of Caspen and how hard his cock was in his mouth. He moved his hips steadily, thrusting into her, coordinating his movements with Adelaide's. She thought of him with the blond basilisk and it only made her wetter.

Eventually, Tem was close. Adelaide had been coaxing her there for a while, bringing her right to the edge but not over it, exercising intuition in a way only she knew how. Caspen was close too; the more Tem moaned, the faster his thrusts became. But just before she could climax, another presence touched her mind.

Apollo.

CHAPTER TWELVE

━•●━✳━••━

H E WAS MOVING ALONG THE OUROBOROS, BRINGING BASILISK AFTER BASILISK TO orgasm, getting closer and closer to Tem.

Temperance. Apollo is—

But Adelaide cut off, and Tem didn't need the rest of her sentence anyway. She could feel Adelaide's pleasure as Apollo's head went between her legs. For a moment, they continued as they had been. Then Tem felt a sudden change in Adelaide's mind. Where before she had been calmly resisting arousal, now she was completely—almost violently—turned on. Heat poured into their shared connection as Adelaide's moaned against Tem's center.

He is very good, Temperance. I am afraid that I—

Tem could barely hear her. Apollo was pushing Adelaide toward climax with brutal insistency, hardly giving her a chance to breathe. Adelaide's motions were less controlled, more desperate. She was losing her rhythm completely, pulling Tem out of her trance.

Can't you hold off? Tem cried. *Please?*

I cannot resist forever. He is…the best at this.

To Tem's horror, Apollo's voice rang through their joined minds, his words directed at Adelaide: *You flatter me.*

Adelaide ignored him, speaking only to Tem: *You are close. I can get you there.*

But Tem was panicking now. If Adelaide came before Tem did, Apollo would be upon her. And what if Caspen left her alone with him? She would have to take the blond basilisk's cock in her mouth while Apollo went between her legs. Neither were acceptable options. Before she could devolve into true terror, Caspen's voice entered her mind: *Tem. My love. Relax.*

But Tem had never been much good at relaxing. She was always overthinking, always worrying. She was not good at being the one thing that would serve her right now: a basilisk. Tem felt Adelaide's presence grow in her mind, joining with Caspen's. They were both coaxing her there, helping Tem ascend in her moment of need. She gave herself over to it, letting her worries and her inhibitions go, letting herself simply *feel.* She felt Adelaide's tongue on her clitoris and Caspen's cock in her throat. She felt the hard stone on her back. She heard the moans of everyone else still left in the ouroboros—their desperate groans of pleasure joining hers.

At last, Tem came.

It was not graceful. It was not elegant. But it was a release nonetheless, and Tem knew not to fight it. She also knew that Caspen had mere moments to finish alongside her—he needed to climax *now* if they were to leave the circle at the same time. Tem sent him a wild vision, completely on a whim: Apollo between her legs, her fingers tangled in his hair.

Immediately, Caspen came.

Unimaginable relief swept through Tem as she felt his release join hers. Adelaide's presence retreated from her mind, and Tem knew she was giving them privacy during their climax. Besides, Adelaide was having her own.

The moment Caspen's cock left Tem's mouth, she opened her eyes to see the view before her. Adelaide was propped up on her hands, her thighs clamped around Apollo's face, sweat dripping down her body. Tem watched as Adelaide came, her eyes squeezing shut as she ground herself against Apollo's mouth. The sight made Tem…jealous. Of Apollo or of Adelaide, she did not know. But for some reason, watching the two of them together made her want to rip them apart. Before Tem could unpack this, Caspen's hands gripped her, helping her stand.

Adelaide stood too, her face flushed, her usually perfect hair mussed from where Tem had been holding it. Apollo grinned up at them both, his lips glistening with wetness. Without wasting a moment he leaned forward, yanked the blond basilisk toward him, and took his cock in his mouth. Another wave of jealousy slammed into Tem. What was *wrong* with her tonight? Was this a symptom of mating season? Perhaps her senses were just heightened, and she was disproportionately prone to possessive emotions right now. Either way, it was becoming unbearable. Without looking at Caspen or Adelaide, Tem walked to the edge of the courtyard, her hands behind her head. Caspen followed her.

"Tem." His fingers brushed down her spine, and she shivered. "What is it?"

"Nothing," she said automatically.

"Tem," he said again, quietly this time. His lips brushed her ear. "It is over. You should be proud."

Pride was the last thing Tem felt. She was tired and overwhelmed, and these infernal basilisks were turning out to be far more than she had bargained for. Tem looked up at Caspen, who was looking down at her.

"Come." He kissed her on the forehead. "Let us watch the rest."

He steered her back toward the center of the courtyard, where the ouroboros had shrunk significantly. Apollo was out now, as was the blond basilisk. They watched until finally it was down to just two basilisks. They formed a circle with their bodies—the woman on top, the man underneath—both bestowing pleasure equally. It was a position Tem had experienced many times with Caspen, and she found herself suddenly aroused by the arrangement.

Caspen's voice came to her quietly: *We will do it later.*

Tem couldn't wait.

A crowd gathered around the couple, watching them as they tasted each other. Eventually, Caspen frowned. *Something is wrong. Neither of them are close.*

Why not?

Tem stared at the basilisks. They looked pretty close to her.

The man is a Seneca. The woman a Drakon. They are fundamentally at odds—neither of them wants to give in first. It will seem like surrender to them.

Tem watched the couple service each other in the middle of the courtyard. But instead of doing it tenderly, there was an aggression to their movements. Clearly it was a challenge, a race to get the other to finish first—one that had greater implications than just the completion of the ouroboros. All around them, basilisks were beginning to murmur. The energy in the courtyard was changing, a hum of anticipation filling the air like a swarm of hornets. Only basilisks could turn a sexual act into an insurgent one. Conflict was imminent; it was only a matter of time before a fight broke out. There had to be a way to resolve this.

I can help them.

Caspen turned to her. *How?*

I can cause a hive orgasm. It will make them finish at the same time. That way neither of them loses to the other. Neither quiver needs to yield.

Caspen shook his head. *Hive orgasms are rare, Tem. They are not predictable; you cannot just choose to cause one.*

They can't go on like this. You said nobody can leave until they finish, and neither of them are going to give in. So do you have any other ideas?

It is not safe, Tem.

But Tem shook her head. She couldn't explain it, but she knew she could do this.

Caspen continued: *Even if you could, it will cause everyone in this room to climax.*

So?

Everyone will transition. But you...

Caspen trailed off. He didn't need to finish. Tem knew what he was going to say: she couldn't transition—she would be in danger. *I'll be fine. You'll protect me.*

He sighed. A muscle twitched in his jaw as he watched the two basilisks battle each other in the middle of the courtyard. Worry clouded his face. Tem knew he was torn between protecting her and doing what was best for his people. The situation went far deeper than just the completion of the ouroboros. This was now a battle of wills, and if they did not resolve it quickly, it would spiral into something much worse. There was no other choice.

Very well. But you cannot leave my side, even after I turn. You must stay close to me.
I will.

Tem looked up at Caspen. He was the other half of the equation, after all. The two of them had caused the hive orgasm last time. It stood to reason that in order to cause it again, they needed to re-create the circumstances.

Without hesitation, she reached for him. Caspen dipped down to grab her legs, lifting her so she was wrapped around his waist. She was already wet, and his cock slid in easily. Tem held onto his shoulders, centering herself as he thrust up into her. After the slow burn of the ouroboros, having penetrative sex felt like heaven. Tem threw her head back, letting Caspen hold her upright, letting him take her over and over.

Immediately the hissing began.

Smoke swirled along the dark stone floors, curling around their feet and skimming up their legs. The temperature in the courtyard rose unmistakably. Caspen's purchase on her waist began to slip as sweat slicked their skin. The basilisks around them began to move. Some merely touched each other; some of them began having sex. Tem was already close to finishing, and she wasn't the only one. The final couple in the ouroboros were about to climax together. She could sense their imminence just as she could sense her own. *We all become one.*

Suddenly, anticipation pricked Tem's spine.

She recognized the feeling from last time—the caustic combination of fear and excitement—the *hunger* that meant the hive orgasm was near. Caspen's breath came in short grunts, his intensity increasing as he thrust quicker and quicker inside her. All around them, cries of pleasure radiated throughout the room. Tem was close. *Everyone* was close.

Just then, Caspen pulled her abruptly off his cock and set her on the ground. Tem gasped at the sudden change.

What are you doing?

She groped for his cock, trying to pull it back inside her. Caspen grabbed her wrist.
Stop, Tem.

Tem stopped. To her surprise, Caspen's tone was panicked—almost fearful. She looked up at him and found that he wasn't looking at her. He was staring around the courtyard, his eyes flicking from basilisk to basilisk. Smoke filled the air, and through it, Tem saw shadows coming into focus. Several basilisks—the same group of men who had eyed her on the first night of mating season—were approaching Tem with a ferocity she couldn't understand. They didn't look aroused, like everyone else. They looked… angry. Violent. A chill shot down her spine at the sight.

"What's going on?" Tem said out loud.

At the sound of her voice, Caspen returned to her. "Do not move." He held her still again, but this time in a different way—this time in a way that was protective, as if he were afraid of what could happen.

Tem pressed her chest to Caspen's despite the heat radiating from his body. It seemed like an eternity passed. But the longer they stood there, the calmer things became. Rather than building toward a collective climax, Tem watched as the energy in the courtyard slowly cooled. The smoke cleared, and the hiss quieted. The frenetic burst of adrenaline that had been crawling relentlessly under her skin retreated, replaced by wariness. The couple in the middle of the ouroboros stood, clearly finished with each other. Tem had no idea who had climaxed first.

Caspen had de-escalated the trajectory of everyone in the courtyard, and he'd done it out of fear. Why? Tem knew just how difficult it was to deny yourself an orgasm. To stop *everyone's* orgasm was a task so impossible she could hardly comprehend it.

Caspen's arms were still locked around her, holding her against him. Tem couldn't have moved if she'd tried. She could only watch as the rest of the basilisks concluded their unions—either completed their orgasms or drew apart—emerging from their partners with dazed expressions. But not everyone was dazed. The men were still coming closer—still staring at Tem like they wanted to devour her. Their eyes were black.

Do not look at them, Caspen's voice commanded.

Tem immediately trained her gaze on Caspen, staring determinedly at his collarbone. *Why are they looking at me like that?*

Caspen didn't answer. It had been a long time since Tem had seen him so tense. His muscles felt as if they were crafted from metal, clamped around her so securely that she was rigid beneath their grip. Something was wrong; that much was perfectly clear. But Tem couldn't imagine what it was.

Before she could ask another question, Apollo appeared beside them. His eyes flicked first to Tem's, then to Caspen's. "You must leave."

"Why?" Tem interjected. "What's going on?"

Apollo ignored her, directing his next words at Caspen. "She is not safe. You must—"

"Do not tell me what to do," Caspen snapped.

Apollo didn't retreat. Instead, he stepped closer, jerking his head at the men, who were coming ever closer. "The Senecas want her," he insisted. "They will take her."

"They will not take anything from me."

"Your arrogance will get her killed."

"Do not speak to me of *arrogance*, Brother," Caspen snapped.

"Caspenon." Apollo glanced once more at her, and Tem saw the fear in his eyes. "You must leave."

"She is *mine*," Caspen said harshly. "And I will do with her as I please."

Tem couldn't help but feel like they were no longer talking about the Senecas.

Apollo stepped closer. "They only reason they have not attacked her is because you are by her side. If she is alone next time—"

"She will not be alone. Clearly, she has you to protect her."

That seemed to shut Apollo up. His eyes flicked once more to Tem's, and this time they lingered. His mind brushed against hers, but she didn't dare let him in. Instead, they stared at each other, Caspen's arms still around her, Tem's body still pressed against his chest.

Apollo opened his mouth to speak again, but Caspen was already pulling Tem away. His grip was unbearably tight as he propelled her from the courtyard and out into the passageway. As soon as they were alone, Tem said, "What just happened?"

Caspen pursed his lips. He didn't answer.

"Caspen," she insisted. "You can't shut me out. Not anymore."

Still no answer.

Tem thought about the men who had been walking toward her, their eyes glazed with want. But what, exactly, had they wanted? Tem shuddered. She needed answers, and she knew Caspen would have them.

"What did Apollo mean? Why would those men attack me?"

"Tem," Caspen said. They had reached their chambers, and as soon as they were inside, he pulled her onto the bed. "I will not let anyone attack you."

"I know that. I'm asking why they would even want to."

Finally, he looked down at her. "They want your power."

Tem wrinkled her nose. "Well, they can have it. There's not much to give."

"You are a Hybreed, Tem. You are the most powerful among us."

A Hybreed. Both basilisk and human. Limitless.

"But I don't *feel* powerful." She could barely transition. Things like the ouroboros still overwhelmed her, and every minute under the mountain was a test of her endurance. Everyone seemed to understand her value but her.

"But you are," Caspen said quietly. "You may be made up of two things, but each of them is whole."

"What do you mean?"

"Your basilisk side does not function at half capacity just because it makes up half of you. The part of you that is a basilisk is fully so. The same with your human side."

"So?"

"*So* you are two things, Tem. You always have been. And you are both of those things fully. Your power is unparalleled."

Tem thought about what Caspen had just said to Apollo: *She is mine.* If she was so powerful, did Caspen covet her power? Tem knew she was safe with him—she always had been. But if Tem was as powerful as he said, perhaps even Caspen could not resist such a draw.

"But how would they get my power?"

"There are many ways. They could crest you. But my guess is they would not dare to do so."

"Why not?"

"Because even my father did not succeed."

Tem remembered the wedding—Bastian's hand around her throat, squeezing. It had taken everything in her to resist, and even then, she'd needed Leo's help to survive.

Caspen continued. "Most likely they will try to kill you."

"*Kill* me?"

"Yes."

"But if I'm so powerful, why would they want to kill me?"

"Because you are more useful to them dead. Whoever kills a basilisk receives their power."

Tem had no idea that was possible. "Really?"

"Yes," Caspen said. "When my father died, I received his."

That was news to Tem. "But you…ate him."

Caspen gave her a grim smile. "Yes, I did. And by doing so, I proved my worth."

Tem stared at him. Basilisks were simply *bizarre.* But she understood, on some level, how Bastian's violent death at the hands of his son might have earned Caspen the king's power. It was no small feat to kill a king.

"So…you're powerful right now?"

Caspen smiled wider. "I was always powerful."

Of course he was. But he was even more so now, and it was something to consider.

Caspen shifted her in his arms, pulling her closer. "Had he lived, I would have had access to his power anyway."

"How?"

"My venom."

"I don't understand."

"The bite of a basilisk is not fatal by itself. My father only died because I…kept going." A beat passed, and Tem remembered the sight of Caspen cannibalizing his father. She shuddered. "But it has a significant effect."

"Which is?"

"Once bitten, the victim is made vulnerable to the basilisk who bit them. The presence of my venom in my father's bloodstream would have created a connection between us."

"What kind of connection?"

"I would have been able to use it to siphon power from him."

Tem frowned. "But I have your venom in my bloodstream, and you've never siphoned from me."

"That is because you merely drank my venom. If I had bitten you properly—with my fangs, while wearing my true form—I would have been able to siphon from you too."

"Thanks for not biting me, I guess."

Caspen smiled. "You are very welcome, my love."

Tem pictured Caspen on the stage, ripping his father's torso to shreds. It was hard to believe that Bastian would want his power to go to the very person who had destroyed him. But such was the basilisk way.

"So…the Senecas want my power. Are they going to kill me or siphon from me?"

Caspen's jaw tightened. "I cannot know that. But my brother was right." It looked like the words pained him to say. "You are not safe when you are alone."

Tem understood Caspen was afraid for her, and she could understand why. It seemed like everyone wanted to take from her. Always, *always* taking. It was exhausting, and Tem was tired of it. There was never enough of her to go around—never enough to make everyone who wanted something happy. It was beginning to wear on her, to rip her at the seams.

Tem sighed. Unlike the other customs basilisks adhered to, this one wasn't sexual at all. It was serious, and it was dangerous. And it put a target on her back. From the way the basilisks in the courtyard had just looked at Tem, Caspen had every reason to be scared for her. She could feel it in the way his hands were gripping her waist a little too tight, as if he feared she might disappear.

"Caspen," she said. "Nobody's going to kill me. They'd be idiots if they tried."

His grip didn't lessen. "And why is that?"

"Because then you'd kill them."

Caspen let out a soft laugh. "I suppose that is true."

It was *certainly* true. Tem might be a tempting source of power, but Caspen was a terrifying source of wrath. She couldn't imagine that anyone under this mountain would dare to touch her. He was already the Serpent King—there was no one more powerful.

No one except for her.

CHAPTER THIRTEEN

———•◦✳◦•———

SUNDAY CAME QUICKER THAN TEM WOULD HAVE LIKED.

The castle was decorated for winter; great boughs of holly were strung along the arch of the entryway, and more still hung in the foyer. White candles had been traded for red ones, and the great drips of wax looked like blood. Tem couldn't stop staring at them.

"It was Evelyn's doing," said Leo stiffly.

Tem frowned at the tension in his voice. Then it made sense.

The decorations were expensive. And unnecessary. Evelyn had spent money on something that had no purpose—something strictly superficial. It was an abhorrent thing to do in a time of financial crisis. Tem couldn't believe where the woman's priorities lay. Who cared about decorations when the villagers were starving? Evelyn, apparently.

As if on cue, Evelyn appeared at the head of the stairs. "Doesn't the castle look beautiful?" she purred.

Neither Caspen nor Tem answered. They were both incapable of lying, and it would have been impossible to say they found this beautiful. Instead Tem took Caspen's hand in hers and squeezed.

This is going to be a long night.

He squeezed back. *Of that I am quite sure.*

Leo seemed to know it too, because he didn't say anything either. The three of them stood awkwardly as Evelyn flounced down the stairs. By the time they were seated in the dining room, Tem was already reaching for her wineglass. If she was in for a long night, she at least wanted to be drunk for it.

"Wedding preparations are going splendidly," Evelyn said, although no one had asked.

Tem downed her wine.

"We've ordered sixty white swans for the occasion. They'll look beautiful in the pond."

Again, no one spoke. Tem couldn't imagine how much sixty white swans had cost them or where they would even import them from. She'd never seen a single swan in the village, much less sixty of them. It was absurd.

"Of course, we're also looking into getting white roses. But those are proving difficult to track down. Isn't that right, darling?" She looked expectantly at Leo, who was staring into his whiskey glass.

"Quite difficult," he said dully.

Mercifully, dinner was served.

The silence continued as the butlers served them roast beef, but at least now there was food to concentrate on. To Tem's surprise, it was Caspen who spoke next.

"Have there been any more protests?"

Tem frowned. Why was he asking? He didn't care about the villagers.

"Yes," sighed Evelyn. "There have been."

Two words flashed through Tem's mind: *Feed us.*

"That is a shame," Caspen said.

"It is." She glanced at Leo, who was still trying to drown himself in his whiskey. "We are exploring…solutions."

Caspen raised an eyebrow. "Such as?"

Ah. That's why he was asking—it wasn't to gauge the situation with the villagers. It was to see what plans the royals had for the future of their kingdom. Those plans would directly affect the basilisks.

Evelyn was still looking at Leo, who was looking anywhere but at her.

"We…haven't decided yet. But we are looking into our options. Things cannot go on as they have been. It's important to leave a legacy for our children."

Tem nearly choked on her wine. "*Children?*"

Evelyn touched Leo's arm. "We want two, don't we, darling? A boy and a girl."

Tem suppressed the urge to vomit.

Tem. Caspen's voice boomed in her mind.

She knew he could hear her thoughts. It wasn't possible to hide them at this point. Tem's displeasure was so loud, she was surprised Evelyn couldn't hear them too.

I'm trying.

You must try harder. You cannot afford to lose your temper.

Tem knew he was right. They had to do this, for the greater good. But he was asking the impossible. Evelyn was *right there.* Her big doe eyes stared at Tem with calculating curiosity, as if she were sizing her up. And how dare she? Evelyn was the one who'd left Leo in the first place.

But was Tem really any better? She'd left Leo too.

The thought only made her angrier. She'd left him *so he could be happy.* And his happiness, for reasons Tem could not and *would not* fathom, hinged on the unremarkable person before her. Evelyn couldn't possibly satisfy Leo. She looked like she'd never had sex in her life, much less be willing to suck his cock in a carriage simply to torture him. Leo required challenge and strength and *power*. Evelyn possessed none of those.

Tem. Caspen's voice came to her again.

What?

Control yourself.

It wasn't an order. It was a warning.

Tem could feel heat rising in her core, the monster within her no longer lying dormant. Her basilisk side felt as if it were clawing for release, climbing steadily up the walls of her insides. Fury was imminent. She'd transitioned only once since the wedding. Yet she felt as if she were about to now, the urge rapidly consuming her like a forest fire.

Tem closed her eyes, trying to take a deep, calming breath. But nothing helped. She was too far gone—too close to the edge.

You are beginning to transition, Tem. I can feel it.

It was true. Tem's skin was crawling—pricks of electricity tingled up her spine, threatening to engulf her. She tried to control her breathing, but she couldn't. The familiar fire burned within her chest, threatening to explode. She couldn't transition here. She had to keep everyone safe—had to keep Leo safe. But at the thought of Leo, Tem only became warmer.

Focus on something else, Tem.

I can't.

Her hands were clenched around the napkin in her lap, which was beginning to smolder. Tem could smell the burning fabric. She was sweating now, great droplets running between her breasts. It was as if she had the world's worst fever.

You must control it.

I'm telling you, I can't.

You can do anything, Tem.

I'm so angry, Caspen. I'm—HELP ME.

An immediate, soothing wave of calm flowed from his mind to hers. Tem leaned into it, pulling it desperately toward her, covering herself with as much of it as possible. It was like dunking her head in a cold bucket of water. Her eyes opened slowly, and when they did, clarity returned.

The dinner had gone on without Tem. Evelyn was still speaking, and Caspen was nodding his head at whatever she was saying. But Leo was staring straight at her, his gray eyes piercing hers. His face was drawn in a frown.

What's wrong? he mouthed.

Tem shook her head. Leo's frown deepened.

She must look like a mess right now. There was no way to hide the physical tells: the sweat, the flush, the shortness of breath. Even the candles couldn't account for the smell of smoke that now hung in the air.

"Tem," Leo said out loud.

The table fell silent as everyone looked at her.

Why had he done that? "Yes?" Tem answered as smoothly as she could.

Leo held her eye contact. "Is everything in order?"

"Of course," she said. "I just need to freshen up. Will you excuse me?"

Without waiting for an answer, Tem stood and left the room. The cavernous ceiling of the hallway loomed over her as she ran for the closest bathroom, ending up in the one with the golden sink. Tem gripped the sides of the mirror, staring at her reflection. Her eyes were bloodshot. A single bead of sweat ran down her temple. She wiped it away with her hand just as a knock came at the door.

"Tem?"

A woman's voice. One she'd heard before, in this very bathroom. Lilly, Leo's sister.

Tem didn't move. She didn't want to see anyone right now. Not only that but she didn't trust herself yet—what if she was still in danger of transitioning?

"Go away, Lilly."

"Tem. Let me in."

A moment passed. Tem had a feeling Lilly would stand there until she obeyed.

With a sigh, she opened the door. Without saying a word, Lilly drew her into a hug. At first, Tem stiffened at the contact. Then she let the embrace deepen, leaning on the woman before her and allowing herself to be held.

"What's wrong?" Lilly murmured. "You can talk to me."

Tem just shook her head. She couldn't talk to anyone, couldn't voice the doubts that gripped her like a vise.

"You still love him, don't you?"

Tears stung Tem's eyes. In reply, she squeezed Lilly tighter.

"Oh, Tem."

There was nothing else to say. Tem simply cried.

Lilly held her for a long time—far longer than she needed to. When Tem's sobs finally quieted, she still held her, gently, Tem's face buried in her ice-blond hair.

"What are you going to do?" the princess whispered.

"I don't know," Tem whispered back. "I don't think there's anything I *can* do."

"You could tell him how you feel."

Tem shook her head.

Lilly pulled away, looking her straight in the eye. "You could," she insisted. "He would be open to it. I know he would."

But Tem had no idea whether that was true. And if Leo would be open to leaving Evelyn, it meant that Tem had made a mistake in sending him away. And Tem wasn't ready to admit that to herself, much less Leo. Lilly knew nothing of the crest—she didn't know this was all Tem's fault. In her eyes, it probably seemed like Tem had simply changed her mind.

"They're getting married," Tem said. "It's too late anyway."

"It's not too late until they've walked down the aisle."

Tem blinked. "How can you say that?"

Lilly sighed. "Because my brother deserves better than Evelyn."

It was difficult not to react to that statement. Tem was shocked to hear Lilly speaking so openly about her brother's betrothed. It was then that Tem wondered whether Lilly knew about the bloodletting. Did she understand that the kingdom was now in dire financial straits because their main source of income had ceased? Perhaps Lilly assumed all was well. The castle was decorated extravagantly, after all, and Lilly hardly ever left it. There was no reason to believe anything had changed.

"He loves her."

"He loves you too."

Tem shook her head. "He shouldn't."

Lilly stepped closer, and the bathroom seemed to shrink. "The men in my family are ruled by their hearts. Do you think my brother is the first to fall for the wrong woman?"

Tem had no idea what that meant. Was she talking about Maximus? Tem knew nothing of the king's love life and certainly wasn't going to start asking now.

"Evelyn came back," Tem said. "They're happy together."

"Are they?"

"She loves him." But the words rang false.

"Do you really believe that?" Lilly whispered.

Another question she didn't want to answer.

Lilly pursed her lips. "Evelyn loves power. And status, both of which my brother can provide." She paused for a long moment before finishing quietly, "I want him to be happy."

The tears were about to return. "I want that too," Tem whispered.

Lilly's hands found hers. "Then tell him the truth. He can't be happy unless he knows how you really feel. He deserves to make his own choice."

But Tem just shook her head. Even if she told Leo how she felt, there was no elegant solution. There were too many people involved—too many marriages. Her union with

Caspen was only one of many things to consider. Tem knew Evelyn would not relinquish Leo—not as long as she thought there was something to be gained from him. She saw Tem as competition, as a player in her sick, twisted game. A game with a prize worth winning. A game Tem wanted no part of.

Lilly dropped her hands. "You'd better get back in there," she said gently.

Tem nodded. She'd been gone far too long. She parted ways with Lilly on the landing, giving her one last squeeze before reentering the dining room. Everything was just as she'd left it, except the dessert had been served now: a chocolate soufflé. But the moment Tem sat next to Caspen, she sensed a shift in his energy.

"Tem?" Leo said. "Would you mind having a word with me after dinner?"

Tem had to concentrate in order to keep her mouth from falling open. Last time Evelyn had wanted her to stay behind, and now Leo wanted the same? What was *with* these two?

Tem's eyes slid to Caspen's. His expression was unreadable, but his body gave him away. His hands were balled into fists. Surely, this was unacceptable to him. Tem wished he would just *say something*—forbid her to go or even yell. Anything would be preferable to his steely silence.

"I... Why?"

Leo glanced at Evelyn, whose expression was a mirror of Caspen's. "There are... matters we should discuss," he said slowly.

"What sort of matters?"

Leo didn't seem to have an answer to that, and neither did Tem. The situation truly couldn't have gotten worse. A meeting alone with Leo was the absolute last thing she needed. Tem had no idea if she could control herself around him. They hadn't been alone together since the annulment, and that had nearly ended with her throwing herself at him. She doubted this would go any better. Before Leo could answer, Caspen stood.

Tem stood too, suddenly afraid of what he might do. But instead of saying anything—or even looking at her—Caspen left the room without a backward glance. The moment he was out of sight, Tem felt him slam the corridor between their minds shut. He was furious. But she would deal with him later.

Evelyn stood too. "Don't take too long, darling," she said, her voice lethally low. A warning.

Leo didn't reply. Tem could see how it physically pained Evelyn not to reprimand him. But to reprimand him would be to shatter the illusion of their perfect marriage. Tem knew that wasn't a price Evelyn was willing to pay—especially not in front of her. A moment later, she swept from the room.

Leo gestured silently toward the library. As soon as they were inside, he went straight for the alcohol. "Whiskey?"

"Please."

Leo took his time pouring them each a drink, and when he handed Tem hers, she noticed he was careful not to touch her.

"Thank you."

"Of course."

They were being overly formal, but Tem didn't know how else to be. This was a foreign situation to her, completely unprecedented. Nobody had the rulebook for this, least of all Tem.

They sat in the leather chairs facing each other. Leo looked tired, as he had last weekend. But he also looked beautiful. Tem couldn't help but stare at everything she so desperately missed: the blond hair, the sharp cheekbones, the long fingers. She could see his heart beating in his temple. Tem wanted to press her lips against his neck, to see if he still smelled like summer. He would be warm. And soft and pliable and alive.

"Tem," he said quietly, breaking her from her thoughts. "Why did you leave the table?"

Tem took a rather large gulp of whiskey. There was no point in hiding it. "I was about to transition."

Leo frowned. "Into a…?"

"Yes."

Leo took a rather large gulp too.

For a moment, neither of them spoke. In the silence, Leo studied her. Tem wondered if he was thinking all the same things she was. Did he want to touch her? To run his lips along her neck? Tem dearly hoped that he did. It occurred to her that they were all alone in the library. Her mind was closed off; no one was here to see them. The only people preventing something from happening was them. She had to distract herself.

"What did you want to discuss, Leo?"

He blinked, as if waking from a trance. "Our kingdoms, I suppose. That's what my father used this room for, anyway."

At the mention of Maximus, Tem gripped her whiskey. She pictured him and Bastian in this very library, discussing politics. It was a bizarre vision. Tem wondered suddenly whether she'd misinterpreted Caspen's anger earlier. She'd assumed he was upset that she was meeting with Leo alone. But now she wondered whether he was insulted that *she* was meeting with Leo instead of him. These discussions were meant for the two kings. Perhaps his ire was actually directed at Leo, not at Tem. Immediately, she hoped it wasn't. Tem could handle Caspen's anger; she wanted Leo nowhere near it.

"Well." She gestured with her hand. "You go first."

Leo set his whiskey on the desk. "Very well. You already know we abolished the bloodletting. All basilisks have been returned to the mountain."

"Yes. Thank you."

"You're welcome."

Still too formal. Tem hated it.

"We are exploring other options for income."

"Such as?"

"The sea is not far away. I thought perhaps fishing."

"Great," said Tem. "Keep me updated."

"I shall."

She took another gulp of whiskey. There wasn't enough alcohol in the world to make this conversation tolerable. Tem wished Leo didn't look so good; it was distracting her.

"There is another matter we must discuss," he said quickly, as if he wanted to pave over the awkwardness.

"Which is?"

"I assume you heard about the incident with the villagers."

Tem nodded. She neglected to mention that she had been there.

"We're attempting to uncover who was behind it."

Again, Tem pursed her lips. She knew exactly who was behind it, and she would never tell. "Do you have any leads?"

"Not at the moment. But we are in the process of investigating."

Tem didn't bother asking what that process looked like. Instead, she made a mental note to tell Gabriel to be careful who he spoke to when he came to work in the castle.

"The villagers are angry, Tem," Leo continued. "And starving. They blame me."

Tem understood his position. It was complicated, like hers. "What do you want me to say, Leo?"

He sighed, his eyes drifting to the fireplace. He didn't answer, and he didn't have to. Nothing Tem could say would fix the situation. They were trapped, both of them, in the circumstances they had created. Tem stared at the fire too. The room was warm— almost uncomfortably so. It reminded Tem of her chambers in the caves. The thought only made her warmer. Every time she was alone with Leo, her basilisk side uncoiled itself, seeking his scent. It was becoming impossible to subdue it.

"My father denies it," Leo said suddenly.

Tem looked over at him in surprise. "Denies what?"

"That he wrote the letter."

It took Tem a moment to understand which letter he was talking about. Evelyn's. "That's…" Tem began but trailed off.

Her conversation with Evelyn loomed in the back of her mind, eating at her like acid. She couldn't tell Leo that she agreed, that she doubted Evelyn's story. She couldn't tell him *anything*.

"Your father is a liar," she finished firmly. "Of course he denies it."

Darkness passed over Leo's face. "He has no reason to lie about this."

What was Tem supposed to say? She had no way to reassure him without lying. So she simply asked, "She came back for you, didn't she?"

Leo shrugged, still staring at the fire. His pulse beat in his throat. "Maybe she thought it an opportune time to return."

"What do you mean?"

"I don't know anymore," he whispered.

It was all he said, and it wasn't enough. If Leo didn't trust Evelyn—to the extent that he'd actually confronted his father about whether or not he wrote the letter that ended their relationship—there was no going back. Doubt had crept in, and there would be no stopping its destructive path.

Tem didn't want Evelyn to be lying to Leo. She wanted Evelyn to be the love of Leo's life. Because if she wasn't, then everything Tem had put them through hadn't been worth it. Tem couldn't bear the thought that his pain was for nothing. She *needed* this to work.

"Leo," she whispered. "She came back. Isn't that enough?"

Leo stared at the fire, his eyes unfocused. He was becoming angry—she could see it on his face. Something was brewing here: something bad.

"I am surrounded by liars," he whispered. "Including you."

His words stopped her short. Because they were true. "Leo—"

"What did she say to you last week? Hm?"

Tem pursed her lips. It was telling that Leo focused on that conversation in particular—as if he knew something significant had happened during it, that there was something Tem couldn't say. He was so intuitive. It was a quality she usually loved about him, but she hated it right now.

"She just—"

"And don't you *dare* lie."

She sighed. He couldn't have it both ways. It wasn't possible for her to tell him what Evelyn said to her last week and also not lie. As a Hybreed, she could lie, though it was painful to—to lie to Leo was painful physically and emotionally. And she knew telling the truth now could sabotage his relationship.

The pause went on too long. Leo leaned in. "What did she fucking say to you, Tem? What did the two of you talk about? Did you talk about me? About *us*? What secrets did my future wife divulge to you that she doesn't care to divulge to me?"

Tem didn't answer. She couldn't.

"Did she tell you why she left me? Did she read you the fucking letter my father supposedly left her?"

At some point during his tirade, Leo stood up. He was towering over Tem, his hands on either side of her armchair, caging her in.

"*What did she say to you?*"

"Leo," Tem cried. "Calm down."

His reaction was immediate. His expression softened and his shoulders relaxed as he sat back down, his hands clasped loosely in his lap. Tem blinked, floored by the sudden change. Then horrible realization struck.

Tem had just given Leo an order. And as the object of her crest, he was bound to obey it.

"I'm sorry," Tem said immediately, scrambling for how to fix it. "You…you don't have to calm down unless you want to."

A moment of silence passed. Then, lightning-quick, the anger from a moment ago returned. He leaned forward but didn't stand. "What's that supposed to mean?"

Tem opened her mouth, then closed it—only she knew the details of the crest. Leo had no idea that what she'd done to him on their wedding day had any long-term implications.

"Tem?" Leo insisted. "What the fuck did you just do to me?"

"Leo," she said as calmly as possible. "Do you remember at the end of our wedding— what you did for me?"

His eyes bored into hers, accusatory and fearful. "Yes. Of course I do."

"You saved my life," Tem said slowly. "And I am so grateful."

"Get to the fucking point, Tem."

She flinched at this tone but didn't let it deter her. "When you saved me, it…bonded you to me."

Leo stared at her expectantly.

Tem groped for the right words. "That bond is significant. And permanent. And it has certain…side effects."

"Such as?"

"Such as what happened just now. I gave you an order—I told you to calm down, and you did it."

There was a moment of silence as Tem waited for her words to land. Then:

"But *why* did I do it? Why did I feel so…?" But Leo trailed off.

Tem couldn't imagine how it felt for him to receive a command and have to obey it. She'd never been controlled like that before. The fact that she'd just done it to Leo—even inadvertently—made her want to cry. He deserved to know the truth.

"The bond makes it so that you must do as I say."

Comprehension dawned on him slowly. Leo had saved her life. Now she controlled his. "I'm…beholden to you?"

Tears threatened to fall. "Yes," she whispered. "Technically, you are, but I would never—"

"Never what?" he snapped. "Give me an order? You just did."

"No, I mean—yes, I did…but not because I wanted to. I didn't mean it like that. I just wanted you to—"

"Wanted me to what? To calm down? So you *ordered me to do it*?"

"I didn't *mean to*."

But Leo just stared at her, his hands clenched into fists. "Your intent is irrelevant," he said icily.

Tem could only sit there and take it. He was absolutely right; it didn't matter that she hadn't meant it. She had done it, and she couldn't take it back.

"I'm sorry, Leo. It was a mistake. It won't happen again."

He only shook his head.

The parallels weren't lost on Tem. She was saying all the things Caspen had once said to her—that he would try his best not to hurt her, that it wouldn't happen again, that he would do better next time. And he never did. And Tem knew she wouldn't either. If a time came when she needed to give Leo an order, she would do it. She knew she would. Her basilisk side would demand it of her, like it demanded so many other things. It didn't matter that her human side hated the thought of controlling someone else. The serpent in her longed for more.

Of all the things she was trying to protect Leo from—heartbreak, Evelyn, his father, the villagers, Caspen—she hadn't considered protecting him from herself. Tem needed to be better for Leo. She needed to be the person he deserved. But it wasn't so simple. *She* wasn't so simple. It was not a matter of will. Tem was resisting the draw of nature, the very thing that brought her to Leo in the first place. It was impossible to resist such a force, and she was powerless against it.

"This isn't the first time, is it?" Leo said.

"What do you mean?"

"This isn't the first order you've given me. At our wedding, you told me to go. You told me to find Evelyn."

Tem bit her lip. Was he going to yell at her for that? "Yes. I did."

She expected him to stand up again—to explode. Instead he simply stared at her, his brow slightly furrowed, as if he were working out a complicated problem.

"Why did you do that?" he asked quietly.

Why indeed. It was the same question she'd asked herself a hundred times since then. There was really only one answer. "Because I wanted you to be happy. You deserved more."

Myriad emotions passed over his face. Tem had no idea what he was thinking and didn't dare ask. Instead she waited for a long moment before saying, "The last thing I wanted was to hurt you, Leo."

This was received with an incredulous laugh. "And yet, that's all you do, Tem."

She opened her mouth to protest but found she didn't have the words. Then, to her surprise, Leo softened.

"I'm sorry," he whispered. "I shouldn't have said that."

He didn't say he didn't mean it—only that he shouldn't have said it.

Without warning, he leaned forward. Tem tried not to flinch, but by the look on Leo's face, she must have. He halted, his body still angled toward hers.

"I would do anything you asked, Tem," he whispered. "Whether I am bound to you or not."

Tears filled her eyes. Of course she knew that—of course she understood Leo's love for her and how he expressed it. She always had.

The only sound was the crackling of the fire. Tem wanted to lean forward too, to close the distance between them, but to do so would mean risking the tentative peace they had just found, and nothing could make her do that. Instead she said, "We can't do this."

"Do what?"

"Meet like this—alone. We should have…a chaperone or something."

Leo let out a dull laugh. "A fucking chaperone isn't going to stop me from wanting you, Tem."

It wasn't going to stop Tem from wanting him either. She had always thought that the pain she felt from letting Leo go was her punishment, that she deserved it. But now she realized she was not the only one being punished. Her selfless act had backfired, and Leo was hurting too. Her attempt to make things right had gone wrong. She had tried to fix something that wasn't even broken, and now they were both paying the price.

"Then what do we do?" she whispered. "How do we control this?"

He shook his head. "I don't think we can."

"We have to, Leo. We *have* to."

"Maybe I don't want to."

"That's not an option."

He didn't reply. It was answer enough.

"If we could just talk it through, then maybe we could figure out—"

"I *can't*," he cried. "I can't *just talk* to you. Talking is the last fucking thing I want to do with you, Tem."

Tem bit back tears. She knew he was right; they shouldn't even be talking as they were now. Technically, nothing had happened yet. But if they continued to do this, it would.

A memory flashed suddenly through Tem's mind: words scrawled in spiky red ink.

"You could write to me," she said without thinking.

Leo blinked. "What?"

Tem leaned forward, ignoring the flash of desire in his eyes. "Everything you want to tell me but can't—you could write it instead."

He shook his head. "What good will that possibly do?"

"I don't know. It might help…get it out of your system."

Leo let out a harsh laugh. Tem knew how he felt because she felt the same: there was no getting each other out of their systems. But they had to do something.

"We have to get through this somehow, Leo," she pleaded. "For everyone's sake."

The problem was so much bigger than the two of them. It wasn't just their marriages at risk. It was their kingdoms.

Leo turned from her, staring into the fire. "Fine," he said eventually, his voice tight. "I'll write to you."

Dull relief pulsed through her. It was hardly a permanent solution. Or even a rational one. But if Leo could express himself in a way that didn't harm either of them, perhaps they would be able to muddle through the rest of these dinners without ruining absolutely everything.

Leo dropped his voice. "Will you read them?"

"If you want me to," she whispered. "Someday. But for now, just…"

"Hide them," he finished for her.

Tem nodded. It was not lost on her that this entire thing was a terrible idea. The thought of Leo expressing how he felt in writing and keeping them anywhere in the vicinity of his soon-to-be wife was surely a recipe for disaster. But there was nothing else to be done. Leo was right; there was nowhere for their feelings to *go*. So perhaps they could go into the letters.

"Will you write to me in return?" he whispered.

"Do you want me to?"

Leo turned back to her. His eyes traced down her body, and Tem knew he was picturing every inch of her curves. In his gaze, she saw everything he couldn't say and everything he would no doubt write in the letters. She saw how badly he wanted her—how much it was killing him to refrain from touching her—how he was mere seconds away from sweeping her into his arms. She saw his pain. So it didn't surprise her when he answered, "No."

Should she be offended? Relieved?

Perhaps it was for the best that he didn't want her to write. Surely, he already knew how she felt. And while keeping love letters around was risky for Leo, it was downright dangerous for Tem. There could be no evidence of her love for Leo—no physical confirmation of their bond. Basilisks were not free with their hearts. No one could read those letters.

Especially not Caspen.

CHAPTER FOURTEEN

———— •◦✦◦• ————

Caspen was not in their chambers when Tem returned to the cave. She knew he was avoiding her, so she fell asleep alone, curled up in the middle of their bed, trying not to think about Leo. But her dreams were filled with him. They always started the same way: with the brush of a pinkie. Except this time, they weren't standing in front of the dungeon door. Now they were in Leo's bedroom, and they were naked.

Leo kissed her first, eager and desperate, his teeth pulling at her bottom lip. Tem received what he gave her, letting him touch her anywhere he liked. They were always a little freer in her dreams than they had been in real life. In her dreams, they were safe.

Will you keep me around?

For as long as you'll let me.

Tem was still alone when she woke.

She'd hardly eaten any dinner; she'd been too busy crying in the bathroom to indulge in the roast beef. The thought of going to the banquet hall without Caspen was intimidating but not impossible. If Caspen was so comfortable leaving her alone, perhaps she should become comfortable *being* alone. Besides, she was starving.

The banquet hall was filled with basilisks from both quivers. It seemed that the tension with the Senecas had abated—perhaps the fact that the ouroboros had ended amicably was enough to appease them for the time being. Tem navigated carefully between the tables, dodging more than one writhing group of basilisks. Mating season was still well underway, and she was still not used to it. Tem tried to be polite—to look at *anything* else—but the only thing happening around her was sex. A man was fingering a woman right in front of her. Beyond them, two women were entangled on a table. Just as Tem was about to give up, she spotted an open seat and collapsed in it gratefully. No sooner had she sat down than she heard Apollo's voice.

"All alone tonight, Temperance?"

It was the exact same thing he'd said to her in the passageway before she slapped him. Apollo was always catching her alone, as if he possessed some sort of instinct for when she would be at her most vulnerable. It was a rather uncanny ability, and she hated it.

"I guess," she said as he sat down across from her.

Apollo smiled, picking up a fork and twirling it deftly between his fingers. "In that case, I shall keep you company."

"You don't have to do that."

"I insist."

"You insist?"

"I beg."

"That's better."

Apollo leaned in, his mouth curling into a smile. "Do you like it when I beg?"

Tem shot him a look of utter disdain. "Only if it's for your life."

"You will never hear me beg for my life."

"No? And why not?"

Apollo smiled, baring his fangs. "Basilisks believe in fate."

"What's that supposed to mean?"

"It means we understand that our deaths are predetermined. If I ever found myself fortunate enough to be beneath your blade, I would welcome it."

Tem rolled her eyes.

Apollo's smile only widened. "It would be an honor to die by your hand, Temperance."

"It would be a privilege to kill you."

Apollo laughed outright. It was always unnerving when basilisks did that. They were usually so serious that anything other than stoicism caught her off guard. But laughter suited Apollo, Tem realized. Despite his wicked tongue, his energy was decidedly lighter than Caspen's. It was the same with Damon—almost as if the brothers were born in descending order of seriousness. Then again, Caspen shouldered the burden of leadership. Everyone else was untethered by such responsibility. Tem would be mirthful too if she wasn't worrying about the future of a kingdom.

"I was impressed by you the other night," Apollo said, still twirling the fork.

"How so?"

"The ouroboros is not for the faint of heart."

"My heart is anything but faint."

"That I know."

Tem snorted. Apollo didn't know anything about her heart. He never would. But that didn't mean he didn't care for her. She hadn't forgotten what he'd said after the ouroboros—how he'd warned Caspen to leave the courtyard when the Senecas were advancing on them, how he'd urged him to take her to safety. It was a side of him she wasn't used to—a side that was compassionate and caring and protective. Of her. Moments like that made her wonder whether his advances were genuine. Moments like that made her falter.

But she could not afford to falter today.

"All you do is flirt with me. It's boring."

Apollo raised an amused eyebrow. "In all my years, no one has ever called my flirting boring."

"It's repetitive. And predictable."

"I see. And what would you suggest I do to change that?"

"I'm not giving you tips."

"Shame. I should like to be in your good graces."

"I'm sure you would."

"I should like to be other places, as well."

"See? Boring."

Apollo threw his head back in laughter. "You are a challenge, Temperance."

"You want a challenge? Go away."

"That will not prevent me from flirting with you. I can still make you blush from across the room."

"Then prove it."

It just slipped out. But Apollo tilted his head thoughtfully. "Shall I?" he said quietly.

Tem didn't answer. She'd said too much already, let this go too far. But Apollo was already standing. He'd been sitting with his back against the wall, already at the edge of the banquet hall, and had to circumvent their table in order to cross the room. As he passed her, his fingers touched her shoulder. Tem shivered at the contact. The moment he left her field of vision, he entered her mind.

Turn around so I can see you.

Tem was frozen in place. What had she just done?

Turn around, Temperance.

Tem didn't think. She just turned around.

Apollo was at the table across from her, seated on the bench, facing outward just as she was. They stared at each other over the aisle. All around them, pairs of basilisks were fucking.

Open your legs, Temperance. Let me see you.

She couldn't believe he was asking her that. Then again, he wasn't really asking, was he? He was *telling* her to open her legs. And Tem was not about to obey.

That's not flirting. You're just ordering me around.

Some would consider that flirting.

Not me.

Most women would. And those women would have let me fuck them by now.

Tem rolled her eyes. She would not be baited into pretending she was unlike most women. She was *just* like most women; she found Apollo blisteringly attractive, and under normal circumstances, she would have fucked him the moment she met him. But he was Caspen's brother, and he was playing games with her. To fuck him would be to let him win. And Tem was not in the mood to lose. It was time to play her own game.

Open your legs first.

A smirk twisted Apollo's lips. Even from across the aisle, she could see how amused he was, how deeply it pleased him that she was flirting back. Apollo was lucky Tem was in the mood to indulge him today. He'd caught her in a moment of weakness—or perhaps a moment of strength. Tem wasn't sure the difference anymore. She only knew that everything inside her wanted to explore this, to see what it would be like to test someone else's limits.

Apollo opened his legs.

His cock wasn't even hard, and it was already magnificent. Tem watched as he grasped himself at the base and squeezed. The muscles in his arms rotated as he tightened his grip, moving his hand in one long stroke. He was rigid by the time he got to the tip.

Kora.

Apollo smirked. *Do you like that?*

Tem had forgotten that he could hear her thoughts. She didn't want him to have any sense of whether she liked that. It was none of his business.

Come here, Temperance. You can have anything you like.

No.

Come over here and ride my cock.

Still no.

It would feel so good, Temperance.

For you, maybe.

For both of us.

I doubt that.

Do you?

She didn't answer. Of course it would feel good. It would feel *amazing*. But Tem couldn't go over there any sooner than she could go to the castle and bed Leo. There were certain things, no matter how badly she wanted them, that she couldn't have.

Anything can be had, Temperance.

His hand was steadily stroking his cock, his eyes boring into hers.

Forget it, Apollo.

He smirked. *It would feel good. I would make it feel so good, I promise.*

You're impossible.

Tem just shook her head. She wasn't ready to take that step. She probably never would be. And even if she was, she had no desire to ruin Apollo's relationship with Caspen.

You will not ruin us.

How do you know that?

Because I know my brother.

What does that mean?

It means you cannot ruin what is already broken.

Tem still had no context. All she knew was that she would not sleep with Apollo today. It was time to take back control.

Slow down.

Immediately, Apollo slowed his strokes.

Use just one finger. Base to tip.

She wanted to watch him trace it—to force him to feel only the bare minimum of what he *could* be feeling. Apollo did as he was told, brushing a single finger first up the length of his cock and then back down. Tem watched him the whole time, noticing how the veins in his hand caught the light as he did it. He really was a beautiful man.

You are beautiful too, Temperance.

So you've said.

Let me guess. That is boring too?

Yes.

If I cannot call you beautiful, what shall I call you instead?

Caspen calls me little viper.

He is right to do so. You are deadly.

His words flattered her more than being called beautiful ever could. And with that, Tem decided she was ready. Slowly, so that Apollo didn't miss a moment of it, she opened her legs.

The moment she did so, Apollo's presence strengthened to the point of pain. His mind gripped hers so tightly, it was as if he were standing before her with his hands on her skull. Tem grit her teeth against the sudden change, forcing herself to maintain eye contact.

Evil woman. You have no idea how good you look.

Tem had every idea. She'd seen herself in the mirror a hundred times; she knew exactly how her center looked—perfect and wet and begging to be touched. She understood how men coveted her body, how she was no longer someone without power. Tem wielded it now, opening her knees even wider so Apollo could see every inch of her.

A wave of pure, untethered lust surged from Apollo's mind to hers. It nearly took

Tem's breath away in its intensity, and she was suddenly aware of the way he saw her. Unlike the desire she felt from Caspen, which was rooted in their deep emotional connection, the desire Apollo felt was purely physical. He wanted to touch her—to *fuck* her. He wanted to grip the soft curve of her hips and yank her body against his until they both came together, sweaty and gasping. The vision was overwhelming; Tem could barely breathe. And yet, she wanted more.

What else, Apollo?

The words were a whisper. A plea. She wanted to know what else he wanted to do with her—how far he would take this. Another scene surged into her mind, so powerful she had to shut her eyes. Her and Apollo, naked together. She saw it from his perspective—how he wanted her on his lap, on his cock, ready for the taking. They were face-to-face, and Tem felt how badly he needed her like that, how he needed to look her in the eye—to force her to be present. He was like his brother in that way; *I want to see your face when you come.* What was it about these two brothers? There was no hiding from them—no deception or concealing. They demanded the truth from her, always, and for once, she was willing to provide it. Tem opened her eyes. She brushed her hand up her thigh, pausing just before her center.

Do you want me to touch it?

Apollo nodded vigorously. Pathetic.

Say it.

Touch it, Temperance. Please.

Why should I?

Because I want you to.

And why should I give you what you want?

It seemed Apollo had no answer to that. His own hand was on his cock, stroking it to the sight of her, far beyond the point of only using one finger. Tem watched him calmly, observing the way he touched himself. It was different than the way Caspen did it—his strokes were steady and sure, confident.

Apollo's were quick and desperate, the muscles in his chest tensing as his arm jerked up and down. Tem watched him for as long as she pleased, contemplating where she wanted to take this next.

There was something satisfying about exposing herself in this way. Tem had always loved the thrill of being seen. She wanted to be perceived as a sexual being, and Apollo thought of her as nothing but. She stared at Apollo, and he stared at her. He was the only one moving—stroking his cock to the sight of her naked body, showing her visions of what he imagined them doing together. Him thrusting between her legs, him holding her down by her wrists, her calling his name. Always, her calling his name. It seemed to be a point of interest for him: Apollo needed to hear her say it. Tem filed that piece of information away for a later date, vowing to remember it when she needed it.

Are you wet for me, Temperance?

She was. Tem could feel it trailing down her thighs, pooling onto the hard wooden bench. How she wished it could pool on something else instead. Apollo's eyes bored into hers. She knew exactly what he wanted her to do: walk across the banquet hall and mount him. But Tem wouldn't mount him. Not today, at least. Today was about teasing him—about showing him what he couldn't have. Perhaps it was time to do exactly that.

Tem slipped her fingers deep into her slick center, wetting them before pulling them out again. Apollo's breath hitched—she could hear it in her mind as if he were right beside her. For once, he didn't speak. Perhaps he had run out of words.

In and out. In and out.

Instead of riding a cock, Tem rode her fingers, plunging them so deep that she nearly lost her breath. With every stroke, Apollo's desire only grew. She could feel it from here—an aching *need* the likes of which she'd only ever experienced from Caspen. What a privilege to feel it from both brothers—to have them both in the palm of her hand. Tem knew Apollo could see everything: the way her fingers dipped in her center, the way her other hand squeezed her breasts. Nobody around them noticed, or if they did, nobody cared. Two people touching themselves was nothing new to the basilisks. This was just another day for them—simply another meal in the banquet hall. Tem's fingers slid deeper, her thumb gently circling her clitoris. It was no different than what she'd done in her childhood bedroom for years. Only this time, someone was watching. Tem thought of the last time she'd enjoyed being watched like this. The ritual.

Had Apollo been there? Surely he had been. And if so, did he remember the experience? Somehow, Tem hoped he did. She wanted him to have seen her that way: naked and sweaty and riding his father before riding his brother.

I was there. I remember.

Apollo sent her a vision: his point of view as he watched the ritual. Tem saw herself on Bastian, her body leaned forward, her ass on full display for everyone to see. Tem blushed. She was so *exposed.*

You were stunning.

Tem couldn't believe Apollo had watched her fuck his father—that it had turned him on—and now he wanted to do the same to her.

She was close now. There was no denying it—no stopping it. What was the point, really, in depriving herself of this? Why shouldn't Tem indulge the way all the other basilisks indulged? They way *her people* indulged? Tem was one of them now. She might as well start acting like it. She drove her fingers deeper, ready to come.

But something stopped her.

Tem felt him before she saw him, his presence pressing against her mind like stone. Caspen was walking slowly—deliberately—taking his time as he approached the table where she was seated. A moment later, he was before her. His eyes roved first over Tem, then Apollo, then back to Tem. She sat frozen, her hand still between her legs, her mouth parted in surprise. Apollo had also ceased his movements and was sitting in silence, watching.

In what felt like slow motion, Caspen sat down next to her.

A beat passed. Then another. Without a word, Caspen turned to the nearest plate, picked up a fork, and began to eat. Tem stared at him. Was he not going to say anything? *Do* anything? Had he even noticed that her fingers were inside her, that his brother was across from her? But he had—she *knew* he had. And he'd ignored it.

Tem had no idea how to proceed. She threw a questioning glance at Apollo, which he didn't return. He was staring at his brother with an expression akin to amusement. It surprised Tem. She would have thought he'd be embarrassed or even apologetic. What could he possibly be so amused about? Before she could ask, Caspen's voice loomed in her mind: *Keep going.*

Tem whipped her head over to look at him. Was he *serious*?

You heard me, Tem. Keep going.

Are you insane?

He still wasn't looking at her. He was looking at his plate, acting as if this were a perfectly normal meal. It was anything but.

Apollo's voice came to her next: *What did he say to you?*

He told me to keep going.

To her utter surprise, Apollo smiled darkly. *You should do as he says.*

You're both insane.

I already told you, Temperance. You cannot ruin us.

Tem processed his words, trying to figure out how she felt about them. Was he saying what she thought he was saying? That nothing she did—even something as wild as this—was worse than what the Drakon brothers had already done to themselves? It was unfathomable. But Tem was done questioning it. She was still turned on—even more so now that Caspen was here. And she wanted to come.

So Tem kept going.

She went slowly at first, tentatively, to see if Caspen would react. When he didn't, she resumed her pace, teasing herself to the sight of his brother. Apollo kept going too. His strokes quickened, his eyes focused on her center, his chest shining with sweat.

My brother does not know how lucky he is.

Trust me, he knows.

Then he does not appreciate it. I would fuck you every day if you were mine.

Too bad I'm not yours.

Yet.

Fuck you.

I would like to.

When she didn't answer, Apollo's eyes narrowed.

Use him.

Tem's jaw dropped. Did he mean what she thought he meant?

Before she could ask for clarification, Apollo said: *Take his hand and touch yourself.*

Hot anticipation shot through Tem. He was asking the impossible. There was no universe in which she would do that.

Use his hand, Temperance.

She couldn't fathom it. It was something out of a dream—a fantasy she would indulge in during the late hours of the night, not something she would do in the banquet hall in front of everyone.

Use my brother. Do it.

Tem couldn't think straight. As if in a trance, she reached for Caspen and took his hand in hers. The moment she did so, a twin wave of desire rushed from Caspen's mind to hers. It was so strong that she closed her eyes, focusing on nothing but how fulfilled she felt, drowning in the ache of need. She felt alive here—she felt *real*. Tem pulled his hand between her legs, tilting her hips to touch his fingers to her wetness.

Nothing about this was normal.

Normal is worthless, Temperance. There is nothing normal about you.

Tem had no idea which brother said it. They were both in her mind, surrounding her—*suffocating* her.

Lick his fingers.

Tem did so, raising Caspen's hand to her lips and sucking her own wetness off his fingers. It was a curious thing to taste herself. She'd only done so on someone else's lips—never straight from Caspen's fingers. It was a mirror of when he'd tried to taste her for the very first time, and she'd been too afraid to let him do it. How long ago that seemed now.

Fuck. I want to taste you.

Only Caspen gets to taste me.

A wave of annoyance flashed through Apollo's mind.

Tem savored it, knowing she still held power over him. It was no small thing to deny a basilisk, especially one as powerful as Apollo. But Tem didn't want him badly enough yet. She didn't want him as much as he wanted her—and she didn't know that she ever would.

Caspen's fingers moved on their own now, returning to her center with such force she could barely breathe. He was still turned away, still facing the opposite direction. But there was no doubt he was participating in this—no doubt he was turned on.

Apollo watched it all. Occasionally his gaze drifted to his brother, but only in an unhurried, lazy way, as if simply checking to make sure he was still there. Tem got the sense that he hoped he was. Nothing would surprise her at this point.

It was a curious thing to be caught between brothers. They were so similar yet also so different. Tem was their commonality: the thing that brought them together. They had done this before, and now they were doing it again with Tem. This was a habit for them—an obsession and a cycle they couldn't seem to break. They worshipped her the way she wished to be worshipped, placing her on a pedestal she may or may not have earned. Tem had no idea whether she was worthy of their devotion. But the fact remained: she had it.

Apollo had followed every order she'd given him. He deserved his reward. But that reward belonged to Caspen. Tem trailed her fingers down Caspen's chest before grasping his cock with her hand and giving it a firm squeeze.

Finally, he turned to her. His eyes were completely black.

If my attention is what you seek, you have it, Tem.

She pulled his length toward her. *Fuck me, Caspen.*

As you wish.

There was no delay. Caspen pulled her onto his lap, slid his cock inside her, and began to thrust. Tem stared over his shoulder at Apollo, who was watching their every move.

She would never get used to this. It was a thrill beyond description—it made her feel like she was breaking the rules, even though the rules explicitly stated that this was allowed. She wanted to feel like this all the time, like she was living on the edge of danger—like she was walking the line between what was right and what was wrong. It made her feel alive, and nothing could possibly feel better. Caspen's cock was deep inside her. His head dropped to her chest, his lips brushing over her breasts.

You kill me, Tem.

It was the last thing she wanted to do.

Without warning, Caspen grabbed her waist, spun her around, and turned them both on the bench so that she was once more facing Apollo—staring straight across the aisle at him as his brother thrust into her from behind. Caspen's hands found her breasts, squeezing them. Tem yelped as he bit her earlobe. Apollo's jealousy burned in the back of her brain like a white-hot brand, forcing her to feel his presence.

Your brother is watching us.

Caspen didn't even pause for a moment—there was no change in his cadence as he replied, *Let him.*

Don't you care?

He is none of my concern.

Tem almost laughed. It should be his only concern. But she was done trying to understand the traditions of the basilisks—done fighting against something she'd only ever wanted to be a part of in the first place.

Caspen drove his cock even deeper. Tem let out a moan, surrendering to his pace, angling her hips so he had full access to her. She leaned forward, her body on full display for Apollo, her breasts pushed together just for him. His cock was rigid in his hand, and Tem knew he was close. So was she. Eventually, she couldn't hold back any longer. It was too much, and Tem was done resisting. She cried out as she came, throwing her head back in triumph, allowing herself to experience it fully. The moment she finished, Apollo finished too. Tem watched as he palmed his cum, his skin already so wet with sweat that the glittering handful blended seamlessly into his hand. Caspen was the last to finish. He held out, thrusting relentlessly, holding Tem at just the right angle so that his cock hit the very deepest part of her. Finally, he came too.

In the aftermath, brother stared at brother.

They were both in her mind; she felt them in equal measure.

Apollo was the first to speak: *It is rude to interrupt, Brother. Next time leave her to me.*

Caspen let out a humorless laugh. *You could not handle her.*

And you can?

I just did.

Barely.

Another laugh. Caspen's grip tightened. *She does not want to fuck you. Surely, she has told you that.*

She has. But who knows? She may have a change of heart.

She cannot be coerced.

Apollo leaned forward, and Tem flushed. *I do not need to coerce her to fuck me. She will come to me, on her knees, begging for it.*

Tem expected Caspen to retaliate—to stand up and yell at his brother. Instead, Caspen's hands went to Tem's breasts. He traced his fingers underneath them before brushing gently over her nipples, which immediately hardened. Then he cupped them and squeezed. His message was clear: *See what I get to do?* It didn't matter what Apollo said. It was Caspen's lap she sat on—Caspen's cock inside her.

Tem saw this suddenly for what it was: a game. She'd thought she was only playing with Apollo. But at some point Caspen had entered, and he had won. Tem shouldn't have been surprised. It was exactly in Caspen's nature to play such a game, one where the ultimate victory was possession. But was Tem interested in being that prize? A week ago she would have said no. But now, with Caspen behind her and Apollo before her, perhaps her answer had changed.

Tem turned her head to look at Caspen.

You used me.

Caspen's eyes met hers. *Did I?*

His words hung in her mind.

Caspen had used her. And she'd used Apollo. Perhaps that made them even.

Without another word, Caspen picked her up. Apollo watched them go, his eyes still on Tem as he wrapped his fingers around his cock and began to stroke it once more.

CHAPTER FIFTEEN

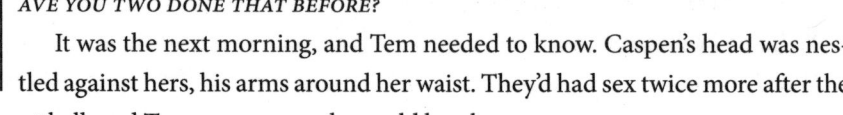

HAVE YOU TWO DONE THAT BEFORE?

It was the next morning, and Tem needed to know. Caspen's head was nestled against hers, his arms around her waist. They'd had sex twice more after the banquet hall, and Tem was so sore she could barely move.

Would it bother you if we had?

No.

That was true. Tem didn't care whether they'd done something similar before. But it would bother her if they'd enjoyed it more with someone else. She wanted to be the only one they loved—the *best* one.

No one could compare to you, Tem. That much I can promise.

Tem didn't know what to do with that information. It meant more coming from someone who had lived a life as long as his, someone who had slept with more people than she could ever fathom sleeping with. Tem hadn't grown up hearing that she was special. When she was a child, she could have been told it a thousand times and never believed it. To be told it now, as an adult, healed something in her that she hadn't known was broken.

It feels like you want Apollo to steal me from you.

Nobody could steal you from me.

"Caspen!" she yelped as his fingers dipped between her legs.

Tem. I am not angry that you have a connection with Apollo.

But you seem jealous.

I am.

I don't understand. Do you…like being jealous?

He stroked her clitoris. Tem was finding it rather difficult to concentrate.

Occasionally.

Was this all a game to Caspen? A play for power? If his brother wanted Tem, that meant she was something worth wanting. Tem could understand that—she felt a similar stab of pride and jealousy whenever other basilisks looked at Caspen. They wanted him. But he was *hers*.

Tem watched him as he fingered her, his eyes never straying from between her legs.

"How many women have you been with, Caspen?"

His eyes flicked up to hers before returning to the task at hand.

"Many," he said.

"I want a number."

He slid his fingers deeper.

Tem tried not to gasp. She was *so* sore.

"I do not know the number."

"Really?" She fought to keep her voice steady. "I thought all men kept track."

"Who told you that?"

"Vera."

Tem had learned nearly everything there was to know from Vera—that all men kept track of how many women they'd slept with, that it was unladylike for women to do the same. Most of her wisdom was baffling at best, sexist at worst. But Vera had been Tem's only source of knowledge on men, and she still found herself drawing on it, even now.

"Hm."

She could tell Caspen wasn't listening. He was doing something new down there—something that was making Tem forget why she'd bothered asking anything in the first place. But she had to know.

"Caspen." She grabbed his wrist, halting his motions. "Tell me."

He sighed, looking up at her. "I do not know how many women I have been with, Tem. I do not keep track as the humans do."

Tem narrowed her eyes. There was only one reason why he wouldn't keep track—because he'd been with so many that it didn't matter. Unfortunately, his answer did nothing to satisfy her. "If you had to guess?"

Another sigh, deeper this time. "Hundreds, Tem. Perhaps more."

Tem nodded. Caspen had been with hundreds of women. Perhaps more. And he had chosen her. She released his hand. "You can keep going now."

The corner of his mouth twitched. "If you insist."

Caspen's tongue joined his fingers. Tem's head fell back onto the pillow, and for a long while, she didn't think about Apollo.

But she thought about him the entire next day. Apollo was all she saw no matter what she did to distract herself. Somehow, he'd managed to sneak his way into the deepest canals of her mind, and her basilisk side nurtured his presence. Tem thought about how she'd touched herself in front of him. She thought about the vision he'd shown her: him holding her down by her wrists, her moaning his name. It was unbearably tempting.

But the action was impossible. Tem couldn't live like this. Between Apollo and Leo, her self-control was at an all-time low. She was drowning in desire.

Caspen was no help. He was off hunting again, and Tem no longer cared to be angry with him for it. She couldn't blame him for putting some distance between them after what happened in the banquet hall. Seeing him was a reminder that she was out of control—that, at this moment, she was not the architect of her own life. Besides, Tem had other things to focus on.

The weeks leading up to Mother's Night were always a big deal in the village. The celebration would begin tonight—on the night of the full moon—with a tradition wherein the villagers set up tables in the town square and ate an abundant feast together. In principle, it was similar to the feasts that occurred in the banquet hall, when all the basilisks were in attendance. But the similarities stopped there. The full moon celebration would be vastly different than the meals Tem experienced underneath the mountain. She rather doubted anyone would be naked.

Tem had planned to meet Gabriel at the Horseman, but by the time she'd scrounged up enough clothing to keep her warm in the winter air, she was woefully late. Instead, she headed straight for the town square, smiling when she saw the familiar decorations: round paper circles strung up on the buildings meant to imitate the full moon. Tem remembered making them in school. Full moon was a time of gratitude, of feast and family. The phase of the moon was symbolic of abundance, of *excess*—of appetite.

Of course, this year would be different.

It only took one glance at the town square to see that the tables were nearly empty. In years past, they were covered in food—loaves of bread, baskets of meat pies. Anything they couldn't grow in their own fields was imported; Tem was used to seeing piles of vegetables and seafood shipped in from far away. Now, with the shortage, the food on the tables was scarce. Fear turned her stomach. A childhood chant came to her suddenly: *full moon, full stomach.* Children used to chant it before the meal. No one was chanting it now.

She moved through the crowd, searching for Gabriel. When she passed the church, she saw that the number of guards had doubled. She also saw that the steps hadn't been cleaned. *Feed us* was still caked onto the marble, covered in a light dusting of snow. The sight made her sick. Tem couldn't believe no one had cleaned it up. Then again, it was meant to be a message. Leaving it there was certainly one way for it to sink in.

The town square was full of villagers. All around her she heard the same whispers:

"Did you hear they're having their wedding on Mother's Night?"

"On Kora's *birthday*? How dare they?"

"Word has it the castle is sparing no expense. Even the flowers are dipped in gold."

"Of course the royals are feasting while we starve. It's shameful."

"It's our soon-to-be queen. She's from one village over. Our queen never would have let this happen."

With a jolt, Tem realized *she* was their queen. She'd spent her entire life as an outcast—chided and ostracized by the villagers. But now that there was a common enemy in Evelyn, they considered Tem one of their own. How quickly the tides changed.

Just then, she spotted Gabriel. He was by the mead, as he always was. But the usual flush on his cheeks from drinking was not there; instead, he was pale, greeting her with a somber wave.

"Gabriel," she said immediately. "What's wrong?"

"Why would you assume something's wrong?"

"Because it's full moon, and you're not drinking."

A small smile twisted his lips. "Maybe I'm on a health journey."

Tem snorted.

His smile faded. "I can't drink tonight, Tem."

"Why not?"

But he didn't answer. Instead, he looked out over the square, and Tem followed his gaze. The villagers were standing in groups, whispering to each other.

Understanding crept into her like frost. "Something's happening tonight, isn't it?"

Gabriel still didn't answer. She stared up at his clenched jaw, wondering just how much had happened since the last time she'd seen him. Gabriel was probably the head of the revolution by now. He'd organized the last protest, and surely he'd organized this one. He was growing into a person Tem didn't recognize. They'd always been close— even though Gabriel was a year older—but now there was distance between them, and Tem had no idea what to do about it.

"Gabriel," she insisted. "Tell me what's going on."

"Tem," Gabriel sighed, placing a gentle hand on her shoulder. "You should go."

"Why?"

"Because you're—" He cut himself off.

Tem found she knew what he was going to say. "I'm what, Gabriel?" she whispered.

For a moment, they simply stared at each other, two best friends who no longer lived their lives the way they used to. "You're one of them."

Tem went cold.

One of *them*: the enemy. And he was right. There were two enemies here—the basilisks and the royals—and Tem was associated with both. She thought about her conversation with Leo, how he'd asked her if she knew who was behind the protests. She could understand how that would put Gabriel in a difficult position, how being seen with her would cast doubt on his allegiance. But she couldn't imagine not being close to Gabriel. He was her only friend—her last true sanctuary. Even when things were going horribly with Caspen or when she was arguing with Leo, he was there. He'd always been there.

"I'm with *you*," she whispered. "I always will be."

He just shook his head. "I'm trying to protect you, Tem."

"And I'm trying to do the same. But you have to tell me what's going on."

"I can't. Not while you're sleeping with a snake."

Tem hated the way he said it—like it was an insult. But of course Gabriel said it like that. He didn't know the basilisks like she did. He only knew their cruelty, their cunning. He had no idea that they were not so different from humans—that they were *exactly* like humans.

"Gabriel," she whispered. "When did you stop trusting me?"

He sighed. Everything she'd told him at the Horseman ran through her mind: how she was a Hybreed, how she was powerful, how basilisks lived and existed under the mountain. Was that information safe with him? Was *she* safe with him?

"Tem," he said quietly. "I'm trying to protect you."

The same thing he said before. It hurt even worse the second time.

The wind rustled his golden-blond hair.

Tem reached for him, brushing a lock from his forehead. "I can't lose you, Gabriel."

He placed his hand over hers, holding her palm to his face. "You'll never lose me, dearest. But you can't stay."

Tem opened her mouth to argue again, but at that exact moment, a cry came from the square. Gabriel's head snapped up.

"No," Tem said, twisting her hands in his jacket. "Gabriel, whatever you do, *don't*—"

But he was already running. Tem ran after him but it was no use; he was far faster than her, and he always had been.

By the time she reached the square, the church was already burning.

Guards sprinted from the steps, dispersing into the crowd as the flames grew. Batons swung. Fists flew. Tem was rooted in place, unable to move, staring in disbelief as pandemonium ensued. She'd already lost track of Gabriel. Was he near the church, feeding the fire? Was he in the crowd, in danger of getting trampled?

The villagers were screaming. Smoke billowed in the air, thick and acrid. It choked her throat and seared her lungs, forcing tears to her eyes. She had to find Gabriel.

Tem pushed into the crowd, dodging flailing limbs.

Cries of grief filled the air—whether over the church or the injured, Tem didn't know. Ash fell on the town square, dusting everything in a layer of gray, including the tiny paper moons. The guards were beating people she'd known her entire life—innocent people—until they bled. Tem was finding it difficult to breathe. This was wrong. *So* wrong.

She groped for Caspen with her mind, but their connection was closed. Panic rose in her chest. Without thinking, she searched for someone else.

He answered immediately: *Temperance? What is the matter?*

I need Caspen. Where is he?

Apollo's presence loomed larger. *He is hunting. Are you hurt?*

No. Not…really.

Where are you?

The village. But I—

Then she saw it: Golden-brown hair. Gabriel.

Tem slammed her connection with Apollo shut, running forward with her hands outstretched. He was bleeding.

"You're *hurt*," she cried, reaching for him.

Gabriel scooped her into his arms, pulling her away from the crowd. The church was ablaze behind them, the flames swallowing everything in its path.

"I'm fine," he panted, still hauling her along. "But we have to get out of here."

"Gabriel, what did you—"

Her words were cut off by the loudest sound Tem had ever heard. Gabriel pulled her immediately to the ground, throwing his body over hers as the cobblestones rattled and rubble rained down over them. Tem knew without looking that the church would be gone, that the damage from the explosion would be devastating—that things would never be the same.

As quickly as Gabriel had pulled her down, he yanked her back up, sprinting down alleyways with intuitive direction, only stopping once they reached the edge of the village. The screams were muted from here. But Tem could still see the blaze, a huge column of black smoke disappearing into the night sky.

"How could you do this?" she cried. "The *church*?"

Gabriel was out of breath, his curls stuck to his forehead with sweat. "It's just a building, Tem."

"But it's…it's…it's Kora's home—"

"We don't need a church to pay our respects to Kora. What we needed was to send a message."

Tem was speechless. They'd sent a message, all right. That they were willing to fight. "People got hurt, Gabriel. The crowd—"

"People are already getting hurt, Tem. We're starving. What do you expect us to do?"

159

Tem shook her head, staring up at him, trying to understand. "This isn't working, Gabriel. You aren't hurting anyone but yourselves. Do you think the royals care that the church burned down? This will only affect the villagers."

"They'll care soon enough."

"What's that supposed to mean?"

"The royals are just the beginning. The snakes are next."

A chill ran down Tem's spine. "When will it be enough?" she whispered.

The wind was picking up now, howling down the alleyway. Gabriel stared down at her, his eyes gleaming in the darkness. "When they give back what they took from us."

Then he turned and left her.

CHAPTER SIXTEEN

———•❉•———

I T WAS THE FIRST TIME GABRIEL HAD EVER LET HER GO WITHOUT KISSING HER ON the cheek. Tem felt a single tear fall, tracing the place where his lips should have been. She stumbled back through the forest cold and alone. Multiple times, she fell along the path, groping her way with no sense of direction. She was crying so hard she barely heard her name.

"Temperance?" Apollo emerged from the forest like a ghost, his bare skin glowing in the darkness.

"What are you doing here?" Tem gasped. She'd never seen him outside the caves.

Apollo stepped closer. "You said you were in the village. You were hurt."

Tem's brain was barely working. She struggled to put the pieces together: Apollo was here. He had come to find her. Apollo was *here*.

"Why are you crying? What happened?"

Tem had no idea how to answer him. Why *was* she crying? Was it because she'd just seen her childhood church burn down before her eyes? Was it because people had gotten hurt, and it was her fault? Or was it because the brother she needed was not the brother before her?

Apollo stepped even closer, brushing his thumb gently over her cheek. "Tell me how to fix it," he murmured. "Please."

Tem closed her eyes, focusing on nothing but his touch, letting it ground her. The intimacy of the moment was crushing. They had to stop meeting like this—alone in the darkness, immediately after something traumatic had happened. It was only a matter of time before it ended in disaster.

"Why the tears, Temperance?"

Tem opened her eyes. "The villagers are angry."

Apollo raised an eyebrow. "Are they now?"

"Yes."

"At whom?"

"The royals. And…" She paused, wondering how much she should say. "Caspen."

Apollo raised his other eyebrow. Tem didn't know how much he knew—if he was aware that Caspen was the one who broke the truce—that he had broken it for her.

"The villagers will not harm us, Temperance. They fear us."

She shook her head. They did not fear them enough. *The snakes are next.*

"If they come near us, we will turn them to stone," Apollo said. "They will not stand a chance. Petrification is our greatest power."

Again, her inadequacy reared its head. Tem dropped her voice to a whisper as she said, "Not for me."

"What do you mean?"

"I've never petrified before."

Apollo blinked in genuine surprise. "Why?"

Tem crossed her arms, suddenly embarrassed.

When she didn't answer, Apollo prompted her. "Are you afraid to do so?"

"No," said Tem firmly.

He furrowed his brow at her tone. "I see. In that case, why have you refrained?"

"Caspen won't teach me."

"And why not?"

"He doesn't want me to kill anyone," Tem grumbled.

The barest flash of amusement brightened Apollo's eyes. "You sound disappointed. Do you dream of being a killer?"

"No," she insisted. "But it feels like…a part of me is missing."

"Hm." Apollo tilted his head, considering something. "I cannot fathom why my brother would not teach you such a fundamental skill. It is unwise. You should know the full breadth of your power."

For once, they agreed on something.

Apollo continued, "Then again, he is…sentimental."

Tem had only heard one person call Caspen sentimental before. Rowe. "Sentimental how?"

Apollo shrugged. "Caspenon upholds a certain concept of…morality."

"What's that supposed to mean?"

"It means that you are a shiny thing to him. And he does not want to see you tarnished."

"Excuse me? *Tarnished?*" Tem was not an object. She was not shiny, nor was it possible to tarnish her. The entire concept was ridiculous.

"Do not hold it against him," Apollo said quickly. "He thinks he is protecting you. Although I rather suspect he is doing the opposite."

Again, they agreed on something. No good could come of Tem not knowing how to petrify.

With perhaps more eagerness than was warranted, Apollo said, "Would you like me to teach you?"

Anticipation pricked Tem's spine. Yes. She would like that. "I…" she started, then paused. Tem knew how she wanted to answer. But she couldn't seem to do it. "Don't know."

Apollo's calculating gaze held hers. "I think you do know."

Of course she knew. She knew *quite* well.

But Caspen had made his stance crystal clear. There was no doubt in her mind that accepting petrification lessons from his brother would anger him, even if it felt like the right thing to do for her—even if she wanted it.

Rather than reply, Tem stared at the middle of Apollo's chest. Anywhere was easier than looking him straight in the eye. He was standing too close. He was selfish, and his desire for her was a strategy. She had no idea whether she could truly trust him.

"Temperance," Apollo murmured, his voice low. "I will teach you, if that is what you wish. You need only say the word."

It was a tempting offer. An *extremely* tempting offer. "I want Caspen to teach me."

"I know you want that. But he will not."

She shook her head. "He will."

"No, he will not."

When Tem didn't reply, Apollo leaned in. Her breath caught in her throat.

"If you think he will change his mind, you are wrong," he murmured. "My brother never changes his mind."

Tem shrugged. "I'll convince him."

No part of her believed it. But she said it anyway.

Apollo scoffed quietly. "If you say so."

A pause. Tem was still staring pointedly at his chest. Apollo raised a single finger, placing it underneath her chin and tilting her face up to his.

"If you cannot convince him, you know where to find me."

Tem just shook her head. Apollo held her gaze for a long moment before dropping his hand. They walked back to the caves in silence, parting in the passageway without so much as a word. Tem fell asleep alone. When she woke, Caspen's arms were around her.

"Caspen," she said immediately, shaking him awake.

"Tem," he murmured into her hair. "It is early."

"I don't care. We need to talk."

At her tone, Caspen propped himself up on his elbow to look at her with a concerned frown. "What is it, my love?"

"Where were you last night?"

"I was hunting."

Of course he was. "You're always hunting."

"Because I need to eat."

"I want to go with you."

"There is no point."

Tem froze. His words felt like a slap. She slumped back on the bed. "I see," she whispered.

Caspen pursed his lips. "Tem," he said quietly. "I should not have said that."

"But it's true."

He didn't reply. Of course it was true. Caspen needed to transition in order to hunt, and Tem had hardly been able to transition at all, even with his help. She was becoming a burden to him. He was right; there was no point in her coming.

"It is only true if you let it be."

"What are you saying?"

"I am saying that you are distracted. And you are not applying yourself."

Resentment tore into her like a thorn. Caspen was no longer her teacher; he had no right to speak to her like that. Against her will, Tem felt the delicate thread that drew her to Caspen tremble. He had been gone a lot lately. He knew it, and she knew it too. Tem tried not to mind, but she did. And his absence had only left her more willing to look for comfort elsewhere. It was killing her, being alone with nothing but her thoughts.

"I needed you last night," she whispered.

Caspen frowned. "I thought you went to the village for the full moon."

"I did, but then something happened."

His grip tightened. "What happened?"

For some reason, Tem hesitated. She couldn't seem to talk about the church. If she said it out loud, somehow that made it real.

"Gabriel got hurt," she said instead.

Caspen said nothing. He didn't care if humans got hurt—he'd made that clear. But he'd also promised to protect Gabriel, and he was breaking that promise right now.

"I told you the villagers were angry," she insisted.

"What do you wish for me to say, Tem? There is nothing to be done."

"There's *always* something to be done."

Caspen just shook his head. What would it take to convince him that this was his problem too? What line had to be crossed in order for him to care? Would it take his own people getting hurt? That line was too far for Tem. She needed him to understand this *now*.

"I told you it would get worse."

"The villagers are none of my concern."

"They are *my* concern," Tem nearly shouted.

Caspen sat up. Tem did too.

His dark eyes were on hers, deep and knowing. He touched his fingertips to her hip, brushing them up her waist, over her breast, and along the column of her neck. They rested beneath her chin, tilting her head up to his.

"*You* are my only concern, Tem."

Tem wished she believed him. But Caspen didn't seem very concerned with her at all. He'd gone hunting without her last night, and now he was dismissing her. Even Apollo had been more attentive than this.

"If I am your concern, then you should listen to what I'm telling you."

Caspen sighed. His fingers traced her lips. His eyes were black; she knew he wanted her. But she would not be distracted by seduction.

"We need to do something about it," she said. "And soon."

"What would you have me do, Tem?"

For some reason, Tem thought of her conversation at the Horseman, how Gabriel had delighted at the idea of sex parties. An wild idea occurred to her, and spoke it aloud before she had a chance to overthink it: "What if Gabriel came here?"

Caspen blinked. "Why would he want to come here?"

"So he could…I don't know…see how we live."

Tem was grasping at straws. She was desperate. But how else could she humanize the basilisks in Gabriel's eyes? He'd expressed interest in coming here in the past. What if he actually did it—what if he saw that the snakes he hated so much acted just like him? If Gabriel came here and integrated with the basilisks for a night, he might understand that their lives were just as worthy as his. Gabriel held significant sway with the villagers. If Tem was able to evoke some empathy in him, perhaps she could put a stop to this. The stakes were too high not to try.

"He's the head of the rebellion, Caspen," she said quietly. "If we can get him on our side, it would help. It could change everything."

Caspen turned to the fire. Tem brushed her fingers along his shoulders gently, savoring the hard muscle beneath his skin. Even now, when they were talking about something serious, she wanted him. She would always want him.

"It is a risk, Tem. One I am surprised you are willing to take."

To be honest, Tem was surprised too. But something in her gut told her that it would be fine—that *Gabriel* would be fine. He was open-minded. He did not harbor deep resentment against the basilisks the way Jeremy, Jonathan's brother, did. The basilisks had not wronged him directly, and yet he led the charge against them. That meant there was still a chance to sway him. It meant there was hope.

"He's my friend," Tem said quietly. "I know he'll see the best in us."

Caspen sighed. "It is dangerous for humans to come here, Tem. Someone may crest him."

"Can't I give him my venom?"

"You can," Caspen said slowly. "But anyone could still petrify him."

"Isn't there some way to protect him from that?"

There was always a loophole, always a way to bend the rules. But Caspen shook his head. Tem knew she was requesting too much of him—searching for exceptions and miracles.

"No. It is permanent."

"I don't mean a way to reverse it. Isn't there some way to prevent it in the first place?"

"Not that I know of. It is our most ancient weapon. We are not immune to it ourselves."

Tem thought about how the villagers had won the war with mirrored shields. If basilisks themselves could be petrified by their own gaze, there was no hope of protecting Gabriel.

"He wouldn't be coming here as an enemy, Caspen. It would be a way for him to experience what I've experienced, a way for him to see the good."

"Are you willing to put his life in danger for that?"

Tem paused before answering quietly, "His life isn't the only one in danger."

There was no other way to say it, no other way to convince him that this was about so much more than just Gabriel seeing how the basilisks lived. The burning church flashed through her mind. This was only the beginning. Tem was sure of it.

She thought of the last thing she'd said to Gabriel, in the cold and windy alley:

When will it be enough?

When they give back what they took from us.

But what had been taken? Did Gabriel mean the food the villagers had lost since the bloodletting stopped? Or did he mean something deeper—the lives of Jonathan and Christopher, something that couldn't be given back? Either way, they had to try.

"I don't know what else to do," Tem whispered.

Caspen took a deep breath, turning to look at her. "If your friend gets hurt, you will never forgive me."

Tem frowned. Is that what this was about? Was Caspen worried about the effect this could have on their relationship if things went badly? It was a worry Tem did not share. She knew Caspen would never let any harm befall Gabriel. Even if he didn't agree with him coming here, he had agreed to protect the people she cared about.

"What if this is our only hope?"

Caspen shook his head. "This is hardly hope. It is delusion."

His words stung. But Tem understood them. "Caspen," she murmured. "It will only get worse—all of it. If we don't try to make peace with the villagers, there could be another war."

He snorted. "We are *far* from another war, Tem."

A few months ago, she might have believed him. But the desecration of the church was an act so extreme, she didn't know what the villagers might do next. "I'm being serious," Tem insisted. "If he came here, he would love it. I know he would."

"I cannot guarantee his safety, Tem."

"But can't you…I don't know…call a council meeting or something? They could guarantee his safety, couldn't they?"

For some reason, Caspen went very still. He looked at her for a long time, so long she became nervous beneath his gaze.

"What is it?" she insisted.

"There is no need for a council meeting," he said quietly.

"Why not?"

His next words were steady and low, as if they required great control to say them. "Because you are a Hybreed. If you wish to bring your friend here, you do not require their permission. You do not require anyone's."

Tem stared at him in shock. The fact that she could bypass the council was news to her. It was also…terrifying. If Tem could bypass the council, could she bypass Caspen? If so, this entire conversation was a formality. Tem's choice, not Caspen's, would be final.

Caspen continued quietly, "It is your decision, Tem. I will not stop you. But if it goes badly, you must live with the consequences."

Things were already going badly. There were *already* consequences.

The snakes are next.

Tem had no idea what the villagers would do next, but she knew it would be terrible. And whether it was against the royals or against the basilisks, she had to try to stop it.

Tem spent the rest of the day deep in thought. To bring Gabriel here would be to take a wild chance—one that could end in death and disaster. But the situation with the villagers was deteriorating quickly. She could think of nothing else to do—no other solution to an impossible problem. Without some other way for the royals to make money, the villages would not be fed and the riots would only get worse. And if they got worse, it was only a matter of time before they became deadly. Bringing Gabriel here might not even be enough to stop the tidal wave that was building. But it was worth a try for a world in which the humans and the basilisks lived in peace.

There was so much that the humans could learn from the basilisks, and vice versa.

Surely if the two sides could coexist within Tem—ceding and wielding power in tandem—they could coexist in real life.

Too soon, it was Sunday.

A carriage arrived to take them to the castle, as always. Caspen's hand was on her knee the entire time. He'd been holding her close the past few days: hunting less, listening more. Tem wondered why. Was it because he sensed the distance between them and wished to prevent it? Or was it because of what he'd told her—that she was powerful—and he wanted to keep that power close? Either way, Tem liked it. She felt more connected to him than she had in days.

They entered the castle hand in hand. But for the first time, no one was there to greet them. No butler, no Leo, no Evelyn. Tem didn't know what to make of it.

"Where is everyone?" she whispered.

Caspen shrugged. "Perhaps they are running late."

"To their own dinner? In their own home?"

In response, Caspen pulled her against him. His mind beckoned to hers. *And how shall we fill the time?* His fingers were already on trailing down her waist.

Tem swatted him away. "Are you *serious*? Someone might see us."

"Let them watch."

"Caspen," she gasped as he wrapped one hand around her thigh, pulling her legs apart and coaxing his knee between them. His other hand dipped into the slit of her dress. "We should go somewhere—the parlor—"

He pressed her against the front door. "We are not going anywhere until you come, Tem."

She couldn't have argued if she'd tried. His fingers slid deep into her wetness, his palm cupping her clitoris.

"*Caspen—*"

Her plea died on her tongue as he covered her mouth with his other hand. Tem arched her back, straining against his grip, but it was no use. He was already working her into a blind heat, distracting her completely. All she could feel was him; all she could smell was smoke. She wanted him to fuck her *right here, right now.*

I thought you wanted to go to the parlor.

She didn't anymore. Not even close.

Now she wanted Caspen.

Tem reached for the seam of his trousers. A moment later they were open, and a moment after that, his cock slid inside her.

Caspen's hand never left her mouth. She moaned against his fingers, their faces an inch apart as he fucked her. They were completely exposed. If anyone walked by—a maid, a stable boy, *anyone*—they would be seen. Tem didn't care. Tem *liked it*. Tem wished she were completely naked and he was taking her in the middle of the ballroom. To do it in the foyer was no longer enough for her. She wanted to be *seen*.

If we are seen here, we will be thrown out, my love.

Even better. No more Sunday-night dinners.

Caspen's amusement lasted only a moment. Then he was thrusting even harder, pushing Tem to the very brink of orgasm. She knew he needed her like this—helpless, his. Tem was happy to be that for him. It gave her pleasure to give him pleasure. It had always been that way between them.

Her dress was off her shoulders. Caspen's free hand found her breasts, squeezing them until she yelped against his palm. She came with a whine that made Caspen's eyes turn completely black. A moment later, he came too, and Tem clenched her center, making sure he felt every inch of her as he pulled out. When they drew apart, they were both panting.

Caspen tucked his cock back into his trousers, and Tem was sad to see it go. She knew he could get hard again in a moment, and she wished they could simply go on forever. But there was dinner to be had.

She was just adjusting her dress when a voice said, "Tem?"

Leo stood at the top of the staircase. His face was pale.

CHAPTER SEVENTEEN

••✳••

TEM STARED UP AT HIM IN SHOCK. DID HE KNOW WHAT THEY'D JUST BEEN DOING? They were both out of breath, both flushed with desire. Tem's dress was barely on—Caspen had yanked it aside so aggressively that her entire thigh was bare, her breasts nearly exposed. Leo knew very well what Tem looked like when she came. Would he recognize it now? If the roles were reversed, she would recognize it on him.

"Leo," she said, because she didn't know what else to say.

Just then, Evelyn appeared. Her eyes ran first over Leo, then Tem, lingering on her askew dress. A cruel sneer twisted her mouth. "Shall we eat?" she chirped.

Nobody answered, but they walked to the dining room in silence, Caspen's hand around her waist. His thoughts were especially loud: she saw him taking her in the foyer, on the stairs, against the dining room table. Tem could barely put one foot in front of the other as he sent her vision after vision of them together, all over the castle, for anyone to see.

You're out of control tonight.

Can you blame me?

Tem couldn't. She sent him a vision back: the two of them in the middle of the ballroom, surrounded by people. Their own mini-ritual.

Do not tempt me, Tem. I will rip that dress off right now and fuck you in front of them.

I doubt that would help relations.

I doubt I care.

They'd arrived in the dining room. Tem sat slowly, aware of the wetness between her legs, arranging her dress to cover her thighs. Underneath the table, she placed her hand on Caspen's and squeezed. *Behave, Caspen.*

He threaded his fingers through hers. *Only if you do.*

The vibe between Leo and Evelyn stood in stark contrast to the one between Caspen and Tem. Things were strained between them. Tense. Evelyn was glaring at Leo as if he'd deeply wronged her. Tem understood suddenly why they were late to dinner. They'd been arguing. The thought thrilled her.

"So," Tem said lightly. "How are you two tonight?"

Leo cleared his throat. Evelyn said nothing.

Tem tried again: "How are the wedding preparations coming along?"

It was the last thing she wanted to hear about. But she was in the mood to push them, and the wedding was sure to get Evelyn talking. Sure enough, she answered, "They are somewhat stalled."

"Oh?" Tem sat up straight. "And why is that?"

"Things are...difficult right now."

"Difficult how?"

Evelyn glanced at Leo, who was staring at his whiskey. "Now that the bloodletting has been abolished, the kingdom is struggling. It was our main source of income."

Income. As if the bloodletting was a job that produced a paycheck. To compare the basilisks chained up in the dungeons to employees was laughable.

"What does that have to do with your wedding?"

"Well," Evelyn tutted. "It has affected our budget, of course."

Rage surged through Tem. The church had burned down, and they weren't even discussing it. The only thing that mattered to her was money.

"Surely there are other ways to pay for it." Tem shrugged.

"None as lucrative as the bloodletting."

A silence fell, the only sound was the scrape of knife against plate. Tem wasn't sure who should speak next, but she decided it wouldn't be her. Beside her, Caspen's hand was still clasped in hers. Only now, he was no longer in a good mood. Now he held her as if her hand were an anchor—a desperate measure to control himself. Tem dearly hoped it was working.

In the silence, Tem considered the implications of what Evelyn was saying.

This was an unanticipated problem. Tem hadn't thought this far ahead—she'd thought that if they could abolish the bloodletting, everything would be solved. It was Leo's job to decide how to run his kingdom in the aftermath, and it was Tem's job to protect her people.

Evelyn broke the silence: "Surely, there is a compromise."

Tem's eyes immediately narrowed. She opened her mouth to speak, but Caspen beat her to it.

"What do you suggest?" The words were icy. Restrained.

Everyone at the table looked at him, but he looked only at Evelyn. He was holding Tem's hand so tightly it was beginning to go numb.

Evelyn shifted, clearly uncomfortable. Then she turned up her nose. "The basilisks could...provide us with a supply."

Tem's mouth fell open. "Of *blood*?"

"It would be on a voluntary basis."

Tem snorted. The basilisks had barely begun to heal from the decades of torture. There wasn't a basilisk alive who would choose to bleed again. And Tem couldn't blame them.

"No one is going to *volunteer* to bleed for you."

"It's not just for us," Leo said quietly, his first words in minutes. "It's for the villagers."

Tem glared at him. "That's not true, and you know it."

Silence.

She needed him to say it—needed to admit that he was doing this for the one person Tem had sacrificed her happiness to give him. To Evelyn, the solution to their problem was simple: bring back the bloodletting. If it had worked for many years before this, why stop now? But it was unthinkable to Tem. Leo had agreed to abolish it. She would not let him go back on it without a fight.

"We have to *bleed* for that gold, Leo. You want us to bleed for your *wedding*?"

Evelyn rolled her shoulders but didn't speak. Her face was a mask of fury.

Leo shook his head. "I don't want that."

"Then why are you asking it of us?"

Leo opened his mouth and then closed it. His knuckles were white around his whiskey glass. Tem stared at him. Then she looked at Caspen. He'd been quiet throughout most this exchange. Tem knew he was controlling his temper, expending every ounce of his energy into staying calm. She also knew it was only a matter of time before his energy ran out.

She turned back to Leo. "Why are you doing this, Leo?" she whispered. "This isn't you."

He didn't reply.

Tem thought about how Evelyn always pursed her lips during dinner whenever the topic of the bloodletting came up. At first, Tem thought it made her uncomfortable to talk about such unpleasant matters. But now she saw the truth: of course she wanted the steady supply of gold to continue. No doubt it was what she'd expected when she first returned to Leo. The royals were known for their wealth, after all. Leo's recent financial change would have been a surprise to Evelyn, and not a pleasant one.

Leo looked at her finally, his jaw tight. "I just want peace."

Tem let out a dull laugh. "Peace is not gained through bloodshed."

Tem couldn't believe this was happening. If she could put a face to the victims—if she could put *her face* to this horrible act—perhaps then finally Leo would understand what this would cost him. There would not be some anonymous basilisk in the dungeon, bleeding for the sake of the royals. It would be someone he cared about. It would be her.

"If you're looking for volunteers," she said through gritted teeth, "you have one. Me."

"*No*," Caspen and Leo said at the same time.

"Yes," Tem insisted. "If you're so eager for blood, you can have mine."

Caspen's grip tightened even more.

"No, Tem," Leo insisted. "Not you. Never you."

Tem straightened. "Why not? I'm part basilisk. I made *that*"—she pointed at the gold claw on Caspen's chest—"and my blood is just as good as anyone else's."

Leo's eyes flicked to Caspen's necklace. His brow furrowed, and Tem wondered what he was thinking. He shook his head. "You're not an option, Tem."

"And why not? I'm no different than anyone else."

"Of course you are."

"No. I'm not. And if you want my people to bleed, that means you want me to bleed too."

"I don't want you to—" But he cut himself off.

Tem leaned forward, staring straight at him, her voice dangerously quiet. "Don't want me to *what*, Leo?"

Leo pursed his lips. He understood. She knew he did.

Tem was making this difficult for him: forcing him to choose between keeping his soon-to-be wife happy and keeping Tem safe. It was a cruel choice but a necessary one. Tem needed to shine a spotlight on Evelyn's asinine idea. Leo was only entertaining it in the first place because he thought some random basilisk would be the one to be harmed. But she wouldn't let him off so easily. If Leo wanted blood to be spilled, that blood would be Tem's.

"I don't want you to get hurt," Leo finally finished quietly.

His words fell on deafening silence.

Evelyn's lip were pressed together in tight displeasure, her eyes flicking from Tem's to Leo's, then back again. Tem ignored her. This was between her and Leo. She already knew where Evelyn stood, already knew she was evil. But Leo was redeemable. Leo was *good*. Tem was going to remind him of that.

She looked him in the eye. "You say you don't want me to get hurt, yet you also want the bloodletting to continue. So which one do you want more?"

Leo's face was pale, his expression strained. Tem could see the toll this was taking on him, but she was not about to let up. She would not let him sit in his privilege and pretend that his actions did not affect others.

"If you want blood," she said again. "You'll need to take mine."

As the silence deepened, Caspen's grip grew even tighter. She could feel him pushing at the edges of her mind, trying to get in. But Tem had shut him out long ago. This was her battle to fight with Leo—her personal mission to make him understand that Evelyn's request was unacceptable. If Leo wanted the bloodletting to continue, he would have to claim it and wear it proudly. If the kingdoms were to backslide, Tem was not going to make it easy to do so. If Leo was going to let this happen, he was going to have to let it happen to Tem. That was the only outcome that would teach him a lesson.

Caspen clawed at her mind. His presence was so strong, she was having trouble concentrating—finding it almost impossible to breathe. His fingers gripped her hand in an ironclad clasp. Still, she did not yield. Tem would face this alone because she did not want Caspen to have to face it at all.

Evelyn blinked her round, baleful eyes. She turned slowly to Tem. "I think it's rather noble of you."

"*Noble?*" Caspen spat.

It was the first word he'd said in minutes, and immediately, the hairs on the back of Tem's neck stood up. She heard the danger in his voice, and it scared her. Evelyn was extremely close to crossing a line, and if she took it any further, there was a very real possibility that Caspen would snap. His presence was a storm, crackling and fierce.

"Noble is one word for it," Tem said as calmly as she could. "Necessary is another. If a sacrifice must be made to keep peace between our kingdoms, I will make it."

"I *forbid it.*"

Tem turned to Caspen. To her surprise, he wasn't looking at her. His gaze was still on Evelyn, his golden eyes narrowed in pure loathing. Her eyes were narrowed in return.

"If Tem is volunteering, then we should allow her to make her own choice."

Caspen and Leo let out identical noises of disbelief.

"Tem is altruistic to a fault. This is not her choice to make," Caspen growled.

"Any choice concerning my body is my choice to make," Tem said quietly.

Silence fell again.

Tem knew she was pushing this too far. Nobody at this table besides Evelyn wanted this for her. But Caspen, despite his intent to protect her, could not prevent this. Only Leo could protect her. And if he was unable to do so, he would suffer the consequences.

Leo's eyes found hers.

Tem had never been able to read his mind the way she could Caspen's. Leo wore his emotions on his sleeve, so it had never really been necessary. But now, in the lingering silence, she wished she knew what he was thinking. Did he understand the gravity of the situation? Did he realize that they were on the brink of complete regression? If the bloodletting continued, everything they'd been through was for nothing. The wedding, the crest, his entire marriage to Evelyn. If Leo allowed this to continue, he was no better than Maximus.

But Leo's loyalty was to his future wife. And that wife was no longer Tem.

His eyes dropped. "Tem can make her own choice," he whispered.

Beside him, Evelyn preened. She looked at Caspen triumphantly, her shoulders thrown back as if she'd just won the world's greatest prize. Then her gaze moved to Tem, who finally understood the loathing in it. This was all about power for Evelyn—she wielded what little she had in order to make it clear that Tem, and the basilisks, were below her. Tem would be disgusted if she wasn't already used to people like her. What disgusted her more was how Leo had allowed it to happen. Progress, when unmaintained, was not progress at all. It was just another lie.

"Then it's settled," Tem whispered. "We can begin next week."

At her words, Caspen stood abruptly.

Everyone stared up at the basilisk, his shoulders squared, his fists at his sides. Tem hadn't felt afraid of Caspen in a long time. But she was afraid now.

"Tem," he said quietly, with no emotion. "I will see you at home."

Tem didn't dare speak. She had no idea what to say. There was nothing *to* say.

They all watched as Caspen left the room. His mind was closed off to her; now he was the one shutting her out. It was the second dinner in a row that he'd stormed out of, and she found it significant that he'd left without her. Did he want her to stay? Did he think *she* wanted to stay? Tem had no idea what else she could possibly accomplish here, especially on her own. She was just about to follow Caspen when Evelyn stood too.

"Leo," she said, somewhat less calmly than Caspen. "Finish this. I will see you upstairs."

Then she left the room too.

Tem and Leo stared at each other. It was only them now.

"*Finish* this?" Tem snapped.

He shook his head. "She didn't mean it like that."

"Then what did she mean?"

When he didn't answer, Tem stood. Immediately, Leo stood too. "Tem, wait—"

Leo reached for her, then dropped his hand. They still hadn't touched since the annulment. Tem wondered if it was deliberate—if he was withholding himself on purpose for fear of what it might incite.

"Wait for what, Leo?"

"Tem, please. Let's just talk."

"I don't want to *talk*," Tem snapped.

"She doesn't know what she's saying." Leo was still standing, leaning toward her. "She's just trying to protect her people."

"Well, that's nice. I'm trying to protect mine."

"I know you are. That's why we're doing this, why we're having these dinners—"

"These dinners are useless if they're just a way to reinstate the bloodletting."

"That's not what they are."

"Aren't they? Then what exactly was that conversation we just had?"

"That was…just a discussion."

"A *discussion*?"

"We're just…trying our best to coexist."

"I don't see Evelyn trying to coexist. I see her trying to bring back the exact thing that caused the problem in the first place. It's almost as if she wants another war."

"That's not her goal. She would never do that."

"She would if you let her."

"Well, I won't."

"Won't you?" The words came out before she could stop them.

But the hurt that flashed across Leo's face was unmistakable. "Do you truly think so little of me?" he whispered.

"I think you've forgotten your priorities."

Leo downed his drink with a grimace. He looked down at the empty glass between his hands, and his next words were a whisper. "*She's* going to be my wife, Tem. She has to be my priority."

The word he'd chosen to emphasize was unmistakable. Tem fought a sudden swell of tears. "I know that," she whispered back. "Trust me, I know."

Their eyes met.

They stared at each other in the dim light of the dining room. It was all too much. She'd tried to do the right thing, and she had failed. She'd tried to protect him, and it was clear she hadn't done that either.

"She's not the same," Leo said, his voice barely a whisper. "She's changed."

"What do you mean she's changed?"

"When I look at her, I—I—" He shook his head, searching for the words. "I don't understand who she is now. She never used to be like this."

"Like what?"

Leo took a long time to answer. When he did, the word was as sharp as a blade. "Greedy."

Tem had no idea what to say to that. It was a shock to hear Leo describe his own fiancée in such a way. But she couldn't pretend she hadn't thought the same thing. Evelyn *was* greedy. She coveted gold and placed value on physical items. Tem couldn't relate to such fancies. And despite growing up in a castle full of them, she knew Leo couldn't either.

"We used to talk for hours," Leo whispered. "Now we barely speak. She never even apologized for leaving."

Tem couldn't take any more. It was all wrong. Evelyn was supposed to be the love of Leo's life. They were supposed to get married and have babies and love each other until their dying day. They were supposed to be *worth it*. But now Tem couldn't shake the inescapable feeling that she'd made a terrible mistake—that in a moment of pity after cresting Leo, she'd damaged his entire future. It was an unacceptable result. His next words only confirmed it.

"I don't want this, Tem."

It was all he said, but it was so much more. It was true that Tem had ordered Leo to find Evelyn. But every decision after that had been his own. She hadn't told him to propose, hadn't told him to bring her back here, hadn't told him to let her seep her way into every aspect of his life. Those were his own choices, and they had nothing to do with the crest or with Tem. He was becoming someone she didn't respect, someone she was not safe around. Tem stepped closer. Leo's eyes widened as she did it.

She lowered her voice, speaking with unquestionable authority. "We are done cutting ourselves open for you."

"Tem," he said desperately. She could hear the tightness in his throat. "Please."

"Please *what*, Leo?"

Tem wanted to hear him say it—wanted him to acknowledge that he was nothing but a horrible, predictable hypocrite. Leo just shook his head.

At his silence, Tem allowed herself to hate him, just this once. She wanted him to feel the pain she felt—to understand exactly what his decision was going to do. There was only one thing she could say that would cut him deep enough:

"Your father would be so proud," Tem said coldly.

She didn't linger to see his shame.

CHAPTER EIGHTEEN

⸱⸱●✳●⸱⸱

ASPEN WAS IN THEIR CHAMBERS WHEN SHE RETURNED, STANDING STOCK-STILL in front of the fire, his fists clenched at his sides. Tem stood next to him but didn't dare speak. There was no point in trying to talk to him anyway—nothing she could say that would soothe his mind. She only wished to be here for him, to let him know she was on his side. They stood there for what felt like an eternity—so long that the fire began to burn low. When Caspen finally turned to her, Tem braced herself for another outburst. Instead, he placed his hands gently on either side of her face, pulling her gaze up to his. His voice was a whisper.

"Do you have any idea how precious you are to me?"

The question wasn't what Tem had expected, and she wasn't entirely sure how to answer. She knew, on a basic level, how much Caspen loved her. But there was no way for her to know how deep that love truly went.

"I think so," she replied. It was the best she could do.

Caspen traced her cheeks with his thumbs, trailing them down along her jawline. "There is nothing in this world that matters to me more than you, Tem. Nothing." His hands stilled, and for a moment, they simply stood there. Then he said slowly, "I cannot allow the bloodletting to resume."

"I know. I don't want it to either."

Caspen's grip tightened. "It is not a matter of *want*. I will not allow it."

Tem realized what he was really saying: Caspen was the Serpent King. It was his responsibility to protect his people. If Leo let this happen again—if he harmed the basilisks again—Caspen would be forced to retaliate.

"I understand," she whispered.

Caspen pulled away. "Do you?"

Tem stared up at him, seeing exactly how angry he truly was. Tem couldn't tell if Caspen was more angry that Evelyn had tried to reinstate the bloodletting or that Tem had volunteered to participate. This was a betrayal of everything he had dared to take a chance on by striking a deal with Leo. What happened tonight reinforced every bad thing the basilisks believed about the humans—that they were greedy, untrustworthy, and cruel. Tem hated that Leo had proved Caspen right.

She tried to defend him. "He's desperate. You would be too in his position."

"I would find another solution. I would not allow blood to be spilled."

Tem didn't bother refuting him, didn't bother pointing out the hypocrisy in his statement. Caspen had allowed plenty of blood to be spilled: all human. Couldn't he see the parallels? Each side refused to see the value in the other. Each side thought the other should bleed.

"This *is* a solution, Caspen. If I'm the only one who—"

"*I do not want you hurt, Tem.*"

Tem tried a different angle. "It's not Leo's fault. Evelyn is the one who wants this."

Caspen turned to look her in the eye. "He is accommodating her wishes. That makes him no better than she is."

It didn't help that he was right. "I know," Tem said, her voice small. "I just..." But there was nothing else to say. Tem *wanted* to argue that it wasn't really Leo's fault. But that wasn't true. He was a person of his own free will. He had agreed to this.

Caspen stepped closer. "He is a problem, Tem. They both are."

Tem shuddered at his words. What little respect Caspen may have had for Leo had been eliminated tonight. At the end of the day, they'd always had Tem in common. But now Leo had Evelyn. If Tem's safety was no longer Leo's priority, he was of no use to Caspen. He was a threat.

"Just let me talk to him," she whispered. "I know I can—"

"We are far beyond *talking*, Tem."

"If I can just—"

"There is only one thing you can do to fix this. And I know you are unwilling to do it."

Tem blinked. "I don't understand."

Now Caspen paused, and Tem wondered if he hadn't meant to say that.

"What do you mean, Caspen?" she insisted. "What am I unwilling to do?"

"What has to be done."

Tem stared at him, trying desperately to understand what he was saying to her. What, in Caspen's eyes, needed to be done? She tried to think like a basilisk, to see things from his perspective. Comprehension dawned.

Leo was bound to her. Tem was the only one who had the power to influence his choices. It was a horrible power—one she wished she could give back—but a power nonetheless. Caspen wanted her to use that power. It's what any basilisk would do.

"You want me to give him an *order*?"

Caspen didn't reply. He didn't have to. Of course that's what he wanted—of course he considered Leo to be so far below him that he deserved to be commanded like a child.

"He's a person, Caspen. Not a toy. I can't just order him around."

"You can tell him to stop the bloodletting."

"I'm not telling him that, Caspen. It won't solve anything. Evelyn will still—"

"It will solve *everything*, Tem. Everything."

But Tem just shook her head. She couldn't believe Caspen was even suggesting this. To give Leo an order would be to abuse the power dynamic created by the crest. Leo trusted her not to tell him what to do—Tem herself had promised him she would never give him another order. She remembered how horrible it felt when she'd told him to calm down and he'd obeyed. Tem never wanted to make him feel like that again.

"I won't do it," she said quietly but firmly.

"Then do not tempt me to do so myself."

Tem froze at the anger in his voice. "What's that supposed to mean?" she whispered.

"It means"—Caspen leaned closer—"that while you may be unwilling to do what is necessary, I am perfectly willing."

Tem's blood ran cold. "He drank my venom," she said. "He wouldn't obey you anyway."

"Would he not?"

In the devastating silence, Tem remembered what Caspen told her about his father, the former Serpent King: *He is the only basilisk with enough power to crest anyone he wants.* As the new Serpent King, that power now fell to Caspen. It didn't matter that Tem had given Leo her venom—it was protection from being crested by another basilisk, but Caspen was the one basilisk who could override that protection. If he crested Leo, the human king would be bound to Caspen instead of Tem. If he gave him any order, he would have to obey.

Tem looked up at him. "You wouldn't dare."

"It is my right."

"Your *right*?" Tem stepped backward, floored by his words. This was a side of Caspen she did not know: a side that scared her. "You can't just do anything you want," she whispered. "You're not a god."

Fury flashed over Caspen's face. "Am I not? He should thank me for my benevolence."

"He's not a plaything, Caspen. He's a person. You can't just—"

"He exists because of *me*."

Caspen's girls were always chosen. He had trained Leo's mother. And his grand-mother, and his great-grandmother. He'd been given the nickname Serpent King for his achievements, and he had earned it. Caspen—and Caspen alone—was responsible for Leo's existence. Without him, Maximus never would have married Leo's mother, and they never would have had children.

Caspen was right. Leo existed because of him.

They stared at each other with an intensity Tem could barely stand. They were far beyond negotiating now. Something had broken between them—something vital. The truth, as it so often did, had forced its way to the surface at last. Caspen expected her to make a choice—to fall in line. It did not matter that she was half-human, half-basilisk. He would force her to choose the same way she'd just forced Leo.

But Tem would not be tamed. She could not control who she loved, and she did not care to try. Caspen, in his infinite, ancient wisdom, would have to bear that. She looked him in the eye as she said, "That doesn't give you the right to control him."

Caspen lifted his chin, looking down at her. He was so regal in that moment—so deeply powerful—that Tem nearly shivered. "I created him."

"Your father created you. Does that mean he had the right to control you?"

That stopped Caspen short. His eyes narrowed. Tem had known the impact her words would have—had known Caspen would not take kindly to the comparison. But it was a comparison worth making. If Caspen thought he deserved to control Leo because he had played a role—no matter how tangential—in his conception, he was wrong.

Tem squared her shoulders, looking her husband straight in the eye as she said, "You will lose me if you crest him."

Smoke was coiling up Caspen's shoulders. The line between arousal and anger had always been a thin one for him, and Tem could sense in on him now. His voice was deathly quiet. "I thought it would have faded by now."

"Thought what would have faded by now?"

"Your infatuation with him."

Tem stared at him. What she felt for Leo was far from an infatuation. It was as real and irrefutable as her love for Caspen. It was the pillar that kept her upright—the force that ensured she was steady. *Fade?* Never. Perhaps Caspen had never fully grasped it the way he should have. Perhaps through willful ignorance, or perhaps sheer denial, he viewed it as a harmless schoolyard crush. A nuisance that would never become a threat. Something fleeting, something that would pass. Caspen hadn't believed that she might actually love Leo. That her heart would forever be swayed in his direction. That it was real.

"It won't fade," Tem whispered. "It never will."

Her words washed over him slowly. Tem watched, in real time, as Caspen understood what she was saying. His eyebrows shot up in surprise before his face turned into a mask of disgust. "Do as you wish, Tem. You always do."

Then he swept from the room.

The following days were long, and Tem spent them thinking.

She thought about the way Caspen had looked at her—like he was seeing her for the first time. Tem had not concealed her feelings for Leo; she had not pretended she did not love him. If Caspen thought otherwise, he had chosen to be blind.

She also thought about Leo and his inability to stand up to Evelyn. Tem had never felt such anger toward another human being before. Evelyn's solution was no solution at all—even if the bloodletting came back, it would never be enough. It seemed like there was no future for them, no path that didn't end in violence and death. It wasn't the future Tem wanted for her people. Surely, it wasn't what Leo wanted either. But it was the direction they were headed, and unless he stepped up to stop it, their fate was predetermined. They would repeat history; there would be bloodshed. And if that happened, what then? Would Leo turn on her, like he turned on the rest of her people? Tem was half-basilisk, after all. She was one of *them*, just like Gabriel had said. The enemy. It had never been easy for Tem to belong to both sides. But now more than ever, she had to find a way to move forward. It was time to take matters into her own hands.

By the next evening, Tem had resolved to do it.

She went to the Horseman alone, ignoring the frigid wind, her curls bundled in a spare blanket. The weather was the least of her worries. Tem focused on the task at hand: finding Gabriel. Something that had started as a pipe dream was now her best option. If Gabriel came to the caves—if he could have a positive experience with the basilisks, it might be enough to change his mind. And if he changed his mind, it could sway the tides. Besides, it was no longer only Gabriel's opinion she wanted to sway. If Caspen could see how a human acclimated—how a human respected basilisk culture—he might change his mind too. She had to try.

Gabriel was in their usual booth. He looked up when she walked in, his eyes immediately searching hers. Wariness. Fear.

"Gabriel," she said quietly as she slid into the booth. "I'm not here to fight with you."

His expression softened slightly. "Then why are you here, dearest?"

"I have a proposition."

"Well, let's hear it."

Tem paused. Was she really about to do this? Caspen was right; it was delusional. But delusional was better than nothing. Delusional was all Tem had. "I want you to come underneath the mountain."

In the silence that followed, Tem wondered whether she'd just made a grave mistake. There was no guarantee that this would work. Even if Gabriel had a successful foray beneath the mountain, that did not mean he would be able to sway the villagers.

She would have put him in danger for nothing. But this was Gabriel—her childhood friend—her greatest confidant. Tem trusted him, even if he didn't trust her in return.

"You want me to come underneath the mountain," Gabriel repeated.

"Yes."

"When?"

Tem had spent the morning working with Adelaide to prepare the quivers for his arrival. When she'd told Caspen what she'd done, he hadn't said a word. But it wasn't his choice to make.

"Tonight, if possible."

Gabriel blinked. "Why?"

The answer to that was slightly more complicated. "Because..."

But how to answer? If she told Gabriel that the future of their kingdoms hung on his visit, he would never agree to it. It was too much pressure for one person—too much to ask of him. But the fact remained that Tem had to ask. So she said, "I want you to experience basilisk culture."

A tiny grin tilted his lips as a shadow of Gabriel's usual spark returned. "Temperance Verus," he said conspiratorially, "are you inviting me to a sex party?"

Tem rolled her eyes so hard, she nearly sprained her brain. "I *told* you. They aren't sex parties."

"Sure sounds like a sex party to me."

"It's *dangerous*, Gabriel. There will be hundreds of basilisks there. If any of them transition, you'll be dead."

"I'm sure you won't let that happen."

"If *I* transition, you'll be dead."

"*Pah.*" He flicked his fingers.

"This is serious, Gabriel. I'm..." She paused, and he held her gaze.

"What, Tem?"

"I'm trying to make things better," she whispered.

It was the least she could say—the least she could do. She wasn't just trying to make things better—she was trying to fix everything in one night. It was an impossible task.

Gabriel shifted closer, his blue eyes holding hers.

"Is this a peace offering?"

Tem nodded.

"And if I go, will the basilisks leave the villagers alone?"

Tem hadn't *exactly* cleared that with the basilisks. But if she was as powerful as Caspen said, she would do everything she could to make that the case.

Again, Tem nodded.

Gabriel leaned back, tilting his head as he appraised her. "So," he said, taking the last dregs of his beer. "What can I expect?"

Pure relief swept through her. Nothing mattered except for the singular fact that Gabriel had agreed to her plan. Tem felt suddenly light as a feather. "You can expect… everyone to be naked."

"Perfect. I love being naked."

"They're naked *all the time.*"

"As they should be."

"*Gabriel.*"

"*Tem.*" He put his hands on her shoulders, pulling her close. "I understand this is an olive branch. But if you're telling me that I'm going under the mountain, I need to know what I'm in for."

He was right, of course. The last thing she needed was for Gabriel to be out of his depth.

"It's a risk," she said honestly. "And I cannot guarantee your safety."

Gabriel touched her cheek. "Surely there is no danger as long as I'm with you."

"That's not necessarily true."

"Well, surely there is no danger as long as I'm with your hot husband."

Tem's mouth fell open. "*That's* not true either. He can't—"

"Tem." Gabriel grabbed her face, looking her straight in the eye. "Am I going to see him naked?"

Tem sighed. There was no containing him. Perhaps it was impossible to anyway. Gabriel's joy radiated off him in infectious waves, and even Tem couldn't help but feel hopeful. It was the happiest she'd seen him look in weeks.

"Yes," she muttered.

"*Excellent.*"

"But, Gabriel"—she placed her hands over his, holding him to her—"you have to take this seriously. The point is to show you how the basilisks live. The point is to humanize them."

Gabriel sobered somewhat at that fact. It was true; this was no lighthearted visit. There might be pleasure involved, but pleasure was not the point. The entire goal of him coming under the mountain was to show him that the basilisks were deserving of respect—that they were kind and worthy and just as important as the humans. Everything was riding on this.

"I understand," he said quietly, his eyes holding hers. "Trust me."

Tem did trust him. She always had. "I have to warn you," she said. "It's mating season."

"Mating season?" He waggled an eyebrow. "What's that?"

"It's a time when any single basilisk seeks a mate. It's a particularly…voracious time."

"*Voracious?*"

"I don't know how else to describe it."

"You described it perfectly, dearest. I await the ravenousness."

Tem rolled her eyes again. He was impossible.

They spent the rest of the evening drinking beers and talking about nothing. They didn't discuss the protests, the church, or anything of substance. It felt like old times, and it felt damn good. But eventually, it was time to go.

They walked to the caves together, Tem's arm looped in Gabriel's. She held him close, keeping his body right next to hers, as if she could keep him next to her heart.

"Don't leave my side, even for a second," Tem said. They had just entered the cave, and Gabriel was acting *far* too excited about what was about to happen. "And don't talk to anyone unless they talk to you first. And *don't flirt.*"

Gabriel's lips turned down in a pout. "What's the point of meeting a bunch of sexy basilisks if I can't flirt with them?"

"They could kill you. That's the point."

"You underestimate my flirtation abilities, Tem. I could charm the clothes off a tree."

"I have never once underestimated your flirtation abilities. I don't think *anyone* ever has."

Gabriel threw his arm around her, pulling her close. "This will be fun, Tem. Lighten up."

"This isn't supposed to be *fun*, Gabriel. This isn't a game."

He became serious. "I understand, Tem. I want this to go well just as badly as you do."

Tem nodded. She knew Gabriel understood the stakes, knew he grasped that the future of their kingdoms hinged on this visit. Still, she was rapidly regretting the entire thing. What was Tem thinking, bringing him around a bunch of basilisks? It was dangerous for him. Possibly lethal. If anything happened to him, she would never forgive herself. And yet, if this could soften him toward them—if meeting basilisks could humanize them in Gabriel's eyes—it would be worth it. Gabriel was the leader of the villagers. His word held real weight.

With a sigh, Tem led Gabriel into the caves.

His eyes slid to the mat in front of the fireplace. He raised an eyebrow but didn't question it. There was no need to tell him that Tem had trained there—he knew what happened in the caves just as well as anyone else.

"You will need to take off your clothes," Tem said.

But Gabriel required no explanation. Before she could even finish her sentence, he was naked.

Tem had never seen his cock before; quite frankly, her best friend's cock was none of her business. So she averted her eyes, keeping her gaze on her own body as she undressed. When they were both naked, she gestured toward the passageway, which they entered together. The deeper they went, the wider Gabriel's grin became.

"Can you *please* not look so excited?" Tem hissed. "They're going to think you're deranged."

Gabriel shrugged. He looked positively overjoyed. "Oh, come on, Tem. Put yourself in my shoes. Wouldn't you be excited?"

"I'd be scared out of my mind. I *was* scared out of my mind."

Tem thought back to the first time she'd come under the mountain—how Caspen had taken her to his chambers after Jonathan and Christopher assaulted her. She'd kept her head down, her eyes on the ground. Gabriel displayed no such qualms. His shoulders were thrown back, his chin held high. He was fearless.

"There's nothing to be scared of," he said. "They're just snakes."

"*Don't* call them that."

"I *won't*. I'm only joking."

"This isn't the time for jokes, Gabriel."

"I *know* that, dearest. Trust me, I know."

They didn't speak after that. Tem guided him through the passageway, trying to quell her anxiety. It was clear she was more nervous than Gabriel was. By the way he peered around every corner, he was obviously eager to spot a basilisk. Tem was not so eager. She was worried this had all been a giant mistake—one that would once again hurt someone she loved dearly. But it was too late to go back now. Adelaide had already told everyone they were coming. They had to do this. When they reached the edge of the courtyard, they stopped.

Tem put her arm around Gabriel instinctively.

"What's the holdup?" he asked, peering down the passageway.

"Caspen said he'd meet us here."

It was true; Caspen had said that, although technically not to Tem. They hadn't spoken since she told him Gabriel was coming, and Adelaide had been the one to coordinate this meetup. Tem was just starting to worry that Caspen wasn't going to show after all when he emerged from the darkness, his skin glowing in the flickering torchlight.

"Gabriel," he said, his voice low. There was a pause, and in it, Tem experienced a bout of minor panic. Were they really about to do this? This was *absurd*. What if Caspen reprimanded them? But to her relief, he said, "Thank you for coming."

To Tem's surprise, Gabriel performed an exaggerated bow, dipping his head nearly to his knees. "Thank you for having me."

Tem pulled him upright. "There's no need to bow," she whispered.

"He's a king, isn't he?" Gabriel jerked his head at Caspen.

"Yes, but—"

"You're supposed to bow to kings."

Tem sighed. Before she could say anything else, Caspen raised his hand, subduing her.

"You are Tem's friend," he said calmly. "There is no need to bow to me."

Gabriel smiled. Caspen turned to Tem. "Did you tell him the risks?"

"Yes, I did." Tem neglected to say that she doubted he cared.

"No flirting." Gabriel piped up, nudging Tem with his shoulder. "Right, boss?"

Caspen raised an eyebrow. Not for the first time, Tem prayed to Kora for patience. She needed Gabriel to behave *just this once*. Too much was at stake for this to go any way other than perfectly.

"Tem's wish is for you to experience our culture," Caspen said. "My people know you are coming, but I must be transparent. Some are not happy about your presence."

For the first time, fear crossed Gabriel's face.

"No harm will come to you," Caspen said. "I will personally guarantee your safety."

Gabriel relaxed, and so did Tem. She understood that this was Caspen's way of making things right between them. He cared about the same things she did, even if he had very different ways of showing it.

Tem tightened her grip reassuringly. "Nothing bad will happen," she insisted. "I promise." She had absolutely no business making such a promise. But she made it anyway, as if by saying it out loud, she could guarantee that it was true. She turned to Caspen. "Will you make him calm?" she asked.

He tilted his head. "You may do that yourself. Remember you are a Hybreed."

That hadn't occurred to Tem. She turned to Gabriel. "I can make you calm, if you want."

But Gabriel waved her off. "I don't need that."

Tem blinked. "What?"

"I'm already calm, Tem. I don't need you to do…whatever you're trying to do."

To Tem's surprise, an amused smile tilted Caspen's lips. Tem wondered if he'd ever met a human like Gabriel before. Probably not; no one had.

"In that case," Caspen said. "Let us begin."

They followed him into the courtyard.

CHAPTER NINETEEN

⋯•◦✳◦•⋯

A LL AROUND THEM, BASILISKS WERE ALREADY HAVING SEX.

It was mating season, after all. They would not control their urges just because a human was here. Gabriel's eyes went wide, his head swiveling from left to right, taking in everything he possibly could. Tem remembered what it was like the first time she experienced all this and knew he had to be overwhelmed, no matter how excited he said he was.

Somewhere along the way, Caspen disappeared. He spoke to her just before he left: *I will remain close by, Tem.*

Tem let him go; she understood that he was waiting to see how this turned out—to see whether her delusional hope hadn't been in vain—but almost immediately, she wished he had remained. The Seneca men were in the corner, watching her. Glaring.

Gabriel nudged her shoulder. "Shall we say hello?" he whispered.

"No," Tem whispered back. "Definitely not."

"Who are they?"

"Nobody you need to know."

The last thing she needed was for the Senecas to get their hands on Gabriel. But they weren't the only ones glaring at them. Evangeline was standing off to the side, her arms crossed, her face twisted in a frown. A fierce protectiveness rose suddenly within Tem. Gabriel was the kindest person she knew. Evangeline had no right to judge him—none of the basilisks did.

"Come on," she said, grabbing his elbow. "Let's go."

"There seem to be a lot of people we're avoiding, Tem dearest."

"There's…a lot going on at the moment."

"Clearly."

"Things are tense right now, Gabriel. It's a risk for you to be here, remember?"

"I remember."

No sooner had she mentioned risk than Apollo appeared in her peripheral vision. "Oh no," Tem muttered.

Apollo's eyes bored into hers before raking over Gabriel. He raised an eyebrow.

"Who's *that*?" Gabriel asked, following her gaze.

"He's nobody."

Apollo grinned, and she knew he had heard her.

You wound me, Temperance.

Oh, please. You're not wounded, you're just dramatic.

For good reason. He moved toward them.

No, Apollo. Stay right where you are.

He stopped. *And who are you to give me orders?*

You like it when I give you orders.

I do. But not this one. I want to meet your friend.

Well, you can't.

"Why is he looking at us like that?" Gabriel asked.

"Like what?"

"Like he wants to fuck you, then me, then both of us at the same time?"

"That's *not* how he's looking at us."

But it was. Apollo was eyeing them like they were his next meal. And Tem was not going to let Gabriel get eaten.

"Shouldn't you introduce me?"

"Absolutely not. He's Caspen's brother, and he's trouble."

She steered Gabriel away from Apollo, only to run immediately into Damon.

"Temperance," he purred, his eyes falling immediately on Gabriel. "So this is your guest."

Tem sighed. Damon was the lesser of two evils. They might as well talk to him. "Damon. This is Gabriel, my best friend."

Damon took Gabriel's hand in his, raising it to his lips to kiss his wrist. It was the same way Apollo had greeted Tem when they'd first met. The similarity was not lost on her.

"It is a pleasure to meet you," Damon said.

Gabriel's face slid into a devious smile. "The pleasure is all mine."

"I can imagine."

A pause. For some reason, Tem felt warm.

"Tell me, Gabriel," Damon continued, still holding his hand, "are you enjoying yourself this evening?"

"I am now."

The warmth increased. The way the two men were looking at each other made Tem feel like she was intruding on something. It wasn't dissimilar to the way she'd felt watching the blood-bound couple make love in front of her.

"I trust Temperance has been an excellent host."

Gabriel looked at Tem. "She's the best. But I'm sure you know that already."

Damon looked at her too. "We are fond of her, yes."

He didn't specify who "we" was, and Tem didn't bother wondering. She knew that not everyone under the mountain was fond of her, but the people who were would do anything to make her happy—including allowing Gabriel down here in the first place.

Gabriel's eyes dropped to Damon's cock. "What else are you fond of?"

Tem froze. She knew that tone; she knew that look. Gabriel was flirting. That was nothing new, of course, but flirting with *Damon* was something else entirely. Something dangerous. Gabriel flirted with everyone—it was his default setting. She held her breath as Damon's gold eyes held Gabriel's blue ones.

A solid five heartbeats passed before Damon turned to Tem and said, "Your friend is charming. Do not let Apollo near him."

"Wasn't planning on it."

"Plans tend to go awry, Temperance."

"Don't I know it," she muttered.

Out of the corner of her eye, Tem saw Apollo moving closer again. Her stomach performed a preemptive swoop. "Gabriel," she said quickly. "Come with me."

Without waiting another second, she hooked her arm in his and pulled him into the crowd. Anything was better than letting him talk to any more basilisks.

"So what's his deal?" Gabriel purred. "He's delicious."

"He's Caspen's other brother."

"Even better." Gabriel grinned, pulling her closer. "We could be in-laws."

"Don't be *gross*," Tem cried.

But Gabriel was already looking back over his shoulder at Damon, who was watching them with his mouth turned up at the corner. If Tem knew anything about basilisks, she knew exactly what Damon was thinking—and she wasn't about to let him act on it.

"Didn't you hear him?" Gabriel squeezed her arm. "He thinks I'm *charming*. Clearly he's got great taste."

"Oh please."

"What? It's not my fault Kora made me irresistible."

Tem rolled her eyes.

They spent the next few minutes navigating the courtyard together. Tem pointed out basilisk after basilisk, explaining their relation to each other and the differences between the quivers. Always, Apollo's gaze followed them. It was as if he had nothing better to do than to watch them traverse the crowd, analyzing their every move.

Caspen was never far away either. Tem saw him on the edge of her vision, his arms crossed, his brow furrowed. She knew he was protecting them from afar, acting as a bodyguard, reminding the other basilisks that they were under the Serpent King's protection.

"What's *that*?" Gabriel pointed at the fountain full of shimmering, white liquid.

"*That* is none of your concern," Tem said firmly. "And you are not allowed to drink it."

"Why not?" Gabriel whined. "Everyone else is."

It was true. But everyone else was a basilisk.

"It's not for humans."

"Do you get to drink it?"

"Yes. But I'm not a human, remember?"

"What will happen if a human drinks it?"

Tem realized she didn't know the answer to that question. All she knew was how the elixir affected her when she'd had it for the first time. She could only assume its effects would be amplified on a human. "It requires a tolerance. Even Caspen can't drink too much of it."

"I've got quite the tolerance, Tem," Gabriel said, pulling her toward the fountain.

"You've got quite the tolerance for *alcohol*," she insisted, pulling him away. "It's not the same at all."

Before Tem could yank Gabriel back, a man approached the fountain. She already knew what he was going to do—she had seen it before, after all. But for Gabriel, the experience of watching someone ejaculate into the fountain was an entirely new one, and the moment the man did so, Gabriel gasped, "It's *cum*?"

Tem sighed. There was no other way to explain it. Besides, it was the truth. "Yes."

"That's *wild*."

She sighed again, pulling him away from the fountain. "Such is the basilisk way."

"I can't believe you've been hiding all of this from me."

"I haven't hidden anything. You're here, aren't you?"

"You could've told me you were drinking from a cum fountain, Tem."

She rolled her eyes again. "You wouldn't have believed me if I did."

Gabriel didn't reply for a moment. He was too busy watching as another man approached the fountain, his cock in his hand. "I want to try it," he insisted.

"Try what? Drinking it, or…?"

"Both."

"No. You get to try neither."

"Tem." Gabriel turned to her and placed his hands on her shoulders. "You won't let me flirt with Caspen's hot brother. You won't let me drink from the cum fountain. And you won't let me come *in* the fountain. What am I even doing here?"

Tem opened her mouth, then closed it. What *was* he doing here? He was supposed to be experiencing their culture; he was supposed to be healing the rift between the villagers and the basilisks. And Tem wasn't letting him. She closed her eyes, trying to clear her mind. A hand touched her shoulder. Damon.

"Your friend is thirsty. You should let him drink."

Tem almost laughed. "He can't handle it."

"Of course he can. You handled it, did you not?"

Tem rolled her eyes. "I'm a Hybreed."

"Which means you are half-human. You should have faith in your own species."

Tem had nothing to say to that.

"Is this not why he is here?"

Tem sighed. It was essentially what Gabriel had just said. She wanted him to experience basilisk culture—to integrate. But letting him drink the elixir was a risk. "Can he really handle it?"

Damon placed his hand over his chest. "I would not lead you astray, Temperance."

Tem rolled her eyes.

Damon looked legitimately offended. "Have you no faith in me?"

What a question. Tem had *no* faith in the Drakon brothers. But this was not Apollo. This was Damon, and he had never given her any reason not to trust him.

"One drop will not hurt him," Damon said quietly.

"Do you promise?" she whispered, her voice nearly breaking.

Damon's expression softened. "No harm will come to him. You have my word, Temperance."

The same thing Caspen had promised. With so many basilisks looking out for Gabriel, Tem was starting to believe it.

"Fine," she said finally. There was clearly no stopping this train anyway. Tem wasn't sure she even wanted to anymore. Why shouldn't Gabriel experience all the basilisks had to offer? If the elixir would contribute positively to the evening, she wanted him to have some.

Damon smiled. "Fine?"

"Yes, *fine*. He can drink it." She turned to Gabriel. "But only a drop. Do you understand?"

Damon nodded eagerly, his face splitting into a grin. He waited until Tem nodded too before turning to the fountain and filling a goblet. He dipped a single finger into the elixir, holding it out to Gabriel, who tilted his head back to receive it. The moment the elixir passed his lips, he smiled. Tem knew that feeling. She knew the heat he was experiencing, the incredible lightness and joy. She also knew the *need*. Gabriel placed his hand on Damon's shoulder, pulling him forward. But he didn't close the distance. Instead, to Tem's surprise, Gabriel's gaze slid to hers, silently seeking permission. She could do nothing but laugh at the absurdity of it all. It was no longer her place to decide what Gabriel could and could not do. He was a human with his own free will, and he deserved to make his own choices. At this point, she knew he understood the stakes.

Tem threw up her hands. "I'm not going to stop you."

At her response, Gabriel let out a delighted noise. Damon smiled in amusement. Then Gabriel wrapped his hand around Damon's neck, leaned in, and kissed him on the mouth. Tem watched as their lips brushed, gently at first, both of them melting into the other as if they'd been waiting for this very moment. And perhaps they had. Perhaps Gabriel, with his unbounded sexual energy, had finally met his match in a basilisk. And Damon, who had a milder disposition than his two brothers, was the perfect complement to a human.

Tem looked away as their kiss deepened. Then she looked back.

She'd always known Gabriel had a healthy sex life—they'd discussed it in excruciating detail since Tem was fourteen years old. But she'd never seen him do anything in front of her, and although her human side was mildly horrified, she found that her basilisk side was *very* intrigued by the sight. She stepped closer, watching them from just a foot away. Damon's hand found hers, drawing her even closer. Gabriel turned to her, cupping her face in his palm. He pulled into him, holding eye contact as he did it. They couldn't communicate with their minds like the basilisks could, but years of friendship told her exactly what he was asking her: *Do you want to do this?* There was only one answer: this was her best friend, the friend she'd had since she was a child. He kissed her on the cheek all the time. This was hardly any different. What was a kiss between friends?

Tem nodded.

Then Gabriel kissed her.

His lips were soft against hers. Tem felt immeasurably light and warm in his arms, her body pressing against his as naturally as it would press against Caspen's. When his tongue found hers, she welcomed it. This was Gabriel, after all. Her closest confidant. Her protector. He was always there for her, no matter the circumstances—no matter the cost. Now it was time for Tem to return the favor. Gabriel was being brave; he was experiencing everything the basilisks had to offer. He deserved to feel pleasure as they did.

A hand touched Tem's shoulder. It was Damon's. He was pulling her away from Gabriel, inserting himself in her place. Tem let him do this, watching as the two of them kissed. Without thinking, she raised her hands, holding their heads together just as Caspen had held her and Leo. She felt the muscles flex in Damon's neck as his tongue dove into Gabriel's mouth. Their arousal was her arousal; it radiated off them in waves, enveloping her in warmth.

Fingers wrapped around her waist. Lips touched her neck.

My love.

Caspen was behind her, his cock against her back. Tem settled against it, arching her neck so she could kiss him properly. His hands found her breasts, squeezing them before traveling up to her neck. Tem let out a tiny moan. She'd missed him *so much* this past week. They may be at odds right now, but they always came back together for this. This was a language she understood—a poem that could be written only for Caspen. They moved together slowly, enjoying the feel of each other's bodies, touching everything they hadn't touched in the past week.

Eventually, others joined.

At first, it was just one woman. Tem watched as her delicate hands brushed over Gabriel's shoulders, tilting his head to hers. She kissed him, and he kissed her back while Damon watched. Then Damon leaned in, joining his mouth with theirs, three becoming one. Tem watched them carefully, letting the event unfold, ready to intervene if necessary. But the time never came. Gabriel was happy.

At some point, Caspen slid inside Tem. He kept her upright, his strong hands holding her so she could keep an eye on Gabriel. But Gabriel hardly needed her help. He pulled the basilisks ever closer, his fingers weaving into theirs, coalescing everyone around him into a gorgeous tangle. His golden hair floated in a sea of bodies.

After a while, Tem said, *It's going well, don't you think?*

Yes, it is. Your friend is capable.

Tem smiled. There was no better compliment from a basilisk. *He was built for this.*

I think you are right.

Eventually, Caspen laid her down. Tem had no idea how many basilisks were around them. At least a dozen, if not more. Others were standing and watching, their hands occupied with themselves and with each other. Power radiated throughout the entire courtyard; Tem was filled with it just as she was filled with Caspen's cock.

His hands gripped her waist, shifting her so she was aligned with the basilisk beside her.

Tem.

It was all he said—just her name. Yet Tem understood he wanted her to do what she had previously thought was impossible—to experience this night as a basilisk would. Perhaps a week ago, such a directive would have scared her. But now, with Gabriel doing the exact thing Tem had always hesitated to do, she was ready to be brave. If he could do it, so could she.

Tem turned to the basilisk beside her. She didn't recognize him, but he was lean and beautiful and already smiling at her.

He brushed a curl from her face as his mind touched hers to ask, *May I?*

Tem nodded. The basilisk leaned in and kissed her. As soon as their lips touched, Caspen's approval rushed into her mind. His cock was still inside her, and she could have sworn he grew harder. Tem parted her lips, slipping her tongue into the basilisk's mouth, tasting what he had to offer. His hands were on her breasts, and so were Caspen's. She was surrounded by skin, surrounded by *sensation.* When the basilisk pulled away, Tem looked up at Caspen and smiled.

I knew you could do it, Tem.

Somehow, she knew it too.

The night went on.

Tem followed Gabriel's lead—when he kissed someone, she kissed them too, performing the steps to a dance only they knew. Caspen was always there, right beside them, helping when needed. His motions were always in service of their pleasure. If Caspen touched another basilisk, it was to push them closer to Tem and Gabriel. The only cock he stroked was his own and only while looking at Tem. Pride flowed from him; it bloomed whenever someone else brought her to orgasm, particularly if they did it quickly.

Basilisks earned their ranking through sex, being with as many people as possible the ultimate goal. Tem could see the ancient cultural pull that these customs had on Caspen—how connected he was to his people and to her. She was becoming a part of his world, learning how to function in it. It brought Caspen great joy to see her like this, and it brought Tem joy too. She felt nothing but warmth and pleasure and bliss, giving herself over to the sheer thrill of it all. She was enraptured. And she enraptured in return. Eventually, she couldn't get enough. Mouth after mouth touched hers, hand after hand gripped her skin. There was no difference between her flesh and theirs, her body and someone else's.

Gabriel was among them, and it was clear that he was just as at home as Tem was. She'd never seen him so happy, so fulfilled. Always, no matter who he was entangled with, he ended up back with Damon. Perhaps that was right; perhaps it was meant to be. Tem had no desire to place judgment or restriction upon his experience anymore. It was his to have in the way he was meant to have it. Eventually, they were before each other once more.

They kissed for a long time in the middle of the chaos, safe and content in each other's arms. There was no one she'd rather see her like this. Gabriel was a lover at heart, and he loved her. There was no better person to be here with.

Caspen was behind her, holding them together.

He is doing well, Tem.

For some reason, it felt like a victory. Tem had been so worried about tonight, so indescribably scared that something would go wrong or Gabriel would get hurt. Instead, the opposite had happened—no one was getting hurt. Not even close. There was only community and climax and pleasure.

Apollo was never out of sight. He was always in Tem's peripheral vision, just out of reach, hovering along the edge of her orbit. She wondered if he stayed away because of Caspen, if he was keeping his distance out of fear of what his brother might do if he tried to come closer. But in the chaos of bodies, Tem allowed herself to indulge in curiosity. She wanted to know how Apollo's skin would feel against hers, if his breath would hitch if she touched him. She wondered what it would be like to kiss him in front of Caspen. It wasn't something she'd allowed herself to think about before—not really and certainly not when her mind was open and she knew Caspen could hear her thoughts.

I told you, Tem. I will not stop you.

There's nothing to stop me from. I don't care that he has first rights. He's insufferable.

Apollo was getting closer.

You say that now. But if I die—

You're not allowed to die. You promised.

I understand. And I will endeavor to keep that promise. But if, for some reason, I break it, Apollo is next in line for your hand.

Suddenly, Apollo was before her—just out of reach, tempting her. Always tempting her.

Kiss him, Tem.

EXCUSE ME?

I want you to kiss him.

But Tem just shook her head. Caspen couldn't possibly want anything of the sort. *You're out of your mind.*

And you are rather feisty tonight, little viper.

I'm only feisty because you're being unreasonable.

I understand. But if my brother ends up marrying you in my stead, you must know that you are compatible.

Tem shook her head. She didn't want to know anything of the sort. And she certainly couldn't believe Caspen was telling her to do so. But Caspen was bound by the traditions of his people. First rights were given to the brother. It was absurd. And yet, her basilisk side *purred* at the thought of kissing Apollo in front of Caspen—to see which brother was a better match. But the answer was Caspen. It had to be. There was no need to search elsewhere, no kiss that would fulfill her in a way she wasn't already fulfilled by him. Apollo could offer her nothing; that much had always been true. Or was it? Apollo challenged her, pushed her, tempted her. Those were qualities Caspen also possessed. *They are quite similar*, Adelaide had said. Tem could see that now. But Caspen was still better.

Kiss him, Tem. Do it now.

Was it a punishment? A test? A way for Caspen to exert control after Tem had gone out of her way to bring Gabriel here? She remembered what he'd said in the banquet hall after he'd found Tem and Apollo touching themselves to the sight of each other: *Keep going*. Caspen had won that day. Tem was not about to let him win today.

Apollo was upon her. His face was right before hers, his golden eyes in the forefront of her vision. He smelled like fruit—peaches—and Tem was utterly unprepared for it.

His voice entered her mind: *My brother wants me to kiss you.*

Tem was well aware of that. Apollo's hand was on her neck. She shook her head. *This is ridiculous.*

I cannot disobey, Temperance.

Don't you have control over your own actions?

Of course I do. But Caspenon is my king as much as he is yours. His word is law.

But *Tem's* word was also law. Tem was the one whose power the Senecas wanted; Tem was the one who could bypass the council. Tem was the one to fear.

Apollo's gaze locked on hers. Kissing him seemed like an admission—like giving in. Tem was aware of Caspen watching her, of Gabriel just nearby. Yet the only thing she truly felt was Apollo's presence before her, his body as it pressed against hers. Their minds were intertwined; there was no escape from him. He leaned in.

Stop.

Apollo stopped, his lips an inch from hers. He smelled *so* good. Yet everything in Tem told her that this was not the right time—that no matter how much she wanted this, it would have to wait. Tem was not ready. Perhaps she never would be. This was a step too far—a step beyond what she was prepared for. The ritual had been different; she'd *had* to do that in order to be with Caspen. But kissing his brother would be a choice made of her own free will, and Tem wanted it on her own terms—not at Caspen's command. Perhaps there would be a kiss for them in the future, but it was not right now. Not tonight.

She turned to look at Caspen. His brows rose in surprise, then furrowed. His eyes flicked from her to Apollo, then back again. They'd both disobeyed their king.

Apollo brushed his thumb over her lip. *You wound me.*

It was not the first time he'd said that. But it was the first time she believed it. There was true disappointment in his tone—genuine sadness that she was unwilling to take this step with him. Any other basilisk would have. Tem was painfully aware that she was the exception to the rule—that once again, her behavior was vexing to Apollo and to his people. But she would not be rushed. Not for something as paramount as this.

Nobody could wound you, Apollo.

It was also not the first time she'd said that. But instead of receiving it with a smile, as he had once before, Apollo gave her a grim look. *Once again, you underestimate yourself.* Then he dropped his hands.

Tem blinked, and he was gone. She turned to Caspen, who was watching her with his brow furrowed.

Are you angry with me?

No.

Are you sure?

Yes.

Then why are you looking at me like that?

Caspen's brow was still furrowed. At her words, his expression softened into gentle understanding. He leaned down to kiss her. *I am not angry with you, Tem. I am just observing.*

They kissed, and Tem tried to believe him. But a part of her felt shame. This was yet another basilisk custom she was unwilling to take part in. She had long ago released feelings of jealousy and insecurity toward Adelaide, but in moments like these, they reared their head once more. A basilisk would be a better match for Caspen. A basilisk would have kissed his brother. That was the truth, and Tem could not so easily forget it.

Caspen kissed her harder. He was inside her mind; he could hear every insecurity and fear that gripped her like iron. It was a confusing mix of emotions. Tem knew basilisks were an ancient species, and she couldn't possibly hope to understand them in one night. But after experiencing something like this, she felt no closer to understanding Caspen than she did before. Tem had no idea how he actually felt. She wished for clarity, but she knew she would not get it tonight.

The rest of the night passed in a blur of sex and bodies and elixir. It was not until the celebration had nearly run its course that Tem found Gabriel again. He was sequestered in a corner, intertwined with Damon.

"Gabriel," she murmured gently, leaning over them. "Are you ready to go?"

Pink cheeks, flushed chests, they both looked at her with dazed expressions.

"Can't I stay?" Gabriel said. His voice was hoarse.

Tem glanced up at Caspen, who was watching their interaction from a step away. "Can he?" she whispered.

Caspen pursed his lips. His eyes slid to Damon's, and Tem saw their unspoken conversation. Tem knew Caspen was asking, tacitly, whether he was safe with Damon.

Damon nodded. Only then did Caspen nod too.

"He can stay."

Relief swept through Tem. All she cared about was that Gabriel survived the night unharmed. If this experience had taught her anything, it was that he could handle himself among the basilisks.

"I will come find you in the morning," Tem said. "We can leave together."

Gabriel nodded, his eyes bright. Tem had never seen him like this. His joy was indisputable; he was glowing from the inside out. It was a distinctly basilisk trait to gain energy from sex, and Gabriel had that in spades. Perhaps he was more suited for this life than Tem was.

"See you tomorrow, dearest," Gabriel said, pulling her in for a kiss.

His lips had barely touched her cheek when a horrible cry pierced the air.

CHAPTER TWENTY

E VERYONE IN THE COURTYARD FROZE.

Tem followed Caspen's gaze to the far wall, where something had been scrawled on the stone. Four words, indisputably written in blood.

Give her to us.

There was a single, hair-raising moment of silence. Then, pandemonium.

The courtyard erupted into chaos as Caspen grabbed Tem by the waist and yanked her toward the passageway. The last thing she saw before the crowd swallowed them was Damon doing the same with Gabriel.

"Where are we going?" Tem cried.

"Our chambers. We will be safe there."

"But Gabriel—"

"Damon will protect him."

Somehow, Tem knew he was right. If the way they'd bonded tonight was any indication, there was no safer person for Gabriel to be with.

"I don't understand," Tem stammered. "What happened?"

"They are warning us," Caspen replied, his voice low. He was still steering her quickly through the passageway.

"Who is?"

"The Senecas."

Tem couldn't help but think of the message on the church steps: *Feed us.* The similarities were striking—both demands, both desperate.

"If we don't give you to them," Caspen continued, "they will take you."

She remembered what Caspen had told her on the first night of mating season: *They feel they are owed your allegiance.*

"How can they take me?"

Caspen didn't answer. They had reached their chambers, and he nearly pushed Tem onto the bed.

"Caspen," she cried as he wrapped his arms around her, crushing her protectively against his chest. He only held her tighter. Their minds were still intertwined, and a torrent of fear and possession raged inside his head.

"Caspen." She touched his face, looking him in the eye. "I'm *fine*. I'm right here. And I'm not going anywhere."

They held eye contact, and Tem saw just how truly worried he was for her. Up until tonight, she'd taken his stoicism for granted. But now she understood how deeply this affected him. Their relationship was constantly under threat—from the Senecas, from Leo, from his own brother. It was a daily battle simply to hold on to each other when everything around them was tearing them apart.

"I cannot lose you, Tem," Caspen whispered.

"You won't. I promise."

He looked her in the eyes.

Everything was always fast and brutal between them—passion in favor of rationality. But now, Tem savored the time between when they locked eyes and Caspen's lips finally touched hers. They kissed like it was the first time: slow and sensual and intimate. Tem missed this side of Caspen. His rough edges were even rougher under the mountain, almost as if his proximity to his people hardened him. She didn't begrudge him his true nature, but sometimes she missed the side of him that was soft with her— she was happy to see that side again now.

He kissed her tenderly, his mind cradling hers. Smoke rose from his shoulders, but he didn't begin to transition. Instead, he moved without hurry, sliding his fingers gently inside her, exploring every inch of her center as if it were brand-new to him. Tem unwound beneath his touch, allowing him to see her as she was seeing him: vulnerable and defenseless.

When she was ready for his cock, he gave it to her.

He was nestled between her legs, his face in front of hers. They both knew they would remain this way, that they would see it through together.

I will not let them take you.

I know. She believed him. She always believed him.

You are mine.

And you're mine.

Tem would not let anyone take Caspen away either. Spending time around the basilisks had changed her too. She was stronger now. Surer. Tem once thought that the ritual was the biggest gesture she could give to Caspen. But now their bond was deeper, and she knew there was no limit to what she would do for him. No height was too high, no distance too vast. Caspen was willing to cross lines for her. Tem was willing too.

Caspen's eyes had long since turned black. His hands were everywhere—skimming over her breasts, brushing down her hips, massaging her clitoris in time with his thrusts. Tem knew they would come together. She knew it as surely as she knew the sun would rise in the morning. When it finally happened, she kept her eyes open so she could see him come too. Tem noticed every detail: the way his neck tensed in the moment just before climax, the way his grip tightened on the back of her head, the sounds he made as he watched her come too.

Everything about it felt right…but something about it felt final.

When they awoke the next morning, Caspen kissed every inch of her body as if he wanted to memorize it. Tem felt his reverence in the way his lips brushed against her skin, reminding her with each gentle stroke that she was loved, that she was treasured, that she was home.

"Caspen," she whispered eventually. "I need to take Gabriel home."

"He is with Damon. He is safe."

But Tem was still worried. The night had ended in disaster. This was supposed to be their opportunity to bring the humans and the basilisks together, to establish some common ground. Instead, Gabriel had seen dissent within ranks—he had been put in danger. It was unacceptable to Tem.

"He could have gotten hurt."

"But he did not. He spent the night with a basilisk on the final day of mating season," Caspen said. "That has implications."

Tem sat up. "What implications, exactly?"

Now Caspen hesitated. "The point of mating season is to choose a mate."

A beat of silence passed.

"So?"

"So…my brother chose Gabriel."

"*What?*"

Caspen placed his hands on her shoulders. "Calm down, Tem."

"Calm *down*? But what does this *mean*? Are they…bound?"

There were so many rules in basilisk society, so many sneaky catches. For all she knew, Gabriel and Damon were practically married now.

"There is no bond other than an emotional one," Caspen said quickly. "Their connection is symbolic. Damon made his choice, but Gabriel does not have to reciprocate. He is free to accept or reject that choice as he sees fit."

It was a disaster. Of course Gabriel would accept. She'd seen the way he looked at Damon, the way they'd looked at each other. It would be the single greatest thrill of Gabriel's life to find out that a basilisk chose him as his mate. There was no bigger accolade.

"Tem," Caspen said, pulling her closer. "There is no cause for alarm."

"Of course there is," she snapped. "I'm *very* alarmed. And I'm angry with you. You were supposed to keep him safe. *We* were supposed to keep him safe. This was not supposed to happen."

"Nothing has happened. He *is* safe."

"He's Damon's *mate!*"

"Only if he wants to be."

But Tem just shook her head. Caspen wasn't getting it. To him, nothing had gone wrong. Gabriel was intact; Tem's friend had survived the night. But Tem didn't want Gabriel to become caught up in her world. The point of the evening had been to mend relations between the humans and the basilisks, not to find Gabriel a mate. She closed her eyes, trying to calm down.

"Tem," Caspen said gently. "I promise you Gabriel is not in any danger. The mating bond is not like the blood bond. It consists only of emotion—there is no magic involved. Gabriel is not tied to Damon in any way. He may walk away a free man if he chooses."

Tem tried to believe him, but panic was cinching her throat. She hadn't expected this, hadn't thought that taking Gabriel under the mountain would mean indoctrinating him into basilisk society. It was the last thing she wanted for him. "Why did you let him stay the night in the first place?"

Caspen gave her a long, knowing look. "Because I could see how Damon felt about him."

"Everyone feels that way about Gabriel, Caspen. He's irresistible."

He shook his head. "My brother's feelings are genuine, Tem. He does not fall easily."

Tem stared at him. He was being sincere; she could tell. But it didn't change the fact that she needed to get Gabriel out of here. "Will you take me to him?"

Caspen nodded.

The journey to Damon's chambers was a short one. Caspen didn't knock on his door; it seemed no one bothered to do that around here. Gabriel and Damon were on the bed, their lanky bodies curled around each other. Tem realized in that moment that she'd never seen Gabriel when he was sleeping. He looked completely at ease, his golden curls tousled, his arm draped over Damon's chest. The sight warmed her heart.

"Gabriel." She touched his shoulder. "Wake up."

His eyes opened slowly. "Tem," he mumbled, his voice thick with sleep. "What is it?"

"I'm taking you home." As she said the words, some part of her wondered if he was already home.

Damon's arms tightened around Gabriel. He pressed his lips to his neck. "Will you return?"

Gabriel looked up at Tem, silently seeking permission. But Tem found no need to give it. She understood that their relationship was out of her hands. Instead, she looked at Damon, speaking into his mind: *Are your feelings for him sincere?*

They are.

Why should I believe you?

Damon looked at Gabriel, who looked at him. Gabriel gave him a dazzling smile, which Damon returned. *He is like sunlight.*

He didn't elaborate, but Tem knew exactly what he meant. Gabriel had been her sunlight her entire life. Perhaps it was time to let him shine elsewhere.

I'm choosing to trust you with him. Don't make me regret it.

In response, Damon kissed him.

Tem watched them together, her heart full, her body warm. When they drew apart, she took Gabriel's hand in hers as they retrieved his clothing in the cave before walking to the head of the trail. Gabriel stood by as Caspen pulled Tem into his arms.

"Will I see you back here before dinner?" he murmured against her neck. It felt like the question Damon had just asked Gabriel: *Will you return?*

Tem had completely forgotten it was Sunday. They would be expected at the castle tonight. And Tem would be expected to bleed.

"No," she said. "I want to spend the day with my parents. I'll meet you there."

For some reason, after the night they'd just had, she craved the comfort of her mother.

Caspen kissed her. Then he turned to Gabriel. "You did well," he said simply. Then he was gone.

Gabriel nudged her shoulder. "Hear that, Tem? I did *well.*"

Tem didn't dare tell him just how well he'd done; she would let Damon tell him in his own time. All she could do was be happy that he was alive and that the visit had done what she'd hoped it would do: make it difficult for Gabriel to turn against the basilisks. After the way he looked at Damon this morning, Tem doubted he would lead another protest.

Tem accompanied Gabriel to the village before setting off for her parents' cottage.

She didn't just crave the comfort of her mother. Tem also wanted to see her father. He was the only person she could ask about the bloodletting.

Her mother was in the garden when she arrived. "Tem," she said. "What brings you here?"

"I…"

How to answer? There were so many questions she needed to ask, and they were all for her father. But Tem was not yet ready to ask them. So she said, "I just needed to get away."

Understanding passed over her mother's face.

They spent the day together, pulling weeds and tending to the garden. Tem found peace in the manual labor, allowing it to lull her into a trance. It wasn't until late afternoon that she finally went inside, leaving her mother to finish the last of the work.

Her father was at the kitchen table. "My child," he said as she sat down. "What ails you?"

Tem found it significant that he immediately knew something was wrong. He may have been absent for her entire life, but he understood her as if he hadn't been.

"The royals are bringing back the bloodletting."

Shock passed over his face. "That…saddens me," he said simply.

Tem saw the grief in his eyes. She was about to make that grief worse. "They asked for volunteers, so I…" She didn't want to say it. She didn't want to sadden him even more.

Kronos held up his hand. "Temperance," he said quietly. "I do not wish that for you."

"I know."

He had suffered for so many years—*decades*—in that cold, dark dungeon. And now his daughter would do the same.

"It's the only option," she continued. "If I give them a supply, no one else has to."

He pursed his lips but didn't say anything. Tem knew him well enough to know that he wouldn't try to change her mind. Her father was not like Caspen, imposing his opinions on everyone; he was reserved and tolerant and kind. He knew why she had done this.

"Will it hurt?" Tem asked. By the look on his face, she already knew the answer.

"At first," he said. "And then your hands will go numb. It is not so bad after that."

Dread twisted her stomach. "Will there be aftereffects?"

Kronos sighed.

She hated that she had to ask him this—hated the fact that she was forcing him to relive it. But she had to know.

"It will weaken you," he said. "It may impede your ability to transition."

Tem shrugged. That hardly mattered. "I can't transition anyway."

Her father frowned. "What do you mean?"

"Caspen has to help me. And even then, I can barely manage it."

Her father straightened. "How long has that been the case?"

"Since the wedding. Why?"

A pause.

"What is it?" Tem asked.

Kronos held her gaze. There was fear in his eyes. It scared her.

"What happened at the wedding?"

She blinked. So much happened at the wedding she had no idea where to start. "What do you mean?"

"I mean"—he leaned forward—"did you crest someone?"

There was only one person Tem had ever crested. "Yes."

"Who?"

"Leo."

"Oh, child," Kronos said quietly. Then he stood, crossing to the window to look out into the garden at her mother. Late-afternoon light bathed his face.

"What is it?" Tem insisted. "What's wrong with me?"

Her father sighed. Rather than answering her question, he said, "It will only get worse."

"What will?"

"Your inability to transition."

"But *why*?" Tem stood too, crossing to join him. "I'm a Hybreed. I'm supposed to be powerful. When Caspen taught me how to transition, it only took me a few tries to do it easily. And then—"

"And then you crested Leo," her father finished.

Tem frowned. "What does that have to do with anything?"

"The crest is extremely powerful magic. Even more so when performed on someone you love."

"So?"

"*So*"—he turned to face her—"it is pulling the two of you together as we speak."

"I don't understand."

"You love him. And you loved him at the time of the crest."

"Yes, but—"

"When you crest someone you love, you must consummate the crest."

Tem's mouth fell open. "*What?*"

"It is an ancient magic, Tem. When you crested Leo, you bound him to you. You must complete that bond. Your ability to transition will continue to deteriorate until you do so."

"But Caspen never had any problem transitioning after he crested me."

As soon as Tem said it, she realized why. They'd consummated the crest mere days later, when she snuck out of the castle to see him. Most likely there hadn't been an opportunity for Caspen to transition between the time he'd crested her and when they'd slept together.

"Why haven't I heard about this?"

"Most people have not experienced it. Basilisks tend to crest humans who they only wish to use for power. They are not often in love with them."

"How do *you* know about it?"

Kronos shifted. His eyes flicked to her mother. He said nothing else, and Tem didn't ask anything further. She didn't want to know whether her father had crested her mother. It didn't matter. All that mattered was the situation at hand.

"I sent Leo away," Tem insisted. "I told him to find Evelyn."

Her father shook his head. "That does not matter, Temperance. Nothing can void the bond of the crest. You cannot circumvent the demands of fate."

So this was it. The catch.

She'd known, somewhere deep in her gut, that something had gone wrong. It was not, as Bastian would say, an elegant solution. Cresting Leo had solved one problem but created another. She had known her inability to transition was strange, that she was not progressing as she should. Now she understood why.

Tem thought about how electric she felt every time she was around Leo, how the air itself was on fire around her. She thought of how polarizing it had felt to touch him, how incredible his skin had felt against hers. It went beyond an emotional connection. She hadn't experienced anything like it until after she crested him. Now it was nearly impossible to be around him, and finally, Tem knew why. This explained everything— her inability to transition, her intense attraction to Leo, her *need*. It had all begun after she crested him. Now she understood why it was torture to be apart from him, why it felt like she was missing a limb when he wasn't around. It wasn't just that she loved him. There was something bigger at play here—something cosmic. The crest was drawing them together, urging her to sleep with him.

Something else occurred to her: Leo had been looking pale lately, worn. If there was a consequence for her, surely there was a consequence for him.

"Can he feel it too?" Tem whispered. "The…bond?"

Kronos tilted his head. "He can."

"In the same way I do?"

"Yes," Kronos said. "Most likely."

The words were said gently, with no judgment. Despite herself, tears filled Tem's eyes.

"You will both continue to suffer until you consummate the crest."

Tem shook her head. "We can't consummate it. He's engaged to Evelyn."

"Yes. But he is also bound to you. You cannot ignore that bond."

"But we can't sleep together."

"You must."

"But we *can't*." Leo was a man of his word. And he'd given his word to Evelyn.

Her basilisk side deemed this a minor detail. But the human side was trapped by its permanence. Leo was not available to Tem even if she chose to sleep with him. There was no appropriate situation in which they could sleep together, nor would there be for the foreseeable future. Tem would never seek to compromise his marriage, never try to seduce him when he was committed to someone else—at least, her human side wouldn't.

Her basilisk side couldn't care less about Evelyn. Her basilisk side felt such *ownership* over Leo that Tem could barely wrangle it into submission. The two parts of her were deeply at odds, forming an internal struggle that was quickly becoming insurmountable. She didn't trust herself around him, couldn't guarantee that she wouldn't do something she could never take back.

Kronos leaned in. "Hear me, Temperance. You must."

"But *why*? *What happens if we never consummate the crest?*"

If transitioning was the only thing at stake, Tem would gladly never do it again.

Her father pursed his lips.

True fear sliced through Tem as he looked her in the eye and said, "The object of the crest will die."

A great weight pressed against Tem's chest. Before she could even begin to process that, a deeper truth hit her.

If the blood bond is broken, a curse is put into effect.

What curse?

Whoever was betrayed must kill the betrayer. My father did not want to kill my mother. But he had to. The blood bond forced him to.

Tem was lightheaded. She needed to lie down.

It was not his choice. My father could not resist. No one could.

Caspen's own mother had died at the hands of his father when she had slept with her true love. If Tem did the same—if she slept with Leo—Caspen would be forced to kill her.

"How long do we have?" Tem whispered.

"Not long," Kronos said. "And the longer you wait, the more discomfort you will both feel. It will eventually progress to pain."

"What kind of pain?"

In reply, Kronos touched his palm to his chest. Tem understood he was holding his heart. "Your ability to transition will only deteriorate. Eventually you will not be able to do so at all. When that happens, it will be too late for Leo."

Tem stared down at her hands, counting the freckles beneath each finger.

"Tem," her father insisted. "You must—"

"I know what I must do," she whispered.

But that did not mean she could do it. Tem had ordered him to find her. There was nothing to be done about it. Or was there? Caspen had threatened to solve it himself. But Tem could solve it too. Leo was bound to her, after all. Tem could order him to leave Evelyn. But it was not a viable solution.

Tem was no god. She did not believe what Caspen believed—that her current position of power gave her the right to control others. She would not mold Leo's future again. She'd done it once and had regretted it every day since. Even if she did it—even if she violated his trust and treated him like her puppet—Kronos had made the terms crystal clear. There was no room for exceptions, no possibility of a loophole.

If she consummated the crest, she signed her own death sentence.

But if she didn't, she signed Leo's.

CHAPTER TWENTY-ONE

·•◦✳◦•·

IT WAS DARK BY THE TIME TEM LEFT HER PARENTS' COTTAGE.

She ran all the way to the castle, not stopping for anything, keeping a breakneck pace even when her legs began to scream in pain. No amount of physical activity could distract her from the torrent in her mind—nothing would quell the panic rising in her stomach, closing in on all sides. By the time she reached the castle, she was out of breath.

Caspen was standing outside the front door waiting for her. Tem could hardly bear to look at him.

"Tem," he said as she approached. "What is the matter?"

Tem only shook her head. There were a hundred things that were the matter. But she wasn't going to discuss them now—not outside the castle, not right before dinner. There would be time to process everything later. For now, they needed to be a united front. For now, she needed him.

"I'm just tired," Tem said, which was technically true. She'd just sprinted all the way here, after all.

A muscle ticked in his jaw. "You do not look well," he said, reaching for her. "I should take you home."

Tem shook her head. They both knew he only wanted to take her home to avoid what was about to happen. "I'm fine, Caspen."

He pursed his lips, but didn't answer. They faced the door together.

"Are you ready?" Tem whispered.

"I will never be ready for you to bleed."

"It's for the best, Caspen."

"Not for you."

"It's not about me. It's for Gabriel and for the villagers and for you."

He furrowed his brow. "I did not ask for it."

"I know you didn't. That's not what I mean. I just mean…" She grasped for the right words, settling on. "It's the right thing to do."

Caspen just shook his head. Tem sighed. He would never be convinced that this was right. And perhaps "right" still wasn't the correct word—perhaps it was simply doing *something* instead of nothing. At this point, Tem was willing to try anything to bring peace, even if it meant hurting herself in the process. Better her than any other basilisk.

"If this is too hard for you," she whispered, "you don't have to come inside."

"Of course I do."

Tem flinched at his tone. At her reaction, his voice softened.

"I must come, Tem. I must protect you."

They both knew there was nothing he could do to protect her. Tem had already made her choice. It didn't matter what Caspen said now—the night would end with her in the dungeon, bleeding.

Tem reached for the door. Before she could open it, Caspen's hand clasped down over hers. He leaned in. "Do not do this, Tem. It is not too late."

She shook her head. "I have to do this."

"You do not," he insisted. "We will figure out another solution."

Tem closed her eyes. If she backed out now, everything would fall apart.

"Tem," his voice was low. "I will do anything to stop this. Anything."

But that was exactly what she wanted to prevent. Tem knew there was no end to what Caspen would do for her—no limit to the people he would hurt. She couldn't allow it.

"I've made my peace with this, Caspen. Why can't you?"

"Because you are precious to me," he said roughly. "When you are in pain, I am in pain too."

"I'd rather be in pain than watch anyone else get hurt."

"That is a beautiful quality, Tem. But you forget that *I* am the one watching *you* get hurt. And it is unbearable."

She didn't know what to say to that.

Caspen's grip tightened. "Do not do this, Tem. Please."

He was begging her. It wasn't a tone she heard from him often. But he used it now, his golden eyes staring deep into her soul.

"It's my choice, Caspen," Tem whispered. "You have to respect it."

Then they knocked, and a butler opened the door and greeted them in the foyer before directing them to the dining room. Tem was about to sit down when Caspen caught her arm. She looked up at him in surprise.

What is it?

Before he could answer, Evelyn and Leo entered. For a moment, nobody spoke.

"Tem," Evelyn said silkily, "I hope you're well."

Tem nearly snorted. She was positive Evelyn hoped nothing of the sort.

"I figured we could enjoy dinner," Evelyn continued. "Before..."

"We are not hungry," Caspen said, his tone nonnegotiable.

Evelyn trailed off. Tem understood suddenly why they hadn't sat down. They would not be enjoying dinner. She was here to bleed—nothing more. There was no point in pretending that this was a regular evening.

Tem's eyes flicked to Leo's. "How does this work?" she asked him.

She wanted him to say it—to spell it out in front of everyone. But it was Evelyn who answered.

"You will go downstairs," she said carefully. "And you will provide your...sample."

So that's what they were calling it: a sample.

Tem fought the bizarre urge to laugh. It was all so *clinical*. In Evelyn's mind, Tem was merely doing them a service—giving something that her body was meant to give. But nothing could be less true.

"Will it hurt?" Tem asked pointedly, again directing the question at Leo. She already knew from her father that it would. But again, she wanted him to say it. She wanted *anyone* to say it, to acknowledge the inhumanity, to put a name to the cruel thing she was about to endure.

Utter and complete silence fell. A slow, sickly expression twisted Evelyn's face. "I... do not know. Surely...it will not?" She looked at Leo.

He looked at the ground.

There was nothing more insidious than cowardice, and that was what Leo was demonstrating in this moment. He had the power to stop this. And yet he stood there silently, staring at his shoes as if they held the answer.

Beside her, Caspen rolled his shoulders. Tem did not condone violence, but right now, she wished wildly that Caspen would rip everyone in this room to shreds.

Do not tempt me, Tem. One word from you and I will kill them both.

You know I would never say that word.

In reply, Caspen closed the corridor to his mind.

Tem knew that his thoughts had likely become so furious that he chose to shield her from them, rather than subject her to them.

Finally, Evelyn broke the silence. "Well," she said. "If we're not going to eat...you... know where to go, I presume?"

Her voice was higher than usual. She was avoiding Caspen's eyes. Perhaps she was afraid the Serpent King would hurt her. The thought cheered Tem enormously.

"Yes," Tem answered. "I do."

Without another moment's hesitation, she stepped toward the door. The second she did, Caspen and Leo spoke simultaneously:

"I will come with you."

"No, you won't," replied Tem and Evelyn at the same time.

A testy silence fell. Both men stared at Tem. Tem stared at Evelyn.

"Darling," Evelyn said through gritted teeth, wrapping her fingers tightly around Leo's arm. "You can't go down there."

"*Darling*," Leo said just as tightly. "Why not?"

"Because…" She paused, clearly grasping for an appropriate end to her sentence. "You shouldn't be around your father."

Tem frowned. It was odd reasoning. She'd expected Evelyn to say that Leo shouldn't be around *Tem*. Leo seemed to think so too because he asked, "And why shouldn't I be around my father?"

Another pause. For the first time since Tem met her, Evelyn looked nervous. "I…"

But the rest never came. The three of them stood in stasis, locked in place.

Leo's eyes slid to Tem's, asking a silent question she couldn't identify. Was he wondering, like she was, why Evelyn was acting so strange?

"I will accompany Tem to the door," Leo said finally. "But no farther."

Evelyn rolled her shoulders as if this compromise caused her physical pain. But rather than make a scene—which Tem strongly suspected she was too afraid to do in front of Caspen—she twisted her mouth into a strained smile and said, "In that case, I will retire for the evening. I'm feeling rather tired."

Without a backward glance, Evelyn turned and swept from the room.

A beat passed. In it, Leo and Caspen looked at each other. They wore the exact same expression that meant the exact same thing: *Are you really going to let her do this?*

Tem didn't wait for their answer. She brushed past them both, stopping only when she reached the door. Leo followed. Caspen didn't.

"Caspen?" Tem whispered.

No reply.

Suddenly, Tem understood. Now that Leo was accompanying her, Caspen was not. It shouldn't have come as a surprise. But it still hurt.

There was nothing else to say. Without another word, they left.

There were a hundred things Tem wanted to say to Leo now that they were alone. But he looked so defeated that, despite her better judgment, Tem decided against it. The last thing she wanted was to make this harder on him. But the threads of resentment were beginning to pile up inside her. *Tem* was the one who was about to bleed out in the dungeon. That was her burden to bear, not Leo's. He should be comforting her.

The rest of their walk was silent. The only thing Tem heard was the pounding of her own heartbeat—and Leo's. His body was warm beside her, his blood pumping steadily through his veins. In the dim lighting, he almost seemed to glow.

Tem couldn't stop thinking about the crest. Her basilisk side called to him like predator to prey, daring her to consummate, daring her to satisfy her urges. Tem stared at the back of his head as they walked single file down the staircase to the dungeon. The urge to touch his white-blond hair was monumental—nearly irresistible. Tem even went so far as to lift her hand, reaching toward him in the darkness. What would happen if she ran her fingers through that beautiful hair? What if she gripped it—*hard*—and yanked his face to hers? Would he resist? Or would he close the distance, pin her against the cold brick wall, and kiss her back?

They reached the door to the dungeon.

Tem thought about how the last time they were standing here together, before they annulled their marriage. Was Leo thinking of it too?

"You shouldn't have to do this," he whispered.

It was an empty sentiment. "Then why are you making me?"

Leo's face fell. He almost looked as if he were about to cry. "Tem…"

Her name evaporated between them.

Tem had never wanted to touch him as badly as she wanted to right now. She wanted it more than she wanted her next breath.

"Leo," she whispered. "You're the only one standing here. *You* are the one letting me walk through that door."

He opened his eyes. They bore into hers. "If I ask you not to walk through that door, Evelyn will leave me."

Tem heard the agony in his voice.

It was horrible. All of it. This entire situation that both Tem *and* Evelyn had created. Leo was trapped now. Perhaps he always had been. Tem thought back to the day she'd found out she was a Hybreed, how she'd come to Leo for shelter. She'd found him in the graveyard that morning. Waiting for Evelyn.

"I don't want this," he said.

"It seems like you do."

Leo closed his eyes.

Tem stared at his blond eyelashes. They were standing so close, she could count them.

"Tell me to stop this," he whispered.

"What?"

"When you ordered me to calm down, I did it. So tell me to stop this."

Tem stared up at him for a long moment before realizing exactly what he was saying to her. All it would take was a single order from her, and Leo would have to obey. If she told him to stop this, he would. It was Caspen's solution, and it was a shortcut, a lie. She was not Caspen; she would not play Kora. Tem was no god.

She shook her head. "No."

"Please, Tem. *Please.*"

"*No.*"

He reached for her, and she flinched.

Unfathomable pain flashed over his face. Surely, it mirrored the pain on hers. But the time for negotiating had passed. Leo hadn't fought for her last week, and he wasn't fighting for her now. He'd made his choice.

"You don't get to take the easy way out. You don't get to cheat. That's not how it works."

"Tem—"

She leaned closed, ignoring her body's scream of desire. "You chose this, Leo. Now you have to live with the consequences."

Tem lived every day with the pain of her decisions, and it was time Leo did the same. Perhaps she had been shouldering the guilt of her choice for too long. Perhaps, despite what her conscience tried to tell her, she had made the right call when she told Leo to go find Evelyn. Perhaps he deserved her, in every sense of the word.

The silence between them was absolute. There was nothing left to say anyway. Tem was prepared to accept this part of Leo—the part he got from his father.

"I will wait for you," he whispered.

Tem didn't believe him, so she didn't reply. Instead, she walked into the dungeon, ready to face her fate with her head held high. The air was freezing—even colder than the staircase. There was a guard here, and he walked over to Tem the moment she entered.

"I'm to assist," the man said.

"I'm sure you are."

"Right this way."

Tem followed the guard down the long row of cells until the very end. It wasn't until she turned around that she realized the cell across from her was occupied.

"What brings you here, Temperance?" Maximus asked.

CHAPTER TWENTY-TWO

⋅⋅◦✳◦⋅⋅

T HE FORMER KING LOOKED WEAK. IT MADE TEM HAPPY.

But any happiness she felt evaporated the moment the guard attached the wires to her fingers. Each wire corresponded with a fingertip, and the moment they touched her, Tem gasped as they welded painfully to her skin. Suddenly she understood why her father could barely speak of the experience. The pain was horrible, but the feeling of being trapped was worse. Even the slightest tug on the wires caused them to pinch painfully. *This* is what her father endured for years? What all the other basilisks who were kidnapped had suffered through for decades until Leo finally made them stop? Tem couldn't imagine ten minutes of this, much less ten years.

This was torture. *True* torture.

The guard turned to leave as soon as he finished attaching the wires. Just before he reached the cell door, he pulled a lever on the wall. Immediately, pain shot through Tem's fingers. Without thinking, she cried out. The wires were *taking* from her—extracting blood from her skin and turning the metal slowly into gold. Through the fog of agony, she heard:

"Does it hurt?"

The question was so idiotic Tem wanted to scream.

"What do you think?" she snapped.

Maximus smiled. It was a disgusting smile, filled with nothing but malice. "Pain is inevitable, Temperance. It makes us stronger."

Tem rolled her eyes. She didn't need a lecture about pain right now. Especially from someone whose specialty was causing it.

"I never thought I'd see you again," Maximus said.

Tem rather wished he would shut up. The bloodletting was punishment enough. "That makes two of us."

"You never answered my question."

"Which question?"

"What brings you here?"

Tem held up her entangled fingers, regretting it immediately when the wires pulled at her hands. "Isn't it obvious?"

Maximus shook his head. "That is not what I mean."

"Then what do you mean?"

"I am asking *why* you are here. You were the one who convinced my son to cease this practice in the first place. And yet here you are, bleeding. Why?"

"Well, apparently I wasn't very convincing because your son brought this practice back."

Maximus let out a low chuckle. "Please, Temperance. You are not some weak creature. You don't do anything you don't want to do."

The compliment wasn't lost on her. But Tem only shook her head. She certainly didn't want to be doing this. "Can you just shut up? This is bad enough without you talking."

Maximus raised his eyebrows, but Tem didn't apologize.

"I am surprised at you, Temperance. You have my undivided attention. There was once a time when you would have taken advantage of that fact."

"Excuse me?"

"Isn't there anything you wish to ask me while we are here?"

Tem almost scoffed but then reconsidered. There was a great deal she wished to ask Maximus. Such as why he'd started the bloodletting in the first place. And why his son was acting like a spineless worm. But one question came to the forefront of her mind, and once she thought of it, she couldn't shake it. Evelyn's words came back to her suddenly: *You shouldn't be around your father.*

"What did you write in the letter you gave to Evelyn?"

Maximus tilted his head. From the look on his face, it was not the question he was expecting.

There was a long silence, in which Tem called upon every ounce of patience she possessed—which wasn't much—to wait for him to answer. When she couldn't take it any longer, she snapped, "Are you listening?"

"Yes, impatient girl. I heard you."

"Then why haven't you answered me?"

"Because your question is nonsense. I have never given Evelyn a letter."

Tem opened her mouth but her next question died on her tongue. Because as long as she didn't ask, she didn't know. And as long as she didn't know, she wasn't keeping the truth from Leo. Before she could decide whether or not to speak, Maximus spoke instead.

"Who told you I gave Evelyn a letter?"

"She did."

"And what did she say I wrote in it?"

Tem pursed her lips. Was Maximus manipulating her? Tem didn't want to give him the satisfaction. But she had no other option. It felt like she was on the brink of the truth. And if there was truth to be found, Tem needed to find it. "She said you broke up with her as Leo."

More silence. Then, to Tem's shock, Maximus began to laugh.

"Is something *funny*?" she cried.

Maximus only laughed more. It was a horrible sound, completely devoid of humor. Eventually, it devolved into coughing, and if Tem's hands hadn't been punctured with wires, she would have clenched them. As it stood, she could do nothing but watch as the former king hunched over in his cell, coughing until nothing came out anymore.

"My son has a type," he said when he was done. "I have told you that before."

"Yeah. Slut."

"*Smart*," Maximus said, correcting Tem. "He falls for smart women. Far smarter than him."

Was Maximus complimenting her again? Before Tem had time to marvel at this, he continued.

"It will be his undoing if he is not careful."

"What are you saying?"

"I am saying that Evelyn is smart. She fooled my son once, and she has fooled him again."

"I don't understand."

"You should. You are just as smart as she is."

Tem heaved a great sigh. *That* was certainly no compliment. "If you don't explain yourself, I'm going to come over there and smack you."

Shock passed quickly over Maximus's face, but Tem didn't bother apologizing. He was no longer king, and even if he had been, she wouldn't have cared anyway. She'd had enough of the men in this family tonight.

"I never liked Evelyn," Maximus continued slowly. "At first my son met her in secret, but eventually she came to the castle. And every time she came, things went missing."

Tem blinked. "What kind of things?"

"Forks. Knives. Cutlery of all kinds."

"So…you didn't like her because she was stealing forks?"

"She was stealing *gold*, stupid child."

All the cutlery in the castle was a result of the bloodletting. Tem stared down at her own hands, which were turning the wires gold. She felt faint.

"She did not leave because of some ridiculous letter. She left because I offered her a higher price than what she could steal from me one fork at a time."

Tem went cold.

Here it was, straight from Maximus's lips: the truth. The thing she suspected but hadn't wanted to face. The thing *Leo* was unwilling to face. Because if what Maximus said was true, it meant that Tem had made a terrible mistake. It meant that she had been utterly wrong in ordering Leo to find Evelyn. It meant that everything they had fought for was for nothing—that the promise of a future for him and his supposed true love was moot. It meant that Evelyn was not who she pretended to be. It meant that nothing would ever be the same.

Tem said the only thing she could think of: "Fuck you."

Another strangled laugh, dark with vindication. "Why do you care?" Maximus sneered. "You left him just like she did. And she will leave again."

"Why would you say that?"

"Evelyn left on the promise of riches, and I have no doubt she returned for the same."

Tem frowned. "What's that supposed to mean?"

"It means she only returned when my son became king. No doubt she thought that status would guarantee her lifestyle. As you can see"—he looked pointedly at the wires attached to Tem's hands—"it didn't. Evelyn did not return for love. She left once. She will leave again."

"You can't know that."

"History will always repeat itself," Maximus sneered. "We do not learn. We do not correct. We forget, and then we repeat the mistakes of our past. It's a pattern, Temperance. One that cannot be broken."

Tem shook her head. She refused to believe that the future was written—that they had no say in the outcome. It was what Apollo believed—that fate was predetermined. But Tem believed that history only repeated itself if you let it. And Tem would not let it.

"Tell me, Temperance. Have the villagers taken kindly to your decision?"

Guilt swooped in her stomach. "What decision?"

"The decision to cut off their food supply?"

The guilt only grew.

"Ah," said Maximus. "You did not think it through, did you? The effects would have been nearly immediate, I assume. We pay for our imports on the day they arrive. Without the bloodletting, there would be no means to pay for more. But that was of no concern to you, was it? You just wanted to stop the bleeding."

"I wanted to protect my people."

"Are the villagers not also your people? Your mother raised you. Surely that counts for something."

Of course it counted for something. But it was not everything. Just because Tem was raised a certain way, that didn't mean it was the only part of her identity that mattered. Tem was made up of two things, both of equal value.

"Don't talk about my mother," Tem snapped.

Maximus gave her a slow, strange smile. "Your mother," he said, "was just like you."

Tem had no idea what to say to that. Of all the things Maximus had told her tonight, that was the least of her worries. "I was trying to do the right thing," she whispered.

"Right is relative, Temperance. You are a fool if you think you can do things better than I did."

"There has to be another way."

"Ignorant child. This is always the way things have been done."

"No." She shook her head. "It's the way *you* do them."

"You know nothing of how the world works, of how adults make their decisions. Power is hard-won and not so easily kept. It takes a miracle to obtain it and a single moment of weakness to lose it."

"I don't want power."

"That is because you already have it. And tell me, Temperance. Would you give it up?"

Tem stared at him. Did she really covet power the way Bastian had—the way Maximus had? It was abhorrent to her. She didn't want to be like them. But perhaps it was unavoidable. Tem had never been powerful until now. She knew what it meant to want something, especially something she would never have. She certainly never thought she'd have power. It was a new thing for her to be like this—to be a Hybreed. *Would* she give it up?

"You think you are so much better than your ancestors," Maximus said, interrupting her thoughts. "You think you can do it all differently. But something always has to give, Temperance. Peace is an illusion."

But Tem was not Maximus; she would not give up hope. She could choose a different path—for the kingdom, and for herself. "Peace is possible."

"There is always a winner and a loser. The cycle cannot be broken."

"You're wrong," Tem whispered.

"I am not wrong. And you will realize that before the end."

But Tem was done listening to men who had no idea what it meant to sacrifice—men like Maximus who were born at the top of the food chain and would always remain there. Even now, imprisoned in his own home, he was sequestered from the outside world, safe from the basilisks he had tortured to get here. There was no justice, no fairness to any of it.

Tem whispered, "*I* will break it."

Maximus didn't reply.

They sat in silence until the guard returned to release her. The stairs were dark; Leo was nowhere to be found.

I will wait for you. More lies.

If Tem weren't so weak from the bloodletting, she might have cared. Instead she ascended the staircase slowly, using the wall to hold herself upright. By the time she reached the landing, she was out of breath.

Caspen was nowhere to be found either. Had he gone back to the caves alone? Was he waiting for her in a carriage? She groped for him with her mind, but the corridor between them was still closed. Tem knew Caspen was angry about her decision. But she'd at least expected him to see her through this—to be here when she got out.

Tem was almost at the front door when suddenly she heard her name.

Leo was before her.

CHAPTER TWENTY-THREE

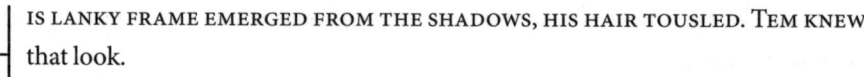

H IS LANKY FRAME EMERGED FROM THE SHADOWS, HIS HAIR TOUSLED. TEM KNEW
that look.

"Are you *drunk*?"

There was no need to ask. Leo was clearly intoxicated—his face was flushed, his
movements loose. Tem had only seen him this drunk once before, during the Frisky
Sixty.

He let out a long breath. "You were down there a long time. I couldn't bear it any
longer."

Tem didn't know what to say to that. She didn't feel like pointing out the inher-
ent privilege Leo held in being able to get drunk while she bled. There was no point.
"Where's Evelyn?"

"Asleep."

Tem almost laughed. Here was Leo, so worried about her that he'd gotten drunk.
Evelyn, on the other hand, slept without a care in the world. Did she know where her
husband was? Did she know he was here, in the foyer, staring at Tem like he wanted to
take her upstairs and fuck her while Evelyn watched?

Leo stepped closer. "I couldn't bear it, Tem," he said again.

The words were a whisper, and Tem believed them. "I'm going home, Leo," she said.

"Please, let me get you something—water, a drink, anything."

"No, Leo."

"Please, Tem," he whispered. "I just want to help."

There was nothing he could do to help, and they both knew it. The time to help was
an hour ago, before he'd let her enter the dungeon. Now the damage was done.

Still. The thought of a bumpy carriage ride was not an appealing one, especially
after what she'd just been through. Tem needed a moment to rest. So she whispered,
"Fine."

Leo's eyes lit up. He extended his hand toward her, the gold cuff glinting on his wrist.
When Tem didn't take it, his face fell. "Very well," he said. "Come this way."

They went to the parlor. As soon as they were inside, Leo poured her a whiskey.

Alcohol was the last thing she needed, but she took it anyway, leaning against the fire-place as she sipped it. In the silence, they studied each other.

The effect of the crest was obvious. Leo was pale. He had bags under his eyes. Tem had a horrible flashback to when she'd watched Caspen deteriorate in front of her in much the same way. Only now it was Leo—the other man she loved—and there was nothing Tem could do about it. Or was there?

She could fuck him right here, right now. The urge was borderline irresistible. Her basilisk side *yearned* to do it—to push him against the wall, undo his trousers, and let him inside her. She wondered if Leo would let her. From the way he was looking at her, she thought he might.

His voice broke through her thoughts. "Why don't you like champagne?"

Tem blinked. It was a bizarre question. "Why would you ask me that?"

"I'm curious. You never drink it."

"It's too sweet."

"Hm." He tipped his glass to his lips. "Evelyn loves it."

Tem snorted. That didn't surprise her.

Leo raised an inquisitive eyebrow. "Something funny?"

"Why does she like it?"

"Ah," he said, swirling his whiskey. "She says it tastes expensive."

Everything Maximus had just told Tem about Evelyn slammed immediately back into her mind. Should she tell Leo what she knew? He practically knew already—he'd called Evelyn greedy once before. But that was not the same as knowing beyond a shadow of a doubt that Evelyn was using him for money. That knowledge was reserved for Tem, and she would not share it with Leo unless she was sure it was the right thing to do. She needed proof before she destroyed a marriage on nothing but Maximus's word.

"You don't like her, do you?" Leo asked quietly.

Of course Tem didn't like Evelyn. But she couldn't say that. Tem would not risk breaking his heart until she heard the truth from Evelyn herself. Instead she remembered what Maximus had said—how Leo fell for the same types of girls.

"I think she's smart."

"No you don't. You scrunch your nose when she talks. Like this." Leo mimicked the motion, scrunching his nose in a passable impression of her.

Tem almost laughed. "So? That doesn't mean I don't think she's smart."

"It means you don't like her. That's what you do when you don't like someone. You always did that when Vera talked."

"That's because Vera is an idiot."

"An idiot you didn't like."

Tem sighed. It was impossible to argue with him when he was this drunk. "Don't you think it's time you went to bed?"

"Only if you come with me."

Tem's heart stopped beating. The air stilled around them. She knew his response was nothing but instinct—pure reflex—but that didn't make it right.

"Leo," Tem whispered.

He held her gaze. There was no remorse in his eyes—no regret. "Let me guess," he said quietly. "I shouldn't have said that." His cheeks were flushed.

Tem wondered just how much alcohol he'd had.

"I meant it, though. And shouldn't you say things you mean?"

"Not those things."

"Why not? We said we wouldn't lie to each other."

But Tem just shook her head. That promise was from a lifetime ago.

Things were different now. They *needed* to lie to each other—it was the only way they could get through this impossible situation, the only way to fix everything Tem had broken. The truth wouldn't help them anymore. Because the truth was that Tem wanted to go to bed with Leo. And if he asked one more time, she was going to do it.

Leo seemed to know this because he stepped even closer. His slender fingers found her hair, twirling the end of a curl. Tem let him do this. She shouldn't, but she did. It felt too good not to.

"I can't stop thinking about you, Tem." The words were rushed, his entire body was tilted in her direction. "You're on my mind every moment of the day. I want you all the fucking time. How can that be? How can you take up so much space in my mind?"

Tem didn't have the answers to those questions. Especially when she had asked herself the same ones. Leo was on her mind all the time—certainly more than he should be…and certainly more than Caspen was.

"Leo," she whispered. "Please."

"It's not enough to see you once a week."

"It *has to be.*"

"It's not. It never will be." Leo's gaze dropped to her hands. "Did it hurt?" he whispered. "The…bloodletting?"

"What do you think?"

Regret flashed over his face. He opened his mouth but Tem cut him off.

"There's nothing you can say."

"I can say that I'm sorry."

Tem shrugged. "I've heard that before."

Leo frowned. "What do you mean you've heard that before?"

"I mean this isn't the first time an apology hasn't fixed the hurt that was caused."

A moment passed. "Are you talking about me? Or about him?"

The silence grew heavy.

"Tem," he said slowly. "Has he ever hurt you?"

She thought of the time when Caspen nearly bit through her lip. It was one of many incidents. But Leo wasn't privy to that information. She didn't owe him any details of her experience with Caspen. "If he has, it's none of your business."

Devastation darkened Leo's face. "You're my fucking business, Tem."

"No. I'm not. Not anymore."

Leo stepped closer. "When did he hurt you?"

"It doesn't matter."

"Of course it does."

"No it *doesn't*, Leo. It's different for us."

"What does that mean?"

"It means we—" But she cut herself off.

"What does that mean, Tem?"

Tem didn't want to answer. But she did so anyway. "It means he can heal me."

"He can heal you," Leo repeated blankly.

"Yes. So it's different for us." Tem had healed Leo once, on their wedding day. He'd called it extraordinary.

"So…he hurts you because he can heal you?"

By the way he asked it, Tem suspected he already knew. Still, she whispered, "Yes."

Leo's face went completely white.

Tem let the silence sit, waiting for him to speak.

"That's despicable," he said finally.

"On whose part?"

Leo's eyes flashed. "His."

"Are you sure?" Tem was pushing him, and she knew it.

"It is despicable on *his* part, and his alone."

But Leo was missing the point. Tem was half-basilisk. She wanted it just as much as Caspen did. She liked it when he smacked her ass too hard, leaving a welt. She liked it when his teeth left bruises on her neck. All basilisks did. She thought of when she'd slapped Apollo, and he'd opted not to heal the mark. *I'd rather have a reminder of you.*

"Even if I'm fine with it? Even if it was my idea?"

"If it was your idea, he planted it in your brain."

"His power doesn't work like that."

"Doesn't it? You told me yourself that he can infiltrate minds."

"Infiltrate them. Not influence them."

"Is there a difference? Because I don't see one."

"That's not what he does. He—"

"He's a *snake*!" Leo yelled.

Tem fell silent.

Leo leaned in, his voice dropping to a strained growl. "He may wear a human form but make no mistake, Tem. He is a monster. You have no idea what he would or wouldn't do."

Tem stared up at him, shocked at the fury in his tone.

"This is not your concern, Leo."

"You do not get to tell me where my concerns lie."

She could feel the warmth of his body. Her basilisk side was fully awake, hungry, reaching for him. Tem couldn't suppress it forever. "And you do not get to be angry that he hurts me when you hurt me too."

Leo froze.

"Your only concern," Tem whispered, "should be your wife."

A muscle ticked in his jaw. "*You* were once my wife."

This was dangerous territory. Tem had to steer them out of it. "Not anymore."

He was still holding the end of her curl. Now he dropped it, touching his fingers to her waist instead. The heat of his skin radiated through the thin fabric of her dress.

Tem didn't move. She could only stand there, helpless, as Leo brushed his fingers slowly across her ribs and up between her breasts. He tugged gently at the front of her dress, deepening the V and exposing her cleavage.

They stared at each other.

Slowly, as if daring either herself or Leo to stop her, Tem raised her hands and brushed her hair away from her shoulders. Leo sucked in a tight breath, his eyes dipping immediately to her breasts. There was no sound except the crackling of the fireplace. A glance between his legs told her that his cock was hard, straining against his trousers. How easy it would be to touch it—to take it in her palm and *squeeze*.

Her nipples hardened at the thought. She knew Leo could see them.

Tem should turn away—she should adjust her hair and cover herself. But she did neither of those things. She *wanted* Leo to see her—wanted him to know exactly what was waiting for him beneath her dress. Tem was starved for his touch. The crest was pulling them together, forcing them to face what neither of them dared to voice out loud. It wasn't over for them. It never would be.

"Tem," Leo whispered, her name barely a breath.

Everything seemed to shrink—the walls contracted, as did the space between them,

Tem's will to resist. There would be nothing left of her if she stayed in this room for one more second.

Leo stepped closer.

Tem stared at his shoulders, his chest, his hands. She saw the sharp bones of his fingers, the deft angle of his thumbs. She wanted those hands on her.

Another step.

He was far, *far* too close.

As if in a trance, Tem's face rose to his. Their lips were an inch apart. She did nothing but breathe him in, feeling the warmth radiate from his body to hers. He was *so warm*, as if the flames that crackled in the fireplace originated within him.

"Tell me you want me," Leo murmured, his voice low and rough.

He smelled incredible. Like summer and cigars and deep, dusty libraries. It was impossible to ignore—impossible to resist.

Tem closed her eyes. If she looked at him for another second she was going to kiss him. "I already did," she whispered.

"No." His breath fanned her face. "You said you missed me. That's not the same."

"It's close enough."

"No," he said again. "It isn't."

Almost against her will, Tem arched her neck.

"Tell me, Tem. Say it."

She opened her eyes. His gray ones were boring into hers, his pupils blown wide with desire. "I want you."

It was only more painful once she'd said the words. Because nothing had changed. She couldn't have him.

Leo raised his hands, touching his fingertips to the underside of her breasts, tracing their shape. Then he went higher, brushing gently over her nipples, the sensation lighter than air.

Tem let out a whimper. She couldn't help it. The moment she did so, Leo pinched both nipples, capturing them between his fingers. As quickly as he did it, he let go. The sudden release left her breathless.

Then he did it again.

There was no proper contact—no skin on skin. Yet Tem's entire body was on fire, as if someone had taken a torch to her bones. She wanted him to rip the dress off her— wanted him to press his lips to her neck and fuck her against the mantle.

"What if I asked to kiss you right now?" he murmured. "Would you let me?"

He was so close, she could smell his cologne—so close she could feel his heat. "Leo," she whispered. "We can't."

He didn't move. "Why not?"

Tem closed her eyes. It was too much. His scent, his skin, his presence. It was becoming difficult to concentrate—to *breathe*. Tem remembered the Frisky Sixty, when all Leo had wanted was to get her naked. Now it was Tem who was staring at the undone buttons of his shirt, imagining what it would be like to rip the rest of them open with her teeth.

He'd been her husband just weeks ago. What was so wrong about touching the man she loved and allowing him to touch her back? Tem knew he wanted to. His pulse thrummed an erratic rhythm. She could *hear* the blood pulsing into his cock, hardening it. She wanted to relieve that tension—wanted to hold him in her hands and stroke him to sweet release.

And why shouldn't she? Evelyn didn't love Leo the way Tem did. Maximus had confirmed as much. Tem was the one who had sacrificed her happiness for his. Tem deserved to indulge. But she couldn't. Because the moment she indulged, Caspen would be forced to kill her. The situation was out of her control. Tem had to get out of this room.

She opened her eyes. "We just can't."

Leo's face darkened. He dropped his hands. It was then that Tem realized just how close they were standing. Their bodies were nearly touching; every time he took a breath, his chest pressed against hers.

"Then leave," he said.

Tem didn't need to be told twice.

Mercifully, there was nobody in the hallway. She rode alone back to the caves, thinking of nothing but what had just happened. When she reached her chambers, the fireplace was lit, but still no Caspen. He was hunting, Tem supposed. Or perhaps he was elsewhere. Did she really have a right to wonder about his whereabouts when she herself had been sequestered with Leo?

Tem curled up in their bed.

Would Leo be thinking of her tonight, as she would surely be thinking of him? Would he return to his bedroom, wake Evelyn, and fuck her the way he wanted to fuck Tem? Brutal jealousy tore through Tem at the thought. It was supposed to be her in that castle. It was supposed to be *them*. What happened in the parlor shouldn't have happened—was not *allowed* to happen. But part of Tem—and she knew perfectly well which part—was deeply aroused by it. Part of her wished they'd taken it even further. She played it out in her mind, how she would slide her palms under Leo's shirt to touch the warm muscles of his torso. Tem could picture it vividly—the way his skin would feel against hers, the way Leo would mutter *fuck* when her hands roamed lower, the way his cum would taste in her mouth.

A moan escaped her lips. She realized she was touching herself, her fingers sliding steadily through her wetness. She imagined they were Leo's fingers, deft and long, bringing her to orgasm. Tem spread her legs. She pictured Leo before her, imagining how he would stare at her center like it was the only thing he ever cared to see. His hands would grip her thighs, pulling her closer until his lips met her skin.

Tem arched her back, moaning. She wanted it. She wanted *him*. It had been far too long since they'd touched properly. The annulment was weeks ago, and that single brush of their fingers had barely sustained her since then. She needed more. She needed everything.

Leo would lick her until she came. Then he would slide his cock inside her and fuck her exactly the way he wanted. And Tem would let him. There was nothing she wouldn't let him do—no part of her that was off-limits to him. She would give herself to him completely, and she would claim him in return.

Her fingers moved faster and faster. Tem missed the way he talked to her—ordering her to be still, to move, to do as he said. She worked her thumb desperately over her clitoris, her other hand moving to her breasts, pinching her nipples the way Leo had. But it wasn't enough. It would ever be enough. Animalistic urge shot through her like a spear. She was on all fours, her fingers submerged to her knuckles, her skin wet with sweat. She imagined Leo taking her from behind, his hands gripping her hips. Tem knew the view would be irresistible, her bent over just for him. Leo deserved every part of her, and more. If only she could give him what she so readily gave to Caspen. If only things were different.

Tem was close. Leo would be too. He would insist on waiting for her, wanting to feel her cum coat his cock before letting himself release inside her. She knew he would fill her up, knew she'd be dripping with him. Tem thought about how beautiful he looked when he came—like an angel brought to life. Her savior. Her Leo.

Here, alone in her bed, the thought was enough to make her finish.

CHAPTER TWENTY-FOUR

T EM FELL BACK WITH A SIGH.

She was *painfully* aroused. If anything, her climax hadn't relieved anything, only made her want Leo more. But there was no way to have him. No solution to this problem. Tem was trapped, as she always had been, only now the circumstances were so much worse than she originally thought. There was no way out. She needed a distraction.

There was only one other person who could provide one.

Surely, it wouldn't be difficult to find him. Tem reached out with her mind, feeling for him. He wasn't nearby. She reached farther, determined. Still nothing.

She was just about to give up when Apollo's voice bloomed suddenly in her mind:

You called, Temperance?

Now that she had found him, she almost regretted reaching out. But Tem was no longer interested in suppressing her needs. And she certainly wasn't interested in feeling lonely anymore. Apollo was here, and Caspen wasn't, and Tem desperately needed to talk to someone.

Yes.

I am honored. What can I do for you?

I'm…bored.

And you thought to contact me? How flattering.

Tem rolled her eyes even though she was alone. Apollo had that effect. *Don't make me regret this.*

And what is this, exactly?

It's… Tem paused. What *was* this, exactly? Was she really about to do this with Apollo? Tem knew what she wanted to say, but it felt impossible to say it. She soldiered on anyway. *It's a proposition.*

I am listening.

Tem took a deep breath. She was about to cross so many lines. Some that Caspen had imposed and some that she herself would rather not violate. But the alternative was stasis, and that was unacceptable to Tem. She was done letting her circumstances determine her fate. She could not have Leo, but she could have this.

I want you to teach me how to petrify.

A pause.

In it, Tem broke out in a sweat. Had she *really* just done that? Was she really asking her brother-in-law to teach her the one thing her husband refused to teach her? It was inappropriate at best. Betrayal at worst. She was a traitor, violating Caspen's trust in an act of pure rebellion. Yet Tem was done being the last to know. It had never seemed right to her that everyone else knew how to petrify and she didn't. It was dangerous, even, for her to be missing this fundamental skillset. Caspen had left her no choice. Surely, he knew that. Surely, he would understand.

Apollo's response came a moment later: *And when would you like me to teach you?*

Right now.

I see. I am afraid I am rather occupied at the moment.

A vision suddenly flooded her mind: Apollo, in his bed, thrusting between the legs of a female basilisk. Tem recoiled in shock.

You're sleeping with someone right now?

Sleeping sounds romantic. I would call this fucking.

Don't be crude.

Crude is my specialty.

Why talk to me if you're otherwise indisposed?

I am extraordinary at multitasking.

You're disgusting.

That is a matter of opinion.

The vision intensified. She watched as Apollo flipped the woman onto her stomach and entered her from behind. The sight made Tem unbearably warm. It was an exact mirror to what she had just imagined Leo doing to her.

Do you like that, Temperance? Watching me fuck someone else?

She didn't want to like it. But she did. *No. I don't.*

You are a terrible liar.

Can you please focus? You haven't answered my question.

I was not aware you had asked one.

I asked if you would teach me how to petrify.

You did not ask that. You told me that you wanted me to teach you. There is a difference.

Tem closed her eyes. Basilisks were simply impossible. Apollo even more so. There were moments, like the one she was experiencing currently, that made her want to throw her hands up and abandon them altogether. *There's barely a difference, and you know it.*

Perhaps. But if I am to do you this favor you so desperately desire, I should like to hear you ask properly.

231

Now Apollo was teasing her, forcing Tem to beg the way she knew he wanted her to.

When she didn't reply, he said, *I have all night, Temperance.*

Tem was well aware of that. There was no shortage of women for Apollo to fuck. He would be occupied until she presented a reason for him not to be. Normally she would never give in to such a request. But she needed this.

Will you teach me how to petrify?

Only if you say please.

Tem resisted the urge to throw up. *Teach me, Apollo. Please.*

There was a long silence in which Tem was subjected to the final moments of Apollo's congress. She watched as the woman came, and Apollo did too, pulling out and releasing himself on her back, splattering the glistening drops of his cum down the sculpted ridge of her spine.

You're a pig.

A pig who is about to teach you how to petrify. You should be thanking me.

I'll thank you once I've learned something.

It is my greatest honor to educate you, Temperance.

Say one more thing I don't like, and I'll revoke this opportunity.

She felt his amusement even through the haze of his orgasm. *Meet me outside. And do not wear any clothing.*

Their connection closed.

Tem sat on the bed, frozen, processing what just happened. It wasn't until now that she remembered that petrification could only occur when a basilisk wore their true form. Caspen himself had told her as much. Tem remembered one of their earliest conversations:

My gaze is not lethal when I wear my human form.

Tem would need to transition in order to petrify. At the thought, a knot of anxiety twisted her stomach. Her father had said that it would only get worse, that until she consummated the crest, her ability to transition would deteriorate. What if she was already too far gone? What if she couldn't petrify at all?

It didn't matter. She had to try.

Tem was already naked, so there was nothing to remove before she made her way outside. The freezing night air immediately raised goose bumps on her skin. It was utterly unnatural to be naked like this outdoors. Tem couldn't stop thinking about what would happen if someone saw her right now. She tapped her foot while she waited, her arms crossed in defiance. Apollo was taking forever; perhaps he had decided to fuck that woman again. Tem was just about to go back inside when suddenly Apollo emerged from the cave. Even in the dark, his beauty overwhelmed her. She stared at his sculpted shoulders, sweat still drying on his skin.

"You came," he said as he approached.

Tem snorted. "*You* came. I saw it, remember?"

"Yes," he said, his mouth twisting in a smile. "I remember."

The last time they were face-to-face, Caspen had ordered them to kiss each other. Tem wondered if Apollo was thinking of it now. She studied his full lips, imagining them on hers. Tem had been naked around Apollo before, but somehow this time was different. Now they were alone, outdoors, and Tem was finding it hard to concentrate on anything except for how perfect his body was.

There is no need to be shy, Tem. You are welcome to look.

I don't want to look.

Lie.

She rolled her eyes.

You are also welcome to touch.

I don't want to touch either.

Another lie.

It was an empty protest. He was inside her mind and knew exactly how much she wanted to touch him. To make matters worse, he wanted to touch her too. Tem could feel the way his gaze traveled hungrily over her body, lingering on her hips, her waist, her breasts. There was an animalistic urgency to his stare. It felt different than when a human man looked at her—different than Leo. Basilisks were harsher in their pursuit, more honest in their intentions. It was something Tem should have been used to by now. But she wasn't.

"Stop looking at me like that," she said out loud.

Apollo smiled, flashing his brilliant teeth. "Like what, Temperance?"

"Like you want to fuck me."

His smile widened. "I do not know how else to look at you."

Tem stared up at the stars—anywhere but at Apollo.

"You are right in front of me," he continued smoothly, his voice laced with amusement. "Where else would you have me look?"

"The ground. The sky. Anywhere."

"Those are not nearly as delectable as you."

Tem bristled, ready to insult him again. "Why do you have to be such a—"

But Apollo pressed a single finger to her lips, cutting her off. They stood there silently, nothing but the murmur of the forest around them. Tem wanted to pull away. She really did. But his finger was warm and soft on her mouth, and she found herself leaning into it, pressing the plump flesh of her lips even farther into his skin. Apollo smiled wider.

What is on your mind, Temperance?

You know what's on my mind.

Yes. But I should like to hear you say it.

Tem sighed. He wasn't going to make this easy for her. He was going to make her admit, to his face, that she wanted him. It was an age-old game, and it was one she had played before. Tem was no stranger to the power struggle, to the way the advantage could switch from one person to another in the span of a heartbeat. He shifted closer, closing the distance between them. He was so tall. Tem craned her neck to look up at him.

Tell me, Temperance.

His presence probed her mind, seeping between the layers of her consciousness and settling at the base of her neck. It felt as if he were holding her head up to his.

Tem still didn't answer. She was too busy adjusting to how close he was standing, how overwhelming he was when he was just inches from her face. He smelled like smoke, just like all basilisks did. But there was an undertone of something else layered within Apollo's scent—something fresh, like the forest. He smelled like wood, like trees. It was intoxicating, and it was all Tem could do not to press her nose to his chest and breathe him in. At the thought, a wave of his hunger crashed into her mind. Apollo wanted her. But more than that, he wanted *her* to want *him*. Tem understood the distinction. It wasn't enough for Apollo just to sleep with her. He needed Tem to initiate it—to *need* it as much as he did. She felt his desire for her grow the longer they stood there staring at each other. She almost wondered whether there was a limit to it.

It was different than Caspen's desire. His was laced with emotion: deep, intimate feeling and care. Apollo's was animalistic, bordering on predatory. He wanted to *dominate* her, to possess her—to *take* her. Sex with Apollo would not be gentle. It would not be loving or intimate. It would be rough and raw and turbulent, and Tem wasn't entirely sure she'd survive it.

It was intriguing, to say the least.

Tem still hadn't answered his question. Apollo still hadn't moved any closer. They were at a stalemate, and Tem knew it was up to her to break it. But did she even want to? Caspen had made it clear he would allow this. He'd practically encouraged it. But men were funny creatures, and as Adelaide had said, they were stupid. Apollo held the power in this moment. But Tem knew if she said the exact right thing, she could take it from him.

I want you to teach me how to petrify.

His eyes narrowed. *I think you want something else.*

Well, I don't.

You are delicious when you are in denial.

The spell was broken. Tem wrenched herself away. "Can we just get on with it already? I don't have all night."

He laughed.

"Forgive me. I did not realize you had somewhere to be."

Tem had nowhere to be and nothing to do but this. But rather than admit that, she crossed her arms and glared at him. Apollo's mouth was still turned up in amusement as he jerked his head toward the forest.

"Follow me," he said.

Tem did so.

They walked slowly. Apollo adjusted his pace to match hers, waiting patiently while she navigated the rough trail with bare feet and a shorter stride. When they passed through the wall, Tem glanced in the direction of her childhood cottage but quickly looked away. They were headed toward the far end of town, into a sprawling field. The night was cold; Tem's breath crystallized before her.

"If I had known we were walking this far, I would have worn clothes," she grumbled.

Apollo let out a soft laugh. "But then you would not have been naked."

"This is ridiculous. Anyone could see us."

"Dawn is still an hour away, Temperance. And we are in the middle of a field."

He was right. But still. "My feet are cold," she grumbled.

"So warm them."

"How?"

To her surprise, Apollo stopped. He turned to face her. "Did my brother not teach you how?"

"How to do what?"

"All basilisks have the ability to regulate their temperature. You are a Hybreed, which means you should be able to as well."

Tem frowned. Caspen certainly hadn't taught her that. Although to be fair, there were plenty of things he hadn't taught her. His resistance to teaching her things was exactly the reason she was here with Apollo in the first place. She wasn't surprised there were other secrets he'd withheld.

"How do I do it?"

"You can use your mind"—he tapped the tip of his finger gently against her temple, and Tem tried to ignore his proximity—"to direct the blood flow in your body."

Tem was barely listening. He was standing *so close to her.*

"How?" she whispered.

"I can show you, if you wish."

Tem nodded. She could do nothing else.

Apollo's hand moved to cradle her face, his palm cupping her cheek. She felt his presence enter her mind, and she welcomed it.

Heat originates in the heart. It travels with your blood. Concentrate on your heartbeat, and you should be able to feel it.

Tem tried to do what he said, but it was difficult when her heart was hammering so loudly, she could practically hear it.

Focus, Temperance.

He might as well have asked her to perform a somersault. The last thing Tem could do right now was focus. She was still cold. The only heat she could feel was Apollo's, and it was driving her insane. Her basilisk instincts were screaming at her to step forward—to kiss him and then some. But she couldn't do that. Not tonight. Tonight, Tem was only here to learn.

So she closed her eyes and concentrated. Apollo was right; when she listened for her heartbeat, she could *hear* where her blood was flowing. From there, it took surprisingly minimal effort to direct it where she needed it.

Warmth seeped from Tem's chest. She could feel it traveling through her bloodstream, spreading through her body. When it reached her limbs, she sighed. Her fingers were no longer numb; she could move her toes once more. Heat probed every part of her—*every* part—right down to her center. Tem was no longer just warming herself. She was turning herself on.

Her face flushed; she gasped for air.

Apollo's voice came to her faintly. *You are so beautiful like this.*

She wondered suddenly if *this* was why Caspen was able to become hard again mere moments after climaxing. If basilisks could direct their blood flow, surely they could control their erections. It was a wondrous thing.

Tem opened her eyes to see Apollo looking at her.

His cock was tantalizingly erect—a bridge between them. Now that Tem knew he had made it that way, it was even more tempting to reward him for it. The warmth was everywhere—flowing beneath her skin with each beat of her heart—surging across every inch of her body. Her breasts felt tender; her clitoris throbbed. Tem imagined, just for a moment, what it would be like to be touched right now. She couldn't even fathom the pleasure.

You need only ask, Temperance.

Tem shook her head.

No.

And why not? You fucked our father, did you not?

That was different.

How so?

I had to fuck him.

Did you?

Yes. Otherwise I couldn't be with Caspen.

I see. But you liked it.

Tem shook her head again, trying to clear it. It was no use. *How do you know I liked it?*

Your thoughts are rather loud at the moment.

The memory of the ritual flooded over her in a brutal wave, exacerbating the feelings she was already experiencing. The altar. The Serpent King. The way Bastian's body was hard beneath hers, how he'd filled her nearly beyond what she could bear. It replayed in her mind; she remembered the warmth she'd felt at the sight of Bastian's naked body— not unlike the warmth she was feeling now—how well she'd taken his cock.

I have no doubt you would take mine just as well.

Guess you'll never know.

Apollo simply laughed. Then he turned away.

Tem stood still for a moment, savoring the heat, before following him. Minutes passed. Now that she was warm, the walk was bearable, but the silence was not. So she asked, "Where are we going, anyway?"

Apollo's dark eyes slid to hers. "We are going to find someone to petrify."

"I know that. But do we need to go so *far*?"

The corners of Apollo's mouth creased. "So impatient."

Tem rolled her eyes. "Shut up."

Apollo let out a bark of laughter. "No one has ever told me to shut up before."

"I find that exceedingly difficult to believe."

He shrugged. "Most find me a witty conversationalist."

"Most are wrong."

Apollo only laughed again.

"Apollo, wait." Tem grabbed his arm, and he stopped. "I…" But she trailed off. She'd hoped that the fear nagging at her stomach would have disappeared by now, but it hadn't.

"I don't want to murder anyone."

Apollo raised an eyebrow. "I see. In that case, I shall take you back to the mountain."

"No." She shook her head. "I want to learn to petrify. I just…don't want to kill anyone innocent."

Apollo took a small step closer. His breath joined hers. "Innocence is not a measurable element, Temperance."

"I know. But can't we pick someone who deserves to die?"

Apollo tilted his head. "Such as?"

"I don't know. A bad person."

"And how would you determine that they are a bad person?"

Tem sighed. She supposed there wasn't really a way to determine that. Truth be told, she hadn't thought this part through. It was true that she wanted to learn how to petrify, but she hadn't thought about *who* she would petrify. If Jonathan or Christopher were still alive, she might've volunteered them. Maximus was the only other bad person she knew, and he was sequestered in the dungeon, his imprisonment punishment enough.

"I don't know," she said again. "But there must be a way."

Apollo considered her. "I see what Caspenon meant."

"Excuse me?"

"He told me you were sensitive."

"*Sensitive?*"

Apollo raised his hand. "Please do not take offense," he said, and the sincerity of his tone surprised her. "I know you are part human. I understand it is important to you that your own kind does not suffer."

At her silence, Apollo stepped even closer.

"I cannot guarantee they will deserve it. But if it will ease your mind, we will choose someone who would be better off dead."

When she still didn't reply, he sighed.

"Temperance," Apollo said quietly. "You can trust me."

They were empty words. What was trust in the face of utter uncertainty? Tem didn't trust Apollo. And she certainly didn't trust herself. Her basilisk side had no qualms with what they were about to do. But her human side was horrified. She was here out of necessity—out of some latent need to…what? Prove that she could do this? Prove it to whom? Tem was the only one who held herself to such a high standard. It was only her own judgment she measured herself against. Caspen himself had made it clear he never wanted her to petrify anyone. She was here entirely of her own volition.

Did that mean she was willing to become a murderer? It was difficult to see it any other way. It was easy to think about petrification in the abstract—to vaguely imagine what it would be like to turn someone to stone. But this was real. Tem was about to voluntarily take a life—a life that didn't need to be taken. Every choice she'd made thus far had been to avoid bloodshed, to prevent death. Now she was choosing to kill. What did that say about her?

"Fine," Tem said. She couldn't seem to manage anything else.

They walked on in silence. Eventually, a structure emerged in the distance: a low brick wall with a run-down cottage just beyond. When they reached the wall, Apollo gestured with his hand. "After you."

Tem rolled her eyes, knowing full well that he only wanted to watch her climb over the wall so he could stare at her ass. But she couldn't care less at this point.

The cottage was crumbling in on itself; Tem couldn't picture anyone actually living here. To their right was a chicken coop. There were hardly any chickens inside, but the sight still made her flinch.

"Why here?" she whispered. For some reason, it felt like she needed to be quiet.

"Its occupant is dying."

"How do you know that?"

"I can tell."

"But *how*?"

Apollo sighed. He looked at her. "I understand why my brother did not want to teach you to petrify. You are extraordinarily impatient."

Tem smiled. They were always trying to teach her patience, these men. It was a skill she had no interest in learning, and if Caspen hadn't succeeded in getting her to master it, Apollo certainly wouldn't either. "He likes my impatience."

"That, I cannot fathom."

She shrugged. "He likes other things too."

Apollo smirked. "Now that I *can* fathom."

Tem pursed her lips. She would not be baited into flirting.

"Impatience is a maddening trait," Apollo continued lightly. "I shudder to think what a task it must have been to train you."

Tem rolled her eyes. "Maybe I already knew everything there was to know before I met Caspen."

Apollo's mouth twitched up at the sides. "Now, now, Temperance. Do not lie. Your heartbeat betrays you."

Tem sighed. She could never get away with anything with the basilisks. She didn't know why she cared in the first place. But for some reason, she didn't want Apollo to think of her as inexperienced. She wanted him to view her as his equal.

"There is no shame in being a virgin," Apollo said. "Even I was one once."

Tem pursed her lips. Apollo was right, of course.

But being a virgin had been the bane of her existence for so long that it was difficult for her to extract herself from that mindset. Vera's cruel taunts still haunted her. It had taken a long time to get over the feelings of inadequacy that had plagued Tem her entire childhood, and now that she was the object of Apollo's sexual desire, she loathed the thought of him knowing how she used to be. It was a victory, somehow, to make someone like him want her. A victory she savored.

"I'm not ashamed," Tem said sharply.

She had no doubt he could tell that was a lie too. But mercifully, Apollo didn't retaliate. Instead, he said, "To answer your question, I can smell the decay. Their body has already given up. It is only their mind that keeps them here. Close your eyes."

"Why?"

A sigh. "Must you question every single thing I tell you?"

"Yes."

Another sigh. "If you close your eyes, your other senses will heighten. You will smell what I smell."

Reluctantly, Tem closed her eyes. At first, there was only the familiar scent of smoke on Apollo's skin. Then something else began to creep in: something *dark*. Decay.

Death was already upon this doorstep; Tem could sense it just as Apollo had. She sensed something else too: suffering. She could *hear* the human inside: an old man. Blood flowed sluggishly through his veins, coagulating. His lungs had corroded; each breath he took caused him excruciating pain. His heart was working far harder than it should to keep him alive—an signal of mortality, an undeniable ode to the fragility of humans. Tem couldn't imagine all that muscle and blood turning to stone. She opened her eyes.

"How does petrification work?"

"It is a matter of transference," Apollo said. "When we take their life force, it makes us stronger. In turn, they lose the flesh that tethers them to life. They become stone."

"Transference," Tem repeated quietly. It wasn't a word she had heard before.

"The power will come from here"—Apollo placed the palm of his hand over her sternum, right above her breasts, and she felt suddenly even warmer—"in your heart. You must pull it from the deepest part of you."

"*Pull*?"

"Yes. The ability to petrify is already inside you. You need only wield it."

None of that made much sense to Tem. She was getting impatient again. "But *how* do I wield it?"

"First you must transition."

Tem wasn't surprised; she'd expected this. Still, it made her nervous. Surely, Apollo would judge her if she couldn't turn. Or worse—he would know why her body was betraying her.

"And then what?"

"And then I will guide you the rest of the way."

Tem nodded. She couldn't do much else. Her stomach was rapidly twisting into a knot.

"Do you still wish to proceed?" Apollo asked.

Tem hesitated. She was grateful he'd taken her here, to this dying man, where the petrification would be a blessing instead of a curse. But Caspen was right: it was a terrible thing to take a life.

"Does it hurt them?" she asked.

Apollo shrugged. "Truth be told, I do not know."

Tem thought of Jonathan and Christopher. She wouldn't have minded if they'd suffered. But she did not want this old man to suffer. She wanted to bring him peace and to do it as quickly as possible.

"Do you still wish to proceed?" he asked again.

Tem didn't hesitate this time. "Yes."

If it had been anyone else in the cottage, she might have said no. But the predator in her knew that this person was beyond life—that they were already as good as dead—that what she and Apollo were about to do would not rob them of anything that wasn't already gone.

Apollo nodded at the chicken coop. "He will come outside to feed them at dawn. That is when we will strike."

Tem nodded too. She was quite familiar with the feeding schedule of chickens. The sky was already beginning to lighten; dawn was not far off. They stood together, Tem watching the cottage and Apollo watching her. If Tem wasn't already used to seeing a plethora of naked bodies beneath the mountain, it would have been downright impossible not to watch him back. But weeks of exposure had trained her for this, and with great will, she averted her eyes from his cock. Apollo, on the other hand, practiced no such discipline. He stared at her openly, shamelessly, and even as the sun rose and dappled the grass with gold, his gaze never wavered. It was only when the door to the cottage opened that he finally tore his eyes away from her to look at the man who emerged.

He was nearly doubled over. They watched as he hobbled toward the chicken coop, his shoulders hunched against the morning chill. He didn't look up—Tem wasn't sure he would have seen them even if he had. His eyes were sunken holes. She could *smell* his age. His organs were rotting, his body nothing but the vestige of a life already lived. His skin was paper thin, draped over his bones like a well-worn sheet. When he reached the coop, he paused. Tem straightened, and so did Apollo.

Wait.

Tem waited.

They watched as the man fumbled with the latch before reaching for the feed scoop. His hands shook so hard he could barely grasp the handle. A great rush of sadness filled Tem, replaced almost immediately by resolve. It was true that they were ending his life. But they were also doing him a favor. Nobody deserved to live like this.

The man was still struggling with the scoop. His fingers were swollen and gnarled—probably arthritic, and certainly painful. It wasn't until he finally secured his grip and turned his attention to the chickens that Apollo said, *Close your eyes, Tem.*

Tem closed her eyes. The moment she obeyed his order, Apollo's presence grew in her mind.

Transition now.

Tem tried to do what he said, searching within her for the thing that yearned to get out. But it was no use. She felt the familiar tightness of constraint—the same thing that had happened every day since the wedding. Tem wished she could shield herself from Apollo. Caspen never judged her when she got to this final, important stage. Now, with Apollo, Tem felt nothing but embarrassment. She was a Hybreed—she was supposed to be the most powerful creature underneath the mountain. And yet here she was, unable to do this most basic thing, helpless.

Apollo was inside her mind, and she could feel his reaction. Unlike the amusement or even cruelty she expected, he felt only gentle sympathy and great understanding.

Do you wish for me to help you?

I don't need your help.

You cannot access your power. I can access it for you, if you wish. Do I have your permission to do so? He was asking to do the same thing Caspen had done many times over.

Fine. Do it.

With pleasure.

Tem gasped as Apollo's presence sharpened, his grip on her—both mental and physical—tightening mercilessly. A great pulling sensation began to form in her chest. It was a familiar feeling; she'd felt it before with Caspen. But this time, Tem was resisting. She couldn't help it. She didn't want Apollo to see her like this, struggling and incapable, like a child in need of assistance.

His voice bloomed in her mind: *Relax.*

I'm trying.

Not very hard, apparently.

You said you would help me.

I cannot help you unless you relax.

His reprimand was so familiar, she flashed immediately back to her training with Caspen. The brothers had the same way of speaking—calmly, with little inflection, as if what was happening was of no concern to them. Tem had always been the opposite: impatient, restless, fallible. There never seemed to be enough time to do what she wanted to do, to learn what she wanted to learn.

Let me help you, Temperance.

It was the last thing she wanted to do. But Tem was at Apollo's mercy. She couldn't achieve this alone. Finally, Tem relaxed. She gave herself over to him, allowing Apollo to do what only Caspen had done, letting him all the way into her mind so he could join it with his. An unmistakable yank tore into the center of her chest, as if Apollo were taking something solid from her. It was not unlike how she'd felt just minutes ago when he'd taught her how to warm herself. But instead of directing her blood, he was directing her power, and finally, she transitioned.

Tem sighed with relief as her basilisk side emerged, clawing its way to the surface until it engulfed first her mind, then her body. Everything was lighter. Everything was *better*. She hadn't transitioned in so long—it was nothing short of bliss to wear her true form once more.

Open your eyes.

Tem did so.

Seeing through a snake's eyes was a singular experience. Certain things stood out: the jerky movements of the chickens, the weak pulse beating at the man's neck. Other things fell to the wayside, like color. Everything was in shades of bluish green; the sun looked as if it were rising underwater. Tem turned her head to look at Apollo. It was the first time she'd seen him in his true form, and he was infuriatingly beautiful. His scales were darker than Caspen's, laced with veins of deep blue that reflected the deepening dawn. Apollo looked at her too, and she found herself hoping he liked what he saw. Faint amusement passed from his mind to hers, and she knew that he did.

Then Apollo said, *Are you ready?*

Yes.

Together, they moved past the wall.

Their transition had been silent, and the man still hadn't looked up. Apollo released a vibration as they approached, a predator's call. The man would sense it, just as any human could sense when someone was standing behind them. Sure enough, as soon as they were close, he turned. The man's eyes widened. They were clouded with white—he was nearly blind—yet the fear in them was unmistakable. Beside her, Tem could feel something happening. Apollo was gathering energy, crystallizing his strength into a single beam of light.

Focus on his heart.

Tem did as he said, focused on the man's heart, which was hammering. She felt as if she were in a trance. There was so much happening, yet also nothing at all. The man wasn't running—he was simply standing there, frozen, an open and willing target. They had all the time in the world to do this, yet time no longer functioned as it should.

What now?

Now we take.

CHAPTER TWENTY-FIVE

H E DIDN'T SPECIFY WHAT THEY WERE TAKING. HE DIDN'T HAVE TO.

Apollo's body rippled, then went taut. Tem mimicked the motion, bracing herself for an exertion of force. Instead, his mind cradled hers.

Take, Apollo said again.

Tem felt for the man's heart, concentrating on its erratic beat, her eyes boring into his. The predator in her recognized that she had won—that her prey was cornered and the man had already surrendered. It was time, at last, to take.

Good, Temperance. Keep going.

Tem kept going, pulling the man's life force toward her, watching it seep out of him like water from a sponge. Petrification was not immediate, as Tem thought it might be. Instead, rigidity crept slowly over the farmer, hardening first his gnarled fingertips before moving to his wrists and disappearing into the sleeves of his jacket. He didn't seem to be in pain, and Tem remembered how Apollo didn't know whether it hurt them. She dearly hoped it didn't.

Blood calcified. Skin became stone.

The last thing to turn were his eyes. She watched as his white, milky pupils turned gray. The moment it was done, a great surge of power slammed into her. It was too much for one person to take; she was crushed beneath its weight.

Apollo's voice came to her: *Control it, Temperance.*

But Tem could barely stay upright. She was not used to being in her true form; she had no control as a serpent. Her skin crawled with a thousand spiders, her entire spine twisted and jerked. Apollo was beside her instantly, pulling her back over the wall. The moment Tem fully returned to her human form, she cried out. Her face was flushed, her nipples peaked. Tem knew without touching herself that she was wet between her legs. The sensation was debilitating—pulsing currents of electricity shot through her center, turning her on to the point of pain.

"Why—" she stammered, trying to catch her breath. "Why do I feel so—?"

"Aroused?" Apollo was also returning to his human form. He was breathing just as hard as she was, a light sheen of sweat glistening over his chest.

"Yes," Tem gasped. She was *so* aroused. Desire tore at her like a feral beast, clenching deep into her core. Stars danced in her vision. Apollo's proximity wasn't helping; she could hear every drop of blood rushing to his cock, hardening it. Tem's lungs contracted rapidly, her breath coming in desperate gasps. "Apollo, what's happening to me?"

His hands were on her waist, holding her upright. "You are feeling the effects of petrification. It requires an extraordinary amount of power to take a life. Power is an aphrodisiac to basilisks."

"But *why*?"

"How should I know? It is simply the way we are built."

We. Tem was one of them—now more than ever.

And as one of them, she was deeply affected by what had just happened. Her entire body felt warm and pliable, as if she'd just stretched it vigorously. She desperately wanted to have sex. *Needed* to have sex. She was so turned on, she was having trouble thinking straight, and in the suffocating blur of desire, she placed her palm flat on Apollo's chest. At the contact, his eyebrows shot straight up. For a split second, neither of them moved. Then he placed his hand over hers, holding them together.

Is there something on your mind, Temperance?

Tem glared up at him. He knew perfectly well what was on her mind. He was *inside* her mind, for Kora's sake.

Would you prefer I was inside your cunt?

Tem blushed.

She shouldn't prefer that. Yet she didn't try to pull away—didn't make a single effort to release herself from his grasp. Instead, she studied the way the rising sunlight hit the slope of Apollo's shoulders, bathing him in a warm orange glow. He was looking at her calmly, his cock completely hard, pressing against her thighs.

"Shall we?" he asked.

"Shall we what?"

"Have sex. Obviously you want to."

"Obviously *not*."

Apollo only laughed. "You are a terrible liar, Temperance."

That was not Tem's concern right now. Right now, she was fighting to stay upright—even leaning against Apollo took too much effort. She was so, *so* turned on. All her mind could think about was sex. Sex with Apollo, sex with Leo—it didn't matter who. The air around her seemed to vibrate with anticipation. It was unbearable.

"It is customary, you know." Apollo's voice came to her through the haze.

"What is?"

"To have sex after petrification."

She could barely hear him.

"Required, in fact."

"Required?"

"Well, not technically. But you must climax."

"What do you mean?"

"I mean, can you not feel the urge?"

Tem could feel the urge, all right. It was tearing her apart. "Yes," she said through gritted teeth. "I feel it."

"You must satisfy it."

"What will happen if I don't?"

He shrugged. "You may find it difficult to come in the future."

"Difficult?"

"Yes."

"What's that supposed to mean?"

"It means that if you do not come now, it will cause a…barrier for all future climaxes."

"*All* future climaxes?"

"Yes."

"As in, I won't be able to come ever again?"

"That is correct."

"Why didn't you tell me this before?"

"I thought you knew."

"How would I know that?"

Apollo was only becoming more amused as this conversation went on. "Surely, my brother told you."

"He didn't even want to teach me how to petrify in the first place. You think he told me the details of what happens after you do it?"

"Clearly he did not."

"Clearly."

Apollo leaned in, and Tem nearly blacked out at his scent. "And here I was thinking you had propositioned our little outing because you knew what would happen after."

"You think I asked you to teach me how to petrify *because I wanted to have sex with you*?"

"I had rather hoped."

"Kora."

247

It was all she could say. It took supreme effort to speak.

Tem had no idea whether what Apollo said was true. The thought of never coming again seemed impossible, especially for a basilisk. But at this point, it was irrelevant. The throbbing between her legs was beyond what she could bear. She felt like water on the brink of boil. If she didn't come soon, she was going to cry.

"Shall I assist?" Apollo asked. She hated how happy he sounded.

"No."

"Are you sure? I can bring you to climax."

Tem snorted. "I can do that myself."

"I have no doubt you can. But I can do it better. And faster."

"I don't need your help."

"I see. In that case"—he stepped back, extracting his body from hers—"proceed."

Anger joined her arousal. Apollo knew how Tem was feeling right now—he knew how cruel it was to taunt her.

"You're going to *watch*?"

"Do not pretend you would not like that."

Tem would like that. There was no way around it. The thought of touching herself in front of Apollo was thrilling. She'd done it before, after all, and she'd certainly liked it then. But they'd been in the banquet hall, surrounded by people, with Caspen overseeing it all. Anything could happen here in this field, alone.

"Don't you need to do it too?" Tem said through gritted teeth.

"Are you asking me to join?"

"No. I'm asking you to explain why you aren't feeling the way I am right now."

"I *am* feeling the way you are right now. But I am much older than you. I have petrified a thousand times, and I know how to handle the urge."

Tem ignored him. He was teasing her, but there was no time to be embarrassed. All that mattered was relieving the sensation in her center. Yet despite the all-encompassing urge to climax, she couldn't seem to do it. Her mind was foggy, her vision blurred. She couldn't form a coherent thought, much less move her fingers between her legs to touch herself. It was almost as if the more she needed it, the less her body retained the ability to accomplish it.

"Let me help, Temperance."

"No."

"It will only get worse if you resist."

"I don't care."

"You will soon."

"I hate you."

"Now, now. We both know that is not true."

Tem shook her head. She didn't have time for Apollo's nonsense right now. She was too turned on, too filled with *need*, to care any longer how it was resolved. She had to release the pressure. And she had to do it now.

"*Fine*," she hissed. A paralyzing moment of silence passed. Apollo's face was infuriatingly smug. "But I don't want to have sex with you."

Apollo tilted his head and smiled. "It rather seems like you do."

"Well, I don't. There are a hundred other ways to come."

His smile only widened. "And which of those hundred ways would you prefer, Temperance?"

"Will you just shut up and help me?"

Apollo crossed his arms. "If I'm going to help you, I would prefer your enthusiastic consent."

"You have it."

"It does not sound like it."

"What else do you want me to say?"

"Something romantic would be nice."

Tem didn't have the energy to argue. The sensation between her legs was crippling her, nearly pulling her to the ground. She'd had enough. "Make me come, Apollo. *Right now.*"

His pupils were already dilating, his eyes turning black. "Are you begging me, Temperance?"

"I'm ordering you."

"Even better." Finally, Apollo stepped forward.

Tem had no idea what he was going to do, and frankly she didn't care. If it meant that the pressure between her legs would be relieved, it would be worth it. She was almost willing to have sex with him just for that. But not quite.

Apollo slipped his hands behind the back of Tem's thighs, lifted her up, and set her on the low brick wall. Despite the urgency of the moment, he took his time spreading her legs, pushing her knees open before nestling himself between them. Her body was naked before him, his warm skin touching hers. There was something so *right* about this position—two people upright, face-to-face, poised to collide. It took every ounce of self-control Tem had not to wrap her fingers around his cock and pull it inside her. But now was not the time for that. Tem had stated her boundary, and she trusted Apollo to respect it. In the end, it was his fingers, not his cock, that entered her.

The moment he made contact, Tem forgot her qualms.

If the circumstances were different, Tem might have been embarrassed about how loudly she moaned. As it stood, she was surprised she didn't orgasm instantly. Apollo's touch was different than Caspen's—less refined, rougher. It was as if he were *pushing* her toward her climax rather than coaxing her there. But Tem didn't care. In fact, she liked it. A push was preferable at this point; she needed to finish as fast as possible, and Apollo was making her do exactly that.

Her hands wrapped around his forearm, drawing him even closer. His face was an inch from hers. They didn't kiss. This was no intimate moment, no tender chance to connect. It was a transaction, plain and simple, and Apollo's breathing was sharp and fast as he fingered her. Tem matched it with hers, allowing herself to moan as loud as she liked. There was nobody here to hear them—the only other soul was dead; no one alive to witness the pleasure he was giving her. Tem could already feel something building within her, and she knew Apollo felt it too. Their bodies were pressed together, the unbreakable expanse of his torso the only thing keeping her steady.

Come for me, Temperance.

Only Caspen had told her to come like that before.

Caspenon would not mind. He would want you to come.

Tem very much doubted that.

Come for me.

She was seconds away. She couldn't hold out forever.

Now.

Apollo's teeth nipped her earlobe. With a helpless whimper, Tem came.

Ten seconds. It couldn't have taken more than *ten seconds* for Apollo to make her finish. She'd already been out of breath, but now she was gasping for air. Pure, unencumbered relief swept through her, followed quickly by total bliss. Oxygen flooded her lungs as the pressure between her legs fell away. She felt *so much better*, her body suddenly limp in Apollo's arms.

But Apollo was just getting started.

He pulled away, trailing his dripping fingers up his cock until they were wrapped around the base. Everything he'd just said to Tem was also true for him, she realized. Apollo needed to come too. His eyes met hers. He gave her a diabolical smile.

Then he began to stroke.

There was no sound other than her wetness around the great length of his cock. Somehow it felt as if Tem were *involved*—as if by fucking his fist, he were fucking her. She watched him as he touched himself, listening to the slick sound of her own cum as it slid against his skin. It felt like she shouldn't be seeing this. But she had to look. Otherwise she wouldn't see Apollo, in all his glory, looking back at her. He alternated between watching his cock and watching her, staring at her with such self-satisfied lust that Tem nearly wanted to slap him. But she'd done that once already, and he'd liked it. The only thing left to do was to allow this to happen—to experience his hand pumping up and down his cock to the rhythm of her heartbeat.

Tem was sorely tempted to join in—to touch herself at the same time. But that felt wrong somehow, as if it were an imitation of what they'd done in the banquet hall. Tem had no desire to replace that memory with this one. This was a new memory. And a good one.

For as intrusive as Apollo usually was in her mind, he was surprisingly silent now. Perhaps that was normal for him; perhaps the imminence of orgasm was the only thing that truly shut him up. It was good information to know, and Tem filed it away for later use.

She decided to fill the silence: *Look how hard I make you, Apollo.*

His eyes darted to his cock, which was rigid in his hand. His mouth twitched, but he didn't reply. Almost as if to dare her to say more. Tem was happy to do so.

Do you like me like this? Wide open for you?

Still no reply. His strokes sped up.

Is this what you look like when you're alone, Apollo? Is this how you touch yourself at night, when you think of me?

Still no reply. His eyes were boring into hers, his irises completely consumed by blackness. It was like staring straight down into a bottomless well. Tem trailed her fingers lazily up her stomach, brushing them over her breasts. Apollo *growled* at the sight, the noise so purely animalistic, Tem immediately got chills.

You want to fuck me so badly. But I won't let you, will I?

It felt immeasurably good to tease him. He was always teasing her, always making her feel slightly out of step. It was a rush she'd never been able to return until now.

What do you want to do to me, Apollo?

It was time for him to be vulnerable, to reveal a part of himself to her the way she'd done so many times for him. She wanted reciprocity. And she was done waiting.

Tell me, Apollo. Tell me what you want to do to me.

He was still stroking his cock, still looking her right in the eye as he said, *I want to fuck you.*

I know that already. What else?

I want to fuck you while my brother watches.

They were approaching the truth of the matter now. It had never been about Tem. It was about power. Apollo wanted to prove something to Caspen, and possibly to himself.

And how will you fuck me while he watches?

Apollo made a noise as if the question physically pained him. And perhaps it did.

This was torture for him, just as so many things were for Tem. She'd finally found Apollo's weakness—the thing that made him lose control. Her.

First, I want you on top.

Why?

So I can see your face.

Just like his brother. Typical.

And then?

And then I will take you from behind.

Why?

So my brother can see your face.

Also typical.

And then?

He sent her a vision—him behind her, his hand around her neck, pulling her face to his. They kissed in his mind but not in reality, and Tem watched as the hand that wasn't around his cock gripped her thigh so tightly it was sure to leave a bruise. Tem didn't mind. She wanted to remember this. His vision sharpened. Tem was crying his name: *Apollo! Apollo! Apollo!*

In front of him, she smiled. So that was what he wanted. For her to say his name—to *acknowledge* him—a level of intimacy she wouldn't allow. There would be time for that later—or perhaps not at all. Tem wasn't interested in giving Apollo what he wanted. She was interested in winning.

Victory was inevitable. Tem could sense it. If she'd been touching herself, she would be close too. Instead she was just blissfully turned on, experiencing this moment right along with him, only this time with the luxury of detachment. It was a new thing for Tem to wield her power in such a way, and she found that she liked it. Distantly, she wondered what else she could make these brothers do.

Tem remembered the woman Apollo had fucked earlier—how he'd painted her spine with his cum. Tem wanted him to paint her the same way.

"Apollo," she said out loud, her voice firm. He'd been staring at her center but now his eyes flicked to hers, devoid of anything but raw hunger. "Come on me."

Equal parts ecstasy and torment flashed across his face. The two were so closely intertwined, there was no difference between them.

"Here." She brushed her fingers over her clitoris. "Come right here."

His eyes glazed over.

"Apollo," she whispered.

The moment she said his name, Apollo came.

He finished with a groan, his shoulders hunching forward as he released himself between her legs. His cum was warm, covering her center with a slickness that shone in the brand-new sunlight. For a single second, neither of them moved. Then Apollo extended his hand and slipped his fingers inside her once more, pushing his essence deep into her center, joining it with hers. Unlike the aggressive way he'd touched her just moments ago, this time he caressed her gently, slipping his fingers in and out, up and down, spreading their combined wetness all over. Tem let him do this, her knees still open, every part of her exposed. When he finally removed his fingers, he raised them to her lips.

Taste us.

Tem didn't need to be told.

She opened her mouth and received his fingers willingly, sliding her tongue through the valley between them. The metaphor wasn't lost on her: she knew he was showing her how good they could be together. Apollo's other hand went to her neck, tilting her head back to push his fingers down her throat. Tem closed her eyes, memorizing the way they tasted, imagining what it would be like to do everything he'd shown her in his vision. But she couldn't do any of that. Not tonight, and possibly not ever. She would not come between brothers—figuratively or otherwise. Apollo's face was an inch away from hers. He was probing her, *testing* her, seeing how deep she could take him.

When she had licked his fingers clean, Apollo grinned.

"Your cunt is exceptional."

"I—what?"

"One of the best I have ever encountered."

Tem closed her eyes. "*That's* what you choose to say to me right now?"

"It is simply a fact."

"Basilisks are insane. All of you—*insane.*"

"I understand why my brother is obsessed with it. And with you."

"Are you trying to compliment me? Because it's not working."

"I am not. I am merely telling you my observations."

"Great. Can you keep your observations to yourself, please?"

"If that is what you wish."

"That is *deeply* what I wish, Apollo."

When she opened her eyes, he was smiling. There would be no hiding from him after this. What had just transpired between them was only the beginning of something—of that, Tem was quite sure. She would have to deal with the consequences of tonight sooner or later. It was too soon to tell whether they had crossed a line. But there was solace in knowing they had crossed it together.

Apollo was still grinning.

"What are you smiling at?" Tem asked.

"I have never met a human like you before."

"I'm not a human. I'm a Hybreed."

"That is true. But you are not a basilisk, that much is clear."

"What do you mean?"

Apollo rolled his shoulders. He was still standing between her legs, his cock still wet with her cum.

"Basilisks give in to their instincts. We are unable to resist the draw of sex. You, on the other hand, do nothing but resist it."

Tem frowned. She'd never thought of that as a distinctly human trait. She didn't usually resist sex. It was specifically sex with Apollo that she was trying to avoid. Then again, she was avoiding it with Leo too. But that was out of necessity.

"I admire your restraint," he continued. "I only wonder how long you can maintain it."

Tem shrugged, the motion far more casual than the conversation. Her answer was not at all what she believed: "Forever, probably."

His smile widened. "I very much doubt that."

Tem very much doubted it too.

There was a day, not so far in the future, when she would break—when she would no longer be able to resist the draw of sex. But she couldn't afford for that day to come. Not when Leo was the one she wanted to have sex with. Not when her own life was on the line. Basilisks were ruled by their bodies; humans, by their minds. Tem was constantly at war with herself, trying to maintain a balance. Caspen had said that her two sides were limitlessly powerful. But Tem hadn't been feeling particularly powerful lately. It had taken tonight—this experience with Apollo, specifically—to feel capable again. Tem wondered if Apollo could sense this, if he knew the effect he had on her.

I do know.

Tem jumped at his voice in her mind. *You can't just eavesdrop on me like that.*

I have already told you, Temperance. Your thoughts are rather loud.

Well, tune them out.

That is impossible.

Tem rolled her eyes.

In response, Apollo took her hand in his, lifted it to his mouth, and pressed his lips to her wrist. Tem didn't know what to make of the gesture—it was the same one he did when they first met. It was oddly respectful, as if he were paying tribute to someone of much higher rank. Then again, Tem was technically his queen. Perhaps that's exactly what he was doing.

"Should you ever tire of resisting," he murmured against her skin, "I am at your disposal."

That, if nothing else, was certainly true. Apollo was always right there, on the edge of Tem's vision, waiting. In some ways, she liked that he wanted her so badly. But often his desire felt like a cage. He was no different than all the other basilisks under the mountain: virile and eager and willing to sleep with her at a moment's notice. There was something to be said for wanting what she couldn't have.

Her thoughts turned to Leo.

He was the *only* thing she couldn't have. Everyone else was available to her; everyone else was hers for the taking. But even now, after sharing this moment with Apollo, Tem could only think of the human king.

Apollo was watching her carefully, as if curious to see she would do next. He had every right to be curious, Tem supposed, after what had just happened between them. But she would not be going any further with Apollo tonight. So she said, "Can you help me down?"

His face resumed its usual smooth expression. "Of course, Temperance." Apollo's arm curled around her, lifting her from the low brick wall and setting her on the ground. He lingered for just a moment, their bodies pressed together.

Tem closed her eyes, savoring it. Then they pulled apart.

"We should return," Apollo said.

Dawn had run its course; it was nearly full daylight.

"What about the body?"

"I shall take care of it later."

Tem frowned. She looked over her shoulder at the statue of the man, his granite hand still holding the feed scoop.

"Won't someone find it?"

"It will not be here for long. I will return as soon as I escort you back."

"I don't need escorting, Apollo."

"I never said you did."

Tem rolled her eyes. She no longer had the desire to argue. The night had been a long one, and Tem was still reeling from the fact that she'd petrified a human being. They walked back slowly, and she knew Apollo was again letting her set the pace. Tem used the time to practice warming herself, finding she was able to direct warmth from her heart to the tips of her toes with hardly any effort at all. With each pulse of her blood, she felt indescribable power, and she knew it was a result of what they'd just done. It was a miracle that basilisks didn't petrify someone every single day just to chase such a rush.

We would leave a trail of bodies if we did that.

Tem was so used to Apollo chiming in by now that she didn't even jump at his voice. Instead, she shared her mind with him, allowing her thoughts to run their course, knowing he was listening. She wondered how the basilisks were able to resist petrifying the villagers when it felt so natural to do so. Even the truce couldn't suppress basic instinct, and Tem couldn't imagine that all basilisks were as careful as they had been tonight, choosing someone who was practically dead already—someone who wouldn't be missed.

We are always careful. The consequences are significant if we are not.

But how can you get away with it? You can't just leave a bunch of statues out for anyone to find.

No. We cannot.

So what do you do with them?

Apollo's gaze slid to hers. *Would you like me to show you?*

By now they had passed the wall and were entering the caves. *Yes.*

In response, Apollo led her down a passageway she'd never seen before. It went deep below the mountain, surely deeper than the lake. Tem was just about to ask where they were going when they stopped before a tall, wooden door. Apollo opened it to reveal a long, dark room. It reminded Tem of the room Caspen had shown her containing the monument dedicated to those who had gone missing after the war. But unlike the room with the monument, which had tall ceilings and intricately carved stone details, this room was bare of any decoration. There were no torches on the walls, nothing to light the way. The ceiling was low and rough, the floor similarly unfinished. It was certainly not a memorial, more like a storage room.

As soon as Tem's eyes adjusted to the darkness, she saw what exactly was stored here.

Row after row of petrified statues stretched out before her, fading away into the distance. People in varying positions, frozen into stone. Some were lying down, as if in sleep. Some were standing, their arms over their heads in clear self-defense. It was cold in here, but for some reason, Tem could no longer warm herself. The sight of so many dead humans made her sick.

"This is…" she whispered.

Apollo finished for her: "Justice."

She frowned. "What do you mean?"

"We do not kill at random. It is retribution: a life for a life."

Finally, Tem understood. If each of these statues represented a basilisk who had been taken for bloodletting, the names on the memorial Caspen had shown her corresponded to the bodies in this room. Tem shook her head in disbelief. There were so *many.*

"How did it go unnoticed?"

"This is the result of centuries, Temperance." He waved his hand, encapsulating the room. "We did not do this overnight."

Tem tried to respond, but she couldn't. She might be queen of the basilisks, but she was also a villager. Today she had petrified one of her own. And if the circumstances had been even slightly different, she could just as easily have ended up in this room herself.

Every action has a consequence, Temperance. You cannot blame us for retaliating.

I don't blame you. It's just…sad.

Apollo didn't answer. Surely, this wasn't sad to him. His sadness was confined to the other room—the memorial, where the names of his people were scratched in stone. But Tem's people were right here.

She turned to Apollo.

"When you said you'd take care of the body, you meant…"

"I will bring it back here."

Tem looked up into his eyes. "Alone?"

He pursed his lips. "Yes."

"Why wouldn't you ask me to help?"

"I do not want you to experience that. Carrying them is…heavy." From the way he said it, Tem could tell he meant the word in more ways than one.

She turned back to the statues, and her next words were a whisper. "You shouldn't have to carry him alone."

A pause. His whisper mirrored hers. "You should not have to carry him at all." When she didn't reply, he said, "It is my choice, Temperance."

A choice he'd made without her. But Tem was used to that by now. Both Apollo and Caspen seemed to think they knew what was best for her. At a certain point, she wondered if perhaps they did.

"Can we please go now?"

Apollo nodded. "Of course."

The walk back through the passageway was silent.

Tem was miserable. Her human side was horrified at what she'd just seen and mourned the man they'd killed. Caspen's words ran once more through her mind: *It is a terrible thing to take a life.* He was right; it was terrible. But there was a fine line between terror and pleasure, and Tem was experiencing both in equal measure. She couldn't help it; the two sides of her were equally involved, as they always had been. Her human side wanted to cry. But her basilisk side felt what Apollo surely felt when he looked at those statues: absolute triumph. Holding both emotions at once was exhausting, nearly impossible, and all Tem wanted was bed.

When they reached the door to her chambers, Apollo turned to face her. "I did not mean to upset you, Temperance. Perhaps it was a mistake to show you that."

"I'm not upset."

"Your thoughts say otherwise."

"Well, I'm not. I'm just tired."

"I see."

There was a pause, and before she could talk herself out of it, Tem said, "Thank you."

A tiny smile twisted his mouth, and a fraction of the heaviness of the evening lifted. "For...?"

"You know exactly what for."

"I should like to hear you say it anyway."

Tem stared up at him, deciding whether she wanted to die on this hill. Apollo had given her his time tonight, among other things. He'd taught her something that Caspen refused to teach her, and he had done it well. Tem wondered if he'd known, somehow, that this was his way in with her. He'd found the one thing that Caspen wasn't willing to do, and he'd stepped in to do it. It was a trait she could appreciate and one she was rapidly beginning to depend on. She relied on Apollo in ways she couldn't rely on Caspen. He was there to fill in the gaps in her knowledge—for better or for worse.

"For teaching me how to petrify."

"*And?*"

Tem rolled her eyes, finishing begrudgingly, "And for making me come."

"There it is."

"I hate you."

"So you have said."

"Can't you just accept my thank-you and let me go to sleep?"

He smiled, baring his teeth. "I accept your gratitude, Temperance. And you are very welcome. It was, as I am sure you could tell, my pleasure."

Then Apollo was gone.

Tem stood there, staring after him, trying to control her heartbeat. As his presence faded from her mind, she found she missed it. They'd been so connected for the last few hours that it hurt desperately to be alone once more.

Tem opened the door to her chambers, wanting nothing more than to collapse onto her bed and fall asleep. But to her shock, the room was occupied.

"What are you doing here?" Tem gasped.

Caspen was by the fire, as he often was. But something in the way he held himself made the hair on the back of her neck stand up. How long had he been waiting for her? Had he been listening in on her conversation with Apollo in the hallway? She'd just thanked his brother for making her come. Out of context, it was a horrifying thing to overhear. Then again, the context was that he'd taught her to petrify—which Caspen had explicitly refused to do. Perhaps that was even worse.

Caspen didn't reply. Instead, his eyes traced down her naked body and a chill slipped down Tem's spine as his gaze landed between her legs. His nostrils flared. An eternity passed.

Then he said, "Tell me, Tem. Why is my brother's cum in your pussy?"

CHAPTER TWENTY-SIX

—••◆✷◆••—

T HERE WAS REALLY NOTHING TO SAY BESIDES THE TRUTH. "HE TAUGHT ME HOW to petrify."

Caspen blinked slowly. "I see."

A deathly silence followed.

Tem knew Caspen would understand exactly what she was really telling him. He knew what had to happen after you petrified someone. Even if *she* hadn't known the implications of that decision until an hour ago, Caspen certainly knew. And Apollo had known too.

"We didn't have sex," she said when the silence lingered too long.

"I see," Caspen said again.

"He just…" Tem struggled to put the experience into words. There was no way to describe what had happened on that brick wall that would make it palatable to Caspen. She decided on "…helped."

A muscle in Caspen's jaw twitched. Tem knew he was picturing them together, imagining everything his brother had helped her with.

"I didn't know," she said quickly.

His eyes slid to hers. He blinked. "You did not know what?"

"I didn't know what happens after you petrify."

No reply.

Tem soldiered on. "You never told me, and Apollo thought I already knew. He thought…" She trailed off. It was pointless to tell Caspen that Apollo thought she'd asked him to teach her how to petrify because she wanted to sleep with him. It was a detail that would only make things worse.

Caspen still wasn't speaking. He was simply watching her silently, his arms crossed over his chest.

Tem could do nothing but try again. "I understand if you're angry but—"

"I am not angry, Tem," he cut her off.

Tem gave him a cautious glance. "It seems like you are."

Caspen sighed. He looked her in the eye. "I am not. I should know you better by now."

Tem had no idea whether she should be offended by that observation.

Another silence followed. A myriad of emotions rushed through Tem's chest, and she could only imagine that a similar set was rushing through Caspen's. Not only had she gone behind his back to learn how to petrify, but she'd done it with his brother. There could be no worse combination of misdeeds.

"Caspen?" Tem said quietly. "Please say something."

"What would you have me say, Tem?"

"Just…tell me what you're thinking."

Tem didn't dare enter his mind. There was a black cloud around it she couldn't hope to penetrate and didn't want to anyway. This was a conversation better had out loud.

"I am thinking that I have never met someone so incapable of following instructions as you."

The words stung. They took her immediately back to the training, when she and Caspen had been student and teacher. It was a time when their relationship was unequal, a time when he made unilateral decisions without her knowledge or consent. Now she had done the same to him.

"I don't understand," she said. "You're always saying how you want me to have the full basilisk experience."

"I have made my stance on petrification crystal clear. Do not pretend you do not understand."

Tem shook her head. "It's not safe for me not to know how to petrify. Apollo said so."

"I do not take Apollo's opinion into consideration when making my decisions. And neither should you."

"But this was *my* decision. You wouldn't teach me, so I—"

"There is a *reason* I did not teach you, Tem," Caspen cried, and Tem flinched at his tone. "I did not want you to kill your own kind. It is a terrible thing—"

"To take a life," she finished for him, her voice a mangled whisper. "Trust me, I know."

"Trust *me*," he snapped, stepping closer. "You do not. You are half-human, Tem. This will haunt you. The basilisk side of you may accept it, but the human side never will."

Tears welled in her eyes. He was right. She was already experiencing the aftermath of the petrification: burgeoning power mixed with horrifying guilt. Caspen had tried to protect her from that. And he had failed.

"It's already done, Caspen. I can't take it back."

He only shook his head, his gaze returning to the fire.

Caspen was furious, that much was clear. But about *what*, exactly? He seemed far angrier that she'd petrified someone than about the fact that Apollo had helped her orgasm. Tem looked at the fire too, and for a moment, there was silence. Then Caspen whispered, "What will your little prince think of what you did?"

A chill ran down Tem's spine. *Little prince.* It was his most demeaning nickname yet. And it was also the first time Tem thought about her actions in the context of Leo. What would Leo think of what she'd done tonight? He would hate it. As he should. She had violated the truce; she had taken a human life. Leo would be horrified if he found out she'd killed a man.

Tem grit her teeth. "He'll never know."

Caspen turned to her slowly. "Won't he?"

His eyes bored into hers. Tem knew he wouldn't tell Leo she'd petrified someone. It would put her in danger, and Caspen would never allow that. She understood what he was really saying: that the truth would always come out—that she would not be able to keep this secret forever, especially from someone who asked her not to lie to him.

Before she could think of a response, Caspen brushed past her, heading for the door.

"Caspen," Tem cried after him. "Don't leave me. *Please.*"

Caspen's jaw tightened. His voice was deathly quiet as he said, "And why should I stay? I have no doubt you can find company if you desire it."

"The only company I desire is yours."

"I find that difficult to believe."

Tem stepped closer. He was not the only one who was angry here. "You don't take me hunting anymore. You've given up on me."

"I have not *given up* on you," Caspen snapped. "I would never do that. But I cannot take you hunting when I require it far more often than you do and it clearly strains you to transition."

There it was. The truth that neither of them wanted to face. Tem could barely transition anymore. Only now she knew it was because of Leo—that her inability was no mere matter of will, that it would continue to strain her until she consummated the crest. But to Caspen, she just seemed incapable.

"And now I find myself wondering whether it truly strains you at all," he said.

"Excuse me?"

"You must transition in order to petrify. Were you able to do so?"

Tem opened her mouth, then closed it. What was he implying? That she was purposefully being a burden to him but not to Apollo? That she was using her weakness only when convenient, wielding it like a weapon to pit brothers against each other? The accusation made her want to scream. She'd just learned that she had to consummate the crest—she was *protecting* Caspen by not doing so. The only reason she'd sought solace with Apollo was because she hadn't been able to seek it with Caspen. He was the one who had driven her into his arms.

Tem squared her shoulders, preparing to defend herself. "It's not my fault that Apollo taught me what you wouldn't."

A moment passed. Then, to her surprise, Caspen relented. The anger left his eyes, and his fists unclenched. He took a step closer. "You are right," he said quietly. "I should have taught you how to petrify. It is no surprise that you sought that knowledge elsewhere. And it is certainly no surprise that my brother was so eager to provide it."

"He didn't mean to—"

"Yes, Tem," Caspen sighed. "He did. And I do not blame him." His eyes raked over her, and she knew he could smell the sex clinging to her skin. "How could he not like what he sees?"

There it was again: the familiar flare of jealousy, the hint of heat that always entered Caspen's eyes whenever his brother tried to staked his claim on her.

Tem took a step closer too. "What about you?" she whispered. "Do you like what you see?"

Caspen clenched his jaw. "You know I do."

Tem's gaze trailed down to his hardening cock. "Show me," she whispered.

An electrifying moment passed. Tem felt the temperature between them rise. Tendrils of smoke curled over Caspen's shoulders, skimming down the curve of his muscles. Pure anticipation shot through Tem as Caspen extended his hand to reach for her, stopping an inch from her skin.

A moment passed. Then another. Caspen frowned.

Fear bit suddenly into Tem. Perhaps he was angrier than he cared to admit—perhaps her seduction wasn't enough.

"Caspen?" she whispered. "What is it?"

His eyes met hers. There was fear in them. "I cannot touch you."

CHAPTER TWENTY-SEVEN

T EM FELT THE SUDDEN URGE TO CRY. "WHY NOT?"

He only shook his head.

She reached for him, determined not to let things end like this, but she found she couldn't touch him either. The moment Tem got near to him, her fingers brushed against something in the air—a barrier keeping her an inch away from his skin. It wasn't solid, exactly—more like a layer of energy that stopped her from moving any closer. Tem groped at it with increasing vigor.

"Caspen? What—?"

But there were no words for the experience. It was as if an invisible wall had formed between them, keeping them apart.

"I don't understand," she cried. "Why can't we—?"

Caspen only shook his head. A moment later, he was out the door.

"Hey!" Tem ran after him, struggling to keep up with his pace. "Where are you going?"

Caspen stared straight ahead. "We must find Adelaide."

"What? Why?"

"She has seen this before."

"Seen what before?"

Caspen didn't answer. He was barreling through the passageway, shoving basilisks out of his path. He could touch them easily; the barrier didn't seem to extend to those in his way.

"Why can't we touch each other?" Tem insisted, already short of breath. "What's going on?"

"I *do not know*, Tem," he snapped, still not looking at her. "I only suspect. That is why we must find Adelaide."

Tem knew Caspen well enough to know when he was done answering questions. Rather than ask any more, she concentrated on her breathing, trying to match his brutal pace. They were headed toward Adelaide's chambers, and Caspen didn't slow down even as the passageway became more confined. By the time they arrived, Tem was nearly doubled over.

Caspen threw open the door. "Adelaide," he began, "we—" But he cut off abruptly when he saw who else was in the room. Cypress and Adelaide were tangled on the bed, Cypress's head between Adelaide's legs. Both of them looked up in shock. As soon as Cypress recognized Caspen, her arm went around Adelaide in a protective embrace.

Surprise, then anger, then determined resolve flashed over Caspen's face in quick succession. He pointed at Cypress. "Leave us, Sister. Now."

Cypress shook her head, her arm still thrown over Adelaide. "I am not your pet, dear Brother. You cannot tell me what to do."

"*I said leave us.*"

Even Tem went still. Caspen's tone was the one he used when he was a moment away from losing his temper. It was a familiar tone to Tem, and surely to Caspen's sister as well.

"Cypress." Adelaide touched her cheek gently. "Please leave us. I will come to you when we are done."

It was her plea, finally, that made Cypress leave. She stood without another word, glaring at Caspen on her way out. He ignored her. The door had barely shut when Adelaide said, "Caspenon. You must understand that we—"

"I did not ask for an explanation," Caspen snapped. "Who my sister chooses to bed is not my concern. I cannot help it if she prefers my scraps."

Hurt flashed over Adelaide's face, but she quickly suppressed it. Her cheeks were flushed, her hair uncharacteristically mussed at the back. Tem had never seen her so vulnerable. She raised her chin. "Then why are you here?"

"I am here because Tem and I cannot touch."

Adelaide raised an eyebrow. Then she sat up slowly, crossed her legs, and positioned herself so she was facing them on the edge of the bed.

"You…cannot touch?"

In reply, Caspen reached for Tem, his fingers once again meeting the barrier between them. An ache ran through her at the sight of his hand an inch from her skin. Out of instinct, she reached for him too, stopping when she felt resistance just before his fingers. She stared at their hands, suspended in the air. The sight made her want to cry.

"*Kora,*" Adelaide whispered.

Caspen dropped his hand. "You have seen this before," he said sharply. "Is it the same?"

Adelaide's beautiful face darkened. She ran a palm over her hair, smoothing it. "I… do not know. It could be." Adelaide stood, crossing to them. She took Tem's hand in her own before grasping Caspen's in the other and raising them. All three of them watched as Adelaide pushed their hands together. A stubborn inch of air remained between them, vibrating with restrained energy.

Tem didn't understand it. But she hated it—and she couldn't take it anymore. "Will one of you please tell me what's going on?"

Neither basilisk answered.

Adelaide released their hands and muttered, "Remarkable. When did it begin?"

"Just now," Caspen replied. "Mere minutes ago."

Adelaide nodded. "I have only seen this once before, and I was very young."

"But you know what it means."

Adelaide bit her lip. "Yes," she said quietly. "I know what it means."

"*Well?*" Tem cried. "What does it mean?"

A perilous pause followed. In it, Caspen and Adelaide looked at each other. Tem saw a myriad of emotions flow between them—first shock, then disbelief, then resolve. What felt like an eternity passed before Adelaide finally answered. "It means that the Senecas have contested your marriage."

Tem blinked. "*Contested* it?" She glanced at Caspen, whose face was a stiff mask of anger. He seemed too irate to speak.

Adelaide continued, "When you married Caspenon, you wed outside your quiver. The Senecas take offense to this. By contesting your marriage, they are invoking an ancient process to challenge your union. You and Caspenon cannot touch each other until it is resolved."

Tem remembered what Caspen had told her: *The Senecas are angry. They feel I am corrupting one of their own.* She pictured the words on the courtyard wall: *Give her to us.* Here, finally, was the retaliation Caspen had feared. The Senecas were done waiting for her to join their side. They had warned her, and she had ignored them. And now they would take her by force.

"And how *exactly* will it be resolved?"

Adelaide's eyes slid to Caspen's, then back to Tem's. "There will be a tournament in your honor. The victor will win your hand in marriage."

The ground seemed to fall out from beneath her. "*Excuse me?*"

"Temperance," Adelaide said steadily. "There is no need to be alarmed."

"No need to be *alarmed*?" Alarm was all she felt.

"It is an honor to have one's marriage contested."

Tem thought back to when Adelaide had told her it was an honor to be pursued by Apollo and Caspen at the same time. *They desire you. You should take that as a compliment.* Tem was a little tired of being told that the inconveniences in her life were an honor. None of this felt like an honor. It felt like an enormous, insurmountable annoyance.

"It means you are a coveted prospect," Adelaide continued. "You are meant to enjoy the process."

Tem snorted. "Enjoy it?"

"Yes."

"But I don't want to be with anyone else. I'm already married to Caspen."

"Yes," Adelaide said gently, and Tem knew she was trying to placate her. "You are already married. But you must remember that basilisks do not conduct themselves as humans do. There is no law that joins you in matrimony. For us, marriage is simply a choice."

"But we're bound together by blood."

"The blood bond is significant. But all it means is that your lives are tied to one another."

Tem felt the sudden urge to scream. It was too much, these ridiculous rules and loopholes and *traditions*. There were not many times when she missed her life before Caspen, but for a single moment, Tem remembered how simple it had all once been. She thought about how her greatest worries were tending to the chickens or weeding the garden, how her nights consisted of nothing more than meeting Gabriel at the Horseman for a drink.

Then she remembered the pain. She remembered the dissatisfaction and the loneliness and the despair she'd suffered during her time on the farm. She was never going back to that. This was her life now, traditions and all.

Tem looked at Caspen. He was staring into the distance, his fists clenched at his sides. She imagined for a moment what it would be like to marry another—to have someone other than Caspen in her bed each night. There was only one man for which she'd entertain the thought, and he was engaged to someone else.

"This can't happen," Tem whispered.

"It is happening," Adelaide said. "The process is already in motion. Now that your marriage has been contested, the tournament must be held. It will determine who is worthy of your hand."

"Caspen is already worthy of it."

"Not to the Senecas."

Stubborn resistance curled in Tem. "But *why*? There are other inter-quiver couples. I don't see anyone else's marriage being contested."

"You are a Hybreed, Temperance. It is an incredible gift. Your loyalty is an advantage to whichever quiver you favor."

Tem hadn't found that being a Hybreed was an incredible gift. Being half-basilisk had caused her nothing but an insurmountable pile of trouble. There was nothing incredible about it.

"Tension has existed between our two quivers for centuries, Temperance. The quiver with a Hybreed has the upper hand. The Senecas know this, and they covet that power. They do not accept that you have married a Drakon. They want you on their side."

"But *I* don't want to choose a side," Tem insisted.

"You chose a side when you married a Drakon."

Now Tem looked at Caspen. His eyes were closed. Perhaps he was processing this in his own time. But Tem needed him right now.

"Caspen," she said firmly. "Say something."

Caspen heaved a great sigh, his chest rising and falling in what felt like slow motion. When he opened his eyes, he looked at her. "The tournament is an ancient tradition, Tem. It is bound by magic. *We*"—he raised his hand to touch her again before dropping it—"are bound by its magic."

A rock settled in her stomach. Tem wasn't used to Caspen admitting defeat. She refused to marry another. Why didn't he feel the same?

"But why now? Why didn't they just prevent us from getting married in the first place?"

"They should have," Caspen said. "But my father placated them. He promised to use you to defeat the royals. Now he is dead, and the humans are still in power. The Senecas are angry he broke his word."

"This is ridiculous," Tem said.

Caspen sighed. "Perhaps to you. But you are a Seneca, Tem. Your quiver has every right to present a more suitable match for you."

"There is no more suitable match for me."

Caspen gave her a small smile. "I agree."

It was unfathomable to Tem that everyone would be so involved in their business. Basilisks were so *nosy*. Everything was a community event—every decision needed approval—everything was voted on and discussed and considered by a great many people before it was allowed. She couldn't understand it. For all the freedoms the basilisks enjoyed in their sex lives, the rest of their society was rigidly structured. It was a bizarre juxtaposition and one Tem would never get used to.

"You said they will present a suitable match," she said slowly.

"That is correct," answered Adelaide.

"So who will they present?"

Adelaide glanced at Caspen. "We…cannot know for sure. Only the highest-ranking male has the power to contest a marriage."

"And who is their highest-ranking male?"

Caspen rolled his shoulders. Tem knew him well enough by now to know that something bad was incoming.

"*Who*, Caspen?" Tem insisted. But she already knew.

There was only one Seneca who would care enough to contest her marriage to Caspen—one man who would do anything to destroy the home she'd built here.

Tem already knew.

But Caspen answered anyway. "Rowe."

CHAPTER TWENTY-EIGHT

———•◦✳◦•———

R OWE.

The very basilisk she wished never to see again, the one who had irreparably hurt her *and* Caspen. The basilisk who wished her dead.

"But Rowe hates me."

"He does not hate you, Tem," Caspen said. "He is envious of your power, and he carries a grudge against me. Marrying you would kill two birds with one stone."

"But he—he doesn't even have a—"

Caspen knew where she was going and answered, "A cock is not a requirement for marriage, Tem."

"It is for me."

Both basilisks smiled, but their grins quickly faded.

"Rowe is not the only factor at play," Adelaide continued. "They will present Eros as well."

"Who's Eros?" Tem interjected.

"Rowe's older brother."

"He has a *brother*?"

"He does."

This was terrible news to Tem. One Rowe was bad enough. Now there were two of them?

Adelaide turned to Caspen. "Eros is known for his bloodlust," she said, her mouth tight with worry. "Rowe would be preferable."

"*Neither* would be preferable," Tem snapped. Caspen had to win. Any other result was unacceptable to her.

"Even if Eros wins," Adelaide continued, "knowing Rowe, he would kill his own brother to enact his first rights."

"Is that *allowed*?"

Caspen sighed, repeating the line he had told her once before: "Everything is allowed here, Tem."

Everyone processed his words in silence. All things considered, it was a disaster. "I won't participate," Tem said. "I refuse."

"Your marriage has been contested, Temperance," Adelaide said firmly. "It is not up to you. You must participate."

"But *why*?" She hated the desperation in her voice.

Empathy softened Adelaide's face. She placed a hand on Tem's shoulder. "Nothing is certain in our society, even marriages. There is always a chance that a stronger option could present itself."

But there was no stronger option than Caspen.

"You and Caspenon cannot touch until the tournament is complete," Adelaide continued. "And even then, you will only be reunited if Caspenon is the victor. If Rowe wins—"

"Rowe will not win," Caspen cut her off.

Adelaide pursed her lips with annoyance. "I said *if*, Caspenon. *If* he wins, Temperance will have to marry him. We must all prepare for that possibility."

Tem crossed her arms. She would do no such thing. The thought of marrying Rowe was abhorrent. She'd kill herself before she let that happen.

Caspen must have read her thoughts because he shook his head and said, "Put that out of your mind, Tem. It is not an option."

"And why not?"

A small smile tipped his lips. "I would rather not die just yet."

Immediately, Tem understood. The blood bond tied them together. If she killed herself, it would kill Caspen too. She shook her head. "This is ridiculous. If I'm so powerful, why can't I call off the tournament? Why can't I make us touch again?"

"It is like Caspenon said: this is a magic greater than you. We believe the tournament is sanctioned by Kora herself."

"It is meant to test our love, Tem," Caspen added.

Tem couldn't think of anything worse to test right now. She was already struggling with her feelings for Leo—feelings that were likely to get her killed. It was not an ideal time to put a strain on their relationship. The last thing she needed was for everything to be out in the open.

"Basilisks take their traditions seriously," Adelaide continued gently. "You must adhere to the results of the tournament. We all must."

Tem wasn't in the mood to adhere to the results of anything. She abhorred the idea of someone else deciding her partner for her. Of all the basilisk traditions, this was the most ridiculous. Why would she ever accept any other outcome than Caspen?

Tem needed more information. She was dying to know what the tournament entailed, how exactly they would compete for her hand. If Caspen was going to beat Rowe, they needed to be prepared. She turned to Adelaide. "You said you've seen this before. What happened?"

"My grandmother was a Drakon, my grandfather a Seneca. The Drakons contested their marriage, and my grandfather had to fight for their love."

"Fight?"

"Yes."

Tem turned to Caspen. "I don't want you fighting anyone. If there's a chance you could get hurt, I don't want you doing this."

"You have already made it abundantly clear that I am not allowed to die."

Tem almost smiled at that.

"But I am afraid it is not up to you," he sighed. "The tournament is binding. I must participate. To do otherwise would be an insult to both our quivers and most of all an insult to you. If I do not compete, I surrender you to the Senecas."

He sounded resolute, as if he had accepted this a long time ago. And perhaps he had. Caspen had seen the warnings—the angry group of Seneca man, the writing on the wall. This was not a surprise to him, even if it was to Tem.

"The goal of the tournament is not bloodshed, Temperance," Adelaide explained.

Tem didn't know whether to feel relieved at that statement or not. If it wasn't about bloodshed, it was probably about something else—something worse. "Then what is the goal?"

"Your pleasure."

Tem snorted. She couldn't imagine anything centering her pleasure less.

"It is true, Temperance. By competing for your hand, the contenders honor you."

"I don't need Rowe or his stupid brother honoring me."

"They...will not be the only contenders," Adelaide said.

"Excuse me?"

She shifted, glancing at Caspen. "Rowe and his brother will not be the only ones competing for your hand in marriage."

Tem stared at her. "What do you mean? Who else is competing?"

"We do not know yet."

"When will we know?"

"When you choose them."

"What?"

"The tournament is for your hand, Tem. It is *you* who must choose who has the privilege of competing. You will select the rest of the contenders."

"The *rest*?"

"Yes."

Dread piled up in her like snow. "How many exactly?"

Adelaide's eyes slid to Caspen's, who gave a stilted shrug that clearly said: *Just tell her.*

"There will be twelve contenders total."

"Twelve?"

"Yes. It is a sacred number to us."

"Sacred how?"

"It is a symbolic number, representative of Kora's lovers."

"I didn't know she had twelve lovers."

Adelaide raised an eyebrow. "Did they not teach you the legends in your human schools?"

They hadn't taught her much of anything in school, except what to expect from the training process. And even that, nothing could have prepared her for. Tem shook her head.

Adelaide elaborated. "It is said that when Kora decided she wanted a mate, she took twelve lovers and had a child by each. Those twelve children were the first of the basilisks."

Tem blinked. She knew the basilisks worshipped Kora, knew they shared the same gods as the humans. But she'd never known that they believed they were descended from Kora herself, that they considered themselves offspring of the gods. Tem thought about her freckles, how there were exactly twelve on each palm. She was beginning to feel lightheaded.

"It's like the ritual all over again," Tem whispered.

To her surprise, Adelaide shook her head.

"No, Temperance. The ritual required you to prove yourself to us. Now it is the opposite. The contenders will be vying for your hand. They will view it as an honor to be chosen by you."

Tem turned to Caspen. "I'm going to choose you."

Caspen smiled. "Yes, that is the hope. But your heart may call to someone else, Tem."

"How would it do that?"

"The tournament demands that you be honest with yourself. When it is over, your heart will call to your true mate."

"Then my heart will call to you."

"You cannot predict the outcome of the tournament."

"Of course I can."

"No." He shook his head. "You cannot. It is not your decision to make."

Tem shook her head. "I don't understand. You said I would get to choose."

"Your *heart* will choose. The heart does not practice logic or reason—it cannot decide who is best for you—it will simply decide who it wants most. It is not a practical choice, but a fated one."

Tem didn't like the sound of that at *all*.

Caspen finished quietly, "If your heart calls to someone other than me, we will both be forced to abide by its choice."

This was a terrible time for Tem to be put to a test of fate. Her heart was in two places; it always had been. What if her heart called to Leo? She could only hope that a human wasn't included in the ancient magic of the tournament. Perhaps her heart would only consider fellow basilisks. Of course, that wasn't good either. Tem thought about Apollo and how close they had been lately. She couldn't deny that there was an intimacy between them. It certainly wasn't love, and it was nothing compared to what she had with Caspen. But the heart often knew things far before the mind did. And based on what Caspen had told her, it seemed there was always the possibility of surprise. *The heart does not practice logic or reason.* That much was certainly true. And it might be the end of her.

"Temperance," Adelaide said. "I know this must be a lot to process. But you will be partaking in a tradition that is centuries old. The tournament has a purpose—one that is bound by fate. It is how we will judge who is worthy of your hand."

"Caspen is already worthy of it. We're *already married.*"

"That may be the case. But two things can be true. You are already married, and that marriage is now in question. Those are the facts."

Tem crossed her arms. As it turned out, she hated those facts. She opened her mouth to protest again, but Adelaide held up her hand.

"It is an honor to compete for you. Our people will be anticipating the tournament."

Tem shook her head. She'd had just about enough of these infernal basilisk traditions. Could they not do anything *normally*? Everything was a ceremony or a tradition or a special process that required a thousand impossible steps. Everything was complicated and impossible. Tem was tired of the course of her life being determined by a group decision. If she couldn't decide who she wanted to spend the rest of her life with, then what was the point of living at all? Perhaps death was preferable to such a lack of control.

"This is ridiculous. I don't want any part of it."

"You feel that way now," Adelaide said gently. "But you may find that the basilisk side of you demands to join."

"What happens if I refuse to participate?"

"It would be unheard of," Adelaide admitted. "But it will not matter whether you choose to participate. The tournament will go on."

"How?"

"The tournament is an avenue for your heart to make its choice. If you choose not to participate, the choice will be made for you."

Tem wrinkled her nose. "And how, exactly, will it be made for me?"

"The twelve contenders would all fight for you," Caspen said quietly. "To the death."

***

The next few days passed in a blur.

Mating season was over, but that did not mean it was quiet underneath the mountain. Buzz about the tournament spread quickly; Tem couldn't go more than a hundred feet in any direction without hearing someone whisper about her or Rowe, or both. Much to her surprise, the general consensus seemed to be excitement. Tem supposed she could understand that; anyone not in her position would have quite the show to watch in the coming weeks. But for Tem, this was the worst thing that could be happening. The tournament would determine who had her heart—something Tem herself did not know. And she was not ready to find out.

As if the tournament was not enough to worry about, Tem dreaded the next Sunday-night dinner. She found herself intermittently flexing her fingers, the pain from the wires still fresh in her mind. Tem had no idea whether the blood she'd given was enough to properly feed the villagers, but there had been no news from Gabriel, and hopefully that meant that, for the time being, it was.

Caspen was gone all the time now.

For some reason, Tem thought he might remain by her side now that the tournament loomed before them. They hadn't been able to touch each other since their marriage was contested, which meant they hadn't had sex either. Instead, Caspen was constantly out hunting, whether to keep up his strength or simply avoid his circumstances, she did not know. Perhaps it was too painful for him to be near her and not touch her. But it was painful for Tem too, and she was in no mood to be alone. By the time Saturday night came around, she was sick and tired of being lonely. Tem groped for him with her mind, pressing against his presence as soon as she found him.

Caspen.

Tem.

Come home.

I am hunting.

But I miss you.

I miss you too. But I am also hungry.

She sent him a vision of them together: his head between her legs, his mouth on her center, showing him what he could eat instead. Equal parts arousal and agony swept through Caspen. Tem knew he wouldn't be able to touch her. But she wanted him anyway.

Come home.

His presence grew in her mind, tightening around the base of her neck. *And what will you do if I come home?*

Anything. Tell me.

Anything?

Yes.

I want you in our bed by the time I return.

What else?

I want you on your back with your legs open.

And then?

I want you soaking wet and ready to come. Can you do that for me, Tem?

Tem blushed so hard, it became difficult to concentrate. She could do that for him. And she would like it. So she said, *Yes.*

She lay on her back, just as he'd asked. She was wet already, and the moment air hit her center, she became even wetter.

Touch yourself.

Tem did so.

She dipped easily into her wetness, playing first with her clitoris before slipping her fingers deep inside. Tem concentrated on how it felt, focusing on the slick sensation, imagining Caspen was doing it instead. It was hard to believe she'd spent so many years doing this alone in her bedroom, and now she was doing it in the chambers she shared with her husband. Tem had spent so many nights in this bed, all of them with Caspen inside her. She thought about those nights, the way they'd moved seamlessly, crashing into orgasm again and again, together. Not a day had passed under the mountain when they hadn't had sex, and Tem hated that the days were passing in the opposite way now. She needed Caspen like she needed air. She needed his body and his cock and his hands all over her. Nothing she did to herself would ever compare.

Deeper, Tem.

Tem went deeper. He was almost back; she could feel his presence growing in her mind as he got closer and closer. Just when Tem couldn't bear it any longer, Caspen walked in.

Her breath caught in her throat at the sight of him. His shoulders were dappled with rain, dripping down his torso and tracing the ridges of his abdomen. Tem wished she could lick it off him. Just the sight of him was enough to bring her to the brink. His eyes were solid black, any trace of gold completely gone. If the circumstances were different, he would fuck her—he would *fill* her. But not this time. This time he crossed to the bed, grabbed his cock, and began to stroke.

It felt like their first time in the cave together—when Caspen had touched himself to the sight of her and Tem had done the same. So much had happened since then. Tem had grown immeasurably, and so had Caspen. They were married now, and they were bound together by blood. Now, when Tem looked up at the man she loved, she saw everything she'd had a thousand times before and she only wanted it more. Caspen was a king, and Tem his eager subject. It was an honor to witness such majesty.

Look at you, doing as you are told.

Tem bit her lip. She would do anything for him.

So good. So beautiful.

She would be beautiful for him.

Both hands, Tem.

Tem used both hands, opening herself for Caspen, making sure he saw everything he deserved to touch. She wished dearly that this could end in sex. But if this was the only way she could have him, they would have to make it worth it.

Deeper.

She went even deeper.

Caspen's cock was hard in his hand, unyielding in its rigidity. Tem would never get used to making him this way. It was a privilege and an honor she couldn't comprehend, and she only hoped she was worthy of it.

Faster, Tem.

Tem went faster.

Again. Just like that.

She was desperate now. Desperate for him.

Again.

His commands were militant. Ruthless. But Tem didn't care. She wanted it this way, wanted Caspen to feel in control. She wanted to give him this, since she was unable to give him anything else. It was her pleasure to obey.

Do not come until I tell you to.

Now *that* would be difficult. Tem wasn't used to timing her climax and certainly not when she wanted it so badly. She immediately held her breath, somehow hoping that might help her resist. But nothing could stop the wave that built insistently in her core, pushing her toward inevitability.

Please, Caspen.

Not yet.

Please.

No. Behave.

Tem writhed on the bed. It was agony to deny herself this. But she wanted to do as

Caspen said; she wanted to behave. Before Tem could release her breath, Caspen was upon her. His knees pushed the mattress down on either side of her. He leaned down, positioning his face right above hers so they were looking each other dead in the eye as he *growled*. Tem heard the hunger in that growl, felt his lust for her in her very bones. She kept her eyes wide open as he straightened, shifting forward and holding his cock by its base.

Open your mouth.

Tem did so, like she had so many times before.

One stroke. That was all it took for Caspen's cum to pour onto her waiting tongue, slipping down the back of her throat. Tem swallowed, but Caspen wasn't done. He leaned back, flicking his cock across her neck and letting the rest of his release splatter onto her skin.

Now.

Sweet relief coursed through Tem. It took just one caress of her clitoris to take her straight into orgasm. She rode the wave gratefully, savoring the pure ecstasy that accompanied release. Caspen watched her proudly, his body still towering above hers. Tem knew he needed this, needed to see her submit. And she was happy to do so.

It was horrible not being able to touch him, and she knew it was even worse for him to resist her. But this was all they could do for now—all Tem could give him was a show. And that's what she did, sliding her hand once more between her legs. The other she raised to her mouth, licking her own wetness from her fingers. Caspen stroked his cock as she did it, making himself immediately hard again. It took everything in Tem not to sit up and take him into her mouth. Instead, she said, *I wish I could taste you.*

And I you.

I want you all the way down my throat.

His hand moved faster.

So did hers.

I want that too.

When you win the tournament, what's the first thing you're going to do to me?

Caspen's mouth twitched. *Touch you.*

And then?

Fuck you.

Tem's smile matched his. She couldn't wait. It was unbearable like this—just like their first time in the cave together, when Caspen told her he wouldn't touch her. That had been a choice; this was forced upon them by Rowe. It felt like wild rebellion to be with each other anyway—in whatever form that took—to refuse to let Rowe win. He could contest their marriage, but he would never contest their love for each other. That was theirs alone.

Her neck was still covered in his cum. Tem took what she could onto her fingers, raising them to her lips. Caspen watched her with complete concentration, pumping his cock through his fist, looking at nothing but her naked body beneath him. Tem knew he was imagining all the things he wanted to do to her. She wished dearly that he would do them.

This time Caspen came all over her breasts. Tem ran her hands through it, spreading it over her skin and rubbing it sensually around her nipples. Then she took herself there, using his essence and joining it with hers.

"My love," Caspen whispered as she came.

They fell asleep facing each other, their bodies an inch apart.

When she woke the next morning, Tem watched him as he slept. She would never get used to falling asleep without touching him and waking up the same. The barrier between them was already devastating, but it was especially horrible today, on Sunday, when all Tem wanted was to be held.

The day passed quickly, and the carriage ride to the castle was silent.

Tem thought of the other carriage rides, the ones where Caspen had touched her and kissed her and teased her. Now they sat six inches apart, completely silent, staring straight ahead. Not for the first time, Tem desperately wished things were different. She wished she hadn't crested Leo. She wished Rowe hadn't contested their marriage. It was all a mess. And it was all hers.

"Caspen," she whispered. She looked at his beautiful, sculpted face—the face she loved so much.

"What is it, Tem?" Always attentive, always tuned in—that was Caspen. It always would be.

"I'm scared," she whispered.

She was scared of so many things—of losing Caspen, of losing Leo, of the bloodletting, of the tournament. The list was growing so long, she couldn't even name them all.

In the darkness of the carriage, Caspen sighed. "As am I."

His admission chilled Tem. Caspen's threshold for fear was much higher than hers. If he was scared, it meant there was truly something to fear. Once again, Tem wanted to reach for him. Once again, she couldn't.

A butler ushered them into the castle and then into the dining room.

Leo and Evelyn were already there, sitting at the table. Leo stood up as she entered, and everything that had happened in the parlor flashed through Tem's mind. She remembered the glow of the fire, the heat of his skin. She remembered how he'd held her breasts and squeezed until she whimpered.

What if I asked to kiss you right now? Would you let me?

"Tem," he said, breaking her from her thoughts. "How are you?"

Tem blinked. She had no idea how to answer it. Rather than try, she said, "Can you just take me downstairs? I don't have all night."

Leo shook his head. "You won't be going to the dungeon this evening."

Tem glanced at Caspen, who looked similarly nonplussed. Evelyn, on the other hand, was fuming. She refused to stand, glaring at Tem from her seat at the table, her hands clenched in her lap.

"Why not?"

"Because we do not require your services anymore."

Tentative hope poured into her chest. Had they found a solution to the bloodletting? Another method to make money that didn't involve cutting her people open? The possibility was nearly too much to bear.

"And why is that?" she asked.

But rather than provide an explanation, Leo fell silent. His hands were clasped behind his back, his chin held high. He looked...resolved. Proud, even. It was the look of a man who had chosen to do the right thing, regardless of the consequences.

Tem looked from him to Evelyn and then back to Leo. Finally, she understood.

They had not found a solution to the bloodletting; she would not be going down to the dungeon for the sole reason that Leo didn't want to hurt her again. Tem thought of their conversation in the parlor—about how Leo had found out that Caspen healed her after he hurt her. *That's despicable*, Leo had said. Tem knew him so well—knew exactly how that revelation made him feel. He would have thought about it all night, racked with guilt, thinking about how, as long as he allowed her to bleed, he was despicable too.

Leo was done hurting her. And now everyone knew it.

"This is absurd," Evelyn said finally, her words stiff. "She has already volunteered. If she doesn't do this, we—"

"We will find another way," Leo said. "As we discussed."

"There *is* no other way," Evelyn snapped.

Beside Tem, something was brewing in Caspen's mind—something dark. She couldn't understand it; Leo was doing the right thing. Caspen should be happy.

"We will find a solution that works for everyone," Leo continued, his voice not quite as steady as before. "Tem and I can discuss—"

"Oh, *please*," Evelyn cried, finally standing. "You don't need to discuss anything. You just want another excuse to meet with her alone."

Tem's mouth fell open.

Leo looked equally shocked, his eyes flicking first to hers then back to Evelyn's. "Those meetings are necessary," he said slowly. "We need to figure out how our kingdoms can—"

But Evelyn was not having it. "Do you have any idea how humiliating this is, Leo? I already have to sit here every week and watch you stare at her. And now you put our kingdom at risk because you don't want her to bleed."

Tem noticed how she didn't say her name. Evelyn couldn't even name the thing that frustrated her—couldn't address her adversary directly. It was the behavior of a coward, and Tem had no respect for it whatsoever.

"I'm not staring at her," Leo said.

Evelyn let out a tortured laugh that sounded like a bird squawking.

Tem knew how much Leo hated lying, knew exactly what it had cost him to say that. This entire conversation was supremely uncomfortable for Tem. Caspen's mood, which was already terrible, had only gotten worse as it went on. She could feel his temperature rising beside her, his hands slowing balling into fists. Tem tried to understand where his rage was coming from.

Realization came to her: Leo may have done the right thing, but he'd done it *for her*. Because he loved her. Evelyn knew it—it was why she was so upset. And surely, Caspen knew it too. Perhaps he had been in denial before this. But now, with Evelyn laying everything out in front of them, there was no hiding it.

It was impossible to ignore the way Leo was looking at Tem. Those stolen glances were the only thing that kept her sane—the only reminder that, at one point, what they'd had was real. They were toeing the line of decency every single time they met together, and Tem wasn't sure how much longer they could keep this up before one of them inevitably crossed it. Most likely, it would be her. Her basilisk side longed to reach for him—to take him in her arms and kiss him senseless. She barely even felt guilt about it anymore. After what Maximus had told her in the dungeon, she almost *wanted* to destroy Leo's relationship with Evelyn. It was a horrible urge—one that was only made stronger by the way Evelyn was speaking to him. But she couldn't do that to Leo. Not without proof.

"You are making a fool out of me," Evelyn said. She pointed at Caspen. "Out of *us*."

Caspen's face twisted with disgust. Tem knew he wanted no association with Evelyn. Nobody could make a fool out of Caspen, and certainly not Tem. He might not like the way she felt about Leo, but he dealt with it in his own way. It was an insult for Evelyn to equate them, and Tem knew Caspen would take it as one.

Still, Leo said nothing.

But Evelyn wasn't done. "And why are you talking to her, anyway? You should be negotiating with the snake."

Caspen's head snapped up, and a chill shot down Tem's spine.

"Do not," he said, his voice deathly quiet, "call me that."

CHAPTER TWENTY-NINE

⸺•◦✳◦•⸺

ILENCE FELL. EVELYN'S THROAT BOBBED AS SHE SWALLOWED. SHE LOOKED ABSO-lutely terrified.

Tem braced herself for what Caspen would do next: yell or possibly break something. Instead he turned to Tem and said, "You do not need me here."

Then he left without another word. Tem stared after him in shock. They hadn't made it through a single dinner without Caspen leaving early. It was his routine. *You do not need me here.* Caspen meant in every sense. If Tem had Leo to protect her, what role could Caspen play?

Evelyn stared at Leo expectantly. He avoided her eye.

"Fine," she said. "You don't need me either. Enjoy your *meeting.*"

As quickly as the evening had begun, it was over. Tem and Leo were left alone again, with nothing to do but look at each other. Tem stared at him in silence, wondering what exactly they were supposed to do next.

"Tem," said Leo quietly.

She blinked. "What?"

"Will you stay?"

Tem sighed.

Evelyn was right; it was inappropriate for Tem to linger. But the fact remained that she wanted to—and needed to. Tem didn't see a world where Caspen would be willing to discuss strategy with Leo, especially after what had just happened. That task fell to her. And even if there was no strategy to discuss, Tem would stay. The crest was still drawing them together—her heart still ached for him. It didn't matter that the world was falling apart around them. Tem wanted to stay.

"Yes," she said.

They went to the library.

Leo crossed immediately to the liquor cabinet and poured himself a glass of whiskey, downing it in one go. The cords of his neck flexed as he swallowed.

He turned to face her. "Do you have to look so good when you come here?"

Tem's mouth fell open. She was so surprised that she replied without thinking, "You're one to talk."

It was true; Leo looked *so* good. The top button of his shirt was undone, revealing the full length of his throat. His hair had started the evening combed back, but after running his fingers through it, blond pieces fell perfectly over his forehead. He looked the perfect amount of disheveled, as if he'd just finished having sex. The thought made Tem immediately wet.

"Don't do that," Leo said.

"Do what?"

"Don't compliment me."

Tem tried to smile. "That's my line."

His frown only deepened. "Evelyn's right. We shouldn't be doing this."

Tem didn't reply. Of course they shouldn't be doing this. But they were doing it anyway.

A long moment passed. Leo poured another glass of whiskey and handed it to her. "The protests have stopped," he said.

Tem took a moment to feel relief, to know that between her session in the dungeon and Gabriel's visit beneath the mountain, there was temporary peace.

"But if there is to be no more bloodletting..." Leo trailed off.

Tem knew what he was going to say. This was just a lull in protests; as soon as the supply from Tem's blood ran out, the villagers would be starving again.

They would be back at square one.

Leo sighed, running a hand through his hair again. "I don't know what to do, Tem. Things are...not good. The villagers are angry. Your people broke the truce. They won't forgive it."

The image of Jonathan and Christopher flashed through Tem's mind.

Caspen had broken the truce. For her.

"My people had a good reason," she said.

Leo's eyes met hers in genuine surprise. "Which was?"

Tem froze. She'd keep Caspen's secret out of fear of what might happen if Leo knew he was the one responsible. But if they were to truly rule their kingdoms in tandem, perhaps Leo deserved to know the full story. Perhaps he deserved the truth.

"Caspen is the one who petrified Jonathan and Christopher."

Leo raised an eyebrow. "And *why* would he do that?"

"It was...retaliation."

The inevitable question followed: "Retaliation for what?"

Now Tem hesitated. How much should she reveal? It wasn't a matter of preserving Jonathan's and Christopher's reputations—they were dead. But Tem wondered how Leo might react to the specifics. It might make him angry. But it also might help him understand why Caspen had done it, so she said, "They hurt me."

A waterfall of emotions passed over Leo's face in quick succession. First shock, then anger, then outright concern. "*What?* How?"

"It's...not important."

"I beg to differ."

"Leo," she said tiredly. "Please."

"Tem." She saw his fingers tighten on his whiskey glass. "Tell me."

She sighed. There was no avoiding this—she knew he wouldn't drop it, and part of her was happy that he cared. But another part of her had no interest in telling him about the assault. It wasn't something she wanted to think about ever again, much less describe in detail.

"They ambushed me," she said, keeping it as simple as possible. "When I was alone on the trail. They...touched me."

Leo's face went white. "Touched you how?"

"It's not important," she said again, firmly this time. Tem meant it. There was no reason for him to know any more.

In response, Leo poured another whiskey, this one significantly larger than the first. "You should have told me," he said through gritted teeth.

"It wasn't exactly dinner-table conversation, Leo."

"I don't mean tonight. I mean you should have told me back when we were—"

His sentence died on his tongue, but Tem finished it anyway: "Together."

The word lingered in the air.

Leo threw back a gulp of his whiskey.

Tem sighed. "There was no reason for you to know, Leo. Caspen handled it."

"I understand he handled it. But that doesn't mean you shouldn't have told me. For Kora's sake, Tem. I defended them in front of the entire village. I said their deaths were *devastating.*"

Tem remembered his speech, how it was meant to placate the villagers. She could understand where his anger was coming from. But she didn't blame him for defending them. It was his duty to defend his people.

"What do you want me to say, Leo? It would have been wrong to put you in a position where you had to choose between your subjects and me."

He let out a bitter laugh. "Please, Tem. You've never had a problem putting me in a position to choose."

His words stung her. *She* was the one who had to choose. "That's not fair and you know it."

Leo merely shook his head. "Unbelievable," he whispered. "You are fucking unbelievable."

Tem crossed her arms. They were getting nowhere. "I'm sorry Caspen broke the truce. And I'm sure he'd apologize himself if you want him to. But you can't blame him for retaliating."

"No, I…" Leo trailed off, swirling his whiskey. Suddenly, his resolve seemed to break. "I would have done the same."

There was a gentle pause. Tem could feel Leo's mood soften, and hers as well.

"It doesn't change the fact that my people are angry," he continued quietly. "A man disappeared a few days ago. He lived alone, on the outskirts of the village. Evelyn thinks it was the basilisks."

Fear pierced Tem's gut. It wasn't just the basilisks—it was *her*.

"If he disappeared, then why would they assume it was the basilisks?"

"Who else would it be, Tem?"

She pursed her lips.

Leo leaned in. "Do you know something?"

Tem didn't answer.

Leo wasn't looking away. Caspen's words ran through her mind: *What will your little prince think of what you did?* Tem knew exactly what Leo would think. He would be disgusted, and he would have every right to be. Tem had become the thing the villagers feared: the thing she herself had always feared. She couldn't tell Leo it was her fault. She couldn't bear for him to look at her any differently.

"Tem." Leo broke her from her thoughts. "What is going on with you?"

"What do you mean?"

"I mean you look…tired. Is everything…well?"

Everything was *not* well. Her body, although exhausted, was fine. Her mind, on the other hand, was a different story. All Tem could think about was everything that could possibly go wrong. It wasn't just the bloodletting; the tournament loomed in her mind like a shadow, threatening to engulf her. Her relationship with Caspen—which was already faltering—was now in serious danger. She should have expected Leo to notice that something was wrong. It was in his nature to notice her—to care. Even when she was no longer his to care for.

"I don't know," Tem whispered. It was too much to explain—too much to bear.

His eyes pierced hers. "Tem," he said, a hesitancy to his voice. "I am always here for you. If you need me."

Tem looked at the fire—it was easier than looking at him.

Leo was out of line to offer himself to her like that. They were not confidants; they were not friends. This was a business relationship now—a political partnership that needed to function perfectly if they were to continue ruling their kingdoms together. Leo knew exactly what his words would do to her, knew exactly how they would make her heart beat faster. Tem hated that she was so predictable. But that didn't mean she wanted him to stop.

She studied the angles of his face, his sharp cheekbones. He looked different than he had even just last week, hollowed out, as if something were eating him from the inside out. She should be asking if *he* was well, not the other way around. But there was no point in asking. Tem knew what was ailing him: the crest. Another problem there was no solution for.

"I'm just…overwhelmed," she said simply.

He nodded. The firelight flickered across his face. "I see. For any particular reason?"

Tem couldn't imagine telling Leo about the tournament. But she'd already told him that Caspen broke the truce, and he'd taken that well enough. What was one more piece of information? Besides, the outcome affected him too. Rowe was violent and unpredictable. He hated the humans. If he won, he would not hesitate to wage war.

"Things are…complicated under the mountain right now."

Leo took a deep breath, as if he were steeling himself. "Complicated how?"

"My marriage has been…contested."

Leo frowned. "I don't understand."

Tem barely understood it herself. "There's going to be a…" She physically couldn't bear to say the word *tournament*, settling instead on "…fight."

Leo shifted. "Are you in danger?"

"No," she said quickly. "Well. Not…immediate danger."

"I'd rather you weren't in any danger at all, Tem. Immediate or otherwise."

She had to smile at that. "I'm not in danger. Caspen has to fight another basilisk for me."

"Why?"

Tem sighed. "In order to explain it, you need to know that basilisks belong to quivers."

"Quivers?"

"They're sort of like clans or groups."

Leo nodded, and she continued.

"Caspen and I are from different quivers."

"I see."

"And the basilisk contesting my marriage is from my quiver."

"So your quiver…"

"The Senecas," Tem offered.

"The Senecas…they don't want you and Caspen to be married?"

"Yes."

Leo looked down at his whiskey. "That's ridiculous, Tem."

That was certainly true. But it didn't mean it wasn't happening. "It's complicated, Leo. Basilisks have all sorts of rules—"

"Who gives a fuck about their rules? You can't just *marry some other basilisk.*"

"I can if he wins the fight."

The look on Leo's face was one of pure horror. And Tem couldn't blame him. When she spelled out this situation like this, it sounded absolutely unhinged. But that was the basilisks for you. Nothing they did was even remotely normal.

"It's not within my control, Leo," she said quietly. "I can't predict the outcome. Caspen is the one fighting for me."

"Well," Leo said through clenched teeth, "he'd better win."

Tem raised an eyebrow. "Do you want him to?"

Leo ran a reckless hand through his hair. "It's bad enough you're with him, Tem. But it would be even worse if you were with someone else. At least I know he loves you."

His words shocked her. They were extremely candid—almost accidentally so. She doubted he'd meant to reveal so much to her. But now that she'd heard it, she had to know: "Do…you love me?"

His jaw clenched. "If you have to ask that, you don't know me at all."

"I know you," she whispered.

"Do you?"

Yes. She knew Leo. She knew him *so* well. She knew that he could never stop loving her, just as she could never stop loving him. She knew that it was torture for him to be standing this close to her, unable to touch her. Just as it was torture for her. She knew that if they had their way, they would both be naked in his bed right now.

"Then tell me, Tem," he looked straight at her. "Do I love you?"

Her answer came as easily as breathing. "You love me. You always will."

Leo was *hers.* They *belonged to each other.*

He was standing too close. They were breathing the same air. The predator in her screamed for release. In another world, they would kiss. In another world, they would get in his bed and never leave it. But in this one, they simply stared at each other, both of them bound by promises they had made to the people they loved. The problem was they also loved each other.

"Is there no chance for us?" Leo whispered.

Tem couldn't answer. She didn't dare.

"Answer me, Tem."

An order. One she couldn't obey.

"You promised," Leo whispered, his lips inches from hers. "Remember? You promised you wouldn't lie to me."

Tem closed her eyes because she couldn't look at him anymore. Of course she remembered. She remembered it like it was yesterday. But she could no longer keep that promise. If she told Leo the truth, that they had a chance—that they would *always* have a chance—it would destroy him. She couldn't do that to him. Not again.

Tem opened her eyes. "Your future wife is waiting for you, Leo."

Darkness passed over him. "And your husband is waiting for you. Although depending on this *fight*, I suppose he might not be your husband for long."

Tem hated how right he was. "Caspen will win," she whispered.

This time, Leo didn't say he wanted him to. "It doesn't matter, Tem. Just fix this so we can move forward."

Tem pursed her lips. It wasn't so simple, and Leo knew it. Things were delicate under the mountain. If one tinder flickered into flame, it could set the entire kingdom on fire.

"I'm trying to fix it," she whispered. "You know I am."

He shook his head. "Don't *try*. Just do it." Leo slammed his whiskey down on the desk. A moment later he was gone.

Caspen was asleep in their bed when Tem returned. Dirt was smeared on his neck, along with blood. He'd been hunting.

"Caspen," she whispered. He didn't stir. She felt for the corridor between their minds, but it was closed.

"Caspen," she said again, louder this time.

His eyes opened slowly. "Tem," he murmured.

"I'm sorry," she said immediately.

Caspen rose an expectant brow. He sat up slowly, holding her gaze. "For?"

"For…"

There was so much to be sorry for. It wasn't just the evening's events that warranted an apology—it was everything that had happened since Tem got married to Leo. Everything had gone wrong, and she was running out of ideas on how to fix it.

"I'm sorry Evelyn called you a snake." It was the least she could say.

Caspen lifted his chin. "*She* is the snake."

Tem had no response for that. Evelyn was duplicitous and scheming and cruel. She moved quietly in the darkness, then lied when she was exposed. He was right; Evelyn was a snake.

There was a long pause, and Tem wondered whether she should also apologize for staying behind to talk to Leo. Before she could decide, Caspen said, "The Senecas will arrive tonight."

Dread twisted Tem's stomach. "For the tournament?"

"Yes. There will be a celebration, at the lake. The tournament will begin tomorrow."

She nodded. A couple days. That's how much longer they had to go without touching each other. She could survive that. Couldn't she?

"Tem," murmured Caspen. "What is on your mind?"

There was only one thing on her mind. "I miss you," she whispered.

"I am right here."

But that was barely true. Physically, he was right in front of her. But in reality, he may as well have been a thousand miles away. It was torture not to touch him—torture to see what she couldn't have. It was the exact same feeling she had every Sunday night when she watched Leo with Evelyn.

"I need you, Caspen."

His expression softened. He shifted closer, his body angled toward hers. "You have me, Tem. You will always have me."

She stared into his golden eyes, trying to find the truth in them. Did she really have him? Would they survive the tournament—would her heart call to his? Tem had no idea what to expect from herself anymore. All she knew was that right here, right now, she missed him.

"Lie down," Caspen said quietly. "We should rest."

Tem lay down. But instead of resting, they talked—about everything and nothing, anything but their current circumstances. Tem told him about her childhood, how the schoolchildren had teased her. Caspen told her about his family and how difficult it was to grow up with Bastian as a father. It was the first time they'd talked like this. Their connection had always been physical. But it was beautiful to connect with him this way as well, on an emotional level. Tem wondered if they ever would have had such a conversation if their marriage hadn't been contested and they hadn't been able to touch. She found it remarkable that the very thing pulling them apart now drew them together.

Tem drank Caspen in: his beautiful body, his dark hair, his sharp jaw. She memorized every inch of him as if it were the last time she was ever going to see him. Caspen did the same, his gaze lingering on every part of her. When they were finally done talking, Tem touched herself, and he watched. Then he touched himself too. When he came, he formed his essence into a claw and set it on her stomach. This, at least, he could still give her. Tem savored its weight. Then she inserted it slowly, her legs wide open so he could see it disappear into her inch by smooth inch. Caspen watched every moment of it, his eyes completely black.

Eventually, they headed to the lake. By the time they arrived, the celebration had already begun. The cavern was even bigger than Tem remembered it, the lake going on for what seemed like miles before disappearing into the horizon. The sloping shore was already packed with basilisks, all of them naked. Tem stared out over the chaos. She shook her head in wonder.

I'll never get used to this.

Yes, you will. It is a part of you.

They walked to the edge of the lake together.

"Do you remember your first time here?" Caspen asked.

"Of course," Tem said.

She remembered it well, how it felt to stand in the lake where Kora had bathed, to feel the same water she had felt. It was a wondrous thing, and Tem did not take it lightly. The same energy she'd felt the last time she was here pricked again within her now: something otherworldly. Divine.

Caspen turned to her. "I was so proud of you that day," he murmured. "You were brave."

"I didn't even transition."

"But you tried. That is what made you brave."

It was typical of Caspen to praise her for accomplishing the bare minimum. But Tem found that she appreciated it, and for a moment, she allowed herself to be proud too. There was something to be said for simply trying. Many people were too afraid to even do that.

They looked out over the water together. The claw pulsed.

"How is it that we were able to transition here?" Tem asked. "Shouldn't the reflection have killed me?"

"I am surprised it took you so long to ask." Caspen smiled. "The lake is sacred. It does not affect us the way other reflections do. It is the only reflective surface that cannot kill us when we wear our true forms."

Before Tem could ask any more questions, Adelaide approached. "Temperance," she said smoothly. "How are you this evening?"

"Fine, I guess," she said.

Adelaide nodded. Then she turned to Caspen. "The council wishes to speak with you."

Caspen nodded. "Very well."

"It is nothing to fear, Temperance," Adelaide said at the look on her face. "This is standard. The council always meets with the spouse the night before the tournament."

Still, Tem worried. Every moment she was separated from Caspen felt significant, as if they might never be reunited. With one last lingering glance at her, he disappeared.

With Caspen gone, Adelaide became Tem's guide.

They moved through the crowd together, and Tem used the time to look at all the Senecas. They were staggeringly beautiful, just like the Drakons, but theirs was a different beauty: more ethereal, less harsh. Whereas Caspen's features were sharp and severe, the Senecas seemed softer somehow, as if they were sculpted by the same artist but from a different stone.

"So how does it work?" Tem asked.

Adelaide raised an eyebrow. "How does what work?"

"The tournament. What's the…schedule?"

It felt wrong to refer to it as if it were a sporting event. But perhaps that was exactly what it was. And if Tem was going to be put through this ridiculous ordeal, she wanted to be prepared.

"It will officially begin tomorrow morning," Adelaide replied. "There will be a feast in the banquet hall. Both quivers will be in attendance."

Tem didn't like the idea of breaking bread with Rowe or his stupid brother.

"You will choose eight contenders at the feast," Adelaide continued.

"Eight? I thought there were twelve."

"Some of them have been chosen for you. Rowe contested your marriage, so he will automatically participate. Caspenon is defending his marriage, so he must participate as well. Each of them will choose an alternate—someone they trust with you should they fail to win your hand themselves. The remaining eight contenders are up to you."

Tem took a moment to process this. Who would Caspen choose as his alternate? Adelaide was already answering her question before she asked it. "Caspenon will choose Apollo. He has first rights to you anyway."

Tem's heart beat a little quicker. "And how will I pick the final eight?" She knew basilisks well enough by now to know that it would not be as simple as pointing her finger.

"Only men whose ranking is high enough to qualify for the tournament will be eligible. You will select from that group."

"Just men?"

Adelaide raised an eyebrow. "Would you prefer to include women?"

Tem considered the question. The only experience she'd had with a woman was with Adelaide, and although she'd certainly enjoyed it, she didn't crave women the same way she craved men. For something as paramount as this—with her entire future on the line—it was probably better to stick with what she knew.

Tem shook her head. "No."

"In that case, the men will present themselves for your consideration," Adelaide continued.

Tem's eyes narrowed. "Present themselves how?"

"They will stand before you," Adelaide continued, her mouth upturned. "To give you an opportunity to compare their…physicality."

Tem's mouth fell open. "I'm supposed to make my decision based on their *cocks*?"

Adelaide smiled. "You are choosing potential mates, Temperance. It is essential that you see what they can offer you."

"Is that all?" Tem asked, by now dreading the answer.

"Once you have made your selections, you will seal your choices with a kiss."

Tem blinked. She would have to kiss each of the contenders?

Adelaide must have seen the look on her face, because she said, "The kiss is only the beginning, Temperance."

Of course it was.

"The tournament will follow a specific structure," Adelaide continued. "There will be three tiers of competition—one based on strength, one based on seduction, and one based on the heart."

Tem waited for details. She already didn't like where this was going.

"The first tier is simple: it will involve only Caspenon and Rowe. They will transition, and they will fight for your hand."

Tem didn't like that at *all*. "And then?"

"The remaining contenders will give a…demonstration."

"A demonstration of what?"

"Of…virility."

Tem crossed her arms. "I'm going to need exact details."

Adelaide smiled. "Is this how you are with Caspenon? Your persistence is rather exhausting."

"Yes."

The beautiful basilisk chuckled.

Tem just shook her head. "Details, please."

Adelaide was still smiling as she said, "The remaining contenders will bring themselves to climax in your honor."

Tem stared at her blankly. "In my *honor*? And what exactly is the point of that?"

"It is meant to impress you. The men who can finish the quickest are the most qualified to wed you."

"The *quickest*? Shouldn't it be the opposite?"

"Not in this case. They will be touching themselves to the sight of you; if it takes them too long to come, you should view that as an insult."

Tem was having a very difficult time wrapping her mind around this. But she supposed that, in some twisted way, it made sense. She wouldn't want to be with someone who wasn't turned on by her. Still, she couldn't imagine a group of men staring at her and stroking themselves all at once. She was just one woman.

"You said there were three tiers. What happens in the final tier?"

Now Adelaide fell silent.

But Tem already knew where this was going. She should have known the moment the tournament was mentioned at all. "Let me guess," she whispered. "I have to have sex with them."

"Yes," Adelaide said simply. "You do."

It was a testament to her indoctrination into basilisk culture that the news didn't faze Tem whatsoever. Her human side might have recoiled at the thought, but the basilisk side nearly *roared* with delight. Warm, lush anticipation filled her center. She thought of the ritual—of how she'd fucked Caspen's father in Kora's palms.

"And how exactly am I supposed to do that?" Tem asked.

"The men will line up and you will take them one after the other."

Tem's mouth fell open. "I have to fuck them all *in a row*?"

"Yes. We do it this way so that it is easy for you to determine who is best. It is meant to be quite straightforward."

Tem almost laughed. The thought of going down a line of twelve men was preposterous. *Nothing* about this was straightforward. But she understood how it seemed that way to Adelaide, how, in her mind, riding one cock after another was the best way to test their worth. Tem had stopped trying to find reason within their customs a long time ago. Now she simply took it as it came and tried not to lose her mind.

"Once you have completed the final tier, your heart will make its choice." Adelaide said.

"I will choose Caspen."

"You may. Or you may choose someone else."

"How can you say that?"

"The tournament is bound by Kora's magic—it is meant to reveal ultimate truths, to allow fate to run its course. While the outcome is technically determined by you, it is not *entirely* your choice."

"I don't understand."

"The main tenet of basilisk culture is that we cannot lie. The tournament will force

293

your heart to reveal its truth. It will call to your best match. No one, not even you, can know ahead of time who that will be."

"You're saying that it could call to Rowe."

"To Rowe, to Apollo, to any of the twelve contenders. Anyone is a possibility."

Tem couldn't fathom how her mind could want Caspen to be the winner, yet her heart might call to someone else. What if it called to Leo? But Leo wasn't even a basilisk—he didn't reside under the mountain; he wasn't part of the tournament at all. Or perhaps he was. She loved him, and she had crested him, and they had yet to consummate it. Perhaps that bond would draw her to him. Before she lost her nerve, Tem asked, "Can the heart call to someone who isn't a basilisk?"

Adelaide gave her a careful look. "I…do not know."

Dread sat in Tem's stomach. She probably shouldn't have asked that.

"I can understand how this may seem frightening to you," Adelaide said. "But to us, this is a momentous occasion. It will be the first tournament in decades. Everyone is looking forward to it."

Everyone but Tem.

"Temperance," Adelaide said gently. "You have nothing to fear."

But of course she did. Tem had *everything* to fear. If the point of the tournament was to reveal ultimate truths, there couldn't be a worse time for Tem to reveal them. She was keeping too many secrets, holding too many lives in her hands.

Before Tem could ask anything else, Cypress appeared beside her.

"Addy," she said. "There you are." Her gaze fell on Tem. "Would you mind if I borrowed her? I will bring her right back."

"Of course." Tem waved her hand. She'd kept Adelaide far too long anyway. "You should go. Enjoy yourselves."

Cypress beamed. Adelaide gave Tem one last reassuring smile before disappearing into the crowd. Tem had no choice but to wander the cavern alone, drinking elixir and watching the festivities. She was surrounded by basilisks, all of them touching each other, all moaning in collective desire.

Eventually, it became too much. There were too many bodies, too many sounds.

Tem walked until she reached the lake, letting out a sigh of relief the moment her feet met the water. The deeper she waded, the farther the relief spread. Eventually she was swimming along the edge of the lake, passing grottos clustered around the perimeter. Tem didn't have to look inside to hear that they were occupied. By the time she reached an empty one, her arms were growing tired. Silence fell as she reached the gaping entrance. A moment later her feet touched stone, and she walked out of the water onto a thick layer of moss. The grotto was tall; she could stand easily with plenty of room. Stalactites hung in glistening points above her, tiny droplets of water seeping from their points.

"All alone again, Temperance?" a voice boomed from behind her. "We really must stop meeting this way."

CHAPTER THIRTY

—••◦✳◦••—

A VOICE CAME FROM BEHIND HER, BUT TEM DIDN'T HAVE TO TURN AROUND TO know whose it was. Apollo immediately entered her mind.

You are without your chaperone.

Is that what you call Caspen?

What else should I call him?

He's your brother, isn't he?

That he is.

Tem turned to see Apollo stepping out of the water, his eyes on hers. He was already on his way to being hard. Tem tried not to stare at his cock, which was staring right back at her.

Apollo smirked. *I always tell you: you may look if you wish. It does not bother me.*

Tem was perfectly aware that it didn't bother him. She could see it in the arrogance twisting his cheeks. *Nothing bothers you.*

He raised an eyebrow. *Is that what you think?*

That's what I know.

Apollo approached her slowly, his footsteps steady despite the uneven terrain. *What else do you know, Temperance?*

The question was a challenge, and Tem was not in the mood to rise to it. *I know you shouldn't be talking to me.*

Talking to you is hardly a crime.

The way you talk, it is.

Another smirk. *Do you wish for me to stop talking? We could do something else instead.*

No.

Her protest was weak. She knew it, and Apollo knew it too. He had nearly reached her side of the grotto. The air was warm—thick and humid—and Tem was having trouble breathing.

Shall I tell you what I know?

I have a feeling you're going to anyway.

Apollo stopped right in front of her. He was shorter than Caspen but still far taller than Tem. She had to crane her neck to look up at him. *I know you like it when I talk to you this way.*

Tem remembered the last time she'd seen Apollo—how he'd made her come in less than ten seconds, his body pressed against hers as the sun rose above them.

Caspen wouldn't like it.

That is not my problem.

Tem sighed. It was about to be hers.

And where is my dear brother tonight?

He's talking to the council.

Apollo raised an eyebrow. A single drop of water slipped from a stalactite above them onto his shoulder. Tem watched as it slid down the expanse of his chest in an endless, wandering rivulet. She repressed the sudden urge to trace its path with her tongue.

Is that right? I am surprised he would leave you alone on the eve of the tournament.

I don't need him to coddle me. I can take care of myself.

I see. And yet, I have cornered you. Would you say that constitutes taking care of yourself?

Tem closed her eyes. Apollo was infuriating her, as usual. It was impossible to talk to him without it turning into something else. *Are all basilisks like you?* she asked.

Like what?

Infuriating. He let out a soft chuckle at that.

You find us infuriating?

I find you infuriating.

In what way?

Tem opened her eyes. Apollo was standing too close, as expected. That was already one way in which she found him infuriating. But the others were more subtle: like the way he turned every conversation into a flirtation or the way he constantly made her feel exposed. Tem settled on: *You keep trying to sleep with me.*

Apollo grinned with unmistakable triumph, his eyes raking over her. Tem was keenly aware that the tip of the claw was visible between her legs. She knew Apollo could see it. She knew he knew Caspen had made it for her.

Can you blame me?

Tem ignored the compliment. *You could at least be discreet about it.*

Is that really what you want?

Yes.

And here I was thinking you enjoyed my advances.

What could have possibly given you that impression?

Instead of answering, Apollo sent her a vision: first of her in the banquet hall, opening her legs in front of him. Then of her in the field, after he'd taught her to petrify, her head thrown back in orgasm. Apollo was right, and they both knew it. Of course Tem enjoyed his advances. If they truly bothered her, she would have left the grotto already. But she hadn't. Her basilisk side *preened* every time he looked in her direction. Only her human side recoiled, and that side was awfully quiet right now.

So tell me, Temperance. What else do you know?

She stared up at him, willing herself to focus. His eyes were a slightly different shade of gold than Caspen's, darker, as if tinted with copper. They were rapidly being overtaken with black. *I know you want me.*

His mouth twitched.

Tem continued. *And I know you only want me because it will make Caspen angry.*

Ah. That is where you are wrong.

Am I?

Yes.

And what exactly am I wrong about?

It will not make Caspen angry.

Tem remembered the possessive pleasure that had flashed in Caspen's eye when he'd realized Apollo was watching them in the banquet hall, how he'd displayed her for his brother.

And even if it did make my brother angry, it would not be the only reason I want you.

Tem didn't dare believe him. *Don't say things like that.*

Like what?

Things you don't mean.

And how do you know I do not mean them?

Because you don't take anything seriously, including this.

This?

Us.

Are we an us now?

No. We're not. I'm just saying that—

You are saying that I do not take whatever it is between us seriously. And once again, you are wrong.

Tem sighed, looking up at him. He was still smiling at her, still being infuriating. It was impossible to have a conversation with someone who was looking at her like that. Apollo was acting as if he were in on some big secret that Tem had no concept of. It was unfair, and she was tired of it.

I take us very seriously, Temperance. How could I not?

Tem didn't know how to answer that. She didn't know the full story of what had happened between Apollo and Caspen—didn't know the details of who they had both been with or what had happened to her. But Tem was not a replacement for that person. She was so much more than a prize in their game, and she refused to be treated as such.

Tell me something, Temperance. Why are you afraid?

Tem scoffed. "I'm not afraid." She said it out loud, as if that would make it more true.

"No?" Apollo matched her tone. "And yet, you demonstrate all the characteristics of fear."

"Such as?"

"Your heartbeat is accelerated. You are short of breath. I can smell your sweat." He smiled, breathing in. "It is sweet."

"Stop smelling my sweat, Apollo."

"I cannot avoid what is offered to me, Temperance."

"I'm not *offering* you anything. I'm just standing here."

"You are standing here afraid."

Despite herself, Tem knew he was right. And why, exactly, was she afraid? Did she fear something in Apollo, or did she fear something in herself? Which, ultimately, was worse? Tem had no idea anymore. Ever since she'd been under the mountain, her sense of morals and what was right had utterly changed. Basilisks didn't act like humans. They lived by different rules here, prioritized different things. It was impossible to tell right from wrong anymore.

"I…" she whispered, struggling to form the words. "Don't want to lose myself."

She knew in her heart that Apollo meant her no harm. But that didn't mean he was safe to be around. It didn't mean that she was safe with him. He was dangerous in the same seductive way that all basilisks were dangerous. He was depraved in a way Caspen wasn't; he allowed himself to walk the line of morality. If Tem allowed herself to walk that line too, she didn't know where it would end. She didn't want to stray from the path of light—didn't want to become something she was not.

"I would not let you stray."

Apollo's words were quiet, and Tem was struck by the meaning of them. She'd never heard him say anything heartfelt and sincere like that before. But if she allowed herself to believe him—to indulge in the fantasy that he had her best interests at heart—she would make herself vulnerable. It wasn't a risk she was willing to take. Before she could decide how to answer, the hairs on the back of Tem's neck stood straight up. Someone else had entered the grotto.

Apollo also straightened, his eyes still on hers as he said, "Hello, Brother."

CHAPTER THIRTY-ONE

❖

ASPEN WAS LEANING AGAINST THE MOUTH OF THE GROTTO. HIS ARMS WERE crossed, but he didn't look angry. Instead, his pupils were wide, his eyes nearly as black as Apollo's. Tem knew that look. Both brothers were turned on.

By *her*.

For a very real moment, Tem wondered what was about to happen next.

"What do have we here?" Caspen murmured.

"We were just talking," Tem said.

"Talking," he repeated, his voice low.

"Yes."

She glanced at Apollo for backup. His eyes were trained on Caspen's, his posture still stiff. Tem had no idea how to proceed. Of all the people in this cave, she hardly felt qualified to determine the course of events. Things were delicate between her and Caspen. Between petrifying with Apollo and the disastrous Sunday dinner, she had no idea where his mind was.

Both brothers stood silently, staring at each other. Tem was just considering breaking the silence when Caspen's presence entered her mind, settling next to Apollo's, as if they were both holding her skull in their hands. It was a strange sensation but not an unpleasant one. Tem's mind accommodated theirs with ease, stretching to take both of them at once.

Then Caspen's voice came to them, deep and languid in the darkness: *Touch her.*

For a moment, nobody moved.

Was Caspen testing her? Testing *them*? If so, why? Was this like when he ordered them to kiss the night Gabriel came under the mountain? Tem had disobeyed him that night. But now, a wave of possibility swept over her. They were sequestered in a grotto, where no one else could see them. Anything could happen in here. Anything *would*, The three of them were not bound by the conventions of human society—they didn't need to adhere to the rules she'd been raised to revere. Here, things were different. Here, they were free.

She looked at Apollo, who was looking at her.

Temperance?

Just her name, nothing else.

Tem looked into his eyes—eyes that were now completely black—as he extended his hand, stopping just short of her hip. A pause. Both brothers stared at her, waiting. They were on a precipice with only Tem preventing them from falling. But what if she wanted to fall? Nothing bad could happen here tonight. Caspen would never let her get hurt, and neither would Apollo. No harm would come to her at the hands of the Drakon brothers. And if that were truly the case, that meant they were here for one thing only: pleasure.

So Tem said, *Yes.*

Just one word. Permission.

As soon as Tem granted it, Apollo reached for her. His fingers skimmed over her skin, tracing up the curve of her waist. Tem's entire body erupted in goose bumps at the contact, and her nipples immediately hardened. Apollo raised his hand to meet them, brushing his palm over her breast. Tem bit her lip. The air of the grotto became so warm, she could feel the gold of her necklace singeing her skin. She was completely wet, and with both brothers in her mind, she knew they could tell.

Another command came from Caspen, this time for Tem: *Touch him.*

Something inside her stirred at his words.

Part of Tem yearned to obey. Her basilisk side had wanted to touch Apollo for a long time, far longer than she cared to admit. But her human side still hesitated. Even as his hands moved up her body, wrapping gently around her neck so his thumbs were cradling her jaw, feeling her pulse. Still, she hesitated. What would it say about her if she touched him? If she were just a human, it would mean being unfaithful. But the man before her and the man commanding her weren't human. They were basilisks. And everything was allowed here.

So Tem reached for Apollo.

When she was within an inch of his body she paused, waiting for Caspen to speak again. But he gave no more commands. Instead, a rush of desire bore down on her mind with such intensity that she winced. Caspen wanted her to *do as she was told.*

Good thing he'd told her to do something so tempting.

Tem's fingers found purchase, brushing over Apollo's impossibly warm skin. He held perfectly still as she touched him, pressing her palms flat against his torso. She slid her fingertips along the grooves of his abs, feeling every plane of muscle, noticing the way they shifted beneath her hands. Tem touched the great curve of his shoulders, sensing the unrestrained power in his body. He was truly an incredible man. Perhaps she hadn't allowed herself to see it until now. But now that she had, she could notice nothing else. There was a small scar on his left bicep. She brushed over it gently. Then she trailed her fingers back to the center of his chest, noticing the way his breath hitched while she did it. As her hands went lower, desire grew ferociously in her mind. Tem couldn't tell if it was Caspen's or Apollo's or her own. Ultimately it didn't matter.

When she reached the base of his cock, she paused. The air, already warm, became sweltering. Smoke was seeping from Apollo's skin and also from Tem's. A hiss filled the grotto, and she knew it as Caspen. Without wasting another second, Tem wrapped her hand around Apollo's cock. There was nothing more thrilling than holding this part of a man in her hand. It was pure adrenaline—pure power. Tem could snap him in half if she wanted to, right here and now. It didn't matter that Caspen was the one giving orders. What happened next was entirely in her control.

Tem dragged a single finger down his shaft in an imitation of what she'd made him do in the banquet hall, watching the way his face changed as she did so. Apollo's jaw clenched; his eyes fluttered shut. It was so easy with them, these brothers. To know one was to know the other. Tem knew what to do because Caspen had taught her but also because she felt an instinctive pull to Apollo in the same way she was drawn to his brother. Perhaps this was always meant to happen. Perhaps the three of them were always destined to end up in this grotto, the air on fire around them. It wasn't surprising to Tem. It was nothing more than fate.

She stroked Apollo slowly, feeling the friction of his skin against hers. His cock was warmer, if it was even possible, than his torso had been. Obsession, desire, and deep-seated hunger surged from both brothers' minds to hers. It was so overwhelming that Tem nearly dropped her hand. The moment the thought occurred to her, Apollo clasped his own hand over hers.

Do. Not. Stop.

Tem stared into his blackened eyes. He *burned* for her—craved her as a starving man craved his last meal. She wondered what it would take to feed him.

Without warning, the claw pulsed. Tem was so wet, she'd forgotten she was wearing it. Now it was the only thing she felt as Caspen sent a long, lingering vibration that throbbed in her center like a heartbeat. Apollo was still gripping her, guiding her motions, stroking himself with her hand. The two sensations combined made her so aroused that she let out a desperate whimper. At the sound, Apollo smiled.

Do that again.

Tem made the noise again, and this time, Apollo's other hand went to her mouth, as if he could catch the sound. He brushed two fingers over her bottom lip. They weren't kissing. But they may as well have been. Tem expected Caspen to approach—to intervene—to tell her they'd gone too far. Instead, he remained where he was, leaning against the grotto entrance as he dropped a single word into her mind: *Kneel*.

Caspen gave no name, but Tem knew the command was for her.

To her surprise, every part of her wanted to follow it. Why shouldn't she kneel before Apollo the way she'd knelt for Caspen? Why shouldn't she bestow the same gifts upon his brother? It was only fair.

Without another thought, Tem knelt.

The brothers' grip on her mind tightened as she lowered herself, digging deep into her brain, seeping into her until she was made up more of them than of herself. Tem was secure between them, nestled within their grasp. Before Caspen could give another command, Tem opened her mouth, and Apollo let out a sigh as her lips met his cock. He laced his fingers through the curls on either side of her face, holding her head in place. Slowly, keeping eye contact, he slid himself just an inch into her mouth before pulling back out. Then he pushed back in. This time Tem took him all the way down her throat; she knew how to do this now, and she knew how to make it feel good.

Again.

Tem couldn't tell if the voice was Caspen's or Apollo's, or both. Perhaps it didn't matter. Perhaps they were one and the same. Tem gave herself over to them without hesitation, trusting the two men to guide her. There was nothing more pleasurable than this, nothing more certain. She welcomed their direction knowing that it was her, ultimately, who held their focus.

All the way in, then all the way back out.

Tem arched her back, letting Apollo as far down her throat as possible. Twin waves of approval shot through her mind the moment she did so. She wanted to show them that she could do this—that she was willing to take direction—that she was capable of more. It was intoxicating to get their approval, to know she was pleasing them both. She wished she could touch Caspen too. The thought turned her on, and she touched her breasts, running her palms over them gently, matching the slow pace of Apollo's thrusts.

Caspen's approval burned in the back of her mind. He was still sending pulses, and they were getting stronger. None of them spoke anymore; Tem couldn't have anyway. Their dalliance had moved beyond words. Pleasure was all that mattered now.

The grotto was so full of smoke, it was becoming difficult to see. So Tem closed her eyes. Instantly, all other sensations heightened. She felt the skim of smoke up her back, the wetness between her legs. The pulses were uncompromising; her clitoris throbbed. It took all her effort to stay kneeling—to stay still for Apollo. Sometimes he was in charge, sometimes Tem was. They took turns initiating the motions, ceding and exercising power at will.

She is extraordinary, is she not?

Caspen's compliment was barely audible. Nothing more than a breath. Apollo's response was similarly so. *That she is.*

Tem's wetness was dripping steadily onto the mossy grotto floor. The claw pulsed relentlessly, and Tem was reminded of Caspen's power. He'd always had this control over her—and she'd always liked it. She remembered how he'd made her come at church, in broad daylight. Now, in the darkness of the grotto, she could submit to it without fear.

Deeper, Tem.

She took him deeper.

So good for us.

Thrust after thrust. Never ending.

Caspen presided over it all. It was his authority that spurred them on, his presence that motivated Tem to perform. She wanted to be *so good* for him. For *them.* She wanted to show them that she was capable, that she belonged here just as they did.

The claw was pulsing; it wouldn't stop. Tem's hands went between her legs, pressing the smooth tip against her clitoris, accentuating what Caspen was already giving her. Something was building deep in her center: something real.

Look at her.

She knew they were both watching her—seeing her take Apollo's cock, seeing her touch herself. Tem was the star of the show, and she wouldn't have it any other way. She wanted to be the only one they watched, the only one they craved. If they were going to be obsessed with anyone, she needed it to be her.

Apollo was thrusting quicker now. He was losing control.

His hand gripped her hair as he leaned forward, tilting her head back even farther. Another pulse came, and Tem moaned around his cock. The sound of his tight, frantic breathing was sending her over the edge. Tem raised her hand, cupping his balls and giving them a firm, dominating squeeze. She barely heard his labored gasp, "Wait—"

But he was already coming. Tem closed her eyes as Apollo's cum filled her throat, poured from his cock in a luscious wave—warm and thick just like Caspen's. Tem swallowed it all without hesitation, and the moment she did so, Apollo's head arched back in relief. She stared up at his exposed throat, chiseled like stone. He was built like a statue, the same way Caspen was—the same way their father was. Tem felt, as she had before, that she was in the presence of a god.

Apollo looked down at her. *If I am a god, you are a goddess.*

His cock was still in her mouth, as strong and commanding as he was.

Tem felt a sudden absence and realized it was Caspen. He was retreating from her mind, relinquishing his grip. He was leaving the grotto as discreetly as he'd arrived, imparting just one final order in her mind before he disappeared entirely:

Do not leave until you are done.

Then Caspen was gone.

Was he telling Tem to fuck Apollo? Or did he mean "done" in another way—that she shouldn't leave until she was done *with him*—until her infatuation with Apollo was over? Tem cursed basilisks and their infernal vagueness. She still couldn't wrap her head around what had just happened. At no point had Caspen come any closer to them—at no point had he intervened. But his involvement was inarguable. Tem may have made Apollo come, but Caspen had *directed* it. And she had liked it.

The next command came from Apollo: *Stay where you are.*

Tem stayed perfectly still, looking up at him. His mind was still joined with hers; they were physically and mentally connected. She was struck by the intimacy of the moment. Caspen's presence had been significant, and now that he was gone, it was only Apollo and she together, alone with what they had just shared. They stayed motionless for just one moment longer. Then Apollo pulled his cock slowly out of her mouth, leaving Tem breathless.

She expected him to leave, just as his brother had. Instead he lowered himself to her level, kneeling so his face was just inches from hers, his cock hard between her legs. He pulled her closer. A single finger touched the bottom of her chin, tilting it up. His thumb brushed over her lips as he said, *May I?*

Two words. Asking permission.

Tem would never understand the basilisks—never comprehend how having Apollo's cock in her mouth was less of an event than kissing him. But perhaps in a way it was. A kiss was intimate; it meant tasting someone's tongue—touching your lips to theirs. To kiss would mean allowing themselves to be soft with one another, to be vulnerable. It was the antithesis of their relationship up until that point, and it felt significant that he had asked. For all their banter, she and Apollo hadn't come close to kissing. Even when Caspen himself had ordered them to—even when Apollo had taught her how to petrify—he'd waited. Here he was, finally. Begging her. Tem found that she enjoyed it, found that it felt right to have him beg her on his knees. If Caspen had taught her anything, it was that her body was worth begging for.

But was it worth it to take this step with him? Tem's heart belonged to Caspen. That was nonnegotiable. But Apollo wasn't asking for her heart. He was only asking to kiss her. If permission was what he sought, Tem was ready to grant it. So for the second time that evening she said, *Yes.*

Apollo leaned in.

His lips brushed hers softly, his tongue dipping into her mouth only after her tongue dipped into his. He tasted like peaches. Perhaps he'd eaten some earlier. Perhaps it was naturally so. Regardless, it was beautiful, and Tem drank it in willingly. Apollo drank her in too, tilting his head to accommodate their height difference, angling his mouth so he had easier access to hers. They fit together perfectly—better than she could have ever imagined. Something in Apollo cradled her—*held her*—in a way Tem deeply needed to be held.

Apollo was good at kissing. He was good at *everything*. Tem couldn't even let herself think about what it would be like to actually have sex with him. The feeling of his lips on hers was already enough to get her halfway to an orgasm. Her thoughts must have been loud again, because Apollo said, *You flatter me.*

You're a good kisser. It's nothing to get a big ego about.

Would you say I have a big ego?

Apollo had her straddling his cock. There was no bigger ego around. Before she could answer, he kissed her even deeper.

It was different than kissing his brother. A little more reckless, a little less careful. The recklessness in him called to the recklessness in her. Caspen was a gateway drug to Apollo—the key that unlocked a passageway to sin.

And yet, the brothers were not so different. Both wanted her for themselves. Perhaps Apollo didn't want *her*, exactly—he wanted to take her from Caspen. There was a difference, and Tem would be a fool to ignore it. But that didn't mean he didn't care for her in his own way.

They kissed slowly, taking their time, their bodies coming together as Apollo's hands slid down her waist to cup her ass, pulling her against him. His cock was between her legs, but neither of them initiated sex. Instead, Tem enjoyed the way it pressed against the claw, stimulating her beyond what she could do for herself. It felt *gorgeous*. She moved her hips, rubbing herself gently along the length of his shaft, chasing that feeling. Their heights accommodated this perfectly; Tem could straddle his cock without inserting it, coating it with her wetness.

I know you want to come, Temperance.

She did want that. She wanted it *so* badly. And she wanted him to see it.

Apollo's fingers pressed the tip of the claw tightly against her clitoris. Tem gasped. Apollo pulled away, smiling. *Do you like that?*

Tem didn't answer. He knew she did. *Can you all make them? The…claws?*

He raised an eyebrow. *Claws?*

I don't know what else to call them.

Apollo seemed amused by that. *Why do you ask?*

I'm just curious.

I see. Yes, all basilisks can make them.

Even the women?

Yes.

Could I?

If you wished.

Tem couldn't imagine making one. At her silence, Apollo asked:

Caspenon never taught you?

No. He didn't.

It seemed there were a great deal of things he'd never taught her. Then again, she'd never asked. But now that Tem was presented with the opportunity, she found she desperately wanted to know.

Shall I teach you?

Without thinking, Tem nodded.

Apollo smiled. *What shape do you wish to make it?*

Tem blinked. *What other shapes are there?*

Apollo shrugged. *You can make them in any shape you choose. The one you wear was made for your cunt. But there are other places they can be worn.*

Tem stared at him. *What other places?*

A beat passed. Then Apollo lifted her slightly off his cock so his hand could go between her legs. But instead of touching her center, he went farther back. When his fingers found what they were looking for, Tem immediately blushed. *Here.* Apollo was touching the part of her she never thought could be used for pleasure. He brushed around it gently before inserting just the tip of his finger and saying, *Some prefer to be penetrated here.*

Tem couldn't imagine that. The tip of Apollo's finger was already substantial—Tem couldn't fathom anything larger possibly fitting inside. The thought scared her, but also made her curious. Before she could talk herself out of it, she asked, *Is that what you prefer?*

Apollo smirked. *Sometimes. If you wish to experience it, I am at your disposal.*

Tem did not wish to experience that. At least not with Apollo. She pushed his hand away. *I don't want you doing that to me.*

Who said I would be doing it to you?

What do you mean?

Without warning, Apollo sent her a vision: him on all fours, Tem behind him. There was something between her legs. A cock—made from the same essence as the claw—held in place by a strap. The vision had no sound, but Tem saw Apollo moan as she entered him. It was like nothing Tem had ever seen before. She should tell Apollo to stop. But the vision was too tempting. Too *delicious*. Seeing Apollo like that, on his knees, vulnerable and at her mercy…it made her feral. Something inside her blossomed at the sight. Something inside her needed more. In the vision, Apollo was close. He was about to come.

Tem wrenched her mind away from his. "Stop," she said out loud. "Don't show me any more."

Apollo's mouth went wide with amusement. "Why? You are aroused by it."

It was true. "That doesn't mean I want to see it."

They stared at each other in the darkness, and not for the first time, Tem understood that she was wildly out of her depth. Apollo was something else entirely, something she hadn't bargained for. It would be so easy to throw herself off the edge with him. To fall. She had to steer herself away from the temptation.

"I don't want to make one in that shape."

"You can make it in any shape, Temperance."

Apollo reached once more between her legs. Only this time, he gathered her wetness in his hand, taking it from her center and the inside of her thighs. Tem watched as her essence solidified, forming the familiar shape. Apollo held the claw out, offering it to her. She shook her head.

I have one of those already.

It is not unheard of to have two.

What would I do with two?

Wear them.

At the same time?

Yes.

Tem blushed. She was used to having Caspen's claw inside her—she couldn't imagine having another beside it, couldn't imagine being *filled* like that. At the thought, a wave of heat came from Apollo's mind. Clearly *he* could imagine it. Tem shook her head.

I don't need another one.

If you ever change your mind, you need only ask.

That would never happen. But she would let him dream.

Tem watched as the claw disappeared before her eyes. They both stared at his empty palm.

If you do not need another, you could make one for me, if you wish.

That was certainly intriguing to Tem. But the shape of the claw inside her made no sense for Apollo. *What form would it take?*

308

Apollo took her hand and wrapped her fingers around the base of his cock. *It would be a ring, to be placed here.*

His cock was already covered in her cum. Tem tightened her grip, sliding her fingers down his shaft to gather what she could in her hand. Apollo watched her as she did it, waiting until her palm was full before saying, *Focus on the shape you wish to make.*

Tem closed her eyes. Apollo gave no further instructions, but she found she didn't need them. She knew exactly what to do, and the moment she set her mind to it, the object began to form. The sensation was similar to how she'd felt when she made the golden claw necklace for Caspen—the same tingle below her freckles, spreading from the base of her fingers, the same sense that she was creating something new.

Good, Temperance. You are a natural.

Tem took the compliment with a smile. Nothing about basilisk culture came naturally to her; she actively felt like a failure every single day. But this, at least, she was good at. She opened her eyes and looked down to see the object fully formed. It was an astonishing thing: a gleaming, opaque ring resting in the middle of her palm. Tem lifted it so that it caught the dim light of the grotto. She turned it slowly, watching it shimmer as if it had its own light source. Tem got the feeling that even if the cave were pitch dark, it would glow.

Her gaze fell to Apollo. His eyes were wide, staring at the ring in awe, its glint reflected endlessly in his pupils. Tem had never seen him so eager—not even earlier, when she'd been on her knees before him. Was this how Caspen had felt when he'd made the claw for her? Tem remembered how he'd looked when she'd inserted it for the first time. It wasn't unlike the way Apollo was looking now: eager to the point of voracity.

She shifted closer.

The moment she did so, Apollo's breath hitched. Tem felt a thrill of anticipation as she placed the ring around the head of his cock and slid it slowly up his shaft. It was a perfect fit, just as she knew it would be. Sharp possessiveness coursed through her as Apollo let out a low, euphoric groan. His pleasure was evident: his already-hard cock hardened even further, straining against the confines of the ring. Tem flushed at the sight. She wasn't even doing anything yet, and he was already at her mercy.

You can make it tighter, if you wish.

Is that what you want me to do?

Apollo didn't answer. Now he was the one resisting. But Tem wouldn't let him get away with it. Why should she be the only vulnerable one? Why should Tem bare herself to Apollo when he refused to do the same for her?

An infinitesimal amount of power shifted back to Tem as she said, *Tell me to.*

A muscle twitched in Apollo's jaw. *Make it tighter, Temperance.*

She made it tighter.

It wasn't difficult to do; all it took was a simple intention in her mind and Tem watched as the ring drew taut around the base of his cock. Apollo's hands gripped her hips so hard that it hurt.

Why not take it one step further?

Tem knew there was one more thing she could do to push him over the edge. She concentrated on the ring, focusing on her connection to it before sending Apollo a pulse just like the ones Caspen sent her. Apollo's reaction was immediate. A shudder passed through him, and he groaned. *Where did you learn to do that?*

Caspen taught me.

Kora.

Almost against his will, Apollo leaned forward and kissed her neck. The moment he made contact, Tem bit her lip in order to hold back a moan. Immediately, he berated her.

Stop that.

Stop what?

Hiding your pleasure.

But it was her instinct to hide from Apollo. She didn't want him to see her pleasure. Perhaps she thought he didn't deserve to see her that way—or perhaps she was embarrassed, somehow, that he was capable of calling such pleasure forth. Whatever the reason, Tem hid from him.

I can't help it.

Yes, you can. You are resisting me.

That, at least, was true. Tem was resisting him, although resistance was rapidly proving futile.

Let me take care of you.

Tem couldn't imagine Apollo taking care of her in any way, shape, or form. *I doubt you're capable of that.*

I assure you, I am.

Still, she resisted.

Your reservation is endearing.

And your arrogance is infuriating.

Do not pretend you do not like it.

I don't like it. She could barely think the words, the lie giving her discomfort.

Lying is a sin, Temperance.

Don't talk to me about sins.

Would you rather I perform them instead?

The answer was yes, of course. But she didn't dare say it.

Apollo's hand reached for Tem's. Out of instinct, she jerked away, and he raised his eyebrows in concern. Tem hadn't meant to do that—it was simply her natural reaction to someone trying to grab her. She couldn't even justify it; they'd just obliterated every barrier between them, and she had nothing more to hide. But for some reason, it felt like what they were about to do was more intimate than what they'd just done, like they were about to cross an unspoken line. Tem wasn't sure if she was truly ready for that.

Apollo didn't say a word—didn't try to coerce her. Instead, he leaned in slowly and pressed a single, tender kiss to her cheek. At the gesture, something inside Tem unwound. It was a reminder: Apollo was telling her that she was safe with him. It was a sentiment she knew but had trouble believing. His lips skimmed gently along her jaw and down her neck. Tem could feel his mind, open and unguarded, filled with attentive care. She wondered briefly if it was all for show. Did Apollo only lower his defenses when he wanted something from her? Tem decided it didn't matter. He had earned her trust tonight.

Then his lips were on hers.

After that, time ceased to exist. Apollo's hands were on Tem's hips, guiding her over the length of his cock. He didn't penetrate her—she wasn't ready for that yet. Instead she pleasured herself on his shaft, rubbing her most-sensitive area along his, teasing herself while she teased him. It was primal and it was simple and it felt *good*. Every time she reached the base, the claw and the ring pressed together, creating an unimaginable sensation. Tem thrust her hips, desperate to feel as much of it as possible.

Apollo was even more turned on than Tem. His presence engulfed her mind, surrounding her from all angles, holding her in place both physically and mentally. He pressed his lips once more to her throat.

How can you feel this good when I am not even inside you?

You feel good too.

Apollo's teeth found her earlobe, and he bit it.

She squirmed, and he only held her tighter.

Come for me.

She would. But not yet. Tem slowed her motions, sliding herself tantalizingly along his shaft before stopping at the tip, the full length of his cock between them. Her eyes flicked to his. *Say please.*

An order. Tem wasn't used to giving those to Apollo—wasn't used to making him beg her for anything. But she was in the mood to test his limits tonight.

Please.

Tem smiled.

His reward was a single flick of her hips. Then she stopped again. Apollo growled with displeasure at her delay. But Tem would not be rushed. She was building to it, enjoying the feel of him between her legs, unwilling to let this be over so quickly. *I want to take my time.*

Is that so?

Yes. And you want to let me.

Do I? And why is that?

Because you like this. And you like me. And you want to watch me get there on my own. Don't you?

They stared at each other in the darkness, their breathing uneven.

Yes. I do.

Apollo's chest was dappled with sweat, and Tem leaned forward, placing her tongue between his pectorals and sliding it up to his neck. His hands cupped her ass as she did it, pulling her completely against him. The moment her clitoris pressed against the ring, she sent a pulse, stimulating them both.

My brother does not know how lucky he is. You are unbelievable.

Trust me. He knows.

Apollo groaned, pulled her face up to his, and kissed her.

Tem threaded her fingers through his hair, participating in equal measure, allowing him deep inside her mouth. She would let him penetrate her this way—not with his cock but with his tongue, tasting her the way she knew he'd always wanted to. There was equilibrium between them: a match of equal value. Tem felt worthy. She felt seen.

Tem sent another pulse. This one was long and lingering, and during the middle of it, Apollo pulled away. She opened her eyes and asked: *Should I stop?*

No. His thumb brushed against the tip of the claw. *You should take this out so I can fuck you properly.*

Tem hesitated. The claw was like a barrier—as long as it was inside her, they couldn't have sex.

Apollo heard her thoughts, because he said, *Have you so little self-control?*

Tem glared at him. She couldn't believe they were having this conversation while naked, intertwined, with his cock between her legs. And yet, here they were. Tem supposed that given their circumstances, perhaps her hesitation warranted an explanation. *I don't trust myself with you.*

To her surprise, Apollo didn't respond right away. Instead he tilted his head, appraising her. *May I ask why?*

Tem barely knew anymore. If she slept with Apollo, it meant that she was slipping— falling slowly but steadily off the path of morality that she'd prided herself on walking her entire life. It didn't matter that sleeping with him was acceptable—and expected—in basilisk culture. It was unacceptable *to her.* Tem couldn't reconcile the way she felt about Apollo with her feelings for Caspen. It was too much to hold in one heart.

And then there was Leo.

If she crossed this line with Apollo, it meant she was capable of crossing the line with Leo. Tem couldn't bear that. So she said, *I just don't want to make a mistake.*

You consider sex with me a mistake.

It wasn't a question. *I consider it a risk.*

A life without risk is not a life worth living, Temperance.

Tem rolled her eyes. It was exactly the kind of thing she expected him to say.

First my brother, then my father. Should I be offended you draw the line at fucking me?

He had a point there. But for some reason, this felt different.

It just seems…wrong.

We will fuck during the tournament. Or did you not know that?

Tem did know that. Adelaide had told her barely an hour ago. But just because she had to fuck him in the future didn't mean she was going to fuck him right now.

When the silence lingered, Apollo said: *I understand you do not trust yourself. But do you trust me?*

What a question. Tem had no idea how to answer it. Instead, she was immediately reminded of the last time she was asked it: standing in a graveyard with Leo. *You don't trust me, do you, Tem?* She hadn't trusted Leo at first. Her trust for him had grown over time, and only after she had allowed him to prove himself to her. Did she owe Apollo the same courtesy? He had taught her to petrify; he had acted as her confidant. They had been naked with each other more than once, and he had acted in her best interests every time. So did she trust him?

Yes.

True joy flashed in his eyes. He pulled her closer. *Then place the burden on me. I vow we will not have sex until you initiate it.*

Tem considered this. *Do you promise?*

His hands tightened on her waist. *I promise.* He pressed once more against the claw. *Now take this out and come on my cock.*

The time for hesitation was gone. Tem was ready.

Slowly, so that Apollo saw every moment of it, she reached between her legs and removed the claw. Then she dropped it, glistening, to the ground. As soon as she was empty, she pressed her center down against Apollo's cock. Without the barrier of the claw, there was nothing between his skin and hers. He was harder than stone between her legs, and Tem settled into position, her hips resuming their rhythm. They moved of their own accord now, rubbing with incessant urgency, creating a friction she had no hope of stopping. She wanted her orgasm, and she wanted it soon. Apollo wanted it too. Tem knew he had waited for this—to see her raw and ready and open for him.

Tem adjusted her position, moving her legs together so she was clamped tightly around him. Where before she'd been sliding luxuriously along his length, now she pumped him quickly through the apex of her thighs, keeping him tight against her center.

Apollo was close. His jaw was tense; his shoulders tight. His arms were locked around her, guiding her every movement. They were working toward it together, helping each other over the finish line. She slid herself desperately back and forth, spreading her wetness along the length of his cock.

There it is, Temperance. I know you like that.

She didn't bother denying it anymore.

One more, Temperance. Just one more. Please.

Again, he begged. A man undone.

Almost there. I know you can do it.

One more flick of her hips, and it was time.

There it is.

It was inevitable, like the dawn.

Apollo held out, watching Tem as she fell over the edge alone. She knew he wanted to see this, knew he needed to know it was his promise that got her here. It was only when her hips began to slow and the last throbbing wave of her orgasm had passed that Apollo gripped her ass with both hands, pumped the entire shaft of his cock along the seam of her center, and came.

Tem watched him as he had watched her, observing the way his eyes closed and his head arched back. His pulse was beating in a vein in his neck, erratic and vital, and wondered what it would be like to bite it. His essence slid down the inside of her thighs, pearlescent and warm, joining hers. They were both soaking wet—with sweat, with cum, with the water that was steadily dripping from the stalactites above them. Tem raised her hands to his face, brushing his hair away from his eyes.

Apollo smiled as she did it. His eyes, which had gone completely black, were still that way even after he finished. He had dimples, Tem realized. They were cute.

He was the first to stand, extending his hand to Tem so he could help her up. To her surprise, as soon as she was upright, he kissed her again. This time felt different than the way he had kissed her before. This time was slow, and he cupped her face gently in his palms as he did it. When he pulled away, his hands brushed down her arms until their fingers intertwined.

Helplessly—that was the way he looked at her.

Tem had been the first on her knees, but somehow, she had brought Apollo to his. He stared into her eyes, his gaze unwavering as he whispered, "You may belong to my brother, but I will protect you as if you are mine."

Tem was floored by his words. Her response slipped out before she could stop it: "Part of me belongs to you."

True euphoria flashed in his eyes. Perhaps he had already known it was true. Or perhaps he had only hoped it was. Either way, Tem said it with a surety she could have never imagined. It was true that a part of her was his. It was a smaller part than belonged to Caspen, for sure. He had nearly her whole heart, and he always would. But why should there not be room for Apollo? Basilisks were free with their bodies. At one time, that had seemed like a burden to Tem. But now she cherished it. It afforded her things she wouldn't otherwise have—it let her live the way she wanted to live. There was no going back for her, and she had no desire to anyway.

"Apollo?" she whispered.

"Yes, Temperance?"

"Would you do anything for me?"

The corner of his mouth twitched. "I would."

Tem found that she knew it already. She knew that if she asked, he would let her bite that vein in his neck—that he would bleed for her. For basilisks, blood was the ultimate gift. But Tem wouldn't request that of Apollo tonight. He'd given her enough. It was time to return to herself—and to Caspen.

Tem was finally done.

CHAPTER THIRTY-TWO

—••●✳●••—

THE CELEBRATION WAS STILL GOING FULL-FORCE WHEN THEY EMERGED FROM THE grotto. Apollo swam beside Tem back to the shore, giving her ass one last squeeze before disappearing into the crowd. She didn't bother smacking him away. They were beyond the point where she could pretend she didn't like the way he touched her.

Tem scanned the crowd for Caspen, but he was nowhere to be found.

She spent time with Adelaide, Cypress, and Damon, drinking elixir and becoming one with the crowd. The drunker she became, the more she thought about what Apollo had shown her: him on all fours, taking him with her own version of a cock. The vision was so tantalizing, it made her ache. Tem had always thought that she was the one who would be taken. She'd never considered that she herself could take.

Both brothers avoided Tem for the rest of the night, keeping their distance. Tem didn't mind the space. For once, she wasn't being pulled in two different directions. For once, she could relax. The celebration went on for so long that she fell asleep right on the sand, her limbs intertwined with Cypress's and Adelaide's.

When Tem awoke, it was the first day of the tournament.

"You will choose your contenders before the feast," Adelaide said. They were heading toward the banquet hall, and Tem's eyes were still heavy with sleep. "After which the quivers will dine together to symbolize their unity. Then at midnight, the first tier begins."

Tem nodded, but she wasn't really listening. She was thinking about Caspen. He hadn't slept next to her, and she had woken up missing him. By the time they reached the banquet hall, she was anxiously scanning the crowd. But something was different.

"Why isn't anyone having sex?" she asked Adelaide.

For the first time since she'd arrived under the mountain, Tem wasn't inundated with the sight of thrashing bodies. There was not a moan to be heard—no intertwining body parts, no ejaculation. Everyone was just…talking.

"They refrain out of respect."

"I don't understand."

"They know you and Caspenon cannot touch. It is a gesture of solidarity."

Tem wasn't sure how to respond. So she settled on "Oh. That's…nice of them."

"Do not be too impressed," Adelaide said with a smile. "It will only last until after the feast. Then you may be shocked at what you see."

A tingle of anticipation slid down Tem's spine. She didn't know whether to be excited or scared.

Before she could decide, she heard "Tem. My love."

She turned to see Caspen looking down at her.

Tem immediately reached for him, but her fingers were stopped by the barrier. She dropped her hand, holding back the sudden urge to cry. Tem thought of what happened in the grotto, how he'd told her to touch Apollo. At first she'd thought it was because he wanted to watch them together. But now she wondered whether it was because Caspen couldn't do it himself. Perhaps he'd used his brother as a conduit—if he could not touch her, at least his brother could.

How are you feeling?

She wanted so badly to touch him right now, to reaffirm their connection in the best way she knew how. For weeks, she'd found solace in his arms, in the pure surety of sex. But now that this barrier had been erected between them, that connection had faded. It wasn't enough to tease each other with their minds or with the claw. It wasn't enough to watch him touch himself in front of her. Tem was losing a part of herself—an important, empowered part—without him. She couldn't bear the thought of not touching Caspen for even a second longer, much less until after the tournament was over. Worse still was the thought of never touching him again.

So she told him the truth: *I'm scared.*

His face softened. He looked at Adelaide, who was watching their interaction sympathetically.

"I will leave you two," she said. "I shall return when it is time for you to select your contenders."

Tem nodded. Adelaide left them.

"There is no need to fear, Tem."

Why did everyone keep telling her that? "That's easy for you to say. You're not responsible for our entire future."

To her surprise, Caspen smiled. "Neither are you."

Tem shook her head. That just wasn't true. "What if I mess it up?" she asked, her voice nearly cracking. "What if my heart chooses wrong?"

"Tem," he said. "It is not possible for your heart to choose wrong. That is the entire point of the tournament. Whoever you choose is your right match."

"How can you be so calm about this?"

"Because I have faith," he said simply.

Tem thought about what Apollo had told her: how basilisks believed in fate. Did Caspen think his destiny was predetermined too? Tem couldn't live in such limbo. She had to believe that she had some agency, that she had a *choice*.

"Tem," he said again, quietly this time. "No matter what your heart decides, know that you are worth fighting for."

She stared up at him. In another world, they would kiss. But in this one, they simply looked into each other's eyes, their hearts beating in tandem, their bodies inches apart. Tem wished she could bottle this moment and keep it forever.

Just then, a murmur swept through the banquet hall.

Tem turned to see the crowd parting to reveal two tall, imposing basilisks. A chill slipped down her spine as she recognized one of them: Rowe. She hadn't seen him since the wedding, when he crested Vera and ran off into the forest. Now he was walking through the banquet hall as if he owned it, his nose turned up, his mouth twisted in a triumphant sneer. Instinctually, Tem stepped closer to Caspen. Then her gaze dropped between Rowe's legs.

Despite herself, Tem's mouth fell open.

The last time she'd seen Rowe naked, there had been nothing but a mangled mound of flesh where his cock used to be. Now gold gleamed between his legs, molded to the space where his cock used to be, fused seamlessly to his skin, flesh becoming metal. It reminded her of what Apollo had shown her—a cock made from essence. But this was nothing like that. Rowe had *bled* for the apparatus between his legs. It was a horrible thing—a thing of power.

Tem turned to Caspen. "Did he…?"

But she didn't know how to finish her sentence. *Make himself a new cock?* seemed far too casual for what Rowe had done. But that was exactly what had happened.

Caspen looked just as shocked as she did. "Yes."

Even from here, Tem could sense Rowe's power. It flowed off him in waves, drawing the notice of everyone around him. The murmurs grew louder. All around them, basilisks whispered to one another in shock.

"I thought what you did made him weaker," Tem whispered.

Beside her, Caspen rolled his shoulders. "It seems he has…found a solution."

Rowe had certainly found a solution.

Light shone on his golden shaft, glowing in the dim lighting of the banquet hall. It was mesmerizing; Tem couldn't look away. She'd been haunted by Rowe's maiming ever since the wedding, but now she couldn't believe she'd spent any time feeling guilty for what Caspen did. The golden cock radiated power. There was not a doubt in her mind that it was a great, terrible thing.

"Has anyone ever done anything like that before?"

Caspen shook his head. "It is forbidden to use your power in such a way."

"Why?"

"Basilisks have always been able to turn their blood into gold. It is one of our most sacred properties. But it is not meant to replace that which was taken. To do something like this is an aberration of nature. There is a reason we are unable to regrow limbs or heal fatal injuries. Once a part of us is dead, it is supposed to remain so. To bring it back to life violates the laws of nature."

Tem shivered. It certainly *looked* like a violation. "But what does it mean?"

Caspen pursed his lips. "It means that Rowe has done something no one else would dare to do. He has created a part of himself *from* himself. It is a source of power for him."

Tem thought suddenly of the final tier, where she was expected to ride the remaining contenders. "Am I going to have to…?"

"Yes, Tem. You are."

"But how am I supposed to—?"

"Just like you do mine."

"But his is—"

"It is still a cock, Tem," Caspen said. "It may not look like one that you or I have seen before, but it is one nonetheless."

Tem stared up at him in disbelief. "How is this allowed?"

Caspen's hands were balling into fists. "It is not allowed. There are supposed to be limits to our power. We can only heal what is broken; we cannot regenerate what is no longer there. This is not right."

Tem couldn't imagine what Caspen was feeling. He was the one who'd ripped Rowe's cock off in the first place. It was his actions that had caused Rowe to do this. Rowe had already hated Caspen for cresting his father; Tem shuddered to think of the depth of his grudge against him now.

At that moment, Rowe's eyes met hers.

Tem froze as his gaze traveled down her body, the desire in it unmistakable. There had always been a bitterness to Rowe, but now it was overpowering. He wore his rage plainly on his face, his expression the twin to Caspen's.

"He's so angry," Tem whispered.

"As am I, Tem."

Rowe turned, heading in their direction. A moment later, he was upon them. "Temperance," he said, his voice like gravel. "Are you enjoying the festivities? They are in your honor, after all."

Tem opened her mouth to answer, but Caspen beat her to it.

"Do not speak to her."

Rowe's eyes slid to his. "And why not? She could be my future wife."

"The day you take her from me is the day I die."

Rowe smiled. "There is no need for such words, Caspenon. I come in peace."

Caspen actually snorted.

Tem's eyes shifted to the basilisk beside Rowe. Eros was taller than his brother and just as formidable. He stared down at Tem with burnished gold eyes that felt like they were looking straight into her soul. She barely came up to his collarbone; his shoulders were so broad, she couldn't see anything behind him.

Rowe suddenly entered Tem's mind.

She gasped in surprise, throwing up walls to block the assault. But she couldn't shut him out—his power was indescribable; it pushed against her like an indomitable force, crushing her like a spider against glass.

You will yield to me, Temperance. And so will Caspenon.

It took everything Tem had to look him straight in the eye and say, "Never."

Rowe's mouth twisted into a dark, amused sneer.

"It is a shame," he murmured. "You are as stubborn as ever."

Tem lifted her chin. "And you are just as cruel."

His sneer deepened. "Cruelty is a necessity in the world we live in, Temperance. Your husband knows that better than anyone."

Tem had no way to refute that. What Caspen had done to Rowe was undeniably cruel. But Rowe had deserved it. And now, with their fight imminent, Tem hoped Caspen would be cruel once more.

Rowe directed his final jab straight at Caspen. "May the best man win."

Then he walked off without another word.

Tem turned immediately to Caspen. He was staring after Rowe with his fists clenched, a vein pulsing in his temple. Tem wanted nothing more than to reach for him, to feel his warm skin against hers, to find comfort in each other. But it was the one thing she could not do.

Adelaide appeared at her side. "Tem," she said gently. "All eligible basilisks have now arrived. It is time to make your selections."

Tem looked at Caspen. He looked at her.

"Will you stay with me?" she whispered.

"Always."

They followed Adelaide to the end of the banquet hall, where a stage had been assembled. On it was a group of twenty or so basilisks, all handsome, all fully erect. Tem remembered what Adelaide had said—how she was supposed to make her decision based on their cocks. She glanced up at Caspen, who gave her a reassuring nod before stepping to the side to join Rowe, Eros, and Apollo. When Tem's eyes met Apollo's, he nodded too.

You can do this, Temperance.

She barely believed him. It was difficult to imagine that any of these men could be her prospective husband. None of them compared to Caspen.

Tem was frozen in place, acutely aware of the crowd behind her, watching her every move. It was too much pressure; she could not perform under the weight of everyone's expectations.

Caspen's voice came to her: *Relax, Tem. Allow your basilisk side to make the decision.*

Tem closed her eyes, resolved to do as he said. She concentrated on the side of her that *liked* being watched, the side that was powerful and bold and brave. She suppressed the human side, pushing away her doubts and insecurities. When she opened her eyes, she was ready.

Tem recognized only one basilisk in the group of men before her. He was tall, with slicked-back blond hair—the man Caspen had pleasured in the ouroboros. Immediately, she was drawn to him. She didn't even glance at his cock; it didn't matter what it looked like. Adelaide's words came back to her suddenly: *You will seal your choices with a kiss.*

Tem knew what she had to do.

The moment she stepped forward, the crowd cheered. She approached the blond basilisk slowly, holding eye contact until she was right in front of him. Then she cradled his face in her hands, stood on her tiptoes, and kissed him. She imagined it was Leo and poured every ounce of longing into their kiss, doing what she could not do with him. When they broke apart, the basilisk smiled widely before bowing to her and moving to the sidelines to stand next to Apollo.

One down. Seven to go.

Tem made the rest of her selections by instinct alone. She didn't care about their cocks—they were all equally glorious anyway—she cared about how they made her *feel*. Tem kissed only the basilisks whose power was compatible with hers—those who she knew, on an instinctual level, could *handle* her. She let the heat between her legs guide her, choosing anyone who turned her on. By the time she'd kissed the eighth man, she was wet.

The crowd roared as the final basilisk joined the line of contenders. Caspen smiled at her, and she knew she'd done well. Adelaide reappeared at her side.

"Now what?" Tem asked.

Adelaide leaned in. "Now there will be a ceremony."

"What kind of ceremony?"

"You shall see."

Everyone except for the final twelve contenders left the stage. Behind Tem, the banquet hall went silent. For some reason, she found herself holding her breath as a woman emerged from the crowd and ascended the stage. Her stomach was swollen.

Tem glanced at Adelaide. *Is she pregnant?*

Adelaide shook her head. *No. She is a new mother who just gave birth.*

Tem looked around for a baby but didn't see one. Then she remembered what Adelaide had told her about basilisk children, how they were raised away from the caves until they came of age and were ready to have sex. Tem couldn't figure out why a new mother would be here without her child. *What is her purpose?*

Adelaide didn't reply. Something was happening; the contenders were kneeling.

What are they doing?

They are paying their respects.

But why?

She represents Kora.

Kora. Goddess of fertility, benevolent ruler of all.

She will touch the person she believes will be the victor of the tournament.

This was all new information to Tem, and it was completely terrifying. The victor of the tournament had to be Caspen. *Needed* to be Caspen. What if the woman touched someone else?

How will she make her decision?

It is believed that Kora will tell her whom to choose.

The woman walked slowly down the line of men, pausing before each one to look them in the eye, as if judging their capability. The men looked up at her with utter respect, as they would have their own mothers, kneeling before her as they would in church.

Tem held her breath as the woman stopped before Rowe. After what felt like an eternity, she continued along, trailing her fingertips through the air as she walked. She moved with undeniable grace, her hips swaying as she approached the end of the line. Apollo was second to last, right before Caspen. The woman stopped before him.

Tem immediately stiffened. *No. She can't choose him.*

Adelaide didn't reply. Tem could do nothing but watch in horrified silence as the woman held out her hand, touching Apollo gently on the forehead. Tem had never seen Apollo so proud. It was clear this was the highest honor possible, that he was receiving a gift of incalculable value. Apollo took the woman's hand in his, raising it and pressing her wrist to his lips.

The crowd erupted into cheers. Beside Apollo, Caspen's face expression was unreadable. Was he angry? Jealous? Afraid? Tem reached for him with her mind, but he was closed off to her. It didn't surprise her. If his thoughts were anything like hers, they were not safe for anyone else to hear.

It will have no bearing on the actual outcome, Temperance, Adelaide said. *It is merely her opinion, nothing more.*

But you said that she was guided by Kora.

That is what we believe, yes.

Have you ever known Kora to be wrong?

Adelaide didn't answer.

You can't possibly tell me that her picking Apollo is a good thing.

Not a good *thing, necessarily. But an interesting one.*

How is it interesting? It seems terrible to me. Caspen will be—

Caspenon will not be angry.

Tem found that hard to believe.

He understands the rules of the tournament, Temperance. He will take it as a challenge.

That was even worse.

It is merely her opinion. Nothing more.

But Tem just shook her head.

"Temperance," Adelaide said gently. "I understand that this is difficult for you. But everything is proceeding exactly as it should. Now that you have chosen your contenders and Kora has chosen hers, the tournament can proceed."

Tem closed her eyes. In her heart, she knew Adelaide was right. She respected the process. It didn't matter if it appalled her; the tournament was happening either way. But that didn't make it any easier.

"Apollo can't win," she whispered. "It's not possible."

"If he wins, it is because he was always supposed to win. We believe our fates are already written."

"But that's—"

"*That,*" Adelaide said firmly, placing her hand on Tem's shoulder, "is the basilisk way."

Tem fell silent. How nice it must be to leave everything up to fate, to believe that your destiny was decided for you. But that was not the way Tem did things. She was too driven by desire to accept that her decisions did not matter. The basilisk way was not her way. It never would be.

The woman descended the stage, disappearing back into the crowd. Tem watched her go, a horrible pit in her stomach. She barely noticed as the crowd dispersed around her and basilisks began seating themselves at the tables. It was time for the feast.

"You will eat at the head of the hall," Adelaide said in her ear, steering her toward a table that was perpendicular to all the others. It was not unlike a wedding table, where the bride and the groom would sit, overseeing the festivities. Only this table had three seats, and two of them were already filled. Adelaide guided her to the seat in the middle.

"If you need anything, I will be close by."

Then she left her alone with the Drakon brothers.

Tem stared straight ahead, utterly unsure what to do with herself. She couldn't touch Caspen, and she didn't dare touch Apollo. There was absolutely nowhere to go.

Finally, she turned to Caspen. "Are you prepared?"

He blinked. "For what, my love?"

"For the fight with Rowe."

To her surprise, he laughed. "I do not need to prepare."

Tem crossed her arms. "If you're going to be fighting for me, don't you think you should prepare?"

"Tem," he said. "there is nothing to be done. I will win."

"How do you know?"

"Because I have more to lose."

"Rowe has *nothing* to lose," Tem said. "That makes him dangerous."

"Tem." Caspen looked her straight in the eye. "*I* am dangerous."

Despite the warmth of the banquet hall, Tem shivered. She turned to Apollo. "And *don't* get any ideas."

He raised an eyebrow at her. "And what sort of ideas might I get?"

"Just because that woman chose you, doesn't mean I ever will."

Apollo's mouth twitched in amusement. "Her choice is not binding. It has no influence on yours." The same thing Adelaide said.

"Still. Don't—"

"Get any ideas? I would not dare, Temperance."

"Good, because—"

Just then, Caspen spoke into her mind: *Enough, Tem.*

Her heart thrummed in her chest at the reprimand. She knew she was lashing out because she was nervous—because she was *terrified.* The fear was beginning to eat her alive. Tem closed her eyes. Somehow, what she needed to say to them was easier that way.

"You can't let Rowe take me."

Silence. Tem opened her eyes to see Apollo's gaze slide to Caspen's. Something unspoken passed between brothers, and Tem wished she knew what it was. Then Apollo placed his hand gently on her waist. She froze at the contact, holding perfectly still as he said, "We will both die before we let that happen, Temperance."

The barest sense of relief flowed through her, followed immediately by horrible guilt. "I can't lose either of you."

Another silence.

In it, Tem felt both of them enter her mind the way they had in the grotto. Only this time, they were not trying to seduce her. This time she felt nothing but an unbreakable wave of reassurance pass from their minds to hers. She understood that they were united in this, that they recognized that the situation was greater than themselves—that they were prepared to sacrifice if necessary. Tem was prepared too.

"It is our honor to fight for you, Tem," Caspen said quietly.

Apollo's hand was still on her waist. His fingers tightened—just barely—in a gesture of agreement. Then he released her. Caspen had retreated from her mind. But Apollo remained, murmuring just a single sentence before retreating too: *You are worth fighting for, Temperance.*

The same words Caspen had said to her earlier. Tem knew Apollo wouldn't say them unless he meant them. Basilisks could not lie, after all. They could only bend the truth, and what he'd said was so straightforward, Tem could do nothing but believe him.

After that, there was nothing to do but eat and drink.

The feast was sumptuous—one of the best Tem had ever had. The food was accompanied by what seemed like endless amounts of elixir. It made sense, she supposed, that the two quivers would need liquid courage in order to coexist. But as a direct result, the banquet hall was rapidly descending into chaos. Adelaide hadn't been kidding when she told Tem she might be surprised at what she would see. All around them, basilisks were fucking. They did it on the benches, on the tables, on the floor. Tem had thought that, given the nature of why they were here, the two quivers would have animosity between them. Instead, the opposite was true. Tem saw Senecas with Senecas, Senecas with Drakons, and every combination in between. Tem stared out at the chaos, in awe of the sheer scope of it.

Only Rowe did not partake in the festivities. He remained on the edge of the banquet hall, not eating or drinking, his arms crossed over this chest. His golden cock was fully erect, and Tem wondered if it was always like that.

"Rowe is staring at me."

Both Caspen and Apollo looked over at him.

"So he is," Apollo said. "Shall we tell him to stop?"

"*Please* don't."

"And why not?" Caspen said. "He is bothering you."

"You already took his cock, Caspen. I don't know what else you could even take."

A dark smile twisted his face. "I would think of something."

"You could take his head," Apollo offered.

Tem smacked his shoulder. "*Stop* that."

Both brothers laughed. Thankfully, at that moment, Adelaide appeared.

"Temperance," she said. "There is someone here for you."

Tem was already sitting next to the only two people who were here for her. "Who?"

In reply, Adelaide simply pointed.

"*Gabriel?*"

CHAPTER THIRTY-THREE

—•◦✳◦•—

H E WAS RUNNING TOWARD HER, HIS CURLS BOUNCING.

"My *dearest* Tem." He threw his arms around her, lifting her from the bench and spinning her in the air. "You didn't think I'd miss a sex tournament, did you?"

Tem rolled her eyes against his chest. It felt *so* good to be held.

When they pulled apart, he kissed her on the cheek, and Tem couldn't stop smiling. Gabriel was here. She had a friend. She was not alone.

Tem looked at Caspen. "Can he be here?"

"He can."

"Will he be safe?"

"Yes."

"How do you know?"

Caspen smiled. "There will be no fighting tonight, Tem. The tournament is a chance for the quivers to get along. It is a sign of good faith—to show their support for the process."

Tem shook her head. Of all the things she'd learned about basilisk culture, this had to be one of the strangest. She couldn't imagine how the tournament could possibly bring people together when it was so clearly designed to divide.

At the look on her face, Caspen smiled. "You still have much to learn."

It was all he said, and it was very much true.

"*Speaking* of learning," Gabriel crooned, turning to Apollo. "Who's *this*?"

Before Tem could answer, Apollo extended his hand to Gabriel, who shook it with enthusiasm.

"I am Apollo," he said. "Caspenon's brother."

"*Brother?* I must say I'm rather fond of the brothers in this family." He glanced over his shoulder, where Damon was watching them with a smile on his face. "Good genetics."

He winked at Apollo, who let out a bewildered laugh. Tem couldn't help but laugh too. Basilisks, with all their life experience, were somehow never prepared for Gabriel.

Suddenly, a scuffle broke out at one of the tables. A group of basilisks were arguing over what looked like a large stone basin, which was filled with scraps of paper. Tem turned immediately to Caspen.

"You said he would be safe tonight."

"He *is*, Tem. They are not fighting, I promise you. They are only taking bets."

"Taking bets on what?"

"On who will win your hand."

"Are you *serious*?"

"It is a lively process, but there is nothing to fear. Gabriel is safe."

But Tem was no longer worried about Gabriel. The thought of people betting on her love life was absurd. She'd always known that basilisks had no boundaries, but this was on another level.

Gabriel nudged her. "Might have to place a bet myself."

She smacked him on the arm. "Don't you *dare*."

"Oh, come on, dearest. What's wrong with a little friendly competition?" He clapped Caspen on the shoulder. "Don't worry, I'm betting on you." To Apollo, he mouthed: *And you.* Then he waggled his fingers at them both before returning to Damon.

"He is really something," Apollo said.

"You have no idea."

The evening only devolved from there. Hordes of basilisks undulated throughout the banquet hall, eating and fucking and laughing in equal measure. Energy was unbelievably high; Tem saw immediately what Adelaide meant when she'd said that the basilisks were anticipating the tournament. It defied all logic, but Caspen was right: this was a way for the quivers to come together. Tem only hoped that their good moods would continue no matter the outcome.

At some point, both brothers left her. Caspen was pulled away by a member of the council, who seemed eager to discuss the impending fight. Apollo was pulled away by sex.

Tem watched as he fucked girl after girl, pulling them onto his lap one after the other. She knew it was part of basilisks' culture—that with every climax, he became more powerful. Still, to watch it in such excess was breathtaking. When the tenth basilisk mounted him, Apollo's eyes met hers.

Care to take your turn, Temperance?

No thank you.

Pity. I would prefer you over her.

I know you would. But it seems like you've already got your hands full.

He literally had his hands on the ass of the blond basilisk riding his cock. Tem's stomach turned at the sight.

I would rather have them full of you.

I'm not an option, Apollo.

Not yet.

It wasn't the first time he'd said that to her. But now that the tournament was immi-nent, Tem knew it was true. She would be sleeping with him in the final tier—riding his cock the same way the blond basilisk rode it now. If her heart called to Apollo, she would have to marry him. Tem tried to picture it: being wed to Apollo instead of Caspen. She couldn't imagine that life.

I can.

His voice was quiet in her mind—barely a whisper—and it was sincere. For once, Apollo wasn't flirting. He was testing the waters, seeing how Tem would react to a genuine display of vulnerability. Truth be told, she didn't know how to react. This was the last thing she wanted to deal with tonight. Her dalliance with Apollo was nothing of importance; it wasn't *real*. Not like her and Caspen.

Without another word, Tem left to find her husband. He was over by the betting basin.

My love. What is it?

Spend time with me.

As you wish.

They stood together, not touching, watching the revelry unfold.

One pair of women were so intertwined, they could have been fused together. When Tem looked closer, she realized they *were*. An object gleamed between their legs, just like the claw Caspen had made her. It was the same color and curved in a similar way. But this object was designed to accommodate them both, double ended, joining them together by their centers so that they experienced dual pleasure. It glistened with their combined wetness, dripping onto the table. The sight made Tem warm. The women were beautiful together—endless curves and soft skin. But it wasn't until she saw two men tangled in an intimate knot that Tem flushed immediately with desire. Caspen's presence nudged her mind.

Do you wish to join them?

The flush deepened.

At her reaction, Caspen said, "Shall I ask them for you?"

Tem hesitated. She only wanted Caspen right now. But perhaps that was actually a reason to do this. Caspen could not touch her; they could not have sex. But he needed to be strong tomorrow, and the only way to gain power was through sex. If he could not have it with Tem, at least he could watch her with someone else.

Before Tem could stop herself, she nodded.

The moment she did so, a flash of pride illuminated Caspen's face. He immediately crossed to the couple, who pulled momentarily apart. Tem watched as they listened, joy lighting up their eyes. Caspen turned to her, extending his hand, clearly indicating for her to approach.

She couldn't believe the enthusiasm with which the men embraced her, lifting her so she was suspended between them, her legs around one, the other behind her. Caught between two men, an illustration of her actual circumstances.

They did not enter her mind. Only Caspen was here with her, and Tem waited for his permission to begin. With a nod, he gave it.

Tem turned her head to the man in front of her. He watched her with anticipation, his eyes wide and trusting, his hands securely around her waist.

She leaned in, brushing her lips against his.

He returned her kiss gently, matching her pace. The man behind her found her clitoris, applying pressure, rubbing in sensual circles.

Good, Tem.

The three of them found a rhythm together, kissing and touching in tandem. Tem felt as secure in their arms as she would in Caspen's, his presence steady and dominating in her mind.

Now let them fuck you.

Tem would have let them do anything. It was her sole goal to obey Caspen in this moment, to let him tell her what to do. She wanted nothing but the simple pleasure of pleasing him. It was the least she could do considering what he was about to do for her.

The basilisk behind her entered her first. Tem didn't stop kissing the basilisk before her, didn't break rhythm even as his cock slid deep into her center, stretching her. She was wet for them; she was ready. Still, it had been a long time since she'd taken a cock that wasn't Caspen's, and she found herself imagining whether it would be like this during the third tier, when she would ride her contenders all in a row.

Tem gasped as the basilisk behind her pulled out suddenly. Then the basilisk before her entered her, and all was once more right in the world. She turned her head to kiss the man behind her, letting them both do anything they pleased. They touched her everywhere: on her waist, her ass, her breasts. Having two sets of hands dedicated solely to her was stimulation like Tem had never known. She leaned into it all, arching her back to meet them, desperate to feel every inch of deliverance.

Caspen oversaw it all, his presence looming larger than the mountain itself, their generous ruler. He touched himself while the men fucked her, stroking his cock to the rhythm of their thrusts. Tem felt his presence in her mind so strongly, he may as well have been inside her. He was just as involved as the basilisks were, directing them with his thoughts. The moment a desire occurred to Tem, they would immediately perform it. When she wanted them to kiss her, they kissed her. When she wanted her neck squeezed, they squeezed it. And Tem returned the favor in kind. When Caspen told her to do something, she did it.

Kiss him.

She did so.

Put your hand on his chest.

She put it there.

Tilt your head back. Let me see your neck.

Tem let him see whatever he wanted to see—her in any position, getting fucked any way he wanted. The basilisks were deliberate, holding her between them as they alternated their cocks, sometimes for minutes at a time, sometimes for a single, sharp thrust before pulling out and letting the other in. All of them moved in sync, existing in a space without time, existing only to feel. Tem could barely breathe, and she didn't want to anyway. She wanted only to be filled—to be taken right here, in the banquet hall, for everyone to see. It would never be enough for Tem: two cocks or even three. Her basilisk side was insatiable, begging for excess, only ever wanting more.

Tem knew Caspen wanted more too. Some part of him liked this—some part of him wanted the tournament to happen. It was an honor for their marriage to be contested—an honor for his wife to be desirable. But most of all, Tem knew he wanted to win. She could see it in his eyes, in the possessive way he watched while the other basilisks brought her closer to orgasm. Every stroke of their fingers made her moan—every brush of their lips sent her straight to the edge. She could stay like this forever, wrapped around their bodies like moss on a tree.

Eventually, Tem couldn't take any more. Caspen's eyes had been black for a long time now; smoke rose from his shoulders. All of them were close, and all of them wanted it. The basilisk behind her was thrusting relentlessly, pushing Tem against the basilisk in front of her, pushing them *all* toward release. Beside them, Caspen's strokes were quickening, his cock straining against his grip. He was so stunning to Tem. She wanted to taste him. She wanted it inside her.

On my count, Tem.

Caspen's mind was guiding hers, pulling her right along with him.

Three.

The basilisk behind her thrust *deep*—deeper than she thought was possible.

Two.

The basilisk before her bit her lip.

One.

It was time.

They all came together, free of inhibitions, free of constraints. Tem knew she'd done everything right—obeyed every order Caspen had given her—done as she was told. His power was undeniable; she felt it even though they weren't touching. She would have felt it from a hundred miles away. The basilisks set her gently on the ground, pressing kisses to her body as they did it. When her feet touched the stone, Tem looked at Caspen. One look at him was all it took; he already knew what she wanted.

"Enough," Caspen said aloud.

The basilisks obeyed immediately, extracting themselves from Tem before bowing deeply to her. "Thank you," they both murmured. Tem heard the awe in their voices, as if what just happened was of paramount importance. Perhaps it was.

"Thank *you*," she murmured in return.

The basilisks walked away hand in hand. Tem was left bereft—utterly and completely empty. She turned to Caspen, who smiled down at her.

"You were so beautiful, Tem."

"So were you."

His smile widened. Then he said, "You should go to sleep. Once the tournament begins, there will be no breaks until it is over."

Tem thought about the structure of the tournament—the three tiers, the endless physical exertion. Sleep sounded nice. "Will you come with me?"

Caspen shook his head. "We are not to see each other over the next few hours."

Anxiety squeezed her chest. "Why not?"

"It is tradition. Think of it as how humans do not see the bride before the wedding."

"Oh," Tem said. "Right."

She supposed that made sense, in a roundabout sort of way. But she needed Caspen right now. The last thing she wanted was to be alone. She couldn't even kiss him good night.

Caspen raised his hand to her chest. But instead of trying to touch her skin, he touched the golden claw hanging from her neck. He moved it with his finger, first up her sternum, then over the tops of her breasts. Tem closed her eyes. It was incredible to *feel* what he was doing to her—to see his body create a motion and experience it with hers. It was the closest thing to touching that they had done in what felt like so, *so* long.

I wish I could kiss you.

Soon.

Tem's stomach clenched. *But what if*—Tem cut herself off, because she didn't want to finish the thought. To her surprise, Caspen smiled.

What if I do not win?

Tem nodded. She couldn't answer.

Then we will take that as it comes, Tem.

She pursed her lips, holding back tears. How could he be so calm about this? How could he be bound to her by blood and not worry about the outcome of this tournament? The thought of being unable to touch Caspen killed her, plain and simple. It made her want to die. But he was not the only man in her life, and he never would be. It had always been this way; it had always been a struggle for her to choose. What if now, in front of hundreds of basilisks, she was forced to reveal something she couldn't even admit to herself? The thought was terrifying.

Caspen looked her deep in the eyes. *I would rather the brutal truth than the sweetest lie.*

Tem barely believed that. *Couldn't* believe that. The truth was not just brutal. It was deadly. *We're supposed to be together forever.*

We will be, Tem. This is not a concern.

Well, I'm concerned.

Tem, I will not leave you. Not now. Not ever.

She stared into his golden eyes, knowing he spoke the truth. But it didn't change the fact that the tournament might force *her* to leave *him*.

Caspen dropped his hand, leaving her cold. *Sleep well, my love. I will see you soon.*

Tem nodded. She couldn't seem to speak. Instead she left the banquet hall, trudging back to her chambers slowly, dreading the lonely hours before midnight. But to her surprise, there was someone leaning against her doorway.

"Going to bed so soon, Temperance?"

Tem crossed her arms. "What are you doing here?"

Apollo straightened. "I came to see you."

"I know that. But *why*?"

"Because you are not well."

It wasn't a question, and Tem couldn't fathom why he would say that to her. "Excuse me? I'm perfectly fine."

"No." Apollo leaned in. "You are not. You have been different since the night I taught you to petrify. You eat less. You do not sleep. Something is affecting you."

Tem stared up at him in disbelief. How had Apollo managed to notice all of those things? Even Caspen hadn't noticed she wasn't sleeping well. Then again, he was gone all the time, hunting. There were some days when Apollo saw her more than Caspen did. And on those days, apparently, he had been watching her closely.

"What ails you, Temperance?"

Tem let out a tortured laugh. What ailed her? Too many things to count. She was worried about the tournament, the crest, Leo. She was worried that everything was about to fall apart. But Apollo couldn't fix any of those things. Nobody could.

"Just go to bed, Apollo."

"It is you who should be in bed."

Tem frowned at his tone. He sounded genuinely concerned. Normally Apollo would have made some cheeky comment about how he wanted to come to bed with her. But not tonight. Tonight he was looking at her as if she were fragile, as if she might break. It wasn't an expression she was used to seeing on him.

"Why do you care what I do?"

"I care because you and my brother are bound by blood. Your emotional bond is significant, which means that your well-being directly affects his. If you are not at your best, he cannot perform tomorrow."

That stopped Tem short. "What do you mean?"

"I mean"—Apollo stepped closer, and she sensed his urgency—"he will need to be strong for the fight, which means you must be strong too."

Tem bit her lip. She was anything but strong right now.

"What ails you, Temperance?" Apollo asked again, softer this time. "If you do not wish to tell me, I understand. But burdens are easier to bear when shared."

He was right, of course. But her burdens were not the kind that could be shared. Apollo could do nothing about the situation with Leo—he could not free her from consummating the crest. He could not even guarantee the results of the tournament. And yet, somehow, his offer to confide in him helped. It made her feel less alone. So she said, "I'm afraid."

"Of what?"

But there were no words to describe it. Tem was afraid of *so* many things. She couldn't possibly list them all right now, and she didn't want Apollo to know them anyway. To know them would be to sit in secrecy with her, and she did not wish that on him.

"Of the tournament?" Apollo prompted.

"Yes," she said truthfully. Among other things.

"You have nothing to fear, Temperance."

Tem closed her eyes, trying to believe him. "That's easy for you to say. Your husband isn't in danger."

"I do not have a husband."

"You know what I mean."

"Caspenon will be fine, Temperance."

"You don't know that."

"I know my brother. And nothing could stop him from fighting for you."

"I can't live without him."

"The tournament presents only a possibility of that. Not a guarantee of it."

A pause.

Apollo's next words came quietly: "I understand you are afraid. But if Caspenon does not win, I will protect you from Rowe. No harm will ever come to you by his hand. You have my word."

Tem opened her eyes, nearly losing her breath when she saw how close Apollo was standing.

"I share my blood with him." Apollo touched his finger to the claw around her neck, the exact same the way Caspen had. "Just as you do." His voice dropped to a whisper as he finished. "We will not let you go so easily."

"It's not up to you."

"Your heart will call to your true match, Temperance. There is no reason to fear that."

"Yes. There is."

"Why?"

"Because I love Leo." The moment she said it, terror struck her.

Apollo frowned. "Leo?"

Tem realized Apollo only knew him by one name. "Thelonius. The human king."

She expected a reaction of some kind. For him to shout, perhaps, or berate her. Instead he tilted his head, looking at her with what could only be described as compassion. His gaze flicked down to her hand, where her silver wedding band glinted.

"I always wondered why you still wore that," he whispered.

Tem twirled the ring around her finger, feeling the cool metal. Caspen had never once asked about it. She was beginning to think he never would. "I...can't bear to take it off."

Apollo tilted his head, as if he'd just understood something. "You are afraid your heart will call to him."

Tears filled her eyes. When he said it out loud, somehow it made it real. "Yes," she whispered.

Apollo sighed. It wasn't an angry sigh—more wistful, as if he felt sorry for her. Most likely he did. Tem had allowed this to go too far, had indulged her feelings for too long. Now she would face the consequences. Apollo could not fix this. No one could.

"We cannot help who we love, Temperance." It sounded like he was speaking from experience. "You are not the first person to enter the tournament uncertain. And you will not be the last."

"I'm not *uncertain*," she said. "I love them both. *That* is certain."

Apollo regarded for a moment before speaking. "I cannot pretend to understand your love for the human king. From what I have seen of him, he looks rather frail."

Tem almost laughed.

"But I can understand matters of the heart," Apollo continued, touching his fingers gently to Tem's chest. "And matters of the heart are never simple."

Tem looked up at him. Apollo said it calmly, in a tone that implied he had extensive experience in the matter. And she supposed he did. Caspen and Apollo had both been alive for centuries—far longer than Tem. She was twenty years old. She was a child in comparison. But nobody here treated her like a child, especially the Drakon brothers. It was a double-edged sword. She was not afforded the grace a child would be in the same situation. Tem had made her bed, and now she would have to lie in it.

"Temperance," he said softly, and she looked up at him. "My brother deserves to know how you feel."

Tem knew what he was trying to say. *I care only that you are loyal with your heart.*

"I shall keep your secret," Apollo murmured. "But I cannot do so forever. Do you understand me?"

Tem nodded. It was all she could ask of him, and it was already too much. "I understand."

They stood in silence. Eventually, Tem couldn't take it anymore. "Do you think I'm a bad person?"

The words were out before she could stop them, and Tem wasn't even sure why she'd said them. Apollo was the last person she should be asking a question like that. She thought about when he'd taught her to petrify, how she'd wanted to do it to someone who deserved it. She wondered whether someone who deserved it was her.

Apollo gave her the slightest smile. "Define bad."

There was no answer to that. Everything was allowed here; nothing was off-limits. Basilisks had absolutely no sense of right or wrong—at least not the way humans did. When Tem remained silent, Apollo touched her gently, skimming just his fingertips along the curve of her waist.

"Why would you ask me that?"

"Because I need forgiveness."

He shook his head. "My forgiveness is not the one you truly need."

Tem knew he was right. She was asking for absolution for what she'd done to Leo. Apollo could not provide it. She sought something that nobody could give her, not even Caspen. Pain pinched Tem's chest. It felt as if she were on the edge of a panic attack, as if the walls were closing in on her. She didn't need Apollo's forgiveness, but she wanted it anyway.

"Answer me," she said, firmly this time.

Apollo raised an eyebrow, considering her. His hand tightened on her waist, and Tem's heartbeat sped up. She knew he could sense it; basilisks could always sense such things. But she didn't retreat. Instead, Tem wondered whether Apollo was a bad person too. He certainly wasn't proper or polite or anything that civilized society would consider good. But he was brave. And fearless. He loved his family, and he protected them when necessary. Was there anything else, really, that mattered? Was it enough to love the people you cared about, to wish the best for them? Tem didn't know anymore.

Apollo's hand trailed up her body to her chin, raising her head to his. Tem almost wondered if they were going to kiss. Instead he whispered, "I do not think you are a bad person."

Tem processed his answer, wondering what to make of it. "I think I am," she whispered.

Apollo's fingers traced her jaw, wrapping around the back of her neck. She was poised, ready, waiting. "That is your choice, Temperance."

She held his gaze. "Apollo?"

"Temperance?"

Her heart slammed against her rib cage. It was all hitting her right now, all at once: the severity of the tournament, the consequences of her actions. If her heart did not call to Caspen, they would never touch again. Tem fought the sudden urge to vomit. She needed comfort, and Apollo was the only one who could provide it.

Before she could talk herself out of it, she said, "Will you hold me?"

Apollo didn't hesitate for even a moment. He simply opened his arms, stepped forward, and pulled her against him. The moment he did so, Tem's mind went quiet. For the first time in days, she relaxed. The tension left her muscles; the anxiety quieted in her brain. She tucked her head against Apollo's neck and closed her eyes, feeling nothing but the steady rise and fall of his chest.

He breathed impossibly slowly, just as Caspen did. But Apollo's body felt different. It was not familiar to her the way his brother's was. Tem had memorized every inch of Caspen's body; she knew every peak, every valley. Apollo's torso had different angles, a different shape to tuck herself against. He smelled of smoke, as Caspen did, but it wasn't the same; Caspen's was dynamic and strong—the smoke of a wildfire as it ripped through a forest. Apollo's was rich and layered and *dark*—an aching ember.

At some point, Apollo's hand cradled the back of her head. His fingers gently stroked her hair, and Tem found herself soothed by the motion. She hadn't realized how much she needed this until it was happening. She'd gone far too long without simply standing still and *being*.

Apollo's mind brushed tentatively against hers. *Is this helping, Temperance?*

Tem nodded, her head still buried against his shoulder. This was the *only* thing that was helping. For the first time in days, she felt human again. It was easy to forget that side of her when she was only surrounded by basilisks. But her human side was the side she had known the longest; she had grown up thinking she was human, and only in the past few months had everything changed. It was too much for one person, too much far too quickly. For the first time, Tem wondered if she had moved too fast, taken on too much in this new life of hers.

She wasn't ready to live like a basilisk. That had only become more apparent as time had passed. She wasn't ready for any of it.

Apollo spoke again. *What else can I do?*

There was nothing else he could do. Not really. There was nothing *anyone* could do.

You've already done more than enough. It occurred to her that there was one more thing she needed to say to him: *Thank you.*

Apollo held her for a long time. Tem let the silence sit, knowing she would not be the one to fill it. When he pulled away, she remained in place, looking up at his carved face in the darkness.

Get some sleep, Temperance.

Then he was gone.

The moment Tem entered her chambers, she saw there was someone in her bed: Gabriel. Tem climbed underneath the blankets next to him, curling her body against his, savoring his beating heart. He pulled her close, the second man to hold her tonight, tucking his head into the crook of her neck. She was so grateful he was here, that he'd forgone Damon's company for hers—that she wasn't alone.

"You'd better not snore, dearest," he mumbled into her hair.

Tem couldn't help but smile. "You'd better not either."

"I would never. I have very delicate airways."

Tem rolled her eyes. Then she fell asleep.

Hours later, her name came to her in the darkness.

"Temperance," Adelaide whispered. "Wake up. It is midnight."

CHAPTER THIRTY-FOUR

⸺•✦•⸺

Tem kissed Gabriel on the cheek before following Adelaide out into the passageway. She didn't bother asking where they were going—she was too nervous to speak anyway. Instead, Tem clenched and unclenched her fists in an attempt to calm herself, thinking about what Apollo had said to her: *We will not let you go so easily.*

But the Drakon brothers were not in control. Neither was Tem. *Nobody* knew what would happen at the end of the tournament. Perhaps not even Kora.

"Everyone is already gathered," Adelaide was saying. "When we arrive, there will be an opening ceremony to inaugurate the contenders. After that, the tournament will begin."

Tem nodded, although it was difficult to absorb this information. She was thinking about the first tier and how Caspen would have to fight Rowe.

"Are there rules?" Tem asked.

"What do you mean?"

They were walking downward—ever downward—and the air was becoming warm.

"For the fight, I mean. Are there rules, or is it just…" She couldn't bring herself to say *to the death.*

"They must fight fair," Adelaide said. "They cannot utilize any weapons nor can they carry objects that might cause petrification, such as mirrors. They are not allowed to bite each other. They will transition in order to begin, and the fight will last until one of them transitions back."

Tentative relief swept through Tem. She was still nervous, considering Rowe's blatant disregard for boundaries. There was no reason to trust him with the rules. But Adelaide had said the tournament was sanctioned by Kora. Surely, even for Rowe, that held some weight. And surely, Caspen would win.

He was the Serpent King—he was the most powerful male under the mountain. But Apollo's words ran through her mind: *Your well-being directly affects his. If you are not at your best, he cannot perform tomorrow.*

Tem was not at her best. She hadn't been for a long time. She was weak and she was worried and she was terrified that it would affect the way Caspen fought. Too much was riding on this—too much was at stake. What if—

Adelaide stopped. Tem stopped too.

They were standing before a set of double doors so tall Tem couldn't see the top of them.

"Temperance," Adelaide said quietly. "Are you ready?"

She would never be ready for this.

When she didn't answer, Adelaide stepped closer. "I will be by your side. You do not have to face this alone."

A wave of gratitude swept over Tem. Adelaide had become a lifeline to her in the last few weeks, ever since the first night of mating seasons. To have her here now was an unimaginable blessing. And she was right. Tem would not face this alone.

"I'm ready."

Adelaide nodded. Then she opened the doors.

What lay beyond them took Tem's breath away. Unlike the contained room with the altar where the ritual was held, they had entered an *arena*. It was broad and deep and oval in shape, with great sloping rows of benches that nearly reached the towering ceiling. Every single seat was filled; basilisks were writhing and cheering and waving from the stands. The same white sand that covered the shores of the lake filled the arena. There, in the middle, was Caspen.

Immediately, Tem ran to him. She didn't care whether it was allowed; she didn't care that everyone was watching. She only wanted to be near him.

"Caspen," she breathed as soon as they were face-to-face.

He smiled. "My love."

Behind him stood the other contenders. Rowe was already scowling at her. Tem didn't even bother looking in his direction, focusing instead on Apollo, who was watching her with a contemplative expression on his face. Was he thinking about her confession? Or was he anticipating what was to come?

"Did you sleep?" Caspen asked.

"Barely. Did you?"

"No." He didn't elaborate.

Before Tem could ask him to, Adelaide appeared at her side. She was holding a large golden chalice filled with elixir. "It is time to begin," she said to the contenders. "Please stand in a line."

The basilisks obeyed, arranging themselves into formation.

"You will each swear to honor the outcome of the tournament. Then you will seal your promise with the elixir." She stepped toward Eros, who was first in line. "Kneel."

Eros knelt.

"Will you honor the outcome?"

"I will," Eros answered.

Adelaide dipped her fingers in the chalice and touched them first to one shoulder, then the other, as if he were being knighted. Then she handed him the chalice, and he drank deeply.

Rowe knelt next, and Adelaide did the same for him.

She went down the line until she reached Apollo, who gave Tem a smile before he bowed his head. Despite herself, Tem smiled back. There were many elements that were well outside her control. But at least she knew the Drakon brothers were on her side. With them in her corner, what did she have to fear?

Finally, it was Tem's turn.

"Will you honor the outcome?" Adelaide asked.

Tem hesitated, suddenly paralyzed. There were too many things that could go wrong, too many lives and relationships at stake. All of it was on her shoulders. And what of the final tier? What if her heart called to another? Would she honor the outcome?

In the pause, Apollo's mind brushed against hers.

Do not be afraid. Let us do this for you.

"Temperance." Adelaide's voice cut through Apollo's. "Will you honor the outcome?"

Everyone was watching her expectantly. They had come to the end of the road. It was time to let fate take its course.

"I will."

Adelaide nodded. Then she dipped her fingers in the chalice, touching Tem's shoulders the way she'd just touched the contenders'. Tem drank the last of the elixir, her entire body warming as it slid down her throat. As soon as she finished swallowing, Adelaide raised the empty chalice over her head, turning toward the crowd to yell, "It is done. Let the tournament begin."

The arena erupted into cheers.

"Temperance," Adelaide said. "Come with me."

But Tem couldn't move. She was staring at Caspen, who was staring at her.

"Caspen," she said. But there were no words—nothing to say to encompass everything she was feeling. So she said the only thing she needed him to know: "I love you."

He smiled. It was a sad smile, and for some reason, Tem wanted to cry. What if this was it? Unless Caspen won the tournament, unless her heart called to him—she would never touch him again. A life without Caspen's touch was not a life Tem could bear. She wouldn't survive without him.

"I love you too."

Adelaide's hand was on her arm, pulling her back. The rest of the contenders were dispersing, leaving only Caspen and Rowe in the middle of the arena.

"Where are we going?" Tem asked as Adelaide steered her toward the stands.

"To your suite," Adelaide said. "You will watch the first tier from there."

They climbed the stairs together. All around them, basilisks reached out to touch Tem—running their fingers along her legs, her waist, her arms—as if they wanted to take some small piece of her for themselves.

The suite was an enormous, ornate balcony. It contained a long bench, from which Tem had a breathtaking view of the arena. Rowe and Caspen stood in the very middle. Caspen's back was to her, and Tem reached for him with her mind, but their connection was closed. She turned immediately to Adelaide.

"Why can't I talk to him?"

"You are not to communicate for the entirety of the tournament."

Tem frowned.

"There is no cause for concern," Adelaide said quickly. "You can still communicate with anyone else. I am at your disposal, Apollo as well."

Of course Apollo was at her disposal. He always was. "Can he watch with us?"

Adelaide raised an elegant shoulder. "You may have anyone here that you wish. You need only ask him. I am sure he would be honored."

Tem reached for the other Drakon brother with her mind, finding him immediately.

Apollo. Where are you?

I am with the other contenders. Why do you ask?

I want you here with me.

A pause. For some reason, she was nervous he would reject her. And then: *I am on my way.*

Tem turned to Adelaide. "Apollo is coming."

"Good."

But even this development was not enough to soothe Tem. "Caspen has no plan," she said, voicing the thing that weighed on her the most. "He isn't prepared. He thinks he will win just because he has more to lose."

"You cannot expect him to prepare as a human would, Temperance."

"That doesn't mean he can't—"

"He will do as he sees best. Do not underestimate his love for you."

Adrenaline pricked Tem's spine. She stared down at Rowe and Caspen, wondering what they were thinking.

"If Rowe starts to win, I'm leaving," she said. "I don't want to watch Caspen get hurt."

Adelaide shook her head. "You cannot leave."

"And why not?"

"When you swore to honor the outcome, you swore on Kora herself. The oath is binding. She will hold you to it."

"What does that mean?"

"The tournament will run until the winner has been chosen. It is not possible to leave before it is over. Kora's magic will keep you here."

Tem put her head in her hands.

Adelaide touched her shoulder gently. "Temperance, listen to me. Apollo and Caspenon will let no harm come to you. They love you."

"*Caspen* loves me."

"Apollo loves you too, in his own way."

"Apollo isn't capable of love."

Adelaide smiled. "You are wrong to assume that. Love can take many forms."

Tem wrinkled her nose.

At her expression, Adelaide smiled. "You do not have to love him back. It is possible he would not respect you if you did. But he loves you, Temperance. And you must allow him to show it in his own way. He would die for you as surely as Caspenon would."

Her mother had once told her that true love was sacrificing your happiness for theirs. Was it a step further to sacrifice oneself? She wanted everyone in Caspen's family to live very long lives that were not cut short by anything to do with her.

"I don't want Apollo to die for me. I don't want *anyone* to die for me."

Adelaide gave her a gentle smile. "That is not for you to decide. We are basilisks, Temperance. The brothers come to this willingly."

A moment later, one of the brothers was beside her.

Tem felt Apollo before she saw him, his body heating the air as he joined her on the bench. Immediately, Tem felt as if she could breathe again. She turned to him. But before she could say anything, Adelaide spoke.

"Look, Temperance. It begins."

The arena roared to life as Caspen and Rowe began to circle each other. Great clouds of smoke billowed from their bodies, filling the air. Pure fear shot through Tem. This was it. They were about to transition. Tem watched as Caspen turned first, his body elongating to release the monster within. She stared at his beautiful obsidian scales, remembering the first time she saw them. Caspen had nearly killed her that night in the cave. Tem almost wished he had. Then none of this would have happened.

Rowe transitioned next.

He roared as he turned, his head whipping up proudly. His scales were pure gold, the exact color of his false cock. Tem had never seen a basilisk that color before. Most were black, like Caspen. Sometimes they varied to green or even dark blue, but never gold. She remembered what Caspen said—how Rowe's cock made him powerful. Did it make his true form powerful too? The thought made her nervous. *Caspen* was supposed to be powerful.

Caspen was supposed to win.

The air was suddenly sweltering. Even in a venue as enormous as the arena, two fully transitioned basilisks took up a lot of room. They circled each other just as they had when they were human, their giant bodies carving valleys in the sand. Then Rowe lunged.

Caspen dodged but just barely. Rowe moved uncommonly fast; Tem didn't dare blink for fear of missing something. She couldn't stop picturing Caspen getting hurt.

"Caspenon is strong, Temperance," Adelaide said. "He will prevail. Try not to worry."

But nothing could stop Tem from worrying. Caspen and Rowe thrashed violently before her, their bodies intertwining, then separating, then intertwining again at lightning speed. It was a wonder to watch, and if Tem hadn't been so nervous, she might have enjoyed herself. Instead she clasped Adelaide's hand so tightly, her fingers went numb.

Relax, Temperance, Apollo's voice said in her mind.

I can't.

You can. And you must.

Why?

Your energy directly affects Caspenon. He will need your strength.

But Tem had barely any strength left to give. She felt completely drained from the events of the last few days. She knew it was an effect of the crest—that Leo was not the only one weakened by her refusal to consummate.

When Rowe advanced on Caspen, Tem's heart jumped.

Put your emotions aside, Temperance. Your husband needs you.

But Tem had never been good at putting her emotions aside. It was the one thing she couldn't master—the one thing Caspen had always tried to train out of her but couldn't. Tem was *ruled* by emotions. There was only one thing she could possibly do to suppress them.

Make me calm.

Apollo hesitated.

Please, Apollo.

Still, he hesitated. It wasn't until Rowe roared—and Tem flinched—that he said, *Very well.*

Apollo's hand went to her waist. The second his fingers touched her, Tem felt calm envelope her. His influence was different from his brother's. Caspen's was gentle, softening the sharp edges of her anxiety. Apollo's was commanding, forcing her into a state of numbness that felt brutally clinical, devoid of anything except for what was in front of her. It was fascinating to experience the differences between the brothers. Of the two of them, Tem preferred Caspen; that was no surprise. But there was a benefit to Apollo's assistance, namely that Tem was immediately able to suppress the panic rising in her chest.

Thank you.

My pleasure.

She didn't have the energy to roll her eyes. He was a little too self-satisfied for her liking, but that would have to wait. Instead, Tem concentrated on Caspen. He was still fighting, and in the wake of her calm, he was winning.

The next time Caspen advanced on Rowe, Tem's nipples peaked. She bit her lip, shocked at her body's reaction. Her basilisk side was fueled by the violence, reveling in the efforts of the suitors before her. The urge to touch herself was so strong, she suddenly had trouble thinking of anything else. Even the importance of the tournament couldn't distract her from how wet she was.

"Adelaide," she whispered. "I'm—"

The roar of the crowd cut her off.

Adelaide turned to her. "What is it, Temperance?"

"I feel…" But how to say it?

Adelaide raised an eyebrow, waiting patiently for her to elaborate. But Tem couldn't find the words. Men were fighting over her, and it was turning her on, and although her human side was horrified at the proceedings, the basilisk side only wanted one thing.

Without thinking, Tem's hand went between her legs. It felt so good to touch herself that she gasped aloud, squeezing her eyes shut in surprise.

"Ah," she heard Adelaide say. "I see."

Tem barely heard her. The sensation of her fingers sliding into her center was enough to make her want to scream.

"You may have sex with someone if you wish, Temperance."

Tem opened her eyes. "What?"

Beside her, Apollo perked up.

"Any of the contenders are at your disposal," Adelaide continued. "They are competing for your hand—it would be an honor if you chose any of them to satisfy you right now."

Tem shook her head. The fight raged before her; blood soaked the sand.

"No."

"Are you sure?" Adelaide's eyes slid to Apollo, who was clearly ready to volunteer.

"I'm sure," Tem snapped. She didn't want to hear how Apollo was at her disposal again. Fucking Caspen's brother while Caspen fought for their marriage was a line Tem was unwilling to cross, even now. With supreme effort, she removed her hand from between her legs, clamping it instead beneath her thighs. She would watch the rest of the fight like this if that was what it took to resist. But it was not so easy. Her basilisk side roared in her mind, grating against her human defiance. Tem was *so* turned on.

I am more than happy to assist with that, Temperance.

I don't need assistance.

Are you sure? It rather seems like you do. Apollo's voice was barely audible over the roar of the crowd, which was so loud it felt as if the arena were shaking.

Arousal turned to fear. Somewhere, in the course of the last few minutes, the tide had changed. Caspen was no longer winning.

Blood soaked the sand, and it was all his. Rowe's golden scales were barbed and sharp, tearing Caspen's to shreds.

"What's going on?" Tem cried. "Why is this happening?"

"I do not know." Adelaide shook her head. "Rowe is impenetrable. I have never seen that before."

"Can you access Caspen's mind? Can you talk to him for me?"

Adelaide shifted in her seat. "That would be…unconventional. You are not allowed to communicate with him during the tournament."

"I wouldn't be. *You'd* be communicating with him. I just need to know what's going on—if he's—"

Caspen let out a roar of pain as Rowe's body struck his. Adelaide pursed her lips.

"*Please*, Adelaide."

"If you will not do it, I will."

The words came from Apollo. His eyes were on Tem, his brows furrowed.

Adelaide glanced between them before holding up her hand. "There is no need. I will do it."

"Thank you," Tem said.

Adelaide turned, focusing on Caspen. Far too long passed. "Caspenon says Rowe is strong—stronger than he should be."

"Why?"

A pause.

"He does not know. But Caspenon has a higher ranking. Rowe should not be able to fight this well."

Tem stared at Rowe—at his hard, gold scales. It was his cock. She was sure of it. He had violated the laws of nature to craft it for himself, and now it had given him some sort of power—power that matched Caspen's.

"Tell him he needs to fight harder—he needs to end this."

Another pause.

"He is trying. But he—"

What happened next was so fast, Tem nearly missed it.

One moment the basilisks were apart, and the next, they slammed together. Caspen pinned Rowe to the ground with his entire body, sparks flying as they writhed in the sand. Rowe's mouth opened. He drove his fangs straight into Caspen's neck.

Caspen let out a tortured roar, lurching backward into the wall of the arena.

"Did he just *bite him*?" Tem cried.

Adelaide's mouth was open in shock. "He…did."

"But—but you said that wasn't allowed—"

"It is not. But Rowe did it anyway."

Everything is allowed here. Even breaking the rules—even going against the one boundary that had been established in this fight.

Blood poured from Caspen's neck.

Tem stared at the wound, her throat tight, her hands clenched into fists. It wasn't just a physical injury. Tem remembered what Caspen had said to her—how the bite of a basilisk created the ability to siphon power from the victim. Caspen and Rowe were now connected. There was a link between them—one that Rowe could use to take his power.

Tem had no idea how it worked, whether Rowe could take it all at once or whether it would be a slow process. All she knew was that Caspen was bleeding, and she would never forgive herself.

Everyone in the arena was on their feet. Tem watched as Caspen transitioned back into a human, still on the ground, still bleeding. Rowe transitioned after, raising his fists above his head.

"What does this mean? Adelaide?" Tem's voice went up an octave. "What does it *mean*?"

Adelaide turned to look at Tem, her face pale. "It means Rowe won."

CHAPTER THIRTY-FIVE

---•••✳•••---

TEM WAS NUMB.

The cheers of the crowd dimmed, as if someone had thrown a blanket over the arena.

"Temperance," Adelaide was saying. "All is not lost."

But Tem barely heard her. Rowe had won. *Everything* was lost.

"You must remember that your heart will make the ultimate choice. All this means is that Rowe has earned a spot in the third tier. That is all."

"That's *all*?"

But that was a disaster. *That* guaranteed Tem would have to fuck him.

How could Caspen let this happen? But Tem didn't bother answering that question. It wasn't his fault. *She* had let this happen. Apollo had warned her; Apollo had tried to help. She was not at her best, so Caspen hadn't been either. She put her head in her hands.

"Temperance," Adelaide said in her ear. "Stand up. You must go down to the arena."

Tem remembered the structure of the tournament—how there were no breaks, and it would run until the third tier was over. It was much like the ritual in that way. Basilisks were not prone to pacing themselves.

"This tier is meant to measure sexual compatibility," Adelaide was saying as she lead them down the steps, Apollo close behind. "The remaining contenders will pleasure themselves in front of you, and the results will determine the order of the final round of the tournament."

"What do you mean?"

"It is a contest in speed," she said. "Whoever finishes the quickest will receive the spot of honor in the third tier."

"And which spot is that?"

"Last."

Tem thought about the third tier—how she would have to ride each of her potential prospects all in a row.

"As soon as everyone has finished and the order is determined, the third tier will begin."

By now they had reached the arena floor. The moment Tem stepped out onto the sand, the crowd screamed. Caspen and Rowe were already gone; Tem saw them in the stands, watching in their human forms. Caspen's neck was still bleeding. The remaining contenders stood in a semicircle, half of them already hard. Tem stared at the blood-soaked sand at their feet, her throat tight with uncertainty as she reached them.

"But what do I…do?"

"You simply stand here," Adelaide said. "They must climax only to the sight of you. You are not meant to do anything that might influence them."

Tem looked at the ten men in front of her. Eros was on the end of the semicircle, closest to Tem. Apollo left her side, taking a spot in the middle. Tem ran her eyes over every basilisk, trying to imagine what they were thinking. They looked back at her eagerly, and she remembered how Adelaide had said this was the first tournament in decades. They had waited a long time for this. The least she could do was let them enjoy it.

Adelaide clapped her hands, and the arena quieted. Then she cried, "Begin."

Immediately, the men began to stroke.

The same urge that had reared its head during the first tier did so again now, her basilisk side desperately turned on by the proceedings. That side loved the way it felt to have the men before her compete for her hand—to prove themselves to her the way Tem had so often had to prove herself to others. For once, Tem was in the position of power. For once, she was not trying to impress anyone. *They* were trying to impress *her*. All at her disposal. All hers. Tem crossed her arms, ready to see who finished first.

It was Apollo.

Not even thirty seconds passed before his shoulders jerked forward and a lumines-cent stream of cum pooled onto his palm. Adelaide's voice entered her mind: *That was impressive. Perhaps the quickest I have ever seen.*

Does that mean he won?

It does indeed.

Tem remembered how the new mother had chosen Apollo to receive her blessing—how he had the favor of Kora. Perhaps that had influenced his performance; perhaps he was driven by forces beyond his control—or perhaps he was driven by Tem.

The rest of the men were still stroking their cocks as Apollo stepped forward, hold-ing his hand out to Tem. She stared at the substance in his palm, her heart hammering. Before she could ask, Adelaide said, *He is offering it to you.*

Am I supposed to…take it?

Not exactly.

Tem didn't bother asking a follow-up question. Somehow, she knew what she was supposed to do. Perhaps it was her basilisk side that desired it. Perhaps she, herself, wanted to do it too. Either way, she stepped forward so she and Apollo were face-to-face. Then she took his hand in hers, raised it to her lips, and licked the cum slowly out of his palm.

It wasn't the first time she'd had Apollo's essence in her mouth. But it was certainly the most public. The crowd was cheering so loudly that Tem fought the urge to cover her ears, concentrating instead on cleaning Apollo's palm. His voice was in her mind:

Are you impressed?

That you finished in thirty seconds? Hardly.

It is not my fault you inspire such speed.

Don't blame your shortcomings on me.

There is nothing short about me, and you know it, Temperance.

Tem dropped his hand and stepped back. Apollo stepped back too, standing to the side so Tem could see the rest of the contenders. Eros finished next. He did not offer himself to Tem, as Apollo had. Instead he stepped aside, standing near Apollo, leaving a gap between them.

One by one, the basilisks before her finished. One by one, they arranged themselves in descending order of ejaculation. Eventually, the line was complete. The crowd cheered, but Tem barely heard them. She knew what came next—knew the third tier would test her in ways she could not comprehend.

She also knew she was ready.

Adelaide's hand was on Tem's elbow, guiding her toward the line of basilisks. She looked up to see Rowe descending from the stands. Caspen remained seated.

"Isn't Caspen coming?"

Adelaide shook her head. "You cannot touch him until the tournament is over. He will not participate."

Tem hadn't considered that Caspen wouldn't be part of the third tier. There was nothing she wanted more than to be in his arms right now. One touch from him would heal her—a single brush of his lips would make this all endurable.

Rowe joined the line of basilisks at the end, filling the gap after his brother and right before Apollo. Tem stared at the three of them, trying not to panic. How was this happening already? The first tier had lasted a lifetime, while the second tier was over in the span of a heartbeat. In the blink of an eye, everything had changed.

"The third tier is symbolic of your journey," Adelaide said, still holding her arm. "Each partner represents the lovers you could have had. Think of them as steps along a path. Each one will lead you to your final choice. You cannot skip a step, and you cannot veer off course. You must follow the path, from start to finish, in order to reach the end."

Tem was barely listening. Her eyes were on Rowe, who was staring at her. His body was bruised and scratched, evidence of his fight with Caspen. The blood on him belonged to Caspen.

"Do not be afraid, Temperance," Adelaide whispered.

Tem almost rolled her eyes. She was asking the impossible.

"You must remember that this is not the ritual. *They* must prove themselves to *you*."

Tem remembered the ritual: the pressure to perform, the endless sex, the horrific crack of her pelvis as it broke beneath Caspen's body. Adelaide was right; this was not the ritual. Nonetheless, Tem still felt similarities between the two events: like how when presented with a willing partner, Tem became willing herself. She couldn't help it. Her basilisk side *roared* at the sight of so many naked men, hers for the taking. She could feel their minds against hers, sense exactly how eager and willing they were for her to ride them.

Tem understood their awe. It was an honor to be ridden by the queen—even more so to be ridden by a Hybreed. Tem had never experienced such a *pull* toward so many people at once before. Apollo and Caspen were just two men. Now there were eleven standing before her, rigid and willing and waiting. Who was she to deny them?

Tem wanted to fulfill her duty. But she also knew what people like Evangeline thought of her—that she hadn't earned her position, that she should abdicate. It made her feel like she had as a child: Not good enough. Incapable. Worthless. But not anymore. Tem was good enough. She was capable. And she had always been worthy.

So she stepped forward.

The crowd began to hiss. Tem recognized the sound, knowing that it meant sex was imminent. She concentrated on the line of basilisks, letting her eyes travel over them one at a time, observing them as they observed her.

Adelaide's voice moved to her mind: *You will start with him*—she nodded at the end of the line, at the basilisk who had finished last in the second tier—*and ride each of them in turn. Everything is up to you: the position, the pace, the duration.*

The duration?

Yes. If at any point climax proves impossible, you should move on to the next contender.

That was news to Tem. *So I don't have to finish with all of them?*

That is correct. The third tier revolves completely around you, Temperance. The point is to find your true match. You should not linger for even a moment if a contender does not bring you pleasure.

Tem's eyes slid to Rowe's. She found it hard to believe he could possibly bring her pleasure, even for a moment. But she was comforted by the fact that their union would be as short as she decided it would be and used her newfound courage to speak a single command out loud. "Lie down."

All the basilisks obeyed immediately.

She would take them like this: on their backs, one after the other. Tem had no interest in other positions, no need for variety. She only needed to be in control. It was her
way of reclaiming the event, of putting them in the same position Bastian had been in
during the ritual—on his back. Only now, *she* was the one who needed to come.

Tem was ready to begin.

The first basilisk had long hair and strong, muscled arms. Tem remembered him
from the night before—how she'd kissed him after she'd chosen him. She lowered herself slowly, stopping just before his cock touched her center. Tem looked up at Caspen
one last time. He was watching her from the stands, blood drying on his neck, his eyes
completely black. Only once he nodded did Tem lower herself completely.

The hiss of the crowd became deafening. Tem closed her eyes, focusing on nothing
but the way this cock felt inside her, moving her hips at a pace that was comfortable.
She felt no pressure—no obligation. She did not moan unless she wanted to, did not
perform her pleasure for anyone else's benefit. The only thing she cared about was
whether or not she could finish. The man's body was warm beneath hers. Tem splayed
her hands flat on his chest, holding him down, using him solely for her benefit. Her
orgasm built slowly, but she had no desire to release it. Before she could talk herself
out of it, Tem stood up.

The crowd screamed.

Some part of her felt badly for moving on. But her basilisk side did not care for the
man's feelings, did not feel like pandering to him when he had not satisfied her. If she
was going to experience this fully, she needed to do it as a basilisk would: selfishly and
with no regrets. She was already here. She might as well make something of it.

Tem rode cock after cock.

After a while, they blended together in an endless wave of penetration. None of
the contenders kissed her on the mouth—that seemed to be off-limits, somehow. But
occasionally they sat up, pressing their lips to her neck, her cheeks, her chest. They
palmed her breasts, groaning as they did so. Tem let them do it. She was happy to give
this to them—to give *herself* to them, just as they were giving themselves to her. It was an
amicable exchange, and she gained something from each of them. It was an impossible
task, and Tem was doing it. This was nothing compared to mounting Caspen's father.
She had enjoyed that, and she enjoyed this too.

Still, she didn't come.

It wasn't that she didn't want to. Tem was *filled* with need—more than any cock
could ever fill her. Yet somehow, the line of contenders was not enough. She was unsat-
isfied with what she had been presented with, even when she had been presented

with so much. It was not enough to simply fuck someone—to jerk her hips on top of a breathing body. Tem required an emotional connection in order to climax. She required something *real*.

It wasn't until Tem reached the blond basilisk that she finally felt it.

He received her willingly, his long fingers grasping her hips, pulling her onto his cock with sharp authority. Tem gasped as his thumb found her clitoris. Now *this* was more like it. She pulled his face up to hers, kissing him straight on the lips. Tem thought about the ouroboros, how Caspen had pleasured this very basilisk, how her husband had this same cock down his throat. The same cock she now rode.

Tem thought of other things. Of Leo and what he would think if he were one of the contenders. She imagined it was his hands on her instead, rubbing her clitoris, twisting in her hair. He would've said *fuck* at least three times already by now. He would have told her she was glorious—that he had to have her. She would have told him the same.

But Tem could not have Leo. She could only have this.

Her hips moved quicker now. Tem threaded her fingers through the basilisk's blond hair, twisting her fists into the icy strands. She chased her climax—as quickly as she could—desperate to feel relief. The basilisk helped get her there, tilting his hips to meet hers, smothering her mouth with his. Tem was almost there. She was almost—

Sweet, gorgeous release.

Her head fell back as a cry escaped her lips. All around her, the arena buzzed with noise. Tem saw the frenzy that was building; all throughout the stands, basilisks had begun having sex. They fucked on the benches, in the aisles, anywhere and everywhere they pleased.

Tem looked the blond basilisk in the eyes. "Thank you," she whispered.

In reply, he kissed her. Tem held her lips against his, as if by kissing him she could kiss Leo. Then she stood.

She had reached the final three contenders—only Eros, Rowe, and Apollo were left. The test was almost over. She had thought that, by now, it would have taken a toll on her. Instead the opposite was true. Tem felt energized by the proceedings, as if with each passing contender, she gained power. By the time she stood over Eros, she was insatiable.

He looked just like his brother—the same proud chin, the same disdainful sneer. Tem had no interest in giving Eros more than a second of her time. So that was exactly what she did. Without hesitation, she sat on his cock, gave him two condescending thrusts, then stood again. Jeers and laughter emanated from the crowd. Eros's face darkened. She knew she had insulted him and she did not care. She turned to Rowe, prepared to do the same to him.

But something gave her pause.

His golden cock was erect, just as the other cocks had been. But his was no ordinary cock. Tem sensed the power in it—a force that matched the force in her. It drew her in, luring her like a siren lured a sailor to sea. It was hardly the first cock she'd ridden, and it certainly wouldn't be the last. But it would be the only metal one—the only one not made of flesh and blood. Her basilisk side could not resist its draw. Rowe was on his back, his eyes locked on hers, daring her to mount him. Whether out of morbid curiosity or actual desire, Tem did so slowly.

She remembered the first time she'd touched Caspen's cock—how warm and hard and strong it had felt. Rowe's cock was nothing like that. His was unnaturally stiff and impossibly smooth, as if she were lowering herself onto a metal pole. Tem strained to take it. It wasn't lost on her that Rowe had made it larger than his original cock had been. *Pitiful.*

Tem couldn't imagine crafting herself a new cunt. Would she make hers differently? If it were up to Caspen, she knew he wouldn't want her to change a thing. Her pussy was perfect; he'd told her that a hundred times. Leo had said the same. Their words had healed the part of her that felt insufficient—the girl who was afraid she'd never be kissed. That girl was nowhere to be found now.

Now she was a woman, and she was fucking eleven men in a row. Now she allowed herself to sink onto Rowe's golden cock with a languid sigh, taking every inch of the metal as if it were the real thing. The moment she was seated, Rowe entered her mind. It wasn't forceful; Tem let him in. She wanted to hear what he had to say.

Do you like my cock, Temperance?

It's not a cock.

Then what is it?

It's a plaything. A toy.

And yet you ride it as if it were the real thing.

I'm required to ride it.

Not for this long.

It was true; she'd already been on him for longer than she'd ridden his stupid brother. *It will never compare to the real thing.*

Rowe's hands were on her hips, gripping her skin, keeping her tight against his body. *It is as real as anyone else's. I draw from it the same way you draw from yourself.*

What do you mean, you draw from it?

By crafting it from my own blood, I created something infinite. Something limitless.

What's that supposed to mean?

It means I am your equal, Temperance.

You. Fucking. Wish. Tem accentuated each of her words with a thrust of her hips. Rowe was not her equal. He never would be. *You are nothing like me. You're pathetic.*

If I am so pathetic, why not stand up? Why do you linger?

Why indeed. Part of Tem wanted to stand up. But the other part couldn't. The other part was drawn to Rowe's cock because it was a source of power in and of itself. It felt inexplicably good in her core, filling her the way the other cocks didn't.

Stand up, Temperance. Show me how pathetic I am.

But she couldn't. She didn't want to, and they both knew it. Tem was going to see this through. Tem was going to come.

She thought of the council meeting—how Rowe had kissed her center until she came. She pictured Caspen's hand on the back of his head, holding him against her. It only made her wetter.

Careful, Temperance. What if your heart calls to me?

It never would.

It might. You are drawn to power, are you not?

You know nothing about me.

I know you love that wretch of a human.

For the first time, Tem paused her motions, too shocked to continue. Why would Rowe say that? How did he know how she felt about Leo?

Ah. Rowe smiled, and terror rose within her. *Perhaps I do know you after all.*

Tem couldn't reply.

Basilisks do not take kindly to affairs of the heart, Temperance. What would Caspenon say if he found out how you feel?

He already knows. He loves me anyway.

Does he truly know? Or will he find out when the final tier is over?

My heart will call to him. I know it will.

Perhaps. Or perhaps your marriage will not survive this. What will happen then?

Tem didn't dare think what would happen then. Everything would fall apart. Everything. *He loves me. No matter what happens, we will survive this.*

Rowe shrugged. He was still holding her on his cock. *It will not matter.*

What's that supposed to mean?

It means I will have my revenge.

You swore you would honor the outcome. You—

The only outcome I will honor is the one where I am given what I am owed.

Tem was caught in the crossfire of a generation's worth of wrongs. This was never about her. Rowe wanted to hurt Caspen, and he did not care how he did it. He'd already broken the rules—already bitten Caspen so he could take his power. Now he wanted to take Tem. There would be no end to his insurgence. Tem knew, without a shadow of a doubt, that Rowe would not stop until he was Serpent King.

Terror engulfed her. This was no longer pleasurable; she was no longer turned on. Desperately, her eyes sought Apollo's.

He was on his back just like the others, watching her with Rowe, his brows drawn with concern. His voice entered her mind: *Temperance? What do you need?*

Tem shook her head. She didn't want to fuck Rowe anymore; she was about to throw up. There was only one thing she really needed: *Help.*

Apollo sat up without a second's hesitation, grabbing her by the shoulders and pulling her off Rowe's cock with undeniable finality. Tem gasped at the sudden emptiness, burrowing herself immediately against Apollo's chest. A murmur swept through the arena, but she barely heard it.

Apollo's arms wrapped around her as Rowe said, "I am not finished with you, Temperance."

Apollo angled his body between her and Rowe. "Do not speak to her."

"Why?" Rowe sneered. "Your brother could not stop me, and neither can you."

"You underestimate my brother," Apollo snapped. "Which is your mistake."

Rowe's sneer only deepened. "You are both fools."

"One more word," Apollo snarled, "and I will kill you."

Tem knew Caspen would have said the same thing. Apollo was no different than his brother in that way, and she almost loved him for it.

Tem stared into Rowe's eyes, which were utterly devoid of humanity. His mind was no longer touching Tem's, and in his retreat, she could once more think clearly. He would not attempt anything here—not during an event sanctioned by Kora, not in front of the quivers. It was in Rowe's best interest to let the tournament continue, regardless of the outcome. His play for power depended on Tem's heart calling to someone else. It could only do that if she finished the third tier.

There was no place to hide, no time to make any decision other than the one she was oath-bound to make. Tem would do the only thing she could do: continue on.

Apollo.

He looked at her. *Temperance.*

Apollo once told her not to come to him for comfort—only when she wanted him to fuck her the way his brother would not. Now she came to him for both.

Fuck me.

356

CHAPTER THIRTY-SIX

—•●✳●•—

SOMETHING PASSED OVER APOLLO'S FACE—TRIUMPH.

His eyes held hers. In them, she saw desire. There was no easier way to wield her power than telling him to fuck her. It was the only thing that trumped everything else—a few simple words that would bring even the most virtuous man to his knees.

Tem wielded those words now, saying them once more: *Fuck me, Apollo. Now.*

A slow smile spread over his lips.

There were so many basilisks watching—including Caspen—so many eyes on what was about to happen. They had withheld long enough—two planets in parallel orbit, existing beside one another but never crossing paths. It was finally time to collide.

Apollo raised a hand to her face, gently brushing a curl from her cheek.

The arena disappeared. Time ceased to exist. This was between the two of them now, and Tem had neither the desire nor the ability to focus on anything else. It was time to see what Apollo had to offer her—to understand him on a carnal level, the way she already understood his brother. She had fucked ten other basilisks. Now it was Apollo's turn.

The previous basilisks had left her dripping. Even Rowe had stirred something within her. Apollo leaned back, exposing his cock, which was already hard for her.

Come here, Temperance.

Tem wanted nothing more. She wanted to come to him—to come *for* him. Apollo was a familiar face in this long line of strangers, and familiarity was what Tem craved in this moment. Here, finally, she let herself fully look at him. Apollo's body was warm and hard, the ridges of his muscle catching the torchlight. Tentatively, Tem touched him, pressing her hand to his chest. He let her do this. After a moment, she trailed her fingers downward, brushing them slowly over the ridges of his abdomen before finally meeting the base of his cock. He drew a breath when she touched it.

Tem had felt this part of him before—she'd rubbed her center along his shaft until she came. But this was different. This time there was a crowd watching, and she sought privacy, speaking a single word into Apollo's mind.

Hi.

Hi?

It's the informal version of hello.

I am aware of that. Do you consider this an informal occasion?

It was anything but informal. But if she thought about the implications of this occasion, she would drown in the uncertainty of it. So Tem did the only thing she could think to do, which was lean forward and press her lips to his.

They kissed slowly. Sensually.

Only the blond basilisk had been blessed with the gift of her lips, and now she gave that gift to Apollo. She wanted him to have this, to know that he was different from the others—to know that he deserved her. It was a completion of a circle that had started long ago, perhaps before she had even met Caspen. The two brothers had shared someone before her. She was not special; she was not unique. And yet, *this* was special.

This was Apollo.

Immediately, her mind emptied of every thought and worry that had tortured her since yesterday. All she knew was the feel of his skin against hers, his tongue in her mouth. She welcomed it, taking his hand and pulling it between her legs, letting him touch her. There hadn't been foreplay with any of the others. She'd simply rode their cocks and moved on. But Apollo was different. He was better. He deserved her body, and Tem wanted to give it to him.

His cock was erect, but she made no move to get on it. This moment belonged to Tem—this *decision* belonged to her. Apollo had promised they wouldn't sleep together until she initiated it. He was like Leo in that way: both men of their word. So different from Caspen, who would break his word if it meant keeping Tem safe. One was not better than the other; they were simply different. But it was working in Apollo's favor now.

How long will you make me wait, Temperance?

She liked the way he said her name. Caspen always called her Tem—he was the only basilisk to do so. But Apollo used her full name every time, and somehow she felt like a different person when he said it.

Not long.

She was straddling him now, both hands cupping his jaw as she kissed him. She couldn't get enough. He tasted like peaches and persimmons and *permission*. It was finally time to do this—to have their moment together. Apollo's hands were on her ass, positioning her.

Without waiting another moment, Tem slid down onto his cock.

Kora.

It was all he said, and it was all Tem could think too. Apollo's cock was like his father's—extraordinarily thick at the base—so it wasn't until he was all the way inside her that she felt the full impact of his shaft. If she hadn't already been so wet and willing, it might have strained her. Instead it was exactly what she needed to satisfy the deep and unavoidable urge in her center—a hunger that demanded to be fed, a craving only Apollo could cure.

Apollo had always been more jagged around the edges than Caspen. He possessed none of Caspen's elegance, none of his grace. His soul was darker and rougher and twisted. He'd taught her how to kill. It was no small thing. Tem felt safe with him in a different way than she did with Caspen. She could tell him any secret, reveal any part of her—no matter how bad—and he would accept her. There was security in being with someone who would never turn you away. Nothing Tem could do would ever scare him off. Apollo did not hold her on the same pedestal that Caspen and Leo did; he did not expect her to be *good* all the time. He allowed her to indulge the parts of her that she needed to indulge. Apollo could sense both things inside Tem: the predator and the prey. It was a unique thing to experience—a unique thing to *be*. Give and take. Ebb and flow. The power in her matched the power in him, and it was a surprise to them both.

Tem's knees dug into the sand as she rocked her hips. Apollo praised her as she rode him, the words murmured into her mind so only she could hear:

Pretty girl. Beautiful, beautiful girl. You are wasted on my brother. I cannot believe he gets to wake up next to you and sink his cock into you whenever he wants. He should fuck you every minute of every day. If you were mine, I would never stop fucking you. I would worship your cunt until the day I died. I would—

Tem rode through it all, barely listening, concentrating on nothing but how good he felt inside her. She wanted to come; it had been building in her since the blond basilisk, and it was pouring out at the seams now. Her thrusts were quick and desperate. She was barely holding on.

Tem sent him a vision—a memory of their time in the grotto. Her on her knees, his cock down her throat.

Apollo *growled* at the sight, his fingernails digging into her so hard they drew blood.

Fuck, Temperance. That was the best night of my life. I will think about it every time my cock is in my hand. I picture you in front of me and it makes me fucking hard. I want you to do that again. I want your mouth on my cock the moment I wake up in the morning and I want it again every night.

They were the only two people in the world. Tem had no sense of time, no sense of space. Her body was his, his body was hers. They used each other with reckless abandon, thrusting and squeezing and yanking and pulling. Apollo knew she wouldn't break; he knew she could take it. Her body was malleable and ready for him—eager to be bent.

Look at you on my cock, Temperance. Such a good fit. So fucking wet for me.

His thrusts were harsh and fast, just like him. It was what Tem wanted—what she *needed*. She had been waiting for so long and now it was finally here. *He* was finally here. Apollo satisfied something in her that neither Caspen nor Leo had ever been able to satisfy. Tem wanted to lose control—to submit to desire—to let herself be free. She had to be perfect for Caspen; she had to be good for Leo. But Apollo didn't want her like that. He didn't want her perfect or good or anything that the men she loved expected of her. There were no rules with Apollo. Tem could do whatever she wanted with him—she could *let go*.

Do you like that, Temperance? Do you like riding my cock?

Tem did like it. But she couldn't answer. She was too distracted by everything that was happening—too caught up in the physicality of sex. So she answered with her body, showing him how much she liked it—showing him that for this fleeting moment, she was his. They were evenly matched, her and Apollo. Each time he held the power, she took it from him. All she had to do was arch her neck, and he would growl. It was so *easy* with him.

Nothing she did could hurt him; he was invincible. Nothing she said would insult him; he had heard far worse. Apollo had seen it all. He'd had every woman, every man. It was impossible to have any impact on him whatsoever. It was freeing to feel like that, to know that nothing could shake him. It had taken Tem too long to come to this conclusion—to realize that he wasn't bad for her. That he wasn't bad at all.

More, she begged.

Apollo smacked his palm flat against her ass—hard. So hard that Tem let out a yelp of surprise and pain.

Too much?

She shook her head. *Not enough.*

He smacked her again, harder and harder until she was weak on top of him.

It is not enough to fuck you just this once, Temperance. I want you as many times as I can have you. I will do anything you want. Anything. Just let me fuck you again. I want to fuck you in my bed. I want to bend you over and fuck you in the banquet hall for everyone to see. I want to lick your cunt. I need to taste you, Temperance. I need to come inside you. I need to come on your back and on your tits and in your mouth and on your hands. I cannot live without those hands, Temperance. I need them on me. I need them on my cock. You have no idea what it is like to look at you and not be able to touch you. Every day I want you and every day I cannot have you. It is agony. You parade around with your perfect cunt and your perfect tits and you do not let me fuck you and I cannot take it anymore, Temperance.

His words were crude. But that was Apollo.

I cannot look at you without growing hard. It was agony to watch my brother fuck you in front of me. I wanted to rip you away from him—I wanted to put you on my own cock instead. You do not understand what it is like to be around you and unable to fuck you. It is all I think about. It is all I need. I think about you every time I am with another woman. None of them satisfy me the way you do. I have lived hundreds of years, and your cunt is the best I have ever touched. I want to run my tongue over it. I want to taste you, Temperance. I want to spit in your mouth. I want to see you take my cock from behind. I want to watch it stretch you until you are begging for more. I want those pretty lips on mine. I want to bite them until they bleed. Are you going to let me do that, Temperance? Are you going to let me fuck you again? Just this once is not enough for me. I need you again and again and again. I need you every fucking day and night. I need you. I need you. I need you.

He was not sentimental, like Caspen, or romantic, like Leo. He was domineering and controlling and he needed her like this—desperate, at his mercy—in order to get off. Tem didn't care. Tem was ready to come. Apollo had only one more thing to say, and Tem could have guessed it in her sleep:

You first.

Tem was already coming. She threw her head back in victory, her fingers gripping him so hard she knew it would cause him pain. But that was the way it was between them: she and Apollo were not soft or tender. They were wild and rough, and it wasn't sustainable, but it was *real* and it was *now* and Tem *needed* it. Apollo gripped her too, squeezing her ass and leaving bruises, pinning her on his cock so she could not escape. She didn't want to anyway. Pain kept her sane; pain meant she was alive.

Kora, Kora, Kora, Kora—

He was calling Kora's name. But for some reason, it felt like he was calling Tem's.

Apollo was nearly there. Just before his moment of climax, Tem placed her lips right against the shell of his ear so there was no possible way he would miss her saying, "Good boy."

Apollo *groaned.* Then he came.

His hips hitched beneath hers, driving his cock deep into Tem's center as his release poured out of him and into her. Tem closed her eyes, feeling the rich warmth, allowing herself to drown in it.

When she opened her eyes, Apollo's stared back at her. She smiled, and so did he. It seemed like the time to kiss him had passed, like their moment was ending. But Tem did it anyway, pressing her lips gently to his. It was the complete opposite of the aggressive way they'd been kissing just moments ago. This was intimate; this was slow.

Tem traced his tongue with hers. *You taste like peaches.*

Do I?

Yes.

Fascinating. He sucked on her bottom lip, pulling it between his. *You taste like the sea.*

Tem shouldn't have been surprised by his answer. Caspen had once told her she'd smelled like the sea. Why shouldn't she taste like it as well?

Does the sea taste good?

He smiled, releasing her lip. *It does.*

With that, their moment was over.

Tem looked around the arena, blinking at the sudden rush of sound. Being with Apollo was like being in a tunnel: close and suffocating. Now Tem felt as if someone had lifted the curtain, and she was suddenly reminded that they were in an arena full of basilisks, in the middle of the tournament.

Apollo lifted her slowly off his cock, and Tem knew he was letting her feel every inch of him as he slid out of her. She realized suddenly that her knees were bleeding; the friction of the sand had torn them to shreds. Apollo pressed his palms against them, healing them with a cooling rush. Then he pressed a tiny, gentle kiss to each one. The gesture surprised Tem. It was not in his nature to nurture. She didn't think they had the type of relationship that warranted aftercare. For the first time, she wondered if she was seeing yet another new side of him: a side of tenderness. He took her hands in his, brushing his fingers over her freckles. They stood together, looking out at the crowd. Despite the deafening hiss, there was no hive orgasm this time. But that didn't surprise Tem. Her and Apollo were not her and Caspen. Their union would not incite the same reaction that she had brought forth during the ritual. A face stood out to her in the crowd: the new mother who had given her blessing to Apollo. She was descending the steps and entering the arena.

The rest of the contenders were all standing, turning to face Tem. Caspen was still in the stands, and something told Tem he would remain there. She looked up at him, reaching for him with her mind even though she knew he couldn't hear her. What did he think of what he'd just seen? Tem would find out soon enough.

Out of the corner of her eye, she saw Adelaide approaching.

"Well done, Temperance," she said. "You have completed the tiers. It is time for your heart to make its choice."

Against her instincts, Tem glanced at Apollo. He was looking at Caspen.

By now, the new mother had reached them. It was then that Tem noticed she held a goblet in her hand, similar to the goblet of elixir. Only this chalice contained a different liquid, one that Tem had seen many times in the village, in bottles held by babies.

The woman held it out to her.

Tem turned questioningly to Adelaide.

"She offers you a holy substance," Adelaide said, "the ultimate symbol of life. Nothing is more sacred to us. Once you drink it, your heart will make its choice."

Tem looked once more at Caspen.

"It will force you to be truthful," Adelaide said quietly. "So make sure you are ready."

The woman nodded at Tem. Tem nodded back. Was her prediction about to come true? Only Kora could tell. She took the goblet, tilted her head, and drank.

Immediately, something *tugged* at her—a physical sensation, yanking her chest in two directions. She felt an undeniable pull toward Caspen—so strong it nearly hurt, straining against her rib cage. It was not unlike the sensation she'd felt before, on the night before the training began. Caspen had come to her in a dream, his presence as warm and as real as a flame. She'd been drawn to him then and she was drawn to him now, her body turning in his direction.

But Caspen was not the only draw.

Something else pulled her heart's focus: *someone* else. As strong as the sensation she felt for Caspen was the sensation she felt for someone who wasn't even here.

She loved them both. She always had.

Tem threw herself into her basilisk side, concentrating on nothing but the way she felt for Caspen, willing it to take over her. She thought of the night they met, how they'd undressed in front of each other; how she'd known, even then, that their paths were destined to cross. She thought of his body and the way it conformed to hers. They fit together perfectly, the way two lovers should.

It was not enough.

Leo crept in, as he always did. She thought of his hair, his laugh, his gold incisors. She pictured the way his hands grasped his whiskey glass: tightly, so his veins stood out. Tem thought of their time together, how she had fallen for him slowly, almost against her will. But she had fallen nonetheless.

Temperance, Apollo's voice came to her. *You are taking too long. What is happening?*

Tem shook her head. It was too much effort to speak.

This wasn't supposed to be happening; her heart wasn't supposed to call to two people. The tournament was supposed to force her to choose—to solve this once and for all.

Instead, it was splitting her in half.

Is it the human king?

It was. But it was also Caspen.

Do you love him more than my brother?

I love them both equally.

That is not possible. You must love one of them more.

But she didn't. They both held equal value to her. It wasn't possible to compare them—to tally Leo's qualities next to Caspen's.

I can't choose.

You must.

I can't hurt Caspen.

Are you saying you want the human king?

She wanted them both.

It will not just hurt him. It will destroy him. I know my brother, Temperance. He cannot live without you.

Tem shook her head. She couldn't fathom it, couldn't imagine doing that to Caspen. She would stop loving Leo—she *had to*.

But she couldn't. Not right now, not ever. Not when his presence permeated everything she did, not when he was always at the forefront of her mind—not when she *didn't even want to*. Tem felt the crest pulling them together, forcing her hand. It didn't matter that she'd sent him away. It didn't matter that he was with Evelyn now. Her heart called to him. Her heart would not be tamed.

Apollo, please. Help me.

You must choose, Temperance.

I can't.

You must.

I CAN'T.

YOU MUST.

But he was asking the impossible. Not even an arena full of basilisks and the pressure of the tournament could change the way she felt about the human king. Tem would sooner stop breathing than stop loving Leo.

And perhaps that's what it would take.

This was killing her anyway. If Tem was going to die, it may as well be at her own hand. All would be solved. Caspen would mourn her, then move on. Leo would be with Evelyn. She would not have to be with Rowe or Apollo or anyone else. Life would go on without her, and everyone would be better off for it.

She looked up at Caspen, who was looking down at her. His mind was closed off, per the rules of the tournament. But she tried to reach him anyway, willing the corridor between them to open. His brow was furrowed. Tem could understand his confusion. Caspen would have no idea why she was hesitating—no context for the battle currently waging within her heart. Only Apollo knew what was going on. He was still here, still in her mind. Tem needed to shut him out.

No, Temperance—do not—

She slammed the barrier between them, concentrating on the urge forming in her gut.

If her human side loved Leo, then that was what she would kill. She would use her basilisk side to destroy it, to extinguish the part of her that was unfaithful. Tem closed her eyes, willing herself to *kill*. If she could crest herself to gain power, surely she could also do the opposite. Surely she could destroy her human side before it destroyed her.

Apollo tore violently at her mind, ripping at the barrier she'd built to keep him out. He was strong—and *so* determined. His roar of disapproval shattered her concentration, forcing her to hear him as he yelled, *If you will not choose, then I will.*

Tem didn't know what that meant. All she knew was that one moment she was fine, and the next Apollo was touching her. Then a knife pierced her heart.

It felt like something had been removed—like Apollo had *taken* something from her. The way she felt for Leo—her *love*—was gone. There was still love left, but it was all for Caspen. The moment it happened, everything in Tem surged toward Caspen. The sensation was so strong that she fell immediately to her knees, her arms clutched to her chest. She screamed his name—whether aloud or in her mind, she did not know.

The crowd roared, and Tem knew it was over.

Adelaide's voice came to her through the noise. "Congratulations, Temperance. Your heart has made its choice."

CHAPTER THIRTY-SEVEN

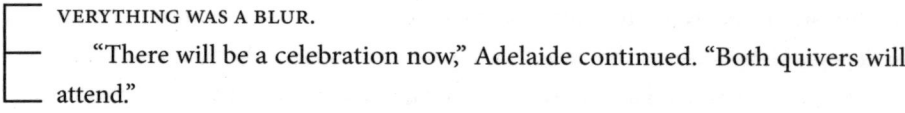

EVERYTHING WAS A BLUR.

"There will be a celebration now," Adelaide continued. "Both quivers will attend."

Tem nodded, barely registering her words.

"You did well." Adelaide's hand was on her waist, guiding her out of the arena. "The Drakons are thrilled."

Tem didn't know what to do with that information. If the Drakons were thrilled, it meant the Senecas were furious. It meant *Rowe* was furious. Victory for one quiver meant defeat for the other. The tournament was supposed to make everything right. This outcome did nothing of the sort.

"I need to see Caspen."

"You will," Adelaide said. "And soon. He will be at the celebration."

It wasn't soon enough. Tem desperately needed to look into his eyes and know that they were going to make it through this, that she had performed adequately—that Caspen did not notice the gap of time between when she drank from the chalice and when she had made her decision. Tem's battle had been silent. To anyone watching, absolutely nothing unexpected had happened. Tem had been given a choice, and she had chosen Caspen. Only Apollo knew the truth. Tem scanned the crowd for him, but he was nowhere to be found. Was he talking to Caspen? Telling him of her deception? Tem still didn't understand what Apollo had done in order to make it so that she could choose Caspen. All she knew was that her love for Leo—the thing that anchored her—was gone. When she thought of him, she felt indifferent, as if he were a casual acquaintance or a friend. It was bizarre to think of him that way. It was wrong.

By now, they had reached the lake. It was already filled with basilisks, all of them holding goblets of elixir. Rowe was nowhere to be found. Neither was Eros. Tem wondered whether they had left already. Before she could ask Adelaide about it, an arm was around her shoulder.

"*Dearest*," Gabriel cried, pulling her close. "That was quite the performance. Who knew you had it in you?"

Behind him, Damon smiled. He'd watched the ritual; he knew exactly what Tem had in her.

"I can't believe you're allowed to fuck your husband's brother," Gabriel continued.

Tem smacked him on the arm. "Gabriel."

"And for so *long* too."

She smacked him again.

"What? I'm impressed. You should be studied. Scholars would marvel at your stamina."

Tem rolled her eyes. Then her heart stopped.

There, walking toward her, was Caspen. Beautiful, stunning, *glorious* Caspen.

The same thing she'd felt for him during the tournament surged through her once more. Tem loved him. That was truth; that was real. She needed to touch him, and now she could. Tem ran toward him with all her might, knowing he would catch her.

The moment she reached him, everything fell away. Caspen's hands lifted her up, his lips pressed against hers. They spun around together, clinging to one another, one body instead of two. Tem could have kissed him forever. Maybe she would.

Caspen set her down, cradling her face in his hands. His skin drew sparks from hers. "I love you."

Tem stared up into his golden eyes. "I love you too."

Then he was inside her.

For the first time, Tem understood just how much Caspen normally catered to her pleasure. Usually there was a buildup, a slow crescendo into sex that started with foreplay and ended with penetration. He did none of that now. Now he fucked her like she was the last person on earth—like he was suffocating and she was the air he breathed. He held her so tightly, she thought she might break. His fingers dug valleys into her thighs. Tem welcomed it all, pulling him only closer, knowing he needed this even more than she did, knowing he needed to claim her. Tem had no idea what it was like for him to watch her with Apollo. But now, with Caspen's cock inside her, she remembered how all other cocks paled in comparison. Caspen filled her; Caspen *fulfilled* her. No one else could fuck her like this. No one else could dive so deep inside her. Tem welcomed him into every part of her body—every part of her soul. Caspen was hers, and she was his. They belonged to each other.

Her climax left her gasping for air. Caspen was out of breath too, his face buried against her neck, his hands twisted in her hair. His mind joined with hers:

We will go slow next time, Tem. I just…needed you.

Tem pulled him closer. *I needed you too. I never want to go without touching again. We will not. You have my word.*

He promised it with every kiss, assured her with every caress. Caspen knew how to make everything better—knew how to turn Tem's world back on its axis. He was still inside her, still hard. He kept his word; this time, they went slow. The celebration raged around them, and they both ignored it. Nothing else mattered; *no one* else mattered. Caspen laid her down in the sand, thrusting into her with limitless patience. Even after she came again, Tem held him only closer, needing him over and over again.

Eventually, she could take no more. Caspen kissed her as he pulled out, both of them clinging to the other with desperate certainty. His fingers laced once more through hers, pulling her up from the sand. Tem wasn't fully present—she was lazy and dazed from sex, her wetness dripping smoothly down her thighs. She didn't bother wiping it away; she had no desire to remove any evidence of her congress with Caspen.

When they were upright, Caspen spun her around before kissing her on the cheek. She was not used to seeing him like this: loose and undone. He was usually so reserved; his joy was rare. But now he smiled freely, his eyes crinkling at the corners as he looked at her with pure, unencumbered love.

"I've never seen you so happy," Tem said.

"I am always happy when I am with you."

"You're acting drunk."

"You have never seen me drunk, my love."

Tem realized he was right. "I'd like to."

He smiled down at her. "Shall we do it together?"

Tem was sorely tempted. She'd tried the elixir enough times to know how it affected her; perhaps it was time to indulge in it properly. After the events of the tournament, she wanted nothing more than to be numb.

"Yes." Tem stood on her tiptoes and kissed him. "Please."

"Very well. Do not move. I will return with elixir."

A moment later, he was gone. No sooner had he disappeared than someone said her name:

"Temperance."

Tem turned. "Apollo," she said quietly. "What did you do?"

A long silence followed. Tem resisted the urge to ask him again; she knew he would tell her. This was too important not to discuss. But Apollo said, "Not here."

Tem didn't bother arguing. She simply followed him out into the passageway.

Apollo turned to face her. "I performed an extraction."

"An *extraction*?" The word was foreign to Tem. It sounded violent. Medical, almost.

"Yes."

"But what does that mean? Why do I feel so…?"

"Empty?"

She looked up at him. "Yes."

"I took your love for the human king."

Tem blinked. "*Took* it?"

"Yes."

"So it's just…gone?"

"I did not say that I disposed of it. Only that I took it from you."

"Oh."

Tem was having trouble wrapping her head around the fact that her love for Leo was something that could be *taken*. But then she remembered how Caspen had once placed his hand on her chest and taken her desire away—how basilisks were able to manipulate emotions and remove them at will. Love was an emotion, was it not? There was no reason why it couldn't be taken like anything else.

"So that's why I was able to choose Caspen?"

"Yes."

"And nobody else knows that I…?"

"Love another?" He turned to her, his eyes dark. "No. They do not."

Tem stared at him. "I can't believe you did that for me," she whispered.

"It is not a permanent solution," Apollo said. "It must be given back. And quickly."

"Oh," Tem said again. There was a pause, and in it, she half expected him to give it back right that moment. But Apollo was looking at her with a peculiar expression on his face, as if he had just figured something out.

"What?" she prompted.

He didn't answer. Instead he stepped closer, his brows furrowed. "You did not tell me the extent of your feelings for him."

"Excuse me?" Tem had told him that she was in love with Leo. That was pretty much the extent of her feelings for him.

"You did not tell me that you crested him. Or that you have yet to consummate it. You did not tell me that his life hangs in the balance."

Tem's mouth fell open. "How do you know that?"

Apollo pressed his hand to his chest. "It is right here."

She stared up at him. He'd gleaned all that just from extracting her love for Leo? If she'd known he was going to find that out, she never would have let him back inside her mind. Up until now, this had been her burden to bear—a secret only she knew the consequences of. Even Adelaide, her closest confidant, was not aware of the extent of it. But now that Apollo knew it too, Tem felt…relief. And also fear. What if he told Caspen? But Apollo would not do that. The time had come, finally, to trust that he wanted what was best for his brother and also what was best for her. Apollo was selfless in that way. He hid behind a facade of carelessness, but underneath it all, Apollo cared about Caspen, and he cared about his family. He was a fierce protector—that much was abundantly clear—and he had done the unthinkable in order to ensure Caspen's victory. He'd placed his brother's feelings over his own—he'd acted selflessly. That was a person she could trust.

"I must give it back, Temperance. I have no desire to hold on to this lie."

Shame flushed her face. When he phrased it like that, it seemed so much worse than it was. But perhaps Apollo was right. Perhaps it *was* worse than Tem had thought it was. Every moment she harbored love for Leo was a moment closer to disaster. Apollo would not be there to take away her emotions every time they became a problem. Tem would have to deal with this head-on, or it would be dealt with for her.

"Besides," he continued, "I could not keep it even if I wanted to."

"What happens if you keep it?"

"It will come out," he said simply.

Then he placed his palm on her chest and closed his eyes.

Unlike when he'd extracted her emotions before—violently and with no warning— this time they seeped back into her chest slowly, warming her the way a crackling fire would. It was as if a flower were blooming in her chest. Tem could feel the petals opening, reaching outward like fingers. Finally, her link to Leo was restored. The moment it was done, Tem sighed. Her love for him might cause her pain, but it also made her whole. She'd felt utterly wrong without it, like she was missing a part of her. And in a way, she was. Despite the fact that this was tearing her apart, it was also the only thing keeping her together. Without her love for Leo, she lost a part of herself.

"You must rid yourself of this," Apollo said quietly.

But Tem couldn't do that. She'd already tried falling out of love with Leo. Nothing could be more impossible. "I can't."

"Temperance." He stepped closer. "You must. If you consummate the crest, your blood bond will be broken and Caspenon will be forced to kill you. He will never forgive himself."

Tem shook her head. "I can't tell him."

"You cannot go on like this. You are tearing yourself in two."

It was only once he said it that Tem realized it was true. She'd been living with these feelings for so long that she'd almost forgotten what it was like to be without them. She had gotten used to feeling like her heart was in two places. The agony was familiar to her now.

"Do you know what I felt when I took this from you?" Apollo asked quietly.

Tem shook her head.

"Pain. Not love, Temperance. But pain. You are hurting yourself by loving them both. You must choose."

Caspen's words came back to her: *The time will come when you will have to choose.*

But Tem didn't want to choose. She *couldn't* choose. She hadn't been able to then, and she was no more able to now. She was at a crossroads, as she always had been, and there was nobody coming to save her. It was untenable. But it was her reality.

"I can't choose," she whispered.

To her surprise, Apollo's eyes softened. "I understand it cannot be not easy for you."

That was the understatement of the century. Nothing about this was easy. It never had been.

"But your current state is unsustainable," he continued, his voice gentle in the dark. "I myself could barely stand it for as long as I did. I do not know how you have been surviving it."

Tem knew. She was two things: basilisk and human. *That* was how she was surviving it. Each side of her loved someone else. It was unsustainable for Apollo; it was reality for her.

"Basilisks are not meant to love more than one person," he murmured. "We share our bodies but not our hearts."

Tem had heard it before. She knew what was happening to her was wrong, that she had crossed a line long ago. But that didn't mean she could help it. And it didn't mean she could change it.

"It is unnatural, this thing within you. I fear it will be your undoing."

Caspen had once called her his undoing. How ironic that Leo would be hers.

"It is breaking your mind, Temperance."

It wasn't her mind that Tem was worried about. It was taking a toll on her heart now, and if things continued as they had been, there was no telling how bad it might get.

"I don't know what to do," Tem whispered.

"I swore I would protect you," Apollo said quietly. "But I cannot protect you from yourself."

Tem nodded because she couldn't seem to speak anymore. She understood exactly what he was telling her. If everything fell apart—if her love for Leo destroyed her relationship with Caspen—it would be entirely her fault. Nobody, not even Apollo, could prevent that from happening, as much as he might want to.

Tem had always known the facts; it was why she'd resisted Leo for so long. But there was no elegant solution here. If she didn't sleep with him, he would die. And if she did, Caspen would kill her. How was that an acceptable outcome? Tem had fallen for both of them, and now their fates were intertwined because of it.

Apollo leaned in, and for a split second, Tem thought he might kiss her. Instead he brushed his lips gently along her cheek before whispering in her ear: "I cannot bear to watch you die."

Despite his heat, Tem felt a chill. She'd never considered how this would make Apollo feel. The pain would be horrific for him. He would feel not only grief but guilt. His role in this was unquestionable now. The last thing she wanted was for Apollo to watch her die, much less at the hands of his brother. The loss would wound them both. Apollo had once told her that she could not break them. But Tem had a feeling she could.

She had just opened her mouth to speak when a voice cut between them: "Tem?"

It was Caspen.

CHAPTER THIRTY-EIGHT

———◆———

F OR A MOMENT, NO ONE SPOKE. IT FELT LIKE A MIRROR OF WHEN CASPEN HAD found them in the grotto. That night had ended in orgasm. Somehow Tem doubted this one would too.

"Tem," Caspen said again. The word was slurred. That's when Tem noticed the goblets in his hands. He'd already started drinking.

"Brother," Apollo said. "Steady."

Tem raised her eyebrows at the warning. She had never heard Apollo chastise Caspen before. Caspen's narrowed. "Do not command me."

The air seemed to go cold. Tem couldn't understand how things had taken such a quick turn. One moment, she was having a conversation with Apollo, and the next, everything felt wrong.

"What are you doing here with her?" Caspen asked.

Apollo rolled his shoulders. "Am I not allowed to speak with whom I wish?"

"There is no reason for you to speak with my wife."

"Possessiveness is unbecoming, Caspenon."

"I did not ask for your opinion on the subject."

"She is not your property."

"She is *mine*."

Here it was again—the implication that Tem belonged to Caspen. He had said it many times before, and it had always been true. But it wasn't the *whole* truth. She belonged to Caspen, yes. But not only him.

Caspen's eyes slid to Tem's. They were turning black. "Unless..." he said slowly, setting the goblets down and crossing his arms. "She is not."

Tem crossed her arms too. "What's that supposed to mean?"

"I saw what happened at the tournament. I saw you hesitate."

Tem's stomach dropped. How long had she stood in the arena, making her choice? She'd hoped that her moment of crisis hadn't been obvious. But if Caspen saw it, that meant everyone did.

"I saw you hesitate," he said again. "And now I find you here, with him."

Tem blinked. "What are you saying?"

"You love my brother."

"*What?* Why would you think that?"

"Because it is obvious."

Tem almost laughed. Nothing could be less obvious. "I don't love—"

"You can admit it, Tem. It will not hurt me."

Tem stared at him, her mouth open. Of course it would hurt him. But it wasn't true—not even remotely. She did not love Apollo. She loved Leo, and it was going to be the death of them all. "I *don't* love Apollo," she said. Beside her, Apollo shifted. Tem had no idea whether she had hurt his feelings by saying that. But his feelings were the least of her worries right now.

Caspen's jaw tightened. "Do not lie to me."

"I never have."

"You are lying right now."

"*No*," Tem said firmly. "I'm not."

In the silence that followed, they both stared at each other. Tem couldn't understand why this was happening. It was *ridiculous*. Caspen had been completely led astray—he'd interpreted everything incorrectly, drawn all the wrong conclusions. But the truth was so much worse. Falling for Caspen's brother would be understandable—acceptable, even. Caspen had said so himself. To jump from one brother to the next was not only socially acceptable, it was expected. Tem *wished* she were in love with Apollo. That would make everything easier. But she was not. And Apollo knew it. And soon, Caspen would know it too.

"I don't love Apollo," she said quietly but firmly, every inch of her spine pricked with anticipation as she gathered the courage to say what she knew Caspen needed to hear: "I love Leo."

A deadly silence fell.

In it, Caspen looked at her with a curious expression on his face, as if he were realizing something for the very first time. Even Apollo did not speak. He glanced between the two of them, clearly bracing for impact.

"You told him to find Evelyn."

"That doesn't mean I don't love him."

"You sent him away," Caspen said.

"Two things can be true," Tem whispered. She had sent him away. And she loved him still.

"You concealed this from me."

"*No*. I didn't."

"You did. You lied."

"I *told* you that I—"

"You did not tell me the whole truth."

Tem fell silent. She had never seen Caspen like this. He was angry, first and foremost. But he was also drunk—she could see the effects of the elixir manifesting on his body. Smoke curled over his shoulders and down his arms, streaming from his fingertips. His eyes were completely black, boring into hers. His next words were a dangerous whisper:

"You did not tell me it was real."

"I was completely honest with you," Tem whispered back. "You were there. You *agreed to share me.*"

"I only agreed because *I knew I would lose you if I did not.*"

Tem's mouth fell open. Was this the truth at last? If they were speaking of lies, this was one of them. It was just as great a sin for Caspen to withhold this from her. It was not what they had agreed upon, and it was not fair.

"You were willing to share me," she whispered. "What changed?"

"Your feelings for him."

"Those have always been the same."

Caspen just shook his head, smoke still curling around him.

"Well, what *did* you think I felt for him?" Tem cried.

Caspen spread his arms wide. "Infatuation. Lust. Either of those I could tolerate forever. But true love is something else entirely."

"I told you I loved him."

"You did not. You told me he meant something to you."

"It's the same thing—"

"It is not."

"I said 'I love you both,' remember? You were there."

"It is not the same."

Tem took a step backward at his words. She couldn't understand this.

"How is it not the same?" she whispered.

Caspen sighed, arching his neck. He closed his eyes, as if it were easier to speak without looking at her. "You can love many things, Tem. Many people. You can love your family and your friend Gabriel. But if you are telling me that what you feel for the human king is the same as what you feel for me"—the muscles in his neck flexed—"that is another matter entirely."

What he meant was that it was an insult. Caspen could not accept that, in her heart, Leo held the same standing, that the two kings were equal.

"There must be a solution," Apollo said finally.

Caspen just shook his head. "There *was* a solution. She crested him, and she sent him away."

Only Apollo knew that the crest was no solution at all. Only Apollo knew the implications of that crest—that it had to be consummated, or Leo would die. Perhaps that would be ideal to Caspen, Tem thought suddenly. Perhaps he would be thrilled to learn that Leo might soon be out of the picture. But Caspen knew better than that. Caspen knew that if Leo died, Tem would never be the same. *A race won by default is no true victory.*

A darker thought occurred to Tem: a world in which Caspen was never on board with their arrangement, that his intent had never been to share her but to encourage her to crest Leo so he became nothing but her servant. It was too horrible to even consider. She refused to believe Caspen could be so cruel. He had sworn to protect the people she loved—that included Leo.

"Caspenon," Apollo said quietly. "You know better than anyone that you cannot control who you love."

Something unspoken passed between brothers. A part of their shared history—a part Tem did not know about.

Then Apollo whispered, "She is in pain, Brother."

Caspen let out a bitter laugh. "She *is* pain, Brother."

"She does not want this. It is killing her."

Wrong. It was killing Leo.

Caspen's eyes narrowed suddenly. He stepped toward Apollo, who subtly angled himself so that Tem was behind him. "And what do you know of it?"

"I know there are things you do not understand."

"Such as?"

It was the first time Tem had seen Caspen be the last to know—a position usually reserved for her. He stepped closer.

"What *exactly* do I not understand, brother?"

Now Apollo looked at Tem. She knew what he was asking—knew he was seeking permission to disclose what he had discovered during the tournament. But if he told Caspen her secret—that she had to consummate the crest—Tem was afraid of what might happen. It was bad enough such a secret existed. Worse still that they had kept it from Caspen.

Tem held up her hand. This was her burden to bear. She would not hide behind Apollo, now or ever. "When I crested Leo, it formed a bond," she said quietly.

Caspen swiveled to look at her. "I am aware of that, Tem. I am the one who told you to crest him."

Tem pursed her lips. "I know. But what neither of us knew was that bond came with a condition."

"What condition?"

"We must consummate the crest."

A pause. And then:

"You have to *sleep with him*?"

"If we don't consummate the crest," she continued, raising her voice above his, "I will never be able to transition again." She dropped her voice, the last words causing her physical pain. "And Leo will die."

In the silence that followed, Tem watched as Caspen processed this revelation in real time. She saw confusion, then disbelief, then pure fury cross over his face. When he finally spoke, it was not the words she expected.

"I do not believe you."

Tem stared up at him. "You have to."

"You are lying to me. You are—"

"I'm *not lying*. My father told me. He has seen it before."

"Why have I never heard of this?"

"Because it's uncommon," Tem said. "How many basilisks do you know who are in love with the humans they crest?"

Of course Caspen hadn't heard of this. No one had. Her own father only knew about it because he'd experienced it himself.

But Caspen shook his head. "I do not believe you," he said again, quietly this time. But Tem knew that he did. He reached for the goblet on the ground, picking it up and downing its contents. Tem looked questioningly at Apollo, who simply shook his head.

The elixir was supposed to make the basilisks merry—Tem had only seen it improve their mood. But now she was sure it was doing the opposite to Caspen. His eyes were glazed over, his skin flushed. Caspen always moved with incomparable grace, his motions carefully controlled. Now he was loose, as if someone had unscrewed his joints. Tem didn't recognize him like this; he was not himself.

"You should have told me how you felt about him," Caspen said roughly.

"I did tell you," Tem whispered.

"I would never have let you crest him if I had known—"

"I *told* you that I—"

Caspen turned and hurled the empty goblet down the passageway with such force, it struck a gash in the stone wall. Tem gasped in shock. She'd *never* seen Caspen react like that before. When he turned back to her, she saw scales dappling his chest. Tem had never seen the look on his face that she was seeing now. She couldn't believe it had come to this.

Beside her, Apollo touched her waist.

"I thought you merely cared for him, which I understood, given your circumstances. But you sent him away, Tem. You *chose me*."

Everything he was saying was true. Tem had chosen Caspen. But her mind had made the choice—not her heart. And the heart was not so easily swayed. "I don't know what to say, Caspen."

He stepped closer. "Say you made the right choice. Say you do not love him."

Only one of those statements was true. "Caspen, please."

But Caspen would not be persuaded. She could see it in his eyes: he was past the point of no return.

"Say it, Tem. Now."

"I made the right choice." It was all she said. The silence hardened between them.

Tem knew Caspen was waiting for her to say the second part. But she couldn't. There was no point in lying. Her body probably wouldn't let her anyway.

It was all coming to a head now. Tem didn't know whether it was ego or denial or sheer hope that had blinded Caspen for so long, but now there was no more hiding, no more pretending that Tem didn't feel the way she felt about Leo.

"This cannot happen, Tem. You cannot sleep with him. If you do, I will have to—"

His voice cracked, and he broke off. The elixir had made him slow—made it so the real conclusion was coming to him now, a minute too late. Caspen's eyes met hers. Tem knew he wouldn't finish his sentence, and she didn't even want him to. She still remembered every word of their conversation—the one where Caspen had told her that his father killed his mother. If Tem consummated the crest, he would be forced to do the same.

Caspen whirled on Apollo. "How long have you known?"

Apollo glanced at Tem, his hand still on her waist.

"Do not look at her. Look at me. When did you find out?"

Apollo sighed. "Recently, Brother."

It was all he said. But it was more than enough.

Caspen's eyes narrowed. "You knew and you did not tell me."

It wasn't a question. It was a statement, and it was true.

Caspen had uncovered the worst of them. He was finally caught up, finally privy to the secret that Tem had been keeping for so long. But even worse than her betrayal was Apollo's. She did not know their history, but she knew enough to recognize that it was playing out again, right now, with her. History would always repeat itself, just as Maximus said.

Caspen turned to her. "It is a shame you do not love my brother, Tem," he said coldly. "You two are perfect for each other." He delivered his last two words as he looked straight in her eyes. "Both liars."

Tem knew he was angry and lashing out. But it didn't make it hurt any less. "Caspen," she whispered. "You said it yourself. I chose you. I haven't slept with him. I haven't consummated the crest."

"But you want to, do you not? You want to more than anything."

She shook her head. "I…"

"It is easy to choose when there are no real consequences. It is not so easy when a life is on the line. How long does he have?"

Tem's throat was tight. She couldn't breathe. Leo did not have long. Her father had said that when she fully lost the ability to transition, it would already be too late. She hadn't transitioned since Apollo taught her to petrify. And he had barely been able to pull her through.

"I don't know," she whispered.

"And if his time is near? What then, my love?"

He said it so condescendingly, she wanted to cry.

"Tell me, Tem." Caspen leaned in. "Will you let him die?"

They both knew the answer to that.

"Perhaps I shall make it easy," he said, his voice deadly quiet. "Perhaps it would be better if I made your choice for you."

Tem looked up into his black eyes, staring at the endless pools. "What are you saying?"

"I am saying that your little human prince is fragile. And I am tempted to break him."

For the first time, Tem truly feared for Leo.

It was one thing for Caspen to be livid with her. But it was another thing entirely for him to direct his ire at Leo. He had already threatened to solve this himself, hadn't he? There was absolutely nothing stopping him from leaving the caves and going to the castle to enact his own revenge. Tem knew exactly what form that revenge would take. She pictured Jonathan's and Christopher's petrified faces. Caspen had already broken the truce. Caspen did not care about the humans.

That could not happen to Leo. She wouldn't let it.

She refused to believe that Caspen would do that to her, not when he knew the heartbreak would surely kill her. Tem was too shocked to speak.

But it was Apollo, ultimately, who said, "You cannot do that."

"Why not? It is a solution." Caspen looked at him wildly. "Just as you said."

"Have mercy, Brother."

"*Mercy?*" Caspen spat. Tem flinched at his tone. "You want me to have *mercy*?"

His words hung in the air. Caspen owed no one his mercy.

Tem did not deserve his compassion or charity. There would be no benevolence for her. She didn't even want it. She wanted to be punished, to reap the consequences of her actions. Why shouldn't she suffer when her actions warranted punishment? Caspen had already suffered, and it had been at her hand. Tem deserved the same.

"It will destroy her," Apollo said quietly. "You know it will."

Finally, Caspen fell silent. A tortured shadow of tenderness passed over his face as he looked at Tem. He did not want to destroy her. It was the last thing he would ever do.

Apollo was truly standing between them now. His back was to Tem, his hand on Caspen's chest. Caspen didn't seem to notice, looking only at Tem.

"I do not want to hurt you," he said slowly, each word drawn out.

"You should," she whispered. "I deserve it."

Incredible sadness passed over Caspen's face. He stepped closer. The moment he did so, Apollo's hand flattened against his chest. Finally, their eyes met. The two brothers stared at each other, and Tem wondered suddenly whether they were speaking using their minds. Both of them were closed off to her—she couldn't listen in. An eternity passed.

At last, Tem caught part of a sentence spoken by Apollo: ...*know when to step aside.*

"She is my wife," Caspen said out loud, his voice dangerously low. "And this is between us."

Apollo opened his mouth again, but Caspen cut him off.

"Leave us, Brother."

Tem expected Apollo to go. Instead, his eyes flicked to hers, then back to Caspen's. He shook his head. "I am not leaving you alone with her."

Anger darkened Caspen's face.

"It's fine," Tem said quickly. "We'll be fine. Just go."

But her words were useless. The situation was beyond negotiation—beyond reason. They were rapidly approaching a precipice and were all out of control. They'd been circling it for days, she realized. Perhaps weeks. It had begun the first night of mating season, when Apollo flirted with her. The tournament had been the final straw.

Apollo only shook his head, directing the same words at Caspen once more. "I am not leaving you alone with her."

Caspen's eyes narrowed. "Do you truly think I would harm my own wife?"

"You are angry with her."

"I am also angry with you."

A long silence passed.

"Or perhaps you are angry with yourself."

Caspen closed his eyes. A vein jumped in his temple as the three of them stood in silence. Tem understood what Apollo was trying to say. It was the very same thing she'd said to herself, in the middle of the night, when Caspen was asleep and the darkness was absolute. Caspen was the one who told Tem to crest Leo. He'd insisted that she do it. It didn't matter that he hadn't known the full consequences of his actions. He'd still been the one who told her to do so. Caspen was culpable in this just as Tem was. Despite what he claimed, Caspen had always known how Tem felt about Leo. He had chosen not to see it.

"No matter how you feel," Apollo said, "you cannot take it out on Temperance."

Caspen's eyes flew open. "Then I shall take it out on *you*."

He moved so fast Tem didn't even have time to blink before they were upon each other.

She flinched as brother met brother, each of them releasing a guttural cry. It was the second time in twenty-four hours that two men had fought over her, and it was just as brutal as the first time. Apollo was a willing target. Perhaps too willing. Tem could do nothing but watch as he absorbed hit after hit, clearly letting Caspen take out every frustration he was feeling.

Tem wanted to scream.

But then, as quickly as they began, they stopped. The brothers stepped apart, and it wasn't until they were fully disentangled that Tem saw Caspen holding his throat. Blood seeped between his fingers, but it was not Apollo's doing. It was the wound from earlier—the one Rowe had inflicted during the first tier of the tournament. Tem stared at it, watching as blood poured down his chest from the two distinct puncture marks on his neck.

"What's happening?" she cried. "The bite—"

"It is Rowe's doing," Apollo said, his breath still coming in short bursts. "He is siphoning from Caspenon."

Caspen clutched his neck. Without thinking, Tem ran forward, pressing her fingers over his, applying pressure in an attempt to stop the bleeding.

"When will it end?" There was so much blood.

"It will not end. The wound will open every time Rowe wishes to take his power. He can do so until there is no power left to take."

Blood was covering Tem's fingers, dripping down her wrists. "Caspen," she said desperately. "Please—"

But Caspen wrenched himself away from her, steadying himself against the side of the passageway. He stared at them both. Then he turned and disappeared into the darkness.

Tem immediately stepped forward, but Apollo grabbed her arm.

"Temperance," he said, his lips on her ear. "Do not go after him."

"But he's—"

"He is drunk," Apollo said, his hand still around her arm. "And he is angry. He will not be convinced of anything right now."

Despite herself, tears rose in her eyes. She pressed her head against Apollo's chest in an attempt to suppress them. "Why is he acting like this?" she whispered. "How can he say those things?"

Apollo sighed. "Because he fears for you."

She frowned. "I don't understand."

"That is because you have not known him as long as I have."

"What does that have to do with anything?"

"Caspenon is…complicated," Apollo continued. "But he is predictable in some ways,"

"In what ways?"

"In matters of the heart."

Here it was again: the intimation that Caspen was sentimental. Tem had heard it before, and she was beginning to believe it. It was hard to believe that someone so formidable could be ruled by his emotions. But that was the case with Caspen. He was driven by his love for her, as she was in return. But their current circumstances were pulling them apart, driving a wedge between them that Tem had no idea how to fix. It was beginning to scare her.

"I can't lose him," she whispered.

Apollo touched the golden chain around her neck. "You will not lose him."

Tem hardly believed it anymore. The blood bond was supposed to keep them together. Now it was ruining everything. Without thinking, she began to cry.

Immediately, Apollo's arms were around her. He pulled her against him, his fingers stroking her hair, her chin nestled in the nook of his shoulder. Apollo had once told her not to come for him for comfort. But he comforted her now, holding Tem as she sobbed, murmuring soft words to soothe her. She allowed herself to collapse against his body, releasing the frustration and pain that had been building inside her for far too long.

Apollo's lips were on Tem's neck, but he didn't take things further. Instead, he simply held her until her sobs quieted. When she was done crying, she simply stood there, wrapped in his arms, listening to his heartbeat, which was far slower and steadier than hers.

Eventually, he asked, *What do you love about him?*

About Leo?

Yes.

Why are you asking me that?

Because I wish to know.

Tem heaved a sigh before settling even deeper against Apollo's chest. She thought about his question and realized nobody had ever asked her that before. What did she love about Leo? So many things. She loved his long fingers. She loved his ice-blond hair. She loved the way he closed his eyes right before kissing her, giving her an extra moment to look at him as he leaned in. She loved other things too—things that had nothing to do with the way he looked.

She loved the way he always made sure she'd eaten enough. She loved the way he stood up to his father even when it meant jeopardizing his privilege. She loved his compassion and his bravery. Leo was always striving to be better than he was the day before. It was an admirable quality and one that Tem coveted. She wanted to be like him: steady and loyal and true. Leo was a better man than Tem had ever given him credit for, and it was her greatest shame that she hadn't realized it until it was too late. Now he was that man for Evelyn.

I love everything about him.

Do you love him enough to forsake my brother?

It was an impossible question and one Tem had no answer for. Forsaking either of them was unacceptable to her. It always had been.

I can't answer that.

Apollo sighed, his chest rising and falling against hers. *Then you must be prepared to lose them both.*

CHAPTER THIRTY-NINE

TEM DID NOT RETURN TO HER CHAMBERS. INSTEAD, SHE SOUGHT SOLACE THE ONLY place she knew she could find it.

Her parents' cottage was dark; it was late—or maybe it was early—and they were surely asleep. Tem knocked on the door anyway, pounding her fist until her father opened it, staring at her with bleary eyes.

"What is the matter, child?"

But Tem did not have the words. Everything was the matter.

"Temperance?" Her mother emerged from the bedroom. "What are you doing here?"

At the sight of her mother, Tem fell to her knees in a defeated heap, sobs racking her body. She was dimly aware of hands on her shoulders, lifting her up. The familiar scent of the sea enveloped her. A mug of tea was pressed into her hands, and she savored the heat. All three of them sat at the kitchen table, in silence, until Tem was ready to speak.

"I think I made a mistake," she whispered. "I've ruined everything."

"You are allowed to make mistakes, my child. They are a part of life. Everyone makes them."

"You don't."

Kronos smiled softly. "Of course I do. I make them all the time. Do you truly think that I have lived as long as I have without making any mistakes?"

Tem deeply wanted to believe him. But she felt so horrible it was difficult to do so.

"It is not your mistakes that matter, child. It is how you fix them."

But Tem couldn't fix them. Not this time. What she'd done was unfixable. "I don't want Leo to die," she whispered.

Kronos sighed, placing his hand on her arm. "Have you been able to transition at all?" She shook her head.

"Then you must make your choice soon. He will not have long."

"If I just had more time, I could—"

But what, exactly, could Tem do? More time wouldn't change her circumstances. It would only prolong them.

"If time is what you need, there is one thing you can do."

"What?"

Kronos glanced at her mother, who gave him a sad, knowing smile.

"The crest must be consummated with sex. But if you do anything leading up to that act, his fate will be delayed."

"What do you mean?"

"If you kiss him, if you do anything other than sex, it will buy him some time."

Tem didn't bother asking how he knew that. She had seen the look between her parents—she knew they had a long history together. She was grateful for that history—it informed her future.

"You must know that is not a permanent solution," her father continued. "The draw of the crest will not wait forever."

Tem stared at her tea, trying to imagine a world in which she and Leo would even be allowed to kiss each other. She doubted Evelyn would ever let them be alone together again. And after what just happened with Caspen, he probably wouldn't either.

"I can't kiss him," she whispered. "I can't do anything else either."

"Then you may have to watch him die."

They didn't speak any more after that. The sun was rising anyway, and her mother went out to tend to the garden. Tem spent the day in her parents' bedroom, alternating between sleeping and eating the meals her father brought her. Eventually, it was evening, and Tem still wasn't ready to return to the mountain. She knew Gabriel had the day off, and she knew where to find him.

"Tem, dearest," he said when she walked into the Horseman. "It's been too long."

It had been barely a day, yet Tem agreed. She returned his embrace, holding him tighter than usual. "Did you enjoy the rest of the celebration?" she asked.

"Of course I did. What about you? I'm surprised you're able to walk after all that."

Tem didn't have the heart to tell him her body had been through far worse than the tournament. She decided to change the subject. "Is Damon taking care of you?"

Gabriel wiggled his eyebrows at her. "As best he can."

Tem shoved him. Some things would never change.

Suddenly Gabriel's eyebrows rose. Tem followed his gaze to see the last person she expected to see: Vera.

She looked rather worse for wear—her blond hair was ragged and lank, her usually pink lips were pale. Tem hadn't seen her since the wedding, and it would appear that the food shortage had affected her as well.

"Rumor has it she's dating Jeremy now," Gabriel murmured as Vera walked toward them.

"Jonathan's brother? Really?"

He gave her a pointed look. "You're not one to talk, dearest."

Before she could retaliate, Vera paused at their table, staring down her nose at Tem.

"Vera," Tem said cautiously. "How are you?"

A quick sneer turned those pale lips. "Better than you."

So nothing had changed, then. Despite her bedraggled appearance, Vera was still a bitch.

"At least I have a husband," Tem said. It was the one thing that might hurt her.

Vera's mouth fell open.

"Close your mouth, Vera," Gabriel said cheerfully. "A bug might fly in."

Tem held back a laugh. Vera leaned in.

"Your husband is a *snake*. It's revolting. You shouldn't even be here."

"Excuse me?"

"Don't think anyone has forgotten what you did. You ruined everyone's chances with the prince, and then you didn't even want him anyway."

She couldn't be more wrong. Tem still wanted him. She always would. "You don't know anything about that," Tem said quietly.

"I know plenty," Vera snapped. "And I know your *husband* should watch his back." Then she flounced away.

Tem turned to Gabriel. "What did she mean by that?"

"I don't know." He stared after her darkly. "But there have been...whispers."

"Whispers about what?"

"A coup."

"A *coup*?"

"Food is scarce again, Tem. Not to mention a man disappeared, and people think it was the basilisks."

Tem's stomach turned. The man again. The one she'd petrified. His disappearance had fanned the flame of rebellion, and it was all her fault.

"Jeremy took over when I...stepped down. He's been leading the charge."

It wasn't lost on Tem the magnitude of what Gabriel had done. To give up his seat as the leader of the rebellion was no small gesture, and it was all because of Damon. She knew without asking that the bond between them was strong. Damon had chosen Gabriel as his mate. It was only a matter of time before Gabriel chose him right back, if he hadn't already. Tem was suddenly afraid that she had made things worse for him— that if the villagers viewed Tem the way Vera did, then they might view Gabriel just the same.

"Gabriel," she said. "I need you to stay safe. If the villagers know you're on our side—"

Gabriel's hands clasped over hers. "Then they'll know I'm loyal to the people I love."

The next few days were agony.

Tem spent hours traipsing around the passageways, trying not to think about everything that was going wrong. She didn't dare seek out Apollo; she didn't want to see him anyway. She only wanted to see Caspen, and he was nowhere to be found. It wasn't until Sunday that Tem truly began to worry. They were supposed to have dinner at the castle. What if he didn't show? What if she had to brave the meal alone? The thought was too much to bear. Surely, he would show. Surely, he would not leave her to suffer Evelyn alone.

But when the carriage arrived to take her to the castle, Caspen was not in it. Tem sat alone on the velvet bench, staring out the window at the stars, wondering where on this earth her husband might be. Had he retreated to the sea, where basilisks originated? Or was he simply hunting, as he always was, trying to regain the strength that Rowe was taking from him? It killed Tem not knowing. But there was nothing she could do about it. All she could do was walk in the front door of the castle and follow the butler to the dining room for dinner.

Leo was already seated. He was alone.

"Where's Evelyn?" Tem asked.

At her question, he flinched. "She won't be joining us tonight."

"Why not?"

"She's not feeling well."

"Is that so?"

"Yes."

"What's wrong with her?"

"She is ill, Tem. What more information do you need?"

"None, I guess. I'm just asking."

"Very well. Shall we eat?"

"Fine."

"Fine."

Tem noticed that Leo didn't ask where Caspen was. He was acting...odd. Restrained, as if he were holding something in. It wasn't like him. Usually, she could read him like a book. But not tonight. Tonight, it was as if he'd erected a shield between them—one that prevented her from seeing what was really going on.

They sat at opposite ends of the table, staring at each other. Tem was quite sure that Evelyn wasn't ill. Surely, she had no desire to see Tem after their disastrous meeting last time. She was probably upstairs, in Leo's bathtub, drinking expensive champagne.

A butler began serving dinner.

Tem studied Leo intently as he ate, trying to determine whether he looked worse than he did last time. She concluded that he did. There were bags under his eyes, and his shoulders were hunched. How long did he have?

"Tem," Leo said, breaking her from her thoughts. "Did the fight happen?"

She'd completely forgotten about their conversation in the library—how she'd told him about the tournament, and he'd told her to fix things.

"Oh," she said. "Yes."

"And? How did it go?"

How to answer him? It had gone terribly, all things considered. "It…" She trailed off.

When she didn't continue, Leo said, "Did Caspen win?"

Tem realized suddenly how it would look to Leo—her showing up to the castle without her husband. "Yes," she said quickly. "He did."

Leo nodded. "Good."

Was it? Tem didn't know anymore. It was better than the alternative. But at this point, that didn't mean it was good.

"There is another matter we must discuss," Leo said.

"Which is?"

He paused, and Tem's heart pounded in her chest. "Will you attend the wedding?"

Tem hadn't expected him to ask that, and she certainly didn't have an answer. With everything going so terribly, she'd forgotten that Mother's Night was just days from now.

"I didn't realize I was invited."

"Of course you're invited. Basilisk royalty is always there."

Basilisk royalty. She'd been human royalty just weeks ago. "Well then, I guess…yes. If we have to."

"You don't seem sure."

"That's because I'm not."

"Why not?"

Tem sighed. Leo was *impossible* tonight—asking too many questions, demanding too much of her. "I don't know, Leo. It doesn't seem like a good idea." Nothing about it was a good idea. And certainly not if she was expected to attend with Caspen.

"I want you there," he whispered.

Tem knew he wanted her there. But why? Because he wanted her to see his union to Evelyn? That seemed cruel—far too cruel for Leo. Perhaps it was because he sought her tacit permission to marry Evelyn, although surely, he knew he already had it. She was the one who had told him to leave, after all. Nothing had changed. Or perhaps he just needed her there. As a friend. It didn't matter. Leo needed her, and she needed him.

"Then I'll be there," she whispered back. It was that simple. She would do anything for Leo. Even attend his wedding to someone else.

"There is one more thing," he said slowly. He sighed. "Evelyn has requested that you and Caspen stay here at the castle the night before."

"*What?* Why would she want that?"

Leo pursed his lips. "She did not give me a reason."

Tem's mouth fell open. She could think of a number of reasons, and they were all terrible. Perhaps Evelyn wanted to punish Tem and, in turn, punish Leo. By bringing her here to the castle, she was rubbing their wedding in Tem's face. There would be no place to hide, no way to avoid what was right in front of her. It would be a special form of torture, crafted specifically for Tem.

"That's an awful idea," Tem said bluntly. "And if she wants us there so badly, she should ask us herself."

"She is not in the mood for dinner tonight."

"I thought she was ill."

Leo didn't reply.

The cracks that had begun to show last week were splitting now. All was not well in the royal household.

The rest of the dinner passed in silence. Tem spent the time picking at her food and staring at Leo, who had long since abandoned his plate and turned to his whiskey. When it finally became unbearable to sit there any longer, Tem stood.

"Well. Good night."

"Wait." Leo stood too. "Stay."

Tem blinked. "Why?"

"Because I…" His eyes flicked to the butlers, who were standing at attention as they always were. Tem understood. Leo wanted to be alone with her.

She sighed. It was a terrible idea for them to be alone together. Tem was surprised that Evelyn had created a situation that would allow it. But another idea nagged at her, one she couldn't shake. Her father's words were running in a circle through her mind: *If you kiss him—if you do anything other than sex—it will buy him some time.*

Before she could stop herself, Tem followed Leo into the library.

He poured each of them a whiskey, as usual. They stood by the desk, as usual. But this time there was an energy in the air that Tem couldn't define—a sense of possibility that made her heart race.

She had already given herself permission for what she wanted to do. Would Leo?

Tem watched him in the dim firelight. The hand not holding his whiskey was on the desk, spinning a letter opener by its thick, marble handle. It reminded Tem of her request to him.

"Have you been writing me letters?"

His eyes flicked to hers. "Yes."

Tem dearly wished to know what was in them. She pictured Leo bent over parchment, scrawling with that spiky handwriting of his. "How many?"

The letter opener continued to spin.

"A lot."

"Where do you keep them?"

The letter opener stopped. "Why are you asking me this, Tem?"

She stared up into his slate-gray eyes, seeking the answer herself. There was no reason to ask him other than she wanted to hear his voice. "Because I miss you."

The same thing she'd told him when she came to the castle just one week after their wedding, to get an annulment. She'd meant it then, and she meant it even more now.

"You don't get to miss me," he said. "You sent me away."

"I wanted you to be happy."

"Do I seem happy to you?"

The answer was obvious, even if Tem didn't want to say it. Leo was a man in crisis, caught between his obligations and his heart. And Tem had put him there.

"Leo…I'm…"

"Don't." He pointed the letter opener at her. "*Don't* say you're sorry."

Tem pursed her lips. It was all she wanted to say. She needed him to know that she was sorry—that she regretted everything. But she understood why he wouldn't want to hear it. It meant nothing coming from her. Tem was the one who did this to him. The fact that she couldn't undo it now was as much his burden to bear as hers. She did not want him to bear that burden any longer. Without thinking, Tem stepped closer.

Immediately, Leo's eyes widened.

Slowly, he set down his whiskey glass. The hand around the letter opener tightened, his veins standing out beneath his pale skin. An unspoken understanding passed between them.

The letter opener gleamed in his hand. When he raised it to her chest, Tem's breath stopped. A moment later cold metal touched her skin as he slid the blade so it was flat beneath her dress strap. Then he lifted the strap so it hovered an inch above her shoulder. They stood there, staring at each other, the air on fire between them. Leo turned the blade on its edge. Then he began to cut.

Back and forth, back and forth. One thread at a time. This was no knife blade; it was not sharp. It sawed slowly through the thin fabric, fraying it centimeter by centimeter until all that remained was a single, tenuous thread. Leo stopped. Neither of them moved.

The thread snapped.

Tem didn't bother pulling the strap back up. It was the last thing she wanted to do anyway. Instead she slid the other strap down her shoulder so that both her breasts were exposed. Then she let the dress fall to the floor.

The moment she was naked, Leo took a deep, strangled breath. It was exhilarating to stand here with him like this, completely exposed, nowhere to hide. Tem looked at him as he looked at her, his eyes traveling over every inch of her body. The last time she'd been naked before him was the night before their wedding. She'd thought about it every night since. Had he?

Leo stepped closer. His entire body was angled toward hers, his tall frame leaning down to enter into her atmosphere as he said, "No skin."

Tem understood what he meant: as long as they didn't touch, it wasn't legitimate—it wasn't *real*. No skin meant no betrayal, no deceit. If this was how Leo wanted to justify this, then who was Tem to deny him? If the only way she could have him was to not have him at all, she would take it. They had to relieve this urge—this horrible, aching need that was driving them both to insanity. No lines would truly be crossed. Not really. Perhaps it was just a lie they told themselves. But Tem needed that lie right now.

She needed *Leo*.

Without a word, Leo raised the letter opener once more to her chest. This time he brushed the blade gently over her breasts, tracing a line from one to the other. Her nipples, already tender, cinched into hard peaks.

With a single, deft motion, Leo flipped the letter opener in his hand so he was holding it by the blade. "Get on the desk."

Tem did as she was told.

As soon as she lifted herself up, Leo stepped between her legs. It was not unlike the position she'd been in with Apollo after he taught her how to petrify, when he'd used his fingers to make her come. Only this time, instead of a finger, the marble handle of the letter opener touched her center. Tem let out an involuntary gasp—one so quiet it was barely audible over the crackling of the fire. But she knew Leo heard it. As if that gasp was the permission he needed, he let out a noise of his own, something between a moan and a growl—something raw and hungry and *real*.

He stepped even closer.

Their faces were inches apart; Tem had to crane her neck to look up at him. Slowly, without breaking eye contact, Leo raised his other hand, grabbed a handful of her curls in his fist, and pulled until her head was arched back. Then he pulled even harder. Tem cried out, jerking her hips so that she nearly fell off the desk. It was *heaven*.

Leo leaned over her, staring right in her eyes as he pushed the handle deep into her wetness. Tem was used to hard objects; she'd already taken Rowe's golden cock. This was no different—the smooth stone slid inside her easily, and she bit her lip in pleasure. Leo bit his own, as if, in doing so, he could feel what she felt. His gold incisors gleamed in the firelight.

He was working her good now—he knew exactly the right cadence to take, exactly the right angle to make her whimper. Leo knew everything about her, including how to touch her even when he wasn't touching her at all.

"Take your cock out," Tem gasped. She needed to see it.

Leo shook his head. "No."

"Why not?"

The smooth marble slid all the way out of her, then all the way back in.

"If my cock is out, I'm going to fuck you."

"I want to see it."

He smiled. "I know you do."

"Please, Leo."

"No, Tem. And don't ask me again."

Tem couldn't beg anymore. There were more important things happening—things that required her attention. The handle was moving quickly now, in and out, exactly as a cock would. Every few seconds, Leo would flick the end up over her clitoris, and Tem would nearly come apart each time.

He was so warm. *All of him.* Waves of heat radiated off Leo—far hotter than the flames in the fireplace. Every dark and luscious urge inside Tem screamed to break free. She wanted to ravage him, to rip him apart and wrap him around her until there was no difference between his body and hers.

The letter opener was still moving. Slipping in and out of her, playing with her, teasing her. Tem moaned through all of it, savoring the unforgiving hardness of the marble.

"Fuck," Leo whispered. "I wish you were mine."

"I am," Tem whispered back.

It was only then that she realized that while he couldn't touch her, she could touch him. Leo was still completely clothed—the only exposed skin were his forearms and his neck, which she could easily avoid. Without waiting another moment, Tem raised her hands and placed them flat against his chest. She felt his torso through his shirt, hard and lean, brushing her fingers over the channels between his abs. She touched his shoulders, feeling his muscles flex as he moved the letter opener inside her. Then she simply grabbed his shirt and held on tight.

"I want to fuck you so badly," he groaned.

That was all Tem wanted too. She wanted him to turn her around and fuck her against the desk, her breasts against the wood, her hair in his hands. She wanted him to fuck her lying down, their bodies pressed together; standing up, their hands on the mantel.

Instead she said, "You can't."

"I didn't say I was going to. Just that I want to."

Tem almost smiled. But the imminence of climax was distracting her. She was *so* close to coming. Leo knew it too. His motions were purposeful and strong, pushing her closer and closer with each passing second.

Finally, it was too much.

Tem arched her back as she came, keeping her eyes wide open, watching Leo as he watched her. Her wetness coated the letter opener.

"*Fuck*," Leo gasped.

Through the violent crash of her orgasm, Tem saw him look down at his hand. A slash of red was on his palm; he'd cut himself at the exact moment he'd made her come. Tem closed her eyes, helpless against her climax. When she opened them, Leo was watching her again.

Tem sat up. She reached for his hand, but he jerked away.

"Let me heal you."

"No."

"Leo, please."

But he only shook his head. Healing him would require touching him, and that wasn't allowed. *No skin.* A man of his word, even now.

They stared at each other in the dim firelight, both of them breathing hard. The effect of their union was unmistakable; Leo looked healthy for the first time in weeks. His skin was flushed, his eyes bright. Tem knew she must look the same. She had bought him time, just as her father said. How much time, she could not know. But enough that, for once, Tem knew she would fall asleep without worry tonight.

Her gaze fell to his cock, which was so hard it was pulling his pants into a taut mountain of fabric. Tem's hand was already rising, reaching for the bulge between his legs. Leo didn't stop her. Something within her exploded with pleasure the moment she made contact, and if she hadn't just had an orgasm, she would've had another. It took everything she had not to slip her hand beneath his waistline, to feel his cock against her palm. But that would mean touching his skin—that would break their rule. So, instead, she rubbed him over his trousers, steadily, feeling just how hard he was for her. Leo's eyes rolled back in his head.

His hand was still curled around the letter opener, gripping it so tightly that blood began to drip onto the carpet. Tem watched him, remembering how well they fit together, how they'd always had such perfect rhythm. She missed their song. She missed *him*.

Tem alternated between rubbing and squeezing, never doing one for too long. She knew by the ragged pattern of his breath that he was close.

"Leo," Tem whispered in his ear.

With a tormented moan, he came. Tem kept stroking until she felt his cum soaking through his trousers. When she was sure he was done, she raised her hand and pressed it flat to his chest, right over his heart. His heartbeat was whip-fast, hammering as if he'd just sprinted a mile. They stood like that for a long time, far longer than they should have. Neither of them said a word. Even when Tem pulled away to put on her dress, they still didn't speak. And when she walked out of the room, holding up the severed strap with her hand, she knew he was watching her go.

On the carriage ride back to the caves, Tem felt as if she were flying. The boost of energy she gained from being with Leo was undeniable. She felt alive for the first time in days. It was sheer heaven to feel so *whole*.

Tem tossed her ruined dress into the fireplace the moment she reached her chambers. No sooner had she done so than she heard someone say her name.

It was Caspen. "Tem," he said again. "Where were you?"

Tem almost laughed. He'd been missing for days and he had the audacity to ask *her* where *she* was?

"The castle," she said. "It's Sunday, remember?"

Before he could reply, she returned the question.

"Where were *you*?"

"I was with Apollo."

"That's not what I asked."

Still, Caspen didn't answer. He merely looked at her, his expression impossible to read. Firelight fell on his neck. Rowe's bite marks were red and deep, the wound opened anew. Tem wondered how long it had been bleeding.

He stepped closer, and Tem braced herself. What came out of his mouth was the last thing she expected him to say.

"You look beautiful."

Tem blinked. "I…" she began but had no idea how to finish. She settled on "Thank you."

The timing of the compliment surprised her, but not the compliment itself. Tem knew she must look radiant—the effect of being with Leo would be unmistakable.

They stood before the fire, the same place they had had so many conversations before. Tem breathed in his scent. She had missed that the most: the way he smelled of smoke. She had no idea whether they were on good terms—no idea who was even mad at who anymore. Tem decided right then to lay down her armor. She extended her hand, touching it to Caspen's warm torso. It was the opposite of the way she'd just touched Leo—through the fabric of his shirt, no skin. Now she splayed her fingers wide, feeling as much of Caspen's body as possible.

A moment later, she was in his arms.

For a long while, all they did was hold each other. Time passed. They breathed.

Eventually, Tem whispered, "I'm sorry, Caspen."

He held her closer.

"When will you understand that you have nothing to be sorry for?" His hands were tracing her spine. "It is me who is sorry. I have always known exactly who you are, Tem. I have always known that you cannot be tamed."

Tem just shook her head.

"It has never been easy with you," Caspen continued quietly. "Most likely it never will be. But I do not need easy. I do not *want* easy." He tilted her head up to his, whispering the rest against her lips. "I just want you." Then he kissed her.

In his kiss, Tem found mercy. His body pressed against her, skin against skin, as solid as the mountain itself. Caspen was gentle with her—so much more gentle than usual—as soft as silk with his touch. In that moment, the only thing she knew was him.

Tem was so swept away in their kiss that she barely heard the dull swell of noise penetrating the back of her skull. She opened her mind, tuning into the collective consciousness of every basilisk under the mountain. It was utter chaos, dozens of voices, all talking over one another, all in a state of sheer panic.

How did it get in here?

We have precautions in place. It should be impossible to—

If there is one, that means there could be more—

How can we get it out?

We must leave, otherwise—

There must be a way to kill it—

Something was wrong, that much was very clear. But Tem couldn't tell what it was, couldn't understand what had happened. The mass panic was pressing against her skull, threatening to crush her. Finally, she heard it. One word, over and over:

Weasel.

CHAPTER FORTY

"Caspen," Tem said out loud. "Listen."

He listened, his brow furrowed. Then his eyes widened.

Basilisks had many weaknesses. Mirrors. The crow of a rooster. The smell of a weasel. There was one here, now, in the passageways. And it was killing her people.

"Who would do this?" Caspen whispered. "Who would—"

But Tem already knew.

She remembered Vera's words perfectly: *Your husband should watch his back.* This was retaliation, revenge for Jonathan and Christopher. The villagers could not reach the royals, so now they'd come for the basilisks, staking their claim in this civil war.

A scream pierced the air.

Immediately, Caspen turned for the door.

"Wait," Tem cried. "You can't go out there. *I'm* going out there."

"*You* are not going anywhere."

"I have to help, Caspen. I'm the only one who can—"

Another scream.

Caspen's face was tight with pain. Whether physical or emotional, Tem didn't know. She grabbed him by the shoulders and pushed him back onto the bed.

"Stay here."

"Tem, I must help my people."

"You can't go near a weasel, Caspen."

He shook his head. He seemed to be in shock. "I must do something."

"*No*, Caspen. I just got you back. You're not going anywhere."

"I cannot just sit here. I must—"

"*You must stay here.*"

She pushed Caspen down again, as hard as she could. This time he sat.

Before he had a chance to protest again, Tem turned and ran from the room. The passageway was utter chaos; basilisks in their human forms sprinted in every direction, trying to sequester themselves in their chambers. Dimly, Tem heard a commotion that sounded like it came from the courtyard. She angled her body in that direction, dodging basilisk after basilisk in the passageway.

Caspen's presence was strong in her mind. Tem kept the corridor between them open, showing him where she was going. As soon as she entered the passageway, the noise in her mind became noise surrounding her. She fought against the stream of basilisks, pushing through the wave of bodies. By the time Tem reached the courtyard, she was out of breath.

Nothing could have prepared her for what she saw.

The courtyard was full of bodies. Basilisks lay in piles along the walls, motionless, in a clear attempt at retreat—all dead. Tem stared at them numbly as she passed, barely seeing them. Husbands shielded their wives, their hands over their noses in an attempt to block the smell. Basilisks had nothing with which to cover their faces, no way to defend themselves against the weapon of scent. It was the perfect attack, and it was unthinkably cruel. With a jolt, Tem recognized the next body she saw. It was the woman in the blood-bound couple: the one she had blessed on the first night of mating season. The woman's mate was nowhere to be found. But Tem knew that wherever he was, he was dead.

Tem blinked away tears. There was no time for that now, no time to grieve.

Anyone who was left alive was screaming and sprinting for the passageways, desperate to get as far away from the weasel as possible. It took less than a minute for Tem to locate it. The creature was in the corner, gnawing on the arm of a woman basilisk. Bile rose in Tem's throat, and she fought to suppress it.

All this destruction from an animal smaller than a cat. Tem couldn't believe that something as formidable as the basilisks could be brought down by something so minuscule. It was some sick joke of nature that they would have such a weakness. They were too powerful otherwise, too dominant. Predators like Caspen had to be controlled somehow. There was always a balance.

As soon as Tem approached the weasel, it bolted in the opposite direction. She ran after it madly, blind with adrenaline, finally cornering it next to the fountain. Her basilisk side recoiled at the smell, but her human side had no reaction whatsoever. She felt much the same as she had growing up on the farm, listening to the crow of the rooster: discomfort but not pain. Tem was the only one who could fix this—the only one who would be safe from the weasel. This time when she lunged for it, she caught it, scraping her elbows and her knees against the rough stone floor as she dove to the ground. The narrow creature just barely fit in her hands, and the moment she caught it, Tem gripped it with her fists and *twisted*. She felt its spine break with a great snap, then it went limp.

Caspen, she called with her mind. *I have it. What do I do with it?*

Do not move. I will tell everyone to sequester themselves. Then you can take it outside.

In reply, a wave of relief passed through her mind. She felt Caspen's presence branch out, reaching for everyone in her vicinity. Tem held the weasel in her hands, staring down at its lifeless body. The sound of screaming slowly quieted as everyone retreated to their chambers until finally it was just her in the courtyard alone. Still, Tem waited to move until she heard Caspen say, *Everyone is gone, Tem.*

Tem nodded even though she knew he couldn't see her. She carried the weasel all the way outside, gasping as the cold air hit her lungs. Sometimes it was easy to forget just how claustrophobic the caves were. But now, under the light of the late autumn moon, Tem felt truly alone.

She looked down at the weasel in her hands. It was bent at an odd angle, its spine cracked. It was still warm. Tem wondered if it was sentient, the way humans were. There was a time, not too long ago, when she'd thought—just like the villagers—that basilisks weren't capable of complex emotion. And yet they were. Perhaps this weasel was too. It was unbelievable to Tem that something so small could have caused such grievous harm. There were countless deaths—many families would be mourning tomorrow. All because of the tiny creature in her hands. Tem paused at the wall. Then on a whim, she walked deeper into the forest.

There was no logic to her actions. This animal did not deserve a funeral. But for some reason, under the naked judgment of the Alpha Serpentis, Tem felt obligated to give it one. She walked until she found a stretch of ground that was untouched by the early frost, setting the weasel down before hacking at the dirt with a stick, her foot, anything she could find until there was a rough hole hewn in the ground. Then she dropped the weasel inside it and spread dirt over it, creating a quick grave. Tem stared at her handiwork. It was a pathetic resting place, even for a weasel. She stood there until she became cold. She didn't bother warming herself; it was time to go back. She could do nothing more for the weasel, and there were more important deaths to mourn tonight. Tem made her way to the caves, dreading what she might find.

The courtyard was once more full of basilisks. Only this time, they milled about in stunned silence, the only sound the occasional mournful wail. Tem cast her gaze around, searching for every face she might know. Relief coursed through her the moment she saw Apollo. Similar relief shone on his face when their eyes met. Tem ran toward him.

He ran toward her too, nearly lifting her from the ground as they collided.

"You were brave, Temperance. We owe you a debt."

Tem just shook her head. A debt was the last thing the basilisks owed her.

Apollo left her when Cypress emerged from the crowd. Tem didn't follow.

Instead, she helped however she could, lending her time and her heart to anyone who needed it. Eventually, Adelaide joined her. They worked into the early hours of the morning, comforting the grieving and counting the dead. In the end, forty-six basilisks fell prey to the weasel. By the time everyone was accounted for, Tem could barely keep her eyes open. She retreated to her chambers with Caspen, and they lay down on the bed together.

Tem stared at him in the darkness.

She had often wondered how he felt bearing the burden of leadership, and she saw that burden now. His brow was drawn, his chest rising and falling heavily. He did not cry, but he might as well have. Caspen had done so much for her, and all Tem wanted was to do something for him. Slowly, so as not to alarm him, Tem touched her fingers to his chest, drawing on the ability all basilisks had to transfer emotions. She knew it was working the moment overwhelming grief slammed into her like a brick wall. Tem gasped from the sheer *heaviness* of it. It was as if she were drowning. Caspen looked down at her in surprise, and she knew he hadn't expected this of her.

The effect on him was immediate. His face softened as the shadow on his brow retreated. Tem knew it wasn't a permanent solution, as nothing ever was. But for now, she tightened her grip on him, holding him against her, taking as much of his grief as she could.

"Thank you," Caspen whispered.

"Of course," Tem whispered. It was the least she could do for him. They fell asleep, Caspen's head on her chest, her arms wrapped around him.

The invitation came the following day.

Temperance Verus,

You are cordially invited to the nuptials of Thelonius and Evelyn in one week's time. The happy couple request your presence at the castle for a celebration the night before the wedding. A carriage will be sent for you. The dress code is evening wear.

Tem looked cautiously up at Caspen. In the whirlwind after the weasel attack, she had completely forgotten about Evelyn's request.

"What does it say?" Caspen asked. He was still on the bed.

"They want us to stay at the castle the night before the wedding."

He sat up slowly. "And why would they want that?"

"I don't know. I…think it's Evelyn's doing."

The look on Caspen's face perfectly matched the way Tem felt.

"We don't have to go," she said quickly.

Caspen held up his hand. "Yes we do."

"But *why*?"

He didn't answer.

Tem stared at him. All night, he had been sad. All night, he had grieved. But now anger crept into his voice, and Tem found herself afraid of what it might mean. Why would Caspen be so willing to go to the castle right after such an egregious attack on his people?

"Caspen," she said cautiously. "It's their wedding."

"I am aware of that."

"We can't…ruin it."

It was all she said, but she knew he understood what she meant. Tem didn't care about the wedding itself. And she certainly didn't care about Evelyn. But she cared about Leo. Nothing had changed: they were still in the same position they had been before the weasel, and there was still no way to fix it.

"Basilisk royalty always attends the royal weddings."

"I know, but—"

"You are the queen, Tem," Caspen said. "You must be there."

At his tone, she fell silent. It was clear he was done discussing this.

Was Caspen testing her? Daring her to say that she didn't want to watch Leo get married? It was a cruel test, but she couldn't blame him for it. The four of them were in lockstep, trapped in a pattern of distrust that was eating them from the inside out. Tem should have known there would be no peace, that these insufferable Sunday-night dinners would eventually lead to this.

They spent the following days in near silence. It wasn't just them; every basilisk under the mountain was grieving the loss of their brethren. Tem felt their collective sadness on a physical level, as if a weight were crushing her chest. Basilisks did everything together, and grief was no exception. Tem spent most of the time in their chambers, lying next to Caspen, running her hands gently over his skin. She could think of nothing else to soothe him; the loss was too great.

"What do basilisks believe happens when they die?" she asked him one night.

"We believe our souls go to Kora."

It was the same thing humans believed.

"When one of us dies, we all feel it," he continued.

Tem could understand that. Basilisks were all connected—all one. "Do you have funerals?"

"We do."

"What are they like?"

"We will burn their remains, then return their ashes to the lake."

Tem nodded. She could think of no better send-off. .

By the time the night before the wedding arrived, Tem was emotionally spent. The carriage ride was silent, and Tem tried not to project her anxieties onto Caspen. He seemed much calmer than her, although she couldn't tell if he was sad or angry. Possibly he was both.

Evelyn greeted them at the door. "Thank you *so* much for coming," she said smoothly, as if this were a regular Sunday-night dinner and not the night before her wedding. "We're so happy to have you."

Tem had no idea who "we" was supposed to be. Leo was nowhere to be found.

"Shall I take you to your room?"

Neither of them answered. Evelyn was acting…strange. Cheerful, almost. It was a stark contrast to her usual mood, and it was throwing Tem off. Was she simply excited about the wedding? Tem could imagine she was thrilled to officially get her claws in Leo. Or perhaps she was eager to rub it in Tem's face. Either way, Evelyn was positively beaming as she ushered them up the stairs. Tem's stomach immediately dropped as she realized where their room was.

Right across the hall from Leo's.

Tem stared at his bedroom door, remembering the last time she was behind it. Leo had asked her to marry him not ten feet from where she was standing. He'd gotten down on one knee and given her the silver ring that was currently on her finger. Tem touched it now, trying to control her rage. Surely, this was purposeful. Surely, Evelyn had done it to be cruel.

Her next words confirmed it: "I put you nice and close to us, in case you need anything."

The only thing Tem needed was a lobotomy.

"Tem?" Evelyn said. "Could I have a word?"

Immediately, Tem's adrenaline spiked. "Why?"

"Oh, you know. Girl talk."

Not this again. Tem had had enough girl talk with Evelyn to last her a lifetime.

"Come," she chirped. "Let's talk in my room. We'll give your husband a chance to settle in."

My room. *Your* husband.

Tem looked at Caspen, who looked disinterestedly around the room. There was nothing in it but a bed, a desk, and a chair. For all intents and purposes, he was already settled in.

Will you be fine here?

I will be fine, Tem. I am not a child. You can leave me unaccompanied.

I know, but…

The truth was she didn't *want* to leave Caspen unaccompanied. Tem had no idea what he would do here in the castle, alone and angry, without her by his side.

Will you be here when I'm done?

I will.

Still, Tem hesitated. She was waiting for something—waiting for him to say—

Go.

At his command, dark disappointment twisted her stomach, and Tem realized she had hoped to hear another word—one that was the opposite of go. But the word didn't come, so she went.

Tem half expected Evelyn to hook her elbow through hers as they crossed the hall. Instead, she proudly opened the door to Leo's room, crossing to pour them drinks from the bar cart. Tem stood awkwardly in the middle of the room, trying not to look at anything. It was too intimate, too personal. And that was perhaps the point. Tem saw their bed, which was unmade. She wondered which side Leo slept on. Her question was answered when her gaze fell on the left bedside table. Tem's heart performed a swoop when she saw the book there: *The Raven and the Swan.*

"Please," Evelyn crooned. "Sit."

They sat in the armchairs before the fire, the same ones where Tem had sought refuge from Caspen before his quiver had given her their blessing. The same ones where she had come on Leo's fingers. *So needy*, he'd whispered. *What are we going to do with you?*

Evelyn handed her a glass of champagne.

With a sigh, Tem downed it. There was no point in asking for anything else, and she was positive she wouldn't survive this girl talk without alcohol.

"I'm *so* looking forward to the wedding," Evelyn gushed. "Wait until you see the swans. They're incredible."

Tem resisted the urge to roll her eyes. Was this the reason Evelyn wanted to talk to Tem? To gloat? Evelyn had won the battle, and this was her victory lap. How Tem wished she could win the war. "Did you invite anyone from the village?"

"Oh, everyone is coming."

"I didn't mean this village."

Evelyn stiffened. But Tem didn't care. If Evelyn was going to insist on girl talk, then Tem was going to push her—to *force* her to acknowledge her time away. "Surely, you made friends while you were there."

Evelyn shrugged. "Not really."

"No? Shame. It must have been lonely."

"I had a good reason to stay."

The words seemed to just slip out. Tem leaned forward. "What reason?"

Evelyn seemed to be considering something. Finally, she said, "You were a chicken farmer before all of this."

It wasn't a question. Tem decided to answer it anyway. "Yes. I was."

"Then you can understand how difficult life can be. You can understand that, when presented with a better option, it's best to take it."

Tem frowned. What better option? Evelyn hadn't made any friends while she was away—she claimed she had taken no lovers. So why had she stayed?

A memory crept in: *She did not leave because of some ridiculous letter. She left because I offered her a higher price than what she could steal from me one fork at a time.*

Tem had nothing to lose. It was the eve of Leo's wedding, and she was at the end of her rope with Evelyn. If she didn't get the truth now, she never would.

"How much?" Tem asked before she could stop herself.

Evelyn raised her eyebrows. "Excuse me?"

"How much did Maximus pay you?"

The rest of her question hung unspoken in the air between them: *to leave Leo?*

Evelyn was watching her thoughtfully. She did not look like an animal cornered in a cage. She was perfectly calm as she said, "Plenty."

There it was. The truth.

All the suspicion Tem had harbored for so long was finally laid bare. Lilly had tried to tell her. Maximus had tried to tell her. But it took hearing it from Evelyn's mouth for her to actually believe it was true. Evelyn had known exactly what she was doing when she left Leo. She'd jumped ship—moved on when she'd realized that Maximus would never accept her and his payout would be more than she'd get if she stayed. She'd only returned when he was no longer king and she could infiltrate the castle the way she'd always wanted.

It was then that Tem understood she had underestimated Evelyn. Now she could see her for what she really was—the worst kind of predator, the kind that looked like prey. Evelyn possessed power indeed. It might not be the kind of power Tem was used to—brash and loud and destructive—but it was power nonetheless. Her sly, wide-eyed innocence was nothing more than an act. She was a wolf in sheep's clothing. A lie.

"You're despicable."

Evelyn pressed her lips into a thin line. "Wouldn't you have done the same?"

Tem recoiled. She thought of how Maximus had tried to scare her off—how he told her to remember her place. There was no price high enough that would have tempted her to leave. He could have offered her anything, and she would have refused. Revulsion swept through Tem. Evelyn was someone who could be bought. It was a disgusting quality, and one that Tem found shameful. Basilisks gave and received in equal measure, and accolades were earned through actions. The only thing basilisks cared about was power—the only thing that swayed them was influence. Money meant nothing to them; they could create gold from their blood. There was no value to something with an unlimited supply.

"No," she said firmly. "I wouldn't have."

Evelyn shrugged easily, as if she didn't believe her. "Anyone in our position would've."

"*Our* position?"

"We come from nothing, Tem. We have to take the opportunities that are presented to us. We owe it to ourselves to be smart."

But that wasn't true. Tem knew what it meant to have nothing—to wish for a wealthy benefactor to come in and fix everything she'd thought was wrong with her life. She knew how it felt to *want*. And yet, when faced with such a benefactor, Tem wouldn't have given in. Evelyn had taken the easy way out—the coward's way. And Tem, like Leo, hated cowards.

Leo would not forgive such a sin. He valued authenticity and integrity. Evelyn had neither. She was a facade—a pretty painting with an ugly canvas underneath. To be one village over and never reach out, to never give Leo closure—Tem couldn't think of a more horrible thing to do to him.

Or perhaps she could.

Nothing was more horrible than what Tem herself had done to him. Tem had *caused this*. She may not have paid Evelyn to leave but she was at least partially responsible for her return. Guilt and horror threatened to swallow her. The only thing left to do was to try to make things right.

"You have to tell him."

Evelyn had the nerve to let out a sharp laugh. "Absolutely not."

"You can't lie to him."

"It's too late."

Tem shook her head emphatically. "He deserves to know who you really are."

Evelyn's eyes narrowed. She leaned in even closer. "Why do you care, Tem? You left too."

Something about Evelyn's challenging tone reminded her of Vera. But unlike Vera, who wielded her cruel words like a sword, Evelyn used hers as a shield, to hide who she really was.

"I trust I have your confidence," Evelyn said quietly.

She had nothing of the sort. Tem would not be silenced—she would not allow the sacrifice she'd made to be for nothing. To keep Evelyn's secret would be to lie to Leo. It would mean betraying his trust—trust that Tem had only recently earned and barely deserved to keep. If she kept Evelyn's secret, she was no better than Evelyn. She was just as much of a fraud. Tem had thought she was doing the right thing, that she was making everything better. Now she knew the opposite was true.

"If you won't tell him, I will."

Evelyn shrugged. "No you won't."

"And why not?"

"Because it will hurt him if he knows. And that's the last thing you want, isn't it?"

Despite herself, Tem paused.

"Picture it, Tem. Picture what will happen if you tell him about me. You'd be devastating him *again*. Do you really think he would survive me leaving twice?"

Tem couldn't believe what she was hearing. But she couldn't deny that Evelyn had a point. She didn't want Leo to get hurt. It was the *last* thing she wanted. To tell him would be to devastate him. Telling him would mean imploding their entire arrangement. It could affect the relationship between the kingdoms, the future of both their marriages—everything Tem had worked to uphold. Telling him would ruin everything Tem had sacrificed her happiness for. It would mean it had all been for nothing.

Evelyn leaned even closer. "And what would happen next?" she said quietly, her voice threateningly low. "If I leave again, would you take him back?"

"I would," she whispered, almost against her will.

Rather than react with horror, or at a minimum disgust, Evelyn replied calmly, "Would Leo even want you to? You already married him, then cast him aside. He must hate you."

He must hate you.

Tem closed her eyes.

Even if Leo still loved her, part of him also hated her. It was inevitable; she'd hurt him too badly for it not to be the case. Evelyn was right about everything. Tem had a husband of her own. She had an entire kingdom to rule; she couldn't do both. Leo probably wouldn't even want her back. Not after everything she'd done to him.

"He doesn't hate me," Tem whispered. She didn't even know if she believed it.

"If he doesn't now, he would if you told him."

Tem opened her eyes. Evelyn was looking at her with *such* pity.

"And what would Caspen think?"

Tem knew exactly what Caspen would think. He'd made his thoughts crystal clear, drunk in the passageway after the tournament. *Your little human prince is fragile. And*

I am tempted to break him. The days of an alliance between the two men were long gone. Their agreement to share her had been a short-lived fantasy. They could never go back to the way things were. She could not command the basilisks and the humans at the same time. It would be impossible. There were too many opposing viewpoints, too many needs that had to be met. Leo deserved someone to rule with—someone who could take on the responsibilities of being queen. Tem had responsibilities of her own.

"Tell me, Tem, even if you had them both—could you love them equally?"

How was it that Evelyn knew exactly what to say to her to make her doubt herself? Tem knew she loved them both. She always had.

"How can you say such things?" Tem whispered.

A sick smile twisted Evelyn's lips. "Because I know you, Tem. We aren't so different. And the sooner you accept that, the sooner you'll understand that this is the way it should be—this is proper. I will get married to Leo. You will remain with Caspen. We both get what we want."

But Tem wasn't getting what she wanted. She wanted Leo to be happy, to choose his future, to be loved in the way that Caspen loved her. Evelyn didn't love Leo. Not the way Tem did. She loved power and money. She loved gold and bloodletting and shiny, pretty objects that would slake her thirst for wealth. There was nothing more revolting to Tem than greed. It was all she heard in Evelyn's voice when she spoke—all she saw in those big doe eyes. She could not condemn Leo to this.

"Leave Leo to me," Evelyn said, leaning even closer. "And we never have to interact again after today."

Tem frowned. "We still have to interact every week."

"Do we? I don't think there's a need for any more dinners, do you?"

The point of the dinners was to cooperate, to ensure their kingdoms were amicable. There was a dire need for them. "And why not?"

"There is nothing more to discuss."

"Of course there is. We need to figure out a way forward that doesn't harm either of our people."

"There is only one way forward, and it is the way things have always been done."

Tem's eyes narrowed. "What are you saying?"

"I am saying we will no longer ignore the resources at our disposal."

"The basilisks are not your *resources*," Tem snapped. "When you abolished the bloodletting, you agreed to enter a new era. If you bring it back—"

"I didn't."

Tem blinked. "You didn't what?"

"*I* didn't abolish the bloodletting. Leo did. Had we been married at the time, I would have advised him differently."

Tem's mouth fell open. "I don't know what Leo sees in you," she whispered.

A slow, vicious smile stretched her lips. For some reason, she looked delighted, as if Tem had just given her an incredible treat. "I know what he sees in *you*."

"Excuse me?"

"Did you know he wrote you letters?"

CHAPTER FORTY-ONE

••●✳●••

TEM'S BLOOD RAN COLD.

"I found them one day when I was wandering the castle," Evelyn said, twirling her champagne glass. She hadn't taken a single sip. "Funny thing to leave lying around, don't you think? Where anyone could find them?"

Tem's heartbeat slammed in her chest. Evelyn had read the letters. *Her* letters. The ones she had told Leo to write—the ones where he had written everything he couldn't tell her now that they were with other people. Fierce jealousy whipped through Tem. *Evelyn* got to read them? It wasn't fair. But more importantly, it was dangerous.

"He doesn't know I read them," Evelyn continued calmly, as if this weren't earth-shattering information. "But I did. Every single one." She leaned in. "He loves you. He always will."

It wasn't new information. But it wasn't something she ever thought she'd hear from Evelyn.

"But *I* have him, Tem," she continued. "He's mine. I won."

Tem opened her mouth, but Evelyn still wasn't done.

"I had him before you, and I will have him for the rest of his life."

Tem almost laughed. Unless she slept with Leo, the rest of his life would not be very long. "You will never have him," she said. "Not as long as he loves me."

Just then, there was a knock on the door.

Both Evelyn and Tem stood abruptly, their conversation immediately abandoned. Evelyn opened the door to reveal the one person Tem wanted to see more than anything.

Leo was wearing a dark suit, his hair slicked back. He looked similar to the way he'd looked for their wedding, and the thought made her want to cry. His eyes went to Tem's before settling on Evelyn's.

"The guests are arriving," he said. "Are you coming downstairs?"

"Yes, of course." Evelyn threw a glance over her shoulder at Tem. "We were just finishing up."

But they were far from finished. So much had happened in the past few minutes that Tem could barely process it. There were a hundred loose ends, a thousand new problems, and no way to solve them. Tem realized suddenly that if there were to be no more Sunday dinners, this might be her last chance to talk to Leo. She had to seize this moment right here, right now.

Tem squared her shoulders, stepping forward so she was right in front of Leo. His eyes flicked to hers as she said, "There is something you must know."

Evelyn's head whipped around, her eyebrows raised in disbelief.

But Tem would not reveal her secret. Evelyn's undoing would be her own. Instead, she would tell Leo the one thing she hoped would make him see reason—the only thing that could convey the gravity of just how bad things had gotten between the kingdoms: "Earlier this week, a weasel was released underneath the mountains. Forty-six basilisks died."

Leo's eyes widened. Evelyn's narrowed.

Tem knew Leo was imagining, just for a moment, what life would be like if forty-six villagers died on his watch. She let the silence sit, wanting him to stew in that thought.

"So many deaths," he said. "From a weasel?"

"Their scent is fatal to the basilisk. Everyone knows that."

Leo nodded quickly. "Of course, it just seems...unbelievable."

"Well, believe it." Her answers were tight. Stilted. Tem was not in the mood to coddle Leo right now. She needed him to see her pain.

"What about you?" Leo asked.

"What about me?"

"I mean...does the weasel...affect you?"

He was asking if she was hurt, if she had been in any danger. Evelyn's lips pursed.

"No," answered Tem. "I'm fine."

Unmistakable joy passed over Leo's face. "Thank Kora."

His words hung between them. It was entirely inappropriate for him to act so relieved. But there was nothing Tem could do about it. It was not her responsibility to monitor Leo's emotions. If he wanted to act this way in front of Evelyn, that was his choice. Tem was past the point of caring.

"I will make sure to find Caspen tonight," Leo continued, "and tell him he has my condolences."

Tem noticed how he didn't say "our."

"You can tell him," Tem said. "But it won't make a difference."

Leo ran a hand through his hair, displacing several strands.

"He's angry, Leo," she continued. "And he has every right to be. The villagers are the ones who did this."

"But why would they do this?"

"It was retaliation," Tem said. "For Jonathan's and Christopher's deaths."

Leo sighed. "I would never sanction such an attack," he said quietly. "Surely, Caspen knows that."

Tem didn't answer.

Silence fell.

Evelyn stood between them, her arms crossed defensively. Tem couldn't read her mind, but it was clear she didn't approve of any of this, that she was upset they were even talking about such things on the eve of her wedding.

"You said that forty-six basilisks died," Evelyn said.

"Yes. They did."

"So…" Evelyn said slowly, her eyes flitting first to Leo, then back to Tem. "Are they buried? Or do basilisks practice cremation?"

Tem blinked. Why was Evelyn asking about basilisk funerary customs? It wasn't like her to care. "They will be burned," Tem said.

"Oh," Evelyn said with obvious disappointment. She seemed extremely put-out.

"Is that quite acceptable to you?" Tem asked.

Evelyn sighed. "Of course. I was merely inquiring."

"Why do you care what we do with our dead?"

She shrugged. "It just seems like a shame."

Leo went pale.

"How is it a shame?" Tem asked. "They will be properly honored."

"It's a waste."

"A *waste*?"

Horrific comprehension crashed into Tem. She finally understood why Evelyn was inquiring about the bodies. To her, there was still a use for them.

"You want them for *bloodletting*?"

"If there are forty-six basilisks available, we should—"

"They're not *available*. They're *dead*."

"I just think that—"

"Evelyn," Leo snapped. "Enough."

Evelyn pursed her lips, then fell silent.

Tem's insides turned to flame. She was beginning to think that Caspen shouldn't have left *her* unoccupied. Caspen, with his centuries of self-control, would be just fine. Tem, on the other hand, was a hair's breadth away from committing murder. She directed her words only at Leo: "The attack must be addressed. And soon."

Leo nodded. "I understand. I will apologize tonight, in person."

Evelyn interjected. "You cannot apologize."

Tem stared at her. "Excuse me?"

Evelyn turned to Leo. "We must show solidarity with our people."

"*Your* people caused this," Tem snapped. "*My* people died."

"Your people are not people at all. They are snakes."

All the rage she'd suppressed toward Evelyn was threatening to spill out at the seams now. Tem wanted to lunge at her, to rip her apart limb from limb. She wanted to throw her down in the dungeons with Maximus so they could both rot together for all eternity. She wanted to kill her. But before she could do any of that, Leo placed his hand on Tem's waist.

Not her arm. Not her shoulder. Her waist.

A moment passed as they all stared at Leo's hand. Suddenly, Tem realized how he was standing: his body facing Evelyn, his shoulder between them…protecting Tem.

"You should leave," Leo whispered to Evelyn. "It's what you do best."

Evelyn raised a singular eyebrow. Her fists were clenched at her sides, and for a very real moment, Tem wondered if she was going to hit Leo. Then her shoulders relaxed, and her lips formed a cold smile. "We will discuss this later," she said. "When we are alone."

Then she swept out of the room.

The moment she was gone, Leo leaned against the mantel, the color drained from his face. Tem immediately crossed to the cart and poured him a drink. He took it, gulping it down without a word. Tem refilled it immediately. This one he sipped slowly, still leaning against the mantel. He looked completely worn down, and Tem wanted to reach for him. But they'd crossed so many lines already—she wasn't willing to cross any more. Instead, she just watched him as he watched the fire, wishing she could make things better. His scent had changed, she realized. Leo used to smell like a summer breeze. Now he smelled heavier. Darker.

"Leo," she whispered.

He didn't look at her. "My guests are arriving," he said stiffly. "I'll see you downstairs."

"Leo, wait—"

But he was gone, leaving Tem alone once more. She cast a single last glance around Leo's bedroom before crossing the hall to hers. Caspen was sitting at the desk when she entered. He stood up the moment she opened the door.

"Tem," he said. He had a curious expression on his face, as if he'd just realized something.

"Caspen."

A pause. "I think it's starting. We should go downstairs."

"Very well. Lead the way."

He didn't ask her about her conversation with Evelyn. Tem didn't know what she would have told him about it anyway. Instead, they made their way downstairs in silence. The ballroom was filled with familiar faces—all the royals who had just been at her wedding mere weeks ago were here again, for this one. Some of them looked rather wary, especially around Caspen, and Tem couldn't help but remember that the last time they'd been here the basilisks had attempted a hostile takeover. She wondered whether they were worried it might happen again.

Notably absent was Maximus. Tem hadn't expected to see him. Still, she found it significant that the father of the groom would not attend his own son's wedding. Even Lilly was here, despite what she'd told Tem in the bathroom with the golden sink. When their eyes met across the room, she gave Tem a knowing look. Tem simply looked away.

The scarcity in the village was nowhere to be found here. Evelyn hadn't been kidding when she said they would spare no expense. Great boughs of holly were wrapped around the columns, framing the ballroom like vines. Table after table was piled high with every type of food imaginable. Tem thought of the barren full-moon feast and fought the urge to vomit.

There were other notable details as well.

White flowers. Just like the ones Tem had picked. At first, Tem thought it might be a coincidence. But then she saw the harpist in the corner—the same one who had played at her wedding. There was no doubt in her mind that Evelyn had asked the maids what Tem had chosen, then chosen it for herself in turn.

Tem broke out in a sudden sweat. She shouldn't be here. It was wrong. But she couldn't leave. Caspen himself had insisted they attend. If she showed her hand—if she displayed any weakness or emotion whatsoever—Evelyn would win.

So she held her head high and stepped into the crowd.

Caspen never left her side. Despite their circumstances, Tem felt a sudden surge of appreciation for him—for just how difficult it was for him to be here. Every royal they passed looked upon him with pure terror. They recognized his height, his golden eyes. They knew he was a basilisk and that he had trained Tem. He was the Serpent King, after all. Many of them had been at the wedding of Leo's mother, and Caspen had trained her too. There was no end to his influence. His legacy was not the only presence the basilisks had here. Tem saw gold everywhere—in the veins of the marble columns, in the grout between the tiles. Caspen's people were tortured here. *Her* people were tortured here. And Evelyn wanted to bring it all back.

They made the rounds of the room, hardly speaking with anyone. Finally, she saw a familiar face:

"*There* you are, dearest." Gabriel bound up to them, wrapping Tem in his arms. "How are we tonight?"

"Could be better."

"Good thing I'm here to cheer you up." He moved on to embrace Caspen, who received it with a bemused expression. "I know where they keep the good booze." He brandished two glasses of whiskey.

Tem took them both, downing them one after the other.

Gabriel raised an eyebrow. "Celebrating tonight, are we?"

When Tem didn't reply, he turned to Caspen.

"I heard about the weasel," he said, his voice uncharacteristically serious. "I'm so sorry."

Caspen shook his head. "You have nothing to be sorry for. It was not your doing."

"I know. But I tried to warn you, and I couldn't."

"What?" Tem asked. This was news to her.

"Vera was in the Horseman bragging about it just before it happened. When I asked her where she got the idea, she said she was just following orders. I ran to the caves, but they'd already sent someone with the weasel."

Tem and Caspen both stared at him, stunned.

"*Orders?*" Tem said. "Who is Vera taking orders from?"

At that exact moment, the sound of clinking glass filled the room.

"I'd like to make a toast," Leo said. He was standing next to Evelyn, who clung tightly to his arm.

Tem turned to Caspen. *We don't have to stay. This is going to be boring. And probably horrible.*

Caspen's hand darted around her waist, as if to hold her in place. *We shall stay.*

They watched as the crowd cleared around Leo and Evelyn, giving them space to speak. Leo raised his glass.

"I wanted to take a moment to thank you all for coming back so soon."

A gentle ripple of laughter. Tem had forgotten how good Leo was at disarming people with his words. He waited until the crowd was quiet before continuing.

"For some, the path to love is simple," he began. "For others, it is not so easy." He paused, turning to Evelyn. "You were my first love, and I was yours. Our paths may have diverged, but we found our way back to each other again."

It was an odd speech—notably different from the lyrical way he usually spoke. He wasn't really *saying* anything. Leo seemed to be listing a series of facts, neither positive nor negative. It was true that he and Evelyn had been each other's first loves. It was true that they had diverged, then come back together. But what Leo neglected to say was how any of that made him *feel.*

He looked straight into Tem's eyes as he delivered his final line. "Somehow I always find my way back to you."

Again, it was simply a statement. But it was enough for the crowd; they erupted into applause, cheering as Leo gave Evelyn a kiss. Tem's stomach roiled at the sight.

Leo raised his glass. "To finding your way back."

The audience raised their glasses. "To finding your way back."

Tem drank the last dregs of her whiskeys. It was all she could do.

The celebration resumed, and Gabriel disappeared to the kitchens. Tem and Caspen found themselves near a group of royals whom Tem recognized from her own wedding. They were talking to Evelyn and Leo.

"We're so excited to start a family," Evelyn was saying. "Isn't that right, darling?"

Leo took a long sip of whiskey. When he didn't reply, Evelyn continued.

"Everything worked out just the way it was supposed to."

"I'll say," one of the royals said. "The last one was a chicken farmer, wasn't she?"

It had been a long time since that simple taunt had made Tem blush. But it did so now, and she turned to Caspen. "Can we go?"

He was looking at the man with fury in his eyes.

Tem placed her hand on his arm, holding him steady. "Please, Caspen. I just want to go."

But the man wasn't done. "Seems like you upgraded. You wouldn't want your children playing in chicken shit, would you?"

Immediately, Caspen opened his mouth to retaliate. But Leo beat him to it.

"Watch what you fucking say about my wife."

Tem's mouth fell open, and hers wasn't the only one.

Evelyn stared at Leo with unbridled fury, her lips a tight, unforgiving line. There was no trace of hurt in her eyes—only anger. She reached for him immediately, clamping her fingers tightly around his arm.

"We're leaving," she hissed. "*Now.*"

Leo didn't protest. He followed Evelyn out to the patio, and she slammed the double doors shut behind them. They were still visible through the glass panes, and Tem could see her beginning to yell. Tem knew she should turn away. But she couldn't. Beside her, Caspen's hand was gripping her waist. Tem felt for his mind, but it was closed off. She couldn't fathom why. Perhaps he felt rage in that moment. Perhaps not. All she knew was how *she* felt, which was utterly enraptured by what was happening before her. She was watching their relationship fall apart. She could see it splitting at the seams like an old winter coat. Evelyn's expression was one of complete fury and betrayal.

"Caspen," she whispered, touching his arm again, repeating her earlier plea: "Can we go?"

He didn't say a word. He merely placed his hand over hers and steered her out of the ballroom. Tem half expected him to take them outside, into a carriage, and back to the caves. Instead he guided her up the stairs, not stopping until they were back in their bedroom. The moment the door closed, he drew her into his arms.

Tem burrowed against his chest. All she wanted was comfort. All she wanted was him.

His mind was still closed. Tem didn't know whether it was accidental or on purpose, and she was too afraid to ask. Instead she spoke out loud.

"He didn't mean that. He just…" But she trailed off.

Caspen was the first to break the silence, finishing her sentence. "He loves you."

He said it quietly. It was not a revelation—merely a fact. Tem didn't know how to respond, so she simply said nothing. She had no idea how long they stood there. It wasn't until a knock came on the door that they finally drew apart.

Caspen opened it to reveal Leo. He looked completely worse for wear. Tem had never seen him so worn down.

"May I…" Leo began quietly. An eternity passed as his eyes traveled from Caspen, to Tem, then back to Caspen. "…speak with Tem?"

The entire world went silent. Tem could hear nothing but her heartbeat, which was pounding like thunder in her chest. Tem looked at Caspen. She braced for impact.

But Caspen was only looking at Leo. He studied the prince with careful intent, clearly drawing some sort of conclusion. His nostrils flared. Tem held her breath.

"That is a question for Tem," Caspen said. Then he stepped to the side.

Leo's eyes met hers. "Tem," he said, even quieter this time. "May I speak with you?"

Her mouth was completely dry. It took nearly all of her effort just to nod. As soon as she did so, Leo nodded back, turning and crossing to his bedroom. Tem looked up at Caspen, who was watching her closely.

"Do you want me to go?" she whispered.

Was she imagining it? Or did a smile cross his lips? "I want you to decide for yourself."

Tem went. Just before she reached Leo's bedroom, she looked over her shoulder to see Caspen one last time. But he was gone.

Leo closed the door after her. Tem couldn't believe she was back in Leo's bedroom for the second time in the span of an hour. This time, it was Leo who handed her a drink, and this time it was whiskey. She wondered wildly where Evelyn had ended up. Was she sequestered in another bedroom somewhere, drowning her feelings in expensive champagne? No. Tem would have bet everything she owned that Evelyn was still downstairs socializing, keeping up appearances, no matter the cost.

Leo still hadn't spoken. In the silence, Tem thought of all the things she wished she could do. She wanted to run to him, to throw her arms around him, to press her lips to his. It was torture not to.

"You look beautiful, Tem," he whispered. He shouldn't be saying that. He shouldn't be telling a woman who wasn't his bride that she looked beautiful. But he was.

"So do you," Tem whispered back.

Leo tilted his head. "Is that so?"

"Yes. Boys can be pretty too."

He smiled. Did he remember when she'd said that to him the first time they'd slept together? Did he know that she still meant it? Tem had to break the moment.

"How are you feeling?"

To her surprise, Leo laughed. "How am I *feeling*?"

"I don't know what else to ask."

Leo crossed to the fire. "I don't know how to answer."

Tem joined him, and they stared at the flames together.

"I feel sad," he whispered.

Tem turned to him. His gray eyes were shining. "Why would you say that?"

Leo stepped closer. "Because I can't breathe when I look at you. Because it hurts"—he pressed his hands to his chest—"right *here*."

Tem's chest felt the same. It had felt that way ever since he'd walked off the stage at their wedding. Nothing had felt good since then. Nothing had felt *right*. There were too many memories here—too many reminders of what she and Leo had been through. Too many things that were no longer hers.

Leo was still talking:

"I think about you all the time, Tem. I can't fucking stop. Nothing distracts me— nothing draws my focus. You're always there, in the back of my mind, watching me."

"I'm not watching—"

"I know you feel it too. I know what you did at our wedding *did something to us*."

Tem stared up at him.

"I'm right, aren't I?" He stepped even closer. She didn't step away. "Something changed. We're different than we were. It's not just that you can give me orders. It's something else—something permanent. Your basilisk magic bound us together, didn't it?"

Tem didn't trust herself to speak. She could only nod.

"I fucking *knew* it," Leo hissed.

The same scent from earlier washed over her. An earthiness she couldn't place.

"What is it, Tem? What did you do to us?"

That question was too vast to answer. What had Tem done to them? She'd ruined them. She'd made it so that Leo's life was at stake—so he was trapped with a woman who didn't love him the way Tem did. The conditions of the crest were clear: it would bind the recipient to her. Tem should have guessed that there would be some caveat, some horrible catch. Nothing with the basilisks was simple—certainly not their magic. There were always complications. Always a cost.

She had tried to do the right thing. And she had failed. "I'm so sorry, Leo."

He closed his eyes as if to block her out. "I don't need an apology."

"Then what do you need?" She shouldn't have asked. Because she already knew the answer.

"You."

The strands of Tem's morality had been fraying for a long time. They were breaking now.

Leo's body called to her. She saw his pulse beating in his neck—the way his fingers flexed around his whiskey glass, accentuating his veins. She had resisted him too long. Tem had thought she could come up with a solution to their problem, that if she bought them enough time, she could solve it. But now, standing here with the object of her crest, she knew she had reached her limit.

Leo opened his eyes. "Tell me not to marry her."

Time stopped as they stared at each other.

Tem wanted nothing more than to tell him not to marry Evelyn. But she wouldn't. She *couldn't.* If she told Leo not to marry Evelyn, the crest would force him to obey. Tem was done making choices for Leo—done trying to dictate his future. The more she did it, the more pain she caused.

Tem shook her head. "It's your choice to marry her, Leo. I gave you two orders, remember?"

She remembered, even if Leo didn't. She remembered the two commands she'd given him on the stage at their wedding: *I want you to find Evelyn. I want you to choose your future.*

"I told you to find her," Tem whispered. "Anything beyond that was your choice."

Leo only shook his head. "You sent me away, Tem. Bring me back now. Bring me back to you."

Tears were forming. She couldn't stop them. "I can't make your choices for you anymore, Leo. I just can't."

"Then tell me something else, anything, that will make it easier to choose."

There was only one thing Tem could tell him. The words were out of her mouth before she could stop them: "Your father paid Evelyn to leave you."

Leo froze, his whiskey halfway to his mouth. For a long moment, he simply stood there. Then he whispered, "What?"

"I can't tell you not to marry her," Tem said. "But I can tell you that Maximus offered her money, and she took it. It's why she left in the first place, and it's why she stayed away."

Leo stood motionless, stunned into silence.

Tem didn't dare break it.

It pained her to see Leo hurting. She had just confirmed the very thing he knew in his heart but didn't want to believe. Tem's heart broke for him. To know that his partner had left him for money was a horrible, awful truth. She wanted to fix it—to patch the wound and stop the bleeding.

"At least she came back," Tem whispered.

"She didn't."

"Of course she did."

Leo looked at her, his eyes finally focusing. "She didn't come back for *me*, Tem. She came back for *this*." He threw his arms wide, encapsulating the room.

Tem understood what he meant—that Evelyn had only returned when it was clear she was returning to the newly crowned king. Little did she know the state of the kingdom and the status of the bloodletting. No one could have predicted that.

"She wants the bloodletting to continue. It's all she cares about."

Tem opened her mouth, but Leo wasn't done.

"I knew." He shook his head. "I knew a long time ago—when I saw how she acted after I told her I freed the basilisks."

"How did she act?"

Leo rolled his shoulders. "She said she couldn't understand why I freed them. She said that the snakes deserved to bleed."

Disbelief passed through Tem, followed closely by rage.

Before she could respond, Leo went on. "She said you deserved it too."

He said it quietly, as if he didn't want her to hear it. But Tem would never forget it as long as she lived.

"Leo." Tem placed a hand on his arm, careful not to touch his skin. "Can't you just talk to her about it?"

He let out a harsh laugh. "I'm done fucking talking to her." His eyes slid to hers. "And to you."

Tem froze at his tone. She knew he was angry at Evelyn. But by extension, he was also angry at her. It was Tem's fault Evelyn was here in the first place—Tem's fault they had reunited. It didn't matter that she'd tried to do the right thing. It didn't matter that this wasn't how she thought things would turn out. Intent was irrelevant.

Leo was still breathing hard. His next word was said with gritted teeth: "Leave."

"What?"

"Leave, Tem," he said. "Go back to the caves."

"But why? What are you going to do?"

"I am going to make my choice."

Then he was gone.

CHAPTER FORTY-TWO

‒‒•◦✳◦•‒‒

TEM STOOD ALONE IN HIS BEDROOM, STARING AT THE FIRE, WONDERING WHAT ON earth to do. Should she go downstairs and rejoin the celebration? Should she stay here and wait? Would Leo return once he'd talked to Evelyn? Or was he even going to talk to her at all? Perhaps he wanted Tem to leave so that she wouldn't have to see him marry Evelyn even after he found out the truth. Perhaps he was ashamed. Tem couldn't think straight. She couldn't even breathe.

Leave. It's what you do best.

The women in Leo's life were always leaving him. And then coming back and leaving him again. The last thing Tem wanted to do was leave. It went against every instinct in her heart. But she also wanted to respect his wishes. If Leo was telling her to leave, he had a good reason to do so. And Tem had never wanted to see this wedding anyway. There was no point in lingering.

So Tem left.

The caves were bustling when she returned to them. Everyone under the mountain was preparing for the funeral. Tem found Caspen at the lake, speaking to a member of the council. She didn't ask him why he left, and he didn't ask her why she had returned. It didn't even matter. It all seemed like minutiae compared to the prospect of laying forty-six basilisks to rest. All Tem knew was that Caspen needed her support, and she was glad to give it. She was by his side as he made arrangements for the funeral. She was by his side as he talked to every single family member of each of the basilisks who had died. She was by his side as he gathered the bodies and placed them in a line on the shore of the lake. The surrounding grottos were decorated elaborately, the entryways wreathed in leaves. It was not unlike the way the castle was decorated for the wedding. Only at this event, the dead would not find their way back.

Every basilisk was in attendance for the funeral, Senecas and Drakons alike. Only Rowe and Eros were nowhere to be found; they had left the night after the tournament. Tem stood next to Apollo, whose hand found hers. She knew he was seeking comfort, and without hesitation, she intertwined her fingers with his.

I'm so sorry for your loss.

Thank you.

Can I do anything for you?

He shook his head.

Are you sure?

There is nothing to be done, Temperance. By you or anyone.

His words gutted her. All Tem wanted to do was fix this—to go back in time and make it so that the last few days hadn't happened.

Adelaide appeared on her other side. Without thinking, Tem reached for her hand too.

One hand held Adelaide's. The other Apollo's. Tem could feel their grief as solidly as she could feel her own. It was not unlike the hive orgasm, but instead of pleasure, she felt pure, unfiltered sadness. It was too much for one person; if she hadn't been standing among the basilisks, she would have collapsed. But here, surrounded by her people, the grief was bearable. Burdens were easier to bear when shared, after all. There was beauty in this—in the collective ability to stand in community, to hold and to be held. Beside her, Apollo's grip tightened. Tem sent him a soothing wave of solidarity. Not enough to alter the way he was feeling—only enough to let him know he was not alone. He turned to her and pressed his lips to her temple.

The crowd fell silent as Caspen approached the line of bodies.

He knelt before each of them, striking a flint and setting them aflame. When all of them were lit, they stood for hours watching them burn, the smoke traveling up into the peak of the mountain. Nobody said a single word. There was only this moment— only right now. When it was finally done, members of the council stepped forward to distribute their ashes into urns made of bright white marble. They became mixed with the sand on the shore, and perhaps that was the point. Tem had lain on this very shore before and surely would again. It was a part of Kora, and so it was a part of them. Tears streamed down her cheeks as, one by one, Caspen took each urn, walked out into the water, and cast his people's remains into the lake.

There was no ceremony afterward, nor any type of speech. Everyone simply dispersed, and Tem followed Caspen back to their chambers in silence. Tem figured they would stand by the fireplace and talk. Instead, the moment their door closed, Caspen picked her up and set her on the bed. His lips were on hers a moment later.

Caspen?

His kiss deepened, his hands threading into her hair.

Caspen. I need to know you're all right.

And I need to touch you.

Tem let him touch her. She let him lay her down on the bed, pull open her legs, and slide his fingers inside her. He did so gently. Intentionally. Tem knew he was concentrating on this instead of what his people had just endured, and she was happy to provide a distraction for him. Eventually, his mouth replaced his fingers. He was so deliberate, so unselfishly soft with her. His hands moved up her body, seeking hers. Tem held on to them tightly, using them to anchor herself, using them to hold him near. Every time she was close to coming, he stopped, lifting his head to kiss along her thighs until she moaned his name. Then he returned to the center of her, going deeper than before, showing her with every stroke of his tongue how much he needed her. Tem arched into him, still holding his hands, still splayed open.

In this moment Tem thought only of Caspen, of how he had always taken care of her, of how he protected her and those she loved. She thought about how he'd been the first to believe in her, the first to tell her she was extraordinary, the first to push her to become what he knew she was capable of being. *Caspen.*

He was her first love. He always would be.

Even after she came, Caspen still wanted her on his tongue. And when he was finally done tasting her, he simply looked at her for a long time, just as he had their first night in the caves. Tem remembered how she'd held herself open for him. She did so again now, letting him see inside her, letting him see what belonged to him. When she became too wet to hold herself, Caspen took her fingers and licked them, one after the other. He bent forward and kissed her clitoris. Then he did it again. Over and over, just as the entire council had, only this time it was just him. He did it until he was satisfied—until she was aching and desperate and dripping. Then he entered her.

They moaned in unison as his cock slid halfway in. When he pulled back out, Tem reached for him.

All the way. I need you all the way in.

Normally he would keep her in check, tell her to have patience. Instead, he did as she requested, sliding all the way in, giving her exactly what she wanted. They were playing no games tonight; neither one of them wielded their power. They pleasured each other tenderly, as only they knew how. It was loving and thorough and real. Tem knew Caspen's body better than she knew her own, and she did every single one of his favorite things. Then he did the same. He did what he had always done—took her to the very edge. Now, they approached it in tandem, their bodies working perfectly to get there at the same time.

They fell over the edge together.

Afterward, Tem studied the sweat drying slowly on Caspen's shoulders. She saw the ridges of muscle beneath his skin, remembering how they flexed when he stroked his cock. Tem shifted closer.

What are you doing, Tem?

I'm just looking at you.

Caspen smiled, adjusting his position on the bed so she could get a better view. *And? What do you see?*

Tem moved closer, tilting her head to study his face. She saw his sharp jaw, his strong brow. Her eyes fell to a single gray hair at his temple. Had that always been there? Was it new? Tem touched it gently, running her finger along the strand. She was so close, she could smell his skin—a tantalizing mix of smoke and sweat and something else, something not quite human. It was almost as if she could sense the magic in him.

I can sense it in you too.

You can?

Yes. I felt it when we first met.

Tem processed this information slowly. Caspen had never talked about that night with her. *How did you feel when you first saw me?*

His mouth twitched. *Aroused.*

That's not what I meant, and you know it.

He sighed, and the smile faded. *I felt surprised. And intrigued. And…drawn to you in a way I could not understand. There was something ancient in you.*

Ancient? What do you mean?

Caspen shrugged. *I cannot explain it. It was just a feeling.*

Tem had no idea what to say to that. She was twenty years old; there was nothing ancient about her. *He* was the ancient one. Before she could ask more questions, Caspen asked one of his own:

How did you feel when you first saw me?

Aroused.

That earned her a proper laugh. Tem laughed too, and for the first time in days, things felt lighter. Caspen shifted closer to her as she continued.

I felt…scared. But also brave at the same time.

Bravery is often the bedmate to fear. One cannot be brave unless one is afraid.

Tem supposed that was true. She'd never considered herself a particularly brave person, but that had changed since meeting Caspen. He was the one who pushed her to do more—to step into who he believed she could be.

I felt afraid too. His admission was so quiet Tem nearly missed it.

You did? Why?

Caspen waited a long time before answering, and when he did, the words were even quieter still. *Because I knew what was to come.*

It was all he said, and Tem didn't press him. Something about the way he said it made her worried, and she didn't want to feel that way right now. Right now, all she wanted was to feel happy.

I'm sorry about the wedding. We shouldn't have gone.

Caspen brushed his fingers gently up her spine. *It was the right thing to do.*

I don't even know if they ended up getting married. Leo…told me to leave.

His fingers stopped. Tem expected him to say something, but he didn't.

Maximus paid Evelyn to leave Leo. I thought he deserved to know the truth.

Still no reply.

Are you angry with me?

No, Tem. I am not.

Are you angry with him?

Silence.

Tem knew in her gut that she would get no more from him tonight. She didn't care to anyway. All she cared about was the feel of his skin against hers. There had once been a time, not so very long ago, when she couldn't fall asleep in her husband's arms.

But she could do so now, so she did.

⸻•◆◆◆•⸻

"I will not go tonight," Caspen said stiffly.

They were lying in bed, intertwined, the fire roaring beside them. It was Sunday evening, and they hadn't gotten out of bed since the funeral.

"Caspen." Tem sat up. "We have to go."

His hand found her hip, pulling her back down. "I do not wish to see the human prince."

So they were back to this. Caspen only called Leo the "human prince" when he needed to create distance between them—when his name was too humanizing. It was doubly insulting given the fact that Leo was now king. And yet, it was also warranted. The weasel had been a step too far, even if Tem knew it wasn't Leo's fault. Why should Caspen forgive the unforgivable?

"Caspen…" But Tem trailed off.

"We have sacrificed enough for him."

"He didn't sanction the attack, Caspen. You believe that, don't you?"

Caspen didn't answer. Perhaps that was answer enough.

"Leo would never approve of anything that might hurt me."

It was a weak argument. The bloodletting hurt her, and he had approved of that.

425

Besides, they were far past that now. The weasel had changed things for Caspen. Too many of his people were dead because of it. Leo's sins were piling up too high, costing too much.

"What will it take for you to forgive him?" Tem whispered.

Caspen rolled his shoulders. She knew she was asking the impossible. But it was true that Leo didn't sanction the attack. He'd been horrified when he found out it had happened. Deep down, Tem was sure Caspen knew that. But Caspen was also angry.

"I will never forgive him."

Tem's heart fell. She wasn't surprised, and she wasn't about to argue. It was well within Caspen's right to never speak to Leo again.

"But I will also not retaliate."

Hope pierced her. "Really?"

"On one condition."

The hope shattered.

"He must apologize to me in person."

Tem nodded. "He told me he wanted to do that. Just come with me to dinner and I'm sure he'd be happy to—"

"No. I will not go to the castle again. He must come to me."

"You want him to come *here*?"

"Yes."

"He could get hurt. He could be *killed*."

"That is none of my concern."

Tem remembered how adamant Caspen had been about not allowing Gabriel under the mountain—how it was too dangerous for humans. Apparently, that caution didn't extend to Leo. "It *should* be your concern."

But Caspen only looked away, as immovable as stone. Tem couldn't stand it when he was like this. She wanted to shake him—to *scream* at him. They were never going to get anything resolved if he chose to act this way. But Caspen had clearly made his choice.

"He owes me an apology. He can come here to give it."

"Why do you even care? His word means nothing to you. You said so yourself."

"Those are my terms, Tem. He does not have to accept them."

"Your *terms*?"

"Yes."

"And what will happen if he doesn't meet your terms?"

Caspen didn't answer. He was staring resolutely into the fire, his eyes narrowed. Any tenderness from their week together was gone. This went far beyond his rivalry with Leo or the recent fatalities among Caspen's people. The weasel had opened a wound that had been festering for centuries—one that an apology from Leo was not likely to heal. Tem feared they were past the point of no return. She feared it was too late.

"Caspen," she whispered. "What will happen?"

He rolled his shoulders, finally looking at her. "There will be consequences."

It was all he said. But Tem knew the meaning behind his words—knew that any allowances he had granted Leo in the past were far gone now.

"This is a mistake, Caspen," Tem said it as calmly as possible. She knew they would get nowhere if she lost her temper. This was a conversation she needed to control.

"It is already decided."

"No. It isn't. You're the only one who has decided, and you can still change your mind."

"I will not change my mind."

"Caspen." She touched his shoulder. "If Leo comes here, he could get hurt. *Please* think about this."

"I do not care to think of anything, Tem. I have already made my decision."

"Think of me."

A muscle in his jaw twitched. Would it be enough? Adelaide had once told her that she held more sway over Caspen than anyone else. Tem was about to find out whether that was true.

"Think of me, Caspen," she whispered, leaning closer. "Think of how this will affect me."

He turned to her. "Your infatuation with the human prince has gone on far too long. You should have learned your place long ago. It is right here, by my side. If you do not understand that by now, I doubt you ever will."

A chill ran down Tem's spine. She'd never heard him speak like that—the way powerful, entitled men spoke to women.

"If my place is by your side, that means we are equals. And I have a say."

Caspen shook his head. "Kora decided your place long ago. Do you think it is a coincidence that you are a Hybreed? You think it mere chance? You are meant for greatness, Tem. It is not your fate to dally with the humans."

For some reason, tears pricked her eyes. "If you hate them so much, it means you hate a part of me."

"I could never hate any part of you, Tem. That, apparently, is my undoing."

His words cut her. "What are you saying?"

"I am saying that you are the love of my life. But I am done accommodating the love of yours." With that, he rose and left.

Tem stared into the fire numbly, wishing she could throw herself into the flames.

It was a disaster beyond what she could comprehend. Things had just begun to heal. And now this. She couldn't let Leo come here. It was impossible. But Tem knew Caspen well enough to know when he had reached the end of his patience. And he was beyond it now. There was no reasoning with him, no talking him down from this. This went beyond mere anger. This was meant to punish Leo and, by extension, punish Tem. If anything happened to Leo, she would be devastated. And Caspen knew it.

Night fell before she was ready. Tem climbed into the carriage alone, trying not to stare at the empty seat beside her. When she knocked on the door to the castle, a butler greeted her, as always. Leo was already waiting for her in the dining room.

He was alone.

The last time they saw each other, he'd told her to leave. They'd had no communication since then; Tem had no idea whether he had married Evelyn or sent her away. She'd been too busy with the basilisk funeral to have any time to communicate with Leo. Besides, she was almost too scared to know. If she didn't know, it meant there was still hope.

"Where is Caspen?" Leo asked as the butler began serving dinner.

Tem considered lying. She could say Caspen wasn't feeling well or that he was tired. But that would solve nothing. "He's not coming."

Leo raised an eyebrow. "Why not?"

"He's angry."

"At…?"

"You."

Leo frowned. Then, slowly, he said, "He holds me responsible for the weasel attack." Tem nodded.

Leo sighed. He looked so defeated Tem almost reached for him. "Did you pass along my condolences?"

"Yes," Tem said. "But he didn't accept them."

"I do not blame him."

The words came quietly. Tem hadn't expected Leo to say that. Before she could react, he continued.

"Did you tell him I wish to apologize in person?"

"Yes," she said again, dreading what came next. "And he's willing to hear it."

"Good." Leo nodded. "I am glad."

Here it came. There was no going back after this. "But he won't come to the castle."

Leo paused with his fork halfway to his mouth. "I see," he said slowly. "Then perhaps I can write him a—"

"He wants you to come to him."

Leo blinked. He put the fork down. "To him?"

"Yes."

"In the caves?"

"Yes."

Silence.

Leo had been to the caves once before, right before their wedding. It was where he and Caspen had agreed to share her, where they had dared to forge a new path together.

But that was a long time ago. And he hadn't *really* been to the caves. Going to the cave where Tem was trained and going underneath the mountain were two wildly different things. Leo hadn't gone where the basilisks were.

"Isn't that…dangerous?" Leo asked finally.

"Yes," Tem said honestly. "Very. But he won't accept your apology otherwise."

Leo frowned. His unspoken question hung in the air. Tem knew he was wondering why she would ask this of him if it would put him in harm's way. The truth was that Tem was torn. No part of her wanted Leo to come to the caves. It wasn't like Gabriel, who was a willing participant. Leo would be coming against his will, forced under the premise of apologizing, with the hope of making peace. It felt like he was walking into a trap. And Tem couldn't be sure that he wasn't.

But if he didn't do this, Caspen would never forgive the attack. And that was too great a consequence to bear. There was no easy option here—no elegant solution to this horrible problem. Tem felt a flare of anger at Caspen for putting her in this position. It wasn't fair. Then again, nothing ever was.

"You don't have to go," she said.

Leo raised an eyebrow. "You just said that he won't accept my apology otherwise."

"That's true. He won't."

Leo frowned. "Then I must go."

Tem felt a surge of affection for Leo. Once again, he was a better person than she was. Once again, he was being brave.

"When shall I come?"

Tem blinked. She'd been so focused on how on earth she was going to convince Leo to come that she hadn't thought about what to do if he actually agreed to it. "I…don't know," she said. "But I can ask."

"Very well."

A pause followed, and it took Tem only a moment to reach for Caspen with her mind.

Leo has agreed to apologize in person. When should he come?

Caspen took a long time to answer. But Tem was used to this; she knew how to wait him out. Finally, he responded.

There is a council meeting tonight. He can attend.

Tem tried to control her expression, but it was impossible. Not only did Caspen want Leo to come to the caves, but he expected him to attend a *council meeting*? That was far and away more dangerous than just meeting Caspen alone, which was already well beyond Tem's comfort zone. A council meeting meant that Leo would be outnumbered by the most powerful basilisks under the mountain.

Are you joking?

I am not. He should apologize to us all.

Caspen. You're being unreasonable.

His presence loomed larger. *Am I?*

His mind overtook hers, and a vision of dead bodies flashed before her eyes. Tem saw from Caspen's perspective as he knelt over them, touching their cold skin. She felt his grief. The sensation was horrible; Caspen's heart was a raw, aching wound. He harbored *such* anger toward Leo—not just for the deaths caused by the weasel attack but for the pain that Leo's family had inflicted on his for generations. Caspen's next words cut through her mind like a knife:

He can come tonight. Or he will not come at all. That is final.

Tem felt as if she were going blind with anger—most of it Caspen's. She closed her eyes and shook her head. *Fine. I'll ask. But I don't know if he'll—*

Caspen cut off their connection. Tem opened her eyes with a gasp.

"Tem? What's wrong? What did he say?"

Tem stared down at her plate, attempting to get her bearings. Caspen was in a volatile mood, and the last thing Tem wanted was for Leo to go anywhere near him when he was acting like this. But she had no choice.

"He wants you to come tonight," she said, looking up at him. "There's a council meeting you can attend."

"A council meeting? What happens at those?"

There was no reasonable answer to that question, so Tem opted to ignore it. "Will you come?"

Leo didn't hesitate. "Yes," he said simply.

Tem was struck by how quickly he'd answered. "Don't you need to run it by Evelyn?"

Tem shouldn't have asked that. It was a blatant attempt to get the answer to the question she'd been bursting to ask all night.

"No," Leo said just as simply.

Tem sighed. Still no clarity.

Leo looked determined—an expression she'd seen on him before. She knew he wanted to make things right. But he didn't really know what he was getting into. His only experience in the caves had gone relatively smoothly, and this time was bound to be different. This time, Caspen was not weakened by the effects of the crest. Leo was. This time, they would be surrounded by not one but many basilisks, in a place where Leo would be at a deep disadvantage. He would have no weapons against them, no defense. Tem was his only ally, and even she had a foot in both camps. Leo's life was her responsibility. It was a precious burden, and one she did not bear lightly. No harm would come to him under the mountain. Tem herself would get hurt before Leo did. She would keep him alive. She would keep him safe.

"When is the meeting?" Leo asked, breaking her from her thoughts.

"Later," she said. "We can go…after dinner."

Neither of them had been eating. Another minute passed before either of them spoke again.

"You should know," Leo said. "That there will be no more bloodletting. It is no longer necessary."

"How is it no longer—"

"There's no need for it."

"But how are you going to pay for things? For food for the villagers? Where will you get your gold?"

Leo shrugged. "I will do what you suggested. I will get a loan."

Tem stared at him. "That wasn't a serious suggestion, Leo. You'd need the world's biggest loan."

"Then I shall try something else."

"What else is there?"

Leo shrugged. "Anything. I will sell my valuables. Do you have any idea how much gold is in this castle?" He lifted up a spoon. "This could pay for a month's worth of food for one villager. It will be quite a long time before we run out. And by then, I'm sure I will have figured out something sustainable."

"Leo…that's…"

"Anything is better than seeing you bleed, Tem."

Tem couldn't argue with that. "And what does Evelyn think of this?" She knew she was pushing him—forcing him to acknowledge the elephant in the room. But it was killing her not to know.

"Her opinion does not matter."

Tem could wait no longer. "Leo," she whispered, "where is she?"

Leo downed the rest of his whiskey. "She left."

A chill ran down Tem's spine. "Leo, I…" But there was nothing to say. Tem wasn't sorry Evelyn left. It was the single greatest thing she'd ever heard. Pure, unencumbered joy swooped through her. "I'm sorry," she said even though she wanted to say something else.

"For what, Tem?"

"For hurting you. I don't want to hurt you anymore. I never wanted to hurt you, Leo. But it's all I do."

In the silence, they watched each other. Tem looked at the bags under his eyes, the pale hue of his skin that seemed even paler than usual. Guilt laced through her. The crest was still in effect. Leo would feel the physical ramifications until they had sex. It would wear on him, as it wore on her. But at least Leo was no longer with Evelyn—at least the very first step to undoing her mistake had been completed. It wasn't much, but it was a start.

Leo looked at her too. Beneath his gaze, she felt peace. Beneath his gaze, she blossomed. They had sat through so many of these dinners—horrible nights with Evelyn right beside them, watching their every move. But now they were alone, and for the first time, Tem wished this dinner could last forever. All she wanted was to look at Leo. It felt as if she hadn't really *seen* him in weeks.

"I'm sorry," she said again.

"You already said that, Tem."

"I'm sorry for something else this time."

"Which is…?"

"That Evelyn turned out this way." Tem was sorry for so much more. But that would have to do for now.

To her surprise, Leo shook his head. "She was always this way."

Tem didn't reply.

After a moment, Leo whispered, "She never loved me. Not like you did."

Tem looked straight at him. "Do," she whispered.

He looked straight back at her. "What?"

"She never loved you like I do."

It was an important distinction. And it was important that Leo knew it.

Tem shouldn't be saying this, shouldn't be confessing her love to Leo now or otherwise. But in light of what was about to happen, it felt like all her cards should be on the table. It felt, somehow, like the moment of truth was finally here.

They didn't speak much after that. Tem picked at her food—she was far too stressed to digest anything properly. Leo opted for a liquid dinner, downing two worryingly large glasses of whiskey before simply sitting and staring at the table. He seemed to be contemplating something, and Tem had no desire to disturb him. Despite the circumstances, he seemed relatively resolved, which could work in their advantage. Tem did not expect Caspen to keep his temper; she was relying on Leo to do so. His safety depended on this meeting going well. If anything went wrong—if the basilisks took offense or if Leo's apology wasn't sufficient—it would mean disaster for both kingdoms. Neither side was willing to bend, and as a result, everything could break.

Eventually, mercifully, dinner was over.

The carriage ride was silent, which was no surprise to Tem; there was nothing left to say anyway. She was struck by how calm Leo seemed. If their positions had been reversed, Tem wasn't sure she would have been quite as calm. Leo had no idea what awaited him tonight. And if Tem was being honest, neither did she.

They exited the carriage together, and Tem led them into the mouth of the cave. It was just as it always was—dark and warm and lit by the fireplace carved directly into the stone. The fire was perpetually burning, and Tem wondered suddenly whether Caspen did that on purpose, so she always felt welcomed when she came here.

As soon as they were inside, Tem turned to Leo. "Take off your clothes."

"I beg your pardon?"

"You won't need them."

"And why won't I need my clothes?"

"Because basilisks don't wear clothes."

He blinked. "Are you saying that everyone is...*naked*?"

"That's exactly what I'm saying."

Leo stared at her blankly. "Tem," he said. "I cannot go in there naked."

She almost laughed at how different his reaction was to Gabriel's. Not everyone was so willing to be nude. "Why not?"

"Because it's...preposterous. And improper."

"*Improper?*"

"You really expect me to make peace with the basilisks without any clothes on?"

"Yes."

"Tem. Please be serious."

"I *am* being serious."

Leo was staring at her like she'd just asked him to recite a limerick. Perhaps that would have been less ridiculous than what she'd actually asked. Leo had no concept of basilisk traditions. Everything that was about to happen tonight would be a surprise, and Tem had no time to prepare him for it.

"You're wasting time. Everyone else will be naked. It will be disrespectful if you're the only one wearing clothes."

"So now it's an *insult* if I'm not naked?"

"Yes. It is."

"*Kora*."

"Would you just take these off already?" She yanked at the leg of his trousers. "We don't have all night."

Leo ran his fingers through his hair before letting out a heavy sigh. "Will you be naked too?"

"Yes."

He seemed to cheer up at that. "Very well."

"Really? *Now* you're ready?"

"I am but a man, Tem," he smirked.

That he was.

Leo undressed first, and Tem watched every second of it. She hadn't seen him naked since the night before their wedding, and she couldn't pretend she hadn't missed his cock. It was as straight and proud as ever, and well on its way to being hard. Tem didn't bother suppressing the rush of warmth that touched her cheeks at the sight. As soon as Leo was naked, he turned to her expectantly.

There was a beat of silence as they stared at each other. Then Tem slowly untied the laces of her dress. She hadn't intended to put on a show for Leo, but it was turning into one anyway. To undress in front of Leo was a pleasure—a gift Tem had been robbed of ever since their wedding. She hadn't thought she would get to do this again for him. She'd only been naked for him once since then—in the library, with the letter opener. But that had been feverish and rushed. Desperate. Now she moved slowly, letting him see every inch of her. She wore no underclothing—there was no use for it under the mountain, and she didn't own any now. Tem held his eyes as she let her dress fall to the ground. There was nowhere to hide—absolutely no mistaking the tight breath that Leo sucked between his teeth the moment she was fully naked before him.

"Tem…"

"Leo," she warned. "Don't say a word."

"And why not?"

"Because I don't want to hear it."

"Hear what? How much I want to fuck you?"

"*Leo.*"

"I'm a *man*, Tem. And you're naked. You can't expect me not to look."

It felt like the conversation with Apollo all over again. He hadn't been able to look away either. "I need you to keep it together, Leo."

"I was keeping it together perfectly fine until you took your clothes off."

"I had to. It's customary."

"Some custom."

"Leo," she said again. They faced each other, the flickering firelight the only thing between them.

"Tem."

It was agony to be this close to Leo and unable to kiss him. Tem studied the angles of his face. They'd become sharper lately—most likely an effect of the crest. Or perhaps he was just getting older and the strain of responsibility was turning him gaunt.

Still. This was Leo.

His body was familiar to her—a body she had seen naked before and didn't think she'd ever see naked again. Tem remembered exactly how he felt inside her, how hard he'd become when she rode him.

Be still, Leo had said the first time they'd slept together. *I want to look at you.*

Tem remembered what it was like to be still on his cock, to sit there and watch him look at her. Now, face-to-face, she knew he must be remembering it too. Did he think of her at night, after Evelyn fell asleep? Was her body a home to him, like his was to her? Or did he prefer Evelyn's? Tem couldn't imagine there was any comparison. Evelyn would never know Leo like she did—never understand what turned him on the way Tem did.

Leo studied her too.

His gaze traveled from her eyes to her neck to her breasts, lingering there for far longer than was acceptable. Tem didn't stop him. She wanted him to look. Leo's gaze dropped to her waist, then her hips, then her center. Tem knew he wanted to touch her. She wanted to let him.

His lips parted. He licked them.

Tem was wet. If it were Caspen before her, he would be able to sense it already—smell it, even. But Leo was human, and he could only imagine how her body was reacting to his gaze—only fantasize that she might be as aroused as he was.

And he was aroused.

His cock was the hardest she'd ever seen it. Tem wanted nothing more than to touch it, to stroke it, to get on her knees and taste it. She remembered the carriage, when she'd told him he couldn't fuck her. Now she mourned the fact that she'd had an opportunity to be with him and hadn't taken it. What a privilege it had been to freely touch him— what agony it was to no longer do so. The only thing she wanted was to press her lips to his, to drag her mouth down his body until she tasted his cock. It was all Leo wanted too. Tem could sense it; her basilisk side was wide-awake, probing for him in the darkness. There was nothing she wanted more than *sex*.

But they could not have sex. They were no longer lovers; they were no longer together. They were just two people who wanted each other so badly that it hurt.

Leo cupped his cock in his palm, holding it as if that would prevent anything from happening between them.

"Well?" he asked. "Now what?"

"Now we make this right."

Tem navigated the passageways with Leo close behind. She tried not to focus on his proximity, but it was impossible. Instead, she focused on what was to come. It was imperative that the meeting went well. Too many lives were at stake if it didn't—not just Leo's but the lives of the villagers as well. Tem knew that Caspen had the power to declare open war. But perhaps as a Hybreed, she had the power to stop it. If they were going head-to-head, Tem had to make sure she would win.

When they reached the doors to the council meeting, Leo hesitated. "Tem, wait."

She waited.

It took a long time for him to form his words, and when he did, they were a whisper. "I cannot die tonight."

"You won't," Tem whispered back. "I'm not going to let anything happen to you. I promise. "

Leo stared back at her, the moment becoming electric. For some unfathomable reason, he smiled. He didn't try to kiss her; he didn't pull her closer. He simply nodded, resolved to his fate.

They entered the council meeting together.

CHAPTER FORTY-THREE

T WAS JUST AS TEM REMEMBERED IT: THE LONG MARBLE TABLE, THE STONE CHAIRS surrounding it.

Caspen sat at the head of the table, his face as hard as the stone around him. Everyone was naked, but this time, a coldness hung in the air that Tem could not escape—it bit into her skin like frost, and she found herself shivering.

Their presence was clearly unprecedented; Tem had no idea whether a human other than herself had ever attended a council meeting before. But Tem was a Hybreed, so in some way, she belonged. Leo, on the other hand, was utterly out of place. Despite this, he held his own. Tem was impressed by the way he carried himself: tall, the way a king should. His shoulders were thrown back, his chin held high. He didn't look scared—only wary. And Tem understood more than ever just how much his life was in her hands. She would not endanger him—she would allow no harm to come to the human king.

As they approached the table, the woman closest to them looked at Leo.

"I have never been with a human," she said musingly, her gaze traveling up and down his body as if he were her next meal.

"And you're not going to start now," Tem snapped, stepping possessively in front of Leo.

The woman laughed softly. "Why do you care? You are wed to the Serpent King. You already have a mate."

"He's my responsibility," Tem said. "And I will protect him."

"Will you fuck him too? Or can the rest of us do that?"

Tem resisted the urge to rip her head from her shoulders.

"Is his cock as hard as a serpent's?" the woman continued, her eyes flicking between his legs. "Or is it fragile, like the rest of him?"

"Enough," Caspen said.

The woman fell silent immediately, and everyone turned to face him. Last time, Tem had sat with him at the head of the table, sharing his seat. This time, she didn't know where to go, so she stayed standing next to Leo. He was a light in this dark room, and she savored his body next to hers.

Tell him he can speak.

Caspen's voice was clipped. Tem hadn't realized that he wouldn't even be addressing Leo directly. It was ridiculous, but it was also his right.

Tem leaned closer to Leo. "He says you can speak."

Leo raised his eyebrows. Tem doubted he'd expected things to start off so abruptly. Neither had she.

"I come before you with my sincere condolences," he began. "I am deeply sorry for your loss."

Tem realized she was holding her breath. If there was ever a time for Leo's words to work their magic, it was now. But Caspen was immovable. He stared not at Leo but at Tem, and she held his gaze despite the rage in his eyes. This was just as much her apology as it was Leo's. Tem was the one who had brought the two kingdoms together—it was her word and her actions that had created the problem they were in right now.

When Caspen didn't respond, Leo kept going, his words steady and true.

"I know you do not think much of me. And I cannot say that I blame you. But you must know that I never wanted this, and I did not order the attack on your people. That is the last thing I would ever do." His gaze flicked to Tem, and she knew he was thinking of how much he loved her. "I understand that your people have suffered at my family's hand. It is my greatest shame to carry that legacy. I only want peace, which is why I abolished the bloodletting."

Leo paused, glancing at Tem for guidance.

"That was perfect," she whispered. "You can stop now."

Leo fell silent.

She'd meant what she said; Leo had done well. Basilisks appreciated straightforwardness, and Leo's speech couldn't have been more sincere. Tem knew he meant every word. She only wondered if Caspen knew it too. She addressed him with her mind. *He's being honest. Will you forgive him?*

Caspen's eyes were still on her. *Will you forgive me if I do not?*

Tem thought about his question. Could she, ultimately, forgive Caspen if he never forgave Leo? Tem understood how difficult this was for Caspen. So much of the basilisks' pain stemmed from the royals—it had gone on too long, and the wounds were too deep. Tem was part basilisk, so she felt that same pain.

But she was also part human.

She had known her human side longer, and that side of her saw the good in Leo and in humans overall. If Caspen chose not to forgive him—or worse, to punish him—Tem doubted she would ever forgive him. She was still processing the fact that Caspen had demanded this of Leo at all. She couldn't blame him, given their circumstances. But it still felt like a betrayal. There was only one answer to Caspen's question. But before she could give it, Caspen looked at Leo and snapped, "You say you abolished the bloodletting. But then you brought it back."

Tem didn't know whether it was better or worse that he was addressing Leo directly now.

"I never wanted to bring it back," Leo said. "And as soon as we did, I put a stop to it again."

"And what will you do instead? Your people will expect a replacement. If they do not get one, my people will continue to weather attacks."

"I will seek a loan," Leo said. "And if I cannot acquire one, I will sell my possessions. There is no need for me to hoard wealth. Generations of my family have long collected gold. I have more of it than I could ever need."

Tem looked cautiously around the table. To her surprise, the basilisks seemed to like that answer. They respected someone who was willing to part with their possessions because they did not have many possessions of their own. Hoarding was not something the basilisks practiced—it was a distinctly human trait to have more than you needed and still think you needed more.

But Caspen would not be so easily convinced. "And when your possessions run out? What then?"

Leo sighed. "I do not know. But I am willing to have many more discussions to come to an acceptable solution for both of us, if you are willing."

Again, an answer they liked. A murmur of approval went around the table, even from the woman who was still looking at Leo like she wanted to jump on him right then and there.

"And you think the villagers will tolerate such a solution?"

"The villagers do not care where their gold comes from. They care only that they have food on their plates."

As a former villager, Tem knew that was certainly true.

"Still," Caspen said, his voice low. "They are angry. They take it out on us."

Leo pursed his lips. He had already apologized; there was nothing more he could do. Rather than fill the space with words, he let the silence sit, letting Caspen dictate where to take this next.

Tem waited, still holding her breath.

The next basilisk to speak was a man from the Seneca side of the table. "The villagers are not the only ones who are angry," he said.

Everyone turned to look at him.

"The outcome of the tournament was unacceptable to the Senecas."

Caspen scoffed. "The outcome of the tournament is sanctioned by Kora. You cannot dispute it."

"I did not say we dispute it. Only that it is dissatisfactory. She"—he pointed a finger at Tem—"belongs to us."

Not this again. The entire point of the tournament was to settle this quiver dispute once and for all.

"You dare question my authority?" Caspen said.

"We question *Drakon* authority. And we are not the only ones. If the attacks continue, why should we trust you to handle them?"

Caspen looked angry. That was nothing new. But something else was clearly present on his face: restraint. He was shifting in his seat, clenching his fists as if he wanted to say something but couldn't. Tem reached for him with her mind:

Caspen? What is it?

They are speaking of rebellion.

I thought most of the Senecas went back to the sea. Are there even enough left to rebel?

They went to the sea to follow Rowe. He has planted seeds of dissent ever since. When the outcome of the tournament was not in his favor, it only made him angrier.

How do you know this?

I have seen it myself.

When?

He didn't answer.

Tem thought about the gap of time after the tournament when Caspen had been gone for days. When she'd asked him where he was, all he'd said was that he was with Apollo. Was this the true answer? That he had been to the sea, that he had seen the signs of rebellion with his own eyes?

But what does this mean, Caspen?

It means that Rowe has become more powerful since the tournament.

Without thinking, Tem's gaze fell to Caspen's neck. The bite mark wasn't bleeding, but it was red and angry, as if it were about to.

He plans to use that power to dethrone me.

You mean he plans to use your *power.*

Caspen didn't reply. They both knew the implications of the bite—how Rowe could siphon from Caspen until there was nothing left to siphon.

The Seneca man was still waiting for his answer.

Finally, Caspen said, "You just heard from the human king. The villagers will be fed; there will be no more attacks."

The man stood. "That's not good enough."

Caspen stood too. "You have my word. *That* is good enough."

The rest of the council stood too. Immediately, Tem stepped closer to Leo.

"Perhaps your word no longer holds weight, Caspenon. Perhaps the time has come to step aside."

"Step *aside*?" Caspen scoffed. "And who would you have take my place? Rowe? He is a disgrace. He used bloodletting to galvanize himself. It is against our laws. He cannot be rewarded for that."

"Perhaps our laws are outdated. Rowe is a visionary. He sees a new way to power."

Caspen's words returned to Tem suddenly: *The royals make their own rules.* So, apparently, did the Senecas.

"That way is wrong," Caspen said, his voice low. "We corrupt ourselves if we allow it."

Basilisks determined their ranking by their sexual prowess. It was how they decided who ascended, who ruled. If Rowe had figured out a way to bypass it—to use his blood to give himself power and to take Caspen's—their entire society was at risk. It would change everything about the way basilisks lived. It made it so anyone, no matter who they were, could fight for the throne. There would be no order, no process. It would be chaos.

The Senecas who stayed were supposed to be loyal, to fall in line. But the basilisks before her were anything but compliant. Tem knew without question that the meeting had spun out of control. Her gaze found Leo's. She wished she could reach his mind.

"The Drakons have ruled long enough," the man said. "It is time for a change."

Caspen opened his mouth to reply. But his words were cut off by the loudest *crack* Tem had ever heard. Everyone in the room looked up at the same time to see an enormous fissure split the ceiling. There was another *crack*, and the crevice split more, fracturing into a lightning bolt. Rock began to fall.

Leo's arms wrapped immediately around Tem's waist, yanking her sharply away from the damage. All around them, the council members were in chaos, some running from the room while others cowered in their seats, their hands above their heads. Through it all, Caspen's eyes met hers.

It has begun.

What has begun?

But Caspen was already in motion, moving so quickly Tem didn't have time to blink before he had corralled both her and Leo into the passageway. The moment they were away from the council room, he turned to Tem.

"You must sleep together. Now."

Leo blinked. "I beg your pardon?"

Caspen ignored him, looking only at Tem. "You must consummate the crest. And quickly."

Tem stared at him with her mouth open. "What are you *talking* about? We can't just—"

"You can. Go to our chambers and sleep together. Do it now."

"You know I can't." She looked desperately at Leo, who clearly had no idea what was going on. "If we do that, you'll—"

"You must, Tem. Right now. There is no time to delay. I did not think the Senecas would attack so soon."

Despite the urgency of the moment, Tem paused. "You didn't think? So you knew this was going to happen?"

"Yes. But I did not know when."

"How could you let me bring him here?" Tem gasped. "If you knew this might happen, then you knew how dangerous it would be for—"

"I did not think they would attack tonight, Tem. But they are. And if you do not sleep together, you cannot transition. You will not be safe if things get worse."

Realization hit her. "Wait," Tem cried, "are you saying you brought him here *on purpose*? For *this*?"

Caspen was the one who insisted Leo apologize in person. He'd forced Tem's hand, demanded Leo come beneath the mountain even though it was incalculably dangerous for him. He hadn't wanted an apology; words were meaningless to him anyway. He needed them to sleep together. And soon.

Another *crack* sounded above them. Dust filled the passageway.

"Tem." Caspen placed his hands on her shoulders. "There is no time. The Senecas are here, which means Rowe is here as well. He will come after you. I do not want him near you when you are vulnerable."

"What do you mean he'll—"

"You will not be safe if you cannot transition," Caspen said over her. "And you cannot do so until you sleep with him."

She shook her head. It was not so simple. There was another side to the coin, another catch. "Caspen," she said as steadily as she could. "If I sleep with him, you'll have to kill me."

"*What?*" Leo cried.

In the chaos of the moment, Tem had nearly forgotten he was listening. This entire conversation would be unfathomable to him—there was no hope of explaining it under such circumstances.

"I could never kill you, Tem," Caspen said, ignoring Leo's outburst.

"I should *hope* not," Leo snapped.

Tem shook her head. "You won't have a choice."

In reply, Caspen stepped closer. He cupped her face in his hand, looking deep into her eyes. "Tem," he said quietly. "Can you not smell it?"

She frowned. "Smell what?"

"The decay."

Her frown deepened. Then tears filled her eyes.

Because she *could* smell it. Leo's scent was no longer summer fields and cigars. Now it was the same smell Apollo had taught her to identify. Tem knew it beyond doubt. Death was on Leo's doorstep.

The tears threatened to fall.

"He can't be," she said helplessly. "Not now. He must have more time. He must—"

"I noticed it at the wedding, Tem. And it is even worse now."

Tem knew he was right. She had noticed it too and chosen to ignore it. "This is all my fault," she whispered.

To her surprise, Caspen said, "It is not your fault. I told you to crest him."

Tem bit her lip.

He leaned in. "*I* allowed this to happen. And now you must allow me to fix it."

She looked up at him. He was resolved. Peaceful.

When he met her eye, he said, "It is time, Tem."

But this was impossible. Tem couldn't do this. It didn't matter how much she craved Leo—how deeply his body called to hers. To go with him would be to abandon Caspen. And that would never be acceptable to her. She needed them both. She always had.

"If we sleep together, you'll have to kill me, Caspen. Apollo told me you won't have a choice."

He shook his head. "There is another way."

"What other way?"

But Caspen was already turning to go.

Tem grabbed his arm, pulling him back. "You can't just leave me."

He placed his hands over hers. "I will never leave you, Tem."

They looked at each other for a single electric moment. Tem saw herself reflected in his pupils. How many times had she stared into those eyes? She remembered the first time she'd seen them, glowing in the darkness of the cave, boring into her very soul. She'd been so naive then. Back then, she'd had no idea what it meant to love two people—to give herself to Caspen and to Leo. Now she understood that love was not simple. It was complicated and treacherous and untamable, just like her.

"Please," she whispered. "Just tell me where you're going."

"As far away as I can."

"But as soon as we sleep together..."

443

He was still looking at her calmly. "The curse will draw me back to you."

"And what happens then, Caspen?"

She needed him to say it—that he would be forced to kill her. Because that was the only thing Tem could see—the only end result to this problem the crest had created. There was no loophole this time, no way out of this horrible mess.

Rather than answer her, Caspen's gaze slid to Leo's. "Take care of her."

Then he was gone.

CHAPTER FORTY-FOUR

N HIS ABSENCE, TEM STARED AFTER HIM. THE PASSAGEWAY WAS FULL OF DUST; THERE were screams in the distance, coming from the direction of the courtyard. Tem didn't know what was happening, didn't know where Caspen would go or how he could break the curse. All she knew was that the fundamental truth she had believed—that Caspen was in denial about her love for Leo—wasn't true at all. He'd known the entire time, and he had known it would come to this.

"Tem?" Leo said. "What do you mean he'll have to kill you?"

"Leo," she said as calmly as she could. "There's a lot you don't understand. And there's no time to explain it. But he's right. We need to sleep together."

"What happens if we don't?"

Tem pursed her lips.

"*What happens*, Tem?" Panic filled Leo's voice.

Tem closed her eyes. Somehow it was easier to explain it that way. "You were right—the crest didn't just make it so that I could give you orders. It created a bond between us. And if we don't consummate it, you will die."

Silence.

She could only imagine what Leo was thinking, how furious he must be with her. He was already angry at her for cresting him in the first place. And now he was learning that the crest had serious consequences—fatal ones.

Tem opened her eyes. "But if we consummate the crest," she finished. "Caspen will kill me."

Leo shook his head in bewilderment. "Why would he do that?"

"He won't have a choice."

"I don't understand. Of course he would have a choice."

"No." Tem shook her head. "He wouldn't. Our engagement is bound by blood. If I betray it, he will be compelled to kill me. His own father killed his mother in the same way. It won't matter whether or not he wants to. He will have to."

"Surely, he can resist."

"No. He can't."

Finally, Leo fell silent.

Caspen had never been able to resist. No basilisk could. The call of nature was too strong—Caspen was bound by forces beyond his control, forces that would make him do things he didn't want to do. Resisting, as Apollo had told her, was a distinctly human trait.

"Tem." Leo placed his hand gently on her waist. "I could never kill you. I am sure it is the same for Caspen."

But Tem just shook her head. Leo didn't understand. And how could he? Tem was his only connection to basilisk culture, and she was hardly versed in it herself. He had no concept of the way things were done beneath the mountain, no idea how strange and different the serpent customs truly were. Why should he believe something so horrible when he couldn't imagine doing it himself?

"You don't understand," she whispered. "It's different for us. There's magic involved—forces you can't comprehend. We are bound by Kora."

Us. We. Tem's wording was not an accident. She needed Leo to understand that, as much as she was a human, she was a basilisk as well.

"But Caspen said there was another way."

Tem shook her head. "I don't know what he meant by that. If he runs away, he will only have to come back. As soon as we sleep together, it will trigger the curse."

"Perhaps he knows something you do not. Perhaps he knows how to break the curse."

"He would have told me if he did."

"Would he?"

His words gave her pause. Caspen was always keeping secrets from her. *Always.* It had, despite the supposed honesty of the basilisks, become a core tenet of their relationship. Why should he treat this any differently? If he said there was another way, then perhaps there was one. It ultimately came down to the guarantee of Leo's death against the credibility of Caspen's word. Tem had to choose to trust him.

CRACK.

Leo once again threw his arms around Tem as the walls fractured around them. Basilisks were sprinting by, barely avoiding collision in the narrow passageway. Some of them were injured. Something was happening—something that, if Tem could not transition, she would be vulnerable to, just as Caspen said. Worse still, Leo was dying before her. She would not let that happen. She had to trust that there was another way.

Caspen was right. It was time.

"Follow me," she said to Leo, grabbing his hand and pulling him through the passageway.

They ran together through the dust, using nothing but Tem's instincts to guide them. The farther they got from the courtyard, the quieter the pandemonium became. When they reached their chambers, Tem slammed the door behind them. For a moment, they simply stood there, the weight of the truth between them. After weeks of wanting each other—of sitting through insufferable dinners and Evelyn's constant, cloying presence—they were about to have sex. But how to begin? Tem said the only thing she could think of.

"Leo," she whispered. "Can I touch you?"

An eternity passed. Then Leo nodded.

Now that she had his permission, she hardly knew what to do. Tem had ached for him every day since the wedding. She'd spent countless nights under the mountain alone, when Caspen was out hunting, thinking of Leo. Touching herself to the memory of him. Now the real thing was before her, and she had permission to touch him. She *needed* to touch him. His life depended on it.

Tem stepped forward, allowing her instincts to lead the way.

She touched only the tips of her fingers to his chest, feeling how his heartbeat hammered beneath his skin. Then she spread her hand wide, so her palm was pressed against his sternum. Just this contact was enough to make her even wetter than she already was. Leo let out a shudder the moment her palm was flat. His eyes were shut, his jaw relaxed. It was as if he was releasing a lifetime of tension, and perhaps he was.

"You're so warm," Tem whispered. It was all she could think to say.

Leo opened his eyes and smiled. "So are you."

They stood like that for a long time, neither of them moving, doing nothing but staring at each other. Tem knew they didn't have time to linger. But she was too enraptured, too engrossed in Leo's eyes to rush this. She wanted him *so* badly. This was the culmination of an urge that had begun the moment she'd crested him. Every day she denied that urge was a day she slipped further away from herself. She could not deny it any longer.

"Leo," she whispered. "You can touch me too if you want."

She'd specifically phrased it so that it wasn't an order. It was an invitation—an opening. Even now, on the threshold of sex, Tem wanted him to know he could make his own choices. She would not coerce him; she would not force him to do this. Tem had no desire for Leo to come to this any way but willingly.

Leo stared at her, unblinking, his heartbeat speeding up beneath his ribs. Tem licked her lips, thinking about that heartbeat. He was so *responsive* to her. It was something she'd taken for granted in the past, but now that they were here, she could appreciate it fully. There was something addictive about having such sway over someone. Even more so when he had the same sway over her.

The moment Leo raised his hand, Tem's heart broke into a gallop. Her vision blurred. He moved in what felt like slow motion, touching just his fingertips to her chin, tilting her face up to his. His eyes held hers. Everything seemed to pulse: the air, the flames in the fireplace, the space between them. Leo's thumb traced her lips. It reminded Tem of the way Apollo had touched her right before he taught her how to petrify. Without thinking, Tem let his thumb slip inside her mouth. He pulled her lower lip down, exposing her teeth.

"Did you think about me?" he whispered. "When you were here with him?"

"Yes."

"Did you think about me while he was fucking you?"

"Yes."

His fingers returned to her neck, arching her head.

"Did you think about me?" Tem whispered. "While you were fucking her?"

Leo's hand tightened. "Every single time."

Tem was done resisting. Her inhibitions left her completely, the last thread of her morality finally fraying to nothing. She did the one thing she should have done every day since they were married.

She kissed him.

Something shattered in Tem when their lips met. There was only this. There was only Leo. To be in agony for so long and to finally feel peace was *ecstasy*. Leo's body conformed to Tem's, his tall frame leaning down to meet her. They had shared so many kisses before, but this one was different.

This one felt like coming home.

They fell onto the bed. Tem knew they would go quickly later. For now, she went slow, running her hands over his body languidly, luxuriating in him as if she had all the time in the world. His skin was soft; his cock was hard. Tem didn't even reach for it yet—she couldn't even imagine touching it after wanting it for so long. The thought of such pleasure made her weak.

Tem sucked on his bottom lip. Leo slid his fingers inside her.

Her gasp was lost in his mouth, carried away by his tongue. Leo fingered her while he kissed her, keeping perfect rhythm for both, tempting Tem to touch him back. Eventually, she did. When her palm found his cock, he shuddered. When she wrapped her hand around it, he bit her lip. They moaned together as Tem began to stroke.

She felt the draw of the crest, second only to the draw of her heart.

It was heaven to touch him again, paradise to see how he reacted while she did it. Leo murmured her name over and over, almost as if to remind himself it was really her.

"Tem. Tem. Tem."

"Leo. Leo. Leo."

He was so hard for her. So willing. Of all the cocks she'd seen under the mountain, this was the only one she felt lucky to hold. It was like holding his heart in her hands. Like holding his soul.

Leo touched her too, his fingers buried in her center, his palm sliding over her clitoris. Every time she drew a gasp from him, he drew the same from her. They were reciprocal forces, moving in sync. His other hand roamed. He squeezed her ass, her breasts, her neck. He worked her nipple between his fingers until it was sore, then he moved on to the other one. Tem reached back to cup his balls. She squeezed. He groaned.

If she didn't get his cock in the next ten seconds, she was going to scream.

Something was rising within Tem—the irresistible urge to take what she knew was hers. Without another moment's hesitation, she rolled on top of him. They were face-to-face, his gray eyes looking into hers. Tem angled her hips. Leo arched his. There was no need for words—no need to grant permission.

Finally, Leo was inside her.

Tem moaned as she slid all the way down his cock, taking him as deep as she possibly could. Leo's neck arched. Tem kissed it. Then she began to move her hips, riding him without a second thought, going on pure instinct alone. There was no time to talk. But there was so much Tem had to say. So she did it while she rode him, whispering the words against his lips in a fevered rush.

"I'm sorry, Leo."

"I know."

"I thought I was doing the right thing."

"I know."

"I thought she could love you better than me, but she can't. No one can."

"I *know*, Tem."

Now that she'd started she couldn't seem to stop. "I never should have let you go. I made a mistake."

"Tem, you—"

"I've missed you every day, Leo. *Every. Day.*"

Tears were coming now, and there was no way to stop them. Her fingers dug into his skin, holding him against her.

"Sunday-night dinners were torture. Every time I saw you with her, I wanted to kill her. But I couldn't do anything. It was like I was trapped. I—"

Her grip tightened. "I'm sorry, Tem."

"For what? *I'm* sorry."

"For the dinners. For making you sit through that every fucking week. I hated it too. But it was the only way I could see you, and I—"

"I know." She brushed his hair from his face, giving him the same reassurance he'd just given her. "I know."

"It felt like I was dying," he whispered.

"You were."

"Every time you left I could *feel* you go, like you were *pulling me* with you."

"I'm so sorry."

"I hated having to fuck her, Tem."

"I know."

"It was nothing like fucking you. I thought it would be, but it wasn't."

"I know."

"All I could do was think of you. Every time I thought of you."

"I'm so sorry, Leo."

They said it all: every unspoken confession, every desperate plea—everything they'd wanted to say to each other since the wedding.

"Nobody will ever love you like I do," Tem whispered. "Nobody."

"I know."

"You're mine, Leo. *Mine.*"

"I know."

"I need you, Leo. I need you. I need—"

His lips were on hers. The time for talking had passed.

Leo handled her the way she needed to be handled—with confidence and utter surety—gripping her hips and yanking them against his. Tem saw how he'd changed, how he moved assertively now, taking what he was owed. He was no longer a prince. It was an honor to see the king he had become.

It was nothing like the last time they'd slept together. That time had been different; that time her basilisk side had been nearly dead. This time the beast within Tem *ached* to get out—to ravage Leo in a way that was sure to hurt him. At the thought of his pain, Tem became so turned on, she had to close her eyes. Suddenly their proximity was unbearable. She wanted to *consume* him, to rip him apart and crawl inside his ribs until they were not two bodies but one. No amount of him would ever be sufficient; nothing would ever be enough.

Was this how Caspen felt when he fucked her? It was so overstimulating—so *excruciating*. Every breath Leo took sounded like a summons just for her. Every inch of his skin was delectable. Finally, after weeks of agony, Tem could feel herself transitioning. The crest had suppressed her for so long. But now she was fulfilling the conditions— now she was consummating her love for Leo—and that came with a reward.

Keep him safe.

It was Caspen's mantra for her, and now it was hers for Leo.

Tem would not allow herself to lose control; she would not endanger the life of someone who was precious to her. Caspen had done it for her, and she would do it for Leo.

But Caspen had not always succeeded.

Tem had been hurt many times over the course of their relationship—sustained many injuries from sex or otherwise. He'd broken her pelvis, for Kora's sake. She'd gotten used to them, over time. Turned on by them, even. But that was because she was part basilisk. The monstrous side of her craved pain—coveted both administering and receiving it. Leo was a human. He did not like pain; he did not deserve to get hurt. He always said to torture him, but he didn't mean it literally. Their battles were mental in nature, their weapons were emotional ones. Tem refused to let him experience even a fraction of what she knew her body was capable of. But it was not easy to hold back.

Keep him safe. Keep him safe.

She understood now how difficult this must have been for Caspen. It was as if she were looking at a delicious meal but unable to taste it. Her basilisk side was ravenous, clawing at the back of her mind with an insistence that was nearly impossible to ignore.

Her hips moved quicker.

"Fuck, Tem." Leo barely murmured it.

But it turned Tem on so much that she pressed her palm over his mouth and said, "Don't."

She'd never wanted someone like this before—never *craved* the flesh of a human in such an instinctual way. Tem wanted to be *inside him*. She wanted to possess him and mark him and ruin him for anyone else so that he would only be hers, for eternity, forever. It was an irresistible urge, and yet she would have to resist.

Tem had no idea how Caspen had done this so many times with her. How had he managed not to hurt her? The effort it had taken just to be in Leo's presence for Sunday-night dinners without touching him was nothing compared to how she felt now with him actually in her bed. The sight of his naked body made her want to explode.

"Tem," he murmured, his lips against her hand. "You feel so fucking good."

"Don't speak. Please."

"I have to, Tem. I have to tell you that I—"

But Tem didn't want to hear it. *Couldn't* hear it. She needed him to stop talking, needed him to shut up. If he said another word, she was going to rip him apart. Smoke was crawling up her back. Her vision was changing—the pink of Leo's cheeks changed to bluish green, the warmth of his skin becoming gray. Every time she blinked, it was like she was seeing more than she should. Her eyes were turning black just as Caspen's did. Her pupils were dilating, her body changing against her will. The call to transition was debilitating. It was too much. *Far* too much. Tem could not resist this—could not resist him. She was no better than any other basilisk. She was just as beholden to her people—to her instincts—as Caspen was.

Caspen.

He was her only hope.

Caspen? Are you there?

Tem. I am.

His voice was distant. She wondered how far away he was, whether he was somewhere in the forest, running from her. Or whether he was already on his way back.

I need your help.

What is it?

There was no time to worry about formalities, no time to present the question in a palatable manner. Tem simply had to know *How do I stop myself from hurting him?*

A pause. Caspen would know exactly what they were doing right now. He had ordered them to do it, after all. If it were only sex, it wouldn't matter. But this was Leo, and Tem loved Leo. This would always be different. Perhaps Caspen wouldn't help; perhaps he wanted her to injure him. But that would hurt Tem almost more than it would hurt Leo, and she knew Caspen would never allow that.

You must concentrate on something else.

But there was absolutely nothing else to concentrate on. Leo's body was naked beneath hers—open and willing and defenseless. Her basilisk side thrilled at the thought.

Like what?

Anything.

I can't think, Caspen. I can barely breathe.

Focus, Tem.

What would you think about?

Another pause. *I would think about how I would feel if you died.*

Tem couldn't imagine thinking about such a thing in a moment like this. The sadness she would feel if Leo were dead—specifically if she were the one to kill him—was unbearable. It overtook any arousal she was feeling, twisting her stomach into a painful knot. Sex suddenly seemed impossible. *But then how could you go on?*

You must allow only your body to experience what is happening before you. Keep your mind under control, and no harm will come to him.

But it was an impossible ask. Tem wanted to flay Leo alive. It was the only thought in her mind, even stronger than her lust. Leo was pliable and vulnerable and *human*. Nothing could be more alluring to her—nothing was more tempting than the open pulse of his throat. Tem wanted to sink her teeth into him—to devour him as Caspen had once devoured her.

Her basilisk side wanted to hurt Leo. Her human side wanted anything but. Her human side wanted him to live a long and happy life, free of any danger or bodily harm, preferably far away from any basilisks at all. It was a dream that would only come to fruition if he lived through tonight. The guilt of killing Leo would be insurmountable. Tem knew she wouldn't survive such loss.

Caspen's voice whispered in her mind: *Your love for him must be stronger than your desire to hurt him. It is as simple as that.*

His voice was fading.

Tem stared at Leo. Caspen had said it was simple. But it was anything but. It was complicated and difficult to suppress her basilisk side—to tame the monster that strained in its cage. But if Caspen had done it for her, then she would do it for Leo. There was no other option.

Tem pressed her hands to Leo's chest, pushing herself up. She looked down at him, concentrating not on how he felt inside her but how she felt *about him*. Tem loved Leo. Always would. It was a basic truth between them, and it would not be tainted or destroyed by this night. Instead, this night was a way for Tem to demonstrate that love: to put into practice the words she'd said so many times. It wasn't enough to tell him she loved him. She would show him instead. She would keep him safe.

"We have to go slow," Tem whispered. "It's the only way I can do this."

Leo nodded, his pupils blown wide with fear and arousal. He looked like a man on the brink. "Then we shall go slow."

For a moment, neither of them moved. Then Leo sat up, bringing his torso to hers and wrapping his arms around her waist. They were perfectly intertwined, their lips an inch apart.

He kissed her gently.

Tem kissed him back just as gently, threading her fingers into his hair and holding him against her. She focused on the way his tongue felt against hers, on the softness of his lips and how they contrasted with the sharp points of his canines. His gold teeth used to bother Tem, but they didn't anymore. Now she understood that they were a part of him—no different than her freckles being a part of her. Leo could not run from his past nor was he trying to. Leo was simply trying to be better in the future. It was all Tem wanted for him, and it was all she wanted for herself too.

Leo's hands were in her hair, tangled in her curls. Tem knew he loved those curls. She pictured the way he always twirled them around his fingers when they talked, pulling them gently so they bounced back up again. She thought of the way he'd gripped them in the library, pulling her head back over the desk. It was his way of touching her when he couldn't *really* touch her—his language of connection when they had been so utterly disconnected.

Tem *missed* Leo.

They'd been robbed of so much together. An entire marriage, to start. But also mornings waking up together, evenings falling asleep in each other's arms, breakfasts and lunches and dinners at the castle. Evelyn had gotten all of those things. Evelyn had gotten everything that should have belonged to Tem.

"I'm sorry," she whispered against his lips.

"For what, Tem?"

"For taking this away from you."

"We have it back now. That's all that matters."

Leo was right; it was all that mattered.

Tem's basilisk side was still there—looming in the background—a quiet observer. With its retreat came clarity and calm.

Keep him safe. Keep him safe. Keep him safe.

Words. Nothing more. Not an obligation or a promise. Just a plea.

Leo's fingers were between her legs, stimulating her clitoris as she moved her hips. They were beyond the point of no return now: two people, in love, having sex. What could be more simple than that?

Leo was talking again, and this time she let him.

"I want you for the rest of my life, Tem. I don't care what it takes. I want you and I need you and I love you and you're mine."

"You're mine too."

"You're fucking mine."

"I know."

At last, they surrendered to each other.

Tem threw her head back in release, gasping as her orgasm took her. Leo did the same, his cry of pleasure the single most beautiful thing she had ever heard. Tem couldn't believe her body could draw forth such a sound from him. She wanted to hear it over and over until he couldn't make it anymore. She wanted to hear it until the day she died. They clung tightly to each other, holding on even after their climaxes ebbed away. Tem brushed the blond strands of hair from his forehead. She kissed one cheek, then the other, then she did it again. All she wanted was to cherish this perfect, exquisite boy. He was her anchor. Her beacon. Her home.

Leo looked dazed, as if he'd just awoken from a deep sleep. He blinked, focusing on Tem. "That was…"

Words seemed to fail him. Truth be told, they failed Tem too. Power was surging through her—power that, up until a moment ago, had been just out of reach. She was not the only one affected. Leo's eyes were bright, his skin flushed. He looked utterly and completely alive.

Tem leaned in to kiss him again. Before their lips could touch, someone pounded on the door. Tem threw herself over Leo protectively, holding him against the mattress.

"Temperance," a voice called from the passageway. "I must speak with you."

It was Apollo.

Tem leapt up, crossing to the door and opening it.

Apollo brushed past her. His eyes flicked over Leo before returning to Tem. His mind was closed off, but Tem felt an unmistakable energy radiating off him. He was afraid.

"Apollo," she said. "What is it? What's happening out there?"

In the haze of sex, Tem had forgotten about the state of things. But now, with her head once more clear, she heard the screams of terror coming from the passageway.

"The Senecas are revolting," Apollo said. "Rowe is on his way."

Tem looked at Leo. He was not supposed to be here in the middle of a revolt. Fear gripped her spine.

"Temperance," Apollo said urgently, pulling her attention back to him. "He seeks you."

"Why?"

"Is it not obvious?"

It took Tem mere moments to catch up. Rowe couldn't marry her. That left him with only one other option—the one way to take her power.

"He wants to kill me."

Tem knew from the look on Apollo's face that she was right. Before he could reply, Leo stood.

"Tem," he said. "I cannot hear about one more person who wants to kill you tonight."

"It's fine, Leo."

"*How* is it fine?"

"Because…" Tem trailed off, trying to think of something that would placate him. There was nothing. She abandoned that train of thought, turning back to Apollo to say, "Where's Caspen?"

Apollo's lips flattened into a tense line. "He is running, Temperance."

Although the update was terrible, Tem felt a strange sense of comfort in the fact that Caspen had confided in Apollo in the first place. It meant that all was well between brothers. That, at least, was some good news.

"Will he come back?"

Apollo's gaze flicked to Leo's. "I assume you consummated the crest?"

"Yes."

"Then yes. He will be back. He will not have a choice."

The implication of his words hung in the air. Tem stepped closer.

"He said there was another way. Was that true?"

Apollo's golden eyes held hers. There was nothing but torment in them. "It is true there is another way."

"What is it?"

Before he could answer, another scream pierced the air. This one sounded closer.

"Apollo," Tem insisted. "Tell me. What is it?"

But Apollo had gone still. "He is here."

There was no need to specify. Tem could feel Rowe on the outskirts of her mind, reaching for her. Already, he was homing in. Already, he was hunting.

Apollo touched her waist. "You must go."

"I'm not going anywhere. I'm the only one who can stop Rowe."

The moment the words were out of her mouth, Tem realized they were true. Caspen, the Serpent King, was supposed to be the most powerful basilisk under the mountain. But Rowe had bitten him during the tournament, and he'd been siphoning that power ever since. That left only one basilisk who could face him. Her.

"No," Apollo said.

"*No?*"

"He is extremely powerful, Temperance. And he is dangerous."

"*I'm* extremely powerful."

There was a pause in which both Apollo and Leo stared at her as if they were seeing her for the very first time. Tem let them look.

"I'm a Hybreed," Tem continued. "And I have consummated the crest. That means I can transition."

She knew without testing her theory that it was true. Power thrummed through her entire body, seeping into her fingertips. Up until now, she hadn't realized she'd been operating at such a deficit, that such a fundamental part of her was missing. But she was whole once more, and she would not waste it.

Apollo shook his head. "You cannot stay."

"I can, and I will."

"You are not safe here. You must go."

"You can't tell me what to—"

"*YOU MUST GO.*"

Tem froze. Apollo had never yelled at her before. Basilisks favored negotiation—logic and reason always trumped outbursts. But Apollo was beyond reason. He was an inch away, his eyes boring into hers. At the look of surprise on her face, he softened his tone, but just barely.

"I will not let you anywhere near Rowe."

"Who are you to tell me what to do?"

"I am someone who loves you, Temperance. And I will not watch you die tonight."

"Excuse me?" Leo interjected.

Tem held up her hand. "He doesn't mean it like that, Leo. He just means—"

"I mean it," Apollo said firmly, enunciating each word. "In the way I have earned the right to mean it."

Basilisks were always being vague. But somehow this made sense to Tem. She understood how Apollo loved her: not like Leo did and certainly not like Caspen. *Love can take many forms*, just as Adelaide had said. He loved her the way she loved him—without expectation or judgment. Freely.

"You must go, Temperance," Apollo said. "Please."

"But I—"

"I know you wish to fight." He placed his hands on her shoulders, steadying her. "But I cannot protect you from my brother and Rowe at the same time."

Tem opened her mouth again, but Apollo shook his head.

"You will not stay here. You will take your human prince"—he jerked his head at Leo, who was watching their interaction with barely contained bewilderment—"and you will get to safety."

Tem stared at him. She thought about their history together, how he had gone from her pursuer to her protector. She hadn't always felt safe with Apollo. But she felt safe now.

"Please," Apollo whispered. "I beg of you. Go."

When just a moment ago he'd been yelling, now she could barely hear him. The words were strained, as if it took great effort to say them. Tem could hear the cries of battle just outside the door.

"I can't just let people die when there's something I could do to stop it."

Apollo's expression softened. "Their choices are their own. Basilisks believe in fate."

Tem shook her head. This was wrong. *Wrong.*

"I—" she began, but before she could finish, Apollo's lips were on hers. He kissed her softly, with more tenderness than he had ever shown her before. Tem heard Leo make a disgruntled sound, but she ignored it, kissing him back as screams echoed down the passageway. The sound of her name pulled them apart.

"Tem?" It was Gabriel. He was accompanied by Damon, who immediately addressed Apollo.

"They must leave. All of them."

"I am well aware," Apollo said. "But they are rather difficult to convince."

"Rowe has infiltrated the caves. He seeks Tem."

"I am *well aware*," Apollo said again. Before he could say anything else, Caspen's voice entered both their minds at the same time.

I am coming back.

Apollo's eyes widened. He looked desperately at Tem. But she just shook her head as Caspen said, *You must leave, Tem. Get as far away as possible.*

No, Caspen. I have to fight Rowe.

You have to do nothing of the sort. Apollo, make her leave.

I am trying, Brother. She will not listen.

She never does.

Will you two stop it?

Tem slammed her connection with Caspen shut, turning to Apollo. "I'm not leaving."

"I cannot protect—"

"I know you can't protect me from both. So choose one. Protect me from Caspen."

The screams were becoming louder.

"Hold him back, Apollo. I will handle Rowe."

Apollo shook his head. But Tem knew he would do as she said. Unlike Caspen, who would never allow her to run toward danger, Apollo had always trusted Tem to make her own choices. Apollo understood who she truly was. "I do not know how long I can hold him."

"Just give me as long as you can."

Apollo didn't reply. But his jaw was set, and so was Tem's. With one last glance at her, he left.

Tem turned to Damon. "Get them both out of here."

He bowed his head. "Of course."

"You can take them to my parents' cottage. They'll be safe there."

"Your Highness." Gabriel winked at Leo. "Ready for a field trip?"

Leo turned to face her. "I can't lose you again, Tem."

"You won't."

"I need you to come back to me."

"I will."

Leo cupped her face in his hands, pulling her close. He kissed her—perhaps a little harder than necessary—and Tem felt how terrified he was for her. He'd just gotten her back. *She'd* just gotten *him* back. If there was to be a future for them, it would start after the events of tonight. And Tem dearly wished to be there to see it. Finally, Leo pulled away. Then he followed Gabriel into the passageway.

"Who was that man kissing Tem?" she heard him ask Gabriel as Damon ushered them away.

"That's Apollo," Gabriel replied. "Caspen's brother."

"His *brother*?"

Then they were gone.

Tem focused immediately on the task at hand, opening her mind to the collective consciousness of the basilisks. It was full of communal pain—all throughout the mountain, her people were dying. Their deaths pressed against her like a thousand grains of sand, suffocating her, closing in.

Focus, Temperance. Find Rowe.

Apollo's voice grounded her. She ran through the passageway, following the screams to the courtyard. The sight before her immediately brought her back to the weasel attack. Bodies were strewn in piles, blood seeped over the floor. The room was littered with severed limbs; the Senecas were tearing the Drakons apart. Tem didn't linger. She didn't wait to see if she recognized anyone. Instead, she kept running, heading for the lake, not stopping no matter how deafening the noise became.

The caverns were utter chaos.

Tem saw the Senecas' strategy immediately; they had corralled the remaining Drakons here, pushing their backs against the water so there was nowhere to run. Here, at the edge of Kora's bathing place, battle raged. Some basilisks had transitioned, whereas others were still human. They collided in horrible tangles of scales and hands and teeth, ripping each other apart. Blood soaked the shores; Tem's footsteps sank deep into the wet, glistening sand. It was impossible to move quickly but she attempted to anyway, keeping to the edge of the cavern and searching for Rowe. It did not take long to find him. She felt him before she saw him, his presence so powerful, it seemed to warp the air. He was still in his human form. Blood covered his bare chest, accumulating between his legs and dripping from his golden cock in a cruel imitation of cum. Chaos reigned around him, but he wasn't fighting anyone. He was standing on the shore, waiting.

Waiting for her.

Tem pushed her way through the crowd, heading straight for him. The moment Rowe saw her, a knowing smile split his lips.

Temperance. How nice of you to join me.

CHAPTER FORTY-FIVE

——•◦─✳─◦•——

TEM PUSHED ANYONE IN HER WAY ASIDE. WHEN SHE REACHED ROWE, SHE STOPPED. He watched her hungrily, his eyes roaming over her body. She thought of the tournament, of the way he'd felt inside her. She was drawn to his cock even now. It was a thing of terrible power, and Tem stared at it as he stepped closer.

"I am surprised at you, Temperance."

So they were doing small talk. Great.

"Why?"

"You are without your husband."

It reminded her of what Apollo had once said: *You are without your chaperone.* Tem no longer needed a chaperone. Tem only needed herself.

"He's on his way."

"Is he? And what condition will he be in when he arrives?"

Tem pictured the wound on Caspen's neck, how it reopened when Rowe siphoned from him. "You tell me."

Rowe laughed. "There is much to take from him, Temperance. I have barely begun."

Tem knew he wasn't just referring to Caspen's power. He wanted to take Tem too. "You'll never have me," she said.

"And why is that?"

"Because you do not deserve me."

Rowe laughed again. "We do not live in a world where we get what we deserve. When you want something, you must take it."

"And what do you want?"

They circled each other as if they were two children in a schoolyard about to fight. And were they not? Tem had a score to settle. And the time to do it was now.

"I want what is best for my people."

Tem cast her gaze around the cavern, where basilisks were brawling and bleeding. "Is this what's best for your people?"

"This is necessary."

Tem shook her head. "No. It's not."

"This is war, Temperance. It will be worth it in the end."

"Even if it means hurting your own kind?"

"It is not the first time I have hurt my own kind."

Tem frowned. "What's that supposed to mean?"

"It means that I gave a warning, and you did not heed it."

She stared at him, trying to understand. What warning had Rowe given? Then she understood. "*You* were responsible for the weasel?"

An evil smile split Rowe's face. "Surely, you did not believe that some idiot human girl could have thought of it."

Tem had thought that the weasel attack was orchestrated by Vera—but it was far too clever of a plot for her. She may be cruel, but she never could have thought of something so deadly. Gabriel had overheard her saying she was "taking orders." Orders from Rowe.

"You can't just use people like that."

"I can. And when I am done using them, I can dispose of them."

Tem felt a sudden strike of fear for Vera.

"But you knew what the weasel would do. How—how could you—*how could you do that to your own people?*"

Rowe shook his head. "I am a Seneca, Temperance. The Drakons are not my people."

"But there were Senecas under the mountain too. Senecas who died."

"They chose their side long ago. They remained after you wed Caspenon. They are traitors."

"They were *innocent*," Tem cried.

"And what do you know of such matters? You do not know what it means to sacrifice, to make choices for the greater good."

"I know I would never betray my own kind."

"You have no kind," Rowe sneered. "You are half-human. A blunt. You do not understand what it means to be a basilisk. You never will."

Tem hated how much his words hurt her. It was exactly what she'd said to herself her entire life—the type of jab that nothing could truly heal because it was true.

"You are a waste, Temperance," Rowe continued, his voice low as he drew ever nearer. "Think of what you could have been. Think of what we could have done together." He swung his arms wide. "We could have been unstoppable."

Tem shook her head. She would never be like Rowe. She hated people like Rowe. She would never do what he had done—would never choose bloodshed over peace. Men like Rowe allowed injustice to occur as long as they could benefit from it. Men like Rowe were evil.

Tem was nearly blind with rage. Nothing existed within her but anger—pure fury threatening to split her apart at the seams. Her entire body vibrated with power; she'd never felt this whole before, as if all the facets of herself were drawing into a single, sharp pinnacle. It was electrifying.

Rowe's eyes locked on hers. "So how does this end, Temperance? What are you going to do?"

They were nearly upon each other now.

"I'm going to stop you."

"Stop me from doing what? From creating a better world—one where power is taken instead of given? A world with one quiver, the superior quiver?"

Tem shook her head. Mass death was not the solution. Wiping out one quiver was not going to solve any problems, only delay them. Tem couldn't predict the future, could not know what the world would be like tomorrow morning. But it would be a world without Rowe.

Without further ado, she lunged.

By the time she reached him, Tem had transitioned. It came easily to her now; there was no more barrier, no obstruction. Now it was as simple as taking a breath of air. Rowe transitioned too, gold spreading from his cock to sheath the rest of his body in gleaming metal scales. Tem barely managed to dodge his gaping mouth as he surged at her with terrifying swiftness. She had very little experience in her true form, and Rowe had had centuries. But Tem was also a Hybreed. And she was not so easily deterred.

Tem lunged at him again, this time from the side. She threw her mouth open, scraping her fangs along his golden scales. Immediately, her skull rattled. The metal was hard and fortified with magic. She could not penetrate it.

Now, now, Temperance. You did not think it would be so easy, did you?

Tem ignored him.

You cannot hurt me, foolish girl. I am beyond pain.

Rowe was right. Nothing could hurt him. Power emanated off him in waves, destroying everything in his path. Whenever another basilisk happened to come into his orbit, he tore their head from their shoulders so quickly Tem almost didn't notice until they fell, headless, to the ground. He was possessed with deadly power—he was an anomaly. Tem threw herself against him with renewed vigor, doing everything she could to catch him off guard. But Tem was not used to this form—she was not used to being this size or this shape.

And then he had her.

Rowe pulled her down onto the sand, wrapping his body around hers, crushing her with his horrible weight. Too late, Tem realized she was trapped. Rowe's head was an inch from hers, his fangs fully bared. Saliva dripped from his open mouth as he berated her with his mind.

How dare you challenge me? I will kill you. And then I will kill Caspenon. And then I will kill everyone you have ever loved, including your little prince.

He's a king.

Rowe laughed, deep and careless. *He is nothing, and so are you.*

His grip tightened. Tem strained against it, doing everything in her power to escape the crushing weight of his heavy gold body. Suddenly, another voice entered her mind:

I am near you, Tem. You must get away.

Caspen, I can't. She was trapped beneath Rowe, their bodies writhing in the sand.

Run, Tem. NOW.

I can't!

You must. I cannot resist for long.

You said there was another way.

I said you must run.

I CAN'T.

But she had to. If she didn't move—if she did not manage to kill Rowe—there would be two powerful basilisks that wanted her dead.

Apollo, she cried, *where are you?*

I am with Caspenon. But I cannot hold him much longer, Temperance.

He sounded out of breath, as if he were under great physical strain. Tem could only imagine what it must be like to try to subdue a basilisk like Caspen, how difficult it would be to fight against the curse that fueled him.

Rowe's grip was tightening. She knew he was siphoning from Caspen, becoming ever stronger. But no matter how much he siphoned, Caspen still had an extraordinary well of power within him: not just his own but his father's.

Temperance. We are almost there. We are—

One minute Tem was on the ground, pinned beneath Rowe, and the next she was free. Tem recognized Caspen's obsidian-black scales as he threw Rowe off her, hurling his enormous body against the wall of the cavern. Tem half expected Caspen to go after Rowe and finish him. Instead, he turned to Tem. Before he could advance, Apollo appeared between them. Tem lurched backward as brother fought brother, each of them barely gaining ground before losing it again. Tem looked wildly around for Rowe, who was already coming back for her.

You cannot avoid me, Temperance. No matter how many bodyguards you have.

Tem didn't bother informing him that Caspen was hardly her bodyguard right now.

It is only a matter of time before you give in. Just give in, Temperance.

Tem would not give in. Tem would fight.

Despite her body screaming in protest, she lunged at him again, and a moment later, they were fighting once more. Every time Tem managed to evade Rowe, Caspen was upon her a moment later. There was no reprieve from the attacks, no moment to rest. Whenever Caspen got too close, Apollo came between them. He threw himself at his brother again and again, taking blow after blow. Eventually, it was killing all four of them. Such violence was unsustainable; someone had to end this.

They were not the only ones suffering. Tem saw glimpses of the battle around them. There was Cypress, fighting two basilisks at once. There was Adelaide, trapped in a headlock. At the sight of her, Tem remembered something she had said long ago:

If the legends are true, it means you can channel Kora.

It had seemed impossible at the time. Laughable, even. But all the other legends were true, were they not? Perhaps this one was too. The next time she had an opening, Tem hurled herself in the direction of the lake. She dove into the water, knowing the other three would soon follow.

Temperance? What are you—?

Tem shut Apollo out, closing her eyes, feeling nothing but the water around her— the water Kora herself had bathed in. She drew comfort from its weight, allowing it to pull her under. There was something here that called to Tem, a vibration that knew her name. Complete clarity overcame her. The others were coming; they were nearly upon her. But time did not exist for Tem. She went deeper, allowing the water to swallow her whole. When she touched the bottom, she finally saw it: a figure in the murky dark.

A woman who looked like her mother was walking toward her.

It wasn't until the woman reached her that Tem realized she herself was human once more. Some part of her knew it was a vision—that her basilisk form was intact at the bottom of the lake. So it did not scare her when the woman reached for her hands, holding them in hers. She turned them so her palms faced up. Twelve freckles. Twelve lovers. Twelve choices she could have made. There was only one choice now, and Tem had already decided to make it. Apollo had taught her how, and Tem had been a willing student. She closed her eyes, preparing herself for the task—preparing herself to *take*. Tem took and took until she was filled to the brim with power, so much that she thought she might explode. When she opened her eyes, the woman before her was gone, and Tem knew it was time to return.

She swam—faster and faster—toward the light. As the surface of the lake approached, so did Rowe. He was powerful—so powerful. But no longer more powerful than Tem. She waited until they had reached the shore before whirling on him like lightning. Tem opened her mouth, bared her fangs, and bit. Unlike last time, when she had been unable to penetrate his scales, this time, her teeth sank deep into his flesh. Rowe let out an agonized roar that shook the entire cavern, forcing waves against the sand. Behind them, Apollo and Caspen emerged from the water. Tem ignored them, focusing only on her prey. When Rowe had bitten Caspen, he'd shown restraint—taking power gradually—subjecting Caspen to a slow descent into decay.

Tem showed no such restraint.

The moment she bit him, she began to siphon, holding his neck between her teeth as she did so. Tem could feel his power joining hers, and with it, the power he'd taken from Caspen. Somehow, she could tell the difference between the two: Rowe's power was hostile, borderline destructive; Caspen's was refined, seeping into her like honey, rounding out the rough edges created by Rowe's. Between them, there was balance—equilibrium. Rowe's mind was not quiet during this process. He thrashed in her grip, screaming obscenities, screaming for mercy. But Tem owed nobody her mercy. She wanted nothing but to watch him die. When he was nearly empty, Tem yanked him into the air with brutal finality. Rowe's neck snapped. His life force flickered. Then it went out.

Behind Tem, the brothers were still fighting. Apollo held Caspen down as he thrashed on the sand, attempting to get to her. Through the hum of her newfound power, Tem realized they were having a heated conversation:

Do not make me do this, Caspenon.

You already agreed.

You ask too much.

It was you who told me to know when to step aside.

I did not mean—

You gave me your word.

I cannot do this, Caspenon.

KEEP YOUR WORD, BROTHER.

Caspen was straining against Apollo's grip, their great bodies tangled in a violent knot. Caspen's eyes met Tem's. If she were a human, she would have been dead. Instead she held his gaze, seeing just how difficult it was to resist her.

What is he talking about, Apollo?

He wants me to kill him.

Tem must have misheard. He couldn't possibly have just said—

He made me promise, Temperance. It is the only way.

Caspen was still trying to reach her, still bound by the curse. It was clearly taking everything Apollo had to restrain him.

You said there was another way—

This is *the way.*

Horrible comprehension struck through her. *NO—*

I must, Temperance. I gave him my word.

Why would you do that?

Because I am in his debt.

I don't understand.

You would not. It is between us.

Apollo, this isn't right. You can't—

I can, Temperance. And it is not your choice to make.

Tem understood, finally, what Apollo had been doing this entire time. Delaying.

There was no other way—no elegant solution. The curse could not be broken. Caspen's father himself could not break it. What chance did Caspen stand?

There has to be a way—some way to fix this—

There is not. The blood bond is our most powerful vow. You broke it when you slept with Leo.

But he told me to. Why would he—

Because he had already accepted the consequences.

But Tem had not accepted the consequences. *Would not* accept them. She tried to come nearer, but Caspen snapped his jaws at her. He was terrifying like this. Tem knew if Apollo wasn't holding him down, he would lunge at her.

He will not stop trying to kill you, Temperance. He will never stop.

We have to figure something else out. Someone must know something—

She cast her gaze around the cavern. Around them, the battle was quieting. Word of Rowe's death had already spread: Tem saw basilisks pointing at his lifeless body, their eyes wide. Their fearless leader was gone.

There is nothing else to be done, and I cannot hold him forever.

No. You do not have my permission—

It is not your permission I need.

He angled himself so he had access to Caspen's neck.

Tem leapt forward. *Apollo, NO—*

But she was not quick enough. Tem could do nothing but watch as Apollo sank his fangs deep into his brother's neck.

CHAPTER FORTY-SIX

———•◦✳◦•———

A PINPRICK. THAT WAS ALL TEM FELT. A PINPRICK IN HER CHEST, RIGHT ABOVE HER heart, as if someone were letting the air out of her. But within moments, that pinprick opened a chasm so deep Tem knew without a doubt what she was about to lose.

NO!

Unimaginable pain was spreading. It gripped her chest, pulling her to the ground. She was transitioning against her will, turning back into her human form. Tem knew in her gut that it would be for the last time.

Caspen was transitioning too. They fell to the sand together, both human, both gasping for air. He was covered in blood. Tem reached for him, pulling his head into her lap.

"Just hang on, Caspen. I'll heal you."

He shook his head with great difficulty. "You cannot heal a fatal injury, Tem," he whispered. "We cannot reverse the path of nature."

"But you said the basilisk bite isn't fatal. You said—"

"A bite to the arm is not fatal. Or anywhere else that would heal on its own. But this…"

Tem stared at his neck. Apollo's fangs had punctured him deep—so deep she knew there was no chance of healing it. The marks were nearly on top of Rowe's.

She glanced wildly up at Apollo, who was also human once more. "How *could you*?"

Apollo was watching them in silence. It wasn't enough for Tem.

"Fix this!" she cried. "Fix it, Apollo."

Caspen's brother only shook his head.

"Tem," Caspen said quietly. "Look at me."

But Tem didn't want to look at him. If she looked at him, she would see the blood. And that would make it real.

"Tem," he said again. "Please."

Finally, she looked at him.

His beautiful face was cradled in her lap, staring up at her. She ran her fingers gently through his hair, brushing it away from his forehead. She traced his strong jaw.

"You lied to me," she whispered. "You said there was another way."

"Basilisks cannot lie."

"We both know that isn't true."

Caspen smiled. Then he coughed, and blood dotted his lips.

Tem wiped it away gently, tears filling her eyes. "I told you you're not allowed to die."

"And I told you I would endeavor not to."

"See? Liars, all of you."

Caspen coughed again, and more blood came out. Tem held him tighter.

"This is horrible, Caspen," she rasped. "You can't leave me alone."

Caspen shook his head. "You will not be alone, Tem."

Tears welled in her eyes as she realized he meant Leo. "Don't do this, Caspen, *please*—"

"You will be happy with him, Tem. He loves you as I do."

"How do you know that?"

For some reason, Caspen smiled. There was blood on his teeth. "He wrote you letters."

Tem stared down at him, her mouth open in shock. "But I—how—?"

"He is your one true love, Tem."

Tem thought back to the dream she'd had before her first night in the caves—how she'd felt Caspen's presence before she'd met him. They'd been drawn together even then. Fate had led them here. They were supposed to collide—they were supposed to be together. He was her twin flame, her other half.

Caspen was her sun. Caspen was everything.

"That's not true."

"It is. The blood bond would not have broken otherwise."

She shook her head, nearly blind through her tears. Evelyn's words ran wildly through her mind: *Could you love them equally?* Tem thought she could. She was wrong.

"I was your first love, Tem," Caspen whispered. "He will be your last."

Basilisks believed in fate. That's what Apollo had told her so many weeks ago. Was this Caspen's fate? To let Leo take his place? Without Caspen, there would have been no Leo, and vice versa. The competition for Leo brought her to Caspen. The things she learned from Caspen brought her to Leo. There couldn't be one without the other. A life without both of them made no sense to Tem. She would be forever off-kilter, forever uneven. Always missing a part of her.

"You can't do this, Caspen. I'm not worth this."

"I decide my worth, Tem. And it is far and away inferior to yours."

"How can you say that?"

"Because it is true."

Tears streamed down Tem's face. She couldn't move—couldn't breathe.

Caspen's thumb slipped into her mouth, then out, dragging along her bottom lip. The same thing Leo had done just an hour ago. "You should only know pleasure," he whispered.

Tem couldn't finish the line. She couldn't. Because this wasn't pleasure at all. This was pain. "Caspen," she whispered. "Don't leave me."

"I must, Tem."

"I can't do this alone. I can't do it without you."

For some reason, he smiled. "You can do anything. Of that I am certain."

Incomparable sadness swept through Tem. This couldn't be happening. But she knew it was. There was no going back, no undoing what had just been done.

Caspen looked at Apollo. Tem watched as something passed between brothers: an unspoken vow. Then Caspen whispered, "Finish it, Brother."

Tem's spine erupted in chills as Apollo bowed his head in an overt show of respect. Then he turned to Tem, as if awaiting her permission. She would not give it; she would have no part in this. This was not the way she wanted them to end. They were not supposed to end. Ever.

She refused to look at Apollo, instead looking at Caspen as his brother did the same thing Tem had just done—siphoned his power until there was nothing left to take. A montage of images flashed suddenly through her mind: their happiest moments together. She saw them meet for the first time in the caves. She saw him slide her own fingers between her legs before tasting them. *As I said. Heaven.* She saw him pull her into his mind so he could see her the way he did. They'd slept together for the first time in his chambers, tangled in his sheets, just the two of them, with nobody watching. She saw how proud he was after she finished the ritual. She saw them transition together for the first time, in the lake, then lie on this very same spot on the shore. She saw him cup her jaw, look her in the eye, and say: *You are perfect, Tem. I will not allow you to think otherwise.*

Through her tears, Tem watched as the power of two kings left Caspen, and with it, his life. Caspen had always felt bigger than her—more important, somehow—more vital. Even now, motionless in her arms, he was magnificent. His golden eyes held hers until they couldn't anymore. The moment they closed, a flash of pain seared her sternum. Tem looked down, and at first, she couldn't comprehend what she was seeing. At first she thought she was injured. Then she realized the liquid on her chest was gold, not blood.

Her necklace was melting.

White-hot metal burned her skin as the golden claw dripped between her breasts in a shapeless mass. Tem cried out, grabbing at the molten charm, burning her fingertips. She ignored the pain, trying to keep its shape in her hands. Caspen's necklace was melting too, pooling in the middle of his chest.

"Caspen," she gasped, staring at the welts on her skin. "*Caspen—*"

The smell of burning flesh overtook her. She doubled over, trying to grasp the necklace with her fingers, but it was too late. The chain sliced into her neck as it melted, cutting and burning her at the same time. The claw was nothing but a mess of metal in her palms. Smears of gold seared her skin before solidifying and dropping to the sand in a waterfall of gentle clinks.

A horrible scream tore her throat.

She couldn't breathe. Couldn't think. Nothing would ever be good again—nothing would ever be right. A great chasm was opening within her, one she knew would never close. Tem stared at her palms, unadorned by constellations of pigment. Her freckles were gone. The blood bond that had tied Caspen's life to hers was broken.

Her basilisk side was dead.

CHAPTER FORTY-SEVEN

—•●✳●•—

LEO GAVE HER NO TIMELINE.

His letter arrived the day after Caspen died, just two sentences written in spiky red ink:

Join me when you are ready.

I love you.

The funeral was extravagant. Adelaide planned the entire thing, and Tem simply showed up. When it came time to release Caspen's ashes into the lake, her hands shook so badly that Apollo stood behind her, placing his hands over hers so she could tilt the urn. She'd been staying in Caspen's old chambers ever since—the ones he'd occupied before he became king, where they had slept together for the very first time. His sheets still smelled like him—like smoke. Tem wondered when that would fade.

Despite the comfort of his bed, she was having trouble sleeping. She spent hours staring at the mirror where he'd first pulled her into his mind, showing her all the things he found beautiful about her. It was the first time Tem had seen herself from his point of view, the first time she'd truly understood how much he loved her. Now, in his absence, she realized what a gift he'd given her that day. So much of Tem's confidence came from Caspen. He'd been the first to tell her she was capable—to insist that she was perfect. It took hearing it from him before she believed it herself, and now she didn't need to hear it from anyone. Now, believing in herself was enough. Caspen had given that to her, and nobody could ever take it away.

She knew Leo was waiting for her—her *future* was waiting for her. But for now, Tem was content to linger in the past. When she left these caves, she would not be able to return; the basilisks had decided to leave the mountain. There were losses on both sides—both quivers had suffered. Rowe's death had ushered in a new era: one with Apollo at the helm. It was Apollo, ultimately, who decided the basilisks would retreat to the sea. Tem did not try to get them to stay. The humans and the basilisks had tried to coexist for centuries, and they had failed. There could be no peace between predator and prey. The circle of life would not allow it. Adelaide had made it clear that the remaining basilisks would wait until Tem left before leaving themselves. "It is a matter of respect," she had said. "They wish to give you time to grieve your king."

But no amount of time would ever be enough.

Tem never thought she would face a future without Caspen—never thought there would come a day when his steady hands were not there to catch her. But that day had come. How could she grieve someone like him? Someone who had taught her everything she knew? Caspen had tolerated her insufferable impatience, her endless questioning, her unwillingness to do things in the order they were supposed to be done. He was the one thing she could never be: patient. And patience, Tem knew, was required in order to be in a relationship with her. She was impossible. What could be worse for a basilisk? Caspen had never quite been able to corral her, and he hadn't wanted to anyway. *You are not meant to be tamed.* He'd meant it as a compliment. Caspen had known, from the very beginning, that Tem was capable of greatness. It had taken her quite a long time to believe it herself. But here she was, finally, fully formed into the queen he had made her, and he was no longer there to be her king.

Eventually, it hurt more to stay than to go.

"Is there anyone you wish to speak to before you leave?" Adelaide asked her on the night she told her she wanted to leave.

"Yes," Tem said before she could stop herself. "Apollo."

Adelaide nodded.

"And Damon."

"Of course. Anyone else?"

Tem shook her head. She had met plenty of basilisks during her time under the mountain. But Caspen's brothers were the only ones she cared to say goodbye to.

"But how exactly do I…" Tem wasn't sure what to call it. "…leave? I mean, what happens now?"

"We will release you from your royal duties. Technically you are already incapable of performing them, since you are no longer part basilisk, but we still need to formally dismiss you."

"Oh." Tem nodded. "Right."

She was about to be dismissed. It sounded so sudden.

"We must do it properly, Temperance," Adelaide said. "It is not meant as an insult. We are rather fond of our traditions, as you know."

Tem nodded again. She knew that basilisks loved their rituals and their ceremonies and their special ways of doing things. She'd never stood in the way of their traditions, and she certainly wasn't about to start now.

Adelaide accompanied her to the courtyard, where the Drakon brothers were standing next to the fountain. Damon embraced her when she reached them. Apollo couldn't seem to move.

Adelaide turned to Apollo. "You have first rights. Do you wish to exercise them?"

His eyes slid to Tem's. They looked so much like his brother's: endless golden pools. "No," he said. "I do not."

Adelaide placed her hand on his shoulder. "You must say it properly to make it official," she prompted softly. "Do you waive your first rights to Temperance Verus?"

Apollo turned to Tem. His eyes gazed into Tem's before traveling slowly down her body, lingering on the scar between her breasts. Adelaide had offered to heal it, but Tem would rather keep the reminder of Caspen.

Apollo spoke clearly, enunciating each word. "I waive my first rights to Temperance Verus."

Tem looked up at him—at his sculpted jaw, so dearly similar to Caspen's, at the eyes that observed her with absolute certainty. *Know when to step aside.*

The Drakon brothers had that in common. Both knew when to admit defeat. It was an admirable quality and not one most people shared. Stepping aside meant ceding your power—it meant admitting that you were not the right choice. Some might consider it defeat. But when done of your own free will, stepping aside was victory in itself.

"Thank you," she whispered.

Apollo nodded. "Of course."

This would have been the perfect retribution for Apollo—the natural conclusion to his long history with Caspen. To take Tem as his own was the logical step for anyone in his position. A part of her couldn't believe he wasn't going to do so. He had left her alone in the days following Caspen's death, almost as if he couldn't bear to look at her. Tem couldn't quite bear to look at him either. But eventually, they had found each other again. She didn't blame him for what happened; Caspen's choice was his own. Apollo had been the one to pull her out of the darkness, to remind her that she had a full life ahead of her. One that was finite. There was value in mortality—a beauty to the fact that Tem was no longer limitless.

There was nothing she could say to properly express how she felt for Apollo. So she said it in the only language the basilisks understood. Tem stepped forward, stood on her tiptoes, and kissed him. Apollo bent down to meet her, wrapping his arms around her waist and pulling her against his chest. They kissed slowly, and Tem breathed him in, remembering just how much he smelled like Caspen. She savored every second, knowing she would never kiss a Drakon brother again.

When they pulled apart, Adelaide turned to Damon. "You have second rights."

Damon didn't hesitate for even a moment. "I waive my second rights to Temperance Verus."

Tem had always known Damon wouldn't stand in her way. His love was blossoming for Gabriel, and they were both going to the sea. It saddened Tem to know she wouldn't see her best friend every day, but if anyone could handle basilisk society, it was Gabriel. Tem touched Damon's mind with hers, sending him a memory of the first night Gabriel came under the mountain. She showed him how their limbs intertwined, how their hands cradled each other's faces. She showed him how it felt to watch Gabriel be with someone who adored him from the moment he met him and how stunningly beautiful they looked together. She left him with one last directive, one she knew he would obey: *Keep him safe.*

Damon bowed his head. *I will.*

An astonishing lightness passed through Tem. Her last worry was resolved. There was nothing left to do.

"Very well," Adelaide said. She turned to Tem. "You are free to go, Temperance."

Adelaide walked her to the cave before embracing her. *Goodbye, Temperance.*

Somehow Tem knew it was the last time she would touch her mind, and the thought made her want to cry. It was a sad thing to leave Adelaide. Their friendship had been an unexpected thing—something that had grown into a bond she truly treasured. Eventually, her presence faded, and Tem stood alone in the cave for the last time.

She looked at the mat in front of the fireplace. So many befores and afters had occurred on that mat. Before she'd been kissed and after, before she'd shared herself with a man, and after, before Caspen and after.

She remembered how she'd felt when she first entered this cave. Nervous. But also ready. Tem had been aching to experience all there was to be experienced, and Caspen had been the one to show her the way. He'd shown her so much. Not just sex—that was merely the beginning. He'd shown her what it meant to stand in her power, to demand more from herself and others, to live a full and joyful life. He'd shown her how to harness her power—how to transition, how to crest. He'd shown her everything.

How long have you loved me?

Far longer than you have loved me.

Her mother had once told her that true love meant sacrificing your happiness for theirs. Caspen had taken it one step further; he'd performed the ultimate sacrifice—the final gesture. He'd done the one thing he could never take back. Tem wondered if she was worthy of such a gesture. Perhaps there was no way to be truly worthy of this.

Tem remembered the first night of the training—how she'd been young, inexperienced, a virgin. She remembered what she'd asked her mother while she spread ylang-ylang and sandalwood oils on her thighs:

What will it be like?

It will be…transformative. You will take the first step to becoming a woman.

I thought I was one already.

Not nearly, my dear. You have barely begun to live. You cannot possibly fathom the journey you are about to embark on.

Tem could not possibly have fathomed the journey she was about to embark on. She could hardly fathom it now that it was over. It was true that back then, she had barely begun to live. Yet somehow, that also felt true now. Somehow, standing here in the cave, Tem felt as if things were just beginning for her. She had an entire life to live with Leo. It would not be nearly the length of the life she would have had as a Hybreed with Caspen. But it would be a good life. It would mean something. Life was something to be cherished. It was better, Tem figured, to do your best with the little time you were given, rather than to do nothing at all with eternity. She would endeavor to live a life she would be proud of—that Caspen would be proud of.

At last, Tem left the mountain.

The night sky was clear above her, the Alpha Serpentis shining brighter than normal. Tem stared up at it, allowing her tears to fall. She walked slowly down the path, one step at a time. Past the makeshift grave where she'd buried the weasel. Past the wall. Past her childhood cottage. She walked all the way to the castle, as slow as she liked, letting herself experience every second of the journey. The village was beautiful at night. All the windows were lit, and Tem could picture how it would look in the coming months when snow arrived.

By the time she reached the castle, it was well into the night. She didn't bother knocking on the door. This was her home now, and she would come and go as she pleased. Instead, she entered the foyer, which was notably empty. Every gold picture frame was gone. The sparkling grout had been scraped from between the tiles. She climbed the stairs to Leo's bedroom, knowing he would probably be asleep. When she reached it, she found that she was right. Leo was in bed, his white-blond hair splayed on his pillow. He looked so peaceful like this. Angelic.

Tem sat next to him.

He woke immediately. "Tem," he breathed.

"Hi," she said quietly.

He touched the very end of her curls, pulling them gently before letting them go. "Can I get you anything?" he whispered. "Are you hungry?"

Tem shook her head. She took off her clothes slowly, letting them fall to the floor. Leo lifted the blanket, and she crawled in beside him. He brushed his fingers gently over the scar on her chest. Then he kissed her.

And thus began their life together.

They remarried in the garden at Tem's parents' cottage, with Lilly officiating. Leo gave her no ring; she had never stopped wearing the one he'd given her the first time. Gabriel came, and so did Damon, who regaled her with tales from the sea. Tem invited Adelaide, who politely declined but sent an elaborate selection of shells. Tem set them on her mother's mantel, where they looked right at home next to the spray bottle of salt water.

Apollo sent his own gift—an enormous bouquet of deep purple and red flowers. The color of a bruise. *Complex. And beautiful. Just like you.*

It was strange to continue her life without the basilisks, to have something taken away that never felt like hers to begin with. But in a way, becoming fully human felt like returning home—like finding something she'd never truly lost. There was no doubt that Tem mourned the loss of her basilisk side. But every time she looked at Leo, she was reminded of what she'd gained.

He was always by her side. Especially in the beginning, he was never more than a few feet away. Tem wondered if he did it consciously, or if it was more for his benefit than for hers. Either way, she appreciated it. Whenever she reached out her hand, he was there. Whenever she needed him, he was there. He would always be there.

Besides, all had not been lost.

Tem retained the ability to manipulate emotions. She often calmed Leo down when he asked her to—when the trauma of what happened became too much for him. She could also still heal wounds—something she'd noticed while gardening with her mother. One moment she'd cut herself with the spade, and the next it was healed. She could speak to basilisks using her mind, although her father was the only one left to speak to. They did it often, and Tem was grateful for that. She had no idea if she could crest and was not willing to find out. There was a constant, insistent thrum of power in her chest at all times, radiating through her skin, warming her even when she didn't mean for it to. It was Rowe's, and Tem basked in the fact that he would hate that she had it. The only thing she truly lost was the ability to transition. But there was no need for that anymore. She would not love another basilisk; she would never again need to embody her true form.

But perhaps, since she was half-human, she would focus on her true human form and Leo. He had also lost a part of himself—he certainly hadn't still been in love with Evelyn, but the reality of her had taken his memories of first love from him.

Evelyn's presence was scrubbed from the castle long before Tem arrived, but Tem swore she still felt her in the hallways, watching her. Her pinched mouth was ever present, even now. Out of sight but not out of mind. Tem wondered where she was—if she had simply gone back to living one village over, or if she had gone somewhere farther away. Surely, she would find some other rich man to take advantage of. Perhaps, in another universe, she would be friends with Vera. The thought amused Tem. They would be the perfect match.

Maximus remained in the dungeons. Leo never mentioned him, and Tem didn't either. But Tem knew Leo thought about his father. Every once in a while, she saw him touch the scars on the back of his neck—the ones Maximus had given him during the Cutting. Four scars. Fourth in his bloodline. Father and son. But Leo was nothing like his father.

He was always there for Tem, comforting her in the middle of the night whenever she woke up to cry. He stroked her spine, murmuring words of comfort until she fell asleep against his chest. They never talked about it the next morning. But she knew he would be there the next night when it inevitably happened again. Still sharing her, even after Caspen was gone. Two men. Two loves. Two kings. On the nights when things got especially bad, Leo read to her in front of the fireplace. She sat curled up in the armchair, soothed by the sound of his voice.

Her scar never healed correctly. Some days it itched so badly, Tem had to take ice baths to soothe it. She'd never enjoyed baths before. But now she savored them. Most nights, Leo pressed his lips to it before he fell asleep. When she asked him why he did this, he answered, "Because it brought you to me."

They visited the graveyard every morning, the same way Leo used to do. They sat on the bench together, facing the old willow tree.

E + L

And then, right below it:

T + C

Love is complicated, after all. It never goes away. Only changes.

Eventually, Leo let her read the letters. It was only fair, considering Evelyn and Caspen had both read them—a fact Tem almost found funny. She was *always*, even now, the last to know.

Leo left her alone while she read them. Perhaps he knew she needed privacy. Perhaps he knew she might cry. But to Tem's surprise, the first letter in the pile was not from Leo. She opened it with trembling fingers to see the words were written in unfamiliar script. The moment she started reading it, tears streamed down her cheeks.

Tem,

It is my understanding that Leo wrote you letters. I thought it only fair that I write one of my own.

At first I found it odd that he would leave such precious materials in the very room in which we were staying on the eve of his wedding. Then, given the content of the letters, I suspected it was not his doing at all. There is a certain type of cruelty that I have experienced only a few times in my long life, and Evelyn possesses it. Even after I knew she left them with the intention of me finding them, I must admit that I read every single one. It was not my proudest moment, and I apologize for doing so. But once I started, it proved rather difficult to stop.

I used to think that my love for you was stronger than Leo's. But I see now that I was wrong. Humans, in all their untidy glory, are capable of emotion just the same as basilisks are. If not more so. You taught me that, and I am forever grateful for the lesson. It is because of these letters that I find myself understanding, finally, what I must do.

It has been agony to watch you love Leo and love me at the same time. I had thought that perhaps you might get over him—that when you chose me, you would forsake the human prince. That was a juvenile hope, and an ignorant one. I should have known that your heart does not work that way. You do not work that way. You love freely and wholly and without apology. You love even when it is inconvenient and infuriating and maddening. You love shamelessly. It is a stunning quality, and it is one I envy.

I love covetously. I love greedily and without regard for others. I swore I would never hurt you, and I have broken that promise many times over. I pray you forgive me. All I ask is that you remember me the way I was—before my anger took my kindness. I should never have married you. I do not say that to hurt you, so please do not take it that way. What I mean to say is that my love for you was selfish. I could not resist you, no matter how hard I tried, even when I knew that loving you meant drawing you into my world. I proposed to you without you knowing. I concealed details of my family, my quiver, my people. You took it all in stride when you should not have had to take it at all.

You came to me new and eager and innocent. I was living in darkness, and the sun came up when I met you. I could not believe how strong you were for someone so young. I have told you before, but it bears repeating: I fell for you the moment I met you. You are bold, tenacious, and unstoppable. You are the most capable woman I have ever met, and I have always wanted more for you. At first, I thought that meant me. But now I understand you are whole all on your own. I have no doubt that the life you live will be sensational. Leo is lucky to live it with you.

When my father died, he bequeathed his power to me, and it has been a burden every day since. Part of me has always known that you are far more worthy to wield it. Leo has always understood that about you. It is I who took too long to realize you do not need me to soar. I understand now why it was so difficult for you to transition—that the effects of the crest were debilitating. I should not have taken my anger out on you. It was never about your ability to turn. It was the reason you could not turn that tortured me. Perhaps, in the depths of my heart, I already knew things would end up this way.

Everything that has happened has been because of me. I am the one who drove you into Leo's arms, all the while insisting you remain in mine. I am the one who demanded you crest him, and now his life hangs in the balance. It is killing you just as surely as it is killing him. I cannot blame you for loving him when I myself could not resist loving you. I understand, more than anyone, how you must feel.

You must forgive me if I am angry when you return from your conversation with Evelyn. You must forgive me if I am angry for a while. But I will not be angry forever, and you will soon know why. What I must do will seem cruel to you. But it is the only way to end this. Kora knows I am not perfect. But you do not need me to be perfect. You simply need me to make the decision I should have made a long time ago. I am sorry you will have to watch me die. But it is so you do not have to do the same with Leo. That would be too great a burden to bear, even for you.

Before you return and I destroy us, I owe you an apology. I should never have asked you to crest Leo. I knew how you cared for him. I knew you loved him. I could not have predicted that you would order him to find Evelyn, but in hindsight I should have known you would try to do right by him. You always try to do right by those you love. Believe it or not, I endeavor to do the same. In fact, I am endeavoring to do so right now.

There is one more matter I wish to mention. You know that I lived a long life before you, and you have often asked me about it. I wish I had answered your questions when you asked them, and now I will no longer be around to do so. But I kept a journal. Apollo knows where it is, and you are welcome to it if you wish. I want you to know everything there is to know about me. I am done keeping secrets from you.

After you consummate the crest, you will be able to transition again. Only then will you be strong enough to defeat Rowe. Only you can do the impossible. You are extraordinary, Tem.

It has been the greatest honor of my life to love you. I only hope I was worthy of your love in return.

Yours,
Caspen

LEO'S LETTERS

Tem,

I am only writing these infernal letters upon your request, and I wish to state for the record that I think it is a stupid idea. But since I have no other ideas myself, I suppose I shouldn't disparage it. Any idea, no matter how stupid, is worth trying at this point. I have to get you out of my head.

Yours,
Leo

Tem,

I told the caterers to make that soufflé tonight—the one we had when you stayed in the castle. Do you remember? Do you remember how I fed you a bite, then you kissed me on the cheek? I swear I felt that kiss for hours.

I would give anything for a kiss like that from you right now. Just one.

Yours,
Leo

Tem,

Dinner was torture tonight, as it is every fucking Sunday. Every time you reached for your whiskey, I thought you might be reaching for me. To make matters worse, your brute of a husband simply sat there and stared at me the entire time. Doesn't he ever eat? Don't answer that. I don't want to think about what he's been eating when it's all I want to eat too.

Yours,
Leo

Tem,

Are you aware that every time you come here, you look more beautiful than you did the time before? How dare you look like that. It should be illegal to be so stunning. And don't think I don't notice when you wear something low-cut. I know you do it for me. And I know you know I know. Stop doing that.

Yours,
Leo

P.S. Never stop doing that.

Tem,

Agony is too kind a word to describe these fucking dinners. I will never forgive myself for suggesting them. Knowing they are my only avenue to see you is the only reason I allow them to continue happening. That, and I like how angry your husband gets whenever I look at you. He practically cracks a tooth when I make you smile. Imagine what he'd do if I made you come.

Yours,
Leo

Tem,

There has been unrest in the village. My people are not happy. I'm being pulled in two directions—toward them and toward you. I don't know what magic you cast at our wedding, but you are always at the forefront of my mind. Even when I'm with Evelyn. All I think of is you.

Yours,
Leo

Tem,

I was late to dinner tonight. And when I arrived, you looked like you'd just been fucked. You know how I know that? Because I've fucked you before, and that's how you looked after I did it. I assume you let your brute of a husband fondle you in the foyer. I swear I could almost hear you moaning for him. I rubbed my cock raw all night thinking of you moaning for me.

Somehow, despite my better judgment, still yours,
Leo

Tem,

The villagers are angry. Evelyn announced our wedding, and it did not go over well. You warned me, and I didn't listen. I thought they would accept her, but they haven't. She's even more convinced that we must bring back the bloodletting now. She thinks it will turn their opinions in her favor. She is probably right.

Yours,
Leo

Tem,

I swear Evelyn doesn't know what she's saying. She's just…complicated. Not unlike you. But that's where the comparison stops. She's nothing like you. She's not even close. I will not let her do this. I promise.

Yours,
Leo

Tem,

Are you ever going to read these letters? What is the point of me addressing them to you if I'm only writing them for myself? What happens if Evelyn finds them? Sometimes I hope she will.

Yours,
Leo

Tem,

It's not enough for me. I can't write to you and pretend it's enough for me. I need to touch you. I need to hear you say my name. Don't you need that too?

Yours,
Leo

Tem,

I think Evelyn is lying to me. It eats at me like a disease. You and I agreed not to lie to each other, and all Evelyn does is lie. I'm beginning to think I hate her for it. I am beginning to think I hate you too.

Yours,
Leo

Tem,

I don't hate you. I could never hate you. I think you know that, so I'm not going to bother apologizing. You won't read these fucking letters, so what does it matter anyway? I love you. I always will.

Yours,
Leo

Tem,

Why is it that every time we look at each other, it feels like stars colliding? What did you do on our wedding—what bond now exists between us? Your brute of a husband was the one who suggested you draw power from me that day. Does he know we're connected like this? He can't possibly. Because if he did—if he knew how I feel when I look at you—he'd kill me on the spot.

Yours,
Leo

Tem,

I hated every moment of that dinner. I hated the way you volunteered for the bloodletting. I hated the way Evelyn smiled when you did it. I hated the way you told me my father would be proud. I fucking do not think he would be. Nothing could be worse than making that monster of a man proud.
    I miss you so badly it hurts.

Yours,
Leo

Tem,

Something is drawing me to you. I can't stop it. I wake up every night thinking of you, and sometimes I'm halfway out the door before I remember I can't go to you. Does your brute of a husband know how lucky he is? Does he understand the paramount privilege he enjoys being married to you? He's the one who gets to kiss you. He's the one who gets to fuck you. At least…in person. You cannot imagine what I've done to you in my dreams.

Yours,
Leo

Tem,

I swear I feel worse every day I'm not with you. It's like I need to touch you, and if I don't, I'll die. Do you feel that too? Or do I yearn alone?

Yours,
Leo

Tem,

I wish you hadn't sent me away tonight.
    I would have sat with you for as long as you were down in that awful fucking dungeon. I don't want you near my father, and I don't want you bleeding because of me. It's the last thing I would ever want.

Yours,
Leo

Tem,

I can't stop thinking about what we did in the library.

    You were so beautiful spread open like that just for me. When Evelyn asked how I cut my hand, I couldn't think of a single fucking thing to tell her. She wouldn't have believed me anyway.

Yours,
Leo

Tem,

My cock was hard when I woke up this morning. Evelyn slid it in her mouth, and I imagined she was you. Then we fucked, and I took her from behind because that's the only way I can fuck someone who isn't you.

    Why are you doing this to me? Do you hate me?

Yours,
Leo

Tem,

I can't bear this much longer.

Yours,
Leo

Tem,

Every day the villagers grow more restless. I spoke to your friend Gabriel this morning as he was arriving for his shift in the kitchen. He says my people are angry, that they resent the inconsistencies in leadership, that they wish you were their queen. I wish that too.

Yours,
Leo

Tem,

It's not working with Evelyn. But I can't leave her. You told me to find her, and I did. And now we're getting married and everything is wrong. I can't stop thinking about you. When I try, I only think about you more. You're in the whiskey I drink, the books I read, the stars I see. You're a part of me.

Is it the same for you? Or did I imagine us?

Yours,
Leo

Tem,

I almost left last night—nearly got in a carriage and went to the caves to find you. What would have happened if I'd done that? Would you have been happy to see me? Or would your brute of a husband have ripped my head from my shoulders? Perhaps that would have been preferable to missing you so fucking much.

I can't keep doing this, Tem. I can't keep writing these letters.

Yours,
Leo

Tem,

Evelyn is here for the wrong reasons. She's obsessed with gold, with money, with power. She wants what I can provide her—she doesn't want me.

She isn't...good. She isn't you.

Yours,
Leo

Tem,

I'm supposed to marry Evelyn tonight. And I swear to Kora if you told me not to, I wouldn't. That's all it would take: one word from you, and I wouldn't marry her. Say that word, Tem. Please.

Yours,
Leo

BONUS CHAPTER

⸻✦⸻

APOLLO

Mating season.

Every year the same lawless indulgence, the same senseless fucking. Normally, Apollo looked forward to it—*reveled* in it. But for some reason, this year was different. This year, he felt...*bored*. Perhaps he had simply outgrown such things. Or perhaps he sought something deeper than a meaningless romp. Regardless, a pit of melancholy weighted his stomach as he circled the courtyard, watching the festivities.

Presently his gaze fell to Adelaide, who was standing next to Cypress. Adelaide was an exceptionally gorgeous woman—tall and lithe with a perfect cunt and a certain proclivity for the Drakon brothers. Apollo had fucked her many times, most notably whenever he was in the mood to make Caspenon jealous. She was excellent in bed, as all basilisks were, but the added dash of spite made their sex even better. Apollo would never understand why his brother had forsaken her in favor of a human. Although Temperance was not truly a human, was she? His brother's new bride was a Hybreed, which made her more powerful than every basilisk here, including himself. Apollo rolled his shoulders. He was not used to being outranked.

Apollo strolled through the courtyard slowly, observing the crowd with detached indifference. Ever since his father died, things had become precarious under the mountain. Caspenon's ascent to power had not been smooth. The Senecas were angrier than ever; Apollo could not walk more than a few yards, even during mating season, without receiving scathing looks, and often, vulgar gestures from them. Bastian had made many promises, and kept none of them. It was a bad time to be a Drakon, and a worse time to be related to the Serpent King.

And then there was Temperance. Apollo had yet to meet her, but he already knew what to expect. Every woman, no matter how strong their conviction, fell head over heels for his brother. Surely this half-human would be no different. Apollo could already picture how she would fawn over Caspenon. Shameful. There could be no worse person to have first rights to—a half-human, half-basilisk blunt. It reflected poorly on Apollo at a time when his family's reputation was already at risk. Of course, that was nothing new; Caspenon had no thought or consideration for others.

Although Apollo could not exactly blame him.

His brother kept him at arm's length for good reason. They had a history, after all, and not a good one. It came as no surprise that Caspenon had waited until tonight to allow Apollo and Temperance to meet. No doubt he was not eager to repeat the cycles of their past. And truth be told, neither was Apollo. This time would be different. This time he would not be tempted by Caspenon's lover, nor would he endeavor to steal her away, as he had done so many times before. Temperance was not a danger to him.

When another round of the courtyard yielded nothing of interest, Apollo finished his stroll at the edge of the cave and waited. Eventually, a woman appeared before him. He did not know her name, nor did he care. He hardly even noticed she was there until she knelt suddenly, taking his cock into her mouth. The woman serviced him to completion, and by the time she moved on, another woman took her place. Mouth, pussy, hand after hand—it did not matter what touched his cock—Apollo allowed it all. It was not until he found himself in the mood for some elixir that he finally broke himself away from the barrage of sex, pulling out of the woman before him, groaning as he did so. Then he made his way toward the fountain. When he reached it, his heart stopped.

There was his brother, seated on the edge of the white stone ledge. Straddling him was the single most alluring creature he had ever seen in his very long life. A cavern opened up in Apollo's chest at the sight of her flushed cheeks, her curly hair. Temperance.

He watched in wonder as she reached behind his brother, extending her fingers so they dipped into the waterfall of elixir. Her other hand wrapped around Caspenon's neck, pulling his face up to hers. When she brushed her dripping fingertips over his brother's lips, Apollo wished she would brush them over his lips instead. His cock went completely hard at the thought, and he immediately began to stroke it, staring at nothing but Temperance, seeing nothing but the wild smile on her face—her eyes wide open, her lips wet with cum. It was a glorious image, one that nearly made him come right then and there. *Kora.*

Apollo had only felt this feeling once before—an aching rush of cataclysmic desire that consumed him like fire. He never thought he would feel that again. It seemed a sick twist of fate that his brother would have access to such a glorious creature, and that Apollo would be regulated to the sidelines, watching.

And watch he did.

He watched as Temperance thrust her hips, riding his brother with unrestrained confidence. He was just close enough to hear her gasps of pleasure, and even from here, they were irresistible. Apollo dared not imagine how good she must feel. He could only pray that one day he might be able to experience her—that somehow, some way, his brother might step aside. Apollo could not understand why this woman called to him the way she did. There had to be something special about her— something magical and otherworldly. Apollo could not believe he had thought that Temperance would hold no allure, that she was not a danger to him. How naive he had been mere moments ago. Now that he was looking at her, he could look at nothing else. Now that he knew she existed, he could want no one else.

Apollo memorized every inch of her body as if it were scripture, observing the way her curls fell down her back in gentle, luscious waves. He wanted to grip those curls in his hand, wrap them around his wrist, and pull. He wanted to hear the noise she would make when he did it. He wanted to understand her carnally—to learn exactly what it would take to make her come. These were not appropriate thoughts. But Apollo thought them anyway, not bothering to shield his mind from Caspenon's. He didn't care if his brother knew. He wanted him to know. There came a time in every basilisk's life when the pursuit of pleasure outweighed everything else. The consequences were irrelevant: if a basilisk saw something—or someone—it wanted, it was compelled to act. And Apollo was compelled right now. He was no better than his brother, no better than any of them.

Apollo was close. And so was Temperance.

Her thrusts were quickening, her grip on his brother iron tight. Unchecked jealousy raged through him, the likes of which he had only felt once before. Now he felt it again, and it fueled him in a way he did not know he could be fueled. There would be consequences for this, but he would face them later. The only thing that mattered was seeing her—observing her—understanding her. Apollo wanted nothing more than to know what made her ache, because he knew it would make him ache too. She existed just beyond his orbit, changing his gravitational pull. Her head fell back, her neck exposed. Apollo's did the same. And when Temperance finally came, all he could imagine was her coming for him.

He finished into his hand with a groan, flicking his cum onto the rough stone floor. In the haze of his climax, he saw Temperance kiss Caspenon on the lips. At the sight, Apollo experienced a surge of envy so strong that, before he knew what he was doing, he was stepping forward. He had nothing to say, but he had to speak anyway. He wanted to meet her—to be *seen* by her. Temperance looked up just as he reached them.

"Impressive," Apollo said, the word barely audible over the pounding of his heart. "But rather swift. Are you losing your stamina, Caspenon?"

His brother's expression turned to steel. But Apollo wasn't looking at him. He was looking at the beautiful woman before him, observing the way she looked right back without fear. There was heat in her eyes—*life* and *beauty* and *sex*. It was a light that Apollo wanted to take in his hands and cradle like a fire, coveting its warmth. Would she ever let him? Surely, she would not. And even if she did, Caspenon would not. But it did not matter. He wanted to anyway.

Caspenon shifted so he was between them.

"Tem," he said. "My brother. Apollo."

Apollo noticed how Caspenon did not use her full name. It was a sign of love, of intimacy. Apollo wanted to call her Tem too. But he knew if he did, Caspenon would kill him.

"Nice to meet you," Tem said.

Apollo took her hand in his, raising it to his lips and kissing the back of her wrist. Her skin was unbearably warm—even warmer than his—as if she burned from the inside out. The wrist was the most intimate place to kiss—basilisks did so out of respect for another's heartbeat. The pulse flowed just beneath the surface, an indicator of life. Apollo lingered for far too long, savoring that vitality, murmuring his next words directly against her skin:

"The pleasure is entirely mine, Temperance."

He dropped her hand. He wanted to tell her that she was stunning—that her beauty rendered him almost speechless. But if he did that, his brother would never forgive him. So instead he turned to Caspenon and said:

"She is beautiful. You did well."

It was the absolute minimum of compliments. Tem's beauty was arresting—*life altering*. Apollo was powerless against it. Caspenon's reply was sharp:

"Her beauty is none of my doing."

Apollo knew that tone—it was the one his brother used when he was barely restraining his temper. It was time to diffuse the situation.

"Of course," Apollo said easily, turning back to Tem. "I meant no offense. Your beauty is your own. And what beauty it is."

Tem nodded as silence fell. In it, Caspenon's voice rang sternly in his mind:

You forget your place, brother. She is my wife.

I am perfectly aware of your marital status.

Then you would do well to respect it.

I see nothing disrespectful about calling her beautiful. It is merely a fact.

A fact you do not need to tell her.

I see. Because you tell her enough yourself?

Because she does not need to hear it from you.

And I suppose you know what she needs?

I know better than you.

Perhaps. Or perhaps you—

Tem's voice interrupted them suddenly:

"Do you seek a mate?"

The brothers finally broke eye contact, both turning to look at her.

"Why would I do that?" Apollo asked back.

"Caspen told me that's what mating season is for."

Apollo smiled slowly.

"I do not seek a mate."

"Why not?"

"I do not desire one."

It was the truth, although just barely. Apollo did not desire the *wrong* mate. But if the perfect woman—like the one before him—were to come along, his answer would be different.

"Then what do you desire?"

Apollo was looking directly at what he desired. But he could not say so. He did not want to anger his brother, and, more importantly, he did not want to make Tem uncomfortable. Or worse, scare her. So he said simply:

"Pleasure."

Another half-truth. Apollo had grown weary of pleasure, of the mindless repetition of sex and climax. The only truly interesting thing to him existed outside the confines of pleasure, in the messy, dark line between right and wrong. Pleasure, if sought with the wrong person, was boring. But when sought with the right one, it was anything but.

Another pause. Beside them, Caspenon shifted, but said nothing. In his silence, Tem continued:

"If you don't want a mate, then why are you here?"

She was asking a lot of questions. More than he would have expected from her. It meant she was curious—an attractive quality, and a potentially difficult one. It did no good to question life under the mountain. There were never any satisfying answers. Apollo considered how to respond, settling on:

"I am here because mating season is an opportunity to experience everything my people have to offer. Surely Caspenon told you that as well."

Tem's forehead wrinkled in a delightful little frown.

"That seems wrong."

Apollo raised an eyebrow in genuine curiosity.

"How so?"

"What if someone develops feelings for you?"

He tilted his head. If only. "Then I will let them down easy."

"What if you develop feelings for someone?"

Caspenon let out an ugly shout of laughter. Tem looked up at him in surprise.

"What's so funny?" She asked.

Caspenon's next words may have been quiet, but their volume did nothing to dilute their strength:

"My brother is incapable of developing feelings. He is only capable of deceit. He manipulates, and he lies."

Apollo raised his chin. They were old insults, well-trodden. He would not bow to them today.

"I thought basilisks couldn't lie," Tem said.

Caspen's lip curled into a sneer. "My brother finds a way."

"Lies are deception," Apollo said in a tone much calmer than he felt. "And I think you will find I am always truthful." His gaze slid to Caspenon's. "Some might say to a fault."

Apollo knew that with every word he spoke, his brother's temper inched closer to its breaking point. And while normally he would not shy away from such a challenge—in fact, he would relish it—for some reason he did not want to do so in front of Tem. He cared what she thought of him. He cared that she thought *well* of him. It would not be wise to cultivate tension with Caspenon tonight. No good could come from acting as his adversary in front of this extraordinary girl. So, without another word, Apollo took one last lingering look at Tem, turned, and left.

The evening wore on. Apollo did everything he would normally do: he flirted, he fucked. But it felt empty now. Meaningless. There was only one person he wanted to flirt with, one person he wanted to fuck. And she was married to his brother.

How could this be happening again?

Apollo shook his head. He would not *let* it happen again. He could not let anything—or *anyone*—come between him and his brother. And yet, it would appear they were doomed to walk the same path, over and over. Basilisks believed that their fates were determined. Apollo believed that too. It meant that ultimately, no matter what he wished, his future would remain unchanged. He would always challenge his brother—he would always fall in love at the worst possible time. It was his nature, and it was his fate. He was resolved to it by now. At some point, he simply had to accept it. Apollo did not mind traversing the same path. Not as long as Tem was at the end of it. If there was one person worth walking the line for, it was her.

Before long, it was time for the main event of the evening. The blood-bound couple stood in the middle of the courtyard, the mattress before them. Apollo had seen only a few of these blessings before; blood-bound couples were rare, his brother's marriage an anomaly. To bind one's life to another required a strength of will that Apollo could only hope one day to discover in himself. It was a rare thing, and a special thing, and it was not something he expected to have in this lifetime. Still, he was allowed to hope for it, and in the dark, quiet moments directly before dawn, he did. Behind his bravado and his strength, Apollo's heart was tender and raw. He did not want more meaningless sex; he did not want another casual lay. He wanted more.

The crowd murmured as they gathered around the couple. Tem looked scared, which broke Apollo's heart. He wished he could comfort her. Instead, he watched as his brother did so, no doubt speaking to Tem using his mind. Apollo knew what they were saying—Caspenon would be explaining how as the new queen, Tem was expected to bless the couple. She would be hesitant at first. Afraid, even. But eventually, he knew she would give in.

Tem stepped forward.

She stood at the edge of the mattress as the couple lay down and began to kiss. Despite their obvious love, Apollo didn't even see them; he could look at nothing but Tem. He saw how unsure she was at first—how difficult it was for her to let herself go, to *indulge*. It was not something Apollo had ever had difficulty doing. But he could understand how strange it would be for a human to adjust to basilisk customs. His people were reckless and wild and free. Humans did nothing but resist.

Finally, Tem knelt.

Such a beautiful creature. So tentative, yet so willing to learn. Apollo did not dare imagine what he could teach her. That was his brother's job—Caspenon, the all-knowing mentor. The Serpent King. It was a title Apollo would never have as long as they were both alive. His father had made it clear he didn't believe Apollo deserved it. But no matter; he did not want it anyway. Apollo did not crave the burden that came with ruling the Seneca quiver. He had no desire to be in charge of other basilisks—to be held responsible for the success or failure of their society. That was a duty reserved for his older brother, the more powerful one, the *better* one.

Tem's eyes were shut tight. Apollo knew Caspenon was talking to her—he could nearly hear it, although not quite. He was encouraging her—coaxing her to indulge. What sweet words Apollo would whisper to her if he could. But that was not his task, not his duty. His job was to stand here and observe, same as all the other basilisks around him. All he could do was watch her as she slipped her fingers in and out of her gorgeous cunt, biting her lip as she did so. Apollo was so hard for her. But it did not matter. He could not take action, he could not do anything to quench the desire that coursed through him like fire. He could only watch.

And then she looked at him.

For a single moment, Tem's beautiful eyes met his. And for a single moment, Apollo knew peace. Everyone was watching the couple. But Tem was watching him. When their eyes met, Apollo's mind brushed against hers hopefully. She didn't let him in. Instead she threw up a barrier to keep him out, one that was far stronger than what Apollo would have expected from her. He could understand her reaction— he knew he did not deserve her attention, her mind, or her body. There could be no overlap between Apollo and Caspenon—no competition whatsoever. Not that Apollo would win if there were. Caspenon won everything. He was the victor, always. But that did not mean Apollo could not compete.

And compete he would. In that moment, Apollo did the only thing he could, which was hold her gaze. His past, or the implications for the future, did not matter. He felt nothing but burning, *aching* desire as Tem watched him as she fingered herself. His brother was so fucking lucky. Apollo could not believe he got to touch this beautiful girl every night. If she was his, he would never let her go. He would touch her and fuck her and kiss every inch of her body until she begged and pleaded for more. He would make her understand that she was the most important person in the world—the *only* person in the world to him. To anyone. Tem deserved to know that she was perfect, that she could do no wrong, that she was an angel and a goddess and an anomaly. Apollo wished to give her that clarity. But for now, his gaze dug into her like a knife, hot and insistent, unrelenting in its intensity. He wasn't touching himself—no one was—that act was reserved for the Serpent Queen. But his cock was hard, and before he could dare to hope, Tem's eyes trailed down his body to look at it.

Then, with a gasp of surprise, she came.

The moment it happened, the crowd erupted into cheers. Caspenon picked her up by the waist and spun her around before setting her down and kissing her straight on the mouth. Tem kissed him back, her eyes shut tight, as if she wanted to forget what she had just seen. But Apollo would never forget it. Nor did he want to. Apollo would play that moment over and over in his head until he had it memorized. He would think about it forever—the way Tem looked when she climaxed: her back arched, her nipples peaked. He pictured the way her lips formed a soft, open 'O', as if she were surprised by how much the sight of his cock affected her. He would replay it forever:

her brown eyes on his—the way her gaze had slid down his body, landing on his cock mere moments before she came. It was something Apollo would pride himself on—a fact that would feed him for months, possibly years. To be worthy of Tem was to be worthy of a queen.

Apollo imagined her on his cock, coming just for him. He did not dare imagine what it would be like to actually give her an orgasm. Nothing could be a greater pleasure. He would die if he never got a chance to do it. He imagined how their bodies would move together—how he would coax her there slowly, then all at once. At the thought of finishing inside her, Apollo felt himself grow even harder. Tem was still kissing his brother, her eyes still shut. What Apollo would not give to have those eyes on him once more, even for a moment.

And just like that, she was gone.

Caspenon whisked her away into the crowd, leaving as easily as they had arrived. Eventually, Apollo left too. The night wore on without incident. All around him, the basilisks celebrated. Bodies churned, legs spread, mouths collided. But Apollo saw none of it. He was bereft. Empty. All he wanted was Tem. All he needed was his brother's wife. How was it possible that he was once more in this position? It was, at best, cruel—at worst, a sick twist of fate. But perhaps there was a certain beauty to such a fate. Perhaps there was peace in predictability. History would repeat itself. Apollo would see to that.

Apollo made the rounds of the courtyard, watching others have sex, yet never indulging himself. Eventually, he found his way back to Tem. She was on the mattress that the blood-bound couple had occupied earlier, intertwined with Caspenon. Apollo knew he should not watch. He knew he should walk away, never to think of her again. Instead he stood there, nearly in the same place as before, and stared. He saw the way Tem's cheeks flushed when his brother penetrated her, the way she gasped as he pulled back out. She did not look at him again, nor did he expect her to. She was occupied with Caspenon, and Apollo knew better than anyone how distracting sex could be. For now, he was content simply to look at her—to indulge in the gift of voyeurism that his culture afforded him.

Apollo watched as she bit her lip, her hands threaded into his brother's hair, her legs tight around his waist. He resisted the urge to step closer—to hear the gasp from her lips as she crashed through her release. Instead he watched from afar, imagining it was him between her legs instead—him thrusting his cock into her perfect, glorious cunt. Would she ever let him? Only time would tell. And Apollo was a very patient man.

Finally, the night was over, and he was alone. Normally Apollo would take someone—or several someones—back to his chambers. But tonight he retired by himself, eager for one thing and one thing only. He wanted to touch himself to the thought of Tem. He wanted no distractions—no falsehoods that would only lead to pain. There was only one thing he desired, and he could not have it. But he could imagine it.

Apollo pictured what she would look like clenched around his cock—her mouth a perfect circle, pink and open and wanting. He pictured the sounds she would make as he fucked her, the way she would gasp desperately as he brought her to the brink. She would bring him to the brink too—Kora, he was already there. Perhaps he had been there since the moment he saw her. It was a fantasy that would never be fulfilled.

And yet, she had looked at him, had she not? Her hand between her legs, her eyes wide and wanting. Only when they had made eye contact did she finally come. There had to be a reason for it—something significant. Something fated.

Apollo had only felt this way once before, and it had ended in disaster. Apparently, he had not learned from his mistakes. Apparently, he was a glutton for pain. And pain was exactly what Tem was. She was hurting him, in her own gorgeous way—slicing him open and cutting him to the core. It was pain he welcomed—pain he craved. It was something he was privileged to feel. There could be no higher honor than being hurt by the Serpent Queen. His brother had no idea how lucky he was. His brother *never* understood how lucky he was. Apollo resented him for it, despite his many years attempting to come to terms with it.

And now, under the cover of darkness, he yearned.

He would always yearn for her.

ACKNOWLEDGMENTS

Not a day goes by when I am not grateful for the support of my parents. Without question, their love has molded me into the person I am today. The same goes for my friends—who know exactly who they are—and who were there for me long before *Kiss Of The Basilisk* was ever published. To Brooke and Shannon especially: I could not do this without you. And to my sister, the most important person in the world to me: I love you so much it hurts.

To my indomitable agent Haley Heidemann: I am forever in your debt. Thank you for taking one hell of a chance on me and this book. Cheers to many more. Thank you to the teams at Bloom, Arcadia, and all my international publishers. Words cannot express my gratitude for their faith in the Split or Swallow series; it would not exist without their efforts. I would also like to thank Suzannah Ball and Celia Rogers for tirelessly championing my books abroad. Split or Swallow is worldwide because of them.

I cannot write acknowledgments without mentioning my readers. If you are reading this, just know that I love you. I cannot believe I get to do this for a living, and it is all because of you. I can only hope that you enjoy reading my words as much as I enjoy writing them. Thank you for taking this wild ride with me. Buckle up, because we're only getting started.

And if you happen to be Team Caspen: I hope the upcoming prequel helps heal the wound that *Between Two Kings* will surely have left. I know I'm Team Leo, but this series wouldn't be the same without our iconic Serpent King. I promise to do right by him, even after doing him so wrong.

Last but certainly not least, I want to thank Chad.

You will never read this. Nonetheless, I wrote it for you.

ABOUT THE AUTHOR

Lindsay Straube is a writer living in Portland, Oregon. She drinks tequila with lemon and watches TV with subtitles on. On any given Tuesday, you can find her at the movies.

Come say hi:

Instagram: @oxfordlemon
Website: oxfordlemon.com

RAISING READERS
Books Build Bright Futures

Dear Reader,

We'd love your attention for one more page to tell you about the crisis in children's reading, and what we can all do.

Studies have shown that reading for fun is the **single biggest predictor of a child's future life chances** – more than family circumstance, parents' educational background or income. It improves academic results, mental health, wealth, communication skills, ambition and happiness.[1]

The number of children reading for fun is in rapid decline. Young people have a lot of competition for their time. In 2024, 1 in 10 children and young people in the UK aged 5 to 18 did not own a single book at home.[2]

Hachette works extensively with schools, libraries and literacy charities, but here are some ways we can all raise more readers:

- Reading to children for just 10 minutes a day makes a difference
- Don't give up if children aren't regular readers – there will be books for them!
- Visit bookshops and libraries to get recommendations
- Encourage them to listen to audiobooks
- Support school libraries
- Give books as gifts

There's a lot more information about how to encourage children to read on our website: **www.RaisingReaders.co.uk**

Thank you for reading.

---

[1] National Literacy Trust, Book Ownership in 2024, November 2024
https://nlt.cdn.ngo/media/documents/Book_ownership_in_2024

[2] OECD. 2021. 21st-century readers: developing literacy skills in a digital world. Paris, France: OECD Publishing.
https://www.oecd.org/en/publications/21st-century-readers_a83d84cb-en.html